Praise for Claire Lombardo's

THE MOST FUN WE EVER HAD

"[A] juicy saga.... Reading about [this family] is a treat."   —*People*

"A sprawling, enchanting debut ... this novel jumps back and forth across time to tell the story of one powerful, complicated, and utterly unforgettable family as they navigate love and loss."
                    —*Town & Country*

"Ambitious and brilliantly written."
                    —*The Washington Post*

"Nicely blends comedy with pathos and the sharp- with the soft-edged."   —*The Wall Street Journal*

"[A] satisfying multicourse feast."
                    —*O, The Oprah Magazine*

"A classy but juicy read that always has one more surprise up its sleeve."   —Shelf Awareness

"[A] brilliant debut."   —PopSugar

Claire Lombardo

THE MOST FUN WE EVER HAD

Claire Lombardo earned her MFA in fiction at the Iowa Writers' Workshop. Prior to writing *The Most Fun We Ever Had*, she spent several years doing social work in Chicago. She was born and raised in Oak Park, Illinois.

clairelombardo.com

THE

MOST

FUN

WE EVER

HAD

THE
MOST
FUN
WE EVER
HAD

Claire Lombardo

VINTAGE BOOKS
A Division of Penguin Random House LLC
New York

The Library of Congress has cataloged
the Doubleday edition as follows:
Name: Lombardo, Claire, author.
Title: The most fun we ever had / Claire Lombardo.
Description: First edition. | New York : Doubleday, 2019.
Identifiers: LCCN 2018036701
Classification: LCC PS3612.O453 M67 2019 | DDC 813/.6—dc23
LC record available at https://lccn.loc.gov/2018036701

Vintage Books Trade Paperback ISBN: 978-0-525-56423-2
eBook ISBN: 978-0-385-54426-9

Book design by Maria Carella

vintagebooks.com

Printed in the United States of America
4th Printing

For Sally and Tony Lombardo,

MY MOM AND DAD

THE OFFSPRING

April 15, 2000
Sixteen years earlier

Other people overwhelmed her. Strange, perhaps, for a woman who'd added four beings to the universe of her own reluctant volition, but a fact nonetheless: Marilyn rued the inconvenient presence of bodies, bodies beyond her control, her understanding; bodies beyond her favor. She rued them now, from her shielded spot beneath the ginkgo tree, where she was hiding from her guests. She'd always had that knack for entertaining, but it drained her, fully, time and time again, decades of her father's wealthy clients and her husband's humorless colleagues; of her children's temperamental friends; of her transitory neighbors and ever-shifting roster of customers. And yet, today: a hundred-odd near strangers in her backyard, humans in motion, staying in motion, formally clad; tipsy celebrants of the union of her eldest daughter, Wendy, people who were her responsibility for this evening, when she already had so much on her plate—not literally, for she'd neglected to take advantage of the farm-fresh menu spread over three extra-long card tables, but elementally—four girls for whose presences she was biologically and socially responsible, polka-dotting the lawn in their summer pastels. The fruits of her womb, implanted repeatedly by the sweetness of her husband, who was currently nowhere to be found. She'd fallen into motherhood without intent, producing a series of daughters with varying shades of hair and varying degrees of unease. She, Marilyn Sorenson, née Connolly—a resilient product of money and tragedy, from dubious socioemotional Irish-Catholic lineage but now, for all intents and purposes, as functional as they come: an admirably natural head of dirty-blond hair, marginally conversant in both literary criticism and the lives of her children, wearing a fitted forest green sheath that exposed the athletic curve of her calves and the freckled landscape of her shoulders. People kept referring to her with great drama as the *mother of the bride*, and she was trying to act the part, trying to pretend that she wasn't focused almost exclusively on the well-being of her children, none of whom, that particular evening, seemed to be thriving.

Maybe normalcy skipped a generation, like baldness. Violet, her second-born, a striking brunette in silk chiffon, had uncharacteristically reeked of booze since breakfast. Wendy was always cause for concern, despite seeming less beleaguered today, owing either to the fact that she'd just married a man who had bank accounts in the Caymans or to the fact that this man was, as she vocally professed, "the love of her life." And Grace and Liza, nine years apart but both maladjusted, the former a shy, stunted soon-to-be second-grader and the latter about to friendlessly finish her sophomore year of high school. How could you grow people inside your own body, sprout them from your own extant materials, and suddenly be unable to recognize them?

Normalcy: it bore a second look, sociologically speaking.

Gracie had found her beneath the ginkgo. Her youngest was almost seven, an insufferable age, aeons from leaving the household, still childish enough that she'd tried to slip into their bed in the middle of the previous night, which wouldn't have been *that* big of a deal had her parents been clothed at the time. Anxiety did something to Marilyn, always had, drew her magnetically to the animal comfort of her husband.

"Sweetheart, why don't you go find—" She hesitated. The only other children at the wedding were toddlers and she didn't specifically want to encourage Grace's already-burgeoning antisocial love of dogs by suggesting that she go play with Goethe, but she wanted a moment to herself, just a few seconds to breathe in the cooling air of early evening. "Go find Daddy, love."

"I *can't* find him," Grace said, the hint of a baby voice blunting her vowels.

"Well, look harder." She bent to kiss her daughter's hair. "I need a minute, Goose."

Grace moved off. She'd already checked on Wendy. Already swung on the porch swing with Liza until her sister had been distracted by a boy wearing sneakers with his wedding suit; already convinced Violet to share four sips of champagne from her fancy glass flute. She was out of people to check on.

It was strange to have to share her parents with others this weekend, to have her sisters back around the house on Fair Oaks. Her father sometimes called her the "only only-child in the world who has three sisters." She resented, slightly, her sisters homing in on her territory. She soothed herself as she always did, with the company of Goethe, curling up with him beneath the purple flower bushes and running her hand through his bristly fur, the part of his butt that looked like it had been permed.

Liza felt a little bad, seeing her younger sister finding solace in the dog while she herself was finding solace inside a stranger's mouth, but the groomsman emanated a smoky vapor of whiskey and arugula and he was doing something with his fingers to the inside of her thigh that made her turn her head away, deciding that Grace could fend for herself, that it wasn't possible to learn that skill too early.

"Tell me about you," the groomsman said, his knuckles grazing the lacy insignificance of the thong she'd worn in the hopes of exactly such an occasion.

"What do you want to know?" she asked. It came out sounding kind of hostile. She'd not quite mastered being flirtatious.

"There's four of you?" he asked. "What's that like?"

"It's a vast hormonal hellscape. A marathon of instability and hair products."

He smiled, confused, and she leaned forward boldly and kissed him.

Violet had never been quite so drunk, sitting slumped, alone, at one of the tables, from which she supposed she'd driven the other guests. The previous night came to her in fizzy episodic sunbursts: the bar that used to be a bowling alley; her blue-eyed companion with his double-jointed elbows, the athletic clasp of his thighs, the back of his mother's station wagon; how she'd made sounds she did not recognize at first as coming from her own throat, porn star sounds, primal groans. How he came first—she'd later felt him dripping out of her, when they climbed back into the front seat—and then made her, with a deft attention to detail, come as well, for the first time in her life. And how she'd made him drop her a block away from her parents' house lest Wendy be still awake.

She watched Wendy, wearing sweetheart-neck Gucci at her backyard wedding to an old-money academic, being spun in circles by her new husband to "You Can't Hurry Love." Her sister had, for the first time, surpassed her, success-wise. She was blithe and beautiful and twirling in circles while Violet was drunk past the point of physical comfort, gnawing at a full loaf of catered focaccia, rubbing the oil on the underside of her skirt. But she felt herself smiling a little at Wendy, at oblivious Wendy getting grass stains on her satin train. Imagined going over to her sister and whispering in her ear, *You'd die if you knew where I was last night.*

Wendy watched as Miles, throwing an apologetic smile at her over his shoulder, was pulled away from her by his toddler cousin, their ringbearer, who had solicited his accompaniment to the cake table.

"There's some good daddy training happening over there," someone said, taking her by the elbow. It was a guest from Miles's side, possibly someone's real estate broker, a silicone goblin of a woman. The people on the lawn at present were probably collectively worth more than the GDP of a midsize country. "It's good you're so young. Plenty of time to flesh out the family tree."

It seemed a crass thing to say for a variety of reasons, so Wendy responded in kind: "Who says I want to split up my share among a bunch of kids?"

The woman looked horrified, but Wendy and Miles lived for these jokes, were allowed to *make* these jokes because neither of them gave a fuck if people thought Wendy was a gold digger; all that mattered was what they knew to be true, which was that she'd never loved another person as fiercely as she did Miles Eisenberg, and he, by some grand cosmic miracle, loved her back. She was an *Eisenberg* now. In the top thirty, at least, of the wealthiest families in Chicago. She could fuck with whomever she wanted.

"It's my plan to outlive everyone and spend my days reveling in a disgusting level of opulence," she said. And she rose from her seat and went to straighten her new husband's tie.

. . . .

The trees, David noted, were burgeoning that day, big prodigious leaves making dancing shadows across the grass, which they'd tried to keep the dog off of for the sake of aesthetic preservation, David and Marilyn rising early in the mornings and pulling on raincoats over their pajamas to walk him instead of just opening the back door like they normally did. He watched as the rented tables and chairs wore their grooves into the pristine lawn, legs melon-balling the expensively fertilized sod in a way that made his gut churn. Goethe was now roaming around the yard like a recently released convict, traversing the verdant grounds with the proprietary confidence of a horticulturist. David took a breath of damp air—was rain coming? It might make the guests leave sooner—and marveled over the sheer number of people that could accumulate in a lifetime, the number of faces in his yard that he didn't recognize. He thought of Wendy as a toddler, when they lived in Iowa, creeping onto the porch where he and Marilyn rocked together in the rickety cedar swing, fitting herself neatly between them and murmuring, already drifting back to sleep, *You're my friends.* He was nearly overcome, standing there, feeling as out-of-place as he had a quarter of a century ago, before they'd married, a chilly December night when Marilyn had lain against his chest beneath the ginkgo. He did a visual sweep, eyes blurring the sea of pale spring colors until he found his wife, a tiny ballast of forest green: hiding beneath that very same ginkgo. He slipped along the fence until he came to her, and reached out an imploring hand to the small of her back. She leaned instinctively into it.

"Come with me," he said, and led her around the trunk, into the shade, where he pulled her to him and buried his face in her hair.

"Sweetheart," she said, worried. "What is it?"

He pressed his face into the crook of her neck, breathing in the faint dry warmth of her scent, lilacs and Irish Spring. "I missed you," he said into her clavicle.

"Oh, love." She tightened her embrace, tilted his chin until he met her eyes. He kissed her mouth, and then her cheekbone and her forehead and the inlet of her jaw where he could feel her pulse, and then her mouth again. She was smiling, lips a flushed feverish plum, and then she was kissing him back, the periphery blurring away. The thing that would always mean more than everything else: the goldish warmth of his wife, the heat of their mutual desperation; two bodies finding solace in the only way they knew how, through the language of lips, his hands along her spine, her spine against the tree trunk, the resultant quiet that occurred when they came together, until she pulled away, smiled up at him and said, "Just don't let the girls catch us," before she buried herself once again against him.

But of course they saw. All four of the girls watched their parents from disparate vantage points across the lawn, each alerted initially to their absence from the reception by that pull, a vestigial holdover from childhood, seeking the cognitive comfort that came from the knowing, the geolocation, the proximity of those who'd created you, those who would always feel beholden to you, no matter what; each of their four daughters paused what she was doing in order to watch them, the shining unfathomable orb of their parents, two people who emanated more love than it seemed like the universe would sanction.

PART ONE

SPRING

CHAPTER ONE

Violet made a habit of avoiding Wendy. Though they'd been inseparable for a time, unbidden contact was now unheard of, and she assumed her sister's most recent lunch invitation pertained either to a favor or to some newly harvested existential crisis that Wendy would want to discuss, at length, regardless of the fact that some people had busy lives that prevented them from taking frivolous weekday meals in the West Loop.

The restaurant was trendy and inconveniently located, and she'd had to valet even though it was 2:00 p.m. on a Wednesday. Wyatt had to be picked up from preschool at 3:30. That was her out, and she planned to present it smoothly to her sister: *There are two children whose lives and pre-K commutes depend on me.* Of course this was ungenerous; of course Wendy found comfort in drama, in midday alcohol, because of all that she didn't have, because she'd never finished college, because of Miles, because she would always win, trauma-wise.

Violet pinched the bridge of her nose, fending off a headache. She was considering a glass of wine. Wendy would have undoubtedly already ordered a bottle, and her sister—despite other shortcomings—had excellent taste in wine, a refined palate for tannins and acidity. Her flats were digging into the backs of her heels. She always felt the impetus to present herself lavishly to Wendy; though most days she was content to ferry the kids around in pricey athletic garb, today she'd opted for a graceful silk butterfly-sleeve blouse and skinny jeans that had fit her better before Eli was born.

She tried to remember the last time she'd seen her sister, and decided that it must have been on Second Thanksgiving, the annual and infuriatingly quirky powwow at her parents' house, over four months ago, and this struck her as absolutely ludicrous, because she and Wendy lived twenty minutes from each other; because they'd shared a bedroom for almost a decade; because Violet, during the darkest time in her life, had moved in with Wendy and Miles; because they were practically *twins*, after all, separated by less than a year.

"Ma'am? Is there something I can help you find?" It was the valet.

"Just getting my bearings," she said, and he smiled.

"If you need a lifeline, just wave and I'll come in and say someone's stolen your car." Was he flirting with her? He was her savior.

"I'll keep that in mind." She fished another ten from her wallet and pressed it toward him. Somehow she'd become one of those people who punctuated everything with a monetary transaction. He took it without missing a beat. "Wish me luck," she breathed, and he winked—*winked! At her!*—and she imagined, perhaps, that he checked out her ass as she walked into the restaurant. She hoped he wouldn't judge too harshly. The hostess ushered her onto the patio in the back and she wished at once she'd brought a sweater then banished the thought as tragically maternal. Wendy was at a table in the far corner, surely so she could smoke without bothering the other patrons, though there *were* no other patrons, because it was early spring in Chicago and barely sixty degrees.

At first all she saw was the back of a head. Presumably a man—and a young one—unless Wendy was going through an exploratory phase and had taken up with some gender-bending yogi from her chakra class. She felt strangely hurt. Of course Wendy couldn't just ask her out to lunch, the two of them: this would, as she should've known, be some sort of look-what-I'm-up-to-now demonstration that would serve to reinforce what a snoozefest Violet's life was, how mired she was in the status quo while Wendy was off doing tantric vinyasa with an androgynous gal Friday.

But then: no.

She would remember, in her car on the way home, after having tipped the valet for a third time, the swelling she'd felt in her chest, a crystallization of *something*. It wasn't that she recognized him. That was the wrong word. And it wasn't anything poetic, no lightning bolts through her temples, no ice in her veins. She barely caught a glimpse of him, really, because he'd only turned halfway in his seat, so her field of vision included little beyond his left ear and the outline of his nose. But it was enough, apparently, on some molecular level, not like the biological recognition she felt when Wyatt and Eli were born but significant in its own right, a sharp uterine tug that almost made her double over. She didn't recognize the boy so much as absorb him. And in her head, in the car, after she'd fled the restaurant and her sister and the person she'd given birth to fifteen years earlier—a boy who now had dark hair that flopped in front of his eyes—she would imagine all of the things she could have said to Wendy. Big things, cinematic things, *how dare you do this to me; you're dead to me, you fucking psycho; how dare you, how dare you, how dare you.* All the reasons it was okay that she left before she really saw his face.

Before Wendy left for the Lurie fund-raiser she went onto the deck to have a cigarette with Miles. She let herself out the back door, Grey Goose in hand, dress hiked up to her knees because she'd settled on an ill-advised black mermaid cut, one Parliament in her mouth and another on the table.

"Today went as expected. Violet booked it before I could introduce them." She lit her cigarette and sighed. "I need your absolution. I didn't know what I was doing when I did it. But he's actually a sweet kid. You'd like him."

Miles didn't reply.

"I'm wearing the dumbest outfit. Your mom would've liked it." She leaned her head back. "I saw my dad yesterday. Retirement seems like kind of a disaster. He told me he was thinking about *bird-watching*. Can you imagine? I can't picture him sitting still for that long."

She'd been doing it since he died. She would talk to him—to some ethereal indication of him that sometimes she felt but most times she didn't. Today was one of the most times, so she just leaned into the side of her chair and smoked.

"Tonight will be a total shitshow," she said after a minute. "The vultures are probably hammered already. Hopefully they won't grope anyone. I, personally, make no promises." She looked upward for some cosmic sign that he was listening to her. There was nothing to see; the sky was overcast and grayish and the stars weren't out yet. Instead she held her cigarette upward, toward where she thought he might be, and exhaled a deliberate jet of smoke. "I hope you're proud of me, dude," she said after a minute. "Because I am really trying to keep on around here, okay?" Somehow she had been without him for nearly two years. She lit her backup cigarette. "I wish I could kiss the inside of your elbow right now," she whispered, almost inaudibly because the people next door sometimes kept their windows open. "But instead I might have to find a Greek shipping heir tonight and let him ravish me a little bit. Not too much. I swear. Fucking fuck, my darling. Man, do I miss you."

She took a few more drags, speaking to him in her head about all of the things she'd done that day, and then when she had one drag left she performed her ritual, which was to inhale as deeply as she could and exhale *I love you* over and over again until she ran out of breath.

A few hours later a man in a tuxedo had his hand on her left breast. She fitted her knee between his thighs and he staggered back, bumping into a table, upsetting a calla lily arrangement.

"Careful," she said.

"My bad," he replied. He was, upon inspection, perhaps more boy than man. He'd told her his name was Carson and she'd actually laughed but when he looked hurt she passed it off as nerves and yanked him down the hall by the lilies.

The man-boy's sweaty hand had adhered itself to her nipple in a way that wasn't specifically pleasant. He kissed her neck. She rubbed her leg a little harder against his groin. Maybe early to mid-twenties. He seemed pretty sure of himself.

"I didn't get your name," he said. Wendy stiffened a little, thought of Jonah across the table from her at lunch that afternoon, the blank innocence of his face, his bald confusion when they both realized Violet had fled. What if this guy wasn't even *legal*?

"How old are you?" she asked, and he pulled away and grinned at her.

"Twenty-two."

She nodded and slipped a hand down the waist of his pants. Just cocky, then, pun acknowledged. An heir, perhaps, of someone who'd invented something that seemed like it had already been invented by someone else. Or maybe the son of a record executive or a spray-tanned Fox correspondent. A boy who would live a life of inconsequence, who would, one hoped, not kill anybody with his car and get away with it. He wasn't a terrible kisser.

"How old are *you*?" he asked.

"Seventy-eight," she said, unfazed.

"You're funny," he said.

She was suddenly irked. "What does your father do?" she asked him, removing her hand from his boxers.

"Huh?"

"Your dad. What's his job? Why are you here tonight?"

"What makes you assume that I'm here with—" He stopped, rolling his eyes. "He's an engineer. Medical software development. Robotics."

"Ah." She'd check the guest list tomorrow, ensure they'd made a sizable contribution. Sometimes the more low-profile guys tried to get away with just buying tickets.

"What's your *name*?" he asked, a little more hostile this time.

She sighed. "Wendy."

"Like Peter Pan," Carlton noted astutely, and it was her turn to eye-roll.

"Its origins have never been explained to me."

Her mom and dad used to call her Wednesday as a nickname, and when she'd confronted her mother about it—just a few years ago—the response had been underwhelming.

"That was mean," she'd said. "Like Wednesday Addams? I was skeletal, Mom; did that really seem like a good joke?"

"Honey, you were born on a Wednesday. Just a few minutes after midnight. I had no idea what day it was and your father— It was because of that."

That was the story of her name, then. *You shattered my conception of the space-time continuum, First Contraceptive Accident.*

She tugged at Carlton's sleeve. "Come on. Let's go outside," she said.

"Wendy," he said. "Hang on. As in—*that* Wendy?"

She turned to see what she'd already known was there: a poster for the fund-raiser, complete with a photo of the cancerous spokesbaby, dotted at the bottom with HOSTED BY WENDY EISENBERG OF THE CHICAGO PHILANTHROPIC WOMEN'S SOCIETY. A robotics engineer would be exponentially less likely to donate if he discovered that the middle-aged organizer was making out with his pretentiously named twenty-two-year-old son. It was the sight of the *Eisenberg* that really got her, though, the prodigious loop of the *g*. It still bothered her to see her name on its own. She backed away from her tailored little charge and tried to smile.

"Do I seem like the hostess of this event?" she asked.

"What's your last name, then?"

"Sorenson," she said without skipping a beat.

"Well, could I—can I text you?" he asked, and she smiled.

"I'd like that," she said ominously. "But I'd better go."

"I thought we were going outside."

"Alas, no time. I'm ancient. I've gotta go. Coaches. Pumpkins. Life Alert."

"Well—okay. This was—um—this was nice."

Ah, he was a sweet one: her prize for taking the high road.

"Do yourself a favor," she said, still flustered, tugging at the heel of her left shoe. "Next time you think a woman's funny? Don't tell her she's funny."

"What do I do instead?" Something about the way his perfect face crumpled in confusion tugged at a place deep in her belly and she couldn't help but smile at him.

"You laugh," she said, and before she realized what she was doing she was reaching to press a shock of hair away from his forehead. "The next time you meet a funny woman, you laugh at her jokes, okay, Conrad?"

"Carson."

"Carson. Good luck, kid."

The room spun again. *Kid* made her think of her parents, suddenly, of her father bowing theatrically to her mother at Wendy's wedding, hearing Otis Redding—"win a little; lose a little"—and declaring, "It's our song, kid." Every song belonged to her parents, it seemed; everything recorded in the last six decades had something to do with David and Marilyn, those two inexplicable people from whom she hailed. She'd thought, when she met Miles, that she'd finally found someone in the way that her mom had.

There were suddenly tears in her eyes, a familiar tightness in her chest. She wasn't supposed to leave this early but she knew that if she stayed things would continue to go south. She left her coat in the checkroom and spun out onto the street.

Some people told you it took a year for everything to get back to normal; other people said things only got worse after a year. She was a member of this latter camp, she supposed, because Miles had been dead since 2014 but she still hadn't cleaned out his nightstand; she still bought things at the grocery that he liked and she didn't; she still operated exactly as she had before, as a member of a unit, as a person who was contingent on the active participation of another person. You couldn't untrain yourself from that. She'd tried. She'd moved to the condo in River North, but she set it up a lot like their house in Hyde Park, and she'd taped up the drawers of all his furniture—his desk, his dresser, his nightstand—so that the movers could transport them intact, full of his possessions.

Some people took a year; it was probable that some other people besides Wendy were still complete trainwrecks after two.

It swept in with the spring like a melting. Quietude, a kind of solace Marilyn hadn't known since—well, ever, honestly; in utero, maybe, but probably not even then, given her mother's penchant for Tanqueray, given the laxity of the 1950s, whichever you wanted to blame. Life was good. *Her* life was good. The hardware store was doing well, and she was sleeping better than she ever had, and her legs had nearly regained the limber give of her girlhood because she rode her bike to work, and her pansies were flourishing, a bright vermilion burst in the built-in box on the front porch.

She, for once, would have been flying high, were it not for the tethers of her family. Marilyn Connolly—who'd've thought? A business owner, a certified nonsmoker for nearly fifteen years, an occasional churchgoer, proprietess of the most beautiful rosebushes on Fair Oaks. She was wondering if perhaps she was in her *prime*, although she wasn't entirely convinced that one was allowed to *have* a prime when one was the mother of four. She was, instead of flying high, like one of those giant kite people they flew outside of the gas station on Ridgeland Avenue, a big vinyl body swaying in the breeze, trussed to the ground by thick umbilical ropes. A few minutes of bliss and suddenly it was the irritating jangle of her phone and an *Oh my God, Mom,* or a knock at the kitchen window with a mouthed *Where's the rake, honey?*

She put her bike on the porch and stopped to pull some dead leaves from her potted plants. Loomis was waiting for her inside.

"Hello, my darling," she said, rubbing deep behind his ears. They'd become those clichéd empty nesters who turned desperately to the Labrador the second the last kid shipped off to college.

"Hey, sweet," David called from down the hall. She followed Loomis to the study, and she paused before she entered, watching her husband's back, the vulnerable fuzz on his neck, the hint of a bald spot spreading from the crown of his head like a galaxy.

She didn't need him: it bobbed around in her head, a tiny infidelity. It occurred to her at that moment, melancholically, as she watched him sitting at his desk before a few books of rare quarters and a pile of pistachio shells. He'd become messy, suddenly, after years of passive-aggressively swiping at the crumbs on the counter with a damp sponge, sighing heavily as he cleared long blond-brown strands of hair from the shower drain. He'd become messy and stagnant and extremely libidinous, and when he rose to kiss her, shaking paper-thin flecks of pistachio skin from his shirt, the thought materialized: *I don't need you.* She moved for a peck on the forehead but he went full-on, running a hand through her hair, looping an arm around her waist, teasing her lips apart with his own.

"Mm," she said, pulling away. "I think I'm getting a cold, love."

It was clearly a lie; they had never cared about colds. They passed germs back and forth with abandon, sharing mugs of coffee, pieces of toast, occasionally toothbrushes when they were too tired to turn on the light and distinguish green from blue. David had an immune system like an alligator and Marilyn, way back when, was always low-level sick anyway, from the girls, their sticky hands and their dirty Kleenexes and their leftover macaroni she'd eat from their bowls after dinner. They weren't afraid of germs. Standing before her, David looked wounded.

Of course she *needed* him, on a molecular level, the deepest kind of human need. But she didn't need his *help.* And she didn't want his body, not really, in a way that reminded her of the times after each of the children were born, the times when the three eldest girls were small all at once, the times when the three eldest girls were *teens* all at once, and she'd been too tired to desire anything that required even a fragment of conscious bodily attention.

It felt like that, except she wasn't tired.

"How was your day?" she asked him, leading the way to the kitchen.

"Oh, you know," he said. "I cut the grass. I walked the dog. Twice." He was quiet for a minute. "How was *your* day?" he asked finally, and she hesitated.

It had started to feel sort of uncomely, countering his Eeyore monologue with a chirpy account of the hardware store's thriving profit margin, her funny teenage employees, the delightful moments of existential introspection she'd been having lately during lulls between customers. You couldn't respond to *I'm depressed and inventing home improvement projects to combat my despair* with *I've never been happier!*

"Just fine," she said. "You going to help me with dinner?"

When they were first married, living in that haphazard green house in Iowa City when David was in medical school, they'd relished the opportunity to make dinner together, trailing each other around the kitchen, making out against the counter while they waited for water to boil, sometimes forgetting the meal entirely and having to fan the smoke alarm with their discarded clothing. Something in his expression now tugged at a sinewy part of her heart; something about the defenseless flop of his graying hair made her go to him and twine her arms around his middle and kiss him. Needing and wanting were different animals entirely.

"I thought you had a cold," he said, pulling away for a second.

"False alarm," she said, slipping her hands into his back pockets, impelling his tongue to engage with hers.

"I can cook," David said, coming up for air. She kissed him harder and felt a flicker of something southward, a gentle reminder of the fact that she loved this man more than solitude. She pushed her hips into his, trying to draw out the feeling, keep it going, but it was gone as quickly as it had come, replaced by stillness, a little ache in her jaw.

CHAPTER TWO

Grace remembered hearing somewhere that small envelopes didn't necessarily mean bad news, but that had been her experience thus far, so when she saw the letter-size in her mailbox alongside a card stock advertisement for dental veneers, she threw both unopened on the table, numb by now to disappointment and numb, as well, to the interior of her apartment, which was the precise color and consistency of shredded wheat. It had a minifridge instead of a regular fridge. The bedroom had cinder-block walls. The shower released a shy stream of lukewarm water that turned to ice if anyone in the building's other units so much as rinsed a plate.

But it was *temporary*. That had been her rationale: tough it out in a cheap hovel for a year (some would argue that sparseness was good for productivity and enlightenment), figure out the logical next step, advance forward at the completion of her lease. She'd kept reminding herself of that over the course of this last year as her college friends, one by one, moved away; as her LSAT scores came back with results she thought must surely be typos: *this is only temporary and everything is going to be fine.* Everything was going to be fine and soon she would find her place in the world, the job she was meant to have and the man she was meant to marry and the little (or, who knew, perhaps not-so-little) plot of earth she was meant to inhabit.

All of this, of course, had sounded great at the time. Catch her breath, save a little money. Jolly, pragmatic Grace, the belated and treasured child of her doting parents.

But now it was nearly April, and her faraway friends were busy with med school and MFAs, with moves to New York or Seattle or Singapore, and her own rejection letters kept rolling in, one after another, and so she continued to be employed for $9.50 an hour as a receptionist at a nonprofit that provided free legal services to woodwind musicians, not herself a woodwind musician and so utterly friendless. Thus she was spending a lot of time in her janky apartment, which was fucking with her morale.

It had been a year since she'd graduated from Reed. The University of Oregon—whose small and unpromising envelope lay on her kitchen table—was her last hope. Not quite a safety, apparently, given the resounding *no thanks* she'd received from everyone else, but definitely lower-tier than the other places she'd applied. It would be ideal, an easy move across the river to the city proper. But it seemed she was destined to remain here with her tiny fridge—which, despite its size, remained embarrassingly empty, containing only a bottle of chardonnay and a few sticks of string cheese.

She lived a little bit like how she imagined murderers lived: sparsely, and with shame.

Her phone rang, and when she saw it was Liza, she grabbed her cigarettes and went out on her balcony. The balcony was theoretically a perk of her apartment, but sitting on it felt like sitting in a playpen, or a jail. Sadistically, she preferred talking to Liza over her other sisters lately because Liza was scads more boring than Wendy or Violet, not married or parenting or haunted by dramatic ghosts from her past, not loaded or adventurous or outstandingly successful. Liza, with her beige home and her seemingly dead-end academic job and her miserly boyfriend, was arguably the third least interesting Sorenson child, beating Grace by only a single slot, and there was a comfort in that.

"Goose," Liza said. "I've got— I have the best news."

Wonderful. She leaned hard against the bars of the balcony and shut her eyes.

"Guess who's a tenured professor?"

She considered making a joke—*Peter Venkman*—but Liza's joy at the moment outweighed her own malaise. "No shit. Lize, that's awesome." Of course this meant that Liza would begin to inch away from her on the interesting scale. She could typically rationalize that her sisters, so much older than she was, had had more time to accrue life experience, but it was tough to minimize the glaring achievement of getting tenure at thirty-two.

"Thank you." Liza was breathless and giddy; it made Grace smile, a surging of sisterly accord. She'd forgotten that your family could occasionally make you forget about the stupid confines of your own dumb life. "I was completely caught off-guard, Gracie. The dean made me a cappuccino. Himself. In his *office.*"

"You're adjusting well to this change in standard of living."

Liza laughed. "I'm— Christ, I feel *high.* I'm so fucking happy."

"You should *get* high. You should be celebrating."

"I'm on my way home. Or, well, I'm—I'm in the Binny's parking lot."

"Where dreams are made."

"Ryan's going to be happy about this, right?" Liza was the only one of her sisters who spoke to her in this way, as though she might possess knowledge beyond theirs.

"Of *course* he is. Don't be nervous. Be fucking ecstatic, Lize. This is so dope."

"I have *job* security."

"Stop bragging." Then, tentatively, because she wasn't sure

she'd ever said the words to anyone, let alone one of her older sisters: "I'm proud of you."

Liza's voice, when she replied, was full: "Thanks, Gracie. I'm— God, I'm so *emotional* about this. I don't think I've felt this way since—like, ever."

"Can you hook me up with stuff now? Like, office supplies? Or emotionally mature undergrads?"

"That's why I signed the contract." Then: "Wait, Goose, what about your applications? Did something happen?"

For some reason, she didn't answer right away. She glanced ruefully, through the door, at her kitchen table.

"Gracie?"

"Actually." The optimistic lilt of the final syllable happened spontaneously. "The letter from Oregon just got here before you called." Technically true. Technically not a massive lie.

"Goose! God, talk about burying the lede. Oh, that's— Gracie, that's fantastic. Oh, I knew you would— Oh my *God*, my little sister's going to be a *lawyer*. You know I used to change your diapers, right?"

"Yes, it's been brought to my attention before." The feeling of having leveled the playing field a bit was definitely not unpleasant, especially after Liza had invoked diapers to highlight their nine-year age gap. Technically she had still not said anything untrue, despite what her racing heartbeat might suggest. Liza had made the leap herself.

"I'm so proud of you, Gracie. Have you told Mom and Dad yet?"

She paused. Then: "Just figuring out the best way to break the news."

"What a great day this is," Liza said. In addition to being the third-least interesting sibling, Liza was also hands-down the kindest, and Grace felt a momentary barb of guilt. "Listen, Goose, I should get home. But we'll talk soon, okay? Mom and Dad are going to flip. You should go celebrate too. I promise not to make you start calling me Professor if you won't make me call you Your Honor. I love you."

"Do what you have to do. I love you too."

When they hung up she rose, creakily—her body suddenly seemed to be rapidly aging—and went back inside to her kitchen table, staring down at the envelope. Perhaps her lie of omission would be validated. Sometimes good things came in small packages; that was something her mom would say. People in Oregon were eco-friendly and mindful. It could just be a couple of sentences. *You're in! Check out the rest on our website.*

She took a knife from the kitchen drawer. Her father had raised them all to open envelopes with dignity, not just tear at the flaps like savages. Her parents were full-throttle optimists as far as her life was concerned; there had never been a doubt in their minds that she would go to law school, buoyed by impressive scholarships, progressing efficiently all the way to the Supreme Court.

She slit the envelope with the knife and pulled out the paper. She read it quickly, with trained eyes, and she dropped it into the garbage. The chardonnay was shitty gas station wine called Hodnapp's Harvest. Though the labels on the backs of trendier and more whimsical wines might say something like PAIRS WELL WITH DELICATE GRILLED FISH AND SPRING RISOTTO—none of the labels ever mentioned complementing string cheese, she noted—this one featured a photo of what was apparently the Hodnapp family crest. She squinted to read the calligraphic inscription below the surname:

THIS WINE PAIRS WELL WITH FRIENDSHIP.

She poured a third of the bottle into a coffee mug and went by herself onto the balcony to mourn her future.

Liza had gotten lucky, she supposed, nearing her house, psyching herself up. Wendy had paved the way for them by dating a bunch of terrible douchebags, blond American Psychos with popped collars and vacation homes on the Cape. She started this processional in junior high and ended it with her comparatively normal, albeit exorbitantly wealthy husband, Miles. Violet's college boyfriend had trouble making eye contact and seemed to be viewing them all as potential lab specimens. By the time Ryan came along, Liza's parents were desensitized, barely batted an eye at the tattoos on his forearms. But she wondered how they would handle his less visible shortcomings: his crippling anxiety, his bouts of severe depression, the way that sometimes she came into a room and didn't recognize him, saw only a man-child with such a despondent expression that she began to question every single happy moment they'd had together.

It had started to get bad last year, when they moved to Chicago from Philly so she could start teaching in the psych department at UIC. Soon, there were days when he wouldn't get out of bed, days when she had late classes but would be up at six and by the time she left the house at two she would have finished grading an entire section's worth of papers and he would still be sleeping. There were the evenings when she would come home late and find that he had eaten toast for dinner and watched six episodes of *Breaking Bad*, and she would curl against him on the couch and he would say things about how he felt hopeless—*existentially hopeless* was a real, actual phrase that her real, live partner had legitimately used—and she would make gentle suggestions that he call an old colleague or one of his friends from grad school. And then, of course, came his excuses: Steve Gibbons lived in L.A. now; Mike Zimmerman had never really liked him; he hadn't turned on his computer in two months.

Eventually she'd stopped suggesting. At some point she'd started coming home and making herself toast for dinner and joining him on the couch. Yet frequently, repeatedly, she found herself seized with the desire to take him by his bony shoulders and tell him to snap out of it. *Stop sleeping so much,* she wanted to say. *Start sleeping a normal amount like a normal person and wake up at a normal time and go make something happen.* It wasn't the lethargy of his depression that she didn't understand: it was her instinct, most days, to sleep through her alarm as well. She loved their bed more than she loved just about any other place in the world. Left to her own devices, without the outside pressures of a mortgage and a classroom full of entitled undergraduate people, she would have stayed in bed all day many days. She would cave, indulgently, to the cloying siren call of instant Netflix and take-out crispy rolls from Penny's and the sweet satisfaction of ignoring her phone every time it rang. That part she got, because she knew what it was like to be tired.

The part that bothered her was his lack of desire to *make* anything of himself. She was bothered by his potential, sitting latent but resoundingly reinforced by a number of intelligent professionals as being a rare and promising thing. She was bothered by his excuses, by his carelessness, by his inability to see in himself what she saw in him.

"You're so smart," she said to him one night, when she insisted that they make a real dinner and eat at the table. "You're brilliant, and there are a thousand things you can do that other people can't. Don't you see that?"

"It's not about being smart," he said. "It's about knowing the right people."

"You *do* know the right people."

"You don't get it," he said. "I'm not trying to be a dick, but you don't."

Sometimes he did things during the day that were nice. He was a meticulous laundry folder. Occasionally, he washed the cars and vacuumed the interiors. He changed lightbulbs and talked to his parents on the phone so she wouldn't have to. She tried to be effusive with her gratitude for these things, kissing his neck and purring that she never would have remembered to get the oil changed, which was *true* but not, she thought, necessarily worthy of any flowery thanks. Mostly, though, when she came home he was watching TV or sitting stagnant before his laptop and it would take her several intensive seconds of cognitive restructuring before she could even say hello to him. Because his salary had helped them buy their house but it was her salary, alone, that was paying for it. Because one of the disgusting grad assistants had made a pass at her and there was nothing she could do given that he was the protégé of the department chair. Because she just wanted to come home and have a glass of wine and talk to someone about these things, but her someone was deeply embedded in a season of *Dexter* and wearing the same gray sweatpants that he had been wearing since December and he didn't want to hear about the pedestrian struggles of functional people because his trials were far direr.

She couldn't explain this to her parents and she couldn't explain it to herself. She couldn't explain how much it hurt— *physically* made her bones ache—when she went to kiss him and he turned his face away and muttered *not a good time*.

Or tonight, when she'd been offered a tenure-track position— at *thirty-two*—and come home with her face almost cracked in half from smiling, bearing ice cream sandwiches from Mumbles and a sixty-eight-dollar bottle of pinot noir (champagne gave her a headache), all the windows on the first floor shut though it was a gorgeous spring evening, to find him pajama-clad and catatonic on the couch. She couldn't begin to explain what it felt like when he looked up at her and could tell she had exciting news and started crying.

"Shit, I'm sorry," he said, now additionally racked with guilt. He leaned into her because she'd gone to him, startled by the bleak lighting and the stale air and how *off* things felt in their home. She'd dropped the ice cream sandwiches in the foyer and set the wine next to them and thrown her raincoat on top of her little celebration to avoid making him feel even worse. She had wrapped her arms around him as tightly as she could and he buried his face in her breasts and wept like she had never seen an adult man cry until she met him. "I'm ruining this, Lize; I'm so sorry," he said, and she rocked him back and forth, now crying a little bit herself despite her near-delirious happiness moments earlier.

"Of course you're not," she murmured, kissing his hair—and she was reminded, horrifyingly, in that moment, of soothing Gracie once after she had tumbled backward out of their Radio Flyer when they were having races up and down the jagged slate sidewalks in front of the house on Fair Oaks. "You're the reason I'm here, love," she murmured, and then she began to worry that he would misinterpret it, think that she meant *You're the reason I'm stuck here;* which surely she didn't, probably. "You could never ruin anything," she added, and knew immediately that this was wrong too, because he might take it to mean *You could never be capable of ruining anything because you're completely insignificant.*

He proceeded, once he'd calmed down, to speak to her in a meandering, disinterested monotone, about how terrible he was feeling, and how it sucked because he had no idea why, but he had a suspicion that his pitch to LemonGraphics wasn't going to be well received and so maybe that was it; he didn't know. Once, early on in their relationship, he had looked at her desperately and asked her, *How can we make this stop happening?* And it had broken her heart because he had been so hopeful that she had an answer, some sort of solution buried in her bullshit grad school textbooks (which described depression as "a condition lasting for two weeks or more in which people experience a depressed mood or a loss of interest in their usual activities"; which said absolutely nothing about thirty-three-year-old men sitting catatonic in their boxer briefs, talking to their girlfriends about how they'd had dreams since age eleven of sitting in the garage with the car turned on because it *seemed like the most humane way to go*). She'd hugged him then, too, at a loss for what to say, and finally murmured something about *getting through it together*, and he'd looked so disappointed, so crushed by her failure to fix things. He had not since then asked her how to make it stop.

Now she whispered "I love you" into the top of his head, and then she just kept saying that, because it left very little room for misinterpretation. They sat for over an hour like that until she desperately had to pee.

"I'm going to go to bed," he said when she got up. "I'm so tired. I'm really sorry, Lize." He was looking at her searchingly, and she knew she had to say something but all she could feel in that moment was *resentment*, because she'd actually had to pee since noon, since her meeting with the dean, which had been followed immediately by a meeting with her department head and then by an ill-planned sit-down with a student in her 324 class who was overwhelmed and overworked and possibly abusing Adderall, judging by the twitch in his left eye. It was now 8:25 p.m. and she was at imminent risk of pissing her dean-meeting cashmere pencil skirt, but she had to stop and take Ryan's head in her hands and kiss his salty wet face.

"Don't be sorry," she said. "It's okay. It's going to be okay."

His face darkened again; his eyes filled. "Fuck. I hate that I'm doing this to you."

"It's okay, love. It's going to be fine." Her declarations became less eloquent as she focused on the agonizing pressure of the thirty-eight gallons of urine trying to escape from her body.

"I just don't know if I . . ."

"Ryan, *please*. I've had to pee for, like, eight hours." She hadn't meant to be so harsh. He looked immediately wounded and she hated him then, for just a second.

She started away from him in an awkward gallop. "Sweetheart, I love you, it's fine; just give me ten seconds, okay?" She dashed off to the bathroom and just as she was releasing a joyful, racehorse-caliber, orgasmically gratifying stream of pee, he appeared in the doorway. He looked like a baby, like a sleepy, agonized toddler, and she felt any annoyance melt away.

He leaned down and kissed her head. "I have to go to bed."

She finished and stood up, not bothering to wash her hands lest he slip away from her in those few seconds. "Good, sweetheart. I'll be up soon." She reached for his wrist and pulled him to her once more. "Get a good night's sleep," she said, rivaling her mother, the parent of four recalcitrant kindergarten dodgers, for most placating send-off ever. He shuffled upstairs and she waited until she heard the squeak of their bed frame to retrieve her mess from the front hall. The ice cream sandwiches, delightful monstrosities the size of human faces, had melted beneath her raincoat in a disgusting, sticky pile, and the liquid had pooled around the bottle of wine so that when she lifted it there remained a coagulated white ring around a stark circle of hardwood.

She came down the next morning to find him making breakfast.

"To celebrate," he said, turning to her, a smile arranged dubiously on his face. "I'm really proud of you, Lize. Congratulations."

Her eyes filled unexpectedly. She came up behind him and wrapped her arms around him. He turned in her embrace, and she cupped his face in her hands, able, suddenly, to see a glimmer of something she recognized.

It was less outright desire than a kind of willed optimism, a possibly pathetic longing for what they didn't have anymore, for the ability to be the kind of couple who easily celebrated each other's achievements over blueberry pancakes. She couldn't remember the last time they'd had sex, for she had not been aware, whenever it was, that they were headed somewhere so dark.

"I'm wet," she said, and Ryan said, "Why?" and she said, "I don't know *why*," and they made love against the kitchen counter with an ease and urgency of better times.

She would try, ardently, not to associate the baby with the day it was conceived.

Wendy had left her numerous voicemails after their failed lunch, but Violet waited three days before calling her back. Wyatt was at preschool and Eli was napping and she paced around her first floor as she mustered the confidence to dial the number. Matt had discouraged it over his Grape-Nuts that morning, telling her that Wendy was unfairly fucking with her and that she needn't engage. And her husband was right, but that didn't change the fact of the boy. Matt had left without kissing her goodbye. She pressed her fingers into the soil of the pygmy date palm. She'd printed up a watering schedule for the housekeeper, but she had suspicions about Malgorzata's English literacy and she was afraid that chastisement would be politically incorrect. She went to fill the watering can, aware that she was procrastinating. There was a chance, of course, that the boy wasn't who she thought he was, but the messages Wendy had been leaving suggested otherwise, as did that feeling in her gut.

She paused midway to the kitchen and dialed Wendy's number before she could stop herself. *Get it over with*, as though calling her sister were the final act rather than the very beginning of what she suspected would be a long sequence of events.

"Am I hallucinating?" Wendy asked.

She bristled. "*You* actually don't get to make jokes," she said to her sister.

"I've called you eighty times. I was starting to think you'd finally transubstantiated."

Violet reminded herself that she had a law degree. That she'd once talked a major airline into shelling out seven figures over a case of rancid in-flight OJ. "You had no right," she said. "You had absolutely no right to put me in that position."

"Did you listen to my messages? I *know* that, Viol, Jesus. I misread the situation."

"Are you fucking kidding me?" Her voice hit the vaulted ceiling of the sunroom and bled down the walls. They weren't a yelling household. She didn't often get upset. It was embarrassing to hear her own hostility. "Wendy, that was— You know how hard that— The universe in which it's even remotely okay that you—" She pressed her forehead against the window glass, looked into the yard, at the custom cedar tree house that had convinced them to buy the main house in the first place. She resented this conversation encroaching upon the fine-tuned landscape of her life. She resented all the ways it would inevitably encroach beyond this afternoon. "Tell me how you found him," she said.

"It's kind of a long story," Wendy said.

"No shit it is."

"I got curious," Wendy said. "A while ago. And I—did a little digging."

"How long is a *while*?"

"Not important."

"I get to decide what's important and what isn't."

"It was a one-off thing, Violet, okay? Christ. I talked to his foster mother once. Ages ago. I never expected to hear from her again. But she called me a few weeks ago, and— God, Viol, if you think *I'm* flaky; this woman's like fucking Joan Baez. And she had this whole thing about how she felt like my calling her in the first place was a *harbinger of change*, and I—"

She quickly lost her ability to follow the narrative thread.

"Wait, what do you mean—it was a closed adoption; what do you mean *foster* mother, Wendy, that doesn't make any sense."

"I told you it was a long story." Wendy's voice softened, sounded suddenly to contain an amount of compassion similar to that of a normal person.

Violet sank onto the chaise by the window and closed her eyes. "What happened?"

"The adoptive parents—died. Car crash. Total freak thing."

There was a feeling she experienced when her sons were sick, an internal weakening, sympathetic infirmity. When Wyatt used to cry before preschool, she would too; she felt Eli's encroaching teeth pressing painfully against her own gums. The feeling originated from a hot mass behind her heart, and she felt the spot pulsing now, thinking of the boy—she still hadn't asked his name—loving other people, people who loved him back and then one day failed to come home. "How old was he when it happened?"

"Four."

"Christ. So he's been—"

"Foster care. Repeatedly. And then a residential place. Lathrop House? Remember there was that kid when we were in grade school who lived there and it used to make Mom so sad?"

Unable to speak, she nodded. *Four.*

"That's where he met Hanna," Wendy said. "Mother Earth. The space cadet. She took him in. They actually only live about half a mile from Mom and Dad."

"Fuck."

"I know; how weird is that? Anyway, he— According to Hanna, it was all just a big bureaucratic clusterfuck. Under normal circumstances he would've been adopted by another family in a flash, but he just—wasn't. Fell through the cracks. He was in a bunch of short-term placements—you know, those, like, child-collecting people who do it for the stipend?—but nothing terrible, Hanna said. She said he's been *lucky*, relatively, and I don't even want to think about what the fuck that means. Then he ended up at Lathrop House, and he and Hanna hit it off, and he's been with them for about six months. Hanna says he's so quiet it's easy to forget he's around, which is pretty much true, from what I can tell."

"Jesus Christ." She tried to picture Wyatt being ferried through the system like that, tried to envision either of her kids experiencing anywhere near that kind of instability. *This is going to open doors you don't want opened, Violet,* Matt had said to her this morning.

"It's shitty, but he seems like a nice kid," Wendy said. "Strangely well adjusted."

"What's his—"

"His name!" Her sister laughed, an organic startling laugh. "Shit, sorry. Jonah. Bendt, unfortunately; like, cool, why not just cement the kid's fate as a pipefitter?"

Jonah. She felt the syllables with her lips. Not the name she would've chosen, but she hadn't allowed herself to entertain the thought at the time, so no name would've been. She tried to fit the name to the face in profile she'd seen at the restaurant, to the ethereal mass she saw on the only ultrasound she ever allowed herself to look at.

This wasn't supposed to be happening. There was not a single element of this that was supposed to appear again in the life she'd worked so hard to build; not a single molecule of this road not taken—though of course she thought of him, sometimes, weekly at least—was ever supposed to find its way back to her, especially now, when her husband had made partner and she had made continual strides among Evanston's social elite, when one of her boys was school age and the other was heading there fast.

"Listen, Viol," Wendy said, "there's—kind of a situation."

"So you said," Violet murmured, feeling spacey and discarnate. "You being a harbinger of change and all."

"That's me," Wendy said, but her voice got serious. Eli appeared on the landing of the stairs, squinty with sleep, clutching his stuffed platypus. She waved him over and he crawled into her lap. "It's this—South America thing," Wendy continued, because of course there was a *South America thing*, because of course there was no such thing as normalcy when it came to her sister, because of course she wasn't entitled to a post-naptime snuggle with her baby boy, not as long as Wendy was around to light fires and push her buttons.

She was stroking her son's back while she forced herself to listen to her sister—rhythmically, ritualistically, like children who comforted themselves by rocking.

1975

The Behavioral Sciences Building was a place where people got routinely, ludicrously lost. The floor plan looked like a genome; the exterior resembled something made from gingerbread; inside, students wandered, wide-eyed, blunted by the windowlessness, looking for classrooms, for bathrooms. All these people getting turned around, dizzied by the double helix of the staircases, yet Marilyn Connolly had just begun to find herself. It was her second semester as a commuter student at the UIC Circle Campus, and though she returned each evening to the house on Fair Oaks, where she lived quietly with her widowed father, during the day she was free to do as she wished.

She quickly mastered the layout of BSB, and there was a particular set of stairs she liked, one that led to a locked classroom between the second and third floors, cold to the touch even beneath layers of clothing, murder on the back, acoustically risky. She was outspoken in her classes, valued and deferred to in a way that she'd never before experienced. Her professors laughed at her jokes; her classmates whispered to her confidentially during lectures. She became, suddenly, very attractive to those around her, not for her ability to hold her head up in domestic crises when her father had had too much scotch or to iron his Oxford collars, but for her mind—and, in the dark corners of this hideous building, her body.

Which was how she ended up on those stairs. Men now looked at her like she was an adult, capable of anything, and it both scared and intrigued her. And she enjoyed the physical part—the deviancy, the feel of the concrete steps beneath her back, the pleasurable filling-in of space that happened with fellow English majors between her legs, their mouths on her neck, her breasts; stuffy Joyce devotee Dean McGillis taught her, somewhat unpleasantly, how to execute a blowjob. Perhaps it was a form of greed, or overcompensation: she'd been deprived for so long—her mother dead, her father broken and firmly opposed to her communing with the opposite sex—of love, of autonomy, of the electric pleasure of another person's hands on her body, and it seemed only fair that she take advantage of the host of willing undergraduates at her disposal.

An unexpected complication showed up one day in March, a bespectacled complication in a raincoat who entered the building when she was hoping to catch one of the TAs from her Theories of Personality class. She knew only the handwriting of the teaching assistants from the feedback they provided on essays: there was Barely Legible Blue Ballpoint, Left-Slanted #2 Pencil, and—her least favorite—High-Pressure Red Pen, whose comments sometimes tore through the paper. She studied the man. His posture was delicate and tense, almost apologetic despite his stature—over six feet, thin but broad-shouldered. She wondered which handwriting was his.

"Excuse me?" She rose from the stairs—a lower and more visible flight, serving, today, a chaste end—and he looked to her, startled. "Hi, are you— I'm—Marilyn Connolly?"

His face opened, a further softening around the eyes. "Hi there," he said.

"I hoped you'd have a minute to talk." She was suddenly

aware of how she'd dressed: a snug sweater with a deep-cut V-neck, suede A-line skirt, and—the clincher—her brown calf-skin go-go boots. But the man had his eyes fixed on her face; he had not once let them dip down toward her breasts. She couldn't decide whether to be flattered or offended by this.

"Would you rather sit out here?" she asked. "Or in your office?" Before he could reply, she continued: "One form of windowless ambience versus another, I suppose."

He smiled at her. "I'm wondering if you—" He paused. "Here's fine."

They sat beside each other—she saw him, finally, notice the exposed curve of her knee. His eyes were dark, almost black. There was a gentleness in the way his neck sloped down to his spine. She was surprised to feel nervous prickles of electricity across her scalp.

"Remind me of your name?" she said.

"I don't think I actually— David. David Sorenson."

"Dr. Sorenson?"

"Not quite yet. David's fine."

"David. Nice to meet you. I wanted to discuss my grade on the midterm paper." She held it out like a summons. "I realize that the mere mention of sexuality apparently makes all of the men in this department melt into puddles of shame, but *Sexual Behavior* was on the list of recommended texts for this assignment, was it not?" Before he could answer, she plowed on. "I didn't choose it provocatively, David. I'd like that to be clear. I chose it based on personal interest, which is what we were instructed to do. I'm an English major. I'm taking this class because I'm drawn to human dynamics. To psychological complexity. So you'll understand that I found the commentary on my paper—and the resulting grade—to be incredibly problematic."

"I—ah, I'm sorry to hear that."

"And I wonder if a male student would have been put under the same scrutiny."

"I couldn't say."

"I'm trying very hard in this class," she said. "I'm a straight-A student." Her biggest fear had been that she'd start crying during her speech. She was horrified to feel pressure behind her sinuses. She was, she *knew*, one of the smartest people in the class, and she felt like she was constantly working twice as hard to assure the people around her that this was even marginally true. A B in an elective class wouldn't be the end of the world. But it might interfere with her acceptance to certain PhD programs, might cause a roadblock on the path she'd been working so hard to lay out. She swallowed. "One of the comments actually contained the phrase *gratuitously indelicate*."

"That wasn't me."

"In any case. I feel like I'm being held to different standards, Doctor. I didn't deserve a B minus on this paper. It was well researched, even if you object to the nature of the texts referenced."

"I'm not a doctor," he reminded her, and she leaned away from him, incredulous.

"That's all you have to say?"

"This is—uncomfortable."

"You're damn right it is. Lord. You want to teach at the college level? I assure you, not everything is always going to fall into some pristine categorical norm where—"

"Not what I meant," David said.

"Oh, God, you're— Oh, if this turns into some convoluted sexual thing, I really can't—"

"I think you might have me mistaken for—someone else."

"What?"

"I—Marilyn, was it?—I'm not— I'm premed. An undergraduate. I came here to talk to my clinical psychiatry professor."

She felt suddenly cold, at once mortified and furious. "I beg your pardon?"

"I'm so sorry. I'm—incredibly sorry. I just— You seemed so upset and I—"

"You *what?*"

He shrugged. "I didn't want to interrupt."

She laughed theatrically—a single, pronounced *ha*. "How many opportunities did I just give you to tell me that I was embarrassing the hell out of myself? Wasting my time?"

"Not that many, actually. You were on kind of a roll." He shoved his hands in his pockets, and he met her eyes again. The kindness behind them annoyed her, the warm agendalessness. "And to be honest, I . . ." He trailed off, looked down.

"For someone who's so sensitive to interruption, you seem to have an oddly faulty grasp on finishing your own sentences."

"I liked listening to you talk," he said. He must have seen the indignant look on her face because he colored. "I didn't mean your voice. Though—I mean, your voice is nice too. I'm not being—you know, some sort of creep. I meant I like the way you structure your sentences. There's something musical about it. I've never really noticed that in another person before."

"Just when I think this conversation couldn't get any more bizarre."

"I really am sorry. And just for the record, I think it's ridiculous that you were docked points on a paper because you wrote about something potentially—erotic." With this, he colored even more deeply. "We'd all get B minuses in anatomy if held to those standards."

She lifted a hand to cover her mouth—she sensed a smile forming—and startled at the heat of her own skin. "Ah, good. I was just thinking the world needs more untoward doctors."

His face fell.

"I'm kidding," she said. "I think. I can't believe you just

allowed that to happen. You easily could have said no when I asked you to sit down with me."

"I don't know that I could have done so *easily*, necessarily." He looked down, then up at her quickly. "It's not every day that a beautiful woman asks me to sit with her." The line flowed from him, oddly, without sounding staged—without, in effect, sounding like *a line*—and this made her face heat up again. "But that's beside the point. I'm a charlatan. I'm sorry, Marilyn. Truly." He cleared his throat. "You don't happen to know where Dr. Bartlett's office is, do you?"

"Your guess is as good as mine," she said. "This building's a labyrinth."

There was no way she could find him charming—this earnestness, this aw-shucks passivity. No way that she was intrigued by this self-professed *charlatan*. She could see that he was older: not much older, but older enough; enough, perhaps, to value her as something more than a stimulated coed with a nefarious mastery of the most confusing building on campus.

"Guess I'll begin my quest," he said. "And again, Marilyn, I—I'm sorrier than I can say. I've never done anything like that before."

"Well, you might want to check and see if the CIA is recruiting, because you had me fooled." And now—damn it all to hell—now she was imagining tucking herself under the arm of his stupid charlatan raincoat and running away with him; now she was imagining herself being somewhere else, with him, or allowing him to *take* her somewhere else. "Here's the deal," she said. "You find this elusive *Dr. Bartlett* before sunset? And manage not to hoodwink some other poor unassuming woman?" Now her heart was in her throat, pulsing to attention. "You achieve that feat, and maybe I'll let you take me to dinner."

"I— Okay," he said. "Deal." He held out his hand to shake.

She could tell that this microscopic act of assertion was hard for him. She would come to find his prudence exquisitely charming, except when she didn't. There was no shock when she took his hand, no cinematic burst of static electricity, but there was a pleasant warmth, the gentle pressure of his fingers around hers. The lightning-quick pulse beneath the thin skin of his wrist; her hand fitting neatly into someone else's hand.

CHAPTER THREE

His mother was, at once, prettier and uglier than he'd been expecting. She had dark hair and big eyes, but she was also pale—almost grayish—and there was something about the pinch of her mouth that reminded him of his math teacher, Mrs. DelBanco, who always told him he wasn't trying hard enough. She didn't fit in their kitchen; the muted blue of her sweater clashed with the red paint over the stove. Hanna kept telling him he had an impressive eye for detail.

"Jonah's got wonderful artistic skill," Hanna said, reading his mind.

Violet Sorenson-Lowell. The name didn't feel right. He'd always thought she would have a more motherly name. Lisa or Cheryl or something. He read the school directory some nights while Hanna cooked dinner, paging through the lines of names, the kid first then usually two parents, *Tom and Beth Costner, Kurt and Carolyn Newberg.* Then an address, a house on a street named after a midwestern state—unless the family was rich, in which case the street was named after a variety of tree—and three phone numbers, home, work, and cell. Jonah was featured in this year's directory, but his last name— Bendt—didn't match Hanna and Terrence's, and they had only one number listed because both of his foster parents worked from home and shared an iPhone because Hanna, as she'd told him many times, was *resistant to technology*. He was staring at Violet's hands, the right twisting the bejeweled rings on the third finger of the left. Hanna wore a plain gold band; she'd told him about blood diamonds. He wondered if anyone had informed Violet but decided that they probably hadn't, since her necklace also bore a number of shiny stones.

"Why don't you tell Violet about that, J?" Hanna said. He looked to her, startled. She fit perfectly in the kitchen with her brown sweater and her messy crumpling of hair. She smiled at him. She was moving to South America.

"What?" he said. He looked to Violet.

"Your— Hanna was just telling me about your ceramics class."

"Oh, yeah," he said. "It's cool."

"Cool *how?*" Hanna asked, prodding him, nudging his foot with hers under the table. "Tell her about the Terra Fiesta exhibit."

"Oh, it's just." He stopped, shook his head once so his hair hung over his eyes. "Just this thing they do where they put your stuff on display and people can—like, buy it if they want."

"But tell Violet how they *choose* whose pieces get displayed," Hanna said.

"People vote," he said.

"The whole *school* votes," Hanna said, turning to Violet. "Thirty-eight hundred students vote, and some faculty, and the person with the highest number of votes gets their work displayed at one of the biggest galleries in town." It was actually the *only* gallery in town, but Hanna was good at making little things sound big.

"That's incredible," Violet said, and she seemed pretty again, brighter. "That's— God, that's huge. You must be— You should be so proud."

"One of his mugs sold for twenty-five dollars," Hanna said. He felt his face heating up.

"Amazing," Violet said. "That's wonderful. Do you have— I mean, I'd love to buy one."

Hanna looked slightly troubled by this. Jonah watched her face for cues.

"We have a number that we— Honey, is there one of our mugs you might want to give Violet?" She turned to Violet. "We're so lucky. He keeps us caffeinated. We'll never run out." *Until we move to Ecuador,* she did not say. He doubted his stupid mugs would make the cut. They were selling the house on Wisconsin Avenue and having a big garage sale for everything that wasn't what Hanna called an *absolute necessity.* "Why don't you pick one out, J?"

He shrugged, happy for an excuse to leave the table, and drifted to the cabinet where they kept the mugs. The red one was Terrence's favorite, and Hanna liked the purple one, the one he'd given her for Mother's Day. The rest were expendable, he guessed, but he was having trouble picturing Violet drinking from any of them. He chose a dark green one with a tiny chip on the rim and brought it over to her.

"Oh, wow." She took it from him as though it were radioactive. "Oh, I couldn't— This is so nice; let me at least give you— God, I must have— Here, please." She had pulled out her wallet and was pressing two twenties in his direction. He looked to Hanna for guidance. She was watching them with what looked like anguish. He eyed the money. This was clearly one of those moments—those *turning points,* as Hanna called them—where he was supposed to choose the right thing. But forty dollars was a lot to him, and Violet seemed pretty rich. Hanna would say those details were inconsequential. He reached over and took the money, pushing it into the pocket of his sweatshirt.

"Thanks," he said. He'd add it to the bank account that Terrence had opened for him, dubbing it his emergency fund. He liked it because it implied that everything in his life wasn't an emergency, that situations might arise where $326—now

$366—could be a gateway to something instead of a depressing reminder of his meager existence.

"Thank *you*," Violet said. He noticed that her hands were shaking; the light from the bulb in the ceiling fan glinted epileptically over the mug's glaze. "It's beautiful."

He couldn't look at Hanna. He went into another cabinet for the graham crackers.

"Why don't you tell us a little bit about yourself, Violet," Hanna said after a minute.

"Oh, me," Violet said. He faced her, tugging open a sleeve of crackers. "Well, there's not a *whole* lot to tell. I—I grew up around here. Not far at all, actually. Over on Fair Oaks and— Over on the north side." He wondered if she was afraid to say her address. Hanna told him that when he wore his hood up he gave off the wrong vibe. "I went to Wesleyan for my undergrad and I got my JD from the U of C." Hanna loathed people who spoke in acronyms.

"What does that mean?" he asked, loyally.

"I'm sorry," Violet said, flustered. "I got a law degree from the University of Chicago."

"Land of the overeducated and underaware," he said, quoting Hanna. He watched both Hanna and Violet turn red.

Violet laughed. "Ouch," she said.

"It's a great school," Hanna said, betraying him.

"You're a lawyer?" he asked.

Violet turned redder. "I mean, technically. I don't practice anymore."

He'd already asked her about her kids, about the little brown-haired kid he'd seen with her in a photo on Google Images. And there was another, she'd told him, Eli, who was two and in preschool and played T-ball already. He knew her husband was some hotshot lawyer and she was, a direct quote, *very active* in her sons' lives. For Jonah, this translated to *I am never taking in some fucked-up kid in a hooded Stewie Griffin sweatshirt*, but

Hanna still seemed hopeful. Lathrop House hadn't been so bad. Sometimes they gave the high school kids their own rooms.

"My parents are still in the area," Violet said, and he watched Hanna perk up. "My dad's retired and my mom—she owns the hardware store over on—"

"Mallory's?" Hanna said. "Oh, we love that place. Is she— She couldn't be the—the blonde with the apron, the one with the dogs on it, the—"

"They're Labradors," Violet said. "Yes. Yes, that's my mom. Listen, if you could—if you wouldn't mind— I haven't actually *told* her that— If you could just—"

Jonah watched Hanna deflate.

"Of course," she said.

"Just for now." Violet resumed twisting her rings. "And I've got three sisters."

"*Three,*" Hanna said. She called this phenomenon *overbreeding*.

"Catholics," Violet said apologetically. "I mean, not *Catholic* Catholics. Just run-of-the-mill, standard-issue, contraceptive-ignorant Catholics. None of the—you know, in*tole*rance."

"Yeah, I've heard fucking without condoms is totally hereditary."

It left his mouth before he had a chance to stop it. Hanna looked like she might cry. Violet did too, but it was harder to tell when people had brown eyes.

"Jonah," Hanna whispered. She didn't even bother to nudge him with her foot again. This was what she meant when she talked about self-sabotage, he guessed.

"No, it's—it's fine," Violet said. "Fair point. It's—absolutely fine. Listen, I— This has been— But I—I actually have to be going. You have my cell number. Call it—you know, whenever you'd like." She rose. Hanna looked at him helplessly.

"Cool," he said. "Thanks for the money."

Violet studied him, adjusting her purse on her shoulder. "It was so nice to meet you."

"You don't have to *leave*," Hanna said, rising too. He felt bad that she seemed so flustered. "He was just— We've got kind of a—an eclectic sense of humor around here, I guess."

"Oh, it's not that. I just have to go pick up the kids."

"I'll call you," Hanna said desperately, and Violet nodded.

"Sure, please. Anytime."

It seemed irreconcilably fucked up to him that he could be regarded as something to be "managed" simply because he'd been born to a mother who couldn't handle having a kid and adopted by people who would quickly get annihilated by a viaduct. He hadn't even known he was adopted until after she died, his mom with the soft red hair and the songs she sang at bedtime about being stuck inside with the Memphis blues. He hadn't asked for any of this, in short, and so his patience was limited, and he wasn't on board with what Violet Sorenson-Lowell had going on, with her pinchy face and her diamonds and her superiority.

"Honey, you should—say bye to Violet," Hanna said.

"Nice meeting you," he said. He felt her evaluating him. She'd forgotten her mug.

"You too," she said. "Really."

And he suspected, after the *really*, that they'd never see her again.

The kindest word Violet could find to describe Jonah's foster parents was *rough*. The mother, Hanna, was that aggressively crunchy kind of Oak Parker where you couldn't tell if unkempt was a tepid political statement or an inevitable way of life. Terrence—who'd emerged, wearing a Matisyahu T-shirt, from a room off of the kitchen—stuck around only long enough to introduce himself and press his hands together in a yogic *what up*. Their house was small and cramped; the people next door had a pit bull chained to a tree in front. She was mere blocks from the fabled, elm-lined streets of her upbringing and yet she couldn't help but hold her purse closer to her body as she waited at the front door. Once inside, she was guided by Hanna into a small, musty kitchen, walls adorned with vaguely vaginal-looking art and splotches of food.

"I'm an artist," Hanna said when she saw Violet looking, and Violet nodded, stretched her face into a smile, hugged her rib cage. "Mixed media, usually, but I'm also interested in artisanal works from the third world."

"Well, who isn't," she said, joking, realizing only when the words had left her mouth that she sounded derisive. "I mean— my husband brought me back this beautiful Nepalese bracelet from a business trip and I couldn't get over the—you know. Intricacy."

"What kind of work brought him to Nepal?"

She kept adjusting her expectations of how hot it was possible for her face to get. "He's an attorney. Intellectual property. And he—well, he actually bought it in New York, but it was a—you know, fair trade. The proceeds . . . I'll have to ask him."

Hanna smiled and it relaxed her. She had been consistently calmed by the woman's phone voice; it was what had coaxed her here in the first place. *We need your help*, she'd said, and Violet had always been powerless before such abject vulnerability.

"Are you ready to meet him?" Hanna asked.

"Am I— Sure. Of course. Yes, please."

Hanna called out his name and Violet heard the dull thump of footsteps. It wasn't until Jonah appeared at the foot of the stairs that she realized she'd been holding her breath.

He was beautiful, in a word. His posture was bad but his eyes were wide and handsome, his hair a russet-coffee color that she knew many of the Shady Oaks moms tried to replicate at the salon. She'd refused to see him when he was born, refused to hold him, allowed Wendy to follow the doctor out of the room and make sure he was alive. Wendy had assured her that he was perfect, exceptionally good-looking for a new-born, not pickled and Margaret Thatchery like some babies. It should've been a seminal moment, seeing him like this, but all she felt was nausea. She rose from her seat and lifted her arms in an awkward approximation of a greeting, a plastic doll's attempt to appear human.

"Hi," she said, woozy. "Jonah, hi again. I'm happy we have a chance to—do this right."

He was beautiful, and then he opened his mouth. "You're skinnier than in the pictures."

Violet glanced uncertainly at Hanna. "Pictures?"

"I googled you. There's a bunch of pictures of you at, like, a preschool. Like, with a bunch of little kids dressed as policemen."

"Career Day," she breathed. Her flagship Shady Oaks event: they'd dressed the babies as adult professionals and raised a shitload of money for a new carpool lane.

"You're a lot skinnier now," he said again. He reminded her a little bit of Wendy, then: lovely to look at but annoying as all get-out.

"That was—" She paused to consider. "Oh. That was right after my son was born. So—yes, I suppose I am skinnier now." She turned to Hanna, hoping for some kind of mediation, but she was just standing there, hands pressed before her, watching them like a tennis match. Hadn't she prepped him? Hadn't she taught him not to comment on women's bodies? Hadn't she taught him to push back his shoulders in order to avoid scolio-sis? Was that a *penis* on his sweatshirt? "That's an interesting shirt," she said.

"It's from *Family Guy*," he said. "You've never seen *Family Guy*?"

"Guilty as charged." Her palms were sweating. She didn't know that was a thing that actually happened to people. Life was so disappointing. You could be reunited with your kid after fifteen years and still find yourself, two minutes in, talking about television.

"Well," Hanna said, finally stepping in. "Violet, would you like some pu-erh?"

"Some—what?"

Hanna was doing something with a big ceramic teapot.

"Oh, no. Thank you. I'm fine." She lowered herself back into her seat and Jonah and Hanna joined her across the table. Jonah hooked his feet between the rungs of Hanna's chair and the intimate familiarity of the act aroused a sick twinge in her gut.

It devolved from there. Hanna did most of the talking and Violet and Jonah both, it seemed, were content to let her. Then Hanna had encouraged him to give her one of his slipshod clay coffee mugs and Violet—she would never forgive herself—had done the worst possible thing in the moment, stammered like an idiot and fished around in her purse. He'd tried to give her a gift and she'd handed over forty bucks like some kind of emotionless Daddy Warbucks; *thanks for the pottery, relinquished progeny, now go buy yourself something nice.* The moment she did it she wished she could take it back. Not the money—she'd be happy to give him money, to give him everything in her wallet; the Danforths didn't seem to be doing especially well financially and research had told her that the monthly stipend paid to foster parents wouldn't even cover a quarter of Wyatt's guitar lessons for a month. It wasn't the money that she regretted but the gesture, the cold emptiness of it. She'd meant it to be nice—every so often when she was a kid her dad would give her a dollar or two for a crayon drawing that she "sold" from a "gallery" at the dining room table. But Jonah was fifteen. Too old to be patronized like that. She was the adult, the *mother,* and she was supposed to know how to be tender and gracious. Her own mother accepted every single one of their half-assed art projects like it was a Vermeer. She should have taken the mug and hugged him and demanded that Hanna fill it with pu-erh, stat. But she hadn't. She'd given him forty dollars, and shortly after that he'd made a terrible joke at her expense and she was certain that the two incidents were directly related. She rose to leave and Hanna followed her to the door, gripped her arm with a fierceness that felt kind of threatening.

"Violet, please don't— He's having a really hard time with our—because we're leaving. He's had so much transition already and he—"

"Why aren't you taking him with you?" Violet asked. They'd already discussed this on the phone, when she'd called Hanna to make initial contact.

Hanna paled. "We're just fostering," she said, like Jonah was a cocker spaniel.

"So why don't you adopt him? Is it about the money?" She felt like someone had taken over her body. "Because if it's about the money, I can—we could—"

Hanna looked briefly disgusted but composed herself. Violet hated her for it. "We never intended to adopt. If we were *staying* here that might be a different story but—I have to do what's best for my family."

"And I have to do what's best for mine," Violet said. She hadn't replied, on the phone, when Hanna had said that Jonah would do much better moving in with an individual family instead of going back to Lathrop House. She hadn't *entirely* dispelled the notion of she and Matt allowing the boy to live with them, though of course, in no uncertain terms, they couldn't. Because she wanted the chance to meet him. She wanted to see him, just once, and now she had. "I never said that I—"

"Tell me you'll at least think about it," Hanna said. "Please. He has so much potential but if he has to go back there he's going to— He's made such progress with us."

"I have two young children."

"Once you get to know him I know you'll love him."

"I already love him," she snapped. "I fucking gave birth to him."

She stilled, feeling the weight of everything she'd been trying to suppress flood into that hot space behind her heart, the space so long reserved for Eli and Wyatt, everything she'd been pretending to forget, the affection she'd felt when he'd been growing inside of her and the jagged-edged agony of losing him. This afternoon had made her aware of a brand-new failure, her failure to act and the fact that she hadn't been aware—shouldn't she have known?—that a person she'd brought into the world was struggling so much to exist in it. That there was something she could do to help him. Behind Hanna, he had appeared in the doorway. He stepped closer when he saw her see him and held something out to her.

"You forgot this," he said, refusing to meet her eyes.

She reached out, the flush in her cheeks matching the one spreading across Jonah's face, and took the cracked green mug.

CHAPTER FOUR

For Wendy, conversations with Violet were rare. They spoke at holidays, brief, wine-drunk, huddled exchanges on the back deck of the house on Fair Oaks when they were both fleeing the oversexed canoodling of their parents. So when her sister's name appeared on the face of her phone, Wendy immediately knew why. She knew Violet well enough—better than anyone, once—to anticipate her next move.

"I take it you met the Danforths." She tried to sound casual, an oracle; *I still know you so well, no matter how hard you try to pretend that I don't.*

"Don't let this suggest for a single second that I'm not furious with you, Wendy. But I— Jesus. You put this in motion and I can't just pretend that you didn't, even though I'd like to. You've put me in an impossible position and I— Look, this isn't—" Violet's voice broke. "He's going to go back to the group home unless someone— It doesn't seem fair that— But I *can't*, Wendy; Matt and I aren't in a position to . . ."

In her pause, she seemed to be acknowledging the vague untruth of this, that she and Matt had three extra bedrooms, that Matt probably billed over a thousand dollars an hour. But Wendy was well aware that having loads of money couldn't solve all of your problems. She lit a joint and leaned her head back, taking in the white expanse of the ceiling.

"I can't subject my kids to that kind of major upheaval, Wendy. And my hands are so full with them already."

Wendy could tell her sister had rehearsed this justification, perhaps even had it written on a sheet of paper in front of her. It didn't surprise her in the least that Violet, the picture-perfect narcissist, was refusing to let anything—even her own biological kid—get in the way of her magnificent life. She was surprised only that Violet had bothered to come up with an excuse.

"Hang on," Wendy said. "What did you think of him?"

"Well. I mean, he's fifteen. I'm not really sure what else to say."

"Acne-riddled? Ungainly? Assholic?"

Violet laughed feebly. "In a sense, yes."

"Don't you think he looks like you?"

She could practically hear Violet stiffen over the phone. "Could you not—say things like that? Please?" *Could you please stop stating the obvious:* a classic Violet ask.

"I just meant— I don't know. He's cute, don't you think? Objectively speaking."

"I don't *look* at teenage boys in that way, Wendy, so I couldn't say objectively whether or not he's *cute* because I'm not a sexual predator." Violet sighed. "But, I mean, sure. Yes. He's still, you know, *growing*, but he seems— He reminds me a little of Dad. Sure, he's cute."

"You're comfortable saying that Dad is cute but not your own kid?"

"He's not my—" Violet stopped. "Look, not that I wouldn't like to hash this out with you but it's actually an urgent situation and I'm— I haven't—"

"You haven't finished a sentence this entire conversation," she pointed out, and she heard Violet start to cry. "Oh, for fuck's sake, Viol. Okay. It's okay. It's going to be fine."

"You did this," Violet said. "I don't understand why you did this."

"I didn't *do* anything. It just happened." But of course she knew this wasn't true. "I could take him, if you wanted," she said, emboldened by the weed, propelled forward by a vague, niggling sense of injustice. For this poor kid with his boring pipefitter name. For all the cracks he'd fallen through. And for the fact that—well, this gave her an upper hand over Violet for once, didn't it? She dragged again, held her hit until her sister responded. And Violet, to her credit, did not laugh or say *what in the holy fuck* or hang up the phone.

"You'd do that?" Violet said, the tears in her voice now accompanied by a fond incredulity. "Wendy—really?"

At her sister's gratitude, Wendy felt unexpected tears spring to her own eyes. "Jesus fuck, you nutjob," she said, exhaling a pale cloud. "Of course I will."

When Violet said she had to speak with them privately, Marilyn's suspicions were activated, perhaps another pregnancy or some kind of marital trouble. She was wrong, though, so treacherously far off-base that she kicked herself for the next six months, ruing whatever alleged maternal radar she possessed for letting her down in such a terrible, critical way.

She'd made them tea and they were sitting on the sunporch in the back, she and David together on the loveseat and Violet across from them in the wicker armchair, her legs crossed so tightly that it was difficult to tell where one ended and the other began.

"This isn't—easy for me," Violet said, and it disturbed Marilyn to see her ever-composed daughter so uncomfortable. "But certain things have—surfaced, and I'm— Of course I thought you deserved to know, even though it's been—difficult."

"What is it, sweetie?" she asked, trying to sound gentle instead of terrified. David had his arm behind her over the back of the couch and he squeezed her shoulder.

"The year I was— Do you remember the year I spent—in Paris?"

"Of course we do," David said, bemused.

In times of uncertainty, Marilyn's mind tended to leap to more ludicrous realms of possibility, and she thought chillingly of the news story about the dead-eyed American girl in Italy who'd murdered her roommate. "Sweetheart, are you in some kind of—"

"I wasn't in Paris," Violet said, as though from a script. "I was here, and I was pregnant, and I had a baby and I gave him up."

Marilyn suppressed the hysterical impulse to laugh, despite the gravity of her daughter's angular face, because though Violet had always been the least *funny* of her children, of course this had to be some misguided attempt at a joke, a red herring, something unreasonably terrible that would soften the blow of whatever the real news was.

"What the hell are you talking about, Violet?" David asked, and the quiet severity of his voice snapped her back to attention.

"I moved in with Wendy," Violet said tonelessly. Her gaze was fixed on the floor. "Right after I graduated I moved in with Wendy and Miles in Hyde Park and I had the baby in January."

Marilyn remembered worrying about her daughter back then, abroad alone. Remembered a specific conversation during which she'd suggested coming to Paris for a visit. Remembered how Violet had demurred, saying she really needed the time to *find herself.* Now it all sounded so theatrically false that Marilyn struggled to reconcile how they had believed her.

But of course they had. Violet had never given them cause for concern. Wendy had been emotionally rickety since she was a toddler, and life had proceeded to pitch itself pitilessly at her anyway. Liza was blithely headstrong—a trait born, Marilyn worried, from her perpetual parking space in the dead-center of their family, where she was frequently sideswiped or rear-ended. And Grace was the baby; she still called them several times a week and asked them for advice and small infusions of money, had just last week had David walk her through changing her vacuum bag over the phone. Marilyn worried about those three, but she almost never worried about Violet. And this, she saw, was a huge oversight, a great disservice to her daughter.

"Why didn't you—" She startled at the sound of her own voice. "Why on *earth* would you— You could've *told* us, Violet, my *lord*. I don't even . . . This doesn't make *sense*."

"He was adopted. We were— Wendy and I were actually quite conscientious about it, given the circumstances. He was adopted by a good family, and for several years everything was fine until—well, they—were killed. In a car crash. I know this sounds ludicrous. But he's been in foster care since then. Living in Oak Park, actually. South side."

"My God, Violet," David said softly, rubbing his forehead.

"I know it's a mess," Violet said. "I know it sounds insane."

"I just don't understand why you didn't tell us," she said. "This doesn't make any sense."

"Saying that three hundred times isn't going to make you suddenly get it, Mom." Violet looked up at them, seeming surprised by herself. "I'm sorry. I don't know what to tell you. I have no good answers. I was really young and it was a really hard time for me. I'm not sure what else you want me to say."

Her two little babies, living under the same roof, executing this madcap strategy, all of it outside of her awareness. What had she even been doing that year? She'd bought the hardware store by then. Gracie was in grammar school. Life as usual, a little crazier than usual, perhaps, but nothing out of the ordinary. She was accustomed to craziness.

"Where is all of this coming from?" David asked. "How did you find him?"

Violet, again, failed to meet their eyes. "I didn't. Wendy did. She said it was—just a lark. Genealogical research."

"But how did she—"

"I don't know, okay?" Violet said. "I've had to force myself to stop thinking about that because now he's here and there's nothing I can do about it."

Wendy. Her eldest daughter was always bobbing around the epicenter of their familial drama.

"It's actually," Violet said, chewing the inside of her cheek. "It's a little more complicated."

"Oh, lord," she breathed. David took her hand.

"The foster parents are moving to Ecuador," Violet said, and Marilyn nearly laughed again. Crazy on top of crazy. "Normally he'd end up back at the group home—that's where he met Hanna, the foster mom; she volunteers there—but she's indicated to me that if there was another living situation in place, it would be advantageous—" Here her daughter began to cry, a display of emotion, finally, that seemed to match the scope of what she was telling them, and Marilyn felt her own eyes dampen. "As I understand it, it's a textbook systemic failure. He was in a series of foster homes, nothing awful, I guess, but nothing lasting, and then he— But he's a good kid, smart. And Hanna says he's made—just astronomical improvements since he came to live with them. There's a chance to keep that momentum if he transitions to another stable family environment. The thing is— Matt and I don't think— The boys, with the ages they are, we don't want to— It could be incredibly disruptive, developmentally, to suddenly have such a major change to our family structure."

"I'll say," David said.

Violet colored. "And so I had the idea that—"

"Of *course* we'll take him," Marilyn erupted, and she ignored the molten heat of David's gaze on her as she focused on their daughter, arranged her most convincing Resolute Mom face.

David would be horrified: imagining bearing the brunt of a new teenage life under their roof just as he'd finally disentangled himself from caring for patients and raising offspring. But of course it would be she who shouldered the burden, washed the boy's clothes, checked his homework, acted as his informal alarm clock. She who stayed awake worrying about his chemistry test, his collegiate prospects; who noticed when he started to outgrow his parka and dragged him to REI for something that covered his wrists. David would be disturbed by the presence of him—his papers cluttering the kitchen table; his shoes tracking mud into the designated mudroom; his youthful indiscretions commandeering the bathroom for hours at a time—but he would never fully experience parenting a teenage boy, just as he had never fully experienced parenting a teenage girl.

"Of course we will," he said from beside her, and everything shifted, fluidly, because of course he'd parented their girls, of course he was the reason that Wendy still spoke to them and Violet raised her kids to be kind to animals and Liza got through a PhD program and Gracie would always stop an elderly person to see if they needed help carrying their groceries. Her hand squeezed his three times, and his hand squeezed back thrice even harder, and they were agreeing to be parents again, during the most unbecoming part of parentage, after the infant sweetness and the toddler charm and the youthful epiphany, straight to the miserable adolescent sludge. Of course she and David would do that. Of course they would handle it together, as they always had, even if her tasks were more concrete and less pleasant.

Violet looked uncomfortable. "Oh, God, you guys, I— That's really nice of you but I—"

"We have the room," David said, running with it. "And we're— I'm free a lot of the time, Viol; I've got—you know, odds and ends." Her heart broke for this, for his *odds and ends*, which were not the official doctorly miscellany he made them out to be but projects that he imposed grudgingly upon himself. "But we can certainly *care* for him, in whatever ways he—"

"He's actually moving in with Wendy," Violet said.

David's grip loosened and then tightened again. "What do you mean," he said, "he's moving in with—"

"How can he move in with *Wendy*?" she interrupted, heart up near her tonsils.

"She's got the room," Violet said. "And the—you know, the time."

"Dad's retired," she said rudely, forgetting her husband's pride. "Dad was dusting the picture frames when I got home today."

"I was *not*," David said. "I was reinforcing the plaster behind the painting of the—"

"We have room *and* time. And we have considerably more experience than *Wendy*."

"Kid, hey," David whispered to her. She extracted her hand from his.

"Wendy's your first choice?" she said. "Over— For God's sake, Violet, I—I was home with you girls until Gracie started *kin*dergarten, I— You don't think that we're—"

"Just—courtesy," Violet said, her face blooming red. "Just because I thought you guys were—you know, done. Relaxing. Enjoying your—"

"I work full-time, you know," she said, muddling her own argument. Was it possible that she'd always been such a terrific failure of a mother? Was it possible that the bonds she'd always felt with her children had been in her imagination all along? That these luminous, freestanding girls in fact had no idea who she really was, saw her as a woman who lived her life ignorant of all of their misgivings?

"I thought it might be nice for him," Violet said. "To spend some time in the city."

"Well, River North's not exactly the *city*, is it?" David asked.

She felt a surging of love for him. "He'll not exactly be slumming it, will he, being taken by Wendy's driver from the nicest part of the city to one of the most comfortable suburbs in the tristate—"

"What he's saying is why not have him living where school is within walking distance? With people who have actually— people who know how—people who under*stand* that—"

"She offered," Violet said helplessly, and Marilyn felt a momentary empathy for her daughter; she had been known to cave to Wendy similarly, to the particular slant in her eldest's eyebrows, the specific downward bow of her mouth. "Mom, she's really— Anyone can *see* that Wendy hasn't been having the greatest time since . . . I think that if she had an extra person in her house she might start to look at the world differently." Violet set her lips in a firm line like David sometimes did. "I think we can all agree that children change our perspective on life."

And what a smug little trump card it was—*parent to parent* from the girl who'd once complained that her lack of Gap jeans was inhibiting her social progress, from the baby she'd carried around in a sling on her chest while helping Wendy learn to walk.

David forged ahead before Marilyn could emote. "Of course they do," he said. His hand again on her thigh. "You really think that this is what's best for him now?" David, so open and credulous and respectful. She could have killed him.

"Honestly, I have no idea," Violet said. "But she's willing and he's desperate and I—*I'm* desperate and I want to give her a chance, if she feels like this is something that she can—"

"Why don't we all calm down," David said. He followed with the question Marilyn should have asked first, the question that had been so far from her mind, pushed aside by her indignation: "Can you tell us what he's like?"

She hadn't even thought to ask what color his eyes were.

Maternal Blunder Number 429. She set the count back to zero at the start of each year.

"We failed them," Marilyn said. Violet had left and they were sitting together on the back stairs, splitting a bottle of wine and watching the sunset as Loomis was being taunted by a squirrel in one of the oak trees.

"We didn't—"

"All the things we've worried about, and this never would have even— *Lord*."

He put his arm around her, though he wasn't feeling particularly comforting at the moment. He had in his mind a nagging miniature memory of a conversation he'd had with Wendy at Violet's wedding. Nearly a decade ago, his daughter had mentioned *something* nonsensical, but of course he'd disregarded it, dismissed it out of hand. Because Wendy was unpredictable. Because she'd been drunk at the time, and grieving, and had seemed determined all day to overshadow Violet's joy. Because he'd never quite understood the ironclad bond between his two eldest girls—their Irish twins, the double helix—except that it was fueled by equal parts love and envy, and made them behave in unpredictable ways toward each other. He'd always assumed it was one of those mysteries of womanhood that he'd simply never be able to comprehend.

"I just don't understand it," she said. "How she— I mean, God, *why* she . . ."

It was nice, in a way, to have his wife's company in this bubble of ignorance, a space where he was so frequently alone.

"I guess the important thing is that he's safe and healthy," he said. "Despite—you know. And Violet—she'll be okay, right? She's always found her way."

"I think that might be part of the problem, though," she said. "It's not always such a good thing to be so resilient."

"Well, I don't—"

"God, we have a *grandchild* we've never *met*."

Loomis trotted over, as though to remind them that they also had a dog that they *had* met. Marilyn scratched his ears and David his hindquarters.

"Doesn't it feel like we should've known?" she said. "Like if we were doing what we were supposed to, we would've been *aware* of this somehow?"

"We *were* doing what we were supposed to," he said gently. "We were living our lives. Doing our jobs. Raising four children."

She was quiet for a long time. "Do you ever think that we didn't focus on them enough?" Her body was tense beneath his arm. "Were we focusing too hard on each other?"

"No," he said, disagreeing with both statements.

"What are we supposed to do with this?"

"I'm not sure," he said. "Just—keep on, I guess."

She smiled faintly. "You and your stubborn peasant stock."

"The girls have it too."

"Uh-huh." She let her head rest on his shoulder. "That's what I'm afraid of."

1976–1977

"Are you sure this is okay?" he asked.

Both of them half-naked under the ginkgo tree in her father's backyard: the house on Fair Oaks, mid-December, the leaves mostly shed but a few dangling due to a late first frost, creating shadows on the lawn that made David jump every time he noticed the movement in his peripheral vision. Their current activity was a scandal by his standards, if not by hers, but her bar would always be slightly higher.

"Would you relax," she said—her voice startling him anew—and the hand she spread across his chest was cold only at the fingertips. She worked her way to his nipple, kneading. She was tucked against his side. He could feel the movement of her smile against his arm. "Look who's worked himself into a *state*."

"Coyotes," he said.

"Yes, here we are"—her hand moved downward—"watching the death toll rise."

He still couldn't get over the fact that she was now a fixed part of his life. That when they were apart, he could close his eyes and conjure the smell of the crook of her neck, citrus shampoo spiked with a salty humanness. That he sometimes imagined the way he would describe their first meeting—*Yeah,*

I just found her on some stairs—jokingly, to future friends, to their future *children*? He was aware of the fact that his fantasies outpaced the normal course of events. They'd yet to sleep together. A shock, still, the warmth of her next to him.

"Calm *down*," she said. "For God's sake." There was a light on in the kitchen of her father's house, the pale bulb over the sink. She squirmed, easing her weight onto his left side, and produced a graying husk of milk thistle from behind her back.

"Woman of the wilderness." But in fact this part of her scared him: the part of her that seemed to derive a thrill from clandestine exhibitionism.

"He's not going to come out here," she said.

"Denying the possibility makes it all the more likely."

"Oh, this logician, all of the sudden." Her breath stirred the hair on his chest. "If you were really that scared, you'd be wearing a shirt."

"You're the one who took it off."

"The martyred saint." Then, more softly: "Hey. Come on." She took his hand and rolled onto her back. "Come keep me warm."

Being with Marilyn felt a little bit like standing in a rainstorm. But like it was with rainstorms—if you had nowhere to be, nobody to whom you had to present your dry form—it was not the least bit unpleasant. He wanted to disintegrate to the sound of her voice. He'd begun to see by then that with her you got a package deal, not only the woman herself but an entire caravan, boxcars full of her love and disdain and expectation. He would not understand the magnitude of this for another year or so—would never fully understand it, if he was being honest—but at that moment, beside her on the ground beneath the ginkgo tree, he had never wanted anything more. He moved tentatively over her, and she lifted her face to kiss him.

"Relax," she said. "You won't crush me."

He almost asked her *how can you be sure*, but he remembered, as he opened his mouth, that he knew how, and that to bring it up would only remind him of her experience, and her of his lack thereof. He eased his weight further. "Still fine?"

"Mm." She kissed him again, wrapped her legs around his thighs. "See? Isn't this nice?"

He was unsure of the next expected move—was he supposed to continue to undress himself? To undress *her*? Was this how it was going to happen, outdoors, under a tree? But she seemed unconcerned with making anything *happen*, anything beyond what they were currently doing, which he had to admit felt pretty great—the heat of her against his chest, the feline familiarity of her tongue, the vise grip of her legs, her hips bucking slightly against his. She guided his hand downward. She was wearing a skirt, and she wriggled her nylons to her ankles. Her underpants were damp, and then, beyond them, a surprising slickness.

"Am I—should I—" It seemed ludicrous that you weren't allowed to stop and ask questions. It had always been his biggest fear that when this moment finally arrived his instincts wouldn't take over—that he would just flop like a fish, show his hand of cards, activate the woman's maternal instinct so she'd walk him through it like a docent at a museum: *Feel this? This is the clitoris.* His face burned, and he was distracted, as ever, by his thoughts, by the thought that if he lost her he wouldn't know what to do with himself.

"Hey." She pressed his hand there, squeezed it once with her fingers, and then left it, like a child at kindergarten, to entertain itself. "You're doing great. My fate is in your hands." She pressed herself against his hand. "A little faster, if you don't mind."

He complied, and he felt her breathing begin to quicken. He opened his mouth to inquire about his progress, but decided to try to trust himself. She didn't seem uncomfortable. She seemed, frankly, ecstatic, head tilted back exposing her throat, eyes closed, a smile playing on her lips. He kissed her, still working, and she reached to squeeze his buttocks. She whimpered.

"Okay," she said, "okay, now you just— Good; I'm— Here, take off your—" She made quick work of his pants. "Here, roll over. I'll be on top."

He realized later that she was doing him a favor, that this position required the least blind navigation on his part. She straddled him, and when she'd gotten comfortable she smiled down at him for just a second, eyes glinting in the dark like a wolf's.

"Feel okay?" she asked him, and he nodded, and she lowered herself onto him—her weight no longer avian but muscular and confident. She kissed him: his chest, his neck.

Neither heard the telltale rusted *scree* of the back door. Neither, despite his earlier vigilance, clocked the footsteps down the worn wooden stairs, the crunch of the frosted grass.

"For cripes' *sake.*"

Marilyn yelped. She clung to David's chest, her legs pressing down on his crotch. "Stay calm, all right?" she whispered to David. Then: "Dad," she said. "This isn't—"

"I thought there was a goddamn animal out here. Oh for— Oh, if your mother could see you like this. Who the hell's there?"

"Hi, sir." He scrambled for his pants, pitied Marilyn for having to navigate her nylons. "It's David, sir." He rose slowly. "Sorenson, sir."

"He's not a *soldier,*" Marilyn said. "You don't have to talk to him like—"

"This is my goddamn house," Marilyn's father said, and as he lurched forward, David could see that he was drunk. Marilyn had mentioned, idly, that he'd begun to drink much more since her mother died, but he somehow hadn't been expecting this. "You think you can just have my daughter on my goddamn lawn like you're some kind of—"

"Daddy." Marilyn had forgone her nylons and was taking hold of her father's arm. "Daddy, everything's fine. We'll talk about this in the morning, all right?"

He was surprised that the man wasn't putting up more of a fight. Marilyn was guiding him back to the house. David heard him mutter something about *goddamn dago* but he was allowing Marilyn to lead him inside without protest.

"We'll talk in the morning," Marilyn repeated, louder this time, apparently for David's benefit, and she jerked her neck once in his direction, urging him down the path around the side of the house.

He was preoccupied, on the drive home to his father's house in Albany Park, not with the fact that he'd just had sex for the first time, and not with the fact that—sex or no—he was reasonably certain he was in love with the woman who'd just taken his virginity, and not, even, with the fact that his girlfriend's father had just erroneously identified him as Italian, but with the look on Marilyn's face as she'd led the man inside. With the strange note in her voice when she'd whispered to him—*stay calm*, just slightly off-key. Not a voice he recognized, nothing of the devil-may-care amusement with which he usually saw her move through the world. And he realized, then, how silly it seemed that you could ever know another person—really know her—and how silly it was to think that he had any idea what it was like to be her, day after day after day.

He was accepted to medical school, conveniently, on a Friday when her father was out of town for the weekend. In her living room, in the house on Fair Oaks, he'd relayed his news—he'd gotten into the University of Iowa; he would be moving to Iowa City—and Marilyn had pushed all dark thoughts of separation from her head and gone immediately to her father's liquor stash to find a room-temperature bottle of Veuve.

David was moving. Not far away, but far enough away that she would no longer have a person in her immediate vicinity who felt like home. On their first date, they'd swapped origin stories: his mother lost to lymphoma when he was five, hers to liver failure when she was fifteen.

"It's a strange feeling to have as a kid, like you're responsible for your parents' happiness," she'd said to him, surprising herself with how frankly she was able to describe the way it felt to be the daughter of her parents. He'd been an attentive audience. "Not that you're the *cause* of it, but instead that there's some obligation on your part to ensure it. I didn't really realize until recently that that wasn't normal."

"Well, who's to say what *is* normal, I guess," David had said, and he'd shrugged.

"Look at the two of us," she'd said, and they'd both glowed at the phrase, *the two of us,* "carrying around all of this emotional baggage." And then, before she kissed him for the first time: "This is the most depressing date I've ever been on, David."

Two motherless children; two young, fumbling people who'd somehow happened upon each other, and until he announced his impending move to Iowa, she'd felt safer than she ever had, sharing a little space on the earth with a person who felt like a necessary element of her being. By the time she returned to him in the living room she was on the verge of tears.

"I'm so proud of you," she said, and immediately started weeping.

He pulled her close to him, stroked at her hair. "All right," he murmured. "Hey."

"I'm so happy," she said, and they both laughed.

"I thought I'd see," he said, "if you wanted to join me."

She moved back from him, appraising.

He rose from the couch and went to where he'd draped his jacket over the rocking chair. He removed a small box from one of the pockets and then he sat down beside her. "So I," he said, and then he took a breath. "I'm nervous."

Unable to speak, she touched his arm.

"I love you," he said. "I hope you know that. I know it's not my—my strong suit. Telling you that. But I'm trying." He shifted to face her, suddenly emboldened. "I think we make each other happy. Not always the same amount, and not always at the same time, but I . . ."

"We do."

"That's what I thought." A smile had found its way onto his face. "Good. That's what I was thinking. So I got you this." He handed her the box. "If you'll have it."

She opened it tentatively and then looked up at him.

"What do you say? Marry me?"

She kissed him, leaned in and kissed his mouth and the vulnerable curve of his left cheekbone and the asymmetrical slope of his right cheekbone, and then she passed the box back to him and offered him her hand.

PART
TWO

SUMMER

CHAPTER FIVE

He'd come with a heartbreakingly meager amount of possessions, a garbage bag of clothes and a dirty JanSport and a Vera Bradley duffel—a castoff from his foster mother, Wendy guessed—which rattled when she carried it to the guest room; she entertained the possibility that it was full of artillery but then reminded herself that he was fifteen and his luggage most likely contained electronics, comic books, and porn. He didn't look anything like the baby she remembered from that dark day over fifteen years ago—a blessing indeed, because the baby she remembered, despite whatever platitudes she'd soothed Violet with at the time, had looked like a cross between Dick Cheney and Gollum. But now, he looked like Violet. The resemblance was undeniable, especially with the two of them standing uncomfortably side by side in her foyer.

"We meet again," she said, holding out her hand to Jonah. He'd been politely quiet the day she'd taken him to meet Violet at the restaurant. Idle chatter about social studies and martial arts. Now she felt her scalp prickling to attention. *I was the first person to hold you,* she thought. *I saw you get born and I sang you a lullaby version of "Shoop" because it's all that I could think of and I counted your toes because your mom couldn't.* This kid would never have any idea how much he'd incited, how much he'd done to them simply by being.

He reached out and shook, a good handshake, a man's handshake. She liked kids this age; they amused her and they were likely to be intimidated by her in ways that adults generally weren't. He was handsome and peevish and awkward and he made her heart ache, both because he was so instantly familiar and because she remembered how much it sucked to be fifteen.

"We should be all squared away," Violet said, like she was dropping off a flower arrangement. "Unless there's— Jonah, is there anything you need?"

He looked up at her like *how the fuck should I know* and Wendy felt a momentary pleasure that he seemed to treat Violet less kindly than he did her.

"The guest room's all ready," she said, addressing Jonah more than Violet. "There's an attached bath. You should have everything you need, at least bare-bones." She'd bought little French goat's milk soaps shaped like anchors for his bathroom. *Bare-bones* was perhaps an overstatement, particularly given his history.

"Thanks," Jonah said.

"Well, I should be going," Violet said. They both stared at her and she twisted her hands together, looking back and forth between them. Wendy enjoyed, as ever, watching her squirm. "As long as there's nothing else you need, Jonah," she said. "I'll—see you, I guess."

Jonah was silent, blinking at her.

"How about if you guys have dinner?" Wendy asked. It spilled from her like vomit. Yes, she had volunteered to take the kid in. Yes, she was happy to have him. But she didn't feel like Violet should be let off the hook *quite* so easily, sweeping in and out with the ease of a summer storm. She didn't feel like she should once again be solely responsible for the fallout of her sister's whims.

Violet looked positively murderous, eyes aglow, teeth clenched so tightly that the hinges of her jaw bulged. "I'm not sure that we—"

"I actually have something coming up," Wendy said. "I'll text you when I pin down the exact date. How about if Jonah comes to your house that night?" She turned to him. "Just so you don't have to spend the evening alone in a strange house right off the bat."

"I have no way of knowing if we'll be free on whatever night it is," Violet said, unsurprisingly trying to cancel the plans before they'd even been made.

"It's important to me. Old friend of Miles's who's going to be in town. One night only." A lie, but Violet always acquiesced when she played the dead-husband card.

Violet breathed out slowly. "Fine, then, I guess. Sure."

"Great." She nudged Jonah. "Wait'll you see the tree house."

"I should go," Violet said. She waved with both hands, like some kind of weird children's show performer. Wendy waited for thanks that Violet declined to provide.

"Bye," said Jonah. As if to make a point, he wandered into the living room.

"Happy trails," said Wendy. But when she watched Violet walk out her front door, she felt a nauseated catch in her throat, fought the urge to leap into the hall and yank her back inside. Instead she took a breath, latched the deadbolt and turned to face Jonah, who was seated rigidly on her couch.

"Make yourself at home," she said ineffectually, and he blinked a few times and rested one of his elbows on the armrest. "Perfect," she said. "It's like you've lived here all your life."

That got a little bit of a smile from him and she buzzed with pleasure.

"You're rich, huh?" he said, pulling nervously at the piping on the couch.

She came to sit across from him. "What makes you say that?"

Though of course it was obvious; she'd chosen the blandest and most cookie-cutter modern construction when she moved from her and Miles's house, a massive glassy expanse, clean white lines and cool gray accents. She found the boring sterility of it soothing.

"Isn't that a first-edition Lord of the Rings?" He nodded to the bookshelf by the window.

"Astute observation. You're a nerd, then? It's my husband's."

"So he's rich," Jonah said.

"He was rich, yes." Her throat felt suddenly dry. "Now he's dead."

Only a second's pause before he replied: "So you're rich."

"I'm comfortable."

"Violet's rich too."

"Yes, turns out marrying Honey Bunches of Snores was quite a lucrative decision."

Jonah watched her.

"Her husband's rich too," she clarified.

"Are your parents rich?" he asked.

"What is this fixation?"

"Are they nice?"

She paused, considering. "They have their moments," she said, but she felt bad and stood up, drifting over to the wine rack. "I mean, yes. They're nice. They're great. They'll love you." She pulled out a bottle, studying the label. When she turned back to him, Jonah was watching her again. "What?"

"How do you know?"

She rifled through the drawer for a corkscrew. "How do I know *what*?" Nobody had prepared her for how irritating it would be to converse with an adolescent.

"How do you know they'll love me?"

"They love everyone," she said.

"Nobody loves everyone," Jonah said.

"That," she said, yanking out the cork with an accusatory

pop, "is the goddamn truth." Jonah looked nervous so she tried to smile at him as she went to the cabinet for a glass. "I'm kidding. They'll love you because you're their grandson and they're sadistic child collectors who delight in seeing their own genealogical inklings on the faces of malleable offspring."

"*What?*"

She tried again. "They're very excited to meet you."

"Are you drinking wine *now?*"

She glanced at the clock. It was not even four, but she'd had a long day.

"My parents had us too early, and they had more of us than they should have had. But they're nice people with nice intentions. Don't you want to know anything about me? About your new house? About—Christ, I don't know. Anything?"

"How did your husband die?"

She swallowed painfully and the wine went down the wrong pipe and she coughed while Jonah stood by, alarmed. "I'm fine," she croaked, eyes watering. "Renal cancer. Way to bring down the mood." She watched him go pale. "I'm joking."

"Sorry."

"Don't be. Life is kind of shitty sometimes. If anyone knows that, it's you, right?"

"Me?" he asked.

"Joking again," she said, realizing her error. "Listen, should we— Want to order some takeout? Boys like food, don't they?"

It took everything she had to not bolt out the front door on her way to the kitchen.

Violet had, previously in her marriage, sensed the acute need for a babysitter, for a night out with her husband where they were both bathed and respectably dressed, where they could speak at conversational volumes without fear of waking sleeping children and where their conversation was unlikely to be interrupted by the bodily effluvia of others. Time alone with her husband was a pedestrian and universal need, understandable by any and all fellow parents if she'd deigned to share her hardship with the Shady Oaks moms.

But it had never felt quite like *this*. Both kids were sleeping through the night and Matt had just made partner and Violet had shed her final pounds of baby weight and everything had been going exceptionally, and if they got a babysitter and went out to dinner it should've been to bask rather than to save their marriage. Except now there was Jonah, and there wasn't a restaurant in the Chicagoland area fancy enough to assuage the effects of his arrival. Matt had known about the boy nearly since they'd met, of course, but he was as troubled as she by the announcement of his return, even if he'd sanctioned Jonah's move to Wendy's house.

She'd donned a brave face on the blacktop at school that morning—explaining why a sitter would be picking up Wyatt—and told the other moms not that she needed an emotional-support dinner with her husband after ferrying her relinquished teenage child to the opulent home of her trainwreck sister, but instead that she and Matt were celebrating their *meetiversary*, May the fifth, fourteen years ago, Logan Center for a lecture on the common man, which actually also happened to be the truth. She'd always insisted, somewhat cloyingly—and, again, with more ease, in better times—that they celebrate the day, even if just with champagne and cuddling once the kids were down. This year, overcompensating, she'd made a reservation at a breathtakingly expensive seafood place in Streeterville and, leaving her car parked in a garage not nearly as far as she would have liked from Wendy's building, walked south to Matt's office on Dearborn.

What were Jonah and Wendy doing now? She hoped not smoking weed or drinking Barolo. The boy had been so silent during their time together that afternoon. He'd given Hanna a hug goodbye and carried all of his stuff himself, dismissing Violet's offers of help. He had decidedly *not* embraced her when she left Wendy's. She hugged her jacket tighter against a nonexistent chill.

Matt's office was one of the few places that made her miss her professional life, populated by a bunch of no-nonsense corporate types, people who rarely stopped to make small talk. She sidestepped Carol, his receptionist—winking, putting a finger to her lips, exaggeratedly indicating Matt's office like she was going to perform some grand surprise—but she paused in his open doorway to watch him, hard at work, writing longhand, shoulders hunched up around his ears. That unbending concentration he had, that ability to power through even the most tedious of tasks. All for the sake of their life together, its steady, comfortable abundance. She'd been drawn to this drive in the first place, this willful blindness he had, all in the service of making their life work.

"Matty," she said, and he startled, dropped his pen. "Hey, stranger." This coquettishness was more for the benefit of Carol.

"What are you doing here, Viol? I thought you were taking—" He stopped.

"I made us dinner reservations," she said pointedly.

"For *tonight*? Sweetie, it's Cinco de Mayo, the pub crawlers are going to be out in droves."

She waited for it to dawn on him.

"Oh," he said. "I— Happy anniversary."

Behind her, she sensed Carol straighten subtly to attention. If a forgotten anniversary could elicit this level of intrigue, she couldn't begin to imagine what state of transcendental bliss a lovechild adoption scandal would send her into.

"Not our *wedding* anniversary," he said defensively. "Just the day we met."

"My husband, the romantic," she said, but only because Carol was there, and not because her feelings weren't hurt.

Matt was right about the pub-crawling, drunken Loyola undergraduates and distressed thirty-somethings with undoubtedly ill-gotten glow necklaces, but the restaurant they arrived at was painfully exclusive and out of the price range of the inebriated masses.

"How'd it go today?" he asked, somewhat stiffly, and she wilted a little, because she'd hoped—unreasonably—that they might be able to make it through dinner as they would've been able to a few months ago, with drowsy conversation about the kids, amusing tales about his colleagues, exchange of bullet points both had accrued about current events. Easy chatter, no-stakes chatter. Matt watched her. He'd seemed relieved, if a bit skeptical, when she shared that Wendy would be taking care of Jonah, that the discovery of her discarded child would not directly upset the landscape of their life.

She sipped desperately at her cocktail, something fruity and strong, the lip of the glass rimmed with fiery red powder. "Fine," she said. "Successful hostage transfer."

He raised his eyebrows at her, fairly: it was an off-color joke; she wasn't sure where it had come from.

"He seemed calm. Wendy was—Wendy. He had the most meager amount of *stuff*, Matty; it was so—like his entire life fit into a couple of bags. And when we left the Danforths' house—Hanna was crying, but Jonah was just—resigned. Like he'd done it a thousand times before. Which I guess he *has*. It just struck me how little I know about him."

"No kidding," Matt said archly. His tone jarred her.

"I don't mean that in like a *sinister* way," she said. "I just mean that he's had so many experiences that I can't even— I don't mean he's *dangerous* or anything."

"I'm not necessarily saying he's dangerous, Viol, but he's— I mean, he's a wild card. You know nothing about him."

"Hanna had nothing but good things to say."

"And yet weeks ago you discredited her as a flaky granola weirdo moving to Ecuador because the spirits moved her."

"Well, she *is*, but . . ." She cleared her throat, sipped her drink. "He's coming over for dinner sometime soon when Wendy has plans."

Matt froze, then closed his eyes and exhaled. "Violet."

"She just sprang it on me—Wendy did, and I couldn't . . ."

"You couldn't *what*?"

"She's— You don't understand how she—what it's like when she—"

"What? Manipulates the hell out of you?"

"She's taking him in, Matty. And I just felt *bad*, leaving him like that, like I was just dropping something at the dry cleaner's."

"But Wendy *is* the solution," he said, as though speaking to a small child. "You didn't want him to get shoved back into the system. But it's not fair to Eli and Wyatt to force a stranger into their lives in this way. Have you given any thought to that? It took Wyatt six months to adjust to a new *cereal* bowl; we can't just expect him to accept out of nowhere that he's got a new half brother. And what if things *don't* work out for him? What if this *isn't* a good fit and he has to find an alternative? What kind of impact will that have on our sons, springing a new family member on them and then having him disappear?"

"Kids adjust to new siblings all the time. I was about Wyatt's age when Liza was born."

"This isn't us having a new *baby*, Violet. How do you plan on explaining this to them?"

"Well, there may be some literature on—"

"On introducing your secret teenage child to your toddlers?" he said meanly. "Never mind the fact that it never occurred to you to *ask* me if I'd be okay with him meeting them."

"It's not as though we have all this time for conversation

lately," she said, a cheap shot. "Matt, this just happened. She just did this. I'm sorry if you feel out of the loop, but I just— This got dumped in my lap and I'm trying to deal with it the best I can and I don't have a chance to run every single thing by you before I do it."

"Wendy didn't just *do* it. You agreed to dinner."

"She put me on the spot."

"And you're putting *me* on the spot. It's not like you to make impulsive decisions like this." He cupped his hands around his tumbler, staring into it. He shook his head once, quickly. "I barely recognize you lately."

Instead of saying *me either*, she said—another sentence formed and uttered of its own accord: "There was always a chance of him reentering my life."

"This isn't about him reentering, Violet. That's already happened. This is about you making responsible decisions that won't completely bulldoze our family. You can't just play the *Wendy's Wendy* card whenever you decide to do something—"

"Something what?"

"We're your family now, Violet. The boys have to come first."

"They *do* come first."

"Until your sister opens her mouth, and then suddenly it's a free-for-all."

"It's one *dinner*, Matt."

"That's not how this works."

"What's *this*?"

"Anything involving this kid, Violet. Nothing's a one-off. Nothing can happen that doesn't affect everything else. We have *one dinner* and he becomes a part of our kids' lives, to some degree, and of course it's not just one dinner, Violet; he's living with your sister; he's meeting your parents; he— Are you really not visualizing the ripple effects? What it means that Wendy's taken him in?" The worst part was that Matt looked worried; his voice was angry but his face was full of a frank apprehension—not about the situation itself, she realized, but about her role in it. About *her.*

"There aren't any rules to follow here," she said quietly.

Matt softened, surprised her by taking her hand across the table. "Are you okay, Violet? Should I be worried about you? I'm not— I haven't seen you so adrift since—"

Her defenses rose quickly, popped up like springs, and she pulled her hand away. "Since *when*?" Challenging him to say it. Daring him to acknowledge what she'd known all along, that things hadn't been quite *normal* between them in years; that they weren't off-kilter as a couple solely because of Jonah's arrival.

Matt looked suddenly tired. "I'd just like for us to tread lightly with this, Violet. In the interest of our children. And— ourselves. Our family."

"I'm *trying*," she said.

They persisted like this, one of those eternal, infernal absurdist conversations, through their entrées, both of them eating quickly, eager to leave. But she'd forgotten that she'd mentioned to the hostess when she made the reservation— as leverage, for a table by the window overlooking the river, which she'd barely glanced at throughout the meal, so engaged was she in this frustrating marital tennis match—that it was an anniversary dinner.

"Compliments of the chef," the waitress said, setting a chocolate croissant the size of a fanny pack on the table between them. "Happy anniversary."

They both stared at it wistfully, a powdered-sugared visitor from a time before.

CHAPTER SIX

En route to her parents' house, Liza allowed herself to imagine an alternative reality, one perhaps occurring at this very moment in a parallel universe: college sweethearts, newly pregnant, showing up at the childhood home of the mother-to-be, some coy demonstration with balloons or sonograms, everyone delighted: laughter, sparkling cider, the works.

Instead she was gripping the steering wheel and staring through the windshield with the grim determination of someone headed to a parole hearing, Ryan quiet in the passenger seat with a bouquet of camellias wilting in his lap. He reached across the console and took her hand, forcing her to look over in his direction. He was smiling at her, a real smile, and she lifted the corners of her mouth in turn, not quite faking it, because the sight of him happy still lightened her. They'd had a few very good weeks after the test came back positive. She'd tried to think of something to say that sounded less binding than "I'm pregnant" and instead said, "I think I might be having a baby," to which Ryan had looked understandably confused, and she'd clarified that she *knew* rather than thought, and the *having* wouldn't be happening until the new year, and Ryan had hugged her with his whole body, like he used to, and kissed her with hunger and confidence, and told her he loved her, that of course it didn't matter that it hadn't been planned, that there had never been news this good in the history of the human race. And for a while he'd seemed to rally, as though the unexpected news were a potion she'd injected directly into his veins, and she began to wonder if it could possibly be this easy, if all it would take to get Ryan back to his old self was a big surprise, a little jolt, an ice pack to the amygdala. Liza had a postgraduate degree that assured her this was impossible, and yet she'd clung to the life raft for days, watching him out of the corner of her eye: the bounce in his step, the energy in his voice.

"You nervous?" he asked her now, and she shook her head.

"Why would I be?"

He was quiet, possibly wounded.

"I mean I'm *excited*," she said, squeezing his hand, approximating enthusiasm. "You going to be okay tonight, do you think?"

She often wondered if this was what it was like to have an alcoholic as a partner, or a Republican; she and Ryan had grown used to their routine, the psyching up during the car ride over, assurances that they wouldn't stay late. They even had a signal, like spies, where Ryan would massage his Adam's apple between his left thumb and forefinger, which meant *time to go*. Because he got tired, or paranoid, or started spacing out.

Of course now, after the post-baby-news honeymoon respite, everything was beginning to get bad again. But she couldn't impart this news to her parents without him; her powers of invention that got him out of family dinners were only so strong.

"I'll be fine," he said. "I'm fine."

"You'll let me know if you—"

"I said I'm fine."

Alternate-universe Ryan would never snap at her; alternate-universe Ryan would say, "The real question is how are *you* feeling, darling?" to his anxious pregnant girlfriend. They might be married, in the alternate universe, she considered, pulling into the driveway. She would definitely be less nauseated.

Her parents were sitting on the porch and the dog came running down the front steps and her mother called after him, halfheartedly, "Loomis, stay up here." Liza bent to pet him. In the alternate universe, as well, this news wouldn't be competing with that of her sister's secret adoption scandal—not a new baby but a teenage boy who'd wriggled out of the woodwork.

"Can you believe this gorgeous evening?" her mother said, rising to hug them both.

"Your mother's officially entered porch mode," her dad said. "She won't set foot indoors again until October."

Liza clung to him when he hugged her, for just an extra desperate second, hoping both that he would notice and that he wouldn't.

"Wendy enrolled us in a *wine of the month club*," Marilyn said. "This month is something white. I know nothing about it beyond the fact that it was dropped on the doorstep this morning like a bomb and probably cost more than our gas bill. Can I interest you?"

Liza paused too long, then said, "Actually," and her voice cracked on the *ack-*, and this wasn't how she'd meant to do it at all, but she'd drawn attention to herself, and she felt blood rush to her face and tears to her eyes.

"Sweetheart?" Marilyn asked.

"We have—some news," she said. She saw her parents exchange split-second eye contact before her mother affectionately took her by the wrist.

"Lize?"

She turned to look at Ryan, but he seemed mortified, toeing one Converse into the other.

"I'm pregnant," she said, for the first time ever, no turning back, and her mother pulled her into another hug—Marilyn's hugs were one of a kind, tight and electric and full of kinetic energy, radiating love—and said, "Oh, *gosh*, honey, what wonderful news."

And then Marilyn moved on to Ryan and Liza again faced her father, who wrapped her in a second hug as well, which immediately activated her tear ducts, and she felt his absorbent polo soaking in her crying, and he pulled away to look at her.

"Liza?" he said softly.

"I'm sorry; they're happy tears," she lied, and she pressed herself against him again.

"Liza-lee," he said after a minute, and the catch in his voice made her wonder if he was shedding some happy tears of his own. "I'm very happy for you," he said, finally releasing the embrace. He offered his hand to Ryan. "Congratulations," he said.

"Thanks, Dr. Sorenson," Ryan said, like a fifteen-year-old who'd impregnated her under the bleachers.

She forced herself to laugh, took Ryan's elbow. "For God's sake," she said. "Call him David." But then, so he would know she wasn't mad, she kissed him, just quickly, once.

Marilyn smiled at them. "Look at these darling parents-to-be," she said. "Goodness. I'll get— Lize, sweetheart, seltzer? Ginger tea? Can you keep anything down these days? I'll bring an assortment. Sit, sit. Tell us everything." She waved her hands as she flitted inside. "I mean, not *everything*," she added, and she left them there, David and Ryan with faces aflame, Liza busying herself with scratching the dog's belly.

"How're things with you, Ryan?" David asked. "Aside from this—boon."

"Fine," Ryan said, nodding vigorously. Hers wasn't one of those provide-for-my-daughter-or-I'll-string-you-up-by-your-you-know-whats fathers, but Liza knew her dad still made Ryan nervous, knew that Ryan hated relaying to David—again and again—that he'd yet to find a job. "Just—doing some—freelance stuff until I can find the right fit for the long term."

Beside him, Liza discreetly took his hand. *It's okay that you're lying,* she meant. *Someday it won't be a lie.* "Tell him about the strange weeds you found around the perimeter of the yard, sweetie," she said. "It looks kind of like—almost like a cactus, Dad."

"Purslane, probably," her father said.

Her mother reappeared with a tray. "Oh, lord, honey, have you moved on to invasive plants already? Before they've even told us when our grandchild is due?"

Help help help, she wanted to say. *This is not going to be okay; Mama, please do something; those weren't happy tears, Dad; I don't know what to do; tell me what to do.*

"I'm eleven weeks," she said. "Due in January." She watched her parents exchange glances again. "What? Is that—bad? What's wrong with January?"

"Oh, no, love," her mom said. "No, I was just—"

"It's a great month," her dad said lamely.

"No, sweetheart, I— It's silly. Jonah's birthday is in January too. Violet just—told us that recently. I just had a little bit of déjà vu."

She watched her mother get teary-eyed and her father wrap his arm around her on the glider. In the alternate universe, it would be *Liza* who got inappropriately weepy over the temperature of her LaCroix, Ryan who put his arm around her and winkingly apologized to her parents, something about *hormones, crazy women, ha ha ha;* there would be nobody to distract from the distress she was in, nobody to divert her parents' attention away from the fact that she and her partner were in serious trouble and that this baby, more than anyone else, would suffer because of it, because Ryan was sick, and his good intentions weren't enough to make up for the reality of it all, the hilly decades that lay ahead of them with Liza, alone, steering the wagon with one hand while the other hung on to her child.

But of course, in the alternate universe, there would *be* no distress. She looked up and saw her father watching her with something like concern.

"I'm sorry, Lize; it just popped into my head," Marilyn said. "Of course it doesn't detract from this fantastic news. It's good timing, semester-wise, is it not? Will you be able to take off the whole spring term?"

"We haven't gotten that far yet," Ryan said. "You guys are the first people we've told."

"Well, we're honored," her mom said, leaning her head against her dad. "And you two have plenty of time to get all of your ducks in a row."

Define ducks *for me, please, Mom. Tell me how the fuck I'm supposed to arrange them.*

"Any pro tips for us?" Ryan asked, which she found sort of endearing.

Marilyn laughed. "For those, you'll need to consult a pro."

"Oh, yeah," her dad said. "We've been floundering since 'seventy-five."

David was a watchful father, but in fairness, his daughters had given him reason to be wary. He could tell that something was askew with Liza. In fact, when she'd asked if she and Ryan could come over for dinner, both he and Marilyn assumed that the two were splitting up. He hoped the hug he'd given his daughter earlier would convey *Hey, just so you know, I'm not a person you ever have to lie to.* He couldn't say these things to his children explicitly; it was an inconvenient caveat of being a dad.

After dinner Liza rose, as she always did, to clear the table, and he rose, as he always did, to join her. They had an easy routine, a trade-off of washing and drying, splash of water and squeak of towel. Some of his most valuable moments with his daughter had occurred while both of them were up to their elbows in Dawn suds.

"How's Gracie doing?" Liza asked. "I haven't talked to her in a while."

He and Marilyn, in their recent twilight porch discussions, had barely scratched the surface of Grace's law school acceptance, so distracted were they by the news of Jonah and, now, their concern about Liza.

"Ah," he said. "You know, Lize, I'm not sure. She'll be fine, of course, but I— She's just sounding a little adrift, I guess. A little lonely. But I'm sure that'll change when she starts school." He fiddled with the taps, waiting for the water to cool off. "Don't you feel like you hit your stride in graduate school?"

She snorted. "I have never come anywhere near hitting my stride."

"Of course you— I mean, Lize, you're—"

"Gracie has nothing to worry about," she said. "Hey, is Mom okay? About—Jonah? Like, she seemed—"

He knew she was changing the subject, deflecting his investigative attempts. "She'll be okay," he said. "It's just been a surprise." He paused. "Lize, you didn't—Jonah—did you—"

"Know about it?" She laughed. "God, no. Dad, I'm the last to know everything. Violet and Wendy have never once let me in on any of their secrets."

Secrets. Plural.

When Liza and Ryan left, he was expecting Marilyn to erupt with speculation. But his wife only half-smiled at him, rubbing at her cheeks.

"You are a god," she said, "for doing the dishes. I'm so tired I can barely see. If I had to tackle all that silverware I think I'd burst into flames."

This was not quite what he'd hoped she would say but he smiled at her anyway. "It's my pleasure," he said. "Are you too tired for a debriefing? How about a nightcap?"

"Oh, honey, you know I'd love to, but I— How about a roundtable over breakfast? We'll go get omelets." She must have seen his disappointment because she came over and kissed him on the cheek. "Or I'll make something. Scrambled eggs on the deck, huh?"

He pulled her against him, and he could feel from the way her body melted into his that she *was* tired. "I forget you worked today," he said. "You go on up. I'll take Loomis out."

She rubbed her cheek against his chest. "Thanks."

The dog, suddenly beside him, wagged his tail expectantly.

Their yard was immaculate, save for the ailing ginkgo tree, stationed in the center like a lighthouse. He descended the stairs to pick a little impromptu bouquet of lilacs for his wife. Loomis, finished marking his territory on each of the bushes David had so painstakingly shaped, sniffed around him as he looked for the best bundle of flowers. She'd given some to him on one of their early dates, picked them from this very bush when the house was still her dad's and pushed them toward him and said, *I'm tired of this antiquated feminine bullshit; girls can bring guys flowers too.* He'd kept them in a coffee mug by his bedside until long after they died, their water giving off a rancid, sewery smell that woke him up each morning. Now he chose a few sprigs and removed them delicately from the branch.

"Spring's upon us, beautiful," he was saying when he entered their bedroom, but Marilyn was dead asleep with all the lights on, curled tightly under their duvet. He set the flowers on her nightstand, undressed and joined her in bed.

"But I think I—" she said, and he felt her kick one of her legs beneath the sheets, preventing herself from falling in a dream.

"Shh," he said. "It's fine. Go back to sleep."

She found him in the dark, wrapped herself sleepily around the length of his body, and he pulled her in closer, kissed the top of her head.

"Sorry I'm such a dud." She shifted, yawned hugely. "I know we always debrief."

He relaxed a little. She knew. She was suspecting all the same things that he was. Their daughters were a mess. Everything was in shambles.

"What's your score?" he asked, his mouth pressed against her neck.

"Oh, nine," she said. "What a nice evening."

He froze, and he felt her wiggle against him, trying to make his body give in to hers.

"What?" she said. "Too low? Too high?"

"*Nine?*" he said.

"Another baby," she said. "How nice. Lize seemed well, didn't she?"

She seemed indolent and regretful and crazy, which—no offense—is how you seemed every single time you were pregnant. And Ryan barely said a goddamn word, and the sleeves on his shirt were too short, and is that really a tattoo of a floppy disk on his wrist?

"You had a nice time," he said instead.

She hummed, and he felt her exhale, halfway to dreamland.

She really wasn't going to bring it up. Nothing about the abruptness of Liza's announcement. Nothing about how Gracie had clearly been smoking while she talked to them on the phone last week, exhaling audibly between sentences. Nothing about how she'd nearly burst into tears remembering that Jonah's birthday was in January. He brushed his hand up and down over her navel, one of the magical spots that seemed to arouse her on contact, but her breathing remained steady. This was arguably one of the life-saving rationalizations for the institution of marriage, one party consumed with worry so the other could sleep through the night.

. . .

"If Miles were here," Wendy said, "he'd be railing on the state of public education."

Jonah had been complaining about his fall schedule, how he couldn't have a study hall because they were making him take a stupid "Exploring the English Language" class that was very obviously for remedial kids, which he wasn't, he just hadn't taken the standardized language test in eighth grade because of the month he'd spent living with the boring animal-figurines people in the ass-fuck middle of nowhere before he moved in with Hanna and Terrence.

"My school's fine," he said, "it's just not been totally, like, accommodating to the fact that I'm not some fucking loaded Gen Y-er who's slated for Princeton." He didn't really get to talk to anyone else like this.

"You could go to fucking Princeton," Wendy said, twirling her wineglass.

"I don't want to go to Princeton."

"Well, I don't want that either, but you shouldn't write it off like you're some kind of bog dweller who can't string together a sentence. Miles would've killed for a student like you."

After a few days he'd stopped being weirded out by how often she mentioned her dead husband. Being married to some-one seemed like a big deal, grand-scheme, and it was pretty fucked up that Wendy's husband had died so young.

"We'll make sure you end up somewhere better than the City Colleges, though," she said, and the indignation in her voice flattered him. "Gracie seemed pretty happy at Reed. It's as expensive as Princeton but not, like, a total doucheville."

"I'm not really thinking about—"

"I'll take care of it," she said, exhaling smoke above her head. "When the time comes."

He wasn't sure what to make of this crew, people who pro-fessed to be ordinary but didn't have normal jobs and didn't appear to worry about taking another person into their homes.

He'd never overheard conversations at Wendy's house like he had at Hanna's, conversations about the grocery budget and dental insurance. Her condo was like the apartment where a wealthy *Batman* villain would live, on the thirty-sixth floor overlooking the lake, nothing but windows, all cool shiny marble and high ceilings and big stark pieces of furniture, a museum exhibit about the future. Wendy had a lot, and he didn't require much. It was the first time he didn't feel like an imposition. Things, for once, seemed to be turning out okay. He was settling into his life with Wendy, the woman who drank wine like it was water and seemed to exist outside of the structure under which normal people lived, a structure where you got up when it was bright out and played by the rules during the day. Better to be living with a rich basket case than to be at Lathrop House. Better to have your own bedroom where you sometimes heard your quote-unquote aunt having sex with men you never saw than to be feigning sleep in the stupidly named Tween Room where your roommates jacked themselves off into unconsciousness and awakened looking for a fight. There was unlimited cereal at Wendy's house, and late-night conversations that felt flatteringly beyond his maturity level. Someone who acknowledged that he was a person instead of a number; someone who'd read too many books, which was better than the opposite.

He remembered that his mom had soft red hair and the sheets on his bed had windsurfers on them. He remembered waffles from the toaster, their squares full of syrup. He remembered running through a sprinkler in his boat bathing suit. How his mom smelled like bread. How people always honked their horns at his dad because he stopped too long at stop signs.

How one day they just stopped being there. How a lady with her hair in a bun said that their car had run into a *viaduct*. How after that he stayed with his first foster family in a town that smelled like cows and at night he fell asleep listening to the cicadas and wondering if his mom and dad could hear them too. How he then went to stay with another family, and then another. How sometimes the people in the families yelled, or were mean to their dogs, or forgot when it was dinnertime. How two years ago, one of them took him to Lathrop House, and he moved into the Tween Room with four other boys.

"You disappeared," Wendy said. She was smiling at him from across the patio, her face soft with wine. "You okay?"

He nodded. There weren't cicada sounds at Wendy's house, just the whoosh of traffic going by below and the gremlin hiss the wind made blowing from the lake. If you went inside and closed the sliding doors, it was like vacuum-sealing a bag; the noise went away entirely except for internal sounds, which meant Wendy, which sometimes meant off-key Mariah Carey songs or occasionally those sounds from her bedroom that he tried not to think about.

"Hey, Wendy?" he asked. "Do you know who my dad is?"

Wendy coughed up some wine. "God, give a girl some warning." But she got serious, fast. "That's a loaded question, J," she said, lighting a cigarette. She dipped her head back and exhaled. "I do know who he is, yes. He came home with Violet for Second Thanksgiving. That's the only time I met him, I think. They dated for a couple of years when she was in college."

He stared at her, waiting.

"The thing is, J, is that this isn't exactly my information to share."

"You're the one who found me, aren't you?" He'd once, eavesdropping, heard Hanna say as much. "Isn't telling Violet about me the same as telling me about my dad?"

"I didn't *tell* Violet about you," she said. "It's not like she didn't know you existed. She was sort of an integral part of your being born."

"You know what I mean."

She took another swig of wine. "I do. And you have a point.

But what say we do this whole thing one step at a time, huh? I don't want you suddenly dredging up God-knows-what when you haven't even had a chance to meet *Gracie.*"

"Can you tell me *about* him, at least?"

Wendy seemed to consider how to proceed. "I don't remember much, to be honest. Not a *bad* guy, just not the most interesting? As per usual with Violet; vanilla's an acquired taste. He was getting a PhD in some kind of science. Are you good at science?"

He shook his head.

"Well. Maybe you'll be a late-blooming physicist. I have a vague recollection of a pasty, awkward guy in a short-sleeved button-down. I don't remember much else, honestly, Jonah. I'm sorry. I wish I did." She sighed. "You know, my husband was raised by his stepmom. His mom died in childbirth. His dad remarried a year later, before Miles could remember anything else. He didn't even know his mom wasn't his mom until he was a teenager."

"That's fucked up," Jonah said.

"Well, sort of. But I guess I'm just saying that—genetics aren't everything."

He was tired of the topic, disappointed that she didn't have more information. "What's Second Thanksgiving?" he asked, and Wendy laughed.

"Oh, what surprises await you," she said.

1977–1978

There was something about the color of their kitchen in Iowa that made Marilyn immediately want to leave it whenever she entered. The cabinets were a sickly chartreuse and the floor a muted mustard; when she made coffee in the morning she kept her eyes in slits, focusing on the task at hand before hightailing it into the beige living room, which she didn't love but could tolerate for long enough to read the paper. She was becoming preoccupied with the ugliness of their house. It wasn't all bad: from the outside it was positively charming: dark green paint, yellow flowered bushes—forsythias? She was trying to learn— and a mailbox at the end of the path with their name on it, a little sticker that read SORENSON that made even picking up the phone bill feel festive and romantic.

She was trying hard to look on the bright side. Their relocation hadn't happened as smoothly as they'd planned. She'd ended up staying in Chicago for a few extra months, easing the transition for her father while David moved them into the house on Davenport Street. She'd lost credits from UIC when she crossed state lines, so she was taking a handful of mind-numbing classes at the community college until she could enroll next semester at the university. Winter had descended early and with it came a months-long anemic pallor that seemed to bleed into every facet of their life, cold air seeping through gaps in the windows and slate clouds covering the sun for weeks on end. It did not lend itself to boosting her morale, though by March most of the snow had melted and the sky was beginning to rid itself of the winter gray. Assuming she was admitted to the university, she would start school again in the summer as a transfer student, but for now she was responsible for getting them settled, hanging funky thrift store art and making curtains for the big windows in the dining room and trying to make their house feel like it wasn't inhabited by a couple of kids. She was finding it harder than she'd anticipated, was starting to realize that she'd taken for granted her mother's eye for design, that drawers didn't organize themselves, that dust could and would accumulate overnight if you didn't keep an eye on your flat surfaces.

She'd imagined married life as a kind of prolonged sleepover, a cozy, athletic marathon where they would spend all their time in bed and eat makeshift meals and break only to spend their evenings outside on the porch, breathing smog-free rural air and befriending quaint neighborhood cats. But David was engulfed in his coursework, a rigorous roster of embryology and neuroscience, left most mornings before she awakened and usually got home after she'd fallen asleep—at first she'd tried to wait up for him, but her intermittent insomnia coupled with her newfound habit of drinking half a bottle of wine at night made it difficult to stay awake. She was bored. Iowa was boring. She went for long walks along the river, alone, and sometimes she visited David on campus to bring him a sandwich, give him a hug, but he was clearly distracted, surrounded by other go-getters and jittery with fatigue. She was ready for her life to settle into something more comfortable—she and David both students, both busy, both useful.

The decision to paint the kitchen was impulsive. She'd bought the paint at 9:00 a.m. and come home and started immediately, and by the time David finished his day, over twelve hours later, she was asleep at the kitchen table, the unimposing pale blue drying around her.

David woke her gently, holding on to her shoulder. "Honey, the fumes," he said. Her head was buried in her arms, her cheek resting against the cool Formica of the kitchen table. "Marilyn, you've got to get out of here." He was opening the windows, waving dramatically at the air with one of his textbooks.

"It's fine," she said. "It's almost dry."

"Come here," he said. "Come out on the porch. Jesus, how long have you been sleeping? Did you pass out?"

"Of course I didn't." She got up and followed him. David pointed to a chair but she sank down onto the stairs instead and after a minute he joined her.

"What's going on with you?" he asked, more candid than she was used to. Another unforeseen downside of marriage: David's sudden comfort with speaking to her openly. "Are you— I mean, you can't just fall asleep in a room full of paint fumes, Marilyn; we haven't even talked about painting the kitchen. Isn't that something we're supposed to talk about together?"

"Don't you like it?" she asked.

"That's not the *point*," he said. "Am I—should I be worried about you?"

"Oh, *God*," she said.

"It's not like you to do something so reckless."

"It's not like I painted the walls with napalm. God, I was trying to do something nice— I was trying to make our house less *hideous*."

"Since when do you think it's hideous?"

"I know you're never around in daylight, so maybe you neglected to notice that our kitchen looked like an insane asylum before I decided to do something that I *thought* you would like; I even tried to match the swatch with the tie you wore at our wedding but of *course* you're only concerned that I acted without consulting you. Is this what I have to look forward to? This chauvinistic husband bullshit?"

"You're kidding," David said. She could see that she'd hurt his feelings. "I was asking you how you're *doing*," he said. "Because in my opinion—yes, as your *husband*, which I wasn't aware was an insult—you're acting a little crazy."

"But it doesn't occur to you why I might *feel* crazy? Because you've set me up in this fucking dollhouse and left me to do all of the boring stuff while you get to go be productive and never spend any time with me?"

"You think I *enjoy* this? For Christ's sake. Are— You sound insane, do you realize that?"

"Perfect," she said. She stood up and went back into the house, surveying her handiwork—she'd need to do a second coat tomorrow—as she went for a bottle of wine, struggled with their cheap corkscrew.

"Just going to start drinking, then? Is that how this works?"

"I am having a glass of wine," she said. "Because my life is incredibly dull and my husband doesn't care about seeing me anymore and I live in *Iowa*, apparently, which nobody warned me would be so goddamn—mid*west*ern." She slammed her glass onto the counter, watching a wave of merlot leap over its lip and bleed onto the drop cloth she'd put on the floor.

"You agreed to this. I don't know what else I'm supposed to say. I'm sorry? I'm sorry. Sonofabitch. Sorry things are exactly how I told you they'd be and you're disappointed anyway. What the hell is it you'd like to hear from me?"

"I'm not *sure*," she said, breathing hard, holding her glass so tightly that she worried it might break. "You've never yelled at me before."

"I'm not *yelling*," he said, which was true.

Later, she couldn't help but pin Wendy's conception to their first fight, to her *I'll show him* decision to forgo her diaphragm after they'd argued over her perceived lack of perspective. She couldn't help but equate Wendy with some convoluted part of her own entrance into adulthood and with the time that David first swore at her—*sonofabitch*. And when she was feeling generous, years down the road, during happier times, she could trace Wendy back to the most primitive expression of her love for her husband: that night, the time that they, too exhausted for anything else, once again found each other.

She was sitting at a table across the restaurant, framed by a halo of hair. David liked watching his wife like this, when she didn't know he was looking, especially in public. Something seemed different about her when she was out of the house; she was less familiar, more composed, pretty in a different way. He went over to join her, bent to kiss her hello.

"Sorry I'm late," he said. "I called the hostess and— Long day." He smiled sheepishly as he slid into the seat opposite her. "I'm happy to see you."

"You too," she said. He took her hands across the table.

"How'd it go?" he asked, though he could already guess, from the droop of her shoulders, that it had not gone well.

"I'm failing," she said.

"Well, I'm sure that's—"

"I'm at a fifty-eight percent."

"Still in the top half," he said feebly.

"My only point of redemption—if I passed it; *if*—would be the final."

"Okay," he said. "Okay, then we'll cram for it together."

"It's scheduled for the seventeenth," she said. The baby, pushing out the gauzy blue material of her shirt, quiet between them, was due on December ninth.

"Okay, but we knew that," he said. "We knew that you'd have to maneuver around finals. You said he'd let you do a take-home. We'll just—"

There was a faintly perceptible shift in her eyes, a little blurry slip from panic to pity, fear to superiority. As in *you sweet misguided thing*, as in *don't even pretend you have any idea*. He almost wondered if she enjoyed it, if she derived some pleasure from getting to play the adult in the situation. He supposed he wouldn't blame her if she did.

"Professor Grady's agreeing to let me drop," she said. "And his wife works in the registrar's office. They took pity on me. They're refunding my course fees." She looked then like she might cry. She deserved to finish college: if he got to, she should too. But he couldn't help but feel a trickle of relief. She made him nervous, working as hard as she was—all-nighters, the full-body panic that seized her before exams—when she was so far along. And were they really going to leave their baby to be raised by strangers, spend money they didn't have on daycare so his wife could get a degree in *English literature*, of all things? These were mean thoughts, fueled by exhaustion.

"You found her, I see," the waitress said, appearing ghoulishly at his elbow. She was beaming at them. People here were so nice that they seemed almost deranged. The Northwest Side of Chicago had never felt like the big city until he arrived in Iowa.

He blinked. "I'm sorry?"

"I talked to you on the phone. Blond wife, blue top, baby on the way?" Was that really how he'd described her? He'd been so startled by the idea of rendering her physically to another person that he'd stalled. It was like being asked to describe his own hand. He studied his wife now. *Beautiful*, he thought. *Irreconcilably sad.* Apparently he'd come up with *blue-shirted blond pregnant lady*. She, the English major, deserved better adjectives.

"That's me," Marilyn said. Only he could hear the sadness in her voice.

"Have you guys decided?" the waitress asked, and for a

moment he wondered if somehow she had entered into their deeper conversation but Marilyn slipped the menu out from under his wrists and opened it. He'd completely lost his appetite but his wife was ordering elaborately, no mayo on her burger, fries *and* a salad, extra dill pickles on the side.

"Eating for two!" the waitress remarked. It drove Marilyn crazy when people commented on her pregnancy. He could tell that if she weren't putting on this show of competence for the waitress she'd be weeping into her iced tea. "And for you?"

He got a deer-in-the-headlights look sometimes, she told him, when people asked him routine questions. *So lost in thought*, she'd say, cupping a hand to his face. *My mad scientist.*

"He'll have the same," Marilyn said, stepping in. "Except *with* mayo, Swiss instead of cheddar, tomato on the side. And no salad. And I'll take his pickle."

"Are you a ventriloquist?" the waitress asked him. "I barely saw you move your mouth."

Marilyn's façade was fading quickly; he saw the muscles along her jawline that appeared when she was grinding her teeth.

"My better half," he said, because apparently they were all in a community theater production together, something cliché about marriage and pickles and barely contained despair. "Thanks," he said, handing over the menus, begging her with his eyes *please, please, please go away*. Her name tag read JANET. It wasn't her fault. Blessedly, she retreated to the kitchen.

Marilyn's eyes had filled. She was playing aggressively with her straw wrapper.

He reached for her hands again. "I'll do your homework for you," he said, glancing around him to make sure no one was listening. He could redeem his ungenerous thoughts by supporting her, whole-hog. "And the final. You'll just copy the answers in your own writing."

"Sweetheart." Her eyes welled up and she smiled a little at

him. "First of all, don't you think it might seem suspicious if I'm suddenly getting As after two months of Ds?"

"Shakespeare's all Greek to me, honey. We'll bring you up to a solid C average."

"Second of all," she continued, "I'd never let you do that. You could get expelled. I'm just going to quit while I'm ahead. Or not—not quite *ahead*, I guess."

"Well," he said. "One less class? It's time for you to start taking it easy anyway."

"Grady's wife reversed the fees for all of my classes. I decided to just call it what it is, David. Think of how helpful that money's going to be."

"You—you already did this? Without talking to me?"

"I figured I'd take care of it all at once."

"You quit school."

"I didn't *quit*," she said sharply, frowning at him. "It's a— It's better for us."

"But it's not better for you; it's— This is the exact opposite of what you wanted."

"I'm exhausted," she said.

"Well, with good reason. But your teachers have been pretty understanding, haven't—"

"I'm—*deeply* exhausted. More than just— It's something more than— It's like my *soul* is tired, David; I know how that sounds but I—"

He'd broached the topic once before, to her dismay, but now he tried again: "Sweetheart, this is why maybe it wouldn't be a bad idea for you to go and—you know, see someone. Talk to someone about—you know, feeling down. Especially given your mom's history."

"My mom drank herself to death because she was chronically miserable," Marilyn snapped. "Just because I'm a product of her genes doesn't mean I have some depressive cross to bear.

Jesus. I'm overwhelmed. I'm lonely. I'm hormonal. That doesn't mean I'm *crazy*."

"I never said— If you're lonely, I wish you'd talk to me."

"We need a crib too," she said, firmly enough that he knew they'd be moving on from the subject whether he wanted to or not.

They'd had it figured out perfectly, an English degree knocked out in five semesters, maybe six. She'd waitress nights, they thought, and then get a more serious job in town, the newspaper or something clerical. Then next steps: maybe a graduate degree for her, a bigger house, a baby. Not until later, those things.

"We'll work it out," he'd said, back in the spring when she told him she'd missed two periods, an absence suggesting a presence, and until that moment, in the too-bright restaurant with Janet, they had been. She'd chewed her way through bottles of chalky antacids while she took a summer class in Irish poetry and she started showing as the fall semester began. She particularly loved her medieval lit class, sometimes read aloud to him from *Sir Gawain* as she marked up the margins in bed.

"What about Arthur for a boy?" he'd ask, trying to tease her, his hand on her abdomen to see if he could feel the baby move. "A daughter named Chanticleer?"

But she refused to engage, just smiled like the Mona Lisa and pulled the covers up to her shoulders; she seemed far less enchanted than he was. "Chanticleer's male, honey," she'd say, or "My body temperature is twice what yours is these days, darling; can I have my space?"

He'd still held out hope that they could find a way to be happy. At the table, while watching her, his confidence faltered.

"I don't want to fight," she said, and her resignation made him sadder than anything. "I'm sorry I did it without telling you. It just seemed like the most painless way." She looked at him with a bitter, greenish smile on her face. "I figure if I'm going to ruin my life, I should at least do it as cheaply as possible. We might as well get a Swyngomatic out of it."

The waitress returned, moon face grinning over the plates balanced along one forearm. He felt another irrational surge of anger, at her smile, her obliviousness, the showy way she was carrying their food though she could have easily held a plate with each hand.

"Anything else I can get you two?"

He watched his wife, smoothing a napkin over what was left of her lap, raking her hair away from her face, already commandeering a dill pickle, starving, powerless before the demands of the half-formed person who would reap the bounty of her disappointment.

"A hundred thousand dollars," Marilyn said. "And a time machine."

The waitress's smile faded. Marilyn bit into the pickle.

"Maybe some extra napkins," he said apologetically, and Janet skittered away. "Next year," he said. He reached for her knee under the table. They'd already planned that—she would take off spring semester to be at home with the baby and head back in the fall. "We'll start again next year. All three of us."

She didn't reply.

When his wife came to join him in bed after putting the baby down, he was already in his underwear, sitting up against the headboard. She turned her back to him and undressed shyly, as though he were not her husband but some kind of predatory swim coach. She pulled on one of his T-shirts, the hem to her knees, before she lay down next to him. She seemed back to her old self, unrested but happy, affectionate in a motherly way—touching the space between his shoulder blades, ruffling his hair, kissing him on the forehead at the breakfast table. Now she hugged his arm to her chest like a stuffed animal. "She's stopped keeping her little hands in fists all the time, have you noticed?"

Wendy was two months old, and he was intoxicated by her, enamored, humbled by all that she demanded of them and transfixed by the unfathomable intricacy of her face, embracing his exhaustion because now he had her to look forward to at the end of each day. He had to confess, though, that he missed his wife, missed her attention and her energy, her surprising ardor, the way she could make him laugh even when she was only half-awake.

He kissed the top of her head. "I'll have to pay attention tomorrow."

"Your Sunday homework," she said, and then she paused. "Is tomorrow Sunday? God, I don't even know what day it is. I haven't known for— I can't think about it."

"Does anybody *really* know what time it is?" he deadpanned, but she had grown serious.

"How tired are you?" she asked.

He wasn't sure how to respond. Their foreplay rarely required dialogue. "Oh, I've got life in me still, I think. How about you?"

She kissed him in a way that felt inquisitive. "Sure. Me too. I was thinking that we . . ."

Of course it excited him, the thought of being with her again. The eight-week marker had just passed; their daughter was fifty-nine days old. He slipped his hand under her shirt and began to feel his way upward, but she stiffened.

"Hang on," she said. "Can I be—can we—" She was suddenly straddling him. "There." She dipped her face to kiss him. "Or I could— If you wanted I could— If you're not . . ." She stilled, above him, and he watched her face turn. "If you wanted me to—I can just—" She sat back astride his thighs.

"What?" he said. "Honey, come here." He took her hands and

pulled her to him once more. They kissed for what felt like only a few seconds, and then she pulled away again.

"But I could also"—she slid her hand into his briefs—"I can just take care of you."

"Hey, sweetie, no, let's— Unless you're—are you nervous? About it being—painful?"

She sat there, holding him in her left hand. She shook her head.

"Honey," he said. "What is it?"

She rolled off of him, pressed her hands over her eyes. "The only reason I know it's been eight weeks is because the checker at the grocery asked me how old the baby is and I realized it had been eight weeks and that's when the doctor said we could start having sex again. But I don't recognize my body right now, David, and I hate feeling that way especially when I'm with you, because it's a real source of happiness for me, our being alone together." She was, strangely, not crying; she sounded impassive. "My body isn't my own anymore. I've lost myself. I know everyone says that happens but I—I guess I didn't believe them. And I'm so tired. I'm sorry. I feel like I'm doing a botched job of this."

But in fact he was in constant awe of how she was with Wendy, how she'd learned to operate with one arm, how she'd resumed her reading of *Rabbit Redux* while Wendy slept against her shoulder, how she sang "Blue Moon" and "Unchained Melody" to Wendy in a voice so soothing that it made him want to fall asleep too. He was blown away by all that her body was capable of, by how immediately, visibly transformed she'd been by motherhood.

He took her hand. "Honey, you're not. You're doing a great job."

"Other people are better at this than I am, I think. I saw this woman at the library today with three kids and the youngest was about Wendy's age and she looked so—*competent*. And there I was wandering around the new fiction, not even *awake*, really, and I realized when I got home that I had one too many buttons open on my shirt and you could see my whole bra, and I feel like I have this *smell* about me—do you smell it?"

Truth be told, he could: her regular perfume had been replaced, after eight weeks of round-the-clock infant care, with something distinctly human. But he found it sort of arousing; he felt like he was getting to know a whole other side of her.

"I'm not *fun* anymore," she said. "I'm not— There's nothing exciting happening, ever, and I'm just—I'm just this *vessel*. I barely *exist*."

"Hey." He chanced to pull her against him again, and she allowed it, and she really believed all of this, he knew; she really saw herself as someone amorphous and inert and unsexy. "You exist," he said quietly. "You're the beautiful, remarkable mother of our daughter, and I've never loved you more."

She looked at him, faces only inches apart so he couldn't make out her expression, only the openness of her eyes, her big olive irises.

He kissed her eyebrow. "Thanks for having our baby for us." And her cheekbone. "Thanks for keeping her healthy." And her lips. "And safe." And her throat. "Thanks for bringing me so much happiness." Her hand now: he kissed the bases of each of her fingers. "Thanks for being here when I get home." He stroked her hair. "You're doing the best job," he said, and she tilted her face up to kiss him.

A few weeks before Wendy's first birthday, Violet was born.

CHAPTER SEVEN

"I never have to worry about you, Lize," her mom had said once, standing at the window over the kitchen sink, looking vacant and exhausted; this was during the Gillian year, the year when her parents had stopped speaking.

"What does *that* mean?" she'd replied, because it was nice to be worried about occasionally; she didn't want her mother so casually validating the rhetoric about forgotten middle children right there in the kitchen, washing a bushel of broccoli.

Her mom had turned to her, face restoring itself to something present and recognizable, and smiled wanly. "I mean you're a good one, honey. That's all I mean."

A good one: Liza, nineteen years later, thirteen weeks pregnant, on her back in the bed of Marcus Spear, PhD, her colleague, her superior; a professor, perhaps ironically, of industrial/organizational psychology, and a superfan, from what she could see of the bookshelves from the vantage point on her back in his bed, of James Patterson. She'd been impressed by the confidence in her own voice, earlier that day, when she'd asked Marcus, with whom she had always shared a light and easy banter, if he wanted to take a walk with her. Marcus Spear, bless his heart, quiet and thoughtful and so soothingly self-possessed, charmingly awkward in bed, so intent on not doing anything wrong that he didn't notice anything askew, didn't notice her swollen breasts and didn't notice afterward that she was trying not to cry. He was deft and careful and she'd wanted it; she wanted it all the time lately, just not with Ryan; she'd masturbated in the handicap bathroom on the fourth floor yesterday, braced against the wall thinking, inexplicably and sort of predatorily, of that kid from the Twilight movies, the boy vampire who drove a Volvo.

Since their dinner with her parents, Ryan had dipped back down, not quite as far down as he'd been but still concerningly low. He slept through her morning sickness and last week had failed to accompany her to her twelve-week checkup; her discussions of the future—maternity leave, things they needed to buy—seemed to overwhelm him. And on a most primitive level, he failed to be there for her, physically; he failed to rub her back when she kept herself up at night worrying; he failed to appear concerned about her well-being as she worked harder than she ever had, burdened with the additional responsibilities accompanying her tenured position; he failed to satisfy her in the most basic way, scratch the itch that surged, she supposed, as a result of her hormones, that caused her to find herself rubbing against the corner of the kitchen table just to feel *something*, that caused her to find herself in bed with a man who enjoyed commercial crime fiction.

She tried to picture herself from a few beats away and found she couldn't get a firm handle on what she looked like, couldn't conjure the image of herself—wide-eyed, mousy-haired, meticulous—doing something so fucking stupid. She'd just been so *horny*, and so desperate for something easy, for the pleasure of doing something simply because it felt good, fallout be damned. She and Ryan hadn't had sex since that disastrous morning three months ago, the anomalous morning that had gotten them into this mess in the first place. His ability to perform had been a one-off, apparently. It seemed radically unjust that the fallout was so tangible, that she was left in another man's bed, swallowing down nausea caused by a baby who likely wouldn't be able to rely on its father.

"That was lovely," Marcus said from beside her, reaching tentatively to pull her toward him. She was considering, now, too late, how stupid it was that she'd approached someone from work, someone who would henceforth be able to accurately X-ray his gaze through her blouse at faculty meetings. But it was late afternoon and the spring semester had finally ended and she was in the roomy Ravenswood studio of a man who had just dipped his face between her tented legs and kissed her until she came. It *was* lovely, except for the inconvenient fact that there was a baby percolating in her belly—still a fetus, she had to argue, as a feminist and a scientist and a woman in deep denial—and the fact that the father of said percolating fetus-baby was at home, probably watching *CSI* in a uniform of depressed-person sweats and a T-shirt from an erstwhile cybersecurity conference.

A good one: she had a suspicion that her current behavior would not earn her such a title.

"It was," she said vaguely, shifting against him. "Thank you." The baby was now, according to the Internet, the size of a Meyer lemon. She was unsure of how this was different from a regular lemon.

Marcus laughed. "Thank *you.*"

Marcus, who'd complimented her shoes the first time she met him so she thought he was gay. Marcus, who'd never been married and who, in the classroom, turned inward and grave, peering up at his students from behind big black frames. Marcus, who had two cats, Sally and Walter, Sally after the *Peanuts* character and Walter after Mondale. Marcus, whose name was Marcus and who went by *Marcus.*

Marcus, who didn't ask questions except for "Would you like a glass of wine?"

To which she said, rousing herself, "Sure, what the hell."

Her mom claimed that she never drank when she was pregnant but the previous generation certainly had: pregnant women all across Chicago swilling Manhattans and chain-smoking. Her parents had turned out all right.

Just a glass. One, after they'd dressed, on Marcus Spear's balcony; she twirled the stem of her wineglass between her fingers, looking down at the sidewalk below, a passing pit bull tethered to a hipster by a retractable leash. Her parents couldn't have been completely happy all the time when they were her age. But there was also no way, she knew, that her mother would ever sleep with another man *ever*, let alone while harboring one of her impending daughters in her belly. Her nausea surged again, and she couldn't tell if it was owing to her pregnancy or her disgust with herself, and at that moment her phone dinged with a text from Ryan—*don't think I'm up for your parents' house tonight*—and she swallowed once more, this time a painful lump in her throat, suddenly life-endingly tired, and she wanted very desperately to have someone take care of her for once, and as she sipped her wine, as it slid pleasantly down, numbing the lump, she turned to Marcus and asked if he'd drive her to the house on Fair Oaks.

One thing Jonah couldn't get over was the common thread in the family of owning fucking ginormous houses, enough square footage combined to accommodate a dozen football fields. The first floor of Wendy's condo was larger than the Danforths' entire house. Now it turned out that David and Marilyn's house was huge, too, but felt more like a home where actual human beings lived, wind chimes and a motley jungle of plants, bikes propped up on the front porch—expensive bikes, Cannondales—and a wooden glider with worn flowered cushions opposite a red porch swing. The house was a stately red-brown brick with stained glass geometry in the windows, a row of purple flower bushes running along the perimeter like a fence. The tile of the porch was terra cotta, the kind that made a terrible chalk noise against the bottoms of his sneakers. He felt the hair on the back of his neck stand up.

"You ready?" Wendy asked him. She'd been entertaining in the car, going down the roster of each of her sisters, describing them physically—"Liza's really pretty but she has that terrible color of hair that's, like, not even a color? *Ecru.* Like a Band-Aid"; "You won't be meeting Gracie but she kind of looks like a Cabbage Patch Kid"—and itemizing their past offenses—"If you ask her she won't admit to it, but Violet unquestionably stole this macramé bracelet my high school boyfriend made for me"—and now, on the porch, she touched his shoulder. "Entirely unintimidating, I swear. They're more afraid of you than you are of them."

"They're afraid of me?"

"Well, no. I mean—no. Poorly phrased." She squeezed his shoulder again and an Infiniti pulled into the driveway, and Violet climbed out. "Where are the boys?" Wendy asked.

"Home with Matt." Violet flushed. "I just figured this might not be, you know, a child-friendly evening."

"Are you anticipating knife fights? Paternity tests?"

He watched Violet turn even redder before she said, "Wendy, can you not? Please?"

"I just think it's weird that Matt didn't come with you."

"We couldn't get a sitter, okay? Jesus. Drop it. Can we just go inside?"

She hadn't even said hello to him, hadn't even bothered to ask if he was enjoying himself in the home where she'd basically abandoned him, but then she was ringing the doorbell, and then the door opened, revealing David and Marilyn, holding hands like those fucked-up twins from *The Shining*, a black dog between them the size of a horse.

"Why did you ring the bell?" David asked, letting go of

Marilyn's hand to push open the storm door. She reached to take hold of the dog's collar.

"I just thought—" Violet faltered. "I just figured because—"

"It's the big reveal," Wendy said. "The grand, dramatic, reality-show premiere."

He liked Wendy, for the most part. She was rich and crazy, but she made him laugh, and she let him watch *The Daily Show*, and she seemed to know the best thing to say, always, like now—even when it deliberately made everyone uncomfortable. They stood frozen for a few seconds, David's arm propping open the door and Marilyn hanging back.

"Come in, come in," Marilyn said finally. "Please. Hi. Come in."

Wendy went first, waving him in behind her. They all stopped again in the front hallway, David and Marilyn still by the door and he and Wendy and Violet over by the big wooden bookshelves that framed the entrance of the living room.

"Mom, Dad," Violet said, stepping forward. She reached out as if to touch him but instead her hand just hovered a couple inches over his shoulder, like he had lice. "This is Jonah."

David came over and extended a hand. He was tall and athletic, grayish black hair, fingers smudged with grease. "Sorry, I was fixing up Marilyn's bike this afternoon."

He took the hand and they shook.

"I'm David. It's a real pleasure to meet you, Jonah."

"Me too," he said. "I mean—you too."

"And this is Loomis," David said, taking the dog's collar.

He instinctively stiffened, backed up a couple steps, bumping into Wendy.

"Oh, no, are you afraid of— Sorry. He's a gentle giant, but we can— Honey, can we—"

His face burned—such a fucking stupid thing to be afraid of, a big dumb horse-dog. Marilyn was studying him with intensity; he wasn't sure but it looked like there might be tears in her eyes. Fucking shitshow—crying, mutant dogs, old people holding hands.

"Right," David said. "Never mind. I'll— Let me just go put him in his room."

"His *room*?" Wendy said. "Jesus. The dog has his own *room* now?"

"Why don't you come see it, Wendy?" David said.

He watched curiously as she shut up and followed her father down the hall, leaving him alone with Violet and his grandmother.

"Mom," Violet said again. "This is Jonah. Jonah, this is—my mom. Marilyn."

"Hi," he said, and the next thing he knew he was being hugged, arms pinned to his sides.

"We're so happy you're here," Marilyn said, finally pulling away. Now he could see that she was crying for real. "Just excuse me for a second," she said, and with that she was gone, disappeared up the stairs, leaving him alone with Violet.

"Christ," Violet whispered, sounding irritated. "Shit. Sorry. Just— She's happy. They're both really happy, I swear. Let's— Why don't we go in the kitchen. Are you actually afraid of dogs? I should've asked. Loomis is harmless though. Coddled and innocuous. Do you want—water? Or—my parents don't really—"

"I bought soda," David said, appearing in the doorway without the dog.

"You bought *soda*?" Violet asked. "You've never bought soda in my entire—"

"Special occasion," David said. "I thought Jonah might like it."

"Thanks, sir," he said, an address that popped into his head from a James Bond movie, and David gave him a puzzled half smile. The next thing he knew, Marilyn was back, ushering them all into the dining room; he could hear her clanging around in the kitchen as the rest of them sat at the table. David rose to go check on her. He watched as Wendy and Violet made elaborate eye contact across the table.

"It's totally fine," Wendy said. "She's fucking insane, but she's totally benign."

"*Wendy*," Violet said.

"Sorry, do you—what, you disagree with that?"

"Knock it off," Violet said.

"This is like the most interesting thing that's happened to her since Grace was born," Wendy narrated to him. "She's a mostly well-intentioned basket case."

"Yes, that's exactly what I meant by *knock it off*," Violet said. She turned to him. "This is just difficult for her. Not because of you. It's because of me. She's fine. Ask them anything you'd like, okay? They're so excited to get to know you."

"Jesus, tone it down," Wendy said. "It's not like they're—"

"The chicken is just a *tiny* bit overcooked, I think," Marilyn said, appearing in the doorway with a platter. He could hardly keep his eyes on her, she was moving so fast, setting the plate on the table on top of a pot holder, messing with one of the tall blue candles, stopping to pick an invisible piece of lint from David's shirt. "Violet, sweetheart, am I correct in my assessment that Matt and the boys won't be joining us?"

"The sitter canceled," Violet said.

Wendy snorted, but Marilyn got to work again, sweeping around the table, lifting three extra place settings. There was a momentary silence and then Marilyn was doing something with her hands; in his peripheral vision, he caught Wendy rolling her eyes.

"In the name of the Father," Marilyn said, "and the Son, and the Holy Spirit."

"Amen," Violet said, and he thought he heard Wendy laugh.

"Liza has a faculty meeting," Marilyn said. "She'll be over for dessert."

"*Dessert?*" Wendy said.

"Dad baked a pie," Marilyn said, and this time Wendy definitely laughed.

"Apple," David said. "With salted caramel."

"Excuse me, Gordon Ramsay," Wendy said. "Are you serious?"

"Your father's an excellent cook. All it took was getting him out of medicine; who knew? Violet, honey, can you start the brussels sprouts?"

"Who's Gordon Ramsay?" David asked, and Jonah, before he realized he was speaking, said, "He's a chef who has this show where there's these people trying to be the best cook and they're all mean to each other and, like, sabotage their opponents." Lathrop House had gotten cable specifically so this one kid with Asperger's could watch it.

Everyone was looking at him.

"Ah," David said. "Maybe we'll have to start watching that, sweetheart, huh?" He accepted the bowl of brussels sprouts from Marilyn. "Are you interested in cooking, Jonah?"

"Oh," he said. "No. I mean—not really, no."

"He's a ceramicist," Violet said, sounding like Hanna. "Aren't you, Jonah?"

"Um, sort of," he said. "I— Do you mind if I go to the bathroom?" He just needed a break from them. Just a minute where he didn't have to be listening to a million people at once. The Sorensons seemed to produce a different kind of chaos from the kind he was used to; a product of having money, no doubt, but there was also an electricity running among the people at the table, facial expressions that meant one thing to a specific person and nothing at all to everyone else, things that made Wendy crack up that didn't seem necessarily funny, the way David and Marilyn always seemed to be touching each other in some way, her hand over his or his arm over the back of her chair. He was used to being the quietest one at the table—

the staff at Lathrop House often cited his *tranquillity*—but he wasn't used to feeling so *observed*; he was the occasion for this dinner; he wasn't sure he'd ever been the occasion for anything.

He was on his way down the hall when he happened to look out one of the front windows where the sun was just starting to set, a radioactive orange. There was a green Subaru station wagon parked at the curb, windows rolled down, and the man and woman in the front seat were kissing. He paused to watch, intrigued. The woman had an orange scarf wrapped around her neck like a flag. Some gross neighbors, he assumed. He proceeded to the bathroom.

When he returned, he barely had time to sit down before another guest showed up.

"Hello?" someone called. "Hey, hi, sorry, I—" The woman from the car—untying the silky orange scarf—appeared in the doorway. Liza, apparently—she was pretty, with bright green eyes and a shiny goldish ponytail; he thought Wendy's assessment of her Band-Aid hair was ungenerous. "Ooh, sorry. Hey, everyone. My meeting ended early and I figured I'd try to make it in time for dinner. Ryan's—busy tonight."

"Jonah, this is my sister Liza," Violet said.

He rose uncertainly, and after he did it he noticed that everyone else was still seated but by then it was too late.

"Great to meet you." Liza leaned in to hug him, which seemed both weird and generous, her way of making him feel less awkward for standing up. "Sorry to interrupt."

"That's okay." He wondered why the guy from the car—Ryan?—hadn't joined her.

"Can I get you a drink, sweetie?" Marilyn asked.

"Water's great; thanks," Liza said.

"Liza's pregnant," Violet explained, as though someone needed an excuse for drinking water.

"Jesus, Viol, he's not an idiot," Wendy said.

"Can you ever just not talk?" Violet asked.

"You're the one who's *narrating* everything to him like he just got out of *prison*."

"*Wendy*," said Violet.

They were all giving him a headache. He felt like he was watching a dodgeball game.

"I feel like I've killed the mood," Liza said, sitting down, frowning. "I didn't mean to interrupt. I hoped you guys might still be getting ready for dinner."

"We're on a weirdly speedy schedule tonight," Wendy said. "Mom's in schizoid mode."

"*Wendy*." This time it was David who spoke up.

"Sorry, sorry," Wendy said, waving a hand. Marilyn returned, and when she'd sat down again, Liza raised her water glass.

"To Jonah. Welcome to the family." Liza seemed kind of insane too—was anyone in this family *not* insane?—but she was friendly.

"Cheers," David said.

He lifted his Coke uncertainly, and a chorus of clinking followed.

Dinner consisted of a series of interrupted conversations. They asked him questions and he tried to sound more interesting than he actually was. Wendy talked about her core barre class and Liza talked about her students and Marilyn never stopped moving, refilling wineglasses and stopping trails of wax from dripping onto the tablecloth. Afterward David rose to clear the plates. When Jonah tried to help, as Hanna had always insisted, Wendy touched his hand.

"No, stay," she said. "Dad's got it." So he was left with the women, Violet and Liza and Wendy and Marilyn all staring at him like a horror-movie coven of unassuming kindergarten teachers who were about to disembowel him.

"I'm sure this is a strange thing to say," Marilyn said, sounding almost kind of dreamy, "but you have my father's nose, Jonah."

He squirmed in his chair. "Is that—sorry, is that a—good thing or a bad thing?"

He heard his grandmother laugh for the first time and he decided, sitting in the dining room of their big weird house, that he liked her.

CHAPTER EIGHT

"If it isn't our lawyer-to-be," was how her dad answered the phone when Grace called home on a Thursday morning in June. Of course she should've nipped things in the bud after she'd lied to Liza. Made up something plausibly stupid, *I was high when I told you that; sorry* or *They sent me an acceptance by mistake.* But she hadn't been able to bring herself to do it, and so when her parents called her the day after Liza had, she'd lied feebly, shyly, as though being humble, while still not quite *fully* lying: *Yeah, so,* she'd said. *Looks like I'll be staying out here.* But since then she'd realized how fucking stupid she was to think she could maintain a fiction of this immensity. She lived in a linoleum box. She made $380 per week before taxes. She had, at present, no viable prospects for future endeavors beyond hermitage and transiency. She had somehow botched her life to an almost laughable degree, and then accidentally lied about it, and this phone call was her chance to set the record straight. Her parents loved her unconditionally, and Liza was pregnant now, so they were likely to be distracted, and so less likely to be too angry when Grace revealed that she'd massaged the truth a bit at the outset. There was a crack above the door to her bedroom that was starting to look moldy, black specks in the bend where the wall met the ceiling. What did asbestos look like? Could you *see* asbestos?

"How's tricks, Goose?" her dad asked.

Tricks are not going particularly well at the moment, actually. She swallowed. "Okay. How are you?"

Her dad paused. "Honestly, sweet?" he said. It startled her. She wasn't aware of her father ever being *dis*honest, but the prospect made her uncomfortable. "There's kind of a lot going on around here." He sounded tired and old. "With your sisters. Plus all these little things around the house. We're having a hell of a time with one of the ginkgo trees in the backyard. A busy time, oddly."

"Oh." Her *how are you*s were rarely met, by her father, with anything but *oh fine, tell me about yourself*s. He didn't usually *talk* about himself. It occurred to her that it must be hard to be the only man in a family of women. Hard to get a word in edgewise. Hard to prioritize your own emotions over those of everyone else. Hard, perhaps, to acknowledge those emotions instead of putting them perpetually on the back burner. She was moved to prod him along: "Is everything . . . okay? With Liza? And—Violet's—"

"Jonah," he said. "Yes. Relatively, I guess. Lize is—healthy. A little—worn out. You heard about her promot—"

"Yes," she said.

"And Jonah—he's a nice kid. Funny. Sharp. You're really going to like him, Goose."

She felt strangely hurt by this assessment, by her father referring to someone else—someone younger than she was— as *sharp* and *funny.*

"We all had dinner last week," he said, not realizing he was rubbing salt in the wound. "Minus you, of course."

She was still—alongside her envy—concerned about the note in her father's voice. She recalled a specific moment in her childhood, riding in the car on the expressway with her dad, her sudden awareness that he was a person, too, capable of doubt and weakness. "And are—*you* okay, Dad?"

But then there it was, the response she'd been expecting earlier: her father laughed. "Oh, sure, Goose. I'm just fine. Enough about me. What's new in your world? Gearing up for school? Mom'd like a coffee mug from the bookstore, whenever you have a spare minute. She recently learned that your mascot is a duck; is that true?"

They'd googled her fake school. They actually believed that she was someone who was capable of normal, upward-moving behavior. Picturing her mom doing image searches on their ancient desktop PC for the beanie-clad and uncreatively named Oregon Duck just about did her in, and she sank cross-legged onto the kitchen floor.

She'd been crying a lot lately. It typically happened at convenient times, when she was away from the concerned eyes of others, but now she felt the telltale throbbing in her throat. Recently she'd felt more achingly alone than she thought was humanly possible, walking the streets alone, waking up alone, making solo trips to the weird off-brand grocery store, where she bought wine and honey and alfalfa sprouts like a biblical widow.

"Grace?" he said, concerned. "Gracie, are you okay? What is it?"

She decided, then, that she couldn't do it, that she couldn't bear to worry her father more, her father, who was always on top of things but who now, for the first time, sounded truly overwhelmed. How could she justify, upon reflection, adding even *more* stress to his life? He'd just retired and was supposed to be doing retired-person things; her dad who was older than everyone else's dad, golfing or day-trading or solving crossword puzzles. Yet he was still clearly devoting all of his energy to her sisters, and would dredge up more energy to devote to her, if she asked, and it didn't seem fair to put him in that position.

How in the hell had she gotten so far off-course? Other people her age were in graduate school. Other people her age were getting engaged, were convincingly sporting business-casual outfits, were romping around exotic lands with boyfriends who were rugged enough to wear the straps of their backpacks clipped across their chests without inciting mockery. Other people her age had *careers*; other people her age had domestic partners with whom they shared pets. And then there was Grace, who had an apartment that looked like the room where Nosferatu kept his victims. Grace, who'd eaten leftover brown rice *with her hands* for dinner last night because she owned only a single fork and was too depressed to wash it. Grace, whose only romantic prospects existed in the form of accidentally answered sales calls and pleasantries about the weather with the hot, red-bandanna-wearing bike messenger who sometimes delivered packages to her boss. Grace, who'd half-assed her law school applications and then—surprise, surprise— been rejected from every single program.

Then again: she wasn't as bad off as *Wendy*. And she wasn't doing anything as serious as Liza was doing, so the stakes were lower. And this *certainly* didn't match the high-level duplicity of Violet's early twenties.

She swallowed down her crying. "No, I'm great," she said. "Just tired."

Other people went to bed at reasonable hours. Grace drank wine in her bed and drifted off watching *Gossip Girl*.

Other people—the crux—probably didn't miss their parents this much. She could picture her dad leaning against the kitchen counter, drinking lukewarm coffee, scratching Loomis's neck with his free hand. And this was what worried her the most: nothing had ever felt as comfortable, as easy, as *good* as being with her parents, her *family*. No one, it seemed, would ever regard her with the same enthusiastic awe as her mother;

the same quiet, feverish pride as her father. It aroused concern within that she was slated for a lifetime of disappointment from the outside.

She wished she was with her dad instead of just on the phone and that she could curl up into the fetal position against him as she had the day she was born, when it was just the two of them, her mother elsewhere, bleeding, somewhere between life and death. It had always terrified her to picture that day but now she thought of her father's side of the story, how he must have felt to be sent into an empty room, without his partner, burdened suddenly with the sole responsibility of Grace herself. He'd moved her into her freshman dorm nearly five years ago.

"It's what I'm here for," he'd said when she thanked him, as she watched him struggle to assemble her assortment of IKEA furniture. "It's in my dad contract."

She wished she had such a concrete favor to ask of him now. She missed being someone's responsibility. But didn't her parents deserve one child they could be proud of? When you were the youngest kid, the bar was set differently, influenced by everyone who had come before. You got points simply for not dropping the ball *quite* as far as your older sisters had. And Grace had always performed accordingly. She couldn't imagine what it would do to them if they learned she'd committed an offense of this level. She needed some more time to think it through, to figure out a smoother way to extract herself. Then, she told herself, she'd come clean.

"I have to get to work, Daddy."

"Godspeed, Goose," he said.

Two days later, a FedEx envelope was delivered to her door. Inside were five brand-new ATM twenties, accompanied by a handwritten note on a Mallory's Hardware Post-it: *Goose, Take yourself out to dinner. Keep up the good work. We love you. Dad and Mom.*

It was written in her father's hand and it made her cry for forty-five minutes.

There was a surprising amount of information to be found on the Internet about arboreal illness. It had become one of David's go-to morning activities, after his wife left for work: cup of coffee with the dog on the sunporch, laptop on the old picnic table, page after page of root-knot nematodes, phytophthora rot treatments, and slugs. Marilyn had been encouraging him to explore his interests, and this made him feel the same kind of energy he felt as a diagnostician, checking things off the list: *vascular, infectious, toxic, autoimmune . . .* He was concerned about Gracie, who'd sounded unusually lost when she called that morning, but he knew what Marilyn would say— that they needed to let her grow up, find her own way—and so he pushed the thought from his mind in pursuit of more concrete knowledge. The leaves on the ginkgo hadn't come in as they normally did; he'd begun collecting leaf samples, lining them up on the kitchen windowsill. He was hesitant to call an arborist—it seemed too bourgeois, a frivolous waste of money—and was trying to solve the mystery himself.

If the tree were dying of natural causes—sinister midwestern slugs, a bad reaction to last year's unusually cold winter—then he would cede one to nature. The ginkgo had been enormous back when he and Marilyn met; perhaps it had simply lived out its time. The quietude of his days afforded him thoughts like these, psychological measurement of organic matter. He didn't *want* the tree to be dead, certainly, but if it was, he would accept it with serenity—he also, sometimes, for something to do, thumbed through his wife's new-agey mindfulness books.

The ginkgo's trunk itself was too smooth to climb, so David set up the ladder against it. He felt young and nimble, the same physical confidence he used to experience when arranging Marilyn's elaborate Halloween decorations on the high eaves of the garage, his wife standing in the driveway below and watching him with admiration.

"Your butt looks really cute from this angle," she'd call up to him, if the kids weren't around.

He continued his ascent, the pruning shears tucked beneath his arm. When he reached the sturdiest-looking low branch he straddled it as though on horseback and paused for a minute, observing the backyard from fifteen feet up.

The dog paced restlessly across the ground beneath him. He held a leaf in his palm, half a dull green, the other half whitish; both sides mottled with tiny black dots. A woodpecker sounded from a neighboring oak. He massaged his shoulder, which was rebelling against his recent foray into elevated landscaping. He leaned his back against the trunk and sighed.

He found the notion of mindfulness irritating. Work made life make sense; it gave it shape and order. And then suddenly you were sixty-four years old, a doctor of medicine, climbing trees like a boy, obsessed with slugs and peculiar strains of mold. It didn't seem fair, this abrupt reversal of his station in life. There should be some sort of middle ground between gainful employment and DiagnoseYourDecidua.com. He'd sent the webmaster an email—the gratuitous *M.D.* punctuating his signature made him feel a spark of pride—pointing out the egregious linguistic error, that *decidua* had, in fact, nothing to do with *deciduous*, that it in fact referred to the uterine lining expelled with the placenta after human delivery. He'd been proud of the email, which contained a patient explanation of the Latin root *decidere*, translatable either to "to cut off" or "to fall off," the latter of which could be applicable, if used loosely, to describe both the shedding of leaves on trees and the shedding of the endometrium formed during pregnancy.

Actually: he'd been proud of the email at the time, but within twenty minutes the pride had turned to shame, shame for the fact that last year he'd been *delivering* uterine linings but now he was schooling an anonymous dime-store dendrologist on Latin root words.

Mindfulness was bullshit. The trim on the house needed painting but Marilyn was adamant that he not do it himself. Perhaps he would remind her that he was a grown man, a once-respected man, a man whose *catlike reflexes* she had previously praised (in bed, albeit, but nobody could argue with the fact that he was fairly coordinated). *I realize this is a cliché*, he would say to her, *but it feels like the world has left me behind.*

He felt an odd moment of vertigo. And then, out of the corner of his eye: something golden. Sprouting from the trunk above him, a cluster of waxy yellow discs, like clamshells. A chill ran up his spine. He'd always hated things like that—corals or sea anemones that the girls would ooh and ahh over when they went to the Shedd, porous, abundant things with lobes growing like cancer.

"Sonofabitch," he breathed.

"Love?"

He startled, grabbed at the branch between his thighs as the pruning shears tumbled to the ground. *"Jesus."*

Marilyn was standing beneath the tree, squinting up at him into the sun. Her hand flew to her chest. "Oh, David, I'm so sorry."

"Trying to kill me, kid?"

"Sweetheart. I'm a menace. I don't know why it didn't occur to me that I might scare you."

The irritation returned, a twinge: "You didn't *scare* me. I just didn't know you were home."

She paused, and he knew she was deciding whether or not to engage with his impertinence. "Here I am," she said, and her voice was effortful, but instead she smiled up at him, her big green eyes creased at the corners but still strikingly bright.

"There you are," he replied. "Honey fungus."

Marilyn cocked her head, bemused. "Sweetie pie."

"No, it's—honey fungus. See on the left there?" He was trying not to betray how upsetting he found this. He'd read enough to know that honey fungus meant the tree was a goner. "If it's on the trunk, there's a good chance it's taken hold in the roots," he said.

"Then what?"

"Then the tree dies. And the fungus can spread to neighboring trees."

"Oh, David." She arched her back and looked upward. "Oh, the poor thing." His wife, who could find it in her heart to have compassion for anyone, anything. "Come on down, love." She held her hands upward as if to spot him. "I haven't kissed anyone all day."

Suddenly eager to embrace her, he descended carefully, so as not to make her nervous.

Violet had begun to view the world, lately, as a nuanced gradient of the degrees to which she wanted to physically harm her sister. If she were measuring murderousness on the one-to-ten pain scale her father had taught them when they were young, she would have given Wendy's latest escapade—inviting her to coffee and then bailing fifteen minutes before, citing a philanthropic emergency, and sending Jonah in her stead—a 7.5. It was not quite the level that Wendy had reached by springing Jonah on her in the first place—that had been an 11; there had only ever been one other eleventh-level cruelty committed between them, and that one had been Violet's doing—but it still infuriated her.

She didn't particularly *want* to hang out with him; that was one of many shameful admissions. She knew she was *supposed* to hang out with him, and to derive pleasure from doing so, from being in his company, from studying the intricacies of his being, from learning who he was, what he wanted from the world, whether there was hope for him yet, despite all the ways in which she and the universe had failed him. Her parents were fascinated by him. Wendy behaved as though she'd known him forever. Violet was deeply uncomfortable with everything he stirred within her, and surely he could sense this. Matt was, understandably, suspicious of him, and keenly aware of the potential ripple effects he could cause, and so she had decided not to tell him about Wendy's last-minute bait and switch.

Wendy had chosen a Starbucks near her house, and Violet hoped it would be annoying enough, atmospherically, to prevent them from staying long. Of course it was awful that she was itching to get away from him before she'd even arrived. But it was true: he made her nervous. She conceded, to herself, angling into a hard-won parking spot on Delaware, that she was kind of a shitty person, but at least she was self-aware in her shittiness.

Jonah was already there, standing outside the Starbucks with a big sweatshirt, hood up, that read, across the front, WE HAVE THE FACTS AND WE'RE VOTING YES, and she stayed in her car for an extra moment to watch him, undetected and objective. He was a normal teenage kid. Bad posture, a nose—not hers—that was still a little too big for his face, a nearly visceral self-consciousness. She fed her meter and crossed the street.

"Sorry I'm late," she called, and she and Jonah both flinched at the high splash of her voice. She lowered her volume. "Have you been waiting long?"

"Uh-huh." Neither yes nor no.

"It's nice to see you. Should we—coffee?"

He shrugged, and she led the way inside.

"Good day so far?" she asked him in line, and when he simply grunted, she said, "Have you ever tried to see how far you can get through the day without using any actual words?"

She'd meant it as a joke, but nobody had ever skewed her off her game like this and she felt somehow not fully in control of her own output.

He just stared at her. Then: "It's our turn to order."

"Oh. Right, I— Hi. I'll do a half-caf cappuccino. Whole milk, but very dry." She turned to Jonah, who was smirking. "What?"

"Wendy and I were just talking about how we hate when people say *I'll do* instead of *I'll have*. It makes it sound like you're, like, boning your coffee."

She reddened. "Well, Wendy's known for her lofty conversation. What would you like?"

"Espresso," he said to the barista.

"Wait," Violet said. "Aren't you a little young to be drinking caffeine?"

Jonah laughed. The barista looked at them expectantly.

"It stunts your growth," Violet said. "It's such a silly thing to become addicted to so young, when your body doesn't *need* it." She'd already read the books on adolescent development, though Eli was still in Pull-Ups. She was nothing if not a good student.

"I've smoked cigarettes since I was thirteen," Jonah said.

If she wasn't mistaken, the barista was fighting a smile.

"Fine," she said. "An espresso. But a single." She paid without looking at him.

At their table, she tried to reset the conversation. "How was dinner with my parents?"

"You were there," he said flatly.

"I meant how was it for you. My mom and dad really like you."

"They're nice."

She smiled, waiting foolishly for him to say more. When this inevitably did not happen, she went on. "So is summer off to a good start? You enjoying being in the city?"

Everything involving this kid is going to lead to something else, Matt had said.

"It's fine." Jonah pounded his espresso in one sip and she tried not to wince. It pleased her, sadistically, to see that he was trying to hide a grimace of his own.

"What have you been up to?"

"Whatever. Netflix. Wandering around. I'm doing this Israeli street-fighting thing."

"*Excuse* me?"

"Wendy signed me up for it."

"For— This is an organized activity?"

"It's called Krav Maga. It's how they train the Israel Defense Forces."

"Wendy signed you up for Israeli military training?"

"They teach it at her gym."

She relaxed, but only slightly. "Is this like—jujitsu?"

"It's actually pronounced ju*jutsu. Jitsu*'s a westernization. And no, it's totally different. It's a lot more—like, intense."

"Intense how?"

He shrugged again, cagily this time.

"Are things going well? With Wendy?"

He seemed to perk up at this. "Yeah, Wendy's awesome."

She wasn't sure whether to feel pleased or wounded. "That's great to hear. I hoped you two would hit it off." Hadn't she? Didn't she? Her cappuccino wasn't dry enough. "I realize I haven't been quite as—*available* as Wendy, but I've got the—" She swallowed. "The kids, and they're—definitely a full-time job." She tried to laugh. "But I'm— Just so you know, I'm available to you in terms of—you know, if you have questions, or things you need."

"Can you tell me about my dad?"

She felt her stomach drop, quickly and heavily, a free-falling elevator car. She remembered, distantly, a lecture from one of her college English classes about Aristotelian poetics, about things being at once *surprising and inevitable*. This was precisely the question she didn't want him to ask, so of course he'd asked it. And he had every right to ask it, so why was she, sitting across from him at a chain coffee shop in the Gold Coast, fighting the impulse to slap him across the face? Though it was hard to describe the latter as *surprising*, exactly.

She must've looked awful because Jonah surprised her again, this time by backtracking. "I just meant—like it's weird that I . . ."

"No, it's—just probably a conversation for a different time?" *Are you free in 2094,* she did not ask. "Things are—complicated, Jonah." He continued to stare at her evenly, not offering an inch, eyes mailbox-blue and unblinking. "We've all got enough on our plates as it is, don't you think? I'm not going to be going anywhere anytime soon. You and I will have plenty of opportunities to discuss this in the future."

The startled relief that crossed his face lasted for only a second, but she caught it, and she wondered, with an increasingly heavy heart, if it had something to do with her offhanded and unintentional promise of longevity, if by saying what she'd said—*in the future*—she had given him the permanence Hanna had begged her for.

This kid across the table from her: once the baby who kept her company. Who made her feel kindly toward the world, if only for a while. To whom she used to whisper at night, this hostage and too-young confidant, her hands on her belly— *Everyone thinks I know what I'm doing but I actually have no idea what I'm doing and that's the cruelest trick the universe plays on people who have their shit together, little one; the people who seem like they have it together are the most overlooked, because everyone thinks those people never need anything, but everyone needs things; I need things; thanks for listening; I'll eat more protein tomorrow.* She was horrified to feel tears in her eyes.

"Oh, I hoped you guys would still be here."

She had never been so happy to see Wendy.

"Jesus, it's like a fucking sauna outside." Wendy slid into the chair between them. "My meeting got out early. Inquiring minds, we decided on the Krug over the 'ninety-eight Dom. Sorry, did I interrupt?"

"Not at all," Violet said. She let Wendy's presence wash over her like a poisonous salve. "We were discussing jujitsu."

"It's actually ju*jutsu*," Wendy corrected her. A couple of peas in a goddamn pod, these two. "Yeah, J's started taking Krav Maga at my health club. He's like a fucking acrobat. It actually seems pretty cool. It's all about situational awareness and channeling aggression. And it's *great* exercise. Show her your triceps, J."

It was a relief to Violet that Jonah seemed to find this instruction as weird as she did, part stage mom and part Mrs. Robinson.

"I'm thinking about taking it up myself," Wendy said. "Core barre's getting a little monotonous."

"Straight from the horse's mouth," Violet muttered.

"I feel like I interrupted."

"No." Wyatt needed to be picked up from sports camp in an hour. Eli was undoubtedly on cloud nine playing Simon Says with Caroline, the babysitter he was supposed to not need because his mother had chosen him over her career. Matt had kissed her goodbye this morning, but in a distant and perfunctory way. And Wendy, good God, her trainwreck sister, had successfully enrolled Jonah in a—albeit dubious—recreational activity because she had all the time in the world to be there for him. And didn't that make sense—*surprising and inevitable*—since he was the boy whose existence Wendy had not only fostered but encouraged? "No, it's nice to see you." She felt as though she'd exerted more emotional energy in the past fifteen minutes than she had in the last decade. She watched her sister and the boy she couldn't bring herself to call her son, and she allowed herself, despite the alarm bells that always accompanied Wendy, to appreciate the ease they had around each other. She swallowed the last of her cappuccino, whose excess milk would sit heavily in her gut for hours to come. "Both. It's good to see you both."

Violet was born four days before Thanksgiving, and David's most selfish thought after she'd arrived was *thank God*. Thank God, obviously, that she was healthy and perfect. But then, next: thank God Thanksgiving could be canceled. Thank God he wouldn't have to go back to Albany Park. Raising a son alone, his father had adhered to ritual with determination; and for Thanksgiving that meant turkey, bourbon, football in the front yard. Whenever he returned from Iowa to visit his dad he was reminded of how much he preferred his new life, the vibrancy and warmth of it, and it made him resent the comparative chill of his childhood. When he called his father from the hospital to tell him about his new granddaughter, his dad had asked the requisite questions, and then: "So, are we still on for Thursday?"

He blinked. Marilyn was drifting in and out of sleep beside him. "Actually, I don't think so. Marilyn's not going to be up for such a long trip. And with two babies now—it's just a lot."

His wife stirred, shifted Violet in her arms. *What are you doing*, she mouthed.

"Well, I wish you would have told me sooner," his dad said.

"We didn't know when the baby was coming, Dad. That's kind of how it works." As though he, newly a father of two, was now the wiser one.

"Let me talk to him," Marilyn whispered. She reached for the phone and David handed it over uncertainly. "Rich? Hi." She smiled into the receiver. She loved his dad, said from the first time she met him that she could tell he had a *good soul.* "I'm doing well," she was saying. "I'm great. We're over the moon. She's David's spitting image." With this she looked up at him, winked. "So I'm not going to be able to make Thanksgiving," she said. "I'll be at home with the little one. But you'll have David and Wendy. The next best thing." David stiffened, reached up his hands in a soundless *what the fuck.* She frowned at him. "I know they're looking forward to it. I wish I could be there, but—" She paused to let him speak and then she laughed. "Exactly. Life has been known to get in the way."

"Why on *earth* did you do that?" he asked when she'd hung up, not quite hostile—she'd just given birth to his daughter, after all.

She fussed with Violet's blanket, cupped a palm over her skull. She was in an idyllic haze, coursing with hormones, high on exhaustion and in love with the world. Next to her joy, he knew he was being childish and obdurate. She just smiled at him. "Honey, it's one day and it'll mean the world to him."

"You just had a baby, Marilyn," he said stupidly.

"Did I? I wondered who this was." She kept smiling at him, then looked down at Violet. "You'll go for the day and then you'll come home. If you won't go for your dad, go for me."

He went for her; four days later, he drove with Wendy to Chicago. She'd been much clingier since Violet was born and she burrowed into his neck as he and his father sat in the living room.

"How's Marilyn?" his dad asked. "The baby?"

"They're great. It's utter chaos but it's— Marilyn's so good with them. I don't know how she does it." Was he doing this on purpose? Rubbing their thriving family life in his dad's face?

Ashamed, he reached for a coin from his pocket, handed it to Wendy to play with.

"I remember your mother transforming when you were born," his dad said suddenly, and David startled. Mentions of his mother were infrequent. "She seemed to know all of these things—just instinctively. Baffled me. I felt like a caveman."

"Yes, it's humbling," he said. He felt his speech change when he was around his dad; his language became more flowery, his jokes more pretentious. He couldn't figure out why or how he did it, but it seemed cruel.

"I was thinking I'd like to do this again in a couple of weeks. If Marilyn's up to it."

"Another—Thanksgiving?"

"Another dinner. Give the little one a proper welcome. Just for the day."

"A second Thanksgiving?"

His father smiled. "Yeah. Sure. Second Thanksgiving."

And this—though the sentiment was nice; though he knew his wife would find it wildly charming—annoyed him as well. "I'll get back to you."

"You shouldn't let her play with that," Richard said. "She could choke." Sure enough, Wendy had the quarter halfway in her mouth. He yanked it away and she started to cry.

"No, it's okay; you're okay," he hummed. Wendy wailed, and he rose, trying to distract her. "Look, little lion, a *mirror.* What's this, kiddo? This is a *box of Kleenex.*" It was ultimately a spool of thread that diverted her attention. Did his father *sew?* He had a sudden image of his father hemming his own pants and it made him so sad that he almost felt dizzy. As he thought about it—did his dad own a pincushion? One that looked like a tomato, like Marilyn's?—he was aware of a hot disgrace swirling around in his belly. How odd that his delight over his new daughter, his healthy growing family, could exist in such close proximity to the sorrow his father had been living with for years. What an asshole he was for avoiding this day, for trying to deprive his dad of one of the few bright spots in his life.

He felt a rough hand on his shoulder: his father, behind him. "You're doing just fine," he said, and he sounded fatherly in a way that he normally didn't, and David felt like a teenager again, he and Marilyn just a couple of fumbling know-nothings, entrusted with two babies, ignorant of all the ways that life could go wrong. "Your girls are very lucky," Richard added, and David just nodded because he couldn't bring himself to speak.

Dinner was a single turkey thigh split between two people, a table with two place settings, a pumpkin pie whose leftovers would be eaten for four subsequent days.

"She'll go down for a nap soon," David said as he cleared the table. "Should we throw the ball around for a while?"

His dad looked surprised, pleased. He nodded. "I'd like that."

His wife was a good actress. He watched her, across the room in a showy three-story neoclassical belonging to the dean of the medical school, Violet wrapped against her chest in a sling, swaying slightly from left to right, sipping modestly from a glass of red wine, smiling in a way that was at once sleepy and beatific as she said, "I just love being a mom. It's the most fun I've ever had."

He begged to differ. At home, she seemed skittish and miserable and crazy, cooing maniacally to either baby or hand-washing bibs and onesies with the demented ferocity of an old-world Italian grandmother. She slept hard and fast, in short bursts, in a way that seemed both deeply unhealthy and innately functional—he did the same thing, working so much that he could no longer distinguish a Tuesday from a Friday, dusk from dawn. She came to visit him at school sometimes with the babies, and she accepted the hugs he gave her like a junkie, clung to him like Velcro and didn't let go until he did. It always pained him a little to pull away from her.

She was talking to one of his professors, a neurologist in his forties. He wasn't sure what version of her Dr. Fletcher was seeing—the charming, beautiful, confident woman who made him feel protective and jealous? Or the sleep-deprived, hormonally flimsy, unoccupied housewife who had the audacity to say things like *It's the most fun I've ever had?*

"High praise," his teacher said, and David felt an immediate stab of pity for his wife. She was still so young and looked it suddenly. He could see her façade starting to buckle, and he excused himself from a circle of classmates and went to her, touching the small of her back.

"Just hearing about the joys of new parenthood," Dr. Fletcher said, smiling in a way that might have been mocking—mocking Marilyn? His wife looked at him with something like desperation: *please don't sell me out, not in front of all these people; I know I was crying in the shower this morning but please just play along.*

"It's the most gratifying, terrifying, wonderful thing in the world," David said, unusually flowery, and Marilyn smiled at him, leaned back into his hand.

"Do you have children?" she asked Dr. Fletcher. Wendy was at home being minded by a neighbor; Violet was ten weeks old and too young to be left with a sitter; it had seemed like too much to bring both girls, but he knew that Marilyn felt Wendy's absence like a phantom limb.

"God, no," the doctor said. "I always thought it would be unfair, given the hours I keep."

Marilyn flushed; David watched her.

"But hey," Dr. Fletcher said. "Some people make it work."

"Indeed," David said.

The doctor leaned in conspiratorially. "I'd advise you guys to stop at two, though. Corrigan's got four kids and he can barely stay upright." He nodded over to one of David's supervisors at the hospital, who was standing beside a woman David presumed to be his wife, both of them looking like the walking dead, wide-eyed and used up, their defeated bodies slouched away from each other.

"Four?" He cupped his hand more firmly around his wife's hip.

"Fell asleep standing up during an appendectomy last week," Dr. Fletcher said as Marilyn excused herself. He couldn't tell what it meant when she squeezed his hand and slipped away.

She was quiet on the way home.

"Nice house, huh?" he asked as they walked across the lighted bridge over the river. "I didn't realize there *were* houses like that around here." Immediately he realized he was opening a door he'd worked hard to barricade closed.

"Yes, such a far cry from our neighborhood," she said, lifting her hand to shield Violet's sleeping face from the passing headlights. Their corner of Iowa City was on the run-down side but it was quiet; there was a park a few blocks from the house where she could take the girls. It was warm and safe. He bristled, but before he could take offense she reached for his arm, wove hers through the bend in his elbow.

"Sorry," she said. "I'm in a mood."

"Fletcher's a condescending asshole," he said. She pulled him closer, their hips bumping together a few times until they found their stride.

"He must think I'm— What did I say to him? *The most fun I've—* What an asinine thing to— Ugh. I just hope I didn't embarrass you," she said dejectedly. She wasn't looking at him, had her eyes fixed on a blinking light down the river.

He shook his head vigorously. "Of course not. Never."

"I wonder if I'll ever have something interesting to say again."

"You're being too hard on yourself," he said.

"You're placating me." She swung her bag around her arm. "I would kill for a cigarette." It was a habit she'd ramped up when they moved to Iowa, though she'd given it up when she'd gotten pregnant with Wendy and was abstaining still, while she was breast-feeding Violet. "Yet another earthly pleasure that would arguably help to keep me sane, and yet . . ."

"We're not earthly?" he asked. "Me and the girls?"

"The girls and I," she corrected. "No. You're ethereal. My intangible everything."

The statement seemed both incredibly romantic and unbearably sad.

When they arrived home, he dispatched the sitter while Marilyn went to check on Wendy. He made a couple of peanut butter and jelly sandwiches, knowing that Marilyn hadn't eaten much at the party. When he brought them to their bedroom, Marilyn was nursing Violet, holding her in one arm while the other hand traced lines up and down Wendy's back— Wendy, who was curled in the crook of Marilyn's knee, breathing deeply. And there she was, his wife, home again, back with her babies, freed from having to needlessly justify her existence to the likes of Fletcher. She raised her eyes to him and he weakened at the knees.

"Would I know if I had mastitis?" she asked him, frowning down at herself. "Also, Wendy needs to be changed if you don't mind."

They would repeat it for years to come in times of strife: *the most fun I've ever had.*

CHAPTER NINE

Violet remembered, from her days as a litigator, the rule of contending with a PR scandal: head it off at the pass and it could remain thereafter within your control. This was the approach she was taking for their dinner with Jonah. Matt was gravely concerned about it; he met every mention leading up to the evening with an *Are you sure you want to do that* look, the kind of look that said, *I'm not going to stop you but only because I'd rather you stop yourself.* For this reason, proceeding with the dinner also gave her a certain satisfaction, that childish fuck-you logic present in most marriages, the contrarian impulse to do something simply because your husband didn't want you to.

There was no extant protocol for how to introduce your relinquished child to your husband, or for how to introduce him to the children you'd had on purpose, the children you'd never given a second thought to keeping. So Violet ordered pizza—everyone liked pizza, didn't they?—and made sure there was an ample supply of wine on hand for herself and Matt, and she explained to Wyatt and Eli, as best she could, that families came in all forms, that she'd been a different person fifteen years ago, that she didn't even know Dada *existed* back then, and that they had a half brother named Jonah who was going to join them for dinner. The boys took the news stoically—though she assumed their quietude stemmed less from acceptance than from lack of comprehension—and Matt, seemingly dissatisfied with this, crouched down before them and said, "Let's keep this between us for now, okay, my buddies?"

"Matt," she said, surprised, because they weren't raising their children to lie.

He rose to his feet and lowered his voice. "You really want this getting out at school?"

She ceded his point, picturing the Shady Oaks moms encircling her like a flock of turkeys marching around a dead body. "Yeah, little loves, this'll be our family secret for now, okay? Like that silly story we heard at the library, how the bear's whole family plans the secret party for him and they all keep their lips zipped?" She made an exaggerated zipping motion across her mouth and Eli laughed, but Wyatt still looked skeptical. "We just don't want Jonah to feel overwhelmed, okay, sweetie? So let's keep this between us. He's got a lot of new things going on in his life."

She went alone to pick up Jonah from Wendy's house, and as they drove back to Evanston, she pointed out their familial landmarks—"We did a fund-raising thing to install that Little Free Library"; "There's the boys' school"—and it wasn't until she looked over and saw his blank expression that she remembered how dull her life had become. She wondered how he would guide her around a tour of his past locales—*This is where I tortured squirrels*, perhaps, or *I almost set fire to this place just for the hell of it.* They spent the rest of the ride in silence.

When they pulled into her driveway, he let out a low whistle. "Damn."

She turned to him suspiciously. "What?"

He smirked. "Nothing. Nice house, that's all."

Of course she was aware that a person she'd created had been living in a group home while she lorded over six thousand square feet of lakeside Tudor swankiness, but it wasn't as though she'd deliberately orchestrated the disparity. "It was a fixer-upper," she said defensively.

Inside, she introduced him clumsily to her family: "This is my—your—a—Jonah."

"A Jonah, huh?" said Matt, who usually didn't have much of a sense of humor. He extended his hand and she wondered what he was seeing, if he recognized her in Jonah's face, if he was thinking about her with someone else, carrying another man's child before he ever knew her. "Really nice to meet you," Matt said, and he sounded genuinely welcoming, and she touched his back gratefully. Jonah had moved on to the kids, giving them each an awkward little wave. Eli hid behind her leg, peering at him between her knees.

"Don't worry," Wyatt said conspiratorially. "We won't tell anyone about you."

Jonah looked over to her and she could see, past the smirk on his face, that of course the remark had wounded him. "Thanks, dude," he said to Wyatt.

He had an ease with the kids, as it turned out. He was the kind of person who talked to children as he'd talk to anyone, a trait she knew her boys admired. They were introducing him to their abundant roster of Lego people, and Matt impelled her into the kitchen.

"You know, I wasn't suggesting that we should tell them to *lie* about him," he said, "just that we don't want them going around telling everyone when we're not even sure—"

She turned to face him, offering him her wineglass. "No, I understand. It makes sense."

"And yet you used the word *brother* when we hadn't discussed—"

"Jesus, Matt. There's no instruction sheet for this. What else was I supposed to say? That Mama and Dada just casually befriended a random high school sophomore?"

"I just think it's better to play it safe. You know how impressionable they are."

"Our children?" she said. "With whom I spend every day? Yes, I'm familiar."

"There's no need to get—"

"Isn't this night stressful enough without us fighting?"

"You're the one who—"

"Mama!"

At the sound of Wyatt's voice she leapt efficiently into panic mode. Was this what she got for opening her home to the boy: peril for her own children? She pushed past Matt, steeling herself for whatever was transpiring in the playroom, hoping that her latent mammalian strength would kick in, whatever it was that helped people save their kids from being crushed by cars.

But in the playroom, Jonah was upside-down in a handstand, a slight outward bend in his elbows, legs splayed in splits, and Wyatt was regarding him with bald admiration.

"Mama, *look*," he said.

She paused to get her bearings. "Honey, you *scared* me. I thought something was . . ." She trailed off when she saw the look on Jonah's face, shades of embarrassment and hurt feelings.

He lowered himself to the floor.

"I didn't mean," she said. "I just thought—maybe someone had gotten hurt." *I thought you'd managed to kill one of my children in the two minutes I left you alone with them.*

"He can do a thing on one hand, too," Wyatt said incredulously. Jonah had since risen and was now standing over by the window, stretching his arms self-consciously against his chest.

"It's a—you know, an accident-prone age. I get nervous," she said, in partial apology. Behind her, she could feel the weight of Matt's silent assessment. "I didn't know you were a gymnast," she said.

Jonah snorted. "I'm not."

"Just a skill you picked up?" she asked. She lifted Eli into her arms and reveled in his solidity. Her children were fine. Everything was fine.

"Yeah, actually."

"No lessons?" She realized the stupidity of the question, dripping with her privilege, a woman for whom *lessons*— gymnastics, viola, whatever her heart desired—had always been a part of life.

"Just things I learned I could do," he said mildly.

"Well, you definitely didn't inherit your agility from me." Again, it was an awkward and conspicuous thing to say, a faux pas of the highest order. Jonah blushed.

"Can you teach me?" Wyatt asked him, and Jonah looked at her quickly before he replied, "I don't think so, dude. Too dangerous."

The doorbell rang. Matt went to answer it.

"Pizza," she said. "I hope that's okay. The universal unifier."

She watched him open his mouth and then decide to close it again.

"Don't tell me you don't like pizza," she said.

"I *love* pizza," Wyatt said gravely.

"I'm lactose intolerant," Jonah said.

"Are you—really? How did I not know that? Wendy should have said—" But of course this wasn't Wendy's fault; it was another orb hanging densely between them, pulsing, winking: *That's just the tip of the iceberg of things you don't know.*

"It's really no big deal. I'm not actually that hungry."

"You're fifteen," she said. "Of course you're hungry. Do you do gluten?"

"Do I— Sure." Jonah seemed to suppress a smile. "Yeah. Gluten's great."

She was so ashamed of the PB & J she made for him that she pretended not to notice, doing the dishes as Matt drove him home, that three bottles of wine were missing from the rack.

Wendy became aware, as the redhead was about to find his target, of another presence in the room. She assumed at first that it was a trick of her mind, fuzzy with Grey Goose, but when she turned her head at the feel of the guy's beard against her clit, she saw the shadow in the doorway.

"Fuck," she said, and for a few seconds there was a kind of slapstick arrangement as she scrambled for the covers, the man's head caught between her thighs, her elbow knocking painfully into the headboard. "Jesus fuck; what're you *doing* in here?" Her pity dinner with Miles's friend, of course, had been a lie; she'd taken advantage of her childlessness to have a night out. She'd heard Jonah come in after dinner at Violet's, but she'd been preoccupied with the redhead. She'd assumed Jonah had gone to bed.

"What the hell?" the redhead said. He was on his feet, hands balled into fists, shoulders tensed like the fur on a dog's back. "Who the fuck is this?"

"No, it's okay," she said, scrambling up, wrapping the sheet around her body. She grabbed his arm before he could approach Jonah. "It's all right; he lives here."

"What the fuck does that mean?" The man looked back and forth between her and Jonah. "Is this your *kid*?"

It hurt her heart that this was the first cognitive leap he made, and with such ease. She'd told him earlier that she was thirty-two. "He's my nephew. Jonah. Jonah, this is—" She was blanking on his name. She waffled constantly between worries about early-onset Alzheimer's and fears of alcohol-induced memory loss.

"Were you *watching* us?" the man asked, his muscles flexing beneath her fingers.

"No, I was just— I came to ask for some Tylenol and—sorry; I wasn't—I just needed—"

"What do you need Tylenol for?" she asked, because— oddly—her first instinct was concern for his well-being.

"I pulled a muscle, I think. My shoulder. I was doing some tricks for Violet's kids."

"Ibuprofen works better," she said. "Downstairs bathroom. Third shelf on the right."

"Thanks," he said. "Sorry."

"Take two, not three," she said.

"Okay. Sorry. Thanks." He skittered away and the redhead pulled his arm from her grasp.

"Well, that was fucking weird," he said.

"It was." She sank onto the edge of the bed.

"He lives with you? You should've *told* me. Jesus Christ."

"Why?" she asked, suddenly defensive. "Why is that your business?"

"Because I'm—we were about to— Don't you think I deserve to know if there's some weird-ass kid who might be watching us from the doorway?"

"He wasn't *watching* us." Though she was preoccupied by the fact that Jonah's initial reaction when he saw them in bed together wasn't to run away in horror.

"I'm really— Shit, I'm sorry, Wendy, but I'm—really weirded out by this."

"We can lock the door," she said listlessly. The little thrill of him was gone, leaving only a light residual slickness between her legs. Steve. His name came to her epiphanically.

"I should go," he said. He wouldn't meet her eyes. "I'll call you."

Because she'd perfected the line herself, she knew it wasn't true.

Sitting on the porch with her mother, Liza asked, "Mom, have you— Was there ever a moment when you thought you might not be with Dad?"

The thing Liza admired about her parents' generation was that they didn't seem to *think* very much. They just did things because those things looked a certain way and looking a certain way was half the battle. You reached a certain age and you found a semiattractive, living, breathing man, and you went through the motions even if he was boring or mean or a sociopath, and you stuck it out to the bitter end. And this was not the most *romantic* notion but she liked the stubbornness of it, the simplicity, the *security*.

Her parents were anomalous, though. They appeared, to this day, ferociously in love. And this stemmed from a mutual feverish adoration, judging by the old photos adorning her father's desk, the kitchen window, the insides of the bathroom cabinets: Marilyn, a twenty-year-old knockout at Foster Beach, wrapped from behind in David's arms; David in a pumpkin patch beside an appraising Marilyn, his arm slung around her waist, her middle swollen with Wendy; Marilyn and David on their wedding day, just after the ceremony, standing to the side of the altar, dissolved with laughter.

"Lord, no," her mother said, and Liza's heart swelled and sank at once, because she liked that those simpler times had existed but knew resoundingly that they did no longer. "I mean," Marilyn continued. She was two glasses of wine deep and Liza stone sober; they both adjusted their posture accordingly. Pregnancy was the cruelest evolutionary fuck-you, filling you with more anxiety than you'd ever experienced in your life while prohibiting you from imbibing anything that might calm your nerves. "Have I ever wanted to punch him in the face? Yes. Has he ever said something that made me question the very construction of the universe?" Wine made her mother poetic. "Of course. But have I ever not wanted him around?" Another sip. "No. In another room? God yes. Silenced somewhere far away? Absolutely."

"But never anything major," Liza said. She and Ryan had met in college. On paper, it was the perfect equation for a simple, stubborn union. Meet someone when you're both too young to realize how stupid you are. Learn all of their oddities and secrets before they have a chance to create more of them beyond your control.

"Never separation," Marilyn said. A light flipped on within the house—David in his office—and they both turned to look, scandalized by the reminder that the subject of their gossip was mobile and mere feet away. "Never anything like that."

"But why not?" Liza asked.

Her mother took another sip of wine and tilted her head, seemingly reflexively, toward the light in her husband's study. "Why would I? God, look at him. Who's better than that man?"

They looked together through the window. Neither had a satisfactory answer.

"Why are you asking me that, sweetie?" Her mother's expression had changed from wistful to concerned.

Liza shook her head, suddenly feeling like she might cry. "No reason." She wanted to ask her mom if this undercurrent of despair was something gestationally ubiquitous that they'd just neglected to mention in the BabyCenter forums.

"How are things at home?"

"Fine. Great."

"You're an endearingly bad liar, Liza-lee." Her mother rose and came to sit next to her on the glider. "I shouldn't have been so glib. We all have doubts." She touched Liza's knee. "Of course we all have doubts. But I think the key is being able to look past them. If you can do that and still feel good, still feel at peace, that's what's important."

"Settle, then," she said.

"No," her mother said emphatically. "*Not* settle. Not at all. I mean take a hard, honest look at the things you're doubting and see if they really matter."

"But how can you tell? How can you decide whether or not—you know, what's a deal breaker, or whatever?"

"That varies with every couple, sweetheart. Not everything has a formula." Her mom put a hand over her thigh. "What's going on with you, Lize? Talk to me."

She opened her mouth and closed it again. What *was* going on with her? To articulate it seemed damning somehow; to vocalize it was to give permanence to what she hoped wouldn't last. "I'm just wondering whether or not you ever had any doubts about Dad." Her mother must have felt this guttural terror at some point, must have experienced moments of revulsion when watching her husband eat asparagus, dreaded the future in which he talked about how it made his pee smell. Of course everyone had those problems, even her parents, who had been married for a hundred thousand years and still winked at each other across the dinner table.

"No, I suppose I didn't. But, Liza, that doesn't mean— It's *okay* to have doubts, honey. It's perfectly fine to feel anxious or uncertain about another person. It's a *huge* thing you're undertaking with Ryan, sweetheart. It's natural to be scared. But it's better if you find a way to be scared together."

Did you ever lie awake worrying what you might be passing on to us through Dad's genes? Did you ever for a second think that he wasn't good enough? Did you ever wonder if it would be your fault if he wasn't? She'd spent a handful of afternoons at Marcus's apartment in the past month, hazy, easy days between his plaid jersey-knit sheets; avoiding Ryan, avoiding reality. She squirmed, feeling a trilling anxiety at the back of her neck.

"It's funny," her mom continued. "I think so much of making a relationship work has to do with choosing to be kind even when you may not feel like it. It sounds like the most obvious thing in the world but it's much easier said than done, don't you think?"

If her mother—her ever-perceptive love guru of a mother—seemed genuinely unworried about Ryan, maybe that was enough of an endorsement. The thing that nobody warned you about adulthood was the number of decisions you'd have to make, the number of times you'd have to depend on an unreliable gut to point you in the right direction, the number of times you'd still feel like an eight-year-old, waiting for your parents to step in and save you from peril.

What she'd been doing with Marcus was cruel, simply put. It was the most textbook kind of cruelty there was: letting him fuck her from behind, letting him make her laugh, letting him drop her off at her parents' house and kiss her in his car while Ryan was at home with his Netflix and his pretzels and his pervasive despondency. It was cruel to Marcus and Ryan both. When her mother went inside to make them some tea, she pulled out her phone and began to type, verging on something novelistic, *This has been really fun but I recently found out that I'm pregnant—it happened before we got together so please don't worry—and I feel as though it's what's best for my health and the health of my relationship and also my libido has really been slowing down in the last couple of weeks but I really do wish you the best and I hope that Walter's hip replacement goes well and that—*

"Everything okay out here?" her mother asked, and she deleted the text before sending it. She looked up—her mom was blithe and optimistic, blind to her daughter's terrible behavior—and resisted asking if Marilyn would be willing to break things off with Marcus for her.

She fired off a quick message—*We need to end things. Personal stuff going on. I'm really sorry. Xx*—and shut off her phone before smiling up at her mother.

1983–1984

Marilyn was beginning to think—more than think: theorize—that her elder daughter was a sociopath. She arguably had too much time to think about it; she was, as one of the many parenting books that now lined the built-in shelves purported, *too close to the problem* to have perspective. But who could judge if not she? She spent every day with the children, was awakened by them each morning and read to them until they fell asleep each night. And she loved those versions of her girls—the warm, sleepy, pajama-clad bodies that tucked themselves next to her at sunrise, breathing their sweet stale breath into her neck, querying about breakfast and telling her about their dreams; the drowsy, heavy heads, trying to stay awake until the end, that lolled against her as she whispered lines of Dr. Seuss.

She liked her children best, then, when they were sleeping. Which perhaps was part of the problem, but she was fairly certain that a larger part of the problem was Wendy, whom she sometimes imagined sending to a boarding school that accommodated distressed preschoolers.

Earlier that day, she had denied Wendy's request for chocolate milk, and then watched as Wendy sank into a ball in the middle of the kitchen floor. Her daughter hugged her knees and started making a strange, fiercely focused face. Her cheeks turned, after several seconds, bright red, and Marilyn realized that she was holding her breath.

"Wendy, stop it," she said. Motherhood had rendered her more fatalistic than ever, and she was picturing blood vessels bursting in Wendy's eyes, in her brain. Her heart started pounding. Violet was propped up on several phone books in a chair at the table, coloring, regarding her sister with curiosity. "Wendy, I mean it. Stop that right now." But Wendy didn't stop; she hugged herself tighter and her eyes bulged a little bit and her face got redder and redder until finally Marilyn dropped to her knees and shoved her fingers into her daughter's mouth, the only thing she could think to do. And Wendy bit her, *hard*, and she hissed, *"Fuck"* and Wendy, breathing laboriously, glared up at her and said, "Mama said a bad word."

She sent Wendy to her room, fighting back tears herself, and she sank into a kitchen chair across from Violet and wept when she heard the bedroom door slam. Violet looked scared, scrambled down from her seat and climbed into her lap.

"It's okay, Mama," she said. "It's okay."

She looked down at her petrified daughter and in an instant realized that this was precisely the kind of scene she had vowed to avoid making as a parent herself, the kind of scene that was completely commonplace to her when she was a child. Her own mother—maybe drinking; probably drinking—would get wild-eyed or melancholy, dissolve before her eyes into a puddle of despair or fury.

"Don't cry," she would say, bringing her tissues, stroking her mother's hair. She remembered these memories as some of her first, from when she was five or six. Or possibly even four, like Violet was now, her own tiny daughter staring up into her face, reaching little starfish hands to her cheeks to dry her tears.

"I'm okay, pumpkin. Mama's okay. I'm sorry I scared you, little bear."

David was not usually home during Wendy's meltdowns and so when she tried to describe them to him in bed at night they came out sounding embellished—though they *weren't*. Her husband would pull her against him and rub her back.

"Just a rough stage, honey. Kids throw tantrums."

But she knew it was more than that. Because sometimes—oftentimes—Wendy got mad out of the blue, not because of any perceived injustice but just *because*. They would be sitting together, she and Wendy and Violet, playing kitchen or making Shrinky Dinks or reading *A Light in the Attic*, and suddenly Wendy would shriek *Stop!* and kick a tiny leg out toward her sister, who would be sitting in complete innocence—Violet was a fervent pacifist from the time she was conceived—and then Wendy would spiral downward. Marilyn would watch this, placed squarely between the girls and certain of Violet's lack of antagonism, watch Wendy's face harden and Violet's face sink. She watched Violet learn, after two or three instances, that Wendy's outbursts would ruin things, at least for a while, that there would be screaming and door slamming and her mother's barely contained irritation or anguish or fury. Marilyn watched her daughter become aware of this, observed her four-year-old's first doses of life's disappointing trajectory, and it would start to break her heart but then she would get distracted by her five-year-old, similarly jaded but much angrier about it all.

The migraines started around that time, too, so sometimes when Wendy made her vociferous exit it was all Marilyn could do to crawl onto the couch and close her eyes.

"Mama has a headache, Violet Rose," she'd say to her younger daughter, and Violet would climb obediently into her lap, resting unimposingly against her and whispering tiny toddler narratives to the Barbies she held in each hand.

Wendy would emerge later, sometimes in minutes and sometimes hours, looking mildly shamed but mostly seeming as though nothing had happened. And she would come over to her mother, lay a soft hand on her knee or curl up against her belly, and Marilyn would have trouble recognizing this tiny model of penance and fall absolutely in love with her daughter again. But the cycle would inevitably repeat itself, and her appeals to David became more zealous.

"I'm *afraid* of her," she confessed one night, near tears, beside him on the couch.

"Sweetheart, she's five years old," he said, not unkind but a little amused. Doctorhood had rendered her husband slightly more irritating; she'd thought he would be immune to the characteristic arrogance but every so often it surfaced in the form of a knowing vocal lilt.

"You don't understand what she's like," she continued. "She— It's like she can't help it. It's— I feel awful, watching her, because I know it can't be fun for her to be so—*anguished*. She's hurting and she doesn't seem to know how to express it and it . . ." She trailed off, her voice wobbling. "It breaks my heart, David. I don't know how to help her."

"Some kids are just more temperamental than others," he said. His indifference infuriated her and she moved away from him.

"You don't *see* her when she does it."

In fact he had seen her: because Wendy's outbursts were becoming more frequent, usually three or four times a day, it was now inevitable that David would bear witness. Marilyn was relieved at first but then saw that he still didn't understand. The first time, Wendy had screamed and purposefully shattered a juice glass because Violet was using the crayon that she wanted, and David had appeared in the doorway, lifted Wendy up under his arm, and started for her bedroom.

"Oh, no you don't, young lady," he said, using the Bad Cop voice that he was required to use only on rare occasions. She was, on the other hand, obliged to be the enforcer simply because she was *around* more, and she despised it, observing her daughters flying delightedly into their father's arms when he got home in the evenings, shunning her because she'd nixed the prospect of cookie baking or a viewing of *Zoom*. David was gentle but stern, and he had a solid grip on Wendy though she was flailing violently as he took her down the hall. "If I *ever* see you do something like that again, Wendy, I'll take away those crayons forever." She continued wailing and after David closed her in her room she pounded on the door with her fists in anguish.

It infuriated her, squatting before the mess of glass and cutting herself in the process, the suggestion that all Wendy needed was a little tough love. That all this time, *all these times*, Marilyn had simply failed to effectively discipline their daughter. She was further infuriated when Wendy appeared twenty minutes later, tiptoed from her room and then flung herself at David's legs in a dramatic act of atonement.

"I didn't mean to, Daddy," she said, wailing, and David swept her into his arms and murmured to her meaningfully about how he understood that *sometimes when we're angry we do things we don't mean, but that doesn't give us permission to break things and hurt our sisters.*

Or our mothers, she thought, finally taking the time to wash and bandage the cut on her palm because it became clear that David wasn't going to notice it. *Just because we're angry about absolutely nothing—because we're five years old and don't want for anything and our every single whim is indulged and what on earth is there to be angry about?—is no reason to break things and make our mothers clean them up.*

There had been several similar instances, instances during which she felt a shameful, agonizing *hatred* toward both her husband and her daughter.

"If I have to wrestle Wendy into bed again tonight I'm going to impale myself on something, David, I swear to God," she'd lamented yesterday, and her husband, obdurate, rolling his eyes, had replied, "Oh, this again. The Antichrist. Good. Great. Let's talk about that."

She knew that she had chosen this life, and yet she would marvel over the fact that less than a decade ago she was making out on Oak Street Beach with Dean McGillis, who once took her skinny-dipping. She would have this same thought each time she was in labor with her daughters and her dopey husband sat by, handsome and ineffectual: *I could be fucking swimming with fucking Dean McGillis.* She could have been there, but instead she was here, sticking a Care Bears Band-Aid to her palm and actively ruing the fact that her husband and elder daughter were having a sweet, lesson-learning moment on the other side of the room. She went into the yard to smoke—trusting that Violet would remain occupied where she sat outside the hall closet, engaged in a heated conversation with her dolls. When she returned, David was sitting at the kitchen table, bluish circles under his eyes, sleeves rolled up to his elbows.

"I think we've contained the virus," he said. "I'm guessing that by bedtime she'll be completely cured."

She smiled at him tightly.

"Oh, come on, kid. I'm just joking."

She sat down across from him and started picking through a pile of papers, intermingled remnants of the girls' artwork. "I'm not in the mood to joke."

He stared at her for a moment, and when she refused to look at him, he rose and started out of the room. "Well, maybe *I* am," he muttered, and then he was gone.

For a moment she allowed herself to feel angry—what a *child* he was sometimes—but then she considered what he'd said. Maybe he *was* in the mood to joke. He was obliging, sometimes to the point of irritation. He was kind and adaptable. He worked twenty-hour days. They had two kids under six. And he *had* contained the virus, this time at least. She missed being able to find something arousing in these kinds of exchanges, though arousal was the reason that their beloved virus existed in the first place. She rose from the table.

He wasn't in their bedroom, as she'd expected, nor was he in the living room. She found him instead on the floor outside of the hall closet, sitting with his legs stretched out in front of him and a Barbie doll in his hand. The other held a tiny pink hairbrush, and he was pulling it through the plastic waves of doll hair with baffling gentleness. Violet was leaning heavily against his side, outfitting another Barbie in a lewd waitress uniform.

"Hi, Mama," Violet said, noticing her first. "Daddy's doing a braid."

David looked up at her equably. "Daddy's attempting to do a braid," he said, his fingers large and inexpert against the tiny doll head. Violet lunged forward and started rifling through one of her many plastic baskets, stuffed to the gills with tiny shoes, tiny hamburgers, tiny aprons and credit cards and spatulas, microscopic half pairs of earrings that had long ago lost their mates. Marilyn met her husband's eyes and smiled.

"I was being awful," she said.

"Only a little." He shrugged. "You had a long day."

She studied his face across the sun-streaked wooden hallway, pinkish twilight rays through the windows rendering his hair a kind of stainless steel.

"I'm going to get dinner started," she said.

"As you were," he said, and when she turned back to look at him, he winked at her.

Bless him, really, for being in the mood to joke. Someone should be.

One night David came home and his wife wasn't around; he was so used to the welcome sound of her bustle, her radio, her running water, that its absence chilled him a bit. Things had been different between them lately, paler, cooler. It seemed so trite that they could fall prey to such banal domestic gripes. Their five-year-old was incorrigible: so what? Couldn't they laugh it off like they had everything else?

He paused at the landing to listen. No hum of her voice soothing the children, reading a book, singing a song. No hiss of water in the shower. He climbed the stairs. His daughters' room was empty. He felt a nervousness settle over him and he held his breath as he jogged down the hall to his own bedroom.

There—he exhaled—was Marilyn, in their bed with a daughter on either side. *The Tiny Seed* was open facedown on her thighs. They were all sleeping soundly, Violet's head resting on Marilyn's rib cage, Marilyn's hand frozen in midworrying of Wendy's hair. His breath caught at the quiet perfection of his family, honey-blond Wendy and dark, serious Violet, tiny bodies in tiny pajamas, their thumbs in their mouths, their legs—little frog legs—twined together. And Marilyn: the girlish smattering of freckles across her nose, the slight leftward tilt of her head.

He noticed, suddenly—a sharpening of vision like Waldo materializing from a sea of striped Vikings—the curve of his wife's belly. He stiffened. It strained against the pale blue knit of her sweater, a swell of maybe eight weeks or ten. Perhaps even more: he tried to think of last time, with Violet, how she'd looked. He could only recall her exhaustion.

Now, sound asleep at 7:30. He went in and sat on the edge of the bed beside her, laid a palm flat between her hip bones, gently. She didn't wake. She didn't know. And it made him so sad; his wife was so lost to herself that—watching her, sleeping—he was sure she hadn't noticed. He thought of her that morning, making breakfast for the girls. Had she looked tired? Swollen? Queasy? He could barely remember what they'd talked about—the weather, the impending need for new tires on the car. He'd gone to kiss her and she'd offered him her cheek.

"Have a good day," he'd said, gathering his things, watching her scramble the eggs. "I love you," he'd told her shyly, and she'd turned to him and given him a drowsy, tolerant smile.

"I love you back," she'd said.

On the bed he considered the substance of her beneath his hand. Maybe she'd just put on some weight. But the bulge under his palm felt muscular, distended: the expanding of her uterus. In her sleep, Marilyn whimpered, the reaction to a dream, and he felt the striking impact of shame, suddenly, for doing this to her, for putting her in this position. It made him feel brutish and oppressive. He had *impregnated* her; he was tying her down, tethering her to a life of laundry and homework and glassy-eyed kid wrangling; he had set her up in a cramped house and filled her womb, again and again and, now, again, with babies, even though she was tired, even though she wasn't herself anymore. But he couldn't take all the blame. She enjoyed sex as much as he did. It was the only way they connected lately, really; sometimes when he came home she was already in bed and they wouldn't talk at all; she would just wrap her legs around him, slip a hand inside his briefs, wordlessly open herself to him, gazing up, even and silent. They made love instead of talking; how could this come as a surprise to either of them?

It would come as a surprise to her. He was positive about that.

He kept his hand on her belly, though, feeling for what he was now sure was another baby, someone to brighten things up, humble Wendy a bit, delight them all. He felt unexpected tears spring to his eyes. Maybe even a boy this time. Another baby.

Marilyn stirred. "Oh," she said. "It's you." She looked at his hand on her abdomen and he rubbed it back and forth over her pelvic bones, like he'd simply been trying to rouse her.

"It's me," he said. "Hey, kid."

Liza was an easy baby, and David honestly didn't know what they would have done if she hadn't been because they didn't have *room* for a difficult one. They barely had room for any baby at all; they were physically at capacity in their little house and they had wedged Liza's crib beside their bed; he tripped over its splayed antique legs in the dark when he was getting ready for work. Of course he and Marilyn both were enamored with her in the dazed, delirious, lovesick way of exhausted new parents, but they had more pressing things—more demanding, high-maintenance children—to which they had to devote most of their attention. It was constant stress, constant chaos, a series of indistinguishable days. He did his rounds at the hospital, he kissed his daughters goodnight, he slept, he fought with his wife. It became harder and harder to justify—he was working, of course, smack in the middle of his residency, to get them to a point of solvency, but that would mean nothing if his family fell apart before the logistical stuff started to come together. Their house was too small, Marilyn was spread too thin, and Wendy had more energy than anyone knew what to do with.

But none of this was Liza's fault, however unexpected she'd been—"It's not *fair*," Marilyn had said, heartbreakingly, when her third pregnancy had been confirmed. He'd heard once that children's personalities adapted to their surroundings, and Liza—apparently sensing, at three months old, that her household could not sustain more turmoil—radiated calm. So he began a new routine with her, one that gave her individualized attention and gave him—selfishly—a dose of tranquillity.

When he got home at night he would bypass his obligations—

the mail, the garbage that needed taking out, the dinner that he needed to eat because Marilyn was constantly lamenting that he was disappearing while she was rapidly expanding—and instead tiptoe into his bedroom, circumvent his sleeping wife, and silently lift Liza from her crib. She usually didn't wake— always a good sleeper, dutiful and disciplined; "a stickler for naps," Marilyn said fondly—and he took her to the living room or sometimes to the porch, if it was warm, and just sat with her, cradled her against his chest and hummed to her, intoxicated by the immaculate sweetness of this tiny new daughter. He sang to her, held her against him and hummed.

His lips pressed against her head, the vibrations of his throat reverberating back to him through her still-forming skull, and she fit against his shoulder perfectly, relied on him to keep her upright. The grass wet with dew and the moon receding and his daughter in his arms, a person in his life whom he'd managed not to let down yet. Wendy remained moody and difficult in school and guilty and belligerent at home, and Violet was the tolerant peacemaker. Liza was, in effect, the *middle child* even when she was technically the youngest. And he would never quite forgive himself or Marilyn for that, for letting her exist as anything other than a welcome member of their family, and so he'd hum to her, rock around the yard with his sleeping baby daughter, "Born on the Bayou" and "Bad, Bad Leroy Brown" and "Back in the USSR," and he had to mollify himself with the possibility that though she'd never remember the humming itself, she might absorb the notion of being loved, that it would somehow take hold in the plates of her tiny skull, that it would accompany her as she grew, as she progressed beyond the confines of her disordered family.

CHAPTER TEN

Liza wondered how much of seemingly normal adult life was simply approximation, effort, good acting. It was the pink stage of morning, the birds going crazy outside, and she was on her side in bed, staring at Ryan, imagining the baby and trying to conjure some tenderness for the two in concert. Perhaps it was less approximation than recognition. Maybe she *was* feeling tenderness and she simply couldn't *tell*. "Hey," she whispered.

Ryan barely stirred.

She took his hand, hot from being pressed beneath his pillow, and brought it to her belly. Perhaps all of these moments had to be orchestrated. Perhaps all that adulthood *was* was repeatedly going through the motions, trying out different arrangements and occasionally landing in cinematic tableaus such as this one, a woman in the not-yet-ungainly stage of pregnancy, *aglow*, maybe, rousing her partner for no other reason than to remind him of the kinetic existence of their child-in-progress.

"Ryan," she said. Then, louder: *"Ryan."*

He startled, regarded her from beneath heavy eyelids. "You okay?"

She tried to smile at him. A precise orchestration of purposefully casual emotion. Maybe that was all relationships were. "I'm fine."

"What time is it?" He moved his hand from her stomach to rub his eyes, not even seeming to notice her.

"It's early," she said. She had it in her head that maybe she could cajole him out with her. She'd read somewhere that one way to help a depressed partner was by urging them to accompany you on manageable trips, brief outings that could yield a sense of accomplishment. They could tackle an item or two on her ever-growing baby list. Maybe wander through the Garfield Park Conservatory. "How about if we venture into the world today?" she said softly.

"Lize, I really didn't sleep well. Could we talk about this in a little while?" His eyes were slipping closed again.

"I made you coffee," she said, and she tried not to be hurt as he sighed laboriously, pushed himself upright, took her proffered mug.

"Is there some reason we have to do this at six in the morning?"

"Is there some reason you're being such a dick?" She closed her eyes. "Sorry, I—"

"No," he said. "I'm sorry. I'm just— I was just awake, for a while, in the middle of the night. I'm just—irritable."

"What if we went furniture shopping today?" she asked. She'd tried to think of the least fraught items on her list, snuggly animal-printed talismans that would not remind them of the baby's constant need or its alarming fragility.

Ryan looked away from her. "Isn't it a little early to be thinking about that?"

"The next few months are going to fly. Wouldn't it be nice to have a few of the big things in place? Just for peace of mind?"

"All that stuff's expensive, Liza. Jesus."

She kicked herself for failing to consider how Ryan would feel to watch her pay for the necessary accoutrements of their baby's well-being. Even worse than he felt watching her buy groceries or pay the mortgage, she realized. And she felt at once shamefaced and resentful, sad that she'd activated his inferiority complex and annoyed that she couldn't enjoy even the most basic parental preparations, that she wasn't allowed to feel excited about cedar cribs or ergonomic rocking chairs because doing so would be yet another inadvertent reminder to Ryan that he wasn't pulling his weight.

"Just a few things, I thought," she said quietly, already backing down.

"That seems like something your mom would be into."

She wouldn't allow herself to cry, mostly because she didn't want to hurt his feelings. "Sure," she said. "Yeah, I'll ask her." She moved onto her back and stared up at the ceiling. "What're your plans for the day, then?"

"Thought I might mess around with the new Halo demo. See what's what."

It saddened her profoundly, his efforts to make playing video games sound like legitimate work, like some kind of professional research instead of just another anodyne outlet for him to sink into for hours at a time.

"What if you asked Jonah to come over?" she said. She wasn't sure where the idea had come from, but it struck her now that it was possibly a good one. "He might like Halo."

"Huh." To her surprise, he did not sound entirely averse.

"Just a thought," she said carefully. "Could be useful to have an—opponent. And I bet it'd be nice for him to feel more included by the family."

"Yeah," he said thoughtfully. "I might have a little insight into where he's coming from."

She turned to look at him again with curiosity. "Because you're also the adopted child of one of my sisters?"

"Because I'm not a Sorenson."

She paused, unsure of where he was heading. "Well, thank God for that, I guess."

"I just mean that I know what it's like to come in blind to your family. It can feel a little—overwhelming."

"Believe me; I'm well aware of how overwhelming my family can be."

"But you're not— There's a caste system, kind of, isn't there?"

"A *caste* system?"

"I didn't grow up how you did."

"So what? What do you mean, how *I* did?"

"There's just an inherent level of privilege that you all have. And that's fine, Lize. It's just life. But it can be kind of an adjustment if you didn't grow up with it."

"I didn't grow up with it. My parents were scraping by before my dad went into private practice. And even now, I mean—sure, they're fine, but they had four of us to take care of, and my dad was a family practitioner; it's not like he was an orthopedic surgeon or something."

"See, even the fact that you *know* orthopedic surgeons make more than—"

"I know that because I don't live under a rock. And I really don't think this is a fair comparison to make. Jonah grew up in foster care. You grew up with stable caretakers in a comfortable home. It's not like you were in, like, the *slums*."

"Are you trying to fight with me?" he asked.

"No, I just— You seemed pretty prepared to make that argument."

"It's a hard thing to not be aware of."

"Fine."

"I think it's a good idea," he said. "To reach out to Jonah."

"Because you feel some sort of brotherly class disparity?" Could it be that she was almost *enjoying* this, the feeling of sparring with him about something as banal and time-tested—something as *normal*—as their differing backgrounds?

"I'm agreeing with you, Liza."

Because it felt sort of good to pretend things were normal,

that they were a normal couple who could trade barbs as a means of gaining or losing prosaic pearls of power, she rolled her eyes at him, suggesting that perhaps she wouldn't—though she *would*, of course—let the subject drop.

David was in his study, glasses slid halfway down his nose, glaring at his computer as he attempted without success to turn it on. There was a message blinking that he couldn't make sense of, white text across a blue screen. He hit blindly at a few keys and suddenly the monitor made an ominous flashbulb noise and the screen went dark.

"God*damnit*," he hissed, tapping the keys a few more times just in case.

"Dad?"

He glanced up, startled, to see Liza standing in the doorway. The sight of his daughters pregnant still unnerved him: the fact that he almost always saw them first, in his head, as little girls was complicated by the reality of them as adults—Liza, now, a grown woman with a swollen belly.

"Sorry, I was going to call, but— Is everything okay with your computer?"

He glanced over at it ruefully as he rose from his desk. "We're having a difference of opinion. What brings you here, Liza-lee?"

"Yeah, I wanted . . . I was hoping I could talk to you." She reached out to hug him and something about the motion seemed kind of desperate.

He put his arms around her, abuzz with the lurking suspicion that had been popping up on and off within him since his daughter had announced her pregnancy. "Is everything okay?"

"I'm not sure."

"Is it the baby?" Alarmed, he pulled away to examine her.

"No. Or—not really. Mom's not coming home soon, is she?"

"She's at work until six."

"Okay. I just—I wanted to just talk to you about this."

This was so utterly *strange*. The girls rarely approached him about anything before they approached their mother, and he'd never taken it personally: he went to Marilyn first for everything too.

"Let me make you some tea." He put a hand on her back and led her to the kitchen, where she sank without protest into the chair unofficially designated hers for the entire history of their family's dining. He rifled through Marilyn's tea bags. "Decaf?" he asked.

"Regular. Please don't judge me. I'd lose my mind if I cut out caffeine entirely."

He smiled and held up his hands. "I don't judge." He regarded her with one part amusement and two parts concern. "Tell me what's going on."

And then she started to cry.

"Oh, honey. Okay." He should have been used to tears, but whenever one of the women in his life began to cry unexpectedly, he couldn't help but act as though she were bleeding, and that he could stanch the flow with his anxious, evasive murmurings of *all right, okay*.

"Ryan's sick," she said. "He's really sick and he's not getting better."

For David, as a doctor, *sick* meant everything from head colds to leukemia. He sat down beside his daughter.

"He's clinically depressed. I didn't know how much you and Mom had sussed out. He's— He never wants to go anywhere, and he sleeps all the time, and I . . . I don't know what to do. I've run out of— I'm running out of ways to pretend like it's not happening."

He'd been at once expecting this and entirely not. "Okay," he said again. He paused. "It— How long has this been going on, Liza?"

"I mean, he's had *ten*dencies since I've known him, but it's been the worst it's ever been since—well, since we moved here, you know, with his difficulty finding work, and his— I think he feels infantilized, kind of, with me as the breadwinner, which— We can all endorse gender equality until we're blue in the face but it's a real thing, Dad; it's really hard to be a woman who makes more money than her partner. I don't know what I'm supposed to—with the baby, and the— He had a good few weeks after we found out, but things are getting bad again, and . . ."

"Breakthrough depression," he said. "Maybe. Stress can cause one to backslide."

"So it's—it's *because* I got pregnant?"

"No, sweetheart." He passed her another tissue. "That's not what I meant at all, Liza."

"It was an accident," Liza said, and he glanced up to see her hands pointedly clasped beneath her little belly and he recognized the act, ruing the arrival of your unforeseen child while trying to be grateful for it at the same time. "I never meant for this to happen. But part of me thought—I thought it might make things better, maybe. But it seems like he's— I mean, of course it didn't fix things; of course it's not going to fix . . ."

"Is he on medication?"

"He's on Prozac but it seems like he needs to be reassessed. I'm hesitant to bring it up because I don't want him to feel even *worse*, like he's so bad off that he's not even *treat*able."

"That seems like a necessary step, sweetheart. The benefits will outweigh the costs." He wished so much that he could emulate his wife, take his daughter in his arms—hum to her, as he used to, or murmur some soothing Catholic adage from his childhood, *sweet hope in the midst of the bitterness of life.* He tried to put faith in his medical knowledge, in its formulae and numbers, but the disappointment on his daughter's face negated any chance of that. He thought of her as a baby, the tiny trusting peanut tucked against his chest. "Are you taking care of your-self, Lize?"

"That's actually kind of why I came here. I mean—I wanted to— This is the first time I've told anyone about this and I— I guess I just needed someone else to know, so I won't feel so—so *alone* with all of this." Her voice broke.

"Hey," he said, and he put his arm around her and she crum-pled against him. "Oh, Liza."

But she righted herself quickly, pulling away, wiping her eyes. "I was hoping I could ask you something. A—favor, kind of."

"Of course."

"I'd like to change doctors," she said.

"Oh. But I thought you— Is your OB not—"

"She's fine. But I—I'd like someone a little more experienced."

"Did they— Is there cause for concern, Lize? Is everything—"

"I'd like some assurance." The line sounded rehearsed.

"Assurance of what, sweetheart?"

"Just—you know. Confirmation." This time he held out, waited for her to continue.

"I'd just like to feel a little bit less unsure. About Ryan. About what his—condition means for the baby. Do you know what I mean?"

He did know what she meant; he'd run the same gamut of anxieties with all four of his children: routine new-parent jit-ters, mostly, enhanced by his vault of professional knowledge and his keen awareness of the tenuousness of human life. But instead he responded in the only way he knew how: as a clini-cian, as a person who relied on research and evidence and data.

"There's no way to know these things before babies are born, Lize."

"I want to know that there's no—" She shook her head. "I want to know which options I can rule out."

"I think those are few and far between, Liza. You're five months along."

"I know that." She looked up at him evenly. "I just want to feel that I'm . . . ready."

"There's no way you can ever be *ready*, honey. Even if you do everything you're supposed to do."

His poor daughter, the one who had found her place in the world after a childhood of being—not *forgotten*, but benched. Perpetually sidelined, waiting patiently in the wings. Their easy one, who was now facing such miserable hardship: an unreliable partner, an unequal coparent. Such a heavy burden for Liza to carry around, on top of everything else. And he could see now that *assurance*, for his daughter, meant ensuring that there wasn't—he flinched at the thought—a way out, a loophole to escape motherhood and its subsequent inextricable ties to Ryan. Not like his wife in the early days after all, then. Liza's concerns were far more potent and her desires much darker. He ached at this revelation.

"I'd like to see if Gillian Levin's taking on new patients," Liza said.

He could've fallen out of his chair. He could've dropped dead right there in the middle of the kitchen, so unswervingly was he not expecting this, the syllables of Gillian's name and all they stood for. Her dark head beside him in the passenger seat of his car. Her eager face appearing in his doorway. Her hand on his arm.

"She was so good with Mom," Liza continued. "When Gracie was born? I mean, wasn't— She was the reason that both of them—made it, wasn't she?"

"She was," he said. It came out sounding stiff.

"So I just thought that— I thought it might make me feel better. To have someone who—played such a big role in our family. And she's—familiar."

He looked up and studied his daughter, trying to assess the level of knowledge behind the statement. *Such a big role.* "That was over twenty years ago, Liza. How familiar could she be to you?" He hadn't meant to snap. "I mean—"

"She knows our history," Liza said evenly. "And about Wendy, everything, you know."

What could he say to this? "You know you don't need my permission, Lize."

"I know, but I figured— I just wanted to make sure you wouldn't mind."

He swallowed. "Why would I mind?"

She seemed to study him for a moment too long. "No reason."

"You should do what you think is right." But, as he considered it: "Except how about you let me tell your mother, okay?"

Liza frowned. "I— Sure, but—why, do you think she's—?"

"No," he said quickly. "Just— Those were hard times for your mom, Lize. With Gracie. And then Wendy. It just might— dredge up some things, you know."

"Oh. Sure, yeah, if you think so."

"I'll take care of it. You focus on yourself, Lize."

She looked down, brow furrowed, nodding. He thought again of her as a baby, then as an apologetically tattooed seventeen-year-old. To the best of his ability, he ignored his unease.

His new Krav Maga instructor talked a lot about living *purely*, which made Jonah start considering his own habits—he smoked only occasionally, because one of the kids at Lathrop House taught him, and he didn't like the taste of beer—and, by extension, Wendy's. He wasn't sure what made someone an alcoholic. He'd looked it up online, and the bar seemed pretty low, like if you went by those standards *everyone* would be considered an alcoholic. And Wendy didn't necessarily exhibit all of the "telltale signs" listed, either; she was usually up before him in the morning, she never seemed to drive erratically, and she was never incoherent, she just sometimes got more animated. She did drink a lot—nightly, for sure—and he'd also come home sometimes to find that the condo reeked of weed, but it seemed like a pretty okay system, as far as he could tell, to be an adult with a sweet house who drank and smoked whenever she wanted and wasn't at risk of becoming, like, a mole person who lived in the gutter.

The sex stuff weirded him out, though; the fact that she seemed to be having so much of it and that she seemed to think she was doing a good job of hiding it from him. He heard her through the walls at night—muffled laughter, a cry, once—and he could hear, too, when she ushered the men out the front door, tenor voices alternating with her alto. He hadn't meant to walk in on her that one time, and he hadn't meant to stand there, but it had shocked him, seeing her like that, and it further intrigued him, that she was so unself-conscious about the fact that she was sort of a dirtbag, bringing home as many men a week as she wanted. But their life proceeded as it had been, dinner together and then Scrabble or rummy on her patio, during which Wendy would nightly finish off a bottle of wine but never get *sloppy*, not like the websites warned about.

"If you don't give your body the respect it deserves, you'll be surprised by the ways it can fail you," his teacher said. They'd spent the full ninety minutes of class time sitting cross-legged on the floor listening to him give a boring Karate Kid lecture about integrity and the inner self and how their bodies were temples. "Ignoring signs of distress can be a fatal mistake," his teacher continued, and this made Jonah nervous because what if Wendy was having signs of distress and she didn't notice because of the wine and the weed? Was he *worrying* about her? It didn't seem like they were close enough to worry about each other, and plus she was the adult, so she was technically the one who was supposed to be doing the worrying.

When class ended, Wendy was waiting for him in the hall-way. She didn't normally pick him up; the studio was just a few blocks from her building.

"I had to run to Whole Foods," she said. "Figured I'd stop in. Who's that horrible Judd Nelson boy who was sitting in the back row? He looks like a school shooter."

"Wendy," he hissed.

"Oh, *God*," she said, handing over her grocery bag. "That's the first time you've done the moody teen voice to me."

"Can we go?" he said. "This is heavy." He wondered if she'd bought more wine. Wendy had a special wine fridge, and a full rack on the wall in the dining room, but she seemed to always be coming home with new bottles.

"Someone's in a snit," she said.

"No I'm not." He was suddenly annoyed with everything, with the weight of the bag in his arms, bottles of wine for his degenerate aunt, who didn't respect her own body, who was too old for him to be worrying about.

"Whoa, whoa," Wendy said. She held the door for him on their way out. "Sorry, dude. Jeez. I got stuff so we could have a cookout, but maybe you want some alone time."

He looked down into the bag, past the length of receipt at the top, and saw a sack of little purple potatoes, paper-wrapped meat, stalks of asparagus like a bouquet of flowers. He felt his face getting red, guilt seeping into his cheeks. "Sorry. Thanks. I didn't— Sorry."

"No worries," Wendy said. She ruffled his hair and he ducked away instinctively, making her laugh. "I was a total asshole when I was your age. This is my comeuppance."

Despite all the time she'd spent thinking about Gillian Levin, Liza could not specifically remember what the woman looked like, so she was surprised by how familiar she seemed when she came bustling into the exam room, dark brown ponytail and delicate features.

"Liza," she said. "The last time I saw you, you were *tiny*."

"No longer," she said, trying to smile.

"Gosh, you look just like your mom," Gillian said. "How's she doing?"

Of course it was suspect that her father wanted to be the one to tell her mother about Gillian, that he'd given any thought at all to who would tell her.

"She's well," Liza said. "Really well."

Gillian nodded, flipping through the paperwork Liza had just filled out. "And your dad?"

Liza couldn't decide if it was suspicious or not that she wasn't making eye contact as she asked it. "Great," she said. "He just retired, actually."

"Mm. Good for him. Tell him I said hello." She uncapped her pen. "All right. Nineteen weeks, is that right? And is Dad going to be joining you?"

She thought for a second that the woman was referring to her father again. "Oh. No, I—he's—he had a conflict. But he's—around, yes. In the picture."

"You didn't say much on the phone about why you've decided to switch providers."

"I just—wanted someone familiar, I guess? I'm having a lot of—anxiety. And I know how wonderful you were with my mom, when my little sister was born. I never— I mean, I thought she was going to die." She was surprised to hear her voice crack. "It was a scary time for all of us. You saved her life."

"I was doing my job," Gillian said, smiling at her. "What happened to your mom isn't something inheritable, though, if that eases any of your anxiety. It's actually likelier for people who've had multiple pregnancies. Do you have concerns about your health?"

"No, I— It's not specifically . . . I just know you—you know our family already. Our family history. And the—familiarity of that appeals to me, I guess; I know I'm being irrational . . ." She felt herself starting to cry. "I'm—scared. I'm terrified of everything. Of all of this."

"About bringing a new life into the world?" Gillian handed her a tissue, smiling still, calm and unruffled. "Why on earth would you be nervous about that?"

"I'm sorry," Liza said.

"You have nothing to be sorry for," Gillian said. "This is a scary thing, Liza. You're about to become a mother."

She realized—tears falling more quickly, rendering the tissue inadequate—that this was the first time anyone had so candidly spoken the sentence to her. *A mother.* Nothing had struck her in quite this way, until now.

"Oh, dear," Gillian said. "Here, come on. A couple deep breaths."

She noted, dimly, that her mother would never omit the preposition. She inhaled.

"It's never my intention to frighten a woman into motherhood," Gillian said. "But I know it's awfully easy to pretend that pregnancy is just something that's happening *to* you. It can be empowering to recognize your role in the process." She paused. She rose from her stool to retrieve the entire box of tissues, and Liza admired her for it, because she'd always hated doctors who rolled around the office like lords.

"How many kids do you have?" Liza asked.

Gillian handed over the tissues, not meeting her eyes. "None, actually."

"Oh. Did you—I mean, you didn't want them, or you— Sorry. Not my—business. Sorry."

"I thought I wanted them," Gillian said. "But time—got away from me. You'll be surprised how that starts to happen."

"Great," she murmured. "So much to look forward to."

"I assure you, Liza: your body, and your baby's body, will be in good hands."

"No, I'm sure you— That's—exactly why I wanted you."

"We're going to take good care of you, okay? But it's also perfectly fine to be scared." Gillian reached out and squeezed her hand. "Why don't you lie back and we'll take a look at the little one?"

"I'm really—grateful," she said haltingly, tensing at the chill of the gel on her belly.

"I am currently being introduced to a brand-new human being," Gillian said, and Liza understood why her father had liked her. "The gratitude's all mine."

CHAPTER ELEVEN

Grace decided to venture across town for her midday coffee because it seemed like an easy way to shake things up. The plight of the youngest child: growing up. Grace had long been regarded as a twelve-year-old by some of her family and as wildly mature by the rest. Liza reminded her to lock her doors and asked for relationship advice in the same breath. Wendy introduced her as her "baby sister." Her sisters had the comparative luxury of growing up in the eighties and had subsequently been successful in pursuit of their Life Plans: law, psychology, and gold digging. She was less certain of her own.

"Well, hey," the barista said. "Look who it is."

It was the bike messenger who frequented her office, minus his red bandanna so she almost didn't recognize him, but of course she recognized him because he was an exquisitely constructed specimen, long-limbed and carob-haired with eyes that were more arresting than eyes had a right to be, oyster gray with flecks of green. He smiled at her. She returned the expression with a horrifyingly uninhibited grin, the kind you couldn't help but make when someone came to pick you up at the airport and you saw them there, in the sea of transient strangers, a familiar face that had arrived at that particular spot on the earth just for you.

"You don't remember me?" he asked.

"You remember *me*?" she replied without thinking. Boys never remembered her. She accepted this on principle, that she would always have to reintroduce herself, at least twice but usually three or four times. Something in her face didn't register with them; perhaps her eyes were too dark for them to clock the dilated pupils that indicated arousal; perhaps she simply looked too much like a potato.

"Grace Sorenson, keeping the world's oboists insured," he said, and she entertained the possibility that she could die there, in that moment. Not only did he remember her, but he knew her *name*. "How could I forget?"

"It's a pretty weird job," she said.

"Normally I would say, like, aren't they all," he said, smiling. "But yeah, yours seems unusually weird. No offense."

"None taken." Orion was the kind of affected hipster coffee shop where you could sit at the counter on a barstool. It was the first time in five years that she felt grateful to live in such an annoying city; she perched before him on one of the stools. "Did you—quit? Your messenger job?"

"Nope. I moonlight as a roasting artist."

"You—what?"

"I'm joking. Messenger work's my side job. Coffee's full-time. What can I make you?"

"I'm not very good at making decisions." She swallowed. "Could you surprise me?"

The crinkling at the corners of his eyes should have been illegal. "I could make you a pour over. We just got this killer Arabica sample from our vendor."

"I am unfamiliar with most of the words you just said."

He laughed—a loud, open, barking sound—and she was flooded with a pleasure that she wasn't used to feeling.

"I just realized I don't know your name," she said.

He extended his hand. "Ben Barnes." Then he asked her questions while he made her coffee; it took an elaborately long time and involved a space-age conical filter. "Chicago, huh?"

"I miss it sometimes. Are you from here?"

"Born and raised." He set a mug before her. "You'll have to tell me what you think."

She unthinkingly took a sip, burning her tongue in the process. "Jesus *fuck*."

"Oh, shit, I'm sorry. I should've warned you."

"That a steaming mug of coffee was going to be hot? God, I'm such an idiot."

He grabbed a clean towel from the stack on the bar, ran it under the faucet, and handed it over to her. "Here. Stick out your tongue. I promise it'll feel good."

She was reasonably certain that you were not supposed to openly display the least attractive parts of your body when trying to entice the opposite sex, but he was insistent and she was in pain. She stuck out her tongue, and he pressed the cool towel to it. She moaned a little without meaning to.

"Told you." Ben smiled. "Milk helps too. When you get home. Cold milk."

"Thank you. You seem to know a lot about tongues." And at this, of course, she wanted to die, because she was so radically ill-equipped for this type of conversation, so disastrously unlearned.

"Occupational hazard. Speaking of which. What's your deal?"

"My *deal*?"

"What's a Chicago girl doing all the way out here?"

"I'm in sort of a—transitional state." She worried it would sound like she was undergoing a sex change. "Like, just between— I graduated last year and I'm just trying to—you know."

"Figure it out," he said. "I hear ya."

"When did you graduate?"

"High school? A while ago."

"You didn't go to college?" She didn't mean to sound so incredulous.

"The horror," he said, but there was an edge to his voice.

"Oh—Jesus. I'm sorry I said it like that. I was never really offered an alternative, is all."

"Strict parents?"

Her parents erroneously thought she was enrolled in law school, and they were proud of her for it, but she knew it wasn't the end-all for them, college, grad school, whatever. They just wanted her to be happy. Thinking of this on her barstool gutted her. "No, actually," she said. She would tell them soon, when the perfect moment arose, which of course, of course, of course it would. "It was more—the culture. You know, the *path*. Just what you were supposed to do."

"Sounds kind of nice, actually," he said. "Expectations." He smiled enigmatically and went to help a customer. When he returned, he nodded at her mug. "Cool enough to taste yet?"

"It's really good," she said, gratefully seizing his change of subject. "Almost good enough to make me ask you to define *killer Arabica*."

They spoke briefly about the weather—she had never known fog could be so arousing—and when she finished the dregs of her coffee she rose to leave.

"How much do I owe you?"

"On the house. I'll tell our vendor that it knocked you on your ass."

"Well, thanks. And thanks for the—towel." She shouldered her bag and steeled her resolve. "I'll see you around?"

He smiled at her. "Here's hoping."

She thought about him during her walk home, and again as

she washed her single fork so she could eat scrambled eggs for dinner. She thought about him, and she thought about what it meant that she was thinking about him.

It wasn't that she hadn't grown up around love. Rather, love was constant, a nearly assaulting presence that confronted her each morning when she came downstairs and her parents were huddled together in front of the coffeepot; in the evenings when her dad was in his office and her mom would yell out, "Darling, the gas bill!" and her dad would reply, "Paid it on Monday, kid." This wasn't the norm, she knew. But her sisters were pretty normal, relatively speaking, and they had each had at least a couple of quasi-healthy longish-term relationships in their history. Grace was growing more and more anomalous by the day, a twenty-three-year-old non-Amish virgin who had never had a real boyfriend. Wendy had Oak Park's high school elite and then Miles, and she was still sexually active, Grace thought, judging by the amount she drank and how often she critiqued the construction of the butts of various strangers she saw on the street. Violet had Matt, and the guy who had come before him, the scientist guy who'd fathered her newfound nephew. Liza had been with Ryan at least since she was Grace's age.

And her parents: her father had loved her mother for decades, and vice versa, but it wasn't like all of those years had been sheer perfection. Her mother was beautiful—she knew this even objectively—but she'd had four children and smoked for the better part of her adulthood and spent much of her twenties and thirties (and forties, thanks to Grace herself) in a state of frenetic exhaustion, things that cumulatively amounted to a sort of protruding belly and veins on her hands and lines around her eyes. None of these things had ever seemed to bother her father, whose own decades of sleeplessness rendered him perpetually heavy-eyed and occasionally bedheaded. And still her mother would rub his shoulder at the kitchen sink or kiss his ear on the front porch and say things like *You missed a spot, handsome,* or *Gosh, do I like you, mister.* All of her memories of her parents' affection consisted of a particular look that her dad often gave her mom, one that said, baldly and inarticulately, *You're the best person ever.*

They were both equally, aggressively sanguine about the imperfections of their union, which meant that someone, somewhere, someday probably had to accept Grace.

Gillian called when Liza was in her office, reading a belligerently boring paper on cognitive ergonomics. She answered the phone, still struggling to correct a faulty sentence.

"Is now a good time?" Gillian asked. "I just got your blood work back."

Liza set down the jaunty green pen that she used to grade her students' most offensive papers and sat back in her chair. "Absolutely. Now's fine."

"All clear," Gillian said cheerfully. "Everything looks very good. You've got a healthy baby on the way. Would you like to know the sex?" It was supposed to be such an exuberant question, *baby boy or baby girl.*

"No," she said. If she knew the sex she would know more specifically who she was letting down. Because that quickening in her belly was supposed to make her feel swelled with love and wonder and fulfillment but instead made her want to cry; because sometimes when she felt that cosmic movement she pushed back at it, insistently. Because a baby meant Ryan, forever. "I'd like to find out with my partner." The bulk of the lie nearly took her breath away.

"Are you okay?" Gillian asked. "You sound a little—down."

"No," Liza said. "No, it's great. I'm fine."

Gillian was quiet for a moment. "You're my fifth phone call today," she said. "And I make the bad news calls first. You and your baby are healthy. All's well, Liza."

All was, of course, *not* well, hadn't been *well* in quite a while, and it was sort of exhausting to be the only one who seemed to be aware of this. Something about Gillian's statement nagged at her. She thought of the way her dad's voice had changed when she'd asked him about Gillian. She thought of him alone in the hospital room when she and her sisters had come to meet Gracie. She thought of that night, two decades earlier, when she'd heard the woman's name, over and over and over again, the smell of cigarette smoke, her father yelling and her mother crying, the night after which everything had changed for her, in a way that was small but distinct, distanced her from her sisters and made her suspicious of her parents.

"Did you sleep with my father?" she asked.

There was a satisfying beat of silence, and then, "I beg your pardon?"

She hadn't meant to ask, of course. But there was satisfaction in suddenly having the upper hand in an exchange for what felt like the first time in ages. *Gillian, Gillian, Gillian.* This looming figure, larger than life, who had left such a lasting mark on their family history.

"I have to say," Gillian said archly, "that's the first time I've ever been asked that question."

It had been fun for a second, the gratification of saying the thing you weren't supposed to say, of so blatantly violating the social order. But she began to lose her nerve. She didn't *want* to know if her father had slept with someone else, she realized. They'd all grown up disgustingly inured to their parents' erotic proclivities. That was enough. Life was hard enough. "I just wondered if—"

"Why on earth would you—" Gillian sounded furious now, and she realized the extent of what she'd said, how stupid it had been, how damning. "Your father was my colleague. Your mother was my *patient.* Not that it's even remotely an appropriate question or any of your business."

"I just—" An incorrigible tear had fallen from her eye right onto a freshly inked correction on the paper before her; green ink bled into a tiny Rorschach. She'd spoken without any thought at all of her child, a kid who already lacked both a stable father and a mother who had any idea what the hell she was doing, a kid who at least deserved a competent and compassionate doctor. "Gillian, I— Dr. Levin, I didn't mean— I'm sorry for saying that; it just— Of course it's not my business."

"No," Gillian said. "It's certainly not."

You're healthy, at least, she thought, a hand on her belly, and when she apologized again, "I'm really, really sorry, really," she wasn't sure if it was to Gillian or the baby.

Forty years: he couldn't quite wrap his head around it. He'd sent his wife an ostentatious bouquet to the store that morning, hydrangeas and tiger lilies and some kind of inedible kale. She'd called him to thank him but she'd sounded distracted and it made him feel like some sad teenage kid sending carnations to the prom queen. She was now, having brought the flowers home, rearranging the blooms in their vase, and she looked up at him and smiled. "These really are lovely," she said. "I feel bad I didn't send anything to you."

She hadn't necessarily forgotten, but she'd left before he awakened and only wished him a happy anniversary when she called to thank him from work, so he couldn't tell if she would have remembered on her own. They'd never been much for holidays like that—holidays that didn't involve the kids—but they tried to do something on the various milestones that accumulated, flowers from him or little notes from her, expensive dinners out, drives along the lakefront. And sex: they always had sex on their anniversary. It was, however crass, one of the few unfaltering pillars holding up their union. But perhaps they'd outgrown that. Perhaps they'd gotten complacent, regarding their decades-long marriage as a point of fact instead of the miracle that it was. Standing at the kitchen counter, they'd eaten swordfish left over from the grill and a salad she'd thrown together; he updated her on the ginkgo tree and she told him about her employee Drew's insistence that they set up a Facebook page for the store.

Now she was making the coffee for the morning, setting the timer. "Any chance you wouldn't mind taking the dog out? I thought I'd jump in the shower before bed."

"Sure," he said, turning to jingle his keys in the direction of Loomis.

"Thank you," she called after him.

He loved Marilyn more, he was pretty certain, than anyone had ever loved another person. It almost suffocated him sometimes. And it was inevitable that one could grow used to that kind of luck, the way you'd grow used to anything, your body adapting around a presence or an absence. But of *course* it was a miracle, of course it was blindly, baldly phenomenal that he and Marilyn had not only found each other—out of all the other people on the earth, in the Chicagoland area, in the Behavioral Sciences Building that day so many years ago—but also that they were still *here*, together, that they hadn't divorced or murdered each other or, worse, fallen into stagnant suburban silence, dead-eyed dinners and separate beds and hostile jokes about the toilet seat. That they still made each other laugh. That they made love, in their sixties, more often than they had in their thirties. That the sight of her at the end of the day still brought him so much joy.

He loved his daughters infinitely, of course. He would die for them, any one of them, for any reason, and he'd known this from the moment Marilyn had guided his hand—his twenty-five-year-old hand—shyly across her belly, swelled with Wendy, and he felt the faint flicker of a kick. He knew from that second that he would love their children with an inexpressible ferocity. And it only became easier, surprisingly, when they emerged from the womb and started to grow into little people. But he loved Marilyn more. He'd accepted this early on. Each one of his children was a singular, baffling miracle, a joy, an utter delight. But they came from Marilyn; he watched each one of them grow within and emerge from her body, he saw her in the subtle nuance of each of their faces, their posture, their frenetic hand gestures. Marilyn held his heart and she treated it with such meticulous care, filled in all of the little holes with her attention and affection and benevolence. Four whole decades she'd been doing this.

Loomis pulled him over to a thatch of milkweed and he allowed himself to be guided, turning back to look at their house, seeing the light come on in their bedroom, letting himself get a little histrionic, thinking of her. He was governed primarily by the part of himself that contained the love for his wife, his love for her endless capacity for love, for her optimism, for the world that she saw in which no one was ugly or evil, just hurting. That part had always been the largest. She was his, and he was hers, and he had never gotten over the mystifying luck of his draw. Some mornings he woke before her and watched her, watched her twitching eyelids, watched her *choosing*, willfully, to spend her life with him, to crawl into bed beside him each night and to kiss him, always, even if they were fighting; to make their bed every morning; to give birth to his children and raise them and regale him drowsily with stories of their troubles and achievements. She promised to love him, and part of his infatuation was sheer confusion. How, why? Why still? How dare they take these years for granted; how dare they pretend it was a night like any other night, dish soap and running shoes, when in fact the universe had allowed him to be with his best friend, his partner in all things, for over forty years? Fatigue be damned, he would wake Marilyn, take her hands, impart this revelation to her. He tugged the dog toward home.

The phone rang as he was retrieving Loomis's after-walk snack, and he smacked his head on the hard edge of the low shelf in the pantry, and so his voice, when he answered—a smarting string of expletives running through his mind, a hand rubbing his head, Loomis sniffing worriedly at his knees—was not quite friendly.

"Yes?" he said, and there was a pause before the caller replied, "Hi—David?"

And she flooded back with ease, Gillian Levin, the woman who had once meant so many things to him and to his family. He'd discovered at some point that it was just easier not to think about her at all. She'd left the office not long after they stopped having their dinners, went to start her own obstetric practice on the Far North Side, and after a while life took over, filled in the spaces that used to be occupied by their friendship. His daughters continued to mature; his wife fell in love with him again; their circumstances were complicated anew by college tuition, by sons-in-law, by grandkids.

Until now, apparently. Loomis shoved his snout between David's knees, still concerned for his well-being. He reached down to rub behind the dog's ears.

"It's okay," he said to Loomis, before realizing the strangeness of it. "I mean—yes, hi, this is David. Hi."

"It's Gillian Levin." The ludicrousness of her feeling the need to introduce herself. "Did I catch you at a bad time?"

"Not at all." *It's my fortieth wedding anniversary.*

"Well, I won't keep you long. I just have— I spoke to Liza this afternoon, David."

And his blood immediately ran cold, thinking that maybe his daughter's dark dreams were coming true, that in fact there *was* something wrong with her baby.

"I'm sorry, that was—poorly phrased. She's fine. Prenatally. But she mentioned something quite upsetting on the phone."

Had he missed something? Should he have been more concerned about Liza's mental state, not just passed it off as the routine jitters of a first-time mother? He thought of Marilyn, asleep among the paint fumes in their kitchen on Davenport Street.

"She asked if you and I had slept together," Gillian said.

The gods were not on his side during this conversation. He steadied himself against the kitchen sink. "She *what*?"

"I told her no, of course. But I— It seemed like a gross invasion of privacy, and I just— I'm not suggesting that you . . ."

"No, that— I can't imagine where she—got that." His heart was pounding. It seemed unfair that the past was just allowed to pop up through the phone mounted on your kitchen wall.

"I've tried very hard to close the door on that part of my life," Gillian said. "I mean, not— Your friendship meant a great deal to me, David."

He swallowed. "Yours too."

"But I never—I'd never— I have a reputation to uphold."

"Of course," he said, dumbly. It was so unexpected, all of this. Was Liza experiencing some kind of psychosis? But no, certainly—she had to have heard something, way back when. *Sensed* something. Their forgotten middle child, easy and unassuming. Could she really have been carrying this suspicion around for nearly twenty years? "I'm not sure what to do," he said.

"I just thought you should know," Gillian said.

"Sure. I'm sorry. I'm not sure— This is perplexing to me. But I'm sorry it happened."

"Nothing for you to apologize for," she said.

"Well." There was a stillness, a long quiet moment in which it would have been normal for one of two friendly old colleagues to propose a future get-together.

"Sweet?" His wife's voice, overhead.

"Marilyn's calling me," he said reflexively. Her name was a grenade.

"Of course." Gillian paused. "Take care of yourself, David."

"I'm sorry, again," he was saying, but by the time he'd finished, she was gone.

When he came into their bedroom, Marilyn was sitting on the edge of the bed in his threadbare old St. Clement's Basketball T-shirt, the one she'd managed to spare from the covetous hands of their girls. She'd let her hair down and she was smiling at him, a kind of smile he hadn't seen for several months.

Life's insistence on juxtaposing darkness and light would never cease to amaze him. That Marilyn was entirely oblivious to Gillian's return seemed like a scientific impossibility. His anniversary gift, perhaps. He decided to seize it.

"Who was on the phone?" she asked.

A little pinprick of guilt. "Food for the Poor."

"Way to bring down the mood, handsome man."

"You're so beautiful," he said simply.

"Forty years is a pretty big deal," she said. "You think I'd let you off that easy?"

He came over to her in a kind of leap, and it made her laugh aloud.

1984–1985

Marilyn had been preparing dinner when she learned that her father had died, Liza on her hip, the ends of her ponytail in Liza's mouth, a bag of potatoes in her free hand, the receiver wedged between her chin and her shoulder.

"Why don't you take a seat?" said the nurse on the other end, but she had already sat down heavily—startling the baby—in a kitchen chair. Liza, sensing her unease, began to fuss.

"Shh," she said. She wasn't sure if she was speaking to the baby or to the nurse.

"Your father's had a heart attack, Mrs. Sorenson."

"I know," she murmured into the top of Liza's head. Because she'd always kind of expected this, since she left Oak Park, hadn't she? "I know, I know, I know."

"We weren't able to resuscitate him. I'm so sorry."

It surprised her anew—as it had when she and David signed their lease, when she wrote the monthly check to the gas company, when the girls were born—how these instances of adult responsibility were just foisted upon you, without preamble or training. Suddenly she didn't have parents, and there was nobody around to tell her what that meant, or how she was supposed to feel about it. In some ways, her father had done her a kindness by allowing her such a swift and clean exit from his life, by failing to express interest in her or his grandchildren.

She tried to picture her own children growing up, progressing into adulthood, and she tried to imagine not being utterly riveted by their every step, as she was now.

"You're wonderful, my lambs," she'd whisper to the girls at night in the weeks after his death, memorizing the parts in their hair. "You're Mama's best things."

Now Violet ambled into the room, having visibly wet her pants, having been too wrapped up in the game she'd been playing with Wendy where their dolls were sea explorers and the dustpan was a boat, which Marilyn had known would happen, because her eldest girls were so tightly wound sometimes that they had to be forcibly extracted from their imaginative world to deal with workaday inconveniences like urination. She knew them so well. So much better, already, than either of her parents had ever known her. Violet's eyes were brimming with embarrassed tears, and Marilyn—her shoulder pressing the phone to her ear as the nurse began to review logistical details, Liza sucking again on the ends of her hair—opened her free arm to her daughter and pulled her close.

She was quieter in the weeks following her father's death, he thought, but it was also hard to tell, because the way their life was structured didn't really allow for a mourning period; he'd offered to take some time off work but she'd just smiled at him and insisted she was fine.

And then suddenly she was back.

"Darling, I hate it here," she declared dramatically one night a few weeks later when he walked in the door, one hand elbow-deep in a rubber glove and the other holding a martini like some kind of missed-bus holdover from their parents' generation; he was pretty sure she was even wearing makeup.

"Good evening to you too," he said. He tripped over a tiny

pair of rain boots as he went to set down his briefcase. He followed her into the kitchen, where she was wiping down the counters, Springsteen playing softly on the radio, which could indicate any number of her moods, from overwhelmed to furious to completely and insatiably aroused.

"There's a dead mouse in the basement," she said. "And the crack in the girls' ceiling is getting bigger; I think it might be from ants. The librarian asked me if I'd *gotten myself pregnant again*. She said she's been noticing that I'm gaining weight."

"You're not gaining weight."

"I *am*, though. I am because there's nowhere to *go* around here and so I'm just always *sitting*. I made you a drink if you want."

"Thank you."

"Sit down. *I'll* get it." She tossed her glove into the sink and spun toward him, stopping to kiss him as she passed; when she pulled away he could taste the waxy sheen of her lipstick. "I'm the one who needs more physical activity."

"For God's sake, honey; you get plenty of physical activity. You're chasing three kids around all day."

"Which brings me," she said, thrusting out his martini, "to the girls' room."

"The ants. You said."

"No. They're going to kill each other in there, David." She sat down next to him, laughing, her domestic façade proving itself to be just that, a theatrical little lilt to make her day more interesting. She still had a sense of humor about it all. She enjoyed their life, sometimes; of course she did. Sometimes he'd catch her humming when she was folding the laundry; her face lit up with pleasure every time Liza did her great hysterical baby-cackle; she'd just planted a row of tulips in the front yard. He reached for her free hand and clinked his glass against hers with the other.

"Oh yeah?" he said. He sipped his martini. "*Lord of the Flies* situation?"

"*Really.*"

"The librarian wasn't right, was she? You're not pregnant again?"

"Christ, no. But I'm losing it here, David."

He often felt guilty when he came home to her, not because his day had been *fun* but because she so often appeared completely drained. He would come over to her on some of those evenings and lean to kiss her and feel afraid when her eyes met his because they were so unfamiliar to him. She'd get this vacant, glassy look, usually accompanied by a weak shell of a smile, and she'd sometimes kiss back and sometimes just let him kiss her, and then inevitably one of the kids would make a noise or the pot she was filling in the sink would overflow and just as quickly she'd snap out of it, wrenched from her rumination by the chaotic onslaught of their household.

He felt bad that he'd never given her the opportunity to get to know herself better. At twenty-nine, she'd become so staunchly, irrevocably *Mom* to three girls that there was no room for anyone else, and even if there had been room, there *wasn't* anyone else, because she hadn't had the chance to discover any of her other selves prior to the births of their children. She'd given up so much and so little when she agreed to marry him, but he had been so fixated on *having* her that he had rarely stopped to consider what it would mean for her to allow herself to be had. This was how he saw it: *getting* her, winning. It wasn't fair. She deserved more.

He observed the room around him: every inch of real estate on the fridge was covered with waterlogged paintings of princesses with pink hair and rainbow-striped dinosaurs. There was barely room at the table for Liza's high chair, and the sink was lined with drying sippy cups and Strawberry Shortcake plates. And his wife, losing her mind in the middle of all of it, in the kitchen she'd impulsively painted blue before either of them had any idea what it meant to be overwhelmed.

"I got a call from my father's lawyer today," she said.

"Oh?"

"We're homeowners." Her voice was tentative. "If we want to be."

The house on Fair Oaks: her father's house, her childhood home, with the lilac bushes and the ginkgo tree beneath which she'd taken his virginity.

He hated Oak Park, and not only because he'd grown up in the city and rued the moneyed profusion of the suburbs— yards that could fit nine of his father's house, fussy cobblestone streets. He hated it because of those things, but he also suspected they wouldn't quite fit there, not like they did in Iowa City. They weren't rich enough and they had too many kids. Oak Park: not north where the Jews lived or south where the *Catholic* Catholics lived, but just west of the city, a land populated by regular, lazy Catholics and agnostics, those who were skeptical or jaded or just liked to sleep late on Sundays. Oak Park: the land of wide lawns and narrow minds, the birthplace of Hemingway and Ray Kroc and home, then, to a bunch of walking contradictions afflicted with what his equally conflicted social liberal/fiscal conservative father-in-law had referred to as "a mean case of NIMBY syndrome." Oak Park, the topography of which David could barely stand to comprehend, such a far cry from the pragmatic gray land upon which he had been reared, not very far away at all but aesthetically unrecognizable, apples and oranges, Frank Lloyd Wright versus the Tom, Dick or Harry who'd mapped out the bland vinyl-sided walk-up in which he'd come of age. Houses with bowling alleys in the basements and indoor swimming pools, houses that had once been inhabited and embellished by Depression-era mobsters but were now owned by white-bread investment bankers and neurosurgeons, people whose kids drove BMWs and had spots on reserve for ineffectual social science degrees from Marquette and Cornell. He hated the thought of living somewhere so precious and affluent.

But his wife—his wife who'd come with him to Iowa and given him this beautiful, chaotic life, made a father and a doctor out of him, loved him amid the tumult—hated it here. And so it was. They were bursting at the seams, and thank God they were still able to laugh about it, but he wasn't sure how much longer that would be the case. He owed her. She would be there, wherever they lived. The rest, he supposed, didn't really matter.

She was watching him with apprehension, and he smiled at her, and the relief that crossed her face made everything worth it; for the simple fact of her hand squeezing his, he would have moved a dozen times over.

The third step from the bottom still creaked as it always had. Marilyn came down from putting the girls to bed and found David on the couch, looking small and uncertain in their underfurnished living room. He saw her and smiled; she came and sat beside him.

"I don't think I ever really realized how huge this place is," he said. "I mean—growing up—I think my entire house was maybe the size of this room."

"My Little Match Boy."

"I'm serious. I think—I would have slept where the fireplace is, and my dad's room would have been the . . . foyer, I guess. Do I have to call it that?"

"You can call it whatever you want," she said, rubbing his thigh.

"You're just going to have to bear with me while I get used to this."

"Yeah, well, likewise," she said, and he looked at her pointedly. "I'll be patient."

Marriage, she had learned, was a strangely pleasurable power game, a careful balance of competing egos, conflicting moods. She could turn hers off in order to allow his to shine. Conservation. Reciprocity. She was allowed to feel confident and excited only when he was feeling anxious and pessimistic. If he worried about everything, she was allowed to worry about nothing. He had given her a gift by agreeing to move here. She curled into him and surveyed the disaster of the living room. They had unpacked the girls' things, some of them at least— her children had roughly seventy times more possessions than she did—and a few absolute necessities; but everything else was still in ruins, haphazardly stacked boxes and furniture left wherever they had decided to set it and rolled-up rugs like fallen bodies and all of the things her father had left behind— the built-in room dividers with the gilt-edged encyclopedias, the antique end tables that her mother had refinished.

"What should we do first?" he asked, sounding drained. He would start work the day after tomorrow, and had just finished at the hospital in Cedar Rapids yesterday, had come home at midnight and meticulously packed up what remained of their kitchen and modest living room; he had gone to bed at three and awakened at six to pick up their U-Haul and play an elaborate game of Tetris with the complete contents of their domestic life, fitting it all into the truck without a centimeter to spare. (She had discovered, after the fact, one box that she had forgotten in the bedroom closet, and when she presented it to him he had looked so dejected that she had decided she could do without the extra set of linens—though they had been her mother's, beautiful Pratesi sheets dotted with lavender fleur-de-lis—and set it on the curb.)

"We should drink a beer together on our porch," she said.

"It's only eight. Tomorrow's our only full day to get settled in before I'm back at work."

"So what?" she said, rising from the couch. "Outside." He looked first at her and then at the carnage in their new living room. "Forget about it for tonight. We've got the next fifty years together to finish unpacking."

At this he smiled, shook his head and rose to go with her onto the porch. They'd yet to unpack the patio furniture and sat instead on old pool rafts they found in the garage.

CHAPTER TWELVE

"Come keep me company," Wendy demanded, calling in from the patio to where Jonah was watching *South Park* reruns in the living room. It was nice to be able to ameliorate your own loneliness, to beckon a person and have him comply. He looked up, one leg thrown over the back of the couch and his neck at a ninety-degree angle over the armrest. He rose without protest, clicked off the television and came to join her outside.

"You want me to bring the bottle of wine?" he said when he reached the screen door.

She stiffened. "What? No."

He paused. "Okay. Just checking."

"How was martial arts?"

"Okay." He shrugged. "I'm still working on the three-sixty defense."

It surprised her how easily they'd fallen into a rapport, how much he'd relaxed around her over the course of a few months. He joked with her, told her about dumb shit he'd watched on the Internet. He inured her to teenisms, *dope* and *lit* and *meme*; and he told her when it would be normal for her to use those words and when it would just seem try-hard.

"If at first you don't succeed . . ." she said idly, lighting a cigarette. Every once in a while he'd bum one from her, but his habit didn't seem serious.

Bring the *bottle*? As though she were some kind of wino. True: if her recycling bin was any indicator, she probably drank more than she should (though at least she *recycled*). And the guy at the bodega where she bought her cigarettes knew her by name, but she also went there for orange juice and Clif bars, which didn't necessarily mean she smoked too much— though scientific consensus pegged all smokers as smoking too much. As for the weed, the evidence in her favor was staggering: reduction in anxiety, possible increase in lung capacity and metabolism. Cancer prevention too; people ignored the research on that. She just happened to live in a state where it had not yet been made legal.

But she was *functional*, wasn't she? She volunteered and went to core barre and showed up to fund-raisers biweekly at *least*, and she'd yet to make a spectacle of herself. And now she was taking care of a teenage kid, and he was still *alive*, wasn't he? And she'd turned her sexual exploits into kind of a game, sneaking around, sparing Jonah from her visitors. There was a pleasant excitement in it, tiptoeing through the halls, muffling her cries in the pillows, silently seeing the men to the front door. And she was surprised by the erotic benefits of this: it felt like when she was a teenager and she'd had to sneak Aaron Bhargava in and out of her bedroom window. She wondered— not to be gross—if her parents had ever benefited similarly from hiding their own romantic exploits. It made her feel illicit and mature, *responsible*, shielding the kid down the hall from witnessing the primal scene.

He'd begun, lately, though, to look at her with a mix of caginess and concern, like nothing that came out of her mouth quite made sense, like anything she said was potentially a joke. She couldn't pinpoint exactly when it had started happening, but now it was all she could see, the way he acted like she was some doddering hag who couldn't be trusted to use the stove.

"Do you think I'm a fuckup?" she asked him.

"What? No."

"Why the fuck did you ask if I wanted a bottle of wine, then?"

He winked. "Because sometimes you ask me that."

"*Maybe* if you're passing by the kitchen I'll ask you to bring me *something*, but it's not like I'm constantly soliciting you to bring me bottles of wine."

"I didn't say that."

"Do you think I'm just a total boozehound?"

"God, no, Wendy. Chill out."

"Honestly." The nausea she felt was another thing that could be assuaged by marijuana, scientifically speaking. "What do you—take me for?"

Jonah frowned.

"What do you *think* of me, I mean."

"I think it's pretty sick, actually, your life," he said, and she felt the blood drain from her face. "No," he said, noticing. "Like, *good* sick."

"Oh yeah," she said, rolling her eyes.

"It's like *lit*," he said. "Like good sick. Seriously. Like you're just this— I don't know. You smoke and drink a bunch and just hang out and you still seem—I don't know, like, okay with everything."

"Just *hang out*?"

"Like you're just a chill person, and it doesn't seem like you're that bothered by all of the bullshit that everyone else worries about. Which is cool, Wendy. It's a good thing." He squirmed. "Can I bum a smoke?"

"No," she said, surprising herself with her anger. "Jesus fuck; you're like a baby. It's not *cool* to smoke; you're fucking yourself over by starting so early." Her father chastened her for it, which made her furious because he was such a fucking hypocrite, because her mother used to keep a pack of Camels wedged behind his workbench in the garage.

"Look, dude, I didn't mean—"

"I'm not a *dude*. God, what the fuck do you— Christ. Forget it. You should go to bed."

"It's like eight-thirty." He looked up at her with surprising clarity. "Wendy, I didn't mean— I think you're cool. I don't need to bum a cigarette. You're good. We're good."

Of course it was common sense, just textbook being-a-person, that you would never appear in someone else's eyes precisely as you did in your own. There had been talk, when she was a teenager, of body dysmorphia, an adolescent mindfuck that added fifteen pounds to her frame every time she looked in the mirror, dishwatered her hair and tripled her chin. But now she worried she'd floated all the way to the other side of the spectrum, that she'd lost perspective on herself in possibly a more detrimental way, one that convinced her she was fine when in fact she was supremely fucked, shoplifting-Winona-Rider-level fucked, merely a mammoth bank account away from being drowned-rat-sewer-dwelling fucked.

"You're too old to be this dumb," she said.

"What?" He seemed like a child again now, fully.

"Stop trying to be cool. You've got enough stacked against you already. Play to your strengths." She convolutedly wished he *had* brought out what remained of the bottle of wine.

He didn't say anything, and it made her feel worse, and she prematurely stubbed out her cigarette and lit another one just for something to do.

"I'm not the cool degenerate aunt who you can just— I'm an *adult*, Jonah; I've been through more shit than— Christ."

"Look, Wendy, I was trying to be nice. I didn't mean anything by it." He rose uncertainly. "You're cool," he said. "You're lit." She heard desperation in his voice, and she felt a combination of anger and compassion, for his apprehension, for his naïveté.

"Sleep well," she said, and she leaned definitively away from him over the railing, staring wistfully down at the lake like some kind of persecuted maritime harlot, listening to the swish of the door as he went inside, feeling an allergic pressure in her sinuses, watching the waves hurl themselves mercilessly against the Harbor Lock.

Later, when everything had had time to sink in, David would marvel over the fact that Wendy had called him first. But when he saw her name flash across his phone on a Tuesday evening, when she responded to his hello not with a reciprocal greeting but with a guttural catch from her throat, his first thought was that something terrible had happened and he wished she'd called Marilyn instead. His wife was reading on the back porch and he had half a mind to bring the phone out to her, deposit it in her lap like Loomis did with sticks and squirrel skeletons.

"What is it?" he asked.

Her voice, when it finally found itself, was more assured than he was expecting. "So this isn't working out," she said. "This— Jonah."

"What do you mean it's not working out?" Of course they could have anticipated this. Of course Marilyn *had* anticipated this, but he'd held out some hope for Wendy, had seen how tender and thoughtful and resilient she could be. She couldn't be getting rid of him *already*.

"There's too much maneuvering. Plus my schedule. It's all too— It's just not meshing."

As far as he knew, his daughter's schedule consisted of various core-strengthening exercise classes and surface-level psychotherapy and a steady stream of cocktails—things to which he'd always considered her entitled, for now at least, given all she'd been through.

"Did something happen?"

"No, I— No, not like one specific *thing*; I just don't think this is an ideal situation and frankly I'm not sure why we even considered it in the first place. You guys are blocks away from the high school. You have the room. You have the—"

"Adolescent strength training?" he asked. It had never been clear to him when Wendy would respond favorably to his jokes but tonight she laughed, after a long minute of quiet.

"It's a lot," she said finally.

No shit, he did not say.

"There's just— I just don't think this is necessarily the best time in my life to—you know, be *sharing* a life with another person. I don't think I'm ready to— I'm *definitely* not ready to have a kid in my possession right now."

He knew that if anyone waited to have kids until they felt ready to have them, the human race would have died off centuries ago. But again he held his tongue.

"It makes more sense for him to be living there anyway." She paused. "I'm sure you think I'm a total fuckup. I know everyone thinks I'm a total fuckup but I— This really just isn't— I just can't right now, Dad. I'm sorry."

"Nobody thinks that, sweetheart. Can you at least stick it out until the weekend?" This poor kid, being ferried around between their homes like a library book.

"Sure," Wendy said. "I haven't told him."

"Don't say anything yet," he said. "In case it— You don't want him to feel unwelcome."

"He's not un*welcome*. I just—"

"I know. Hold tight. Let me talk to your mother."

Marilyn was curled up on the wicker couch on the back porch with Loomis beside her, his head nestled into the crook of her knees. David paused in the doorway to watch her, the wave of hair that fell over the curve of her neck, the way one hand idly traced soothing lines down the dog's back. He came up behind her and laid his hands on her shoulders, making her startle.

"Just me," he said.

"Hey, you. Who was on the phone?"

"Wendy, actually." He sat down beside her, placing a hand on her knee. "So, guess what?"

She held a finger in her book and looked up at him expectantly. He remembered getting a call from her during his rounds at the hospital in Cedar Rapids, her voice wobbling, uttering the very same line: "Looks like we're going to be having another baby."

He should've known before he said it that it wouldn't make her laugh.

"Mom called me," Violet said, and Wendy, phone pressed to her ear, felt a surging of bile in her throat. "God, you really are fucked up, aren't you?"

"I—"

"I should have fucking known," Violet said. "Of course you don't feel any kind of *anything* about this because you're a goddamn sociopath."

"It just wasn't—"

"I asked you one thing," Violet said. "I asked you for one *thing* and I— Christ, I didn't even *ask*; you offered, and all you had to do was the bare minimum and you lasted the *summer*? You're the one who started this, Wendy. You're the one who started *all* of this and you've never given a single thought to the fact that these are people's actual *lives*. Jesus. Do you not get that other people exist and have feelings and needs and— God, he's fifteen. He's a fifteen-year-old kid with a fucked-up life and you had the *effortless* opportunity to make things suck a little bit less for him and you couldn't even pull it together for that?

Do you realize how much instability he's had in his life? Do you get that I *told* him you'd be happy to have him for as long he wanted? Which you said to me, by the way. Verbatim. I wrote it down because I was so fucking shocked to hear you sounding like a psychologically reasonable person."

Violet never spoke to her in this way, never dared to be so candidly cruel. She was so busy trying to compose herself, to speak past the thickness in her throat, to not feel life-endingly hurt, that she didn't give any thought to what came out of her mouth in return: "You know, Violet, I seem to recall someone else in this family being the direct cause of his fucked-up life."

"Fuck you," Violet said.

"Perhaps our most entitled member, who refused to even *look* at him when he was born. You couldn't even make sure he was *alive* and you're throwing around the word *sociopath*?"

"Don't ever talk about that to me," Violet said. "You have absolutely no— It's not yours, okay? That experience isn't yours. It never has been. Just because you were there doesn't mean that you get to add it to your fucking—your—"

"My what?"

"The—your—the roster of suffering you keep. It's pathetic, Wendy. We get it; your life sucks. So does everyone else's. That's just life."

"Roster of suffering?"

Had this been a different conversation, they might both have laughed.

"It's not a game," Violet said. "None of this is— You treat other people's lives like they're— Not everything is about entertaining yourself."

This, for whatever reason, filled her with a hot purple shame.

"I want nothing to do with you," Violet said. "I want you to stay as far away from me as possible, okay?"

"There's something profoundly wrong with you, Violet," she said, because she had always found combat easier than crying. "Like, for whatever reason you're able to pass as a normal human being but there's something *deeply* fucked about you, like core-level fucked."

"Coming from you," Violet said, before she hung up, "that's actually a compliment."

PART
THREE

FALL

CHAPTER THIRTEEN

"This isn't anything personal," Wendy said to him. They were stuck in traffic. She wasn't looking at him. He had his ugly flowered duffel in his lap, a bag someone sadistic had donated to Lathrop House. He shifted to look out the window. Out of the corner of his eye, he saw Wendy glance over at him. What the fuck did he care? She didn't *owe* him anything.

"It just makes more sense," she said. Then: "I'm really sorry, Jonah."

She actually sounded sorry, but he just rested his head against the window, staying silent, because he was sick of telling people that he was willing to settle for their shitty behavior.

Marilyn watched the boy—whom she could not quite bring herself to call her grandson—shuffling around their house, poking his toe tentatively against the floorboards whenever he stopped, breathing in that phlegmy way he had, and she was reminded—problematically—of when they'd brought Loomis home from the shelter, of how reluctant and skittish he'd been, surreptitiously sniffing their scents when he thought they weren't looking.

"So this is it," she said, throwing her arms out expansively. She colored. She'd meant it as a joke but she realized, standing in her kitchen, amid its disarray and utter familiarity, that their house must seem huge to him; that—without four girls sharing the space anymore—it *was* huge. "It'll be nice to have a teenager in the house again," she said, and she meant it, though the idea of uttering such a statement back when she'd *had* teenagers in the house was laughable.

"Are you hungry?" she asked. "What could I make you? A sandwich? Some—" She opened the refrigerator and faltered. She knew only the culinary catalogs of her own children— Liza liked strawberry jam but not grape; Violet liked peanuts but not peanut butter; Wendy, for all those dark years, refused to touch anything white; Gracie favored grilled cheese sandwiches cut into four vertical strips—most of which had been rendered obsolete by the maturation of their palates. What did teenage boys eat?

"I'm good for now," he said.

"Well, help yourself whenever. There's—you know, whatever's in the fridge, and we keep snacks in the pantry." They'd kept snacks in the pantry when the girls lived at home. Now it was mostly full of Loomis's accessories and frightening, expensive bits of other animals, livers and lamb shanks, that had been freeze-dried and sold to them by an upscale "canine marketplace" in downtown Oak Park. She would send David to the grocery later for human snacks.

At the dinner table that evening, they eyed each other warily, exchanged shy smiles over the salad. Loomis watched them, forlorn, from the doorway, sequestered there behind a baby gate because she didn't want him scaring Jonah away from his dinner. The boy didn't look malnourished, exactly, but his skin had a mushroom pallor and she couldn't tell if it was because of his diet or the fact that he, like many kids today, spent all of his time indoors.

"I never had a dog growing up, either," David said. "But they really— You'd be surprised how they grow on you."

Jonah smiled tightly, examining Loomis out of the corner of his eye.

She checked on him later that night, stood in the doorway of Liza's old room. She had the strange impulse to tuck him in, though he was neither in bed nor of an appropriate age.

"So sleep well, okay?" she said. He swiveled back and forth in the desk chair. "There's extra blankets if you get cold. Can I wake you for school?"

"I have an alarm on my phone," he said.

"Well, what time do you normally get up, just in case?"

"In case what?"

"In case your alarm doesn't go off. Or you sleep through it."

Suddenly, blurred beneath the contours of his face, she saw a familiar amusement, the same exasperation with which the girls used to regard her when she tried to coordinate their morning routines.

"Mom, it's not like a NASA mission," Violet had said once, and David, later, when they were alone, had supplied gently, "Well, honey, it's just that you have a tendency to over*plan*."

"Seven-thirty," Jonah said.

"Do you snooze? Is there an absolute latest time you want to be woken up?"

"I don't snooze," he said. There was the hint of a smile again.

"Seven-thirty, then."

"Thanks. But I'll set my alarm."

"Sure." She nodded. "Yes. And David can drive you to school, if you want."

"I'm fine to walk. Thanks."

"Well, you can decide in the morning." She looked around the room, the biggest bedroom in the house besides hers and David's. It still smelled like Liza, still featured the most taste-ful of her Smashing Pumpkins posters and the antique dresser that she had painted a garish shade of acrylic green during a fit of teenage rebellion. "You should make the space your own.

Let me know if there's anything you'd like. A different desk. Or a reading chair."

"No, this is all good. Thanks."

"You don't have to thank me," she said. "I think you've filled your quota."

"Oh, I wasn't—"

She smiled, and—at once unthinking and entirely calculated—she bent to kiss his forehead. He smelled waxy, like old bar soap.

"Nobody in this family credits me for having a sense of humor," she said, "but it's my personal opinion that I'm far funnier than the rest of them."

His grandparents were doing something in the kitchen that it seemed like he shouldn't be watching. He'd just gone to get a snack. The house was, suddenly, filled with snacks, the good kind that Hanna would never buy, granola bars with chocolate chips and fresh pineapple in clear plastic vats of juice and non-gluten-free pretzels and unfathomable varieties of Little Debbies—oatmeal creme pies and the chocolate-covered wafers with peanut butter. He could have snacks whenever he wanted, though if Marilyn caught him while he was looking she would offer to make him something healthier and more substantial, and he had trouble saying no both because he felt awkward and because she made good sandwiches, cut up apples in a triangular way that made them taste better. He'd just wanted some sesame sticks, maybe, or a can of seltzer, but when he reached the doorway he saw them together, having what seemed to be a normal conversation—he heard David say, "They seemed like weeds but I wasn't sure so I just left them"—except Marilyn was leaning against the sink and David was pressed into her, closer than he ever saw Hanna and Terrence get.

"Aster, probably," Marilyn said. Her arms were looped

around his back. "Or maybe white snakeroot, but I've never really seen those around here. There are some in Columbus Park, I think. Never in our yard. But you never know."

"We can look together tomorrow."

Their mouths seemed uncomfortably close. He thought of Wendy in bed with the redhead and felt his face get hot. David bowed his head and kissed Marilyn's neck, not like the goth couple in his gym class but just quickly, once.

He was frozen in the doorway, unsure of whether he should hightail it back upstairs or go into the kitchen or just stand there until someone noticed him. The back stairs creaked conspicuously. The hallway to the front stairs creaked too. He was stuck, watching, and a weird part of him didn't want to move, wanted to see what happened, wanted to understand this new faction of human life where people willingly stood so close to each other, consciously chose to talk about weeds with their crotches touching. They were old, definitely, but they didn't *seem* old.

"The martyred saint, shouldering the burden of the weeds," Marilyn said. He was glad that he couldn't see David's hands.

"What does that mean?" David's hands were suddenly at his sides, and he took a step back so Marilyn's arms straightened a little at the elbows.

"Oh, God, honey, I'm kidding."

"I was weeding your garden for you."

"I know that. Lord. Sweetheart, I know. You're an excellent weeder. It's a huge help. Knock this off. I didn't mean anything. I was joking."

"An excellent weeder?"

Now Marilyn unlocked her hands and crossed her arms in front of her chest. He wished he'd made the decision to leave sooner. Walking in on a fight was way more awkward than walking in on whatever had been happening before it.

"I think I've earned a little bit of credit," she said. "You know what I meant. You're deliberately misconstruing what I said because you're in a mood."

"I'm not in a mood."

There was a silence, a moment during which Marilyn reached her hand up and ran it through David's hair.

"You know I appreciate everything you do during the day." Jonah tested his weight backward to see if he might still be able to sneak upstairs. "And at night." Her voice had changed. She tilted her face up to kiss David, and this time it lingered, and he watched as her knee appeared through the line between David's legs, and at that point he knew he had to go but when he actually made the leap the floorboards creaked louder than he thought possible and he froze again and when he looked up they'd pulled apart and were staring at him, wide-eyed.

"Oh, honey," Marilyn said. She picked up the dish brush from beside the sink, holding it weirdly in her hand like a wand. "Hi. I didn't see you. Did you need something?"

"No," he said. "No, I just— I was looking— I was going to get a snack."

"Sure," Marilyn said. She turned on the tap and started scrubbing at one of the pans from dinner. "Don't mind us. Just catching up. Can I make you something or are you—"

"No," he said. "No, I—just wanted—some fruit or something."

"There's apples," Marilyn said. "Or plums, but I'm not sure they're ripe yet."

"An apple's fine," he said, going to the fridge, just trying to get it over with.

"How's the homework coming?" David asked. "Chemistry's good?"

"More or less."

"If you're having any trouble, you've come to the right place," Marilyn said. "Someone in this room got me through a couple of brutal physics exams." Jonah turned from the fridge just in time to see them looking at each other again in this sort of dazed, goofy way.

"Not sure how much help I'll be, but I'd be happy to take a look," David said.

"Thanks. I'll let you know." In fact his chemistry homework was going terribly; the only thing he remembered from the semester was the day his teacher turned vials of liquid a bunch of different colors while playing "The Rainbow Connection."

"I have a feeling you're both downplaying your strengths," Marilyn said.

He exerted a single, forced *heh* before he hightailed it back upstairs with his apple.

1992–1993

It was David's suggestion; they were sitting up in bed and Marilyn had presented him with a gamut of boys' names, and he said, "How about Grace?" It came to him, his mom's name, surfaced from the repressive caverns of his memory, and Marilyn, who had just suggested Christopher, smiled grudgingly at him and said, "He might get made fun of at school."

"We should have something on the back burner. Just in case your ability to see the future proves faulty. Which of course it shouldn't, considering your glowing track record."

She laughed, leaning into him. The pregnancy was making them both feel youthful and giddy. "Fine," she said. "On the off chance that I'm wrong—which I'm *not*, ye of little faith—you can choose a girl's name."

"Grace." His grief over his mother cropped up only occasionally, usually at the most bizarre and least opportune times, and saying her name aloud then felt weighty and sad. His early memories were composed almost exclusively of sterile hallways in state hospitals; of his mom, toward the end when they'd deemed the cancer terminal, reaching out a stick-thin arm to touch a hand to his forehead. His own children, extant and as yet unborn, aroused this kind of nostalgia—the ability to look beyond the day-to-day and see the inextricable ties that looped back generations, like dipping wires between telephone poles. Marilyn picked up on it immediately, her intuitive wifely radar kicking into high alert. She kissed the side of his head next to his ear.

"I love it." She rested her head against his shoulder. "It's a beautiful name." She allowed them both a moment—she knew he felt more comfortable when she was the one commandeering their collective ability to emote. After a minute she squeezed his knee. "It's a shame we won't get to use it on our little accident." It was his turn to laugh at the joke that neither of them dared to make unless they were alone in their bedroom. Their secret: that this baby had *not* been an accident. Everyone assumed so, considering the nine years that had elapsed since their last child, considering Marilyn's age. It was assumed—*reckless Catholics*—that they had simply *had an accident*. He didn't like the word, had been glad when his wife started to make light of it, but of course *Liza* had been an accident. Violet, conceived when Wendy was only two months old, had been an accident. And Wendy—well.

But this baby—*Grace*—had not been a slipup. The idea of her had been conjured between them as they sat on the front stairs, a late summer evening when the girls were playing basketball together in twilight. He watched his daughters getting along, playing Horse. These little almost-women. Even Liza, their baby, seemed to have awakened one day suddenly sporting long coltish legs and the wide, knowing eyes of an adult. He felt an indistinct sadness.

"They're all so tall," Marilyn had said, and he knew at once that it was a loaded declaration; her voice was both woeful and contemplative. "I don't think I'm ready for them all to be so tall."

"Me neither," he'd said, and she'd turned to look at him. They had, over time, developed this sophisticated secret language in which his simple declaration of *me neither* actually meant *I agree, let's have another baby, kid*, and neither of them had to say the words.

"Really?" she said, and he shrugged.

"Yeah. Let's give it a go."

In bed, now, beside his wife, their twelve-week-old new baby in her belly beneath his palm: the result of their *giving it a go*. And he felt unprecedentedly unburdened, blessedly solvent. Unworried, not like he had been any of the previous times. They had a big house. He'd settled into a spot in a private family practice in the neighborhood, regular hours and appropriate compensation. The lines in his wife's face had receded—were beginning to be filled in by her pregnancy, though she, for the first time, had been sick in the mornings—and they were old enough, finally, at a comfortable enough station in life that they could reasonably make decisions like this one. A tiny baby, one who would keep her parents young and unite her older sisters. Grace. He imagined his mother proud of him, father of daughters, stable provider. His most tangible memory of her was the smell of the hospital: lemon cleanser, human secretions, and rot. His kids would have more than that, and he knew she would be glad for it.

"Oh, lord," Marilyn said, tensing suddenly next to him as though privy to his olfactory memories. She rose from the bed, hand over her mouth, and made her way to their bathroom. He followed, squatted beside her and held back her hair.

Their joy over the news was tarnished somewhat the following week, when they sat down to tell the children.

"A baby?" Liza asked. "I don't—get it."

Beside him on the couch, Marilyn gripped his hand. There was a ludicrous book in the waiting room of his office called *How You Were Made*, which contained startlingly graphic depictions of female anatomy—blood-red uteri and a cervix like a gash—alongside utterly cartoonish renderings of the male counterparts. Could they show that to Liza, those bow-tied sperm with optimistic smiley faces journeying valiantly into the depths?

"Some gross tadpoles came out of Dad's penis and swam in between Mom's legs," Wendy said casually, "and that's what makes a baby and then it grows really big like a watermelon and Mom has to push it out of her butt and there's all this blood and stuff."

"Wendy," he said, just as Marilyn was saying, "Oh, gosh, honey, no."

"Aren't you kind of *old*?" Violet asked, her gaze on them narrow and sharp.

"Lize," Marilyn said, "when a—when a mother and a father love each other . . ."

"Men and women have sexual intercourse, sometimes, honey, and when they do that, sperm come out of the man's—"

"*David.*" Marilyn beckoned Liza into her lap. "Pumpkin, this is a really great thing, okay? Mama and Daddy are so happy about it. The baby grows in here for a little while—" His wife deigned to rest a hand in the general vicinity of her uterus. "And then he's going to come out and we're going to set up the bedroom next to yours with a crib. And you can take him on walks, and hold him, and read to him. Doesn't that sound like fun?"

"I'm not sure," Liza said, frowning. "How do the—tadpoles, how do they . . ."

"You're almost *forty*," Violet said, studious now in her appraisal.

Marilyn squeezed his hand in desperation. He looked at her helplessly, surveyed his triangle of daughters with their varying amounts of angst. After Liza was born, they'd marveled at the odds—*another girl.*

"We're thinking a boy this time," he said now, squeezing Marilyn's hand, in return, three times. He nudged Liza with a playful elbow. "Huh, Lize? What do you say?" He could feel the weight of Wendy's and Violet's judgment. He cleared his throat. "Tip the scales in my favor."

Gillian, through Marilyn's entire pregnancy, seemed to get livelier and prettier as Marilyn grew older and larger. She was on the young side given all that she'd accomplished, energetic and successful in the same way David had been early in their marriage. And Marilyn noticed moments of youthfulness in the woman that reminded her of her daughters—how when she came into the room for the prenatal appointments, Marilyn sometimes felt like her mother or her teacher, firing off a bunch of nervous questions: How was the new apartment? What had she been up to lately? And Gillian, only four years her junior, divulged her dating mishaps and her reluctance to acclimate to the suburbs, lengthy reviews of restaurants in Wicker Park and Roscoe Village that Marilyn and David would never be cool enough to visit.

Odd, perhaps, to seek medical care from a woman who'd attended Christmas parties at your house. But David had been singing her praises since she'd joined the practice and Marilyn felt bad objecting, because to do so seemed like an affront to her husband's medical expertise. So she signed on as a new patient with Gillian, enduring marginal prickles of impropriety each time the woman queried her about hemorrhoids or discharge. Gillian was professional and hyperintelligent and Marilyn tried to be grateful for this, but she wasn't entirely comfortable with the fact that her onetime dinner guest had given her multiple pelvic exams.

The one appointment David had to miss, Gillian swept into the room saying, "Heard our favorite superhero doctor got called to the ER." He had: one of his patients had had a stroke.

Marilyn knew this because David had called her. It irked her that Gillian knew as well.

And, oh, what happened next. Because, alone, without her husband, in the company of another woman, she'd gotten weepy; as Gillian prodded at her, looked off into the distance, frowning, listening to overlapping heartbeats, Marilyn started to cry. She surprised herself: she hadn't, previously, been aware of feeling unhappy.

Gillian was unfazed. She got a few tissues from a box by the door, pulled the gown back down over Marilyn's belly, and dragged a chair next to the exam table to sit with her. "You want to talk about it?" she asked. "It's okay if you don't. Take a few deep breaths."

She supposed it was because David wasn't there that she did it—she felt a simultaneous license to disclose and a profound loneliness, exposed like this, solo, in a doctor's office, though she knew her husband was just a mile away, knew he'd be there if he could be.

"I'm sorry," she said, but her efforts to speak just made things worse.

"In through your nose. Out through your mouth. It's okay. Go ahead and cry."

She mimicked the doctor's breathing a few times, feeling herself settle. "I'm so embarrassed," she said. "I don't know what's gotten into me."

Motherhood was the loneliest thing in the world sometimes. And pregnancy was isolating, exhausting; her fatigue distanced her from her daughters and their lives; it made her forgetful and distracted. What made this time so different hadn't been clear to her until that moment in Gillian's office, with her husband missing in action. David had always been the one she could go to when she felt alone. It never mattered how disconnected she felt from the world around her, because

David was always there. When she was tired or sore or hyper-emotional, he'd show up, rub her back, give her a hug, make her laugh. But it didn't feel that way this time; he was working late hours; the girls were all at varying stages of intolerability; she was thirty-eight years old and had started going to bed before nine some nights.

"I've just been feeling very—old, lately, I guess. And David isn't— Oh, this feels like a betrayal to say when he's not here."

"You're my patient, Marilyn. It won't leave this room."

"He's not *attracted* to me anymore, it seems. This was never a problem before. He's just so— We haven't made love in—since February. We've never gone that long."

"Well," Gillian said. "It's a transitional time, you know. Physically, obviously. Emotionally, very much so. It's not uncommon in the least."

"We've done this three times." She smiled ruefully. "It's never been a problem."

"You're a little busier this time, though, are you not? A little older."

She started crying again. "I don't— I mean, I *am*. I'm a lot older. And I just wonder if I—if maybe I'm not making myself available enough to him? I feel like I'm in this other world and I'm not even sure how I got there but I'm not doing anything *well* right now and I . . . I just wonder if we've made the right decision."

"About what?"

She startled, realizing what she'd said. "I don't even know why I'm saying any of this. It's not— I haven't even really been thinking about it."

But of course she had. Because Wendy seemed to be on a downward spiral, worlds more vitriolic and afflicted at fifteen than she'd been at four; and Liza was regressing, tiptoeing around with her little hands linked through Marilyn's belt loops, asking about babies, asking about Santa, asking whether or not she could sleep in their bedroom because she was having nightmares about the characters from *Zoobilee Zoo*; and she was shocked by her own exhaustion, so much more crushing than it had been with any of the girls. Because she had, on more than one occasion, wondered if things might be easier if they'd decided to keep their roster at its barely manageable three.

"I feel like I don't have enough of myself to go around," she said.

"If I may?" Gillian touched her shoulder with a cold hand. David always had cold hands too; they turned up the heat only in the exam rooms to cut costs. "It's become sort of a running joke around the office. He's so— I mean, you know. David's the most professional guy in the room, always. But he starts talking about you and it's like he's fifteen years old. His *voice* changes. I heard him on the phone with you once—I was eavesdropping, shamelessly—and I didn't know it was him at first. God, the amount of *love* he has for you."

"Oh," she said, embarrassed in a different way now, having moved beyond caring about her coital drought. "You don't have to say that."

They were interrupted by a knock on the door. She blotted at her face with the tissue.

Gillian frowned, rose. "Just a minute. One of the nurses, probably."

But when she opened the door—first a crack, for privacy, and then all the way—it was not one of the nurses but David himself.

"Well, look who's here," Gillian said, smiling at them.

David noticed her tears, came to her, squatted before her with a hand on either of her knees. "What is it, sweetie?" He turned to Gillian. "Is something the matter?"

"I'm fine," she said, putting her hands over his. "Everything's fine. Hormones." She laughed, ashamed, and she felt the fluttering in her belly, their innocent afterthought responding already to the sound of his father's voice. David rubbed at her thigh over the gown.

"The baby's okay?" he asked.

"The baby's wonderful," Gillian said, betraying nothing. "Everything looks great."

Wendy had signed up for the spring production of *1776* not because of any particular interest in musical theater but because a boy she liked was on the stage crew. She earned an ensemble role in the front row of the Continental Congress and on opening night she "forgot" her breeches and so was bare-legged beneath her waistcoat, and so finally attracted the amorous attention of swarthy stagehand Aidan O'Brien, and it would've been a perfect night were it not for her family, who had insisted on attending the production. She was so mortified by it all, by her motley family: clingy Liza, Violet in her dumb Frank Lloyd Wright vest from her new volunteer job as a Home and Studio tour guide, and her mom, the most embarrassing of all, enormously pregnant, wearing one of her dad's button-down shirts through which patches of her belly were visible when she moved in certain ways. Wendy had avoided looking at them for the entire production: the obscene swell of her mother and the awkwardness of Liza, who insisted on sitting in their father's lap even though she was almost *ten*. Afterward, when everyone was supposed to be paying attention to Wendy, other parents were instead asking her mom about the baby. Her mother, at some point, produced an inexplicable bouquet of lilies from behind her back and presented them to Wendy, stooping with difficulty to kiss her hair.

"We're so proud of you, Wednesday," she said, but the niceness of the gesture was overshadowed both by those awful patches between the buttons of the shirt and by the fact that

Aidan O'Brien had overheard the dumb nickname her parents called her sometimes.

At dinner, Wendy noticed her mother wincing, squirming, clutching her belly like a kickball.

"You okay?" David asked her. They'd been talking about Wendy, finally, about how pretty she looked in jewel tones, what a coordinated dancer she was, how exciting it had been to see her onstage. She'd been waiting for the inevitable interruption.

"Mm, fine," her mom said. She made some secret face at their father, half eye-roll, half smile. "Tell me again, Wendy; who was that young woman who played Thomas Jefferson?"

"Summer Frank," Wendy said. "She's a ho." She started talking about her classmate, making scandalizing use of the words *skank* and *grody* to her father's gentle tsking, but then her mother made a quiet groaning noise. She nodded, trying to seem like she was still listening. "*Mom*, God, what's the matter?"

"Nothing, honey, sorry," she said. Now everyone was watching Marilyn with concern, especially Liza, who looked like she might cry. Her mother noticed this and—she was sitting next to Liza; Liza always insisted on sitting next to one of their parents—put her arm around her. "Practice contractions," she explained apologetically. She kissed Liza's head.

"You sure?" her father asked.

"Positive."

"What does that *mean*?" Liza asked tearfully.

And then she'd launched into an explanation—one that was watered down for Liza's benefit but still gross—about her cervix and her uterine muscles, about all of the strange private things her body was doing while they were out to dinner, allegedly celebrating Wendy's stage debut. She smiled at Wendy, finally. "I had these for almost two months before Wendy came along. I'm fine. I'm perfectly fine; keep telling me about this wretched Summer Frank."

The food arrived, interrupting them again, but by then her stomach had turned, thinking of contractions and kickballs and her own irrelevance, how easily her mother had forgotten her. She wasn't large, but she was the proportionately biggest person in her family, bested by her mother now only because of her pregnancy. There was the most damning story about how Wendy weighed nearly 10 pounds when she was born, that her birth had nearly done her mother in, her mother who weighed, on a bad day, maybe 115. Wendy's origin story: the tale of a giant mutant baby hell-bent on wrecking her tiny elfin mother from the inside out. She watched Liza, stick-thin and birdlike, surreptitiously smash three pats of butter onto a piece of bread before shoving it into her mouth. She watched Violet, prissy like Summer Frank, eating the salad she'd ordered in imitation of their mother, undoubtedly in an attempt to seem reasonable and adult. Wendy had ordered penne alla vodka in an effort to appear mature, and she pushed the creamy orange mess around her plate again and again. She thought of her parents naked, her father pumping over her mother; she thought of her mother straining to give birth; she thought of the salad her mother was eating traveling through secret, bloodied channels to feed the new baby. She felt sick. Her father, so tall and thin, had finished his cavatelli quickly and she moved to push some of her food on his plate.

"Eyes bigger than your stomach, Wend?" he asked, joking, accepting the ration.

She forced herself to laugh, felt her mother's eyes on her, ignored them. It was the first meal she successfully avoided eating.

The Mother's Day that fell just a week before Grace was born: she awakened to the feel of David's mouth on her shoulder, kissing a line from the nape of her neck, and she was so disoriented by the notion of being roused by anything romantic that it took her a minute to register him. She shifted and he moved his kisses down into her clavicles and she moaned a little before remembering the unforgettable fact of her girth, remembering that the last time she and David had had sex there had been snow on the ground outside.

"Honey, what are you doing?" She couldn't roll over without considerable assistance so she flopped artlessly on her back. He was propped up on his elbow, his hair in one of its more comical states of disarray, and she couldn't help but smile at him.

"What do you think I'm doing?" he asked, laughing, and it occurred to her that she'd forgotten what it felt like to have her husband desire her, and she felt her eyes filling hotly, felt the jab of the baby against her ribs, felt the sheets beneath her, damp with a mammalian but decidedly unconnubial sweat.

"Oh, for God's sake," she said, pressing her face into her pillow.

He moved closer to her, a tentative hand on her side. "What is it?"

"*Look* at me," she said into the pillow, her words coming out like marshmallows.

"I am," David said, running his hand up and down. "I am looking at you."

"Well, stop." She looked up and they both laughed. "What's with us? When did this become so foreign to me? Am I— Something's *off*, David, don't you feel like something's—" Beneath his hand on her side, the baby kicked hard, and he met her eyes, smiling.

"Things are a little different these days," he said. "I know we can't—" He paused, blushing. The idea that they *couldn't* was new, specific to this pregnancy; she was convinced that late-term carnal indulgence was what had put her into labor with all three of the girls. "I was reading about— I thought that maybe I could—*service* you."

"Service me?" She was horrified. The wave of emotion had passed, its only evidence a salty wetness on her cheeks, cooling in the breeze from their window. "Like a *car*?"

"No, not like a *car*," David said. "Open your legs." This, whatever it was, sounded suspiciously like a pelvic exam, and she watched him, thighs clamped together. He leaned in and kissed her and then scooted his way down the mattress by her feet and put a hand on her knee, pulling gently. "Come on. Let me do something for you."

"David, what are you—"

"Shh."

She shifted somewhat doubtfully and he reached to slide off her underpants. She considered their beige unsexiness, the urine that had probably leaked into their crotch every time she'd sneezed or moved too suddenly since putting them on.

"Do you want an extra pillow?" he asked, and she shook her head, too curious to interrupt him. "Okay," he said. "Just try to relax." He reached for her knees again, parting them tenderly. He kissed the inside of each of her thighs and her breath caught in her throat.

"I know you love me," she said. "I know we'll have sex again—maybe when the baby's in college. You don't need to do this to prove something. You don't want to put your *face*—"

She stopped speaking because apparently he did; she suddenly felt his tongue, its rough, catlike warmth between her legs, exploring, venturing shallowly inside her.

"Oh," she said, more of a gasp than a word. She thought, shamefully, of Dean McGillis, in the sand on Oak Street Beach, their bodies shielded by the boulders. Her life before David. She felt the blood rush to her cheeks. She sank back onto her elbows. "Honey."

The sensation abated and his face appeared, rising like a moon over her belly. "Everything okay?"

She felt herself flush and she nodded. "Yes." Resting weakly against her pillow, she added, "Thank you."

He grinned. "You don't have to thank me, kid."

"I might," she said dizzily. How was it possible they'd never done this before? She did the equivalent for him on occasion— much less frequently since they'd had the children—but she always felt a low-level gag reflex as she did, persevered only because she could see how much he enjoyed it. But this: what *was* this? She pushed the thought from her head with surprising ease as she felt a quickening low inside of her, David's tongue—that chaste, gentle tongue—working its way around the sacred space that she hadn't shared with him in months. Or that he hadn't wanted her to share. She stroked his neck.

When she came, it was different than other times, at once ethereal and violent, accompanied by the movement of the baby in a way that maybe should have shamed her but she was too taken. She pressed her face again into the pillow, this time to muffle her own sounds.

"How was that?" David asked, continuing to stroke her with his hand. She inhaled raggedly and nodded. His face was slick with her and it embarrassed her for just a fraction of a second because the look in his eyes was unmistakable, his love for his hulking, unsexy, animal wife and the fluid from her body that he now wore unabashedly on his own skin.

"Come here," she said, and he crawled up next to her and she kissed him, wiped the wetness from his mouth. "You're really something, you know that?"

He tucked her hair behind her ear. "Better than the alternative."

"There's a decent chance I'll be less encumbered by Father's Day."

"I'll look forward to it."

"I love you madly; you know that too?"

He kissed her in another line, this time down her throat, over her breasts, her belly, and then back down between her legs. "There she is," he hummed, like he was soothing a baby. "There's my girl." He was back to work and she was letting him, her hands in his hair. This man, with his surprising tenderness, his care for her. There he was.

He was on his stomach between her tented knees, trying again, when they heard the girls in the hallway, a chorus of giggly whispering. She stiffened, snapping her legs shut as David leapt away. When the door opened she was beet-red and covering herself with a much-too-warm blanket and he was standing ten feet from the bed in an unconvincing display of nonchalance.

"Is it a good time?" Violet asked, as Liza was shouting, "Happy *Mother*'s Day." Her children had not quite mastered the clichéd tray of charmingly shambolic pancakes, but Violet held a plate of toast while Wendy and Liza clutched, respectively, a box of Crispix and a bouquet of tulips pulled from the front yard.

"Look at all this," she said, glancing at David, trying not to laugh. "Come here, loves."

"I'll get some coffee," he said, and he patted her knee under the blankets.

"Come on up," she said, wondering where he'd thrown her underwear, hoping to God it wasn't anywhere visible. Liza mounted their bed first, crawling up and snuggling against her. Violet followed more shyly, coming to kiss her on the cheek. "How sweet are my girls," she said, scooting over to make room for Violet. Now only Wendy remained in the doorway, pulling out a handful of dry cereal and letting it rain, one piece at a time, back into the box. "Wednesday, humor me today. Let me have all three of you in the same bed." Wendy fought a smile. "Come on. Come placate your big crazy mother." Wendy advanced into the room and curled herself demurely at the foot of the bed. "Did your dad help you with this?"

Violet shook her head. "No, it was our idea."

Liza draped herself over Marilyn's belly, dropping the tulips and their accompanying dirt into David's spot on the bed. "Oh my *gosh*," she squealed. "He kicked me."

And suddenly she had three pairs of hands on her stomach, even reluctant Wendy's, prodding, reacting to the movement from within, laughing, murmuring to one another. She allowed herself to rest back against her pillows again, contented in an entirely different way. Your family could do that to you sometimes, catch you off-guard with their charm and their normalcy. Those rare moments—like this one—were the reason that she was pregnant again. That she and David would soon be celebrating their seventeenth wedding anniversary. That these three girls, wearying as they often were, were currently making her happier than she'd possibly ever been. This was the point of having a family, these fleeting moments of absolute pleasure. Stockholm syndrome. They kept her coming back for more.

She shifted beneath the weight of the baby and the six small hands. She reached to stroke Wendy's hair and her heart swelled when Wendy let her. This was the point.

"God," David said when he returned. "I leave for ninety seconds and look what happens."

He couldn't recall ever seeing so much blood. Things with Marilyn went very wrong very quickly and he was taken to the far corner of the room with the baby; still nameless, she received a rough bath and a perfect 10 on her Apgar all while he considered the knowledge he had accrued in med school of placenta accreta, which he had heard Gillian say, not to him but to someone else in the room. Gillian was suddenly shouting out orders that he could not bring himself to process. The baby was swaddled and placed in his arms and he stood dumbly, staring at a ravaged, bloodied version of his wife, until Gillian noticed him and stopped, red hands poised above the glossy gushing of Marilyn's uterus, and said, "She'll be fine, Dad. Go introduce yourself to your daughter."

Another girl, he thought dimly, but he had no one to tell. One of the nurses—Kathleen, who was both no-nonsense and mystically intuitive—laid a hand on his back and led him out.

"Come on, Dr. Sorenson."

Marilyn had been admitted at 3:00 a.m. and he was wearing jeans and a Cubs T-shirt, unshaven and wide-eyed. He knew some of the nurses who had tended to Marilyn over the twelve-odd hours and they looked at him knowingly, fondly, not as Dr. Sorenson but as a soon-to-be new dad; as a man who, when prompted, made up a story to entertain his suffering wife, something Arthurian that he remembered from an undergrad lit class; as a man who took it stoically when his wife shot down the story, hissing, *No knights. Nothing medieval. Don't talk to me about the fucking patriarchy right now, and don't ever touch me again.* He'd suddenly felt ridiculous, schooled, completely foolish about the fact that these nurses—far more capable than he, conversant in the baffling language of women—had ever deigned to call him "doctor."

"David," he corrected her hoarsely, and Kathleen patted at his shoulder.

"Chin up, David. She's in good hands. Look who you've got there."

It was then that he finally looked down at the baby.

"Do you have a name picked out?" Kathleen asked, leading him back to Marilyn's hospital room, from which she had been whisked at such speed that he had barely been able to hang on to her hand—a room where he didn't want to go; a room whose walls held the memories of his wife vocally and animally in agony. Kathleen led him gently to the chair next to the bed, where he had spent the better part of the last twelve hours. The bed was gone, wheeled away with his wife still attached.

"Christopher," he said wryly, feeling the ironic weight of the name.

Kathleen smiled, handed him a cup of water. "Sounds like you've had a few shockers today, hmm?" He looked up at her again and felt the muscles of his face lighten a bit; he wasn't sure if he was about to smile or cry. "You didn't have a girl's name picked out?"

"Grace," he said, studying his new daughter's face, rumpled and reddened and damp. He touched a wisp of hair on her forehead—dark like Violet's, dark like his own—and she flinched, but she still wasn't crying, had quieted almost immediately after they cut the cord.

Let's give it a go. This was what he got for being impulsive: his wife slit open and bleeding without getting to see their beautiful new baby; facing single fatherhood of four daughters. The last word he'd heard Marilyn utter—on all fours, writhing—was *motherfucker.* He felt himself starting to cry and he felt Kathleen's warm hand again on his shoulder.

"It's a beautiful name," she said, and she turned to leave him alone. "I'm praying for Marilyn," she added quickly before she slipped from the room. And he looked down at the baby and she looked back up at him, met his eyes, it seemed, though he knew she wasn't yet capable. He started praying then too—first halfheartedly to the ominous Catholic God of his childhood and then to something larger. *Just please don't let her die,* he thought. *Please, anyone, whoever, I don't mean anything without her; I can't do this without her.*

"Please please please," he said aloud to anyone, everyone, to his daughter, who didn't deserve to be burdened with this kind of responsibility but who deserved more than anything to meet her mother, the woman who'd been joking, hours earlier, between contractions, about how mole rats were known to give birth to two dozen babies at once, about how lucky she was to have it so easy. "Please," he whispered to the baby, but she had fallen back asleep.

"I thought you said it was a boy," Wendy said with some amount of distaste, peering skeptically at the bundle in her father's arms. Liza was worriedly examining the dry-erase board on the wall. *Mom: Marilyn*, it read in loopy cursive, a heart over the *i* in her mother's name. *Goal: healthy baby!* Her dad's dad had driven them to the hospital after staying with them overnight, and though he'd been extra jokey in the car, she could tell something was wrong, was deeply suspicious of the fact that her mother was absent from their introduction to their new sister and of the fact that her father wouldn't quite meet any of their eyes.

"What's dilation?" Liza asked.

"We did say she'd be a boy," her father said. "We were wrong." Then, to Liza: "Ask Mom about that some other time."

Wendy relaxed slightly. Their mother must not be dead if Liza was being encouraged to ask her irritating questions.

Her mom had come in to say goodbye in the middle of the night; Wendy had awakened to find her sitting on the edge of her bed.

"Sweetheart, wake up for just a minute," she'd said, her voice gentler than usual but also weirdly awake-sounding, given that it was still dark outside. "Wendy. Hey."

"*Mom*," she said, trying to sound exasperated, but in actuality her heart was pounding. She didn't want her parents to leave. She couldn't admit this, because she was fifteen, but she wanted their family to stay exactly as it was.

"Darling, I'm turning on your lamp for just a second, okay?"

Wendy heard the click and suddenly the blackness of her pillow was edged with eye-watering yellow light. "Oh my *God,*" she said.

"Honey. It seems like this baby might be trying to join the ranks. Daddy and I are going to go to the hospital."

She didn't react.

"Grandpa's downstairs," her mom said. "He'll get you guys off to school, all right?"

"Fine. Can I go back to sleep?"

"Want to wish me luck first?" Her mother's voice had changed. Wendy chanced to look at her, just for a second, and saw, beyond her anxious smile and the exhausted puffiness around her eyes, something almost frightened on her mom's face.

"Good luck," she said. "Can you turn off the light?"

Her mother seemed to deflate. "I— Sure. We'll call soon. I love you."

She hadn't said it back, had yanked her blankets up and rolled away and buried her face in the mattress. She hadn't said it back, and now her mother had disappeared and her father looked epic levels of weird, his hair sticking up in the back and his eyes big and hollowed-out like Beetlejuice, gazing down at the baby.

"It kind of looks like a boy," she said disdainfully.

"No she doesn't." Violet crept closer. "She looks like Mom."

"I think," he said, "that she looks a bit like all of us."

Liza took a step toward them. "Like how?"

"Well." Their father settled back in his chair, tucked in a corner of blanket around the baby's neck. "Mom's nose. The same little hands that you had, Viol. Wendy's mouth. And Lize's long legs, which you'll see when she's not swaddled."

He'd told them their mother was resting and that they couldn't see her because of germs.

"She's going to have her feelings pretty hurt if no one volunteers to hold her," he said. "She may begin to develop some kind of a complex."

"I will," Liza said.

"Remember to support her head," Violet said, her voice lowered to baby volume in a way that made Wendy want to punch her in the face. Their mother had been giving them lessons in infant care in the last few weeks but Wendy hadn't really paid attention.

"Remember to support her head," Wendy mimicked.

"Dad," Violet said, "can you tell her to stop being such a—"

"Girls," their father said flatly. "Please."

"Don't drop her," Wendy said. She brushed Violet with a sharp elbow as she went to sit on the windowsill. Her dad rose and rested the baby in Liza's arms.

"What about you, Dad?" Violet asked. "What part of her looks like you?"

He suddenly looked like he might be sick. She'd never seen her father throw up before.

"Dad?" Violet asked. "Are you okay?"

He smiled weakly. "I'm great. Of course. Just have to take a leak."

Wendy wrinkled her nose. "Dad, gross."

He laughed too forcefully, making his way toward the bathroom. "I want three pairs of eyes on that baby, okay? Mom'll kill us all if we let someone kidnap her." He closed the door behind him and turned the water on, but beneath it Wendy could hear a strange noise, not a throwing-up noise but a shuddering sound that she did not recognize immediately as crying.

"I want to see Mom," Liza said, holding the baby with a prim, infuriating exactitude.

"Shut up," Wendy said. Through the door she now heard the distinct heaving sound of a sob, and it made the hair on her arms stand up.

"I don't have *that* many germs," Liza said thoughtfully.

"Shut *up*," she said again. She couldn't stand her mother, but she didn't want her to die, didn't want their last exchange to be the one they'd had last night. She started cataloging all of the mean things she'd said to her mom in the last year, in the last three years. All the times her mom looked at her like she'd just floated down from Pluto. The way she hadn't said *I love you* back.

Her father emerged a moment later, patting at his face with a wad of paper towels. "Girls." His expression was grim. "We've gotta talk about Mom."

CHAPTER FOURTEEN

Violet was on her way out the door, headed to Wine Night at Jennifer Goldstein-Mayer's, when she was waylaid by—pulled to, magnetically—the dishwasher. The nature of domestic life, she mused, a suburban inevitability: at some point, you were going to find yourself having a heated argument over which end up the forks should be in the silverware basket. The subjects of her fights with Matt had become progressively pedestrian, achingly trite. She remembered laughable debates from their early days together—heated, vitriolic shouting matches about politics (oh, the Romney days!) and propriety (Matt still didn't understand why it was iffy that he used *Jew* as a conversational noun) that usually ended in fantastic sex.

Things had become more complicated, of course; their alone time was virtually nonexistent, especially since Matt had made partner. They had two young children and a mortgage; they had wealth to be managed and a house to be maintained; and, now, they had the insertion of a controversial teenage person who threw a wrench into the well-heeled maintenance of all of those things. It bore revisiting, the Jonah subject, but instead it had become their unvisitable thing, the taboo topic that they edged their way around and pretended they weren't bumping into.

So there she was, fuming instead over the fact that when her

husband had loaded the dishwasher he'd put all of the silverware blades and tines up, making the emptier prone to minor
stabbings, even though she'd told him last night for the seventeenth time to always put the blades down.

"I thought you were leaving," he said, appearing in the doorway. She watched him register what she was doing—carefully,
pettily, unloading one piece of cutlery at a time, to make a
point. He squared his jaw. "You really want to do this, Violet?"

She bristled. "I didn't even—"

"Can't you just go drink wine with your friends? Is it not
possible for us to have a single night where you don't freak out
about something completely inconsequential?"

"I'm not *freaking out*," she said. "It's just that we talked about
it yesterday." If she really listened to herself she would be
appalled by how she sounded, but she sort of wanted to kill
him at the moment, and perhaps this was one of the problems
with constantly talking about things other than the thing you
actually needed to talk about, because she was reaching a level
of anger about the silverware that was appropriate only for
something much more apocalyptic.

"I was distracted," he said. "I won't forget again."

"What's going to stop you from forgetting again?"

"I can't give you a scientific analysis, *babe*," he said, his
final syllable bordering on hostility. "But I'll give it my all to
remember, okay?"

The smartest girl in the room, Matt had said of her once. How
false it was. How sick she made herself. She'd opted for all of
the decisions exactly opposite from her mom's; she had done all
of the things that her mother had chosen not to do. And she was
no better off. She was, arguably, *worse* off. Her mother, at least,
had a sense of herself, despite being a college dropout who'd
followed a man to the middle of nowhere, let him pursue his
passion while she exercised her gravity. Her mother's story,
for all she'd judged it, resisted it, was far more poetic than

her own. Look at where they'd arrived: the mundane started out being ironically exciting and suddenly you were sexlessly fighting about silverware while your children watched *Wonder Pets!* in the next room. Something was shifting; something had blown in through the front door and they were both breathing it in, losing ions of love by the second. Never mind the unacknowledgeable fact of Jonah. She shuddered involuntarily.

"It's dumb," she conceded. "It's such a dumb thing to be fighting about."

"You're the one who brought it up."

"I *know*," she said. "I'm apologizing. That was me apologizing for bringing it up."

"Ah, I missed that. Have fun at Jennifer's."

He went off in pursuit of the kids without looking at her again. She carefully removed the rest of the knives from the dishwasher before following him into the den. She stood in the doorway and observed. Matt was on the couch with Wyatt's socked feet in his lap. Eli, who she had just laboriously bathed, was absorbing his father's postworkout sweat. She took a deep breath. *Let it go*, she told herself. *Drop it, drop it, drop it.* She exhaled louder than she intended to, with a bovine hum, and Matt looked up at her.

She smiled at him, trying, really. *Invite me over*, she willed. She could ditch the Shady Oaks moms, join her boys and snuggle and be snuggled and they could have an extremely photogenic family evening that concluded spiritedly with a romantic reunion with Matt, possibly some kind of avant-garde union in an obscure place—the kitchen table?—after the kids were in bed. She could see it vividly, could feel the pleasurable dampness of her husband's Double Door shirt and the smooth, electric cool of her sons' little feet and the sleepy complacency of a night in with your sedate young children, watching a show where hamsters wore baseball hats while the man you loved traced lines up and down your spine with his fingertips. They could find themselves again, get back on track, erase some of the tension of the previous months. All he had to do was smile back; all he had to say was *Get over here, darlin'*.

Instead he looked confused. "Are you still mad?" he asked.

"Am I—?" She stopped, hurt. "No."

"You look mad."

"I was smiling at you."

"Mama, I can't hear," Wyatt interjected politely.

She pressed her lips together. "Forget it," she said, and the crack between them widened further, the Matt-shaped hole grew larger, and another day would go by with them failing to connect. *I'm lost*, she wanted to say. *Help me, Matty; help me, help me.* She wanted to tell him that the accretion of these kinds of days could be fatal to a marriage. She wanted to tell him that the entire *point* of being married was so neither party would ever have to go through times like these alone. She wanted to tell her husband that she missed him a lot, but that she missed herself even more.

"I'll see you guys in the morning," she said instead.

Driving to Jennifer Goldstein-Mayer's, she started feeling anxious, the kind of anxiety she could feel burning through her sternum and lifting the hair on her arms. She became suddenly aware of the terrifying responsibility of driving a car, navigating two tons of steel at forty miles an hour, how easy it would be to turn the wheel a little and end up wrapped around an elm tree or floating in Lake Michigan. The thought startled her so much that she missed the light turning green, causing the car behind her to honk, which made her even more anxious, and so she flipped on her blinker and turned onto a side street, parked the car, rested her forehead on the steering wheel.

This kind of anxiety was disturbingly familiar to her. She tried to slow her breaths. She'd never been good at relaxation exercises; in yoga classes, during corpse pose, her mind always raced wildly from her grocery list to the deadline for summer camp registration to whether or not her sports bra was giving her back fat. Now she felt as though her lungs weren't filling completely with air, like she had to yawn but couldn't quite finish. This was supposed to be a fun night out for her, a foray back into the Shady Oaks social set, pinotage and petty gossip, but the more she fixated on not being able to take a full breath, the harder it became, and she also couldn't stop thinking of her car, barreling down McCormick Boulevard; how quickly things could change; how easily things could end. She rolled down her window and tried to remember the rules of nadi shodhana breathing, which nostril was supposed to be the calming one. Who knew what would come tumbling out of her in a routine Shady Oaks conversation? *I'm celibate now! And a pathological liar! And prone to panic spirals!*

She had nowhere to go—not back home, where her husband didn't recognize her, and not to the opulent Goldstein-Mayer residence, where her friends weren't really her friends, and not to her parents, or her sisters, because she'd isolated herself from them, too, hadn't she, by her failure to embrace Jonah, the boy who'd lived inside her and whom she was never supposed to see again. She felt like a teenager, not the teenager she'd actually been—the one who was bright-eyed and forward-looking, the one who brushed her hair seventy-five times each night and volunteered on the weekends at the Frank Lloyd Wright Home and Studio—but like an average teenager, aimless and contrarian and confused. It astounded her now, how uncomplicated her life used to be, a mere six years ago: jogs along the lakefront with her husband, their charming Edgewater apartment, litigating cases against major and victimless corporations, earning more money than she knew was possible for an individual person to make, climbing dutifully up the ladder. But then Wyatt had come along, and his arrival was accompanied by a new darkness, and she couldn't, at the time, justify abandoning another child.

She texted without being fully conscious of doing so, an effortless lie: *E is projectile vomiting; have to take a rain check; cheersing you in spirit!* She sent a vague heavenward plea that her son would enjoy his night with his dad and not be karmically hindered by her using him as a pawn in her social avoidance. Jennifer fired back a message right away, a sad face alongside a festive champagne emoji.

1993

Liza woke with a panicky feeling, that few-second twilight stage where you weren't sure whether or not you were dreaming. But then she felt the hot wetness, already turning cool on the pilled fabric of her Sleeping Beauty nightgown. She had been bumped up the totem pole of their family, which was not nearly as fun as it sounded. When her mom had returned home from the hospital with the new baby—her mom, who seemed smaller, slower, sleepier now—the bed-wetting started to happen, like clockwork, every night. She squirmed. The house was quiet, the baby sleeping and thus her mother sleeping—a rarity, she knew, judging by how her mom sometimes poured orange juice in their cereal or milk in the dog's bowl, how she packed them lunches that consisted of an apple and a pudding cup, sandwiches forgotten on the counter or unmade entirely. She slipped from her bed, holding the wet nightgown away from her body, and tiptoed into her parents' room.

Her mom was sleeping so soundly that Liza had a momentary worry that she was dead. She inched over and watched, looking for signs of life. Her dad wasn't in bed: she remembered he'd been called to the hospital after dinner to fill in for someone overnight. She remembered she'd heard her parents fighting after she'd gone to bed, her mother crying, "So I'm just supposed to get up with her four times my*self*?" and her father rebutting, "What is it you'd like me to *do*?" and her mother replying, disintegrating into tears, "I just want to *sleep*," and her father leaving, slamming the door out to the garage. She had fallen asleep concerned that her parents would get a divorce.

"Mama," she whispered. She hadn't called her mother Mama in months, either. She and Violet had taken to calling her Mom, while Wendy called her Mother with a very specific disdainful inflection. "Mama." She poked apologetically at a shoulder. "Mommy," Liza whispered, worried she might cry. *"Mommy,"* she said, loudly this time, and her mother startled.

"God," she gasped, blinking, like she'd just narrowly avoided hitting something with her car. She squinted, reached a hand out, pushed herself up on her pillow. "What is it, honey?"

"I peed in my bed."

Her mother seemed to register the announcement and then visibly deflated. She sat up completely, disoriented, looking for the clock. Their eyes found it at the same time: 2:32 a.m.

"Sorry," Liza said. "Sorry, sorry, sorry."

"Oh, sweetheart, it's okay. Don't apologize for that."

For some reason then she started crying. Her mom reached out to hug her, pee-nightgown and all. She was softer since Grace was born and Liza snuggled against the pillow of her belly.

"You can always wake me up, little one," she said. It was the first time she had called anyone besides Grace "little one" since she'd gotten home from the hospital. Grace was pretty easygoing, but she demanded attention in a way that Liza found shocking—how was it possible for a person to be so helpless? She needed their mother for everything, and there was an obvious shift, the noticeable insertion of a tiny extra person into everything they did.

"Let's get you cleaned up, Liza-lee." Her mom stood slowly and they went into the bathroom and she started running a bath, not her usual remedy for nighttime accidents—usually she just stripped and remade the bed, still half-asleep, like a robot, and had you change into new pajamas. "Want bubbles, darlin'?" she asked, and Liza nodded, feeling a smile bloom onto her face, and climbed into her mother's lap, towel-wrapped, as they waited for the tub to fill, and her mom began to hum into her forehead, her voice husky with sleep. Usually it was "My Bonnie Lies over the Ocean" or "Big Rock Candy Mountain," but tonight she was singing something else, something folky and sad.

"What's that song?" she asked, and her mother paused.

"It's—" She faltered. "I can't for the life of me think of the name. Isn't that funny?" She gave Liza a feeble smile. "I'm just tired, not crazy, honey, I promise."

Her mother proceeded to give her a bath, the longest she'd taken maybe ever, humming and engaging in dialogue with the various rubber animals they kept on the ledge—a cow, an elephant, a penguin. When they finished she poured warm cups of water over Liza's head to rinse her hair, and Liza shivered with pleasure.

"Hop out, Lize," her mother said, and she held open the towel. She wrapped her tightly and kissed her wet hair. "You know I'm still here, sweetheart, don't you? I'm always here. I know things are different now but I'm always, always around."

"I know."

"Some times are easier than others," her mom said oddly, and she nodded, uncomprehending. Her mom kissed her forehead. "You're my old soul." She dried Liza off and helped her into new pajamas and guided her into her own bedroom, where she pulled back the covers on her father's side. "You sleep in Daddy's spot tonight, pumpkin." She thought this a fantastically exclusive invitation but realized later that they were probably just out of clean twin-size sheets; her mom had been doing about half as much laundry as usual lately. Her mother crawled in next to her and held her until she fell asleep.

Her dad ended up coming home early, slipping in just as her mom was finishing with the baby's 4:00 a.m. feeding, and Liza watched them woozily from her place in her parents' bed.

"I called Lacey and had him take over for me," he whispered to her mom, taking the baby from her arms. "Go back to sleep."

"Liza's in our bed," she said.

"I'll sleep in her bed."

"She peed in her bed."

"I'll sleep on the couch," he said, and there was a long quiet, a kissing noise.

A trademark of her parents' dialogue: they rarely apologized. Fights were resolved via some mystical, unspoken understanding, concessions made and forgiveness granted through what seemed to be a scientific combination of eyes and mouths and lenient spirits.

"No, we'll just squeeze in together," her mother said.

So they did. She remembered feeling her parents on either side of her, remembered the cool antiseptic smell of her dad and the powdery sweetness of her mom, and she remembered thinking that it wouldn't be possible to feel safer than that.

Wendy referred to her parents as "a physician and a home-maker" to make them sound loftier, when in fact her father spent much of his time at a clinic on the West Side, sometimes wearing *jeans*, and her mother wasn't "making" their home so much as she was barely maintaining it, keeping the cacophony to a medium-high roar, often also wearing David's jeans.

"If we're really *so* embarrassing," her mom was saying, methodically tearing up a pile of junk mail, "perhaps we should just move to a new house without you guys. Send your bills through the mail." She was offended because Wendy had mentioned, just *offhandedly*, that she would prefer it if they took their homecoming photos at Scott Pratt's house, a massive

Colonial on Euclid. His dad worked for Wells Fargo and his mom legitimately wore an apron sometimes; it was just different. She couldn't explain this to her mother.

"It's just prettier," she said. "There's just—like, a lot of *leaves* in the front yard here."

"You know, despite historical convention, leaf raking isn't an explicitly masculine job, Wendy. It wouldn't kill you girls to help Dad out with some of those things."

"Can't *you* do it?" she asked. She immediately knew she shouldn't have.

"I'm a little busy, actually," her mom said shortly. "I actually have a few other things going on."

She had never known her mother to *not* have a few other things going on. She was a crazy person, in constant motion, her hair always swept back with various barrettes and her hands dotted with little notes she'd written to herself on the backs, against the grain of her veins.

Beneath the table, Wendy palmed her hip bones. They jutted against her sweater like wings.

"I forgot," she said—the real reason she'd come to the kitchen: "I need my dress fixed."

Her mother looked up at her tiredly. Grace was napping, had just begun to take regular midday naps—they had all heard about it in ecstatic detail. Her mother frightened her lately; she'd returned from the hospital after Grace was born looking pale and diminished and skinnier than ever; she'd walked for a month with a stoop because of her stitches.

"We had it tailored a month ago," she said. They'd gone together to Marshall Field's during a big sale for her homecoming dress.

"You look absolutely gorgeous, my grown-up girl," her mom had said in the dressing room. And then, the clincher: "Are you losing weight, honey?"

Since they'd bought the dress, she'd lost six pounds. She felt her mother's gaze.

"I'm worried you're not eating enough."

"I *am*."

"You look thin."

"I'm not. I just— I forgot I had my period when we got it tailored the first time." She blushed, at the lie, at the subject matter. "Now it's just a little too loose."

Her mom studied her. "I didn't make you a lunch today," she said suddenly.

"It's fine." She'd been elated to see that her mother had forgotten, elated that she didn't have to throw away the brown bag like she did every other day—the PB & J, the baby carrots, the granola bar—because it always made her feel guilty. "I shared," she said desperately. She could see that her mother was preparing to make her a snack. Marilyn turned to look at her skeptically.

"Well, that was four hours ago. And I'm going to see how long Gracie'll sleep if I don't wake her, so dinner's going to be later." Her mother was cutting up an apple, going to the cabinet by the sink to retrieve the jar of Nutella.

"I'm not hungry," she said desperately.

"Don't argue with me." Perhaps feeling guilty for how sharply she'd spoken, she added: "This is possibly the first time in history that a mother has bribed a child to eat chocolate."

At this, she forced herself to laugh. She ate while her mother watched, because apples were easy to throw up if you chewed them enough.

On the morning after Wendy's homecoming dance, he came home from a night shift to find Marilyn awake at 5:00 a.m., hugging herself before the coffeepot.

"What's going on?" he asked. She raised her eyes to him slowly. The fine dusting of blond hairs on her cheekbones was visible in the strange light and the purple circles beneath her eyes seemed to have carved themselves permanently into the structure of her face. They were both still adjusting, neither sure how to behave as parents to both an infant and adolescents.

"You're home," she said oddly. "Wendy's drunk."

He glanced behind him, never entirely sure of who was lurking where in the caverns of their enormous house. "Our Wendy?" he asked. It had moved him, the previous evening, seeing his daughter in a long shiny dress and high-heeled shoes, on the arm of a classmate—a junior, the boy—who seemed far too old for her, for the young girl who'd once seemed to be the tiniest baby he'd ever seen.

"She came home drunk at midnight, just in time to throw up all over our bed."

"She was in our bed?"

"I brought her there to keep an eye on her," Marilyn said defensively.

"She was drunk?" He felt his body stand to alert. "Where did she— On what?"

"We didn't get that far. I'm assuming someone snuck booze into the dance." She sighed. "I'm not ready for this."

"Ready for what?"

"For our *girls* to be *drinking* at *parties*, David," she said, like a poem.

"Well, everyone experiments." This wasn't what he wanted to be saying. He wanted to say, *who in God's holy hell got my daughter drunk?* and *she is only fifteen years old, for Christ's sake*, but he saw that his wife was already fielding these thoughts and so decided to take the laissez-faire approach, one that would either pacify or exasperate her.

"There is vomit in my *hair*," she said, and he saw that she was choosing the latter.

"Do you want to shower? I can get up with Grace if that's what you're worried about."

So much of marital misunderstanding stemmed simply from trying to keep the peace. They both did it. Efforts to ameliorate resulted, 75 percent of the time, in fights, simply because annoyance was the most easily accessible emotion.

"She won't be up for an hour," Marilyn said. She poured a mug of coffee, sipped it, winced.

He went to the freezer for an ice cube, dropping the cube into her mug before he kissed her temple. Then he reached past her to pour his own cup of coffee.

"There's not a chance in hell you're having caffeine right now," she said, and she intercepted him with such vigor that coffee sloshed onto the counter. "You've been up since yesterday. Go upstairs. Now. Sleep."

"Do you know where my blood pressure cuff is?"

"Your— Oh, for God's sake, David."

But he was already looking, rifling through the multiple junk drawers in the kitchen. It felt pressing, suddenly: his daughter asleep under the influence of something other than fatigue. He squatted before the Tupperware cabinet, pushed aside stacks of plastic bowls. Marilyn left the room.

Wendy in his arms, legs looped over his forearm, having fallen asleep in the car on the way home from a family day trip to the Warren Dunes. Wendy at two, riddled with fever, draped listlessly over his shoulder, delirious and trusting him to fix things.

"Hey." Marilyn was back, and he turned, came face-to-face with his pressure cuff, dusty with misuse. "It was in the mudroom."

He touched her arm before he went upstairs. Their bedroom didn't smell like vomit—he wasn't sure how Marilyn did it—but it felt different with his daughter there, her small unconscious form illuminated by his wife's bedside lamp. He sat on the edge of the bed and unwrapped the cuff—he winced at the Velcro sound, deafening in the quiet room, but his daughter didn't stir—and then secured it around her arm. He was never this close to her anymore, and he saw how thin she was. He'd asked Gillian about it at work last week, about his daughter's weight loss, her moodiness, about whether or not it sounded like cause for alarm, and she'd suggested that they not over-react, chalk it up to routine adolescence but keep an eye on her. She told him the situation would likely right itself, and that they shouldn't worry unless she began to display signs of malnourishment.

He primed the pump—waiting, all the while, for his daughter to awaken, to mock him for his hypervigilance, his dorky dad concern. But she remained sleeping as he pumped the cuff to bursting and then released the air, watching the gauge. A little higher than normal, but an increase that could be attributed to the alcohol. He pressed his fingers to her wrist. Sixty-four beats per minute. He thought of her falling asleep on the couch on Davenport Street between him and Marilyn, begging to stay up later with them, her feet in his lap and her head in Marilyn's. The acrobatics required to lift her from the couch without waking her. Now she was pale against their sheets—the fancy flowered sheets that Marilyn had forgotten to pack when they were moving to the house on Fair Oaks, that she'd seemed so sad to lose, that he'd rescued from the curb and stowed in the cubby with the U-Haul's spare tire.

He brushed her hair from her face—her forehead felt temperate—and scooted up beside her, leaning back against his own pillow so his ear was near her mouth. He looked at his watch and listened for her exhalations, vaguely asthmatic. In and out, as her breathing should be. A little curtain of hair fell over her face and he pushed it back, studying her features, so like her mother's, but—now, yes—gauntly angular, not fleshed out with adolescence. There were circles under her eyes, bookending the familiar freckles on her nose.

People said the infant stage was the hardest but he had never found that to be the case. Gracie, almost five months old, was sound asleep in her crib, zipped snugly in her little pajamas. Liza, on the other hand, was standing outside the entrance to puberty, refusing to step over the threshold. Violet's type A personality, so promising in young childhood, was converting their daughter into one of those insufferable, solitary students, propelled unpopularly forward by the promise of extra credit that would give her a leg up into the Ivy League.

And Wendy: tiny and vulnerable, but not in the same ways as Grace. She was hard to love and exceptionally easy to worry about and it was an exhausting combination. He felt unexpected tears in his eyes.

"Sweetie?" Marilyn was watching him from the foot of the bed.

He blinked rapidly, willing the tears away, aware of the fear in his wife's eyes. "It's okay," he said. "Respiratory rate is normal."

She nodded, came over and lay on the other side of their daughter. She propped herself up onto an elbow, cradling an arm around Wendy's head, and he pushed himself up too, curving around their daughter, a couple of protective apostrophes. As they'd done when she was a baby, curled around her in their bed, her mom and dad, marveling over the mere fact of her being.

CHAPTER FIFTEEN

When Jonah had finally met Ryan, all he could think of was seeing Liza kissing the guy in the Subaru at his first dinner at his grandparents' house, before he knew who she was, when she was just a random lady in an orange scarf making out with a gross Rivers Cuomo–looking guy in a green station wagon.

He was surprised that the guy he'd seen in the car wasn't Ryan, unless Ryan had lightened his hair and lost a bunch of weight and gotten tattoo sleeves in the months since then. But Ryan and Liza were both so friendly to him—inviting him over to play Halo with Ryan, telling him he was welcome anytime, Liza once bringing them a tray of pretzels and grapefruit seltzer—that he just decided to go with it, figured it was just some weird adult thing he hadn't encountered in person until now. He forgot about this pretty quickly, because Ryan had more video games than it seemed normal for an adult to have. He hadn't been allowed to play video games at the Danforths' house because Hanna thought they "promulgated violence and misogyny."

Hanging out with Ryan felt more like hanging out with someone his age, though Ryan was actually *twice* his age and about to become a dad himself. Plus, Liza and Ryan's house was regular-nice—way more normal than the other Sorenson homes—and Liza would pop in sometimes to bring them snacks or ask Jonah about school, and Ryan was funny, and really fucking good at video games.

"What'd you think of that last level?" Ryan asked, doing a Spartan Charge like it was no big deal.

"It was cool," Jonah said. "I liked the—you know, blue clone lady? With the bowl haircut?"

"Right? She's a total badass. She's confident, and she has a sense of humor, *and* she's, like, proportionate, more or less. The bar's not very high, but she's better than most of the others." Ryan laughed. "Liza would disagree."

He was curious about Liza, though she wasn't often around because she had a job. He'd never known anyone pregnant before, and of course Liza was planning to keep her baby. He'd been moved out of foster placements so many times that he couldn't help admiring someone's willingness to commit to a kid before she'd even met it.

"Hey, man, how have things been going for you lately?" Ryan asked suddenly. He'd get like this sometimes, awkward and scholarly, like Jonah was someone he was studying in a lab.

"Good," he said.

"Things are okay at David and Marilyn's?"

In fact, Jonah had been spending a lot of time with David lately, doing random projects around the house—rehabbing the gnarly shower in the basement, putting winterizing plastic on the windows, climbing on low branches to trim the trees in the backyard. And it felt like how he'd always imagined it would feel to hang out with your dad, long stretches of silence that weren't awkward at all, oldies playing on the radio, David every so often stopping whatever he was doing to explain something to Jonah—"Try to find a faucet with integrated shutoff valves, if you ever find yourself doing this again."

"Yeah," he said. "Really good."

"This family can be a little intense," Ryan said. "The first time I came home with Liza for Christmas, Wendy and Violet were in this big fight at dinner about—God, I don't know, one of those tiny things they're always fighting about. And then I walked in on David and Marilyn in the pantry. I remember I just ended up sitting on the floor with Grace and petting the dog for most of the night."

He unpaused the game and Jonah sat back to watch for a minute, considering. It *was* kind of intense how Marilyn was always making sure he'd eaten enough, slept enough, gotten enough fresh air, gotten enough attention from his teachers, but it was a nice kind of intense. And Wendy and Violet were definitely intense—a less nice intense—but he'd successfully avoided both of them when they'd stopped by in the past few weeks.

"I didn't mean that in an asshole way," Ryan said. "They're good people. Just kind of—a lot. You know? I definitely didn't grow up like Liza did."

"Me either," he said, though it occurred to him that Ryan already knew that, that everyone in this family had a weird level of knowledge about his upbringing while he was still learning about each of them bit by bit.

"Just letting you know I'm relatively objective," Ryan said, performing an elaborate series of commands on his controller that made one of the swords emit a cloud of sparks. "If you ever need—you know, a nonjudgmental audience."

It was nice, even if he wasn't entirely sure what Ryan meant. "Thanks, man."

"For sure," Ryan said. "Everything else okay? School's good?"

"Uh-huh."

"You dating anyone?"

He colored. He had never kissed a girl, which he knew was pathetic. He tried to imagine reaching a point in his life where he could meet someone pretty and mature who would know where to find pale blue curtains like the ones on Liza and Ryan's windows. Where he could feel connected to another human being like that. Because, the truth was, since the viaduct, he had never felt legitimately tied to another person, a parent or a sibling or a girlfriend. He had never, since then, felt like he couldn't be returned at a moment's notice.

"Uh-uh," he said, noncommittally. Ryan seemed to fit in well enough with the Sorensons, even though he wasn't around much, didn't show up to family dinners. He'd managed to convince Liza to have a baby with him, apparently, which seemed like a pretty permanent decision. "How long have you and Liza been married?"

"Almost ten years. But we're not married, actually."

"You're not?" He thought of the Rivers Cuomo guy again, Liza's orange scarf.

"Nope. We just haven't— I mean, we are in every sense of the word but legally." Ryan glanced at him. "I mean—we're just not really into labels. And it's—whatever, marriage is just a social construct anyway."

"How'd you guys decide—like, is it some hippie thing?"

"No, we just—" Ryan shrugged. "We're not into that boring cookie-cutter suburban thing. The nine-to-five; the picket fence. We go our own ways. I'm trying to get into the agribusiness software game; Liza's got her teaching gig. She does her thing and I do mine."

"That's cool," he said. Ryan was talking to him sort of how Wendy used to, like he was mature enough to understand, like he was worth trying to impress. "I'm not really into labels, either."

Ryan laughed at that, and Jonah felt embarrassed all of a sudden, diminished and little-brotherly. Ryan was more fun to hang out with than his aunts, and playing SoulCalibur was cooler than pruning the lilac bushes with his grandfather. He scrambled to regain the equal footing he'd felt earlier. "Does it weird you out to have an open relationship, though?" He thought that was what it was called. "Like, when Liza hooks up with other people?"

"What?" Ryan snorted. "No, man, I— No, I meant, like, we file our taxes separately. We aren't like *swingers*."

"Oh." But it must have taken his face a second to catch up because Ryan was suddenly not smiling anymore.

"Why did you ask me that, man?" Ryan asked, and Jonah could hear that he was trying to make his voice sound casual.

"No reason," he said. "I just thought you meant that, like . . ."

"Did you—are you asking me this because you—did you see Liza with someone else?"

He shook his head, very much wishing he were scraping mold from a shower stall with David instead of sitting next to a guy whose pregnant wife was apparently cheating on him. He was a terrible liar; the staff at Lathrop House used to find it totally adorable.

"No, no, I just thought you meant—when you said—like, she does her own thing, I thought you were talking about . . . not that she . . . it just made me think of when . . ."

"When what?" Ryan looked kind of afraid now.

"Just a time I saw—Liza. Just once. Like a really long time ago. Like the summer."

It was weird to say something that made another person look so crushed.

"Saw her where?" Ryan asked.

"Just outside. At my grandparents' house. In a car."

"Doing what?"

"Um. Kissing. Some guy."

Ryan dropped his controller into his lap. "What did the guy look like?"

"I couldn't really see him. Kind of dorky. Glasses. Dark hair."

"What kind of car?"

"A station wagon. A green one. It was quick. It was just—"

"What kind of kiss? Like—just on the cheek? Or—"

He didn't reply to that, mortified, and Ryan's face fell.

"I'm sorry, Ryan, I didn't mean to—"

Ryan abruptly got to his feet.

Jonah stood too. "I can go, if you—"

Ryan nodded, and while this didn't surprise him, it was disappointing.

"I'm sorry if I—"

"All good," Ryan said briskly. He wasn't making eye contact; his hands were balled in fists at his sides. "But you should probably just—"

"Yeah."

"The guy. Was he old or young?"

"Oh. I— Medium, I guess? Like—your age, maybe?"

Ryan smiled faintly at that, but Jonah wasn't sure why.

Violet had come to regard the weekday arrival of three o'clock, kindergarten pickup time, with the live-wire wariness of a death row inmate. The inside of her Infiniti, she was certain, was rank with anxious sweat. It was 2:58 and she watched the others gathering, Genevieve Wilmot's mother and bouffanted alpha mom Gretchen Morley and Jennifer Goldstein-Mayer in her floral visor, tailored and bushy-tailed and chomping at the bit. She hadn't had sex since June. Her hair was in the same ponytail she'd slept in. And Eli was in the backseat singing "Shop Around," which she would normally find endearing but was currently setting her molars on edge.

"Sweetie," she said. "Let's use our inside voices."

In his defense, Eli dropped his singing to an adorably low whisper. *My mama told me.*

"Thank you," she breathed.

"Mama," Eli said, interrupting himself. "A lady."

"Yes, sweet pea, Mama's a lady," she said. *Don't ask Dada*

about Mama being a lady; the jury is out at the moment on that particular verdict. Ashton Treslo's mother was walking across the parking lot cradling a newborn; Violet hadn't even sent her a card; in a past life she would have made several dozen of those killer fontina risotto cakes and brought them over along with a copy of that heartbreaking Iron & Wine album that had lulled Eli to sleep in his early days. Not so long ago at all she'd been the first one on the asphalt at pickup, lipsticked and North-Faced and caffeinated, Eli strapped to her chest like an adorable bomb.

"No, a *lady*," Eli said. She looked up and her heart sank. Gretchen Morley was coming toward the car, face ablaze with an unnaturally white smile.

"Fucking *hell*," Violet hissed, her face trying to arrange itself into something similar, some alarming shell of a grin that would throw the vultures off her scent. "I'll give you ten Oreos if you start crying in a minute, buddy," she whispered in Eli's direction, but he had already started singing again. She pressed the button for her window.

"Violet," said Gretchen. "If it isn't our favorite recluse!"

It seemed odd—and sad—that the removal of Violet's social life from her overall life hadn't had much of an impact on her. The Shady Oaks moms—Gretchen! Jennifer! Ashton's mom, whose name she could not currently remember!—had once been vital cogs in the machinery of her days, filling the blank spaces with pottery-making birthday parties and lakeside cappuccinos. They were her *friends*, weren't they, so why didn't she care more that she never saw them anymore? There was a distance, now, between the life she'd built and the one she was currently living. A Jonah-shaped distance; a Wendy-shaped distance; and, smartingly, the Matt-shaped distance.

"So good to see you," she said to Gretchen, her face still frozen in a ghoulish approximation of a smile. "We've been so busy."

They'd worked so hard, she and Matt, to get where they were. And yet her reflection, in the torso-only recessed walnut mirror opposite their California king, had begun to startle her, its athletic thinness and the dark circles beneath newly prominent eyes, big brown orbs that had lost their inquisitive luster and produced only a fraction of the laugh lines that she assumed would have accreted over the course of thirty-eight years. She'd skipped her Bikram class five weeks in a row and her children had eaten bunny-shaped pasta for dinner the last three nights, though she had ample time to make them something greener and higher in protein. *I have never felt so lost in my entire life, Gretchen Morley.*

Gretchen seemed to grin harder and leaned in closer to Violet through the window. "I didn't want to say anything in front of the other moms," she said.

I know I forgot the cupcakes for the Sudanese bake sale. I know my roots are showing. I know it's my turn for book club and I know I'm supposed to pick something "less dark" than Flannery O'Connor.

"I just wanted to say congrats," Gretchen said. "And offer you *any* of Harrison's old stuff if you want. I'm sure you have plenty from Eli but just in case there's anything you gave away."

"Any—?"

"Wyatt told Harry he's getting a new brother," Gretchen said, and then, horrifyingly, she winked, closed one big tastefully shadowed eye and opened it again. "You still look so *thin.*"

No, no, no, but also *of course* this was happening, surprising and inevitable, of course her darling, enthusiastic kindergartener had been unable to keep the lid on their "family secret." Of course they never should have asked him to lie, of course Matt had been right to be reticent, of course she'd done a botched job of all of this, but fuck if she wasn't gobsmacked to be confronted with it now, in her very own car, by a woman holding her bouffant in place with a forty-dollar Lululemon headband. "Well, thanks," she said. "I— That's because I'm not—"

"I figured it was probably early. That's why I didn't say anything in front of the ladies."

"I'm not pregnant," she said, and Gretchen paled. *Wyatt's new brother is my illegitimate lovechild and he hails most recently from a rustic trash heap in south Oak Park.* She swallowed. "We had a— Um, it didn't work out." Who cared if it was bad karma? It was also bad karma to shove your big coiffed head into someone's car and ask her if she was pregnant.

"Oh," Gretchen said. "Oh, honey, I'm so sorry."

"Well." Her quick-thinking litigator brain again: *tortuous fallopian tubes.* She'd read about them in *Us Weekly.* "It's this awful condition. Tortuous fallopian tubes."

"Oh, I—" Gretchen squinted. "Torturous?"

"Tortuous," Violet corrected her, keeping an eye on the dashboard clock.

"Well, that's—that's so terrible, Violet. I had no idea. I'm so sorry."

"Yes, well," she said. "It's been really hard on all of us, so if— if Wyatt says anything, it's best to just—not give it much credence. It's confusing to the kids." *It's confusing to the kids when Mama throws them directly under the luxury party bus of Gretchen Morley.* For a bizarre handful of seconds, she found herself missing Wendy, the wildly creative liar who'd cooked up the yearlong Parisian farce that had gotten them into this mess in the first place. Certainly this news would travel further. Certainly Gretchen—who'd very likely already shared the news of Violet's phantom pregnancy with the other moms, despite her insistence that she hadn't—would go slithering back to her entourage and share, with mock sympathy, the tragic tale of Violet's imperfection. The Shady Oaks moms were her friends only as far as surface-level life analysis, Pilates and Mini Boden. Social currency was everything in this world, but it could gain or lose value in an instant, and someone could steal your shares right out from under you if you weren't paying close attention.

From the backseat, Eli whimpered.

"Just a second, honey," Violet said.

"Well, listen," Gretchen said. "I know you're supermom, but . . ." Violet was sure she wasn't imagining the condemnatory glint in the woman's eye as she said this. "If you need *anything*, if you need me to take the boys so you can go to—the doctor, just say the word."

She smiled. She'd choose Jane Austen for book club and bring a case of wine. For a brief moment, she even imagined one day confessing the epic fallout of her youthful imprudence, sharing that Wyatt's brother had not, in fact, been quashed by her reproductive organs and was currently enrolled in very expensive Israeli military training on her sister's dime.

Behind her, Eli began to wail.

"Oh," Gretchen said, and she backed away from the car. "Okay, well. I'd better go. Anyway—sorry about—you know. I mean—I'll text you!"

She watched Gretchen bounce back across the blacktop and then she turned to her son. "Sweetheart, what is it?"

Eli stopped crying as abruptly as he'd started and grinned at her. "Ten Oreos!"

She started laughing, the kind of laughing where you were also partially crying; she had always associated it with exhaustion and psychopathy and her mother.

1994–1995

Wendy had crept downstairs to use the adult line—following the unceremonious disconnection of the kids' line once it was discovered that she'd used it to call Spencer Stallings, who was, *yes, technically,* a cocaine dealer but also just her *friend*—but she froze three stairs from the bottom. In the living room, a movie was playing—*Malcolm X;* obviously her mother's choice—but her parents were not asleep.

It was a moment during which every molecule of her physical composition impelled her to look away, but something combative in her brain resisted, a perverse piece of genetic makeup that said, *my parents are making out on the couch; another time my parents were making out resulted in me.* "Making out" was an understatement. This was not *kissing.* They'd all seen kissing: their mother gravitationally suctioned to their father when he came in the door from work; their father leaning over to peck their mother on the cheek waiting at a stoplight; Marilyn curled against David on the loveseat in the backyard, her head tilted up like that of a marionette or a movie star, kissing with such vigor that the balsa creaked. They kissed at Little League games and the grocery; they kissed each other's elbows and necks and hair; they kissed with their hands in each other's pockets and their arms slung around each other's waists; they kissed good morning and goodnight and hello and goodbye; they kissed just because.

This was not kissing. This was something else, something more. On the stairs, she watched, frozen. Save for the ragged keening of her mother, steady and coarse, like the rhythmic hiss of a long freight train, the house was quiet. Her father made a gasping noise. He was so much larger than her mom, so much taller and broader and darker; she almost looked like a doll pressed against him like that. Her mother had mounted him—that was the most accurately disgusting word for it— and he was lying half-down on the couch, the couch where they sometimes watched *Seinfeld* together *as a family*, where little Grace had, hours earlier, in her tiny, unsullied Batman pajamas, been turning the pages of *Guess How Much I Love You*, where Wendy herself sometimes *ate*. It was sacrilege; that couch was a chaste, communal space.

There was a kind of reciprocal grinding activity taking place. Her mother moaned. They were both still clothed—*thank all the heavenly bodies above*—but her mother's shirt was lifted in the back, lifted by her father's hand, and Wendy could see the white horizontal slash, like a painted traffic line, of her bra.

What to do? If she startled them, who knew what she would see? She couldn't tell what the situation was with her father's pants; her mother was blessedly impeding her view. She crept back upstairs. A major benefit to weighing 101 pounds at five foot eight was stealthiness.

She went to her sister's room, not bothering to knock before she opened the door. Violet was stretched out on her bed, still wearing the ugly plaid headband she'd had on at school that day, following the text of her ethics book with a pencil. She looked up blearily.

Wendy slipped inside. "In case you wanted to know, I'm dead."

"Doors were invented for a reason."

"I just *died*, Violet."

"Can I have your hair dryer, then?"

"Something's happening downstairs. Something . . . *sick*."

"A dead mouse?"

"No. Like, *obscene*. I think Mom and Dad are having sex."

Violet frowned.

"I mean, not like *sex*-sex, but like—a prelude." The word felt lewd and disgusting in her mouth, an extra tongue. She couldn't help it: she laughed.

Violet was just trying to finish her homework. Violet was *always* trying to finish her homework; finishing your homework was a difficult endeavor when you lived in the loudest house in Illinois. It was a noble pursuit, she thought, this aspiration toward academic accolade.

And now, apparently, her parents were having exhibitionistic sex. It did not surprise her in the least. She couldn't wait to go to college, to leave behind all in her life who were indulgent and anorexic and carnally motivated.

"There were noises," Wendy said, "that I will never unhear."

Her parents' bedroom shared a wall with her own. Violet had heard the unhearable. She turned, skeptically, to that west wall, which prominently featured her framed induction certificate from the National Honor Society, and an unframed, thumbtacked poster of Whitney Houston.

"On the *couch*," Wendy said. "In the *living room*."

The thought of anyone—let alone her haphazard, pragmatic parents—having sex on a sofa was unfathomable. Ethics in journalism, chapter 6: Wendy was an unreliable source.

"Mom made a noise too," Wendy said.

"Like a snoring noise?"

"There is nothing less like snoring than the noise I heard," Wendy said.

Violet sat up. She marked the page in her book and regarded her older sister, emaciated and sensationalistic and sporting new bangs that didn't suit her face. "What kind of noise?"

"Like—" Wendy made a face that made her laugh. Wendy, the most annoying, wonderful person she knew, could always make her laugh. "Like *pleasure*. The most horrifying kind of pleasure." Then Wendy laughed too, and it lightened her, and for a few delightful seconds they were both dying of laughter, whinnying like ponies, a scandalized, limitless duo.

"Mama?" A tiny voice broke the blissful sibling respite like an alarm. All the girls had developed a motherly radar for it, several pitches above the voices they were used to hearing, sometimes crying but more often than not imploring, solemn and curious, through the darkness of their house. *Mama, is there water? Daddy, are you here? Anyone; is anyone there?* Wendy turned to open the door. Grace was there, foot-pajama clad, thumb a few centimeters from her mouth. Wendy was still laughing. Violet opened her arms to her littlest sister.

"Shh," she said. "Mama's busy, Goose." Which, of course, incited a fresh torrent of cackling from them both as Grace made the arduous journey of a two-foot-tall person onto Violet's mattress.

"Where's Mama?" she asked. It was her most-oft asked question.

"She's downstairs," Violet said. "What do you need, Goose? It's late."

Grace shrugged, jamming her thumb into her mouth and pulling her arms tighter around Violet's waist.

"Is it weird that I kind of want to see?" Liza asked, and Violet and Wendy both jumped.

Wendy turned to her. "Jesus fuck; you're such a ghoul. Did you *float* here?"

"I mean, you've kind of *intrigued* me," Violet admitted. "I'm a little curious."

"You know what?" Wendy hissed. "Fine. Let's go see them."

They all met eyes in a complicated, giddy web across the room. Violet rose from the bed and transferred Grace to Liza's arms and then Wendy led the way downstairs. The third stair creaked with the combined weight of Wendy and Violet, and their parents—it was true, twined together, their father splayed and their mother writhing—both startled.

Marilyn, usually content to exist in her husband's castoff Oxford shirts, had chosen to make an effort for Gracie's graduation ceremony, one of her old sundresses, navy with little green flowers. Wendy wasted no time in making her feel self-conscious about it.

"God, Mom, are you wearing *that*?"

"What's wrong with it?" she asked, looking down at herself. Standing across the room from her teenage daughter—who had a full face of makeup and dramatic highlights in her hair—Marilyn suddenly felt matronly, dowdy and old compared to the startlingly sexualized young woman who allegedly shared half her genetic material.

"What *isn't* wrong with it? No offense, but you sort of look pregnant, for one."

How was it possible that she had birthed such an insufferable aesthete?

"I know you feel this license for verbal abuse because I'm just your *mother* but it's really a bad way to go about your interactions." She faltered. "Listen. I'm asking you for one hour of your time. For your sister."

"I have *plans*," Wendy said, sitting before a closed trigonometry book, staring at her with a bald-faced hatred she'd grown very used to over the past year.

"It's her graduation."

"It's *preschool*," Wendy replied.

"What's the biggest difference between the first kid and the fourth?" someone had once asked Marilyn, and she'd actually said, "Hopefully everything."

"I'm busy," Wendy said.

She made a fist, digging her nails into her palm. "You said that," she said. "But Dad was busy, too, and he traded shifts with someone. And Liza's skipping her water polo practice."

"Liza sucks at water polo." Wendy was now painting her nails a dark, vampy red; the smell wafted across the room. "Oh my God, is your life really so pathetic that this is the only thing you have to focus on? She's *two*."

She had to admit that Wendy had a point. Gracie attended "school" for ninety minutes on Tuesday and Thursday mornings. She was less "graduating" than she was moving from one group of tiny uncoordinated people to another, slightly older group, advancing from the Pineapple Room to the Grapes Room across the hall. But there were so few opportunities left for their family to unite, and this microscopic milestone seemed like such an easy, innocent way to bring all her girls together.

"It would mean a lot to Gracie."

Wendy snorted. "Mom. *Rugrats* means a lot to her. Her stupid eraser collection means a lot to her. She's not going to care whether I watch her graduate from a fake school or not. She doesn't even know what graduation *means*."

"That's not the point."

The real reason, she suspected, that Wendy didn't want to go: because David had proposed that they all go out for ice cream afterward. It made her at once indignant and devastated, defensive of the life she'd created and hopelessly sad for her daughter, for the pain she was in, for the extremely unbecoming way that pain manifested itself, a way that made her impossible to comfort. What if she hugged her? What would happen if she came into the room and wrapped her arms around Wendy?

"I'm not going," Wendy said.

"Would you go for me?" It was laughable: Wendy doing something for her was about as likely as her eating a boxful of ice cream sandwiches, but she thought it was worth a shot. Occasionally pockets of humanity shone out of teenagers.

Wendy, predictably, started laughing. She rose from her desk chair and traipsed over to her dresser. "Are we pretending to be in a Lifetime movie now?" she asked. "God, Mom. You can't be a totally shitty mom for like a thousand years and then suddenly try to guilt me into watching a bunch of toddlers sing Phil Collins songs."

It was like being slapped. "That's an incredibly hurtful thing to say."

Wendy shrugged and she fought the urge to seize her daughter by the shoulders and shake her; she remembered the anger she used to feel when Wendy was a toddler and she longed for that kind of anger now, benign and manageable, though it hadn't felt to be at the time.

"You're grounded," she said, though she would've liked to say *What the fuck did I ever do to you?* and *Do you understand how much worse you could have it?*

"I already have plans," Wendy said.

"That's too bad."

"Mom, Aaron is *literally* going to be here in less than—"

"You're grounded, Wendy." She left it at that, slammed the bedroom door on her daughter's openmouthed protest. She went into her own room and lay back on the bed, letting tears leak from the corners of her eyes and drip down past her temples and into her ears. Growing up amid chaos had tamed her, she supposed. She didn't have it in her to yell at her children, usually. She was instinctively submissive around her teenagers; they made her nervous.

Eventually she composed herself, reapplied her mascara and changed first into jeans and then, ultimately, defiantly, back into her sundress. She went downstairs in search of Grace. Her youngest was still always excited to see her, to touch her. It was a cheap form of gratification but she seized it. She heard Wendy's voice and stopped just before the kitchen doorway. Grace was in Wendy's arms, her toddler pudge making her sister look even thinner.

"Are you *so* excited to graduate, Goose? Are you the vale-dic*to*rian?" She bounced Grace a few times and Grace cackled, throwing back her head. "Are you gonna give a *speech* and throw your *hat* and get a di*plo*ma?" With each syllable she bounced Grace again and with each bounce Grace laughed anew. "Are you gonna be the cutest graduate *ever*?"

"Yeah!" Grace said.

"I'm going to see you tomorrow," Wendy said. Marilyn noticed then that her daughter had her purse slung around her shoulder. "I'm going to see you in the morning and you're going to tell me *all about it*, okay?"

"Okay," Grace said.

"Should we put on your gown? Wanna put on your hilarious gown?"

At this, Marilyn stepped into the room. "I've got it."

Wendy slumped visibly at her entrance. "I was just—"

"I told you you're grounded, Wendy. It's unclear to me why you look like you're on your way out." She wished her voice were more measured. She was the adult; she was supposed to be able to table her pettiness, her hurt. She reached for Grace, who clambered eagerly into her arms.

"I told you I already made plans," Wendy said.

A horn honked outside.

"Wendy, I swear, if you walk out that door—"

Wendy reeked of perfume; she leaned in to kiss Grace on the cheek, surprisingly tender. Marilyn wanted to nuzzle her, to wipe away some of her eye shadow, to kiss the sweet peach fuzz on her cheekbones. Wendy stepped away. "Good luck, Goose," she said. "Knock 'em dead." And she was out the door before Marilyn could counter.

Grace would repeat this phrase, *knock 'em dead, knock 'em dead, knock 'em dead*, while Marilyn helped her into her tiny polyester ensemble, while she herded the girls into the station wagon and drove them to St. Edmund's. At the ceremony, she wept as the iridescent glob of gown-clad toddlers swayed around, "the bright blessed day; the dark sacred night." David put his arm around her, thinking her sadness hormonal nostalgia. And she supposed that was part of it—the simple sweetness of the song, the heartbreaking innocence of her little girl trying to mouth along to the words, graduation cap pushing her bangs down over her eyes; this ascent, suddenly, onstage, from baby to young person. But as she cried against her husband—attracting some attention from fellow parents, a few moms who looked on with bemused empathy and a couple of fathers who just looked concerned—she was thinking, overwhelmingly, not of her youngest daughter but of her eldest.

"Knock 'em dead, knock 'em dead, knock 'em dead," Grace said in the car.

"Knock it off," Marilyn snapped, and everyone—she herself—was surprised.

Three hours later, after crayon-drawn diplomas and sprinkle-doused ice cream, after David had returned to work and Liza and Violet were, in a rare moment of sisterly generosity, pulling Gracie around the block in the Radio Flyer that had been left in the driveway, Marilyn pushed open the door to the laundry room to find the most horrific scene she'd yet witnessed as a parent: her daughter spread-eagle on top of the washing machine, connected at an invisible point to the lithe Aaron Bhargava, whose muscled buttocks—she had to admit—were a sight to behold.

"Mother of *God*," she said, and though both bodies stiffened to attention, Wendy met her eyes languidly across the room and held her gaze as Aaron scrambled for his clothes. This composure stilled her further, as did the ladder of her daughter's rib cage, pale and stark beneath her near-nonexistent breasts. She couldn't remember quite what she'd said after that. She averted her eyes as they scurried into states of dress, Wendy moving at a more leisurely pace than her companion.

She'd previously been grateful for Aaron Bhargava, her daughter's on-again/off-again boyfriend. Every few weeks Wendy would bring a different boy home, one who was blonder or broader or more brainless, but Aaron seemed to be a mainstay, a boy who was charming in comparison to the roster of others—"the Hitler Youth," David called them behind closed doors. Aaron was polite and straitlaced, an athlete (good heavens, those glutes!). He was goofy with Gracie; he'd bonded with David over their shared affinity for the Cubs. He was a boy whom she could envision progressing successfully into adulthood. He'd probably never look her in the eye again.

Because of her own father's complete denial of her as a sexual person, Marilyn had high hopes of being more engaged with her children, encouraging open lines of communication and providing strings-free contraception, rearing a crop of psychosexually healthy young women who knew what they wanted, knew how to say no, and grew to find sex a point of pleasure rather than confusion or shame. She wanted them to know the comfort of stable relationships and have partners who cared about them and found joy in their bodies. She didn't want them to end up, as she had, being schooled in the art of fellatio on an abandoned staircase at a state university.

She wanted to be the kind of mother they could come to with questions, with stories, with Mama-is-this-normals. Or so she thought, until her daughters started growing into women and she watched warily as the transformation began: the languor of their long-legged gaits; their pert breasts and the declension of their hips; the loss of baby fat in their faces, how this made their eyes at once wider and wilier. They began to surpass her in height and, it seemed, in knowledge of the outside world; they gave knowing smirks when she asked how their days were and what they were doing at so-and-so's birthday sleepover. She told herself she was overreacting, that of course this was a traumatic transition for her as a mother, to see her tiny girls sprouting up from the ground like orchids, growing striking and graceful like ponies. Of course it was hard to watch, at times, and tugged cruelly on the parts of her insides that remembered them as newborns, as chubby oblivious toddlers.

After Aaron fled, she went to Wendy's room and found her daughter sprawled on her stomach on the bed, bikini top tied around her neck and cutoffs baring long tanned legs. From this angle, she seemed like a healthy, glowing girl, a little on the skinny side, but David had been lanky too. And Marilyn stilled for a moment, watching her from the hallway, face buried in a weathered copy of *Frankenstein*—Marilyn's own copy, she realized, from college. And she remembered, before she thought of the partying, the dieting, and, now, the *fornicating*, the goofy, eager eight-year-old Wendy had been not so long ago, playing at the beach with her little sisters, reading herself to sleep with The Baby-Sitters Club.

"Is this like linger-in-the-doorway day or something?" Wendy asked, startling her. "I know, I'm still grounded. Am I more grounded than before? Is there, like, a grounding gradient?"

"Wendy, you— I had no idea that you—that it had gotten that serious. With Aaron."

"What serious?" Wendy asked.

"Put the book down." She inched into the room and sat down in Wendy's desk chair. "Are you using protection?"

"He pulls out," Wendy said, and a chill ran down the insides of her arms.

"Oh, lord, sweetheart, that's not—that is *not* a reliable— Oh, Wendy, have you been—"

"Jesus Christ, Mom, I'm joking. I'm on the Pill," Wendy said.

"You—what? Since when? How?"

"Just a couple months."

"Honey, I wish you'd—" This in no way resembled the open communication she'd envisioned herself having with her daughters; she'd pictured genial late-night conversations and meaningful hugs, not this stilted, clumsy navigation after she'd caught her daughter in the act. "I know it's uncomfortable but one of my primary jobs as your mom is to teach you how to—"

"Have sex? I'm good, but thanks."

"I didn't have my mom around to talk to me about this stuff. And you don't know how much I wish I did."

"Mom, I've got it covered, Jesus," Wendy said.

She rose, her knees shaking. "My father would've killed me if I talked to him the way you're talking to me."

Wendy glanced up at her once, quickly, darkly. "Sorry."

"I don't— I'm not sure what to say about any of this, Wendy, but we'll have to discuss it again at some point."

"Wow, promise?" Wendy said meanly, changing on a dime like she did, leaping from being genuine to being cruel in the span of a few seconds. "I have absolutely zero desire to get chlamydia. Or to get pregnant with demon spawn like you did. God, Mom, we literally *all* walked in on you and dad boning on the couch a few weeks ago. It's not like you're this virtuous model for how to live."

"You could do so much worse than me as your mom," she said. She turned to go.

"It— Mom, seriously. I'm being safe. I swear."

"Thanks for telling me," she said, and she left her daughter's room.

It didn't fully sink in until later, when she was folding laundry and Gracie was sitting at her feet, tiny pink tongue sticking out of the side of her mouth, scribbling with page-tearing ferocity in a Muppets coloring book. She was not thinking of *them*, specifically; her attention to Aaron's physique had been passing; she wasn't some sort of predator. She was preoccupied by their *ardor*, their urgency, the extent to which they seemed to be enjoying themselves. She and David didn't have that anymore, not quite like they used to. That kind of desire was so far removed from the routine of marital lovemaking, which was certainly *nice* but so often either drowsy or militant, a means to an end, a final act—like locking up the house—before they fell asleep. That kind of desire—the sweet substance of their intimate encounters before they married—took too much time.

A terrible mother. Was it all her fault? she wondered. Sitting astride David on the couch, the world around them fuzzed into static, right in the middle of the living room, where anyone could see them, *did* see them: her daughters, lined up on the landing of the stairs like a firing squad, watching them with the kind of intensity they usually reserved for *The Real World*. And then—even then, with the children in the room!—she'd been sharply aware of the parts of her they couldn't see, the mellow throbbing in the cleft between her legs, the intensity with which she wanted to drag her husband upstairs and let him have his way with her, a lights-on, unapologetic physical union with the ropy muscles of his legs and the broad solidity of his chest, with his gentle strength, the sweetness of the inside of his mouth, the limitless click that happened when he entered her, how it always felt good even though she'd known him for a hundred million years.

What kind of example were they setting for their children? Certainly a better one than her own parents had for her, wasn't it? Gracie, who craved physical contact like a sloth, leaned against her shins, and she reached down to stroke her little graduate's wispy dark hair, woven by Liza into tiny French braids, and she decided that if she was guilty of anything in this particular parental gaffe, it was of still being attracted to her husband, and as far as motherly transgressions went, this one seemed fairly innocuous. NPR bled into white noise and Gracie returned to her picture and for a while she was left alone with her thoughts, with a dull stirring between her legs.

"Mom?"

Marilyn's eyes had been sagging closed but she roused herself at the sight of Wendy. She'd stopped waiting up for her eldest out of physiological necessity; Grace ran her ragged all day and slept fitfully at night and her body's need for sleep occasionally eclipsed vigilance. David was working late. She held her place in her book—why did she unconsciously make these efforts to seem preoccupied when she was around Wendy? Wasn't her real preoccupation enough?—and pushed herself up against her pillows.

"What's up?" she asked.

"Can I come in?" Wendy asked, and it tugged at something in her heart, something that radiated downward, a millisecond twinge of digestive churning that she recognized immediately as a particular kind of overwhelming, unrequited love.

"Of course, honey."

Wendy climbed into David's side of the bed, surprising her further. She collapsed a little bit, shoulders caving inward, pulling up the covers over her knees. She smelled like beer and burning leaves, the remnants of a bonfire. "Mom do you ever feel like—like you're a lot older than everyone else your age and you just want to either go ahead without them or just find a bunch of people who—like, *do* act your age?"

Marilyn set down her book. "I— Sure. Sure I've felt that way. Did something happen?"

Suddenly she felt the weight of Wendy's head on her shoulder.

"I just had a really bad time tonight," Wendy said. She could smell the alcohol on her daughter's breath, a sick saccharine odor that reminded her of old men on the CTA, the desperate ones who drank mouthwash. She made the swift decision, closer to Wendy than she'd been in ages, that this particular fight could be fought tomorrow. She put her arm around her oldest daughter.

"I'm sorry," she said, both because it was what she would've said to the others and because she *was* sorry: sorry for the state of her daughter's life, sorry she didn't know how to fix it.

"*I'm* sorry." It was the first time she'd heard Wendy say the words since she was microscopic, apology edging its way out of her mouth around the impediment of her thumb.

She pressed her lips into Wendy's hair and kept them there, feeling like she'd felt when they'd adopted the dog last year, her daughters and her husband looking to her to be effortlessly affectionate when in fact Goethe—who'd seemed like a beast at the time—initially made her nervous. She caught herself comparing Wendy to their yellow Lab and reddened but she didn't change positions, only moved her hand to tuck some of Wendy's hair behind the warm flimsiness of her ear, over and over, and then she took a breath and spoke: "So, honey, what happened?" It was what she would have asked the other girls, what she wouldn't have had to ask David because he'd already know she was interested. "Why was tonight so bad?"

But Wendy, it seemed, was already asleep, and she would blame herself forever that it wasn't until several hours later—early Sunday morning, David asleep on the couch, Wendy beside her, her breathing alarmingly feeble—that she tried and failed to wake her daughter up.

CHAPTER SIXTEEN

Ryan was packing up his trunk when she pulled in behind him in the driveway, and it struck her that she would have to move her car in order to let him out.

"What's going on," she said, not quite a question. Ryan slid a box into a snug space, reminding her, for just a second, of her father. "Ryan."

He turned to face her. "I'm not sure what to say."

"Say about what? What's all that stuff?"

"I was hoping I'd be out of here before you got home. I know it's not good for the baby when you get stressed out. But I'm not sure I have it in me to be civil to you, Liza, so maybe you should just— Could you move your car?" There was an energy in his voice that she hadn't heard in a long time, and a hard-edged anger that made her incredibly nervous.

"Ryan, you're not making any sense."

"That guy in your department, right? The one I met at the Christmas party?"

She was so caught off-guard that she had the impulse to sit down in the driveway. She steadied herself against the car, tried to breathe normally. "How do you—

"Glasses?" Ryan said. "Dark hair?"

"Wait, no, Ryan, how do you— I never meant to—" She gathered herself. "It just happened a few times. And I'm not—

We're done. It was only—over the summer. And it's—over. It was never even— Let's talk about this, please."

She could see, from the way his face fell, that he'd been harboring some hope that he was wrong, and that she'd just showed him a hand he hadn't expected her to be holding.

"Is it—is there a chance it's his?" He motioned to her belly.

She would never forget how this gutted her, would never forgive herself for putting him in the position of having to ask such a devastating question. "No," she said. "It didn't start until after I got pregnant." This sounded much worse aloud than it did in her head. The onus was on her to explain herself, but it struck her simultaneously that she hadn't given any thought to an explanation. Her mind was vexingly blank. She opened her mouth and closed it, twice, like a guppy.

"Was it to—what, punish me?"

"No, of *course* it— Ryan, how did you even— We need to *talk* about this. Would you—come inside? Please? Let's—"

"I'm sorry I haven't been here for you," he said flatly.

"Ryan, *please*, it was just—a stupid thing, a stupid hormonal thing, and I'm sorry; I'm so sorry I did that to you but it's *over*, and if we can just *talk* about this . . ." She didn't realize she was crying until she tasted salt. She wiped her cheeks. "How did you—know?"

Ryan studied her evenly. "I put two and two together." He cleared his throat.

"I'm sorry," she said. "I'm sorry you—however you figured it out."

"Least of my concerns."

"Ryan."

"I'm not sure what else to do," he said. "It's not fair. To either of us. To—" He gestured vaguely at her. "To the baby, either. If I'm dragging you down and you hate me enough to hurt me like this—it's toxic, Liza."

"I don't *hate* you, Ryan, Jesus."

"I think this is the decision that's going to be the least harm-ful to everyone."

"What decision?"

"One of the guys I knew at LemonGraphics is doing a wind energy thing in the Upper Peninsula. He's got a spare room and he said he could use a hand with some of the tech stuff. He actually posed the idea a few months ago, but I didn't even mention it to you because—well, at the time I was thinking of—the two of us." He rubbed his forehead. "The three of us."

She felt both very sad and very angry, and because she couldn't decide which was more appropriate she grabbed the one that allowed for less guilt. "I'm sorry," she said, "you're moving to *Michigan*? You think you're in a good enough place to be moving by yourself to *Michigan*?"

He narrowed his eyes. "You really think you're in a position to be asking me that?"

"I just mean that you haven't been in the healthiest—"

"You *cheated* on me," he said evenly. "I'm humiliated and I'm furious and I'm fucking *devastated*, Liza, because of you. So I'd argue that alone makes Michigan a healthier place for me to be, given the alternative." He raised his eyebrows expectantly and she was almost proud of him for challenging her.

But then she remembered herself, their life together for the past few years, the baby in her belly. And Ryan, catatonic on the couch, his impenetrable misery. Was this not, in its own way, the escape hatch she'd been seeking when she first came clean to her father? Was this not—unintended and wholly unexpected—a version of what she'd wanted? That it might be better this way, without him—hadn't that been what she was thinking all along, caring for her child without having to worry about its father, allocating all of her resources in one direction instead of spreading them around? She hadn't cheated on him so he'd leave her, and yet here he was, leaving her, freeing her, in a sense, from all she'd wanted to get rid of. But she wanted, to some degree, to feel in charge, to hang on to some of the indignation she was entitled to as the partner of a seriously troubled man. She wanted them *both* to feel responsible. Because, yes, she'd done something awful, but he was leaving her to care for their baby by herself. The shift from hypothetical to actual struck her with vigor and she was suddenly terrified. She was alone—expansively, islandically alone.

"You don't think we should break up?" he asked.

"Well—no, I guess I'm not saying that." *I don't know what the fuck I'm saying. I don't know what the fuck I want. I don't want to be the only one responsible for making decisions.*

"I don't know what else to do, Lize," he said, and she didn't recognize the smallness of his voice, and in the smallness she realized his desperation.

In a weird way, Ryan's suggesting that they split up was the most mature, unselfish thing he'd done in years. But she started crying anyway because *she* knew better; she would always know better and her kid would not; her kid would never awaken at night and join them in bed, sleep between its parents; her kid would never catch them making out on the living room couch and turn its head away in prideful disgust; her kid would never come down in the mornings to find them together, leaning half-asleep against the kitchen counter in each other's arms, waiting for the coffee to brew; her kid would never feel the ironclad suburban security that accompanied any of these things, the comfort of offhandedly telling some embarrassing story to friends beginning with *"Ugh, my mom and dad"; mymomanddad*, her kid would never get to say that.

"So you're just going to bail," she said.

"Fuck you for making it sound like I'm the bad guy. Jesus Christ, Liza. This is one of the worst things you could possibly do to someone else. I'd *never* do something like this to you. I know I haven't been the easiest person to live with but I'd *never* hurt you like this. And I've never felt fucking worse than I have in the last few hours."

"I'm sorry," she said again. She'd lived with him for eight years. Woken up beside him nearly every single morning for the last decade. He met her eyes, and she examined the loveliness of his face, the face she'd known since she was nineteen, those kind gray eyes.

"Maybe this'll be good for us," he said. "I don't know. I don't know if I— But I guess it's hard to picture things getting much worse. Nowhere to go but up." He shook his head. "I'll send money when I can. And I hope you'll—keep me in the loop."

She nodded. He could have reminded her of her culpability, that technically all he'd done wrong in the last few years was suffer, that his suffering was largely beyond his control and her punishing him was barrel-bottom cruelty, that his genes might predispose their kid to depression but hers might predispose it to unkindness, and that suffering of your own making was a different animal entirely.

"I love you," he said instead, and when he came to hug her before abruptly releasing her, before driving off without a backward glance, she had no choice but to hug back, the baby pressed between them, the little person they'd already failed.

1995

When Aaron Bhargava showed up at the front door, Violet was annoyed, because Wendy had people checking in on her even when she wasn't home to be checked in on.

"She's still in the hospital," she said, not quite flatly, because he was the kind of boy to whom you just couldn't be unkind; his eyes radiated warmth; his smile made her stomach hurt. He was holding a bouquet of tiger lilies.

"No, I know. I just thought I'd bring these for—your family. And see how Wendy was doing." He handed over the flowers.

She looked down at them, pressed her nose into one of the blooms. It had a dense sweet smell and she imagined her nasal passages filling with pollen, pollen that Aaron Bhargava had bought from Jewel-Osco. "Thanks," she said. "She's—I'm not really sure. Okay, I guess?" Aaron was the only boyfriend of Wendy's who said hi to her in the hallways at school, who stopped to chat when he was leaving their house in the evenings. She sat down on the porch swing and, without thinking, anchored her feet so he could join her without it rocking.

He sat. "Have you been to see her?" he asked.

She shook her head. She and her sisters hadn't been to the hospital yet. None of them had specifically asked, and their parents had not specifically offered. She and Liza had put Gracie to bed together, lulling her to sleep with renditions of songs their mother loved, "Please Mr. Postman" and "Harvest Moon" and "The Night They Drove Old Dixie Down," and after that they'd watched a rerun of the Tom Petty *Rockumentary*, which should have been fun and illicit because their parents didn't allow television on school nights, but the balance felt off without Wendy there; there were four of them and to be three felt sacrilegious, even though she knew that when Wendy returned, she would consume their family entirely, because that was what always happened with Wendy.

"You holding up okay? With her—not around?"

Which of course reminded her of Wendy's dramatic exit, of the ambulance in their driveway, of her mother like she'd never before seen her, like some kind of terrified animal.

"One day at a time," she breathed to Aaron, feeling beleaguered and mature.

"She talks about you a lot."

"Ha. That I'm a total square?" she intoned, imagining. "That I stole her Black Honey lipstick?"

"She did say that about the lipstick, actually." He laughed. "But otherwise, she mainly talks about how smart you are."

And that made her even sadder, because she'd always been sort of curious as to why her sister—her headstrong, adventurous, go-against-the-grain older sister—even bothered with her: prissy, predictable, uncreative Violet. It was the first time, throughout the whole ordeal, that she felt like crying. A good sister would never enjoy—even if it was only for half a second—the soothing hush that fell over the house when her Irish twin wasn't in it. But she would not allow herself to cry in front of her sister's hot boyfriend, a boy who loved Wendy enough to come check on the rest of them when Wendy herself was out of commission.

"You guys need anything?" he asked. "A ride to school tomorrow?"

"Our grandpa's taking us," she said, but couldn't resist imagining how it would feel to show up at school like Wendy did, with a boy who drove a car, how it would feel to be Wendy, gorgeous and brave and dynamic, coveted by all.

"Hey, she's going to be fine," Aaron said. "Wendy's Wendy. She's resilient."

"Thanks," she said, and she tried to think of something she could say that would make him stay a little longer, but he was already standing up. She smoothed one of the flower petals between her middle finger and her thumb. "Thanks for the flowers."

At the hospital, his wife had fallen asleep next to Wendy's bed, hands steepled together and back rounded forward, her head lolling at a sickly angle, as though she'd dropped off while praying. Wendy was asleep, an IV in her left hand. He leaned to kiss his daughter's forehead. She was bare-faced and limp-haired and looked like a child in a way that she hadn't in years. He turned away from her, thoughts of those years suddenly too much to consider. He went around the bed and squatted before Marilyn. "Sweetheart."

She startled; he heard a distinct crack from her neck and they both winced. She turned quickly to Wendy's bed as though to ensure she hadn't escaped. It was a heartbreaking gesture; they both knew that neither one of them had possessed, for several years, the ability to prevent their daughter from going anywhere.

"We should go home," he said, although he knew it was probably best that the girls didn't see much of her: their mother was barely recognizable, savage, circles under her eyes like bruises.

"I'm not leaving her here by herself."

"Marilyn, you haven't *slept* since—"

Since Saturday night, he couldn't say, because they were currently not talking about Saturday night, nor were they to discuss early Sunday morning, when Marilyn had awakened to find Wendy unresponsive beside her in their bed. Even if he'd wanted to discuss it he couldn't bring himself to consider the specifics: the weight of his daughter's body in his arms, how sallow and scary she looked. She'd been at a party; there was a mix of alcohol and a startling cocktail of pills featuring traces of MDMA and ketamine. These were the things he couldn't think about. He could think only of Sunday morning—waking up on the couch having found his daughter in his spot in bed a few hours earlier—and the noise his wife had made, an unearthly screeching.

"She's going to be fine," he said, squeezing her knees. They both looked over at their daughter, who had—owing to the nurses—bathed more recently than his wife. Some of Wendy's color was coming back. Marilyn turned away as though in pain.

"I wish everyone would stop saying that."

Their daughter hadn't been *fine* for a long time. And here they were.

"At least come down and get something to eat."

He saw her glance over again at Wendy's bed.

"Sorry," he said. "Come on. Something simple. I'll buy you some frozen yogurt." He rose from his squat. She opened her mouth as if to argue but then sighed. He offered her an arm, rather archaically, and she took it and leaned into him, but not before stopping at Wendy's bedside to tuck in her blanket and kiss the angled curve of her cheek. They rode silently down to the second floor in the eerie calm of the hospital in the evening. Seated across from her at a cafeteria table, he took her hand.

So strange to be here with her, vampiric orderlies milling about, the familiar odor of disinfectant and pizza overpowered by his wife's unmistakable skin-sunshine-vanilla combination, a scent that had persisted despite her hygienic laxity. He held her hand to his lips and met her eyes. She held his gaze for only a second before looking away.

"Do we trust Dr. Carlson?" she asked. "I'm not sure I trust him. He doesn't make a lot of eye contact. I just don't— I don't like how they talk about her like she's this textbook *case* of something, like she's . . ." She started to cry and he squeezed her fingers.

"Eat something, honey; you'll feel better."

She pulled her hand from his and pushed her cup away. "For God's sake."

"Marilyn." The three feet separating them felt legion; he couldn't quite recognize the look on her face.

"I'm so fucking tired of all of the—*rhetoric* they use here; they talk about her like— I'm not an idiot. There's something to be said for the fact that I'm her mother. I could stand to not have a bunch of strangers psychologizing my daughter."

"They're doctors, Marilyn. There's precedent for how they're evaluating her."

She smirked. "Spoken like an overeducated man."

Overeducated man? When Marilyn got upset, she pulled unfathomable and previously unmentioned barbs from some bottomless bag within her; she said things that made him question her love for him, their life together. He knew his wife was insecure about her education, resentful that she'd never finished school, but she was smarter than anyone he'd ever met.

"*Your* daughter," he said. "As though I haven't—"

"You know what I meant."

He'd never been a parent without her. He couldn't remember the last time he'd been a *person* without her. But he was angry, angry at her cruelty, and he didn't have the energy to try to connect with her; he lacked the vocabulary to communicate with his wife for the first time since he'd known her. "Don't you think this is fucking killing me?"

"Of *course* it is, but it's not— You're not *with* her every day, David."

"Well, fine, you are. And look what happened."

She looked up at him lethally. He'd never before seen this white-hot anger on her face, mixed with an unrecognizable level of hurt. "You think I haven't spent the last seventy-two hours blaming myself for this? I'm the one who found her, David. If it's unclear whether or not I'm completely *shattered*, let me elucidate."

"She of the ten-dollar words," he said after a minute. She stared at him, stirring her yogurt into beige paste, her sprinkles bleeding their dye into the swirl. "I'm sorry."

"I just sit there watching her and I—I would hand over anything in the *world* if I could make things okay for her."

"That's not how it works," he said, and he was trying to be pragmatic—she usually appreciated this—but it came out sounding harsh. But of course he agreed. His desire for his child to be okay was stronger than anything he'd ever felt, stronger, even, than his love for his wife.

"Do me a favor," she said, "and don't talk to me like I'm *impaired* in some way, would you?" And he saw it on her face too: the myopia of her want, all of it siphoned off to Wendy, none to spare for their other girls, least of all none to spare for him. He acknowledged the newfound blank space between them and grieved for what had previously filled it. Marilyn rose from the table, her chair squeaking on the linoleum. "I shouldn't have left her," she said. "I'm going to go back up there before I say something awful to you. Apparently if one of us isn't being careful about that, the entire thing can completely implode." She said it conversationally, but her face, slack and wan, left no room for uncertainty. "Are you coming up or not?"

He rose to follow her. "I guess I should get home and check on the girls."

She gave him a nauseated half smile and hurled her yogurt into the garbage. "Liza has band on Wednesdays," she said, which translated loosely to *I'm three steps ahead of you, you asshole.* "Make sure she has her clarinet tomorrow morning."

They stood in the hallway outside of the cafeteria, facing off.

"Kiss Gracie for me," Marilyn said finally, gently. She studied him for what felt like a long time and then, to his surprise, she leaned against his chest and hugged him tightly. "We're being terrible to each other because we're terrified, right?" she asked.

He put a hand to the nape of her neck and another at her waist. "I imagine so."

She finally pulled away, wiping her eyes. "Drive safely. Kiss the girls. Remember the clarinet." She straightened her posture, sniffled.

"I love you," he ventured, and she nodded.

"Yeah," she said. And then, ambiguously: "Me too."

CHAPTER SEVENTEEN

Through the sliding doors, from where she was preparing their lunch, Wendy watched her mom on her patio, her face tilted up to the sun and her eyes closed. Her mother was tiny and freckled and blond, the kind of Irish that looked more like Elfish, and her father was tall and broad-chested with an angular face and eyes that were good at winking. Wendy had good-looking parents. This did not, she argued, necessarily amount to good-looking children. The Moore-Willises and Brangelina proved incontrovertibly that impossibly attractive people scientifically failed to produce appealing offspring. It was, thus, in her opinion, a curse to have beautiful parents. And her parents were catalog-model pretty, not even a JCPenney catalog but like the Ralph Lauren section of a Macy's catalog.

"Your father," Marilyn said once, proudly, watching a sweaty David on the roof, hanging Christmas lights, "is the reason so many women wear lipstick to the Pancake Breakfast."

She'd invited her mother over on a whim. After her eviction of Jonah, Violet was no longer speaking to her. Liza was pregnant, a state that Wendy found intolerable to be around for several reasons. And her father was always suggesting that she and Marilyn make more of an effort to spend time together. So her mother came over on a Wednesday, right after Yesinia had power-buffed the floors.

"I don't know how you keep things so clean," said her mom. "Even with just me and Dad, things have a way of—accumulating."

"Just different priorities, I guess," she said, and what an awful, prissy thing it was to say—she would never say something like that in front of her father.

Her mom looked at her for a long minute. "I'd almost forgotten what it was like to live with a teenager, though," she said. "Talk about accumulation."

It didn't seem to be quite a dig. Her mother was well schooled in the art of passive aggression, but she wasn't mean. They hadn't discussed Jonah since he'd moved out of Wendy's house. Now she met her mother's eyes steadily, waiting for the harshness she felt she deserved. But Marilyn said nothing more.

"I've never met a person whose being emanates so many stray socks," Wendy said finally. "And they all smell like death. I never even see him wearing them."

This elicited a wisp of a smile.

"Would you like a glass of wine?" Wendy asked.

"Well." Marilyn glanced at the clock. "Well, sure, why not."

Yes, I get it, Mom, she thought. *I get that I make you uncomfortable enough to want to day-drink.* She made sure her mother's eyes followed her over to the rack in the dining room, followed her manicured fingers touching the necks of a few bottles.

"I just got a really lovely Chablis from a friend of ours at the American School."

"Don't waste any of your fancy stuff on me, Wend; I'm a rube."

If she were feeling especially ornery Wendy would have said, *All I have is "fancy stuff,"* Mom, but she wasn't, so she pulled down the Chablis.

"That's a very pretty bottle," her mom said.

"I'll give it to you to use as a vase when you leave."

"Oh, well, I doubt we'll finish an entire *bottle*."

Again, if feeling ornery, she would have said, *You bet your ass we will.*

Instead: "I'll give you some of the hydrangeas. I know how much you like them."

She brought out a variety of small plates—olives and pita and hummus and some soft cheeses, a dish of ceviche, all bought in little plastic tubs from Whole Foods but served now with garnishes to make it look like she'd prepared them herself.

"I don't think I realized how hungry I am," Marilyn said. "This looks wonderful."

A little smug, maybe, as she set down the last plate, one containing tiny slices of bruschetta, like *Look at me, Mom, look how normal I am.*

Vestiges of her teenage habits appeared only fleetingly for her now—she still, on occasion, flirted with the idea of purging, and once in a while she'd try a diet that she read about in *Us Weekly*. But she became comfortable with her body in adulthood—after her husband, after her abbreviated pregnancy—in a way that surprised her. She grew out of the part of herself that worried obsessively about things like that with so little holdover that it made her suspicious.

She regarded those days primarily with embarrassment. Common wisdom would say her dalliances with cocaine and extreme dieting were the manifestation of some larger psychological shortcoming, but Wendy disagreed. She'd disliked her family. She'd wanted better things. This, as she saw it, was a marker not of psychological distress but of upward mobility. She was ambitious, like her father. He'd gone to medical school and she, conversely, had made herself appealing to men who were also planning on going to medical school (or law school, or parentally funded gap years in Amsterdam). Except, of course, people like her father were respected. She recalled one evening, in the basement of an enormous house by Thatcher Woods, during which coke-peddling Spencer Stallings said, in front of three other boys, in front of one girl named Autumn, who was also very rich and flawlessly honey-haired, with an air of entitlement specific to blond boys reared in sprawling Colonial Revivals: "Suck my dick, Sorenson."

And Wendy had done it. That was the worst part. She got down on her knees and did it right there, with other people watching, because you had to have *something* to remain on the inside with these people, and she had mousy hair and a motley Catholic family and a swan-like body that was maintained only because she was exceptionally good at making herself puke, and none of those things were enough. Her position in that basement was tenuous, so she'd unzipped his pants. Spencer had spoken to her with such authority both because he was an insufferable prick and because he knew she would do it; because Wendy, when receiving direction from anyone other than her parents, did what she was told.

She'd since been able to reconcile those degrading adolescent days with the life she led now, a life with a temperature-controlled wine rack and a two-story unit in a high-rise overlooking Lake Michigan, a life in which she could boss people around and meet a twenty-something at a bar and take him home and then kick him out in the middle of the night if she was so inclined. She'd endured years of being treated badly in order to fashion a version of adulthood in which she could do the same to others. There were worse things. This was survival.

"So," she said, going to work on the wine. "How is everyone?"

Marilyn sighed. "Oh, *everyone*. They're fine. We're fine. Your sisters are—you know, status quo, I think. Lize seems a little worn out, but I suppose that's— Well, you know how it is." Her mother stopped, realized what she'd said and glanced up at her with apology. "Jonah's doing quite well. Getting acclimated. He's really a lovely boy; his resilience is—astounding, honestly, don't you think?"

She sipped her wine, declining to answer.

"Honey, are you and Violet—is everything okay between you two?"

"Uh-huh," she said, reminding herself a bit of Jonah.

"Because I can't— I imagine these past few months have been—overwhelming. For both of you. And I can't help but notice that— Well, I don't know. It's just a feeling I get."

"I'm fine. I don't know about Violet."

"You and I haven't discussed it, actually," her mom said carefully. "What—happened. That year. The year Violet was living with you."

"We came, we saw, we conquered," she said idly, though the intensity of her mother's attention was making her nervous. "Jesus, Mom, what more do you want to know? Violet was pregnant. Violet had a baby. The baby went home with other people. Violet returned to her same robotic self at an alarming speed. Violet went to law school. The end." But of course that wasn't true. Of course that had been just the beginning, as far as she and Violet were concerned.

"I just wonder why you wouldn't have called me. I just don't get why either of you thought you'd be even remotely equipped to handle such an enormous life decision."

"You were as old as we were then when you had me and Violet," she pointed out.

"Well, yes, but I— Times were different back then, Wendy, and I had your father and we'd always planned to have children. Just because you came a little earlier . . ."

"Gosh, Mom, did you get pregnant with me before you planned to?" She rolled her eyes. "I'm totally *shocked*; you've never mentioned it."

"Oh, lord, Wendy, I didn't mean—"

"We're sisters, Mom. I can't explain it any better than that. You wouldn't understand."

Her mother laughed. "How on earth do you argue that someone who's given birth to four daughters still doesn't understand sisterhood?"

Wendy shrugged. "I don't know. You just don't."

Her mom, after a moment, apparently decided to let it go. "How about you? Are you as hopelessly lost as everyone else?" It was possible that this was some kind of convoluted compliment. Wendy, with her two floors and her widowhood and her organic prepared foods, was now situated more comfortably into the fibers of the world than her sisters. Survival. Her mother leaned her head back in her chair and closed her eyes, not seeming particularly eager for a response. She was struck again by how lovely her mom was, by the way that all the wrinkles on her face seemed to be laugh lines, by how her hair—uncolored and neglectfully cut—still looked a bit like gold Christmas-tree tinsel.

"No, Mom. Status quo. I'm a marathon of disappointment as usual."

"You've never disappointed me," her mother said, eyes fluttering open. "If you're unhappy with how things are, then I—I'm sorry for that, and I wish you felt differently, but you've never been disappointing. Not ever."

"Could've fooled me," Wendy said.

"Is this some kind of—what, reckoning? Because I wish you would've warned me if—"

"This is what you always do. You start to be sincere and then the second I reciprocate you shut down."

"You made a joke, Wendy. That's not sincerity."

"It's my kind of sincerity."

"*That* you get from your father." She sighed. "Wendy, honey, I— You'll have to forgive me if I'm caught off-guard when you just all of the sudden lash out at me with—"

"Oh my God, Mom, it's not all of *the* sudden. You're the only person I've ever met who says that. It's all of *a* sudden. Didn't you get, like, a significant portion of an English degree? Before I showed up and ruined your life?"

"Wendy, you didn't ruin my life. Lord."

"I'm just saying. Do you mind if I smoke?"

"Not in the least." She blinked. "Well, I mean, of course I *mind*. But smoke away. Blow it right in my face. It's criminal how much I love the smell."

Wendy lit a cigarette and exhaled away from her mother.

"I was asking because I was genuinely curious about what's going on with you, Wendy," she said. "I *am* genuinely curious."

"Well, forgive me if I didn't recognize that because it's literally the first time I've ever seen you be curious about me."

"You fascinate me," she said. "All you girls. You're miraculous. There's nothing in the world I care about more."

"All I'm *saying*," she said, filling their glasses, "is that you seem particularly *fas*cinated by those of us who've achieved certain milestones. Liza has a PhD. Gracie's—whatever, like an adult baby who we feel affection for by default. And Violet has *kids*."

"I adore the boys," she said. "But I hope none of you ever felt any pressure from me to— Nothing about that makes Violet any more legitimate in my eyes."

"You act like she's the fucking Blessed Virgin."

"Violet's fragile," she said, and Wendy was surprised by the ease with which she spoke. "Violet needs to be treated like that."

"Bull*shit*."

"You're the strongest of my kids. I know I'm not supposed to say things like that."

"And yet," Wendy said, but she was intrigued.

"Maybe I didn't coddle you enough at the outset," she said, and Wendy snorted. "I definitely didn't. Fine. But don't you think there's a chance that you're better off because of it? Don't you think it's possible that I was teaching you how to be—resilient? Self-sufficient?"

"Not intentionally."

"Nothing you do as a parent is intentional."

"Which I'd know if I'd done what I was supposed to?"

"Which you'd know if things happened the way you deserved for them to happen."

"What about *God*?" Wendy asked meanly. "Isn't *God* supposed to give us what we *deserve*?"

"That's not how it works," she said flatly. "Life's hard for all of us. Life's terrible, a lot of the time. It's not about deserving things but we— I think we're entitled to feel angry when we're deprived of things that other people take for granted."

"Well, hey, thanks," Wendy said. "Thanks for the permission."

"Would you like me to leave? I can't—I can't ever seem to do anything right, by your standards. Would you just like me to leave you alone?"

Wendy sipped her wine and squinted at a spot past her mother's shoulder. "No," she said finally. "I'm not sure what I'd like."

"Well, settle in," Marilyn said. "Because it takes for-fucking-ever to figure that out."

Wendy raised her eyebrows.

"Fine," her mom said, taking a drink of her wine. "Let me bum a cigarette."

"Excuse me?"

"I'm unused to having this kind of fraught existential discussion over lunch," she said.

Wendy handed over the pack of cigarettes.

She took one, lit it and inhaled deeply, coughing on her exhalation. "Well, it's been a while, hasn't it?" she said.

"Disgusting?" Wendy asked.

She shook her head. "The most wonderful thing I've experienced in months." She took another drag. "I get why you did what you did. With Jonah. I get it. I've wanted to tell you that. Nobody's ever ready to be a parent."

"I wasn't going to be his—"

"Nobody's ever prepared to care for a child full-time, is what I mean. Nobody understands what that means until they do it for themselves. We're all just holding our breath and hoping nothing catastrophic happens. And how deeply you get *hurt* doing that! It's constant pain. It's a parade of complete and utter agony, all the time, forever."

"You're selling it well," Wendy said.

"It takes such a long time to realize that it's worth it. I wonder why we're engineered that way. We're sleep-deprived to the point of madness those first couple of years and then one day you wake up and you see the little person you've created and she says a *sentence* to you and you realize that everything in your life has been an audition for the creation of that specific person. That you're sending freestanding beings off into the world and it's entirely on your shoulders."

"So when you fuck it up . . ." Wendy said.

"Please, my dear," her mom said. "Don't put words in my mouth."

The secret of her mother: she wished she'd been willing to learn it earlier. Give her an ounce of yourself and she'd give herself to you in totality, metric tons of love and amusement and conviction. Wendy pulled her knees to her chest, fifteen again, and shoved a triangle of pita into her mouth.

"In my desk," Wendy called. "In the middle drawer on the left."

In her daughter's bedroom in search of Advil—their conversation had given her a headache; the cigarette had made it worse—all Marilyn heard was *left* and she pulled open the top left-hand drawer and was confronted with a number of files.

Medical—2009; Dental—2012; Tax Exemptions—07–08. And then, the fourth folder in: *Ivy*.

The sight of the name still made her so sad, and she stared at it now, the smallness of it, three letters, Wendy's familiar looping tail on the *y*. How much it must have hurt her daughter to do something as pedestrian as labeling a folder, to have Ivy relegated to the shallow depths of a file cabinet. She slipped her hand inside the file to open it and peered in the crack. A few ultrasound photos, a hospital bracelet, and a pale blue slip of paper. She removed it, holding her breath. ILLINOIS BUREAU OF VITAL STATISTICS. DATE OF DEATH: 09/10/2005.

"Did you find it?" Wendy called.

She forced the air out of her lungs, slid the paper back into the file, and opened the middle drawer. There, among paper clips and Post-it notes: the Advil. She shook the bottle for validation. "Found it," she called.

She had so many regrets about Wendy. She regretted that she'd had her so young, during a time in her life when she was so lonesome. She regretted that she'd never really given Wendy her full attention, overcome first by delirious exhaustion and then by preparations for the unexpected arrival of Violet, the born-too-soon second child who kicked everything into such chaotic overdrive. She regretted—not *Grace*, certainly, but the impulsive moment during which she and David had decided to try again, when she perhaps should have been noticing the increasing moodiness of her eldest, the troubling relationship Wendy was developing with food. She regretted whatever she had done to make her daughter loathe herself so. She wondered what she'd done to make Wendy so entranced by a life loftier than the one she was living.

She was disturbed by the way their lunch had unfolded, by Wendy's accusations, by the swift dexterity—indicative of bad habit—with which her daughter had opened the bottle of wine. And it occurred to her for the first time that she was maybe the only person in their family who knew uniquely the kind of loss Wendy had endured, that she hadn't lost a husband and a baby but she'd lost her mother before she'd had a chance to figure out who she was as a person. That there was no way to measure suffering, of course, but that she—whose entire childhood had been an exercise in settling—knew better than anyone else what Wendy was going through.

She could see herself in all of her children, most often things about herself that she disliked. Violet knew how to put on a brave face, even if to her own detriment. Liza regarded her parents with undue reverence in the same way that Marilyn once had, watching her own parents—likely both extremely intoxicated—waltzing around the living room together one Christmas Eve, blind to the things both of them had to swallow in order to continue their relationship. Grace was malleable and conflict-avoidant. But Wendy had the strongest hold on her. Her daughter was impulsive, compulsive, turbulent. She spoke her mind as Marilyn had before she had children. She was self-conscious and self-critical and self-destructive.

She'd never say it—for fear of ruining a good thing in a way that only a well-intentioned mother can—but Wendy's marriage to Miles reminded her the most of her own, the way that her daughter seemed to come into herself only after she'd met her husband, a man who was older than she and more serious—as David had been in 1975. And this made everything harder. Wendy was harder to approach, harder to soothe, harder to pity. She thought of all the times she'd tried to comfort her as a teenager, all the times her daughter's sticklike limbs had remained flaccid beneath her touch, all the times Wendy had sneered at her mother's efforts to connect.

Wendy: that first baby, that first person who demanded that she love the world around her in addition to and on behalf of the tiny person in her arms, who woke up a part of her heart whose existence she had not previously known and who made her realize its potential, those infinite and ever-shifting thresholds. Wendy: strong-willed and infuriating. Wendy, the first person on the earth in whom she had seen her husband's exact same eyes.

She could never explain this to her daughter. *You made me recognize that my heart is in fact a bottomless hole of simultaneous pleasure and despair.* She could never say, *You gave my life meaning and ruined it at the same time.* She spent six months with her firstborn, conjoined, buried in blankets against the long winter, noticing *You got my mom's nose* and *Other people may not think your eye contact means anything but I know that it does.* But then Violet came, along with the excuse to say, *I am now the mother of two infants and any mistakes I make can be chalked up to exhaustion.*

And then Ivy had died. She'd been in agony for her daughter, for the grandchild she'd never get to meet. In the office, she steadied herself against Wendy's desk. All these years she'd thought her granddaughter had lacked a middle name in the same way that Grace did—she'd never faulted David for the oversight, picturing him making a knee-jerk decision, holding their newborn, certain his wife was dead.

There was a fullness in her chest. Perhaps Wendy didn't hate her as much as she'd always assumed. IVY MARILYN EISENBERG, on the certificate she'd just tucked back into its resting place in Wendy's desk, just above the date.

When Wendy walked her to the door later, Marilyn surprised them both by throwing her arms around her daughter.

"I hope you know how much I love you," she said, and Wendy stiffened.

"God, Mom, melodramatic much?"

"You didn't ruin my life, Wendy. Quite the opposite. I can't say that enough."

"Okay, but, Mom, I was kind of a monster," she said.

She studied Wendy's face, the parts that hadn't changed since those frigid mornings in the house on Davenport. She watched her daughter, the strangely sure-footed woman she'd become, and was suddenly able to see all incarnations of her, infancy onward, in a bizarre tessellated flip-book that disappeared as quickly as it had materialized.

"I would've *killed* me if I were you," Wendy said.

"You wouldn't have." She brushed a strand of her daughter's hair away from her face. "You would've done your best and powered through and then, decades later, gone to your firstborn's house for a lunch of wine and cigarettes." Who'd've thought that Wendy would emerge victorious in the measurement of her daughters' current performance? Her first baby, who'd figured out, herself, how to power through. "And you would be just as*toun*ded by what a remarkable woman she's become."

1996

Gillian Levin had saved his wife's life. This seemed somehow to advance their relationship to a new plane, a liminal level between collegial and concomitant. One evening, she appeared in his office, her lab coat replaced with an incongruous little motorcycle jacket.

"Going home?" she asked.

He paused, holding one of the clasps of his briefcase. "Not quite," he said.

"I was going to go grab some dinner. You don't want to join me, do you?"

He dropped the clasp, uncertain. "Join you?"

"No pressure." She smiled at him and he felt his face get redder. He spent so much time in the company of women, but none of them—not even his wife, not anymore—looked at him like this. They had one seriously distressed kid and three other statistically average high-maintenance ones. They'd returned to their lives like soldiers from battle, atrophied, squinting, sun-deprived hostages. He'd never felt as distant from her as he did lately.

"Oh," he said. "Well—sure. I just have to make a quick phone call."

She held up her hands. "I'll go lock up the supply closet. Take your time."

He and Marilyn had now spent months in an exhausting union, monitoring Wendy's doctors, her food intake, the number of times she left the house, her visits to the bathroom (standing outside the door, listening for retching—it felt like such a violation). They'd spent months handing Gracie back and forth and reminding each other to check in on Violet and Liza, reminding each other to be enthusiastic when Violet won the nebulous Trapeze Prize for her hard-hitting English essay on "Hills Like White Elephants," when Liza, against all odds, made the water polo team. They'd spent months falling into bed beside each other and drifting immediately into deep sleep, never touching. Their interactions weren't hostile, but they weren't talking beyond businesslike exchanges about the children, about the dog, about the house, and this made him more nervous than anything else. They had weathered years and years together, winging it, but nothing had prepared him for this, for the illusion of normalcy when in fact everything was precisely how it wasn't supposed to be.

Gillian probably assumed that he was calling Marilyn. But instead he dialed the clinic, where he'd been volunteering extra evening hours for the past few weeks, cited a minor emergency at the office and told them he wouldn't be coming.

He chose a table by the window so it would be clear he wasn't hiding anything. He was *allowed* to have dinner with a colleague. Just because he and Marilyn had never really had a vibrant social life outside of each other didn't mean that he couldn't have a *friend*. Gillian was telling an elaborate story about her brother, a news anchor in Cincinnati, and he was trying to pay attention, trying to act casual.

"It's just tough," Gillian said, "constantly being in that shadow. Even though we're both adults. But I guess it's— Well, you know all about sibling rivalry."

"I'm an only child, actually," he said.

She smiled. "I meant your daughters."

"Oh." He felt his face get warm. They'd been so far from his mind for the first time in months. Liza had a friend who lived in an apartment building on this side of town. He pictured Marilyn driving by in the Volvo, catching sight of him through the window. But he *wasn't doing anything wrong.* And would Marilyn even care if he was? He sipped his scotch.

"You seem agitated," Gillian said.

He shook his head. "Just a little—underslept."

"How's Wendy doing?" she asked gently.

When he'd taken the day off to be with her in the hospital, right after her overdose, he'd simply told their office manager that one of his girls was sick. But he'd told Gillian the full story upon his return; Gillian, who'd been the first person he went to when Marilyn started expressing concern about Wendy's weight; Gillian, who understood women in a way that he never could.

"Getting there," he said. She watched him, waiting, and he found himself continuing: "Wendy, actually, is almost back to a hundred percent. As for the rest of us—well. A lot left to be desired." It was astounding how suggestive everything could come to sound when you were having dinner with a woman to whom you weren't married.

"Are your other girls having a hard time?" Gillian had stopped by the house one night when Marilyn was in the hospital, after Gracie was born, to drop off Chinese food and a little bag of presents for the older girls, *Archie* comics and slap bracelets.

"Oh, no," he said. "They're all—well enough. Kids are resilient." He realized that one could apply the process of elimination: subtract his daughters from "us" and you were left with him and Marilyn and the dog. He cleared his throat. "Tell me about you. What's it like in the outside world?"

Gillian shrugged. "Same old. I'm noticing lately that I don't have *hobbies.* Do you have hobbies?"

"Does sleeping count?"

She smiled. "I feel like I used to be more interesting. I used to *do* things. Rollerblading. Crossword puzzles."

"*Roller*blading?" He couldn't help it; he laughed, and then she did too.

"Don't knock it till you try it," she said. "Maybe your kids could teach you."

"Oh, they'd have a field day." He smiled, shook his head. "You're a successful doctor," he said. "You have a good excuse for not having hobbies."

"Ah, but at what expense? I never imagined it would be so hard to find someone who I'm just happy to *be* around. Because that's really what it comes down to, don't you think?"

"Sure. Among other things. But that's a— Yes, I'd say that's a pretty important one."

"You and Marilyn knew each other before you started med school, right?"

To have his wife suddenly on the table between them surprised him. "We did."

"That must be the way to do it. I don't have the time anymore. I don't know when I'm supposed to meet anyone normal. Ask my patients to set me up in exchange for delivering their babies? This is the first time I've been out socially in months. It's a nice change from microwave popcorn and *ER*."

Of course it was a nice change for him too—a change from not loneliness but its opposite: the chaos of his household, his ever-present daughters and the constant demands of family life, and the newfound estrangement from his wife, who was his only source of shelter from the bedlam. "A doctor watching *ER*'s a bit of a cliché," he said.

"Did you love anyone before you loved Marilyn?"

He coughed. Then: "No, actually. We got very lucky."

Her eyes dimmed a little. "That's sweet," she said. "I'd just like to at least find someone who—I'm not sure. Feels lucky to be with me."

"That's critical," he said. "Having a partner who knows you're the most necessary element in his life." These were things it would never make sense for him to say to Marilyn; there was no place for them between drowsy goodnights and grocery lists. "You deserve to be with someone who can sit across the table from you and understand that it's the best thing that'll ever happen to him."

Gillian's eyes were shiny. "That's a high bar."

"There's no reason to settle for someone who isn't nuts about you."

She laughed. "No offense to your gender, but you're awfully insightful for a man."

"Well, I—"

"You're making good use of having daughters," she said, smiling at him, and it confused him, his children being invoked in a sentence that seemed flirtatious.

"We'll see about that."

"Any interest in doing this again?" she asked.

He could rearrange his clinic hours again, free up another evening. "Yeah." He grabbed the check before she could try to split it. "How's Thursday?"

Violet was obsessive about college, about where she would get in and what she would study. And yet her mother seemed sort of bored by the whole affair, making little asides about her determination and patting her gamely on the head as she took SAT practice tests. She'd gotten tired of it—tired of the dysfunction around her, of the hypersensitive focus on Wendy and of the subsequent fact that this was the most important thing she'd ever done and her mother didn't even seem to care.

"Mom?" Her mother was filling out camp registration forms for Liza, and she kept jumping up to check on something in the oven. She could never just sit down and have a conversation;

she was always holding Grace or a pile of laundry or a pot of water or one of her garden tools or sometimes combinations of those things, balancing Gracie on her hip while folding towels with a trowel sticking out of her back pocket. She inked in Liza's middle name and looked up.

"What is it, honeybunch?"

"Why didn't you finish college?"

They'd heard bits and pieces about their mother's wild undergraduate days, information characterized primarily by Marilyn's embarrassment and David's teasing. That evening her mom frowned, rising to get the Wite-Out from the drawer by the phone.

"A slight hitch in cosmic timing." She squinted, blotting at the paper with the tiny brush.

"But why did you— I mean, you were so close to finishing, weren't you?" Her mother had always seemed highly intelligent, well read; last week she had come up behind Violet and, peering at the pages of *Jane Eyre*, said, "Oh, she hasn't learned about Mr. Rochester's *wife* yet?," ruining the surprise. "You had— Didn't you *want* things? Why did you just—stop?"

"I wanted a life with your dad," she said, and it struck Violet as wildly narrow-minded, old-fashioned, *sad*.

"But you could have finished college in Iowa, couldn't you?"

"Almost none of my credits transferred, as it were. And we were broke. And then Wendy arrived." She spoke as though Wendy had orbed down from a star or staggered through their door on the run from a refugee camp. She'd stopped filling out the form, set down the Wite-Out. "Does it embarrass you, Viol? I'm— I have to say, I don't know where this is coming from. It just wasn't in the cards for me. I've thought about going back since, but I— Well, things got in the way. I didn't finish college because I chose not to finish college."

"But *why*?" Not going to college, for Violet, was a decision akin to relinquishing a limb.

"What kind of a question is that, sweetheart?"

She was trying to picture the fact that her mother had once been her same age, that she'd once been in high school, the world at her fingertips. She knew her grandmother had died when her mom was a teenager, and that her grandfather had worked a lot, but her mom had plenty of options regardless; she'd grown up with money, certainly more money than they had now, especially with four kids instead of one.

"But didn't you want *more*?" she asked.

"More what, Violet? For God's sake."

"Like more—for yourself?"

Her mom looked down at the form in front of her, twisted her wedding ring around her finger. "There were times when I wanted that, sure. But you can't— Sweetie, it all looks so black and white right now, I know. But that's not how life ends up being. There's— It's mostly gray areas. It's not *this* versus *that*. It's just—things come at you, and you twitch in one direction or the other, and suddenly you're graduating from medical school." She drummed her fingers on the kitchen table. "Or you're an exhausted mother of four, trying not to burn the pork chops while your teenage daughter grills you about your lack of tutelage."

"I didn't mean— I just meant that I don't understand why."

"I'm crazy about your father. I'm nuts about the whole lot of you. That's why."

"Because you're insane?"

Her mother, having regarded her previously with testiness, laughed, hard. "Well, that's what it comes down to for all of us, isn't it? God, where did any of you girls come from?" The spell had been broken; her mom had risen again to look in the oven.

CHAPTER EIGHTEEN

When the doorman called Wendy to tell her that her sister was in the lobby, she was momentarily excited, envisioning Violet with her tail between her legs—or, better yet, Violet in combat mode, ready to have a candid conversation with her, finally, for the first time in over a decade. But it was Liza to whom she opened her door a minute later, wan and wide-eyed.

"Hi," her sister said. "Ryan left me."

And while she acknowledged the parallel—Violet had said as much to her, fifteen-plus years ago, *Rob left me and I'm pregnant*—this was, of course, entirely different, and it was actually kind of chilling because she and Liza got along well enough, but they'd never been close, certainly never show-up-in-crisis-unannounced close.

"Strong lede." She ushered Liza inside. "Do you want—water? Decaf? Arsenic?"

Liza shook her head, folding her legs up cross-legged on the couch. "I'm sorry for just showing up like this. I didn't have anywhere else to—"

"What's that?" Wendy said, joking, as ever, to avoid betraying that she was hurt. "I'm your first-choice sounding board in the event of any emergency? I'm the most sage and levelheaded person you know?"

Liza smiled dimly.

She sat down beside her. "What happened?"

"I'm not—sure. A lot of things."

"Like, he just left, physically, now?"

"Last night. He's moving to the Upper Peninsula."

"Shit," she said. *"Why?"*

"He has a friend who's a wind scientist or something." Her sister shook her head hard, like a little kid adamantly denying blame. "It was— It's complicated."

"Does it have anything to do with the fact that you smell like men's deodorant?"

Liza colored. "I've been wearing Ryan's. The smell of his makes me feel less nauseous than the smell of mine."

"Nause*ated*," Wendy corrected her, their decades-old joke, gentle mockery of their medically precise father. She recalled Miles correcting her in the same way, in the early days of their marriage, and he'd sounded so like her dad that she'd laughingly threatened annulment. "Look at you. Knocked up. Wearing Degree for Men."

Her sister smiled feebly, but she could tell she was being too jaunty for Liza's taste. People had this reaction to her more often than not.

"Tell him to come back now. If he doesn't get why that's important, I'll tell him for you." She paused, Miles on her mind now, not that he wasn't always, not that he hadn't taken half her mind and left her with half of his. "Miles and I got into a huge fight when I was pregnant. About humidifiers." She saw herself, across from him in their under-construction nursery, Richard Scarry–themed; she'd been not quite as pregnant as Liza was now and was railing at her husband about the potential toxicity of humidified air; Miles had printed an article from the Internet and was waving it in her face, how the air wasn't *toxic* but *pur*ified, that they'd all sleep better if they put one by the crib. "It was dumb," she said. "But he left for, like, six hours, at eleven o'clock at night, and when he came home I told him that if he left us, he'd be a biological coward."

"A biological coward?"

"If you leave someone when she's pregnant with your child you're solidifying the fact that you're evolutionarily weak. Which most men are, in my opinion, but not quite so overtly. But shit happens. The important thing is coming back."

"I'm not sure I want him coming back," Liza said quietly. "I'm not sure either of us wants that. I'm starting to think that it— I don't know. I think maybe this is how it has to be."

"Pretty fatalistic thinking."

"I'm trying to be *real*istic, actually."

"Could be the same thing." She squeezed Liza's knee. "God, it's hard to be a person in the world, isn't it?"

Her sister nodded blankly.

"I can't fucking handle it sometimes," Wendy continued. "Everything's so miserable, and we're all just a bunch of giant narcissistic babies wandering around pretending we know what the fuck we're doing. Everyone except Mom and Dad, who are so fucking happy they make me want to put my head in the oven."

"Are you—being serious?" Liza asked, suddenly straight-spined and teacherly.

"Define *serious*."

"I just mean that nobody would blame you," Liza said.

Wendy registered the statement in all its humorlessness, then looked up at her sister, who was staring at her like some kind of Vision-Questing interventionist. "Jesus Christ, Liza, are you fucking joking?"

"No, no—I mean—of course we would all—I just mean you've been through a lot, and it would be an entirely natural reaction to that level of—you know, *trauma*, to just shut down. To lose the will to . . ."

"Are you saying you'd understand if I lost the will to live?"

"*No,* I just mean that it wouldn't be— God, you're boxing me into a corner here, Wendy."

"You don't counsel people, do you? Like, at your job?"

"Not really."

"Good," Wendy said. "I'm not being serious. Jesus. And we're talking about you. Whose life, for once, seems to be more fucked up than mine."

And her sister broke down then, another single pregnant woman self-immolating on her sofa. "I can't do this my*self,*" she said. "I thought I wanted Ryan out of the picture because he's been—well, a mess, really, lately; he's been really struggling, Wendy, for a while, like totally catatonic, and it's felt kind of like I already *have* a kid, so I've been worried about him being able to be a father to his *own* kid, but now that he's actually *gone* I don't know what I was thinking. And God, the timing couldn't be worse with work; it looks like I got pregnant to take advantage of my benefits as permanent faculty; you should *see* how my department chair looks at me now, like I'm fucking radioactive."

"You're going to be okay," Wendy said.

"There's a *person* inside of me that I'm supposed to keep *alive.*"

She watched Liza's brain catch up with her mouth, and her sister reached first to touch a hand to her belly, as though in apology to her baby, and then for Wendy's wrist, squeezing it like their mother sometimes did when she felt emphatic about something.

"Oh, my God, Wendy, I'm sorry. I didn't mean—"

"Don't worry about it."

"I just meant that—"

"You're fucking terrified," Wendy said. "Of course you are. But you *are* going to be okay. And you're not going to be by yourself. Mom and Dad are super-stoked and they're going to be all over you to babysit. And Violet will seize any opportunity to inundate you with smug parental wisdom and remind you she's smarter than you. And I'm also not, like, a total miscreant. I can spoil it rotten. I keep walking by these fucking ludicrous newborn culottes in the window of the Dior boutique. I might be just a ridiculous enough person to buy them for you."

Shortly after she'd gotten pregnant, Miles had come home with a Cubs onesie he'd bought from a street vendor by Wrigley Field, and everything had felt real, then, for the first time, her baby and its devoted, doting father. She swallowed. "There will be tons of people to love your kid, Liza. You know that, right?"

"I just had this—image. Like we grew up so—like how you *want* your kids to grow up."

"That's a matter of opinion, I think," Wendy said. "And things usually don't turn out exactly how we imagine they will."

Liza paused. "I didn't mean that nobody would blame you."

"If I offed myself? Thanks, Lize."

"You know what I meant?"

"I took it to mean that you think I've been pretty violently fucked. But that plays to my point. Shit happens, people leave, and you can still end up being rich enough to live in the same building as Oprah."

"I thought she left Chicago."

"I mean, she *allegedly* did."

"Oprah does not live in your building, Wendy."

"You can forget about me buying a Burberry trench for your baby if you keep up that attitude."

Liza smiled. "I came here because I was hoping you would temporarily lure me into the illusion that everything's going to be okay."

"And?"

Liza reached for her hand again, but this time she held it, didn't let go. "Thank you, Wendy."

. . .

An upswing: Grace had a crush on a boy and she made just enough money to pay her rent and buy a quarterly avocado and/or nongeneric tampons, if she was feeling decadent. These were the important details, and the ones on which she chose to focus. She'd started going to Orion with regularity, stopping after work on days when Ben was there. She'd quickly grown familiar with his schedule, which seemed like either a step in the right direction of a romantic relationship or unequivocal stalker behavior. And she'd sit across from him at the counter, legs swinging from the high stool, and they'd talk about anything—the underratedness of *Pete & Pete*, her weird oboist boss, interpersonal dramas within Ben's pickup soccer league—and that wonderful thing would happen where hours would pass by in seconds; she'd look at her watch and see it was suddenly 10:00 p.m., a phenomenon anathema to her lately, because every other area of her life seemed to be creeping along, slouching toward nothing at all.

She was most acutely reminded of how royally screwed she was during contact with her family. When they weren't on the phone, she was able to ignore many of the details of her circumstances, let everything blur at the edges a little like when she watched Netflix without her contacts. She'd begun to limit her communication with her parents and her sisters—the latter was much easier than the former, because all of her sisters seemed to be at peak stations of selfishness; but her parents called her at least once a week, usually more.

"Gosling," her mom said when she answered. "I've missed the sound of that little voice."

It was a Saturday evening and she had just done a hair mask with her two remaining eggs that were a week past their sell-by date. She sat against the wall next to her refrigerator, where her service was the strongest. "It's not *little*; it's just a regular voice." She paused. "Sorry."

"Is now a bad time, sweetheart?" her mom said, laughing uncertainly.

"No. No, it's fine. Sorry, Mom. It's good to hear your voice too."

"Dad and I just spent much of our dinner discussing how much we miss you. Are you bogged down with school work? I saw it's been raining there for almost a week."

"I'm—pretty bogged, yeah. How did you know it's raining here?"

"Dad and I added you to the weather trackers on our phones."

It was the nicest thing she'd heard in some time, the fact that people existed on the earth who gave a shit whether or not she was enduring excessive precipitation. She combed her fingers through her hair, trying to decide if it felt softer, wondering if Ben would notice its shine, wondering what it would feel like to have *Ben* run his fingers through her hair, down her back. They'd go have a beer sometimes, after his shift, and last night he'd flicked a piece of lint from the sleeve of her shirt. She'd panicked, at the time, so unprepared for intimate contact, and Ben, laughing, had apologized for startling her, but now she felt the ghost of his touch on her arm while her mom yammered on about the hardware store and Jonah's martial arts.

She swallowed. She'd become preoccupied with sex for the first time in her life, surreptitiously borrowing D. H. Lawrence and Catullus and *Lolita* from the library. She had once gone so far as to type out the single, shameful word—*porn*—before slamming her laptop closed in terror. She'd become obsessed, from afar, with the construction of Ben's body, with the way his shoulders looked straining against the back of his T-shirt, with the dark hair she'd seen once on his lower belly as he reached to get a bag of coffee beans from a high shelf, with the smell of his sweat when he got close enough. She'd read that some boys could tell when they were having sex with virgins, which of course made her terribly nervous.

"Before I forget," her mom said, jolting her back to attention. "I wanted to give you the new credit card number so you could get your flight home for Christmas."

She'd forgotten the inconvenient fact of holidays. She'd managed to evade Thanksgiving by citing a crushing midterm exam schedule, but she felt somehow blindsided by the existence of Christmas. It wasn't that she didn't *want* to see them. In fact, she was wildly homesick, would've loved nothing more than to spend a week or two kicking around at the house on Fair Oaks, snuggling with the dog, sleeping until noon and eating her mom's grilled cheese. She wanted to hear from Liza, no holds barred, what it felt like to be pregnant; she wanted to drink fancy wine on Wendy's couch while her sister tipsily bought her expensive handbags online. She would've liked to go grocery shopping with her dad and to play Candy Land with her nephews and to finally meet Jonah, her sister's mysterious progeny, who'd already seemed to have been absorbed wholeheartedly into the fibers of the family, who was spoken of so highly that it made her kind of jealous. One of the few perks of being the youngest kid was the fact that you didn't have little siblings to be jealous of, but Jonah was a game changer, and it seemed ludicrous that she was the only one in the family who hadn't met him, a fact that only made everyone feel farther away.

But as she pictured how these things would unfold—eating the grilled cheese would mean sitting with her mother at the table, having to lie to her face; everything she would say about herself to her newfound nephew would be at least slightly false; her sisters had an uncanny ability to extract the truth from her—the risk of it all started to feel enormous. She couldn't keep this up forever, of course—things would inevitably implode, she knew, and probably soon; she couldn't believe she hadn't told them yet; she couldn't believe that she didn't have a plan for the coming year, a *real* plan involving some kind of forward motion, another go at the LSATs or a lower-bar round of law school applications or a ballsy move to San Francisco to live with her rich friend Caitlin and get an entry-level marketing job. But she hadn't done any of those things, and every day the lie was growing like mold, furring her judgment.

"Mama," she said without meaning to, her voice now truly pathetically small.

"What is it, Goose?" Her mom sounded concerned, but then interrupted herself: "I'm on the phone with Gracie, sweetheart; could you ask David?"

She had to be talking to Jonah. Her replacement, filling the place she'd once inhabited and of an appropriate age to actually *need* parenting.

"Love? You okay?"

She cleared her throat. "I'm fine. I— Actually, I feel so terrible about this, but I . . ."

"Of course you're coming home," her mother said, the statement part question.

"It's just that I—got an offer I kind of can't refuse." She conjured up an image of some pedigreed friends, hearty souls who vacationed in wood-paneled chalets. "I'm going skiing. With a few friends from school."

"Which friends?"

She tried to ignore the way her mom's voice had wilted. "Um. Emily." Emily she'd mentioned before, a made-up bisexual Wisconsinite from her fictitious study group. "And Sharon." She froze. Where had *that* come from? Who, other than those born before 1960, was named *Sharon*? But she just had to go with it. This was one of the drawbacks of living a lie, the constant need to be ten steps ahead of where you thought you'd need to be. "Her parents have a house in the Alps," she said.

"The *Alps*? In *Switz*erland?"

Fuck, fuck, fuck. "I meant Aspen," she said. "Sorry, I'm super-tired."

"Wow, sweetheart." Her mom's voice was undeniably wounded, despite the fact that she was obviously trying to be enthusiastic. "That sounds like a wonderful vacation. But of course we'll— Gosh, I feel like I haven't seen you in forever, honey. I miss you."

The niggling sense again of *how easy* it would be to collapse right now, confess, take a red-eye home and let her parents take care of her. But then her phone buzzed with a text message, and she pulled it away from her ear to look at it: *You around? Up for a drink? Comeback, 8ish?* Every time her screen glowed with his name she felt a tiny door opening up inside of her, one through which she could enjoy little pockets of her life.

She returned to her call. "I miss you too," she said. If she paused too long to consider anything, she felt a sickly vertigo. "And I'm really sorry to miss Christmas, but I—like, I feel like it's important to be making friends, trying to find my footing here again since almost everyone from Reed left, and I . . ."

"Of course," her mom said. "Of course that's important. We'll be a skeleton crew anyway; Violet and Matt will be in Seattle. You live your life, Goose. Dad and I will be here whenever."

There was a downside, guilt-wise, of having the most wonderful parents known to man. She swallowed the lump in her throat. *I'm sorry I am such a garbage person-slash-daughter,* she did not say. "I've got to go, Mom. I'm meeting a friend for a drink."

"Sure. Have fun, sweetheart. I love you."

"Love you too," she said, and she hung up the phone, texted Ben back *Be there in 20*, and flew out the door and into the chilly evening mist before she could fully digest what a monstrous asshole she'd become.

1996

It was rooted in chivalry, his offer to drop Gillian off at her car, because the windchill was twelve below, but David felt something else taking hold with her beside him in the passenger seat, something that quickened his pulse and left an acidic sickness at the back of his throat. They'd been stealing away to dinner after work for weeks, meandering meals with tacked-on rounds of drinks.

"Of all the places to live in the world," Gillian said, blowing big dramatic puffs of air into her cupped hands, "we've chosen the Midwest." The *we* struck him as odd, as though he and Gillian had, together, planted a flag in the soil of Illinois.

"Insanity," he said absently, angling out of his parking space. Her presence contracted and expanded next to him, filling the car like monoxide, scent of cold air and kinetic energy, static and spearmint. He'd learned a great deal about her, their meals together allowing an impressive coverage of ground: she'd spent a year abroad in Italy when she was in college and had retained bits of the language and an affinity for the country's dry red wines; she'd voted for Perot because she had a soft spot for crazy underdogs; she'd broken her right clavicle while cycling and the bone had been improperly set, resulting in a visible notch beneath her skin. He tried to allow himself to experience their conversations without any real-time introspection. On his way home after their dinners, he ticked off reasons why they weren't doing anything wrong.

"I'm parked right up here," she said.

He pushed the gearshift back into park beside her little gray Honda. She didn't move.

"If you could live anywhere else," she asked, "where would you choose?"

"Huh." He fiddled with his heating vent.

"I have a list," she said.

"I guess I've never thought about it."

"You've never thought about living somewhere else?" The note of surprise in her voice shamed him. Was it so unheard of, that he'd never envisioned an alternative? His family was here. The rest was white noise, as far as he'd always been concerned.

But now, in the car, he considered it. He'd always liked the winter—the ground had been white on the days both Wendy and Violet were born; one evening in Iowa City, before the children, the furnace had broken, and he'd come home to find Marilyn waiting for him, naked in a nest of blankets on the living room floor. The best thing about the cold was the comfort that came from escaping it. The warmth pulsed from the vents while the air outside the car crackled with the bone-numbing negatives of early February. He wondered if it ever got this cold in Italy.

"Siberia might be nice," he said, but Gillian didn't laugh. "Have I given you my hearty endorsement of snow tires yet? We've got at least a couple more months of precipitation."

"David."

"They really make a difference." Nothing had happened between them. He reminded himself of this at intervals each time they went to dinner. But he knew how to order a glass of wine for her, and he knew she'd always felt estranged from her parents, and he knew she'd gone on a series of unsuccessful dates in the fall with a high school math teacher who was an

amateur parasailor. He'd grown accustomed to her conversational rhythms, to the weight of her silences, to her wit, which
was often so dry as to be overlooked.

Gillian shifted incrementally closer. "I'm not—imagining
this, am I?"

"Imagining what?"

"Come on, Mr. Observant Feminist. Help me out here." She
leaned in—his heart stopped; she smelled—he could finally
experience it himself, from a point of remove, the scent his wife
loved—like the grainy silt of latex gloves. She put her hand
over his.

He exhaled, and it wasn't until he did that he realized he'd
been holding his breath. "I can't," he said. It almost felt more
intimate than kissing, the breath of his words so close to her
face, the chapped skin as her fingers laced between his own.
"I'm sorry."

"I'm not looking to interfere with anything," she said. "I just
thought . . ."

"I didn't mean to—mislead." He still hadn't moved his hand.

An inch of charged particles between their faces. Warm
boozy breath, and he couldn't tell if it was his or hers. The dull
shock of her hand moving up to his forearm.

"You're not imagining it," he said after a minute.

The smile that bloomed on her face was sudden and girlish.

"But I'm not—that man."

"What man?" She put her hand on his thigh, and he was so
used to the gesture, one his wife made often when they drove
together—her little proprietary hand just patting his leg hello,
an idle expression of affection—that it took him a few beats to
realize what was happening.

"Gillian . . ."

"I just— I need to— I like you so much. I'm never happier
than when I'm with you, lately," she said. And though he realized the same was true for him, he knew he could never admit

it, that to do so would be damning, forever, even if Marilyn never found out. "It's just *easy* with you, you know?"

"I'm married, Gillian." He couldn't remember the last time he'd felt so anxious. "I can't— This isn't—" He reached down and took her hand, lifted it away from his leg. "You're my friend. I'm flattered. But—"

"I'm not crazy."

He swallowed. "You're not crazy."

She smiled at him sadly. "You're too nice for your own good."

"I should get going."

She hadn't yet moved. "Back to the Arctic." Eye contact that lasted a second too long. She leaned in closer. "Thanks for your company, David."

She kissed him—dry, quick, like a goodnight—and was gone.

When he got home he was surprised to find Marilyn awake, reading on the couch in what didn't seem like enough light.

"Hey," he said. The house was quiet. She didn't look at him. He was unused to seeing her stationary like this; lately when he came home she was either going full speed—packing lunches, keeping an eye on Wendy, trying to assure the other girls that their parents were still wholly extant beings, still available should they, too, God forbid, find themselves in crisis—or dead asleep. "Hi, sweetie," he repeated, and finally her eyes traveled upward, slowly, like they could just barely be bothered to register him.

"I called you," she said finally, flatly, and his heart immediately started racing.

"Oh."

"Six weeks," she said. She set down her book. "Adrian said you switched to volunteering at the clinic in the *mornings* six weeks ago."

"Why were you calling?" he asked, still trying to hang on to some modicum of normalcy, though he knew, then, that he had irrevocably ruined something, he hoped not everything.

"I put Gracie to bed early. The girls are out and about. I was seeing if you wanted to have dinner." Very few things that she possibly could have said would have made him feel more terrible. He came into the living room and sat in a chair across from her. He could see, through her indignant playacting, that she was trying not to cry.

"Sorry," he said. "Sorry, honey, I was . . ." He stopped. Changing his schedule without telling her was one thing, but outright lying was another entirely. "I'm sorry."

"Sorry for what? What have you been doing?" She didn't sound angry so much as wounded. "You've been getting home so late."

He'd never been able to lie convincingly. "I went to get dinner with Gillian."

"With—*my* Gillian?"

He paused. Of course it made sense for Marilyn to identify her that way: her doctor. Because while Marilyn saw Gillian maybe ten times a few years ago and he saw her nearly every day, Marilyn's ten times had been far more intimate. *My Gillian.* Her Gillian, *of course*, because Gillian had delivered their youngest daughter.

Oh, Christ, he was an asshole.

"Just dinner," he said quietly.

"It's after eleven." She now sounded decidedly hurt. "That's kind of a long dinner." It wasn't a long dinner for him and Marilyn; on rare nights when they had a sitter they would meander sweetly into the wee hours, drinking wine and then walking it off languidly around the city before they drove back to the suburbs. It was a long night for him with anyone but his wife.

"We were just talking," he said. "Lots of—just stuff at the office. Lots to talk about."

In fact they hadn't talked about work at all. And this was worse. He knew it with certainty now, looking at his tired, pretty wife, wounded on their couch, imagining the worst for possibly the first time in their marriage. Because it was the same at their four-year anniversary or their fourteenth: he was never concerned that Marilyn would stray, and vice versa.

"I'd argue that *we've* also had quite a bit to talk about," she said. "Perhaps you and I would benefit from an hour or five of conversation over dinner." And then she seemed to notice herself, her submissive posture and the weakness of her voice, and she sat up straight and met his eyes. "You know I trust you," she said evenly. "But you get why this might make me feel—not great?" A conversational ease had crept back into their dialogue and he started to relax.

"It was really nothing, honey."

"Has it been going on for six weeks?"

He froze again. "Well," he said. Her face fell. "We just kind of fell into a habit," he said. "We've both been really stressed out."

She laughed meanly. "Well, in that case," she said.

"Marilyn."

"No. By all means, if you're the only two *really stressed-out* people left on earth, go ahead. Spend all the time you want with her. Don't bother coming home; it's like a goddamn Buddhist retreat around here so I can see why you wouldn't feel comfortable bringing your stress to me. I probably wouldn't recognize it if it punched me in the face."

"In fairness, it's not like you've been so forthcoming with me."

She paled in her lively Irish way, a deathly whiteness with two spots of color high on her cheeks that betrayed she was livid. "Because you won't *listen*," she said. "I've tried to talk to you and you don't want to hear it. And *in fairness*, I haven't found a replacement who goes out to dinner with me."

Again he clammed up; Marilyn's anger was extremely rare but lethal when it did make an appearance.

"Do you understand why that offends me?" she asked. "Do you get why that *hurts* me? That you'd rather go talk to a colleague than to me? Because all I want to do lately is talk to you, David. And if the feeling isn't mutual, then—fine. I don't know. But I wish you could at least do me the courtesy of telling me that." She was clearly on the verge of tears but still wasn't crying.

He had rebuffed Gillian's advances. He'd been so close to being with another woman and had chosen his wife instead. He had a pleasant, easy outlet, a friend with whom he could spend unencumbered evenings, and it was so much more palatable than the stress of their home, and yet here he was, with Marilyn, as ever. And suddenly something gave way and he was *furious*, all of his guilt and sadness overpowered by a potent and specific anger. He'd done everything he was supposed to. He'd *always* done everything he was supposed to, especially tonight, especially when there was another woman in his car and he'd played his Marilyn card; he'd chosen Marilyn over everything else, like always, and so what the hell did he have to feel bad about?

"You don't understand why I haven't felt able to talk to you lately? You're like a ghost, Marilyn. You're the one shutting me out. You're the one who refuses to acknowledge that anything's happening. And you're such a fucking martyr that even if you *did* admit that, all we'd hear about is how hard things are for you." He froze then, acutely aware of the sensation in his bones, the feeling of having overstepped his bounds, *their* bounds, unspoken bounds that they'd erected years ago and agreed not to cross. He'd risen from his seat at some point during the last minute and was aware of himself looming over her, face warm from the two cocktails he'd had during dinner. "Shit," he said softly, weakening. He would have apologized then, but she had untangled her limbs and was sitting up straight, rigid, on the couch. She was watching him with such distinct hurt but also with her own breed of anger, and he knew that it was too late to take back what he'd said. After a minute she stood up and went to the kitchen and he heard a drawer slam and then smelled the unmistakable indoor scent of a cigarette.

He followed her. She was leaning against the sink and had the window propped open and was smoking mechanically, severely, eyes still threatening to spill over.

"This is the problem with you," she said finally. "You're so nice until you're not. And then you're the biggest asshole on the planet. Why have I never heard any of this before? If I've just been consistently fucking things up, why haven't you *mentioned* it?"

"I didn't mean that," he said, and she regarded him curiously. "I mean—I meant some of it. But not— Jesus, honey, I'm over-whelmed, okay? I don't know what to do with that."

"I have a couple of ideas that don't involve you dating my obstetrician."

"I'm not *dating* her. Jesus Christ, we've had dinner a few times." Gillian's lips on his: the thing he decided, right then, that he would never mention. But then: "Talking to her is a hell of a lot more pleasant than *this*."

"So sorry I haven't made things more fun for you." She turned her back to him, smoking out the window, and then she told him flatly, drama-free, to sleep in the guest room. "Or on the couch. I don't care. Sleep on the lawn. But if the kids see you, you're explaining it to them."

"What am I supposed to—?"

"You're on your own, David. Just try not to traumatize them."

He had not slept in a room without his wife, save for eve-nings when the children encroached upon their space, in nearly twenty years.

"But tomorrow—" *Help*, he wanted to say. He wanted her to hear it in his voice. *Help me out here.* Nothing on her face indicated that she registered his desperation. "Honey." *Look at me, honey.* They didn't do things like this. They never fulfilled those faddish clichés of their bored, swanky neighbors. They fought sometimes, sure, but they never slept apart. It never seemed worth it to sacrifice that part of their day, when they were safely, warmly together, the part when they could kiss and grope and *talk* like teenagers if they wanted, unafraid of the discerning youthful filters of their children. She started upstairs and then stopped, not turning to face him.

"Tell them we had an argument. Don't tell them why. We can deal with that later." She went up another stair and then paused again. "This isn't an argument, though." Another step. "For your own reference." She paused for just a second, and then she disappeared from his view.

Long after she had fallen asleep, he crept into their room and was sitting on the edge of the bed, careful not to wake her. Her face was puffy from crying, he assumed, though she hadn't shed a single tear in front of him. (That pack of cigarettes in the junk drawer, though: that had surprised him.) It was all he could do not to wrap himself tearfully around her body, like Gracie did after a tantrum. The instincts his daughters had in childhood were actually often not far from his own feelings toward his wife—to hug, to grab, to allow her to bury and protect and engulf; because despite what he'd just said, she was the most comforting presence he had ever known.

He let his eyes wander around the room, adjusting to the darkness. There was a board book on the nightstand, which meant that she'd let Gracie come into their bed for her story time. Militant stacks of laundry in a basket in the corner, waiting for distribution. In the window: a few of his shirts hanging from the curtain rod, back from the dry cleaner's. Though they were fighting, though things between them were worse than they had ever been, though those things were clearly pervading the atmosphere of the house—quieting their daughters, making them anxious—she was persisting. She was taking care of their children and their clothing, their quiet life, all manners of tucking in and folding and cuddling and driving, picking up and dropping off, and he was lying to his wife and his children and his patients so he could go have cocktails with a woman who was kind and capable, whose company brought him undeniable pleasure, but who didn't have the same ties he did, a single woman who reminded him, in fact, quite a bit of his wife, but who would only ever be his friend. A single woman who seemed more aware of this tension than he was. He rested a hand very gently on his wife's shoulder just to remind himself of her, the person who'd brought him to life. No wonder she'd been crying. No wonder she kept secret cigarettes more than five years after she'd quit. No wonder she'd relegated him to the living room. He was a child. His wife was married to a child.

He remembered feeling a similar inadequacy the night Wendy was born. Marilyn was twenty-two and more frightened than he had ever seen her, terrified of motherhood and its ironclad accompanying responsibility—but the minute Wendy arrived, the very second he laid her, squalling, on her mother's chest, Marilyn shifted. She came of age instantaneously and suddenly she was *Wendy's mom*; she was in her element and everything clicked. And he stood there, his eyes filled with tears, a brand-new and unexpected panic roiling in his gut. And it had been the same thing three times over—*another girl, another girl, another girl*—despite mounting responsibility and the steady accumulation of debt and details and obligations and *years*, simple numerical age. Each time his wife shifted fluidly into the mother of two, then three, then four; into a homeowner, a bookkeeper, a crisis counselor, a chauffeur. Caring for their house and their children while also tending to his aging father—Richard now declining, on dialysis, and in need of at-home nursing care—to their rambunctious dog, to him. She did this, and the structure of his daily life remained relatively unchanged, and yet he was the one fucking things up. He, on this terrible night, had given her one more enormous crisis, a ten-foot wave of malicious ineptitude. And she—his lovely wife—had cried herself to sleep, landing in a contorted position that would have been funny under better circumstances.

Liza had been planning on going to a friend's house that night, but in fact she was home, home to hear her father come in from the garage; home to hear her mother's voice, scary in its cool measurement, say the name Gillian again and again; home to smell cigarette smoke from the kitchen; home to hear her mother retreat to her bedroom and sob, the most frightening noise she'd ever heard.

Gillian, Gillian, Gillian. She'd heard her name dozens of times: her father's partner, her mother's doctor, the woman who'd saved her baby sister and her mom. But she was more than that, clearly, the catalyst for something. A major player in this terrible year they were having, during the time that Wendy was under informal house arrest and their entire family was abiding by a ridiculous meal plan that prominently featured red meat and fish, though Liza had been contemplating an experiment with vegetarianism. Their house was chaos; after Wendy's "incident" with the pills her dad began working more and her mom threw herself full-throttle into Wendy's care. Was her father having an affair? It was unthinkable, but she also couldn't come up with another reason for her mother to be crying like she was. To be smoking cigarettes in the house—to be smoking cigarettes *period*—like she was.

Her parents had spent that night apart—*Gillian, Gillian, Gillian*—her father on the couch and her mother weeping in their bedroom, and Liza curled, sleepless, under her covers, wanting to tell her sisters, afraid to tell her sisters, utterly confused.

CHAPTER NINETEEN

"*Bas*tard."

Liza heard her father's voice sharply from the kitchen, not muted like the lilt of her mother, a harsh bass note over the melodic rise and fall of *David, please* and *Keep your voice down.* She'd just delivered the news of Ryan's departure to her parents and was seated on the couch, hands folded primly in her lap, feeling like some kind of defiled virgin, a ruined high school sophomore. She'd made a feeble joke about *conscious uncoupling* that neither seemed to understand. Her mother's face had drained of color and her father's, compensating, reddened vividly, and her mother had risen from her seat in the rocking chair and come over to sit beside her and said *Oh, sweetheart,* and held her hand; her father, meanwhile, had stood up, paced a few lengths back and forth across the living room, the dog rising with intrigue to follow him.

"Let's get you some tea," her mom had said finally, squeezing Liza's knee before she rose. "Come help me make some tea, honey," she'd said pointedly to David, stopping him midstride. She'd seen, in profile, her mother's raised eyebrows, and her father had consented, compliant as a child, and followed her into the kitchen. He still hadn't met Liza's eyes.

Which led to the "*bas*tard" and the clink of mugs and Liza sitting alone, the dog coming over to her to shove his wet black snout between her thighs. He glanced in both directions and then loped onto the couch, long limbs like a horse, and settled next to her. Pets on the furniture were strictly forbidden in her parents' house, but Loomis was nimble and wily, their final child at home, and he got away with more than most. The dog rested his head in her lap and she stroked the soft bristles of his fur. She was good with dogs; dogs had always liked her; she would be fine as a single parent; why wouldn't her father look at her?

She thought of the word *bastard* and applied it—though of course her father had been referring to Ryan—to the feeble movement inside of her: she was, technically, now carrying a bastard child, was she not? She heard the teakettle whistle and then her father returned.

"Loomis, get *down* from there," he said, and the next thing she knew her dad was sitting next to her in the dog's spot, placing a rough hand on her head, petting the hair at her crown. "It's going to be fine, you know," he said, and something about this made her start to cry, something about the familiar weight of her father's hand and the fact that he'd broken from his repressive masculine shell to come and comfort her. It made her at once want to submit to his touch—move back in with her parents and let them raise her baby and live forever as a child in an adult's body—and feel completely convinced that it *was* going to be fine. "You're a wonderfully capable person, Liza. This baby is very lucky already because of that alone. Let your mother make you some tea and we'll go from there, okay?"

She laughed in spite of herself into the familiar cottony human smell of his shirt.

"Are you two mocking me?" her mother asked, appearing in the doorway, the dog gravitating to her. She smiled kind of sadly at Liza as she rubbed Loomis's ears.

"Never," her dad said, jostling Liza gently against him.

"Come sit with us, kid. I was just about to ask Liza to explain this *conscious uncoupling* thing."

She talked, sandwiched between her parents, about various divorced celebrities and the faculty daycare she was looking into. After a while she felt herself getting lethargic and her mother leaned away to look at her.

"Are you eating enough, sweetheart?"

"I eat constantly. I think I'm just tired."

Her mother lifted a hand to her cheek. "Of course you are. Why don't you go lie down?"

Naps were against Liza's nature, even more so after she'd met Ryan—because logistically speaking, not everyone could take naps at all times—but as soon as Marilyn mentioned it she found she could barely keep her eyes open.

Her mother rose. "Come on, honey." She led her to Violet's old room and tucked her into bed like she was a kid. Maybe she could stay here forever. Maybe her parents could help and her kid wouldn't have to go to the faculty daycare after all; maybe they were in the market for another second wind as they'd been with Grace, and now with Jonah; maybe she could sell her house and languish rent-free on Fair Oaks for the rest of her life. "I'm going to leave you a snack on the nightstand in case you wake up hungry. Try to eat something, okay? You'll be doing yourself a favor."

She murmured in response, halfway to sleep, and the last thing she remembered was the faint whiff of lilacs as her mother leaned in to kiss her.

Wyatt was preparing for his upcoming kindergarten musical performance with the fervor of someone headed to Carnegie Hall. In a month's time it would be his turn to be his classroom's Star of the Week, and during his reign, he got to showcase a special talent. So they were sitting together in the living room, and her son was strumming the opening chords of "Have You Ever Seen the Rain?"

"Mama, could Jonah come to my concert?" he asked, interrupting himself.

She froze. He'd been smitten since they'd had Jonah over for dinner, brought up his name with alarming frequency— "Do you think Jonah likes pad thai too, Mama?"; "I'm going to draw Jonah a horse." She'd been careful, popping by her parents' house solo when she could, avoiding family gatherings. But there had been a few times when she'd been forced to take the kids with her, and Wyatt seemed to grow only more enamored. But, Jesus—to have Jonah show up somewhere other than the house on Fair Oaks? The thought made her dizzy.

"He'll be in school, sweetheart," she said, wondering if her son would one day recall her voice and recognize the strain in it, a strain indicative of deep unrest, just as she'd done with her own mother's voice, one trying to save face, *I'm sorry I scared you, little bear.* "Just like you."

How could she possibly explain his presence at Shady Oaks? *This brooding young man just sprang, full-grown, from my tortuous loins. Domestic adoption of recalcitrant adolescents is all the rage; hadn't you heard?* Wyatt was staring at her with such earnest inquisition, her sweet tiny boy who never asked for anything. She reached to brush some hair from his forehead.

"You like Jonah, huh, pumpkin?"

He was arranging his little fingers into a chord position, tongue sticking out of his mouth in concentration. "Uh-huh."

She couldn't think of anything nice to say. "What is it— *about* him that you like so much?"

He strummed the strings. The pick was not much smaller than his hand. "He's funny," he said. "He's nice."

Why didn't it please her more to hear this? Why wasn't she *leaping* at the chance for her forgotten teenage kid to bond with her little boy? Why didn't that fill her heart with something glowing and warm, the fact that you could fuck up everything in your life, make all the wrong decisions, and little bits could somehow still work out for the best? Because she was cognizant of the reality, she supposed, one that Matt had repeatedly articulated: that one thing would inevitably lead to another, that things with Jonah were unfolding whether she wanted them to or not, that she couldn't stay in this pleasant limbo state forever and that there was no way her life—her *family*—could be spared from change.

"Should we practice again?" she asked.

Her son: heartbreakingly shy, cripplingly anxious. He was too nervous to perform on his own, so she'd agreed to provide vocal accompaniment. She and Matt had laughed about it in bed, but when she actually practiced with Wyatt, his frank concentration and the waver in his tiny voice almost brought her to tears. He strummed the first chord and she tapped at the coffee table for percussion. He moved his fingers around the frets to form the opening progression. This little body she'd made, now making music of his own. Her voice wavered, too, when she started in with the vocals.

When they finished, she applauded wildly.

"Mama, why are you crying?"

She shook her head. "I'm just happy, honey. I'm proud of you."

He clambered over, tucking himself under her arm, smiling as though this were the silliest thing he'd ever heard. "Why are you *crying* if you're *happy*?"

She stroked his forehead, breathed him in, contemplating the autonomous intricacy of him, all the things he would learn to do beyond her influence. It was a fair question, but one to which she didn't have an answer.

1996

When Marilyn tried to imagine David and Gillian together, she had to admit she couldn't. Her husband had been a virgin when she met him, and this gave her confidence, an upper hand that neither of them ever acknowledged. She'd never worried about David straying, and part of that was because—stupidly, she thought now—she'd been his first. His only.

He was, objectively speaking, a good-looking man. But he seemed so oblivious to it, so mired in his own head—though she supposed wandering around the grocery with your wife and toddler was a different animal than going to work each day as a handsome free agent. She had always felt a little jealous of this woman with whom her husband spent every day, especially because Gillian had seen her at her most primal, watched her through a difficult labor, reached her gloved hand repeatedly inside of Marilyn's body and, then, eventually, cut into her belly to retrieve a distressed baby Grace.

She wasn't sure what to *do* with this new business of not trusting David. It was nothing she'd ever had to do before. He'd started sleeping in their bed again but she was mostly ignoring him—though not entirely, because to do so would have been too much a comical mimicry of their teenage daughters. She tried to be composed and polite and diplomatic. He still seemed rattled. Once, they'd gone upstairs together and he'd said, in the dark, "Honey, you know I'd never . . ."

And she'd said, impatiently, "I know. It's beside the point."

She did know. But it *was* also beside the point. And those things in concert brought her to his office one afternoon a few weeks later when she knew he had his clinic hours. Gillian was her doctor, but she had also, once, been her confidante. The woman had to know that going out to dinner with David meant something more than *friendship*. She had to know that Marilyn was an adult with feelings and agency, not just the woman on the other end of a phone call who turned *Dr. Sorenson* into a lovesick buffoon. And at the front desk, leaning over the receptionist's shoulder to look at something on the computer, there she was: Gillian.

"Marilyn." She sounded surprised but not incriminated. She came from behind the desk and Marilyn was taken aback when she reached out for a hug. "You look fantastic. It's been so long. Are you here for an appointment or to see David? He's in Englewood this afternoon."

"Not an appointment," she said. Gillian was smiling at her blandly, looking a little confused, not like a woman standing before the wife of the man she'd had an affair with. Confirmation, then. Why didn't it feel better? "I had—ah. Gracie threw something of mine into his briefcase this morning. He said he'd leave it on his desk for me. Do you mind if I run and—"

"Of course," Gillian said. "Come on back." She led her down the long, familiar hallway, past the scales, past the posters on infant nutrition. "How's Grace doing? I haven't seen her since—God, I couldn't tell you. She was in diapers."

"She's great. Out of diapers. Talking nonstop. She's the most energetic human being I've ever had the pleasure of meeting. I don't know where she gets it."

"She's beautiful. That photo on David's desk kills me. Those eyes."

"What photo? When did you— I mean . . ."

Gillian turned to her uncertainly. "You'll see it when you go in there. Front and center."

"Oh, sorry, I—I was going to show you one. But I think it's the same one. So."

Gillian pursed her lips, squinted at her, touched her arm. "How's Wendy doing?"

"Well," she said firmly. "She's doing really well."

"I'm so glad to hear it."

"I don't mean to be rude, but I've got to pick up Grace in a few minutes."

"Of course," Gillian said, holding up her hands. "It's great to see you, Marilyn."

She watched the woman walk away, imagined how she looked through David's eyes.

On his desk: a surprising number of photos. One from their wedding. Wendy and Violet at Christmas in the early days, tiny and velvet-clad. The girls crowded around a newborn Grace. One of Marilyn in her garden, a candid taken by Violet, where she was wearing ridiculous overalls but laughing, happy in a way that she could no longer remember. One of her with Wendy, minutes after she was born, exultant and exhausted. She imagined him purchasing the frames, picking up the prints. It endeared him to her. How she loved him, missed him, wanted to kill him. If someone asked her to poetically describe her marriage, she would articulate that particular feeling, one of simultaneously wanting him pressed against her and also on another continent.

The picture Gillian had mentioned was indeed in the front. David had taken it about a year ago; Grace was cuddled in Marilyn's lap on the couch. She'd been reading *Frog and Toad Are Friends* to their daughter and had stopped to smile tolerantly at her husband, charmed by his initiative and his affection. Gracie had been startled by the flash, looking into the camera with wide, dark eyes. Such a mix of the two of them. Wendy and Liza appeared to be direct descendants of Connolly lineage—photos of Liza now made Marilyn think unequivocally of her own mother. Violet was, without question, the Czech from David's mother's side, not a lick of Irish visible in the dark swoop of her hair or the unseasonable tan of her skin. But Grace: a perfect split, David's hair and forehead and eyes and Marilyn's nose and chin, her mouth a charming combination of both.

All the times they'd fought in the last months. All the times they'd argued over Wendy's treatment, Violet's obstinacy, Liza's isolation, Gracie's arrested development. The house, the dog, the oil in their cars. All the times he'd yelled and she'd wept, or she'd yelled and he'd sat there, stock-still and expressionless, in his collected way that drove her crazy. All the times they'd spoken to each other through the children without even realizing it—"Tell your father you need a ride" or "Ask your mom that, Gracie." All the times they could have been kind to each other and had instead chosen ignorance, solitude. She missed him so much.

"Find what you were looking for?" Gillian asked, appearing in the doorway.

She brushed a wrist across her eyes—was she almost crying? Who *was* she lately?

"You know, I'm remembering now that he said he'd bring it home for me. When you get to be a trillion years old and married for half that, you'll notice things start to slip. Cognitively."

Gillian laughed, and it bothered her, even though she'd been the one to make the joke, because, again, she wasn't *that* much older than Gillian; her husband wasn't coming home each night to a withered crone; she still had energy and verve and a sense of humor, and even if she had *none* of those things, she'd produced and raised his children and made him coffee in the mornings and had the decency not to *poison* it.

"I was lying," Marilyn said bluntly.

"About what?"

"I didn't need something from his office. I came here to talk to you. I lied."

"To me?" Gillian frowned. "Should we— Do you want to go in my office? Is everything okay?"

"I know about you and David," she said. "I know that you've been—seeing each other."

Gillian looked suddenly smaller. "Oh, Marilyn, I—"

"I'm not accusing you of anything. I just came to talk to you about it. I don't want to anymore, but I—I guess I thought, initially, that maybe you'd be able to tell me more. Because he's not telling me anything. This is so inappropriate. I feel like such a—fool."

"It's not—what you think," Gillian said.

"Oh? What do I think?"

"Nothing's . . ." Gillian pulled the door shut. "I know it's a chaotic time for you guys."

"Ah, yes, well." She waved a hand. "The steady accretion of years."

"You have a lot going on."

"What do you— Has he—*said* anything?"

Gillian looked uncomfortable.

"Right," Marilyn said brusquely. "Confidentiality. I'm not a patient anymore."

"David's not my patient; he's my friend."

"Your friend."

"Look, Marilyn, I'd prefer to not—" Gillian's face grew redder by the second; her voice wobbled. "I'm just saying David knows where the lines are. If I've learned anything from talking to him, it's that. He—"

"I *really* don't need to hear reassurance from you that my

husband loves me." She pulled her coat more closely around her and started toward the door.

"I wasn't going to tell you that. I was just going to say that he's a good man."

Marilyn stopped. "I know he is."

She supposed that was part of the problem. Her husband *was* a good man. It was hard to get mad at him. And perhaps it was this—the anticlimax of it all—that frustrated her so much. He hadn't had a traditional affair. She'd confronted first him and then his alleged mistress and both had sincerely denied it. But what they weren't denying was their closeness, the fact that David had actively chosen to spend hours and hours of his limited time with another woman, to confide in someone else his worries and observations. She felt—as she had three years ago, crying in the exam room—so far from him. She could identify that as the problem—not just the distance but the fact that it had grown so much since then, that it was so much more dire than it had been—and there was nothing she could do about it.

"I'm sorry, Marilyn," Gillian said. "I confess I've always envied you. But I also really like you."

The perfect ridiculousness of all this, to be debasing herself for no real reason, to have arrived at this point in her marriage.

"Listen, if you could not— I mean, I can't stop you from— I'm embarrassed, Gillian; I'm mortified by all of this, and if you could not mention to him that we had this conversation, I'd—"

"Of course I won't," Gillian said.

"I owe you my life," she said. "Literally. I realize that. And I'll always be grateful to you for that. But I need you to stay away from my husband. I don't—" She opened her mouth, closed it again. "There's more to it than me."

It was Sunday, and David was home when Marilyn left to go into the city, mowing the lawn in the backyard while Gracie played on the swing set. She came out to say goodbye and found Grace at the top of the slide by herself and immediately dropped her purse and sprinted across the lawn, David oblivious to his surroundings beneath the roar of the mower.

"Honey, what'd we say about no climbing when you're alone?" she asked, breathless.

"Daddy's here," Grace said, smiling at her, ignorant or impish; she had a hard time telling with her youngest daughter: she was either an evil genius or the exact opposite.

"David," she said, but he didn't hear her. He kept walking away from her, finishing his row, and it wasn't until he got to the end and turned around that he saw her staring at him. He turned off the mower and waited for the motor to die.

"Something wrong?" he asked, and she gestured at Grace. "What? I'm ten feet away."

"She's too little to be on the swing set alone."

"No I'm not," Grace chimed in from behind her.

"Oh, for Christ's sake," David said.

"You need to be watching her. I have to *go*, David; your dad's expecting me."

"I'm *not* too little," Grace protested, a quickening in her voice, a tearful breathlessness, and she swung boldly from the bar at the top of the slide, making Marilyn physically convulse.

"Gracie, get down. This second. The right way. On your bottom. Feet first."

"You're turning this into a *scene*," David said. Grace was now crying in earnest, the telltale signs of a tantrum oozing into her little limbs—stiff arms, an indignant stomp of a sneakered foot. She *had* turned it into a scene; she'd found them enjoying a pleasant afternoon in the yard together and she'd come out and ruined it. But when she saw Gracie, alone, at the top of the slide, her head had immediately morphed into a flip-book of gruesome injuries. She couldn't set foot in a hospital again, not anytime soon. There was a time when David would have understood this. But now she'd taken a stance and she had to follow through; all of the parenting books she'd read over the years drove this home. Be firm in your punishments. Don't back down. Don't let your spouse undermine you, even when he is being a childish asshole.

Grace slid despondently down the orange slide, weeping; it would have been funny if Marilyn had been in the mood.

"Honey, come here," she said, but her daughter ran instead to her father. David stooped to pick her up and Grace buried herself in his threadbare polo shirt.

"Thanks for this," David said sarcastically, looking at her over Grace's head.

"Don't talk to me like that," she said. "I'm leaving. I don't know how late I'll be. She needs a bath after dinner tonight."

"No I *don't*," Grace wailed into David's chest, kicking her legs.

She felt suddenly jealous of her daughter for her position in David's arms. When she touched Grace's back, her daughter stiffened, crowed anew. She flicked her eyes up to David.

"Bye," he said, and she thought it might have hurt her too much to reply, so she didn't.

A home health nurse cared for David's dad three times a week, but Marilyn had been spending her Sundays puttering around his house and making him dinner. In Richard's living room, she thought of how much she seemed to annoy David lately, of how he had moved fluidly from guilt and attempts at redemption to this kind of perpetual disdain for her. He hadn't looked at her like that since they lived in Iowa City, when they had the first three girls and were both constantly exhausted and embittered and within arm's length of both a baby and two small children. At least then it made sense; at least then they commiserated, once the kids were in bed. At the house in Albany Park, she was hot and irritable. She held her ponytail away from her neck. She'd just helped Richard with his washing-up and he'd requested a recess before they dove into their requisite marathon of Scrabble. He was in his armchair with his eyes closed and she decided, feeling her own fatigue settle over her like a fog, to rest as well. She hadn't been sleeping much lately. And David was working more. She knew his evenings with Gillian had ceased but in their stead he had picked up extra clinic hours in earnest, as if to karmically atone.

"Rich?" she asked, lifting the material of her shirt and dropping it, creating a breeze. She was going to ask him for something about David as a little kid, some story that might awaken some tenderness within her. She paused. "Never mind."

"Everything okay?"

"Sure. Fine." She felt tears in her eyes but blinked them away.

"You have so many wonderful qualities, Marilyn, but you're a worthless liar."

She laughed, felt one of the tears snake its way down her cheek.

"My son's treating you well, isn't he?"

"Of course." She hadn't told anyone about her distance from him, about Gillian. David's father would hardly be the appropriate audience, but she indulged the thought: *Your son's found himself a girlfriend. Your son's a philistine.* She pictured Richard cuffing David on the side of his head, telling him to pull it together. "Rough patch," she allowed herself to say.

"How's Wendy doing?" Richard asked.

"Oh. She's—" She studied him and tugged a few times at her ponytail. If David were here she would say something blithe and noncommittal about her passable grades or her renewed interest in literature. David was decidedly not here, though; David was at home bonding with their three-year-old, who she hoped would have already forgotten that she hated her mother just like Wendy did. "Her weight's up. Her spirits are—not quite as up. She's pretty miserable at school, I think, but possibly less so than she is at home. We're keeping her to a curfew because I think if she didn't go out we'd all lose our minds, and I have no idea what she's *doing* when she's out but at least she comes home. She's just—existentially unhappy, I think is the problem, and I'm not sure what to do with that, so I'm just trying to make sure that I don't make her *more* unhappy, which is hard because she hates me, but overall she—she's doing better than she was."

"I'm sure she doesn't hate you."

Unable to look at him, she said, "I would place your bets elsewhere, Rich."

"God, if those girls had any idea how lucky they are to have you as a mom."

"That's kind of you to say."

He shifted stiffly and cleared his throat. "I should tell you she's been coming here."

She glanced up, uncomprehending. "Pardon?"

"She comes here sometimes."

"She comes here? Like, *here* here?"

"She showed up once after she got out of the hospital. And she's just kept coming. We talk. We play Scrabble. She's almost as good as you."

She studied him.

"Okay, not almost as good. But not terrible. She's a formidable opponent."

"I'm sorry, Rich, I— Wendy, we're talking about?"

"I think she's needed a place that wasn't home. Don't we all need that sometimes?"

She was going to counter with something about how she herself had never been afforded such a respite, but she supposed that her own visits to Richard's were not entirely altruistic. It was a place where she could go without her children; it was a place where she could go to help her father-in-law that had the convenient side perk of giving her the upper hand with her husband. It was a place where she could be alone and adult.

"I suppose so," she said. "How does she get here?"

"Takes the train," Richard said. "Green to Brown."

"What does she— What do you talk about?"

"Nothing," he said. "Anything. Little things. Her classes. The dog. You."

"Me?"

"You and David. Historical stuff. She calls it her 'origin story,' I'm assuming because of that new-agey socialist school you're sending her to."

She smiled at that. "It's a public high school, Rich."

"I was telling her the other day about the first time I met you. How shocked I was that my son had happened upon such a knockout."

"Well, obviously," she said, blushing.

"How you saved him. You can't know how relieved I was when he found you."

"We found each other," she said. She felt dangerously close to crying. She looked away, but his gaze was so persistent that she finally met his eyes.

"David's a good man," Richard said. "But he's as flawed as the rest of us. He has good intentions but he doesn't always do the right thing. None of us do. If you're unhappy with him, Marilyn, you should talk to him."

"That doesn't work if he's not talking back." It was the closest she would ever come to betraying him.

"I was telling Wendy about those two *kids* sitting at my kitchen table that first time you came over. You were both so young. He didn't take his eyes off you the entire night."

Her throat throbbed. "Rich, really, this is sweet of you to mention but—"

"He's lucky to have you, and he knows it more than he knows anything in the world, and sometimes you just have to remind him. I think you owe it to yourself. If you're even one-tenth as miserable as you look, sweetheart, you've got some real problems."

"I'm not—" she started to say, but she stopped, because she was.

By the end of May, Wendy had lost all of her acquaintances and all of the acquaintances had acquired coveted slots in incoming freshman classes. She had refused to participate in the collegiate rat race, and her parents had stayed quiet about it until one afternoon when she came home and her mother was sitting on the front steps. She hoisted her backpack higher on her shoulder and turned up her headphones, preparing to walk straight past her.

Her mother held up a hand to stop her. "Hi," she said. "Have a minute?"

"Homework."

"You're a second-semester senior," said her mom. "High school is behind you. Your homework is pointless. Aren't you the one supposed to be making these arguments?"

Just when she'd decided to hate her mother forever, she made a joke like this.

"I know you despise me," her mom said lightly, and the easiness of her tone pierced Wendy through the ribs. "But please just sit for a couple of minutes. I want to talk to you."

Wendy, compromising, leaned back against the built-in flower box on the porch.

"*I could never despise you, Mom,*" her mother said, playacting now, embarrassing herself. Pretending they were a normal mother and daughter, that jokes like this could be thrown around casually between them. She seemed to realize that Wendy wasn't going to smile and she dropped the act. "We need to talk about the college thing, Wendy."

"What's to talk about? I'm not going."

"*Yet*. You're not going yet."

"I'm not going ever. It's stupid. I'm not going to go spend another four years with a bunch of maladjusted brats just so I can get a crazy-expensive piece of paper and become, like, that narcoleptic lady who does the filing in Dad's office."

She couldn't be sure, but she thought her mom might have almost smiled at that last bit.

"You can become whatever you want, sweetheart." Her mother almost never called her "sweetheart" and they both seemed to realize this at the same time; Marilyn blushed and Wendy scowled. "We'll do some research. You can apply for next year. Maybe take a community college class. Take some time to get your bearings and figure out what you'd like to do."

"I don't want to do anything."

"I know that's not true," her mother replied. "Look, honey—" Again they both bristled at the *honey*; her mother was off her game. "I had no idea what I wanted to do when I started school. And then I discovered how much I loved to read. And once you find that thing—it can be the tiniest thing, Wendy— possibilities start opening up. You start thinking about your life in a different way. For me it was— There was teaching, or editorial work, even *writing*, I thought about. There were options. Things that I never would have seen had I not gone to college."

"Quoth the woman who dropped out of college to follow a man," Wendy said, and she watched her mother's face fall, a familiar expression that suggested she'd just been cracked over the head with a baseball bat. "I'm just *saying*, like, you're not exactly a paradigm for why college is the answer. Fine—you found some stuff you thought was interesting. But then you left it all behind and married Dad and you—whatever, you have us." It occurred to her that if anyone ever presented a similar situation to her—*forgo typical young adult dalliances and look: you could be living a boring-as-fuck middle-class life with the world's biggest asshole as your teenage daughter!*—she would slit her wrists.

"There's more to it than this," her mom said, raising her hands to indicate the spread surrounding her, the brick and the geraniums and Grace's finger paintings taped to the front door. "Of course I don't regret any of my decisions. But I'm grateful I got those few years as a student. They did me a world of good."

Wendy saw, before her mother, that Grace was at the front door, trying to bust her way out, fumbling with the knob.

"Mom," she said, just as her sister tumbled outside, ponytail askew, awash in that three-year-old energy that Wendy found at once adorable and exhausting.

"Mama," Grace said, throwing her arms around their mother's neck. She was surprised to see her mother's face fall again. She'd never really seen her get annoyed with Grace.

"Hey, my pumpkin." She touched Grace's arm. "We're right in the middle of talking."

More surprising still: her mom apparently considered this conversation more important than whatever Grace was bringing outside.

"Mama, I can't find Scotty and Liza said he's in the laundry but he's not." Grace buried her face in their mother's shoulder, and Wendy wondered if she herself had ever been so offhandedly affectionate as a child.

"He's in the dryer, sweet thing, but Wendy and I are talking right now and I need you to not interrupt."

"What are you talking about?"

"Gracie," her mom said, her voice suddenly stern. That was more like it, more like what Wendy had been reared on. "Honey, your sister and I are having a private conversation and you just interrupted. I need you to go back inside. I'll be in soon and I'll get Scotty out of the dryer."

Wendy and Marilyn both watched Grace with apprehension: she was unused to being scolded. Grace looked hurt at first, and her eyes widened in a way that might have been tearful, but then she righted herself, one tiny hand still resting on their mother's shoulder.

"Okay," she said, stepping back.

"Give me a hug, gosling," Marilyn said, and she twisted to pull Grace into her. Wendy watched them, intertwined, and wondered again whether her mother had ever made the same request of her. *Give me a hug, Wendy.* It didn't seem likely. "Good waiting, sweetheart. We'll be in soon." Grace tiptoed inside and Marilyn fixed her gaze on Wendy again. "Here's my proposal," she said. "Stay home one more year. Apply anywhere that interests you. Wait and see what happens. And I've thought about it and I'd like to pay you to babysit Gracie a few afternoons a week during the school year, if you're interested."

She was never asked to babysit Grace. "Are you joking?"

"I'm not," said her mom. "You've had a long year, honey, and I think it could do us all some good to take a breather on this one."

It was a surprisingly gentle approach, but she couldn't bring herself to express any kind of gratitude. Another year at home sounded like hell. She would still always be the fuckup who'd not bothered to apply to college the first time around. "Alternately, I could just leave," she said.

"Alternately with what money?"

She shrugged, raised an eyebrow, tried hard to suggest to her mom that perhaps she had secret and untoward channels of income, that perhaps she had entrepreneurial inklings after all.

"Try it through the summer."

And because she didn't have a rebuttal, because she didn't have any connections or anywhere else to go, because it seemed for the first time in a long time that her mother didn't actually hate her, Wendy agreed.

CHAPTER TWENTY

Liza was trying not to dwell on the complete egregiousness of the fact that she had been asked to stay at the house on Fair Oaks and keep an eye on Jonah while her parents had one of their clandestine sex weekends. She was trying not to get riled up over the fact that her parents had not asked either of her sisters—because though Violet, the boy's mother, had maintained a sociopathically troubling lie about his existence for fifteen years, and Wendy, jobless and loaded, could barely be trusted to care for a cactus, both were technically more able to step in than Liza, who was eight months pregnant, six weeks single and deep in the throes of a hellish fall semester. And yet her older sisters had won again. She was curled in her parents' bed, trying to focus her thoughts on something serene—the sunrise, the snuffling of Loomis's exhalations from where he lay on the floor beside her—when her morning sickness reared its head again, a familiar, belated and unwelcome guest.

She knelt before the toilet in her parents' bathroom, waiting for the next eruption. The last time she'd been sick here had to have been in the nineties. Adolescent stomach bugs and her mother's washcloths on her forehead, blessedly cool. Simpler times.

"I—uh—sorry." There had never been any doubt that Jonah

had Sorenson genes; they appeared constantly in the form of his social inelegance.

She turned to the door. "Oh, Christ, it's Friday. It's your Krav Maga day, isn't it?" She was unused to having to consider the schedules of others. "Listen, I—I'll take the train to work. You can take my car." Distracted by the buzz in her esophagus and the bladder acrobatics of the baby, she didn't notice his second's hesitation before he nodded. "Keys are on the table by the door."

She practically fanned him out, and when she heard the door click behind him, her stomach reacted compliantly, heaving, bringing her once again up onto her knees, the baby romping carelessly somewhere southward.

Lake Michigan in late fall: too cold for swimming, of course; an oversight on Marilyn's part (though she'd tried, valiantly, wading in to midcalf) but fabulously unpopulated, pitch-black by a quarter to six, quiet save for the rhythmic rolling of the waves against the beach. The house they'd rented was old and drafty, and as David made a fire their first night, she stopped what she was doing to watch him, kneeling before the hearth, poking at the pile of wood with a raccoonish curiosity. She was giddy with the freedom of being somewhere different, alone with him; she awakened him at sunrise to make love and then dragged him out to the pier, despite the cold, with a thermos of coffee and an armload of scratchy afghans from the bedroom. She built them a sort of nest on the atrophied boards and coaxed him down beside her, pink light beginning to bleed orange onto the horizon. She shivered, and he pulled her against him.

"Someone's in high spirits," he said.

"What, is your coffee not strong enough?"

He laughed. "I just haven't seen you like this in a while."

"Oh, God. Are you in a mood?"

"No, I'm not in a *mood*," he said, "I'm just not feeling as carefree as you are, I guess."

She moved away to look at him. "What the hell is that supposed to mean?"

"Oh, for God's— Honey, I wasn't— Forget it, okay?"

"Do you realize this is the first time in my life when nobody *needs* anything from me? Aren't we supposed to be enjoying these years? Haven't we earned that? We've raised four kids into adulthood. Can't we feel a little bit smug about that?"

"Well, but they're not exactly— I mean, have you taken a look at them lately?"

"They're adults."

"So we're celebrating the fact that we didn't kill them during their upbringing? That's a pretty low bar, kid."

She laughed in spite of herself. "I guess I feel like it's up to them now," she said. "The onus is— I mean, we can coddle them until we're blue in the face but the fact is that they're all on their own. There's not much we can do anymore but love them and hope for the best."

"Big talk from the woman who walked Gracie into her classroom until she was ten."

"*Gracie* was having terrible anxiety. And now she's getting a law degree, which is precisely my point. We did all we could and now I feel some license to take a backseat."

"While our single, pregnant daughter takes care of the teenage boy our other daughter secretly gave up for adoption?"

She closed her eyes. "We've been through this, haven't we?"

"I'm worried about Liza," he said. "And Jonah. And Violet. So my ability to enjoy this *freedom* is hindered by that a little bit, yes."

She was, of course, tempted to shake his shoulders and say, *Cede me this one; let me enjoy a single goddamn sunrise.* Because if you opened the gates to Liza and Jonah and Violet, Wendy and Gracie would come flooding through as well, all the girls, and their partners and their children and their anxieties and shortcomings, every lie they'd ever told, every mistake they'd ever made, and how those things could somehow be traced back to Marilyn herself—their progenitor, the easy target—and the wave would engulf her entirely, disastrously, forever.

"I'm sorry," he said, surprising her, pulling her close again. "Liza's been on my mind."

She imagined the fluctuating dynamics in their marriage flying around them like molecules, shape-shifting genetic code. *You're worried. Now I am. Now it's your turn again.* Colorful protein pearls rearranging at a moment's notice to accommodate David's nerves or her own.

"She's going to be okay, isn't she?" he asked.

"I assume so," she said mildly. "Though you know what they say about assuming." She paused. "Oh, she will, won't she?" The pearls, glittering between them, reflecting off the surface of the lake, shifting once again. "Lord. They're all going to be okay?"

"You're allowed to enjoy yourself," he said.

"*We* are," she said after a minute. "Forty-eight hours without us isn't going to kill them."

He smiled. "Come here," he said, maneuvering upright and tugging at her hand. This necessary reminder, so often forgotten, that they existed beyond their children. When she rose, he kissed her, pulling her to him against the November cold. The waves lapped around them. She wove her arms into his coat. Together, they went inside.

Liza never left her phone on during class, trying to set an example for her sea of dead-eyed Millennial drones, so she was delayed in seeing the line of missed calls—*Mom, Dad, Mom,*

Dad, Dad, Dad—and the series of all-caps and unnecessarily signed texts from her father.

CALL ME PLEASE, LOVE DAD
URGENT, CALL ME OR MOM . . . DAD
WHERE ARE YOU? DAD

She felt suddenly faint and sank into her desk chair. Someone was dead. Everyone was dead. She could feel her pulse like it was another body sitting on her chest. She dialed her father, whispering *no no no no no* while she listened to the ringing.

"Liza, thank God."

"Dad, what's going on; why are you— Is Mom— I didn't— Daddy, is everything—"

"Everything's okay, Liza. Calm down. Everything's fine."

"Is Mom—"

"Mom's right next to me on the couch. Lize, honey, did you let Jonah use your car?"

"What?" The room was spinning in a different way now, more whimsically, routine dizziness instead of the fatal kind. "Yes. I was— I wasn't feeling well this morning."

"He's fifteen, Liza. He doesn't even have his learner's permit. They took him to the police station. They thought he'd stolen it, for Christ's sake."

"But he's okay?"

Her father softened. "He's fine, sweetheart. Not a scratch on him. You just need to call and let them know you let him use it. Then he needs to be picked up."

"Are they— Is he in trouble? Are they going to— This is my fault, I shouldn't— Dad, I'm so— I didn't— I was so tired and I didn't even—"

"I know that, Lize. It's all right. Should we come home? It'll take us— The drive's about four hours from here, honey, so you'll need to go get him regardless, but we're happy to—"

"No, it's— Jesus. Couldn't Violet be taking care of this?"

"She's not answering her phone," her dad said.

Liza breathed out slowly. "Of fucking course she's not."

The whole thing was so fucking stupid, and *embarrassing*; he hadn't seen the person pulling out of the gas station parking lot, and when he did he'd jerked the wheel instead of just trying to stop, and so he'd hit the mailbox, and the cops were acting like he was some kind of hilarious anomaly, like a dog or a baby in a business suit driving a car instead of just a fifteen-year-old without a license, and to add insult to injury they also seemed to suspect him of stealing the car, which, no offense, but if he was going to do that he would set his sights elsewhere, because while Violet and Wendy both drove super-tricked-out, totally-worth-stealing luxury cars, Liza's was a fifteen-year-old Camry with hand cranks for the windows.

He wasn't hurt, and once his grandparents and Liza had had several phone conversations with the cops, all seemed to be resolved, and it was then that he realized how frightened he was, how you could get kicked out of foster care for way less than crashing someone's car, and plus Liza was like the most sympathetic victim ever, pregnant and vomiting, single because Jonah had accidentally spilled the beans about the Subaru guy. It was totally possible that Ryan had already told Liza what he'd learned. It was possible, even, that Liza would pass on that news to her parents, the news that Jonah was a total dick who couldn't keep his mouth shut. He wasn't locked up or anything, at the police station, just sitting on a stool behind the front desk with a lady wearing a sweatshirt that said GIVE ME CHOCO-LATE AND NO ONE GETS HURT. It occurred to him that maybe he could leave—Jesus Christ, should he leave? David and Marilyn had been so nice on the phone, but then again it hadn't been their car that he wrecked. He was considering this—he could pretend to go to the bathroom, skip out a side door, figure out the rest later—when he heard a woman's voice, high and anxious: "I'm here to pick up my nephew. He was in a car accident."

He was in a car accident, not *He totaled my car*. He looked past the chocolate lady. Liza was near tears, stark white. When she saw him her face lit up.

"There he is," she said.

"You be careful out there, Evel Knievel," the chocolate lady said.

"I'm really sorry that I— I didn't mean— Liza, I'm—"

"Jonah, *I'm* sorry," she said, drawing him into a hug, soft and warm and motherly, and he felt the trembling almost turn into crying, and he wasn't used to feeling this emotionally reactive to people; with every family before the Sorensons it had been easy enough to say *not worth it* but with them there seemed to be more at stake. "Hey, hey, hey," Liza said. "It's okay. Everything's fine. Gosh, what a day we've had."

She took him home and he fell asleep that night counting his lucky stars.

1997

He had never before fully experienced how long a year could feel. They had so much going on, which tended to make days fly by but currently seemed only to bog them down. He and Marilyn barely spoke; their separate existences barely brushed against each other. Weeks passed, then months, as a pall hovered over their household; Wendy was mopey and Liza was moody and Violet had her sights set on the East Coast once she finished high school. And his father's decline was speeding up; Marilyn returned from her Sunday visits with puffy eyes and he envisioned her crying in the car, which is what he did when he stopped by the house in Albany Park after work on Tuesdays and Thursdays to bring his father meals he didn't have the energy to eat.

When the inevitable news arrived, Marilyn was in the next room—they had become highly, strategically adept at avoiding each other—but when she heard his end of the call she came in immediately.

"Peaceful, like an angel," the home health aide said to David over the phone, and he marveled, sitting next to Marilyn at the kitchen table, because his father had been many things, but *peaceful* and *angelic* had never been on the list. Marilyn had taken his hand for the remainder of the call.

This was what marriage could be, he learned: months of intensely powerful loneliness, nearly a year of isolation that at first felt unbearable but slowly melted into routine. But mostly it was this, the amazing reality of Marilyn's hand in his, the seamless return to form after such a long stretch of adversity, the weight of his wife against his arm when she knew he needed her. That was the kind of love he had never known until her and, at that moment, remembered how lucky he was to have. He put his arm around her, pressed his cheek against the top of her head. Her hair was thick and silky, citrus-scented. He inhaled her and held her and let himself be held and that, he knew, softened the blow of the news.

His father had been a steady, quiet presence in their lives, but one who existed mostly at a point of remove, an occasional visitor, the stalwart of Second Thanksgiving, and a sporadic babysitter or bleacher occupant at floor hockey games. At the wake, Liza and Violet sat at the back of the room, leaning unhappily together, occasionally looking up when prompted to respond to some stranger from their grandfather's past. Wendy was at home with Grace; she had been profoundly upset by the sight of Richard's body and volunteered shakily hours earlier to go relieve the sitter. He was proud of them, his little crew, his beautiful, mature girls, and his wife, sweeping around from older to oldest guests and doing her thing: touching forearms, listening attentively, providing brief and charming stories about Richard to his old friends, neighbors, work buddies.

And then Marilyn came to his elbow, rested her head gently against his bicep, touched the back of his neck with an intimate, insistent pressure in just the right spot that made him feel protected and invigorated. *She picked me*, he wanted to say. *She picked me and we did this.* His dad had to have been proud of him, of the choices he'd made, of the kind, brilliant women with whom he'd surrounded himself. David felt the newfound warmth of his wife's hand as he stared at the waxy replica of his dad situated in the casket, and he marveled over all of the things he would never know about him.

This awful year they'd had. This terrible, off-kilter alternate universe in which everything was quiet and loaded with resentment and terror and a savage stubbornness. He and Marilyn were now utterly orphaned, and that required a kind of standing up. Concession, the high road, bitten bullets. All of which seemed smaller now, alongside the magnitude of loss. Her hand in his—the cool metal of her wedding ring now growing warm against his palm—felt the same as it had a year ago, as it had when he had first gripped it in the hallway of the Behavioral Sciences Building.

He squeezed her hand three times quickly, their Morse code, *I love you.*

She looked up at him again—confirmation, that loaded click that made this eye contact different from the fleeting glances they gave each other over the children's heads in the kitchen in the mornings—and then she lifted her face to kiss him.

That, too, felt as familiar to him as breathing.

When they got home that night, he went in to check on Gracie. He was so tired, suddenly, picturing his dad leaving for work in the evenings, navy Dickies and a T-shirt, off to oversee one of the major trolley fleets for the 85 Central line. Picturing him showing up for his high school graduation, leaning against the doors of the gym at St. Clement's, his dark, hardened face looking almost malleable.

He found Gracie still awake, snuggled in her bed against Wendy.

"Okay but," Grace was saying, "where *is* he?"

He should've stepped in—it was their job, as her parents, to field these kinds of big questions—but something stopped him. Curiosity, maybe. Fatigue.

"It's not so much a *where*, Goose," Wendy said, and David saw then that his daughter—that *baby*, that first baby who had shaken up his and Marilyn's life together with such delightful, frenzied, terrifying fervor—was unquestionably an adult, a woman, nineteen years old. "He's everywhere, I think. Kind of. And he'll be there forever."

Grace's eyes were wide. "But I don't—"

"It's not scary, Goose. It's actually really nice."

"But what do you mean *forever*," Grace said. "How long is that?"

"It's a really long time. Like the longest time ever."

"Hey, girls," he said softly. "You want me to sub in for you, Wednesday?"

She nodded, seeming relieved, and kissed Gracie's head before she got up. "Sweet dreams, Goose," she said, and she touched David's shoulder as she walked past him out of the room. "You okay, Dad?" That was what you got when you were the only man in the house: his wife and daughters sniffed out potential weaknesses with acute drug-dog noses, suspicious, nurturing German shepherds who could spot his oncoming head colds or emotional fragility in a way that seemed almost superhuman. Or perhaps this was what happened when you became an adult orphan: the slippage started, the shift where your children began to parent you.

"I'm just fine, honey," he said. He sank onto Gracie's tiny bed and stroked a hand over her hair and she moved groggily to rest against him. "Hi, polar bear," he said, his throat full. She'd always looked the most like him, which by extension meant that she looked the most like her grandfather: dark hair, wide eyes. One of his aunts had presented him with an envelope full of old photos, the first baby pictures he had ever seen of his dad.

It was eerie how familiar he looked in some of them; he couldn't tell if he was recognizing his father or himself or his daughter as a baby. His eyes welled up; Gracie wasn't a baby anymore, was no longer the androgynous little bundle staring up at him in a vacated delivery room.

"Papa, what's forever?" she murmured, but he could tell she was drifting, headed to limbo. "Why are you so fancy?"

"Shh," he said. "Everything's okay."

"Are you sad?" She stuck her thumb into her mouth, her other arm across his rib cage.

"No, Goose," he said finally, and he hugged her to him for another minute before he settled her back in bed. "Dada's fine, little one."

He changed out of his suit and went to join his wife, who was seated cross-legged on the couch with a glass of wine, still in her dress, heels kicked off before her, leaning her head back.

"The food should be here in twenty minutes," she said without opening her eyes. "Violet's on the phone. Lize's in the shower. Wendy's out back. She's thrilled I ordered pizza; she claims that all she's eaten today is the body of Christ."

"I'm going to go check on her."

"The most energetic man in Illinois," she said, smiling. "Kiss me, Doctor Strange."

He came over and kissed her; she smelled weakly of her perfume and strongly of the holy-water scent of the funeral home.

"I like you better in your street clothes," she said.

It was, presumably, as far as her family was concerned, a walk in the park for Wendy, away from the soulless processional of the wake, away from the inquisitive relatives, away from the bloated frightening body of her grandfather, to whom she hadn't been able to say goodbye. Her grandfather, who'd been her friend during a time when no one else wanted to be. And now he was dead, and she'd accidentally told her four-year-old sister about infinity, a concept that she remembered having endless nightmares about when she was a child. This was one of the great injustices of being an older sister, these occasional times the universe challenged you to not traumatize your siblings for life—a task that, under normal circumstances, should belong to the parents. But it was hard to be mad at Grace, who was warm and microscopic and so genuinely unwitting. And her dad had come to rescue her. How weird it must be for him, that his own dad was in a box. That he'd never see him again.

"Hey, Wednesday," he said, startling her. She was sitting on the back stairs, wishing she had a cigarette. This was the first time she'd ever been concerned about her dad's emotional vulnerability, about the fact that he could be hurt by something that didn't pertain directly to their immediate family. He sank down beside her. "How goes it, honey?"

She shrugged, nodded.

"I know today was hard for you," he said. "I'm sorry."

"I just—" She shook her head. "I just don't . . ."

He wrapped an arm around her shoulders. "Oh, honey," he murmured. "It's okay, Wendy. Hey, it's okay." He rubbed her arm. "It's kind of a shitty day, isn't it?" he finally said. She nodded into him and he rested his head against the top of hers. "Today sucks."

"Hey, Dad? You know how they have—like, people? To hold the—like, the casket?" She moved slightly away from him, straightening her spine, readying her case.

"Pallbearers," he said. "What about them?"

"Who's doing that tomorrow?"

"Me," he said. "A few of my cousins. A couple of men from the funeral home."

"People who didn't *know* him?"

"Your grandpa's friends are mostly octogenarians. We take what we can get."

"Do women ever do it? Hold the casket."

"Not that I've seen."

"Is it allowed?"

"Whatever we want to be allowed is allowed with this stuff, I think. Why do you ask?"

"Maybe I'd like to do it," she said.

Her father's voice sounded strangled: "You would?"

"Yeah," she said. Then: "Yes. Daddy? Is that okay? Would that be . . . like . . ."

"Of course," he said finally. "I'd love that."

It had been a strangely nice few days, given everything. She and her sisters were all being kinder to each other, and she'd walked into the kitchen earlier to find her parents kissing for the first time in months. And it was weird, she thought, feeling adult and aware, how a thing so terrible as losing someone could yield goodness in the ones who were left.

PART
FOUR

WINTER

CHAPTER TWENTY-ONE

A brisk knock, one that was less question than announcement, and then Gillian entered the exam room, not quite smiling but with a face pliable enough that it seemed a possibility.

"Liza," she said. "How are we feeling?"

Who was the *we*? She and the baby? She and Ryan? She and *Gillian*? "Fine," Liza said, though the word didn't necessarily apply to any of the possibilities.

Gillian set down her chart and pumped her hands with sanitizer. "I'm a little surprised to see you."

She had been avoiding Gillian since their disastrous phone call, had arranged to see other doctors in the practice for her intervening prenatal visits. But her recent change in circumstances had made her edgy and anxious, and she craved, again, what she'd sought Gillian out for in the first place: familiarity. The knowledge that she was *lucky*. And, perhaps, absolution for her behavior.

"I wanted to apologize," she said.

Gillian raised her eyebrows.

"My partner left me recently," she said without planning to. "The baby's father."

Gillian paused. "I'm sorry to hear that."

"It's not an excuse, but I—I've been—going through a lot lately."

"Shall I point out that that *sounds* like an excuse? And a flimsy one, given what you accused me of?"

Her biggest fear, initially, had been that Gillian would tell her father what she'd asked, but he hadn't mentioned it, and she'd relaxed. In the room with Gillian now, practically writhing with shame, she realized she'd been too hasty in assuming she was in the clear.

"I have pristine ratings, you realize that?" Gillian continued. "I have a wait list for new patients through next year. I don't need to sell myself to you. Your being here is contingent on me, Liza. Let there be no ambiguity about that. So before we move on, two things: firstly, as I believe I mentioned, before you hung up on me: it is entirely unprecedented for me to have someone accuse me of what you accused me of."

"I was just—"

"Second of all, though I'd normally never dignify such an accusation with any type of response, I feel obliged in this case, because your dad's a wonderful man. I'm telling you this because of that. Not because I feel you deserve an explanation. David was my friend. He was my friend during a very difficult time in my life."

She regarded the crests of her knees beneath her belly. "I really am sorry," she said. "I don't— I feel terrible for acting how I did. But it's been a—particularly awful time for me. I'm facing down being a single parent and that would be hard enough on its own, but when you grow up with parents like mine—parents who are in *love* like mine . . . God, these stable, perfect, desperately infatuated— It just . . ." She shook her head. "I'm falling so short of the mark."

"Yes," Gillian said mildly. "It was hard for me too, when I was your age. Trying to figure out my own life while bearing witness, every day, to such an idyllic marriage."

Liza looked up to find Gillian staring at her squarely. It

occurred to her that this woman may have been one of the few outside of their family who understood the magnificent albatross that was her parents' love, who had suffered her own pains in its wake.

"My sole requirement is that we don't discuss your parents. Beyond the genetic necessity. Understand? This conversation is our last on the subject."

The indoor smell of cigarettes. *Gillian Gillian Gillian.* The woman had been such an enigma to her for so long, a ghostly fragment of her childhood that never fully went away. How odd to realize she hadn't been so different from Liza herself: navigating a demanding work life, and juggling that, with varying degrees of grace, alongside a quest for personal fulfillment.

"All right," she said. "Thank you, Dr. Levin. Really."

"And your mother's aware that I'll be the one delivering this baby?"

"Oh, yeah," Liza said. "My dad told her when I first started seeing you."

She'd offered Christmas in a moment of weakness because Wyatt wouldn't stop asking about Star of the Week, if Jonah could come, if she thought Jonah would know the song, if Jonah knew how to play any instruments, could Jonah *please* come, Mama, even just for *four* minutes. She'd thrown out a noncommittal "He'll be in school but maybe you can show him during the holidays" before realizing that it was their year to go to Matt's family in Seattle for Christmas, but during the three-second delay her son had already darted up the stairs to practice the chord progression again, and so she'd called Matt at work and told him, tonelessly, that she hoped he wouldn't mind but they were going to have Jonah over for a pre-Christmas dinner. And her husband's clenched-jaw acquiescence was worse than any fight they could've had, as though he no longer possessed the ability or the desire to dialogue with her, the kind of quiet acceptance that one used to placate a padded-cell maniac.

Matt had driven to Oak Park to pick up Jonah, and after some cajoling from Wyatt had taken the boys with him—"We get to ride in our *car* with him?" Wyatt had said, awestruck—and when the four of them returned, she couldn't help but marvel at the sight. If anyone had told her, fifteen years ago, that she'd be standing in her foyer watching the baby she'd given up teaching her sons how to do the "blow it up" fist bump while her husband looked on, she—what *would* she have done?

"Merry Christmas," she said. He seemed to have gotten taller since she'd last seen him. It still made her uncomfortable to have him here against the opulent backdrop of all she'd failed to give him. She willed herself not to think about the housekeepers, the landscapers, the hours of free time that stretched before her like luxurious carpets. The way she filled those hours with book clubs and Bikram and bake sales that were needlessly raising money for elective things that any parent at the preschool could've funded out-of-pocket in the blink of an eye. Of course it was silly—worse, obnoxious—to rue the emotional dearth of a materially prosperous life. But Jonah was a salient reminder of the contrast: her excess with his have-nots. She felt sick to her stomach.

"Thanks for having me," he said.

"Of course. Are you hungry?"

"I— Sure," Jonah said. "I mean, whenever. Not starving."

"Dinner's ready now," she said. She had orchestrated it this way, timed it so she was pulling the pork chops out of the oven when she heard the car in the driveway. If they ate early, they could usher him out with the excuse of needing to put the kids to bed. She didn't care if it was cruelly controlling. His presence in her house made her feel a bit like she was drowning.

"Mama, can I play my song first?" Wyatt appeared on the landing with his tiny guitar.

She swallowed. "Sure, honey. I'm just going to— I'll be listening from the kitchen, baby. I just have to whip the potatoes." So what if 80 percent of the things that came out of her mouth were utterly ridiculous? So what if she wasn't like her own mother, warmly bustling and open-armed? "Matty, I'm just going to— Could you just—" But her husband was already leading the charge into the living room, Eli in his arms. He'd been vehemently opposed to their first dinner, and he'd remained silently opposed to this Christmas celebration she'd sprung on him, and yet now he was behaving with absolute decency, making casual conversation with the boy—the tilt of Jonah's head reminded her, for a second, of her father. It wasn't Jonah's fault. She knew that. He hadn't asked to exist. And he'd done nothing wrong, nothing at all except for *being*, and she could acknowledge candidly that it wasn't so much the *boy* she resisted as it was all that he represented, and all that he threatened to unravel, but acknowledging that didn't make a bit of difference.

In the kitchen, she poured herself far more wine than was socially acceptable and drank it down to an appropriate amount and then leaned against the counter, trying again to remember which nostril you were supposed to breathe out of when you were about to lose your shit. She was just trying to do the right thing, but that wasn't so easy, because everyone in her life had a different conception of what the right thing was, and she herself was caught somewhere in the middle, trying to give Wyatt what he wanted and heed Matt's concerns and extend some modicum of *something* in Jonah's direction, though she knew she owed him more than she could ever give. She wasn't a bad person. She was, of course, as had already been well established, not the *warmest* person, but she was a good mom, wasn't she? Hadn't she given everything she had, every single ounce of herself, to her children, and weren't they growing into fantastically vibrant boys? Didn't she, for the most part, do what she was supposed to?

What would happen if she had a full-throttle panic attack in the kitchen? Or passed out, everyone ignorant to the thump of her body because Wyatt really wailed on his guitar strings? What kinds of memories would nights like this imprint upon her children? *Remember when Mom's illegitimate lovechild came for dinner and we found her in the kitchen throwing back a bottle of carménère? Remember that fucked-up Christmas before Mom and Dad got divorced?*

She heard Wyatt playing the chorus and she swallowed, impressively, the rest of her wine. This evening was making her child wildly happy. Wyatt, to whom she was bound in a deeply intricate way, more deeply even than she was to Eli, because of all she and Wyatt had been through together at the outset. Because Wyatt had, simply by coming into being, helped her find herself again, a new self, the one that was his mother, after so many years of being lost.

He was on the final repetition of the chorus, she recognized, so she poured and pounded another inch of wine before turning the mixer on the potatoes, the sound of which, conveniently, also drowned out Jonah's applause.

In a tone that sounded, to Jonah, not totally *inviting*, Violet had invited him over a few days before Christmas to have dinner with her family, and while it didn't sound fun to him—like, at *all*—it wasn't like he could tell her he had other plans, because besides school and martial arts pretty much all he did was hang out with David and Marilyn, both of whom encouraged him to go. So he found himself sitting at their dinner table for the second time in his life, almost *enjoying* himself, having just plodded through an awkward meal, playing this dumb game with Wyatt and Eli where he tried to guess their ages and kept intentionally guessing wrong.

"Forty-seven," he said, and both boys totally lost it, laughing in that infectious kid way where you couldn't help but laugh, too, even if your dumb birth mother was staring at you from across the table like you were teaching her children how to masturbate. Violet rose from the table with her empty wineglass. The last time he'd been there he'd shoved a few bottles of wine in his backpack. Just for fun. Just to *see*. They were still in the duffel bag in his bedroom closet. He wondered if Violet had noticed them missing.

"Can Jonah come to Star of the Week?" Wyatt asked.

Jonah turned to the kid, making a face. "Like, a real star? In space?"

Eli and Wyatt both cracked up at this, but their laughter was not enough to distract him from the fact that Matt had blanched at Wyatt's question, and that Violet had reappeared in the doorway, glass filled and mouth pinched, as it had been when he'd first met her.

"I'm Star of the Week in January," Wyatt explained, oblivious to his parents and the horror on their faces, which was plainly obvious to Jonah.

"Dope," he said. "Congrats." He pictured himself showing up at Wyatt's fancy school, an outsider with three hundred dollars to his name, being run off of the grounds by armed guards.

"Wy, sweetheart." She came over and kissed the top of Wyatt's head. They both stared at him from across the table, two identical sets of dark brown eyes. Violet must have the recessive gene, Bb; this meant, of course, that his dad had blue eyes. "We talked about this, baby."

Jonah must've looked hurt—he *was* hurt; he wasn't the fucking Unabomber; he hadn't fucking asked for any of this— because Violet softened again.

"It's during the school day," she said. "Just some— Dada and I don't think it's a good idea for anyone to miss school because of this, right, Dada?"

These fucking bizarro cyborg people. Matt nodded stiffly. Violet pressed her lips again into Wyatt's hair and he could tell, watching them from across the table, that she was a good mom, that she was nuts about her kids, would always be nuts about Wyatt and Eli in a way that she would never be about him.

"Okay," she said with what sounded like forced enthusiasm. "What if we get our jammies on and then read *The Grinch*?"

"Can Jonah put me to bed?" Wyatt asked.

Violet stiffened. "Oh, I—"

Jonah watched with interest as Violet and Matt exchanged some exaggerated pantomime across the room, Violet lifting her eyebrows all the way up on her forehead and Matt cocking his head to one side, scratching an invisible itch on his cheek as he mouthed something.

"Have you read *The Grinch*?" Wyatt asked him, clambering into the seat beside him.

"For sure," he said. "*Every Who down in Who-ville*, right?"

"Mama, he *knows* it," Wyatt said, incredulous.

"Yeah, sweetie, that's impressive, but isn't it—"

"I'll read to Eli," Matt said in a tight voice, and then, turning to Jonah: "You can read to Wy."

Violet spun from the room, and he followed Wyatt and Matt and Eli uncertainly up the stairs and down the hall.

"Teeth and PJs first," Matt said, and Wyatt skittered off to the bathroom, Eli toddling behind him. "You all good with this?" Matt asked him, like Jonah was about to fly a plane or something.

"Sure," he said. "Yeah, no problem."

"I'll be right across the hall," Matt said, and Jonah took a second to stew in the *gall* of these people, their acting like he was not only an inconvenience but a sketchy Stranger-Danger predator too.

"Got it," he said, but only because Wyatt had appeared again, having changed into his pajamas in approximately three seconds. Wyatt took his hand and pulled him into his room. It took a few minutes—Wyatt giving him the tour of his bedroom, showing him his gargantuan arsenal of Matchbox cars; God, their abundance of *stuff*—but he finally got the kid into bed.

"Lie down with me," Wyatt said.

"Oh—I'm good." He sat upright at the foot of the bed with Wyatt's copy of *How the Grinch Stole Christmas!* on his lap. He looked up at the ceiling, its elaborate skyscape of glow-in-the-dark planets, and thought about how fucking nice it must be to be these kids, growing up like they were, with racecar beds and guitars and parents who loved them.

"You live with Loomis, right?" Wyatt squirmed under the blankets. "Do you like dogs?"

"No," he said.

"How come?"

Violet always referred to Wyatt as shy, but this seemed less and less true every time he saw the boy. He wondered if Violet would be mad if they didn't read. If she tried to fill a quota every night, a hundred thousand words per kid, stuffing their tiny brains with brilliance. If he'd ultimately be to blame if Wyatt wasn't accepted to Yale.

"Will you come to Star of the Week?" This kid was so earnest and hopeful it was ridiculous. "It's on January fifth at ten o'clock."

He thought of Wyatt with a tiny date book like Violet's and almost smiled. January fifth: his birthday was January seventh. He wondered if Violet remembered. Marilyn had it written on her calendar, had insisted on having some kind of celebration, a dinner out or with some of his new school friends. He'd told her he'd prefer to have it just be with her and David. Was picturing, with a kind of dorky excitement, how nice it would be to celebrate his birthday with people he liked. To celebrate it, period.

"I'll try, dude," he said.

"Could we sing instead of read? Mama sings to me sometimes."

He couldn't picture Violet singing. "That's out of my wheelhouse, man."

"What does that mean?"

"It means I don't sing. You can sing if you want."

Wyatt was quiet for a minute. Then: "Is Santa real?"

Oh, *shit*. Of course this was happening to him.

"Jax told me Santa's not real," Wyatt said.

"Who the hell is *Jax*?"

"He's in my class."

"Tell him he's got a stupid name."

"Is he right?"

He felt like he was on a reality television show where they put unassuming people into uncomfortable conversations with child geniuses and left them to dig their way to safety.

Wyatt watched him expectantly.

"How old are you?" he asked. "Five?"

"I'll be six in the summer."

He'd been seven when he learned the truth about Santa, from an atheist manic-depressive kid in one of the foster homes. Before that, though, he'd always been skeptical of Santa, conceptually speaking, and a little creeped out, too, by the idea that there was an adult man in a fur suit who broke into your house at night and watched you sleep.

"Santa's not *not* real," he said. "Not exactly. I mean, technically, no, he's—"

"Where do the presents come from?" Wyatt sounded less

traumatized than he did curious, wide-eyed and tenacious under his covers, hungry for intel; his face reminded Jonah, again, of Violet, the mother he shared with this kid. He wondered if any of his own expressions resembled hers. He wondered if he'd inherited from Violet this stupid tendency to say precisely the thing he wasn't supposed to say, like he'd done when he accidentally told Ryan about Liza and the Subaru guy. It took him a few seconds to realize that the creepy feeling at the back of his neck was because someone was watching him. He sat up halfway and saw Violet in the doorway, her face white with anger.

"Jonah's teasing you, my tyrannosaurus," she said, entering the room. "Say goodnight."

The kid must have been tired, because he just waved listlessly from his pillow, eyes already drooping closed. Maybe he wouldn't even remember their conversation in the morning. Violet wouldn't look at him, even as she sat down on the bed beside him. He stood up to go.

"Of course Santa's real, sweetheart," she whispered to Wyatt. "And he'll come down the big chimney at Grandma and Grandpa's house in Seattle."

He wasn't sure what to do so he just stood in the hall watching them, the way Violet rubbed circles on Wyatt's chest, how her voice had dropped in both octave and volume so it became the perfect bedtime voice. She leaned in to kiss him and Jonah looked away.

"I love you, my pumpkin," she crooned. "Sweet dreams, sweet thing." Then she rose and clicked off the lamp and tiptoed out of the room. He moved out of her way and she pulled the door shut. Then she turned to him. "What the fuck was that about?"

He froze. He'd always suspected Violet was capable of meanness, but so far he'd only seen her be subtly bitchy. "He asked. I wasn't sure what to— I didn't want to, like, *lie* to him."

"Ninety percent of talking to children is lying."

"Violet, hey." Matt appeared, closing Eli's door behind him. "Keep it down."

"He just told Wyatt that Santa isn't real."

"Let's talk about this downstairs," Matt said.

"I mean, he *asked* me," Jonah said, ignoring Matt. "He said *Jax* already told him. He was *confirming.*"

"He's five years old. He would've believed you over another kid," she snapped. "Jesus Christ. I'm sorry if you were forced to grow up more quickly than you should've, but you're almost a fucking adult. There's no reason for you to try to ruin it for my kids."

"I didn't—" *My kids.*

"I think you should—probably go. Matt, can you take him?"

"Honey, hang on a second; let's—" Matt went over to Violet, dipped his head toward hers, whispered something, *Calm down, Viol.*

"It's fine," he said. "I'll go ruin things for David and Marilyn. Set fire to the house or something. Old Christmas tradition from the mean streets."

"Do me a favor and don't raid our wine rack again," Violet said acidly.

Matt glanced up at her, not with anger but suddenly wary, alert, and Jonah could tell that he was worried about her, legitimate crazy-person-level worried, like she was about to catch fire.

"Matt, if you could just—" Violet said, turning away from her husband's grasp and disappearing through the bedroom door behind her.

"Come on, let's get you home," Matt said, not unkindly. How fucking weird these people were. How you could burn your bridges with one half of a couple and not the other. It was exhausting to be with them, with their stuffiness and their secrets. He still didn't understand how Violet had come from

David and Marilyn, how it was possible for someone to be such a total fucking android when her parents gave off so much warmth it was unseemly; how when he worked on the trees or the plumbing with his grandfather, the silence between them contained more kindness than he'd ever experienced from Violet for a single second.

"Whatever." He pulled out his phone to text his grandparents a warning that he was coming home early, just in case they were having old-people sex in his absence.

1998

In the span of a single weekend, Wendy had, unbeknownst to them, found a studio apartment near the Briar Street Theatre and a job waiting tables at a steak house in the Loop. The only favor she'd asked from her parents was use of the station wagon to transport her possessions. Marilyn's first reaction to this had been to firmly object to Wendy's moving out, but the more she thought about it, the more she couldn't help but feel proud. Her daughter was taking initiative, making a bold move that would force her life forward. She'd hugged her daughter goodbye in the foyer, feeling almost sadder than she had when they'd dropped Violet off at Wesleyan that fall, though Wendy was moving only twenty minutes away. Wendy had never quite fit in in the world in the way that Violet had. Wendy forging her own path was a far more terrifying prospect, she thought, at the time, than anything Violet would ever undertake.

Standing at the window, the Volvo's taillights having long since left her field of vision, she both missed her daughter and didn't. She was both proud of her and hopelessly worried about her.

"Mom? Lurk much?"

She startled and turned to Liza, who'd appeared at her elbow. She smiled faintly. "Apparently so."

"What are you doing?"

"Just contemplating my half-empty nest. Just missing your sister a little."

"Mom, she's an *adult*. She's *twenty*," Liza said, as though that were the oldest age imaginable. Marilyn had gotten married at twenty-one; by the time she was twenty-four she had a husband and two kids and free rein over her own household. And yet saying goodbye to Wendy had felt a bit like dropping her off at preschool for the first time.

"I'm allowed to miss twenty-year-olds," she said. She put an arm around Liza's shoulders. "Or fourteen-year-olds."

"She'll be fine, Mom," Liza said gently. At some point your children crossed a threshold from being children to being real people and it never seemed to announce itself dramatically but rather in quiet moments like this one. Marilyn said goodnight and went upstairs, forwent putting on pajamas and instead stripped down to her underwear and climbed between her sheets in the dark. Her own children slipping from her in increments, she pressed the cool knob of her wrist against her forehead, willing away either the dregs or the beginnings of a headache. When the door creaked open she rolled instinctively toward the light from the hall.

"You awake?" David whispered. He shut it behind him and the bright blade disappeared.

"How'd it go? Was she okay?" She and David could talk about Wendy to only a certain degree of honesty; their first-born was emblematic of too much for them both—too much heartbreak, too much tension, too much earth-shattering love.

"Fine," he said. She knew him well enough to know that it was not gruffness in his voice but gloom. He crawled in next to her, his knee grazing her thigh and his hand getting tangled in her hair before they settled together, an old, tired pair of spoons. *Forks*, David called them, because he was tall and she was slight and their limbs sometimes seemed to get stuck together like interlacing tines.

.   .   .

At some point, Marilyn had let go of the notion of going back to school. And while she never quite stopped resenting that fact, she held the anger back, stored it in the space behind her molars, biting down, every so often, and allowing herself to revel in the injustice. But mostly she just kept going. Kept dropping off the girls at school, kept going to their water polo games and piano recitals, kept signing their permission slips and hemming their skirts and fixing their dinners. It was all-consuming, as it had always been.

She was headed to the hardware store on Chicago Avenue in pursuit of new pruning shears one morning, but when she arrived, she found the front door locked and a small sign taped to the window announcing that the business was for sale.

She was less haunted than one might think, raising her family in the place where she herself had been so distressingly reared. Most of the time she focused on the creation of new memories—choosing the guest suite instead of her parents' room for her and David's bedroom; covering the nauseating yellow floral wallpaper in one of the bedrooms with an infant-appropriate animal print when she was pregnant with Gracie; urging the girls, when they repaved the driveway, to imprint the concrete liberally with their initials and handprints. The house on Fair Oaks had been a saving grace for them, of course, but that didn't mean Marilyn wouldn't approach it like she had their house in Iowa, with the blue paint in the kitchen: with a penchant for change and renewal.

There were parts of life in her hometown that tugged at her pleasantly, though—the familiarity of the trees, the muscle memory that kicked in when she walked down the street, and the way she could enter any of the old shops and be transported back decades by the sick-sweet milk of the ice cream parlor or the chlorinated sawdust of the hardware store. She had a distinct memory of herself—one of few not marred by her parents' emotional detritus—riding on her father's shoulders, him dipping down in order to enter Mallory's Hardware without bashing her head against the frame, the jangle of wind chimes, the fishbowl full of Dum Dums.

"Marilyn Connolly? Where are all those babies of yours?"

Now, on the sidewalk outside Mallory's, she turned to see an old friend of her mother's from Sundays at St. Catherine–St. Lucy (her father called the cumbersomely named parish St. Mouthfuls Aquinas). She couldn't for the life of her remember the woman's name.

"Not babies anymore, I'm afraid," she said and was surprised to feel real emotion in her throat after she said it.

"They can't all be in school?"

"Every single one," she said, forcing a smile.

"What are you doing with yourself, then? Luxuriating?"

She hadn't stopped to consider her own forward momentum. Gracie was only in kindergarten; she still wore Pull-Ups to bed. Liza required constant chauffeuring and surveillance. But her days were notably quieter, and she hadn't given much thought to what was next for her.

As an adult, she visited Mallory's Hardware with no real regularity, but it was where they went when they needed potting soil or birdseed, tools for David's one-off home improvement projects. It wasn't that she had any deep-seated attachment to the place, but it held pleasant associations, and sometimes she believed in signs, and there was a bit of money left over from her inheritance from her father, and while there was no such thing as leftover money when you had four children, it seemed only fair that she should be able to spend some of it on herself. She and David would never be able to leave for their children what her parents had left for her, fiscally speaking, but she hoped they would provide a legacy of happiness, or at least the earnest pursuit thereof.

She stopped by David's office on the way home, shamefully aware of Gillian's absence—she had recently left the practice to start her own in Andersonville.

"Hey, sweet," he said, and she remembered what Gillian had said about how his voice changed when he was talking to her. She closed the door behind her and went to sit in his lap behind his desk, cognizant of the ridiculousness of the gesture but wanting to be near him. She wrapped her arms around his neck.

"I'd like to do something kind of radical," she said.

His hands cupped her waist. "Overthrow the government?"

"I'm serious," she said.

He furrowed his brow, trying to hide amusement. "Noted."

"Do you support me?" she asked.

"I don't know what it is that you're—"

"Generally, historically speaking. You trust me?"

"More than anyone on the planet, kid."

She kissed him. "Thank you."

"You're welcome?"

"I'm not crazy."

"I never said you were."

"A new chapter, I think, maybe."

"You going to enlighten me, sweetheart?"

She stood up, held out her hand. "Let's take a walk."

For as long as Wendy could remember, she'd wanted a house with a quiet garage. When she was growing up, the telltale crunch of the garage door had signaled impending doom: her parents' arrival home from a PTA meeting or dinner or work, which would mean a Chore List or a lecture on how she had ditched school. She wanted a quiet door that swooshed open, a quiet door through which some quiet, humming European car would glide, driven by a man who was just slightly alternative, who smoked and drank but not too much, who had read *Crime and Punishment* and burned incense.

It was a fairly simple request. Quiet garage, interesting life. With Miles she got everything she wanted, though not exactly in the way she imagined. He was, for starters, fifteen years her senior. And this was *fine*, despite the reactions of her family. She was twenty and he was thirty-five. And—okay, her teacher: that was another detail that her parents weren't crazy about, but that was barely true, an inconvenient fact of no more than an hour's duration. She met him in a Foundations of Economics class that she was taking in the Continuing Education program at Harold Washington (she saw an ad on the Halsted bus; she shelled out her saved tips and found herself taking two night classes). She'd had to leave home eventually. Violet was immersed in her Connectican liberal-arts situation with the vigor of someone far more purebred. Grace was adorable but maddening, always sneaking into the room when Wendy was watching *The Kids in the Hall*. Liza was a weird, temperamental quasi adult who misused words like *quasi* and didn't get why that was funny. Wendy had been sick of it all, so she'd left.

She watched Miles come into that first class and quickly turned to the people seated around her, expecting her female classmates to be abuzz. Instead she saw indifference. She glanced up to the front of the room again. There he was, pulling a few books from his bag, running a hand through floppy, graying hair (prematurely, surely), and—ah—shoving a pack of American Spirits deep into one pocket. Why wasn't anyone else noticing?

She pulled out a legal pad and pushed her hair from her face. It was then that he met her eyes, and Wendy knew, immediately, that he was going to be hers. She couldn't help but smile, and it horrified her. She was smiling like those terrible people who just couldn't wait to get to the punch lines of their bad jokes. *Grinning*. Repulsive. But she couldn't stop. She watched him clear his throat and chew the inside of his bottom lip (a nervous habit, she later learned).

"Hey," he called, rapping on his desktop with his knuckles. Slowly, the room quieted. He sat on the edge of his sad linoleum desk and shoved his hands in his pockets. She noticed a watch, at once delicate and imposing, on his right wrist. Cartier. She had, after years of entertaining the suburban elite, an eye for luxury. "I'm Miles Eisenberg. I'll be your instructor for this term." He suggested that they start out with an icebreaker and his eyes fell, again, on Wendy. "How about you? Would you mind starting us off?"

Wendy was born for such situations and sat up straighter in her chair. "Me? Sure."

"Great. If you could pick a partner, get us started pairing off. We're going to interview one of our classmates. Just to make sure we're all acquainted. Would you choose someone?"

She swallowed, crossed her ankles, and looked up at him. "Can I pick you?"

There were a few titters from neighboring chairs. Miles Eisenberg flushed a deep red.

"I—well, sure. Sure you can. Why doesn't everyone else partner up and we'll talk for . . ." He glanced at the clock. "Five minutes." It was an uncomfortably long time but she was ecstatic. She went to join her future husband at his desk.

She went home with him that night and they made it to his foyer—he had a *foyer*, a whole brownstone, in fact, in the desirable part of Hyde Park—before things started to get weird. She sat back on her haunches, straddling him.

"If you say one more thing about how young I am, I'm going to leave right now and go find a willing fifteen-year-old boy." She made him laugh; he reached to brush her hair from her face.

"Wendy, you're my *student*."

This had already occurred to her. First, in class, perched

on the edge of his desk telling him about her job at McCormick & Schmick's. And it had occurred to her again a half hour ago when they were making out in his car—an *Audi*; such kismet that she'd settled for a community college instructor only to find out he was secretly loaded.

"Why the *fuck* are you teaching Misfits 101 if you can afford a car that's worth like a billion times more than all your students' sold plasma combined?" she'd asked him in the front seat, when they'd risen for air.

"I find it fulfilling," he said.

There was something unendingly satisfying about this answer: a person doing something because he could, because it brought him joy. In the foyer, pressing herself teasingly against his groin, she thought of him in the front of the classroom, the awkward grace of his presence.

"I'll drop your class," she said. "There. I'm not your student anymore."

He leaned his head back. "This is so fucking surreal, you know that?"

"If you want me to leave, I will," she said, and she hoped she sounded convincing.

CHAPTER TWENTY-TWO

A Christmas miracle: Ben appearing on her doorstep in the early afternoon, the hood of his parka pulled up against the gray drizzle. She was so happy to see him that she forgot she was wearing her raccoon boxers and a T-shirt commemorating her middle school graduation.

"What are you doing here?" she asked, stepping aside to let him in.

"What are you *wearing*, Sorenson?" He tugged playfully, once, on her ponytail, and she saw him observe her just-vacated nest on the couch: a knot of blankets and a splayed copy of *The Haunting of Hill House*. He turned to smile at her. "I was sort of hoping you'd be caroling or something. Or dressed as a shepherd."

"Sorry to disappoint."

Hanging out with Ben was one of the only things she enjoyed lately, apart from true-crime documentaries and going for occasional drinks with a dorky flutist named Candace who was her age and worked part-time doing payroll in her office. Her life was mostly a mundane marathon of work and sleep, except when it wasn't, except when Ben made an appearance.

She wasn't sure how to take initiative. She'd submitted, with a great deal of pleasure, when he kissed her—precisely two times, both when they were both reasonably tipsy—but she also found herself consumed with worry while it was happening, wondering where she was supposed to put her hands, whether or not her body felt lumpy or subpar beneath *his* hands, how to know if she was overstaying her welcome in his mouth, if he was ready for it to end but she was still going at it. And he hadn't pushed it beyond those two pleasant but minor encounters. She was astounded by his patience and good nature, by the fact that he kept inviting her out, again and again, by the fact that he was willing to just spend time with her, beers at the Comeback or walks around Berkeley Park, nights that had twice ended with nice-but-awkward kissing.

And now he was in her house, on Christmas, bearing witness to her weird hermitage. "Anyway," he said, looking again at her Shirley Jackson nest, "you seem busy, but if your day frees up, I was hoping I could take you out."

"Like, murder me?" she asked. She was not wearing a bra and she hadn't showered or brushed her teeth and her hair was pulled back into what she hoped resembled a chignon but was in fact just an unwashed ponytail that she'd sort of smushed into an orb with her hand.

"For Christmas," he said. "It's bumming me the fuck out that you have this giant adoring Kennedy family across the country and you're spending Christmas alone wearing raccoon shorts."

Tears sprang to her eyes. "You're Jewish."

"So what? I'm not taking you to mass." He smiled at her. "Unless you're into that."

"Let me just change," she said, but first she threw her arms around him, seized by a force beyond her control. "Thanks, Ben," she said, releasing him immediately, face aflame. She skipped into her bedroom before she could clock his expression.

They ended up, no surprise, at the Comeback, which was empty save for the usual Irish bartender and a couple of regulars at a dark booth in the corner, people whom Ben had once genially described as having been "rode hard and put away wet."

"That's going to be us in like forty-seven years," she said, a few drinks in, clumsy-tongued and giddy. "Lonely old barflies. What would you be doing today if you weren't here?"

"Today I had a couple of options. There's a pickup soccer game at the rec center. A family dinner at my aunt and uncle's house. A few friends from high school are camping in Lazy Bend. A couple of people from—"

"Jesus Christ, I get it. You're wildly popular."

"I meant it as a compliment," he said, and when she glanced up at him his expression was less impish than she'd been expecting. "I'm having fun with you."

They hung out a lot, but they both seemed to have agreed that their conversations would not cross certain barriers; it was okay for them to make out a little bit under the striped awning of the head shop next to the Comeback before they went their separate ways; they were allowed to die laughing, sitting by Crystal Springs Lake with their feet in the water, about one of Ben's high school classmates—who had started a crowdfunding page for her "artistic lifestyle," asking for $1,900 per month in donations to support her pursuit of rendering, in polymer clay, what she referred to as "fractal goat likenesses"—but the second the laughter started to fade, it had become a point of fact that Grace would make a self-deprecating joke ("I, like goats, lack the necessary degree of self-control that should prevent me from eating tin cans") and defuse any romantic tension that threatened to overtake their platonic camaraderie.

Ben was awkward too, so she assumed she was doing him a favor, sparing him further unfolding. But now he was complimenting her, *having fun*, being *sincere*, it seemed.

Her phone began to buzz on the table between them.

Ben read from the screen. "I get to witness communication with Mama Sorenson?"

Grace, flustered, declined the call. "Sorry about that."

"Jesus. Did you just hang up on your mom?"

"I sent it to voicemail." She cleared her throat. "It's impolite to answer the phone at the table."

"Okay, Queen Elizabeth. But it's Christmas. You should talk to your mom."

"She's not expecting me to answer."

Ben studied her. "I don't want to pry, but is there some bigger reason you didn't go home? Other than the cost of plane tickets? You speak so highly of your family, and . . ."

She pounded what was left of her vodka soda. The bartender looked up from his Sudoku and, seeing her empty glass, saluted her and set about making her another drink. Despite their afternoon walks, the wee-hours beers, the caffeinated chatter about Christopher Guest and Camera Obscura, she'd never actually told him about the lie she was living. Only Ben knew the truth—that she'd been rejected from law school, that she had a weird-as-fuck job answering infrequent phone calls from struggling saxophonists, that she had never felt as lost as she did now. Ben was the only person in her life who knew the substantive truth, but she hadn't told him that she'd been lying about that truth to everyone else who mattered to her.

"Nobody in my family has any idea what the fuck I'm doing right now," she said. "They don't know that I'm a receptionist and they don't know my house looks like a residential treatment facility and they don't know that I'm spending Christmas in an abandoned bar with a boy who has a whole roster of better offers."

"What the fuck does that mean?" Ben asked. "You— What do they think you're doing?"

"They think I'm in Aspen," she said. "Or, no, the Alps. Which one's closer?"

"I can't tell if you're joking."

"I'm not," she said. "But could we pretend I am? For the purposes of my not weeping in a bar on Christmas?"

Ben studied her, then raised his glass. "To far and away my best offer of the day," he said, and she felt her face ignite.

A shitty frenemy from Reed had once drunkenly asked her, "Is it hard? Having such pretty sisters?"

She knew her sisters were beautiful. But she had always harbored some hope that she was the same way, that she was similarly alluring and just had low self-esteem. She was *fine*-looking, she had always assumed. She had nice hair. She had good skin. She had teeth perfected by years of costly suburban orthodontia. Her breasts were large but not obscenely so (plus didn't guys like that? Weren't they supposed to? Wasn't that just *biology*?). She had her mother's defined waist. She had short, bitten nails like a fourth-grade boy and prematurely jiggly upper arms but her eyebrows were striking, full and dark, and as far as she could tell there was nothing wrong with her labia, no unnaturally large "wings" or anything, which she had learned about (and wished she could *un*learn about) in an unsettling documentary about cosmetic vaginal surgery she watched in GWS330: Psychology of Feminine Self-Perception, and her butt was whatever. She had always skirted the topic in her mind, avoided thinking about the fact that maybe no man would ever want her, because she figured something would eventually click.

Her sisters were sexually interesting. At least she thought they were: Violet was take-charge and fierce; men seemed to like that. And Wendy was—well, not a *slut*, but adventurous, free-spirited, and that had to translate into some kind of prowess, didn't it? And Liza was just *good*—a very complicated, intense kind of goodness that radiated from her, made both men and women stop what they were doing and just *smile* at her, lightened somehow by her presence.

Grace, conversely, was profoundly uninteresting. But if

there was such a marked difference between her and her sisters, wouldn't someone else have pointed it *out* by now? Wouldn't Grace be more aware of a grave disparity? If you were the Hobbit in a sea of Sirens, wouldn't you *know* it? Her mom thought she was pretty, would sometimes get teary-eyed and contemplative and say, "You're so beautiful it hurts me, Goosey." But moms *had* to say those things, Grace supposed. And they probably especially had to say them if their children were homely, to fatten them up with compliments before they unleashed them into a dark world of people who were not their mothers.

"So, it's almost 2017," Ben said, beside her, nicer than he had to be, blessedly quiet on the subject of her major and troubling confession about her family. "What's in store, Sorenson?"

"New leaves?" she said. "Leafs?"

"What's the one thing you most want to have happen?"

She paused, considering it. "I'd like to find my *destiny*," she said, boozy and sentimental. "I'd like to transcend all the bullshit. I'd like to be . . . happy."

"You're not happy now?"

"I—I mean, like, *right* now I am. Here." She blushed. "But broad-scale, there's not— I mean, there are things I wish were a little less . . . you know. Up in the air." She wasn't sure what to do with her body. She wasn't sure what to say. She put a hand on his thigh—loosened, lively—and he looked up at her, smiling.

"Less up in the air sounds good," he said.

She raised her glass again. She felt like she had as a little kid when she had to present in front of her class: aware of being on the precipice of something, unsure of how to make the final leap, of what it would mean if she did. "To being rode hard and put away wet."

"Hey." He laughed. "I'm game if you are."

But she didn't know how to navigate this space. Didn't know what on earth she could say beyond *I both bodily and psychologi-*

cally want this, but I need you to tactfully and generously navigate our course from here on out, because I just can't take the initiative myself. Didn't know why Ben would ever possibly choose to go further with her; out of—what? Kindness? Pity? Some trippy altruistic mind-meld, like when her sisters would invite her along to the movies, impelled by their mother, forced to go see *Air Bud* or *Harriet the Spy* instead of what they actually wanted to watch, *Fight Club* or *The Ice Storm*?

"You don't have to—like, flatter me," she said abruptly.

His face fell. "What? I'm not."

What's it like to have such pretty sisters? Her heartbeat quickened. "I know I'm not, like, a catch." She forced a smile, reached for her drink.

Ben didn't say anything, and when she looked up at him he was staring into his beer.

"What?" she said.

"Why do you talk about yourself like that?"

She blinked. She was truly not one of those people who said self-deprecating things as a means of fishing for compliments. She took another swallow of her drink. How could she articulate this to him, this handsome, inexplicable person sitting beside her drinking a Leinenkugel's? How could she convey to him that she *knew* how embarrassing it would be if she were pursuing him romantically and that knowing was half the battle, that neither of them had to feel embarrassed, that they could keep on with their platonic union without his ever having to worry that she would one day awkwardly break the rules and try to kiss him? She just wanted him to know that she *got it*. She wanted to stay friends and keep talking about Jeff Tweedy and *Twin Peaks* and taking bets about when Justin Bieber would have an emotional breakdown.

"I just don't want you to think that I have, like, some kind of agenda," she said finally. "I'm Eleanor Roosevelt, and I'm actually super-stoked for my spinstress hovel in the woods, because I bet there'll be a bunch of deer and stuff, and I've always wanted to live in a tree stump."

Again, he was quiet, and he took a long sip of his beer. "How do you know *I* don't have an agenda?" he asked, and she chewed the inside of her cheek, disappointed that her preemptive strike had not, in fact, deterred them from this excruciating topic.

"Because. God, Ben. You're *normal.* You're, like, a regular person."

"I guess you've got me figured out," he said after a minute, looking up at her sharply. He didn't sound like himself, first because he wasn't calling her Sorenson and second because he sounded mad; he had never been mad at her before. "First of all," he continued, and his voice still had a distinct, uncomfortable edge to it. "I'm not sure if *normal* is supposed to be some kind of insult, but you're as normal as the rest of us, and I don't know why or when you decided that you weren't. You're not weird, and you're not Eleanor Roosevelt. And it's really hard for me to listen to you characterize me as basically some douchebag who's looking for a *catch*, and it's hard for me to listen to you say that you're *not* a catch, and this entire exchange is making me feel like maybe we don't actually know each other as well as I thought we did." He met her eyes once, quickly. "Which really fucking *sucks* for me because I've wanted to ask you out for like a month, like on an actual date to an actual place like an actual adult person, not just fucking around at a bar like every other dumbass around here. I've wanted to feel like this is—*something.*"

A large percentage of her was trying to determine whether or not this was actually happening—and, if it *was,* how she was supposed to respond. Her first instinct was, she was almost positive, joy, complete elation and delight, but in the passenger seat sat the usual skepticism, the constant, hyperactive court reporter who transcribed her interactions with a healthy dose of cynicism: BEN EXPRESSES HIS AFFECTION FOR GRACE BECAUSE

HE FEELS SORRY ABOUT THE FACT THAT SHE'S A MALADJUSTED
ADULT CHILD WITH A JUST-OKAY ASS AND A SHAMEFULLY FAULTY
GRASP ON NORMAL SEXUAL MATURATION.

"You don't have to . . ." she started to say without thinking, and she immediately stopped herself but Ben was already
standing up, pulling out his wallet, dropping a couple of twenties onto the bar. He was apparently paying for her drinks
while simultaneously walking out on her.

"Thanks for letting me off the fucking hook." Who knew
boys could be so dramatic? Who knew that Ben would wear it
so well? "I'm going to go. Do you have money for a cab?"

It occurred to her, then, that she didn't. Much to her father's
chagrin, she never carried cash on her. "I'll go to an ATM. It's
fine." She mentally slapped herself—she should have just lied—
because Ben pulled out his wallet again. "No, Ben, it's—"

But the look on his face silenced her, and she reached out
and took the money. She watched him go, and suddenly the
bartender was at her elbow again.

"You doing okay?" he asked. He was always there; she'd seen
him a million times before but tonight was the first time she
stopped to take stock of him, youngish, and Irish, and ruggedly
not-quite-handsome, sort of big and outdoorsy, like a bear.

"Not—especially."

"That your boyfriend?"

"No." She sipped her drink, hated herself. "Not really."

So elusive, her girls, Marilyn thought, preparing a little bowl
of Christmas leftovers for Loomis, who was waiting eagerly
at her feet. Gracie hadn't answered the phone when she called.
Violet had responded to her novel-length Merry Christmas
text—featuring an account of the day's activities at the house
on Fair Oaks, a photo of Loomis eating a rawhide candy cane,
and a reminder of the time that Wendy and Violet had got-

ten matching roller skates from Richard and had spent the entire holiday gliding around the basement to the histrionic soundtrack from *Ice Castles*—with a cold and abstruse *xo*. The day had been quiet; they'd done low-key present time and pancakes with Jonah in the morning, and then she and David and Loomis had taken a snowy walk through Thatcher Woods, and then Wendy and Liza had arrived for dinner, and it felt like any other day of the week, utterly devoid of the infectious delight that came from celebrating holidays with children. Her kids weren't kids anymore. She stooped to kiss the dog's impatient head.

"What are you doing?"

She turned to see Liza in the doorway. She'd reached the point in her pregnancy at which her size was almost preposterous. Marilyn thought of Grace again, her most belated baby, who'd been technically, physiologically ready to be born, fullterm, for ten days before she actually arrived. She was, still, that sweet, dawdling girl, unwilling to enter the world.

"Nothing." She set the bowl before Loomis. "Sweetie, why are you even still upright?"

"I'm not an invalid. If anyone should understand how irritating it is to have people telling you to sit down every eight seconds, it's you, Mom. How the fuck did you do this four times?"

"Darling," she said, chastising. "Bodily discomfort took a backseat to the livelihood of a bunch of little kids, in my case. I'm sorry I'm micromanaging. I worry about you."

"You talk to Gracie?" Liza asked, sitting down, after all.

"Mm. No, I left her a voicemail. You haven't talked to her, have you?"

"Not in forever, actually. She's okay?"

"I guess so? I hope so. It's still so hard for me to look at her as anything but a child."

"Does it always feel that way? Do your kids ever stop seeming like kids?"

"Entirely? Never." But she smiled, realizing the need to falsely reassure her immensely pregnant and undeniably single daughter that she would not live out the rest of her life seized with worry. "But it all sorts itself out, Lize. Truly."

"No offense, but that's easy for you to say."

"I—beg your pardon?"

"I just mean—look, Mom, we're not all you and Dad, okay?"

She recoiled, wounded. Didn't her daughters know that what she and David had took work, had always taken work?

"It's not— God, Mom, you talk about it like it's totally normal, but I've literally never met anyone who has what you have with Dad."

"That could be said for any relationship."

"Not *truth*fully."

"Yes, truthfully. Every couple has their own—everything. Highs and lows."

"Of course, but not every couple has those with absolute certainty that no *low* is going to be low enough to derail them."

She wasn't sure what to say, wasn't sure whether to invoke her mental ledger of all that had gone wrong in her marriage, all that had been propelled by anger or fear or ignorance. Her daughters had fanned out: to different cities, to different states; to different planets, it seemed sometimes.

"We're all emotionally stunted because you and Dad love each other more than you love us," Wendy added conversationally. Marilyn hadn't noticed her standing in the doorway, and now she came to sit beside her sister at the table, twisting her limbs yogically, her gorgeous and radically unpredictable eldest, the button pusher.

"Lord, what a thing to say. Is this some kind of intervention? *Merry Christmas, Mom.*"

"Do you disagree?" Liza asked, the two of them tag-teaming her now, apparently, her two sharp-eyed, honey-haired daughters.

"Of *course* I—"

"It's not necessarily a bad thing," Wendy said. "I'd rather be fucked up because my parents are hot for each other than because they're, like, keeping me chained to a bike rack overnight and feeding me raw oats. But you have to admit that there's a gradient of preference."

"That's not how love works, Wendy."

"Who are you to say how love works, though?" Wendy asked. "Just because you've been married for like eight centuries and you still check out Dad's butt when he's mowing the lawn?"

"Who *made* you girls this way? Dad and I were lucky to find each other, but I don't love him *more* than— It's a whole different thing. A different ball game. An entirely different *kind* of love, your love for your kids."

"I'm not talking about the kind, I'm talking about the amount."

"I thought my heart was going to burst open when you were born, Wendy. Both of you girls. *All* of you girls. If you want to talk about *mag*nitude—"

"Babies don't count," Wendy said. "Everyone loves babies."

"I feel—lucky, actually," Liza said. "It made for a wonderful childhood, you have to admit. But it feels like a pretty fucking insurmountable bar to reach as an adult."

She didn't chastise her daughter's language this time.

"We all *desperately* want your life," Liza said. "And we all know we'll never have it."

She considered—openly, for the first time—the sheer amount of luck she and David had happened upon, and the fact that she, forty years married, despite everything, knew that he would always be her person, in some important capacity; that they were mutually exclusive.

She studied Liza, her third-born daughter, who would set all sorts of examples for her own child about fortitude and flexibility, who would someday sit before the baby in her belly like

Marilyn was sitting before her now, accountable for any number of questions about how she'd made her life work. And her firstborn: tenacious, resilient, unsparing Wendy.

"Am I allowed to play the *I birthed you* card here?" she asked them. "In an effort to spare myself from further holiday abuse?"

"Are you girls giving your mother hell?" David in the doorway now; David, who'd never not been around; David, who took Wendy's blood pressure and hummed Springsteen songs to baby Liza when he thought his wife was sleeping; David, whom she'd chosen, who'd chosen her back. "On Christmas, of all days?" He came over, put his arm around her waist, and the girls watched them. These vexatious little mysteries they'd created, imperfect and endlessly exquisite. She knew she and her husband were, then and there, reinforcing all of the accusations Wendy and Liza had just made. *Not necessarily a bad thing*, Wendy had said, though. She wove her arm around her husband, and she decided, in the moment, that she didn't really care.

2000

One night when everyone was back for a weekend, Grace, six years old, woke up to laughter from the living room—her sisters awake together, without her, making jokes she didn't understand. She was drifting back to sleep when she heard her mother's voice, different but distinct.

"Well, that's what I *mean*." Her mom and her sisters all beside themselves about something. She tiptoed to the top of the stairs, listening. Little bits of leftover laughter. A creak of the living room floorboards. She advanced down the stairs, her nightgown brushing her legs. She paused at the bottom. Liza and Wendy were curled up in armchairs. Across from them, her mother and Violet were on the couch, her mother's feet up on the coffee table. She had a ponytail and her dad's old baseball shirt with the red sleeves and she looked like someone Grace had never met before; she looked like Wendy. There was music in the background—*I'm a fleabit peanut monkey and all my friends are junkies*—and Wendy bobbed her head a little to the beat.

"The perils of the collegiate lifestyle," her mom was saying.

Then Liza spotted her, smiled and crossed her eyes and stuck out her tongue. Liza was usually pretty nice unless she was in what their mother called "one of her moods."

"There's a ghost in the hallway," Liza said, and everyone turned to look.

She would remember the thing that happened to her mother's face forever. It started out one way—girlish, glowing, ready to tell a story—and turned another, melted a little in disappointment. She knew she'd interrupted something sacred—this meeting of women—and she felt profoundly left out and guilty at once, butting in when her mom looked so happy. Her mother had been a girl in one second and herself again in another; she was still wearing the baseball shirt but everything else had changed. Sometimes Grace felt like she had two moms, the one who was kind of older than other moms and the one who was about as old as her sisters. The face fixed itself quickly, turned into the face that Grace saw four million times a day, the freckled, sleepy, smiling face with big green eyes that always looked happy to see her except when she was whining.

"A goose," her mother said, moving her legs from the table, opening her arms. "Not a ghost at all. Come here, sweet one."

She crept in and then made a beeline for her mother lest she'd aroused this same kind of disappointment in her sisters. She didn't want to see their faces. She crawled into her mom's lap and tucked her face against her warm sharp collarbone.

"Hey, pumpkin. Were we too loud down here?"

"Yes, enlighten us, buzzkill," she heard Wendy say. She felt her mother stiffen.

"She's not a buzzkill."

"What is that?" she asked, curiosity piqued, lifting her head from her mother's chest.

"Someone who shows up to a party four hours late wearing an Ariel nightgown."

"What are you doing?"

"Having a little girl time, honeybunch," her mom said, her breath warm against the part in Grace's hair, the waxy white line between two brown sides.

"I'm a girl," she said emphatically, and she watched as her mother and sisters made eye contact, all of them smiling. Wendy snorted.

"Of course you are," said her mom. "I meant my older girls. A little older girl time."

"We're talking about grown-up stuff, Gracie," Violet supplied.

"It's so late, little darling," her mom said.

"I'll put her to bed," Liza said. "Come on, Goose."

She felt suddenly indignant; her feelings were hurt and she *was* a girl, too, and she didn't want her sisters to have this new distorted version of her mother if she didn't get to have it as well. She rested her head defiantly again on her mother's chest. "No," she said. "I want Mama."

Her mom opened her mouth, closed it again. "It's past my bedtime anyway," she said. "All right, all right. Up we go, gosling." She rose from the couch and Grace tightened her legs around her waist. She regarded her sisters over their mother's shoulder. Liza looked disappointed and Wendy and Violet both looked annoyed. "Sweet dreams, honeys. Don't stay up too late." Marilyn blew a kiss to the room and started up the stairs with her. Grace rested her face on her mother's shoulder and closed her eyes, pretended to sleep so she wouldn't have to see the aftermath of the gathering she'd disrupted. *Buzzkill.*

Liza decided to get the tattoo because it seemed like it would make a good story. Dorky girl makes a bold move; is immediately noticed by all important outsiders; life changes color. She was not yet eighteen, so she had to maneuver, legally speaking. Her parents had not specifically forbidden tattoos but she knew they would say no if she asked. So she waited until her mom was going to visit Violet at Wesleyan for the weekend, yanked Wendy's old ID from her sister's abandoned bedroom, and went to Blue Moon Ink on Division. She was clutching a folder with the artwork in it; she had meticulously sketched the design using the Smashing Pumpkins album cover, the star, sans baby-angel. She braced herself against the leather chair as *Dirk*—at first she thought that the ironic fifties-mechanic cursive on his shirt spelled out *Dick*—seared the image onto her skin.

It took her three painful days to realize that her tattoo was infected. She discovered it on Saturday morning, when she awakened feeling feverish, and she ignored it for several hours, curled up on the living room couch watching *The X-Files*. The pain was worsening, though; the skin at the nape of her neck was swollen and tender, and there was also the undeniable earthy smell of her bandages. This was, she decided, probably something you could not will away.

Who to call, though? Liza wasn't *un*popular in high school so much as she was *a*popular; she got by each day with few peer interactions and left in the afternoons without any inkling of being disliked. But she had no one upon whom it would be normal to call in a time of crisis—when, for instance, you'd developed an infection after you went by yourself to get an illegal tattoo. She knew her father would come home from work in a heartbeat, furious and mildly cursing ("sonofa*bitch*, Lize") but present nonetheless. But then Wendy appeared in her head, materialized like an irritating swami, her older sister who was just across town in her swanky new Hyde Park townhouse with her ancient boyfriend. She took a deep breath and dialed the number.

"Liza," Wendy exclaimed, sounding strangely excited to hear from her. "Thank God. I need some advice." As though Wendy had been the one to place the call. "We're having this party tonight for a bunch of terrible people from Hong Kong and I'm freaking out about what to wear. There are some Asian people in Oak Park still, right? Are any of them not totally prudish?"

"What?" Liza sank into a chair by the phone.

"Can I wear something that's above the knee? Or are all Asians super-conservative?"

"I don't think all of them?" Liza squeaked, incredulous.

"It's black, so it's understated," Wendy said. "We got it in Milan. It sounds okay, right?"

"I don't . . ."

"Thanks, Lize. Shit, they're going to be here soon. I have to get ready. Did you need something, or were you just calling to say hi?" No one in their family called *just to say hi*. That was not how they operated. She swallowed a few times to prevent herself from crying.

"No, just calling to say hi."

"You're sweet. Thanks for your help, Lize. Wish me luck tonight, huh?" And then she was gone, the line dead. Liza chewed the inside of her lip and picked up the phone again.

Her father came into the living room and sat beside her on the couch. She was crying but trying not to cry, staring at her toes and refusing to look at him.

"I'm sorry," she said, and that seemed to break the spell; he shifted back a few inches and lifted her ponytail. He seemed just to be staring at her neck for what felt like several minutes.

"It's definitely infected." He didn't quite touch the area and she stiffened involuntarily. "It's painful, I take it?"

"Yeah," she said. Then: "I mean, kind of."

"Turn around."

She faced him and he cupped his palm over her forehead, frowning.

"I can't tell if you're warm. Come here." This coveted maternal gesture: David sometimes felt their foreheads in the way that Marilyn did, bowing his face down to rest his cheek above their eyebrows. He hadn't done this to her since she was a child. "You're not too warm, but you're warm. I'll call in a script for an antibiotic and we'll go pick it up."

"Thanks."

"Liza, *why*?" he asked, still holding up her hair, still studying the inflamed ring. "Do you realize how close this is to your spinal cord? How dangerous that is?"

"I wanted to," she said, still trying not to cry, trying to sound petulant and careless instead of like the most pathetic, lonely person in the world. "It's my body."

"For Christ's sake, Lize, this is such a cliché." Something in his voice sounded sad, which made her feel a trillion times more terrible. "Just talk to us. It's much less contrived."

She, though quite sarcastic herself, could not appreciate her father's humor. She scowled.

"What can I do?" he asked gently. "Tell me what I should be doing."

"Nothing." She spun away from him, ran up the stairs and slammed her bedroom door.

The next morning he came into her room early. She felt him sit next to her on the bed and as she awakened she became aware of the hot ache on her neck.

"How much does it hurt?" he asked. Their father had been employing the pain-scale method on all of them since they were tiny. They had learned early not to abuse it when ten-year-old Violet declared her sore throat a 9.5 and David sat them all down and talked to them about terminal illnesses, about how lucky they were, and about how if they had to think about whether something was a 9.5 or not then it was definitely *not* a 9.5. That morning she considered, weakly, the pulsing at the back of her neck. It was unpleasant, yes, but was it as bad as a third-degree burn? As bone cancer? She decided that this, however uncomfortable—and likely exacerbated by her shame—was probably no more than a 4.

"I'm just going to take a look, okay? It might hurt a little when I take the gauze off." She braced herself but her father was gentle and meticulous, slowly peeling away her bandage. "Mm," he murmured, and she felt the tips of his fingers touching the very edges again. "Well, it looks okay. I mean— considering the fact that someone accepted money in exchange for branding a giant star onto my daughter's neck. It doesn't appear to be getting worse." His voice was almost playful and she felt the familiar curiosity about her father, about who he used to be, before her, before her mother, before any of them. It seemed like her dad had always been someone's *dad*, kind and soft-spoken and austere. "Stay still for a second, sweetie." She felt a tiny point of pressure, not so different from the tattoo gun.

She tensed. "Daddy—"

"Sorry, sorry. Just making a pen mark so I can measure if the area's shrinking or not."

All this knowledge he had that she'd never considered. He reached into her nightstand for the anti-inflammatory cream and a Q-tip and he applied it to her skin and covered it with a new bandage. "This would kill Mom, Liza-lee," he said. She blinked, and he stroked her hair, a little awkwardly. "So we'll take care of it, okay? You stay on top of it and I'm going to check on you until it's healed." She shifted to face him, ignoring the pain in her neck. "We'll keep it between us." It was rare— extraordinary—to hear him speak like this; she knew he loved her, loved all of them, but he was not a very talkative man and even less of an emotional one. He reserved that for their mother. "If you want to tell her, feel free. But I'm not going to. It's not my place. It's my job to make sure you're safe. I'll do that part." She opened her mouth to speak but found herself unable. He leaned down and kissed her forehead. "You're a good egg, Lize. Let me know *immediately* if it starts to feel worse than a four."

"Okay," she croaked, and she watched as the silhouette of her father disappeared again into the hallway.

It had been surprisingly easy to become someone's wife. Wendy moved in with Miles not long after they met and made sure she left her mark throughout his house—soy milk in the fridge, box of tampons under the sink, surreptitious spritzes of her Bulgari musk on the sheets. A year later, they married in her parents' backyard, surrounded by Gatsbyesque strangers and awash in Dom. And after that it was like someone had flipped a switch; suddenly this three-story townhouse in Hyde Park belonged to *her*, and Miles carted her along to cocktail receptions and donor recognition dinners, and after two awkward times she figured out the dress code, what was okay (wrap dresses; pashminas) and what wasn't (knits or anything strapless), and suddenly it was like she was meant to be there. She chatted up his older colleagues, charmed the pants off of them, and was pretty good with their wives, too, murmuring things like *I'm older than I look, trust me* and *Bunny, I have a lot to learn from you*. And it was work, but she *fit*. Finally, somewhere, she fit. She was young and beautiful and everyone thought she was quick-witted and sharp and it was just assumed that she was *keeping Miles in line*, though in actuality he was the one who kept things going. He was rich, from his grandparents, had happened upon his wealth by genetic chance, and he shared readily, adding her to his accounts without a second thought.

His job at Harold Washington gave texture to his gobs of money: his parents had, of course, wanted him to take something at Northwestern or the U of C, and certainly would have been able to make it happen for him, but he'd demurred, explaining to Wendy that spending his days teaching students whose parents could afford forty-grand-a-year tuition—students like he himself had been—would only fuel his well-oiled hatred of the American elite, into which he had undeniably been born. Her husband had a complicated relationship with his privilege, working constantly against all that he could easily be taking for granted. And he had fun with his students, she could see; he took unfathomable amounts of time grading their papers and prepping his lectures. He took his job seriously, even though technically he didn't have to, and there was a beautiful dignity to that, she thought.

Other than his course load, he sat on the boards of a few nonprofits, but he mostly spent time with her. She started getting involved in charities and social clubs and once she had enough of those things to make a *schedule* she no longer felt bad about quitting school or her job.

She started owning it, her new life with her Audi and her checkbook and her badass contrarian husband. She was finally able to shed the part of her that was fucked-up and anxious and deficient in comparison to her unyieldingly middle-class, moderate-to-high-functioning family. She was in love, and someone loved her back.

And then one day, by some miracle, she answered the phone and it was Violet, the only person missing from the newfound wonder of her circumstances, but before she could get too excited, her sister started talking, her voice unrecognizably uneven, and everything started to slip after that, down down down, gaining speed, lightpost-bound, like a doomed kid on a sled.

CHAPTER TWENTY-THREE

She and Matt had survived Christmas with his parents by banking on their limited acting skills, using their children as a distraction, and avoiding each other as much as possible. If his family noticed the chill between them, nobody mentioned it. There was a fog delay for their flight out of Sea-Tac so they didn't return to Chicago until nearly midnight, and Violet, by the next morning, was so desperate to be alone that she took the boys through the drive-through drop-off lane, derided by most Shady Oaks moms as being taken advantage of by the lazy or employed.

Her mother called just as she was walking in the door.

"Are the weary travelers back?" Marilyn asked when she picked up the phone.

"Just barely," Violet said. She made a point to sound beleaguered sometimes when talking to her mother, to drive home the point that just because she'd had half as many kids didn't mean that her life wasn't still stressful.

"Well, merry belated," her mom said, sounding a little short.

"Is everything okay?"

"Yes, fine. Well. I mean, everything *is* fine, but I— Listen, *please* don't take this out on Jonah, Violet, because he didn't volunteer the information without my prompting, but I heard what happened at your house that night he came for dinner."

"What did he tell you?" she asked carefully.

"Just that— Well, he told me what happened with Wyatt, the whole thing about Santa Claus, but he also told me that you'd gotten quite upset with him, that you asked him to leave."

"I'm sorry, how exactly did you *prompt* that specific information from him?"

"He was upset when Matt dropped him off. I kept asking him what had happened and he finally told me. There's no reason to take that tone, Violet; it was clearly an accident . . ."

"I don't have a *tone* and he didn't *accidentally* tell him; Wyatt asked him and he easily could've talked his way out of it."

Her mother was quiet.

"God, Mom, what?"

"No, it's— I'd hoped maybe he was . . . I hoped he'd misinterpreted your anger, I guess."

"Did you call to scold me for getting mad because Jonah ruined Christmas for my son?"

"Jonah is also your son, Violet."

When she wasn't ruing it, she envied her mother's ability to speak about the world with such frank obviousness. But right now she just wanted a few fucking minutes to catch her breath after the Christmas from hell with her frigid husband and her hyperactive children.

"Oh my God, Mom, you can't just— You don't have any right to—" But she recognized her anxiety as the kind that came with being caught, and she was afraid of what her mother was going to say next. Her mother, the pacifist. Her mother, who gave her such a long leash. "Christ, Mom, I never *wanted* this. I don't have room in my *life* for this."

"*This* being Jonah, you mean." It was jarring to hear her mother sounding angry.

"Sorry we don't all quite have your free-love, open-door policy, Mom. Sorry some of us actually *like* for elements of our lives to not be utter chaos all the time."

"It's my free-love open-door chaos that's the reason Jonah isn't getting shuffled through the child welfare system anymore, Violet. A fact that you've never acknowledged or expressed an ounce of gratitude for. This whole *family* has rallied to care for this kid, and I don't think it's unreasonable to wonder where you've *been* the last eight months. You're his mother."

"Look, Mom, if you want to be worried about one of us? Wendy's been on the edge of a cliff for decades. Liza's pregnant by a man who's never going to be remotely her equal in terms of maturity or functionality. There are plenty of other directions for you to focus your attention."

"I'm going to get off the phone before I say something I regret," her mother said, her voice clipped. "I'll be here to talk if you decide you want to, Violet." Her last few syllables wavered, and she hung up.

She never fought with her mother; to have Marilyn—loving, patient, easygoing Marilyn—be angry with her felt uniquely awful. It dawned on her, as she went to curl up in the armchair overlooking their side yard, wrapping a blanket around her shoulders, feeling her eyes and nose leaking beyond her consent, that she had felt as lonely as she did lately only twice before in her adult life: the weeks following Jonah's birth, and the weeks following Wyatt's. She couldn't talk to Wendy. She couldn't talk to Matt. She could barely bring herself, anymore, to engage in the most base-level small talk. And now she'd driven away her mother, too, and this felt like the most damning thing of all. She wanted to call Marilyn back and tell her this—*I'm sorry, I'm lost, I know I fucked up*—but she'd left her phone in the kitchen, and she was suddenly so tired she could barely move, and so she just lay there, knees to her chest, crying in the way she'd resisted for months until she didn't have anything left, until— empty, utterly depleted—she fell blackly asleep.

. . .

Jonah went to Wyatt's school less to spite Violet than because he thought it would be nice to be a little kid and have an adult promise you something and then actually do it. He had never had that, though he was starting to understand how nice it was, because David was never late—not even by a minute— picking him up from Krav Maga, and Marilyn remembered that he hated asparagus but was okay with broccoli. So he ditched second period and took the Green Line to the Red Line to the Purple Line and then followed the directions he'd printed and jogged thirteen blocks to Shady Oaks Academy, and he arrived, both freezing and sweaty, only eight minutes after ten. He hadn't talked to Violet or Matt since the night he'd ruined Santa. He wondered if Violet had put him onto some prep-school no-fly list and he'd be turned away by security. But he was banking on the fact that she would be too embarrassed to cause a scene and would explain him away as some poor little street urchin whom she would allow to watch her son's performance as an act of charity. He wasn't looking forward to seeing her again.

When he told the secretary he was there to see Wyatt, her face broke open in relief.

"Oh, thank *God*," she said. "He's been a wreck. Poor thing. Are you— Wait, I'm not sure I have you on the list. Are you a new babysitter?"

But suddenly there was a blue blur coming toward him, and then Wyatt was in his arms, wrapped around his torso like a koala.

"I'm his brother," he said, the words clumsy in his mouth. Wyatt was weeping, again that sad quiet kind, almost like an adult. "Whoa, okay." He patted the kid's back. Then—so the secretary, whose *list* seemed pretty official, didn't call the cops—he added: "Half brother." He tilted his head down. "Wyatt, buddy, it's okay. It's all right."

"What on earth is going on?" A woman in a skirt-suit had

appeared behind the secretary's desk, along with a scary-looking tall-haired Spandexed lady.

"This is his . . . brother," the secretary explained.

"I wasn't aware that Wyatt had an older brother," said the principal.

He took an immediate dislike to these two women. "Violet's my mom." It was the first time he'd ever said it and the last thing he'd been expecting to say, and he could only imagine Violet's reaction if she were here, the fury he would incite simply by stating the obvious. And then, with a bit more authority: "What's going on? Why is he so upset?"

"Mr. Lowell is in a meeting," the principal said. "And Mrs. Sorenson-Lowell is—running late, apparently."

"Just a little case of stage fright," the secretary said more tactfully, patting Wyatt on the back. "How'd you feel about doing your song now, with your brother here?"

"I'm sorry," Spandex said, jutting out a hip, giving Jonah a once-over like Violet sometimes did, like he was spewing bad intentions and environmental toxins. "Who *is* this person? How did he even— Is this how lax our security has become, that we just . . ."

Jonah stared at her and she trailed off. "*I'm* sorry," he said, "but who the hell are you?"

"I'm Mrs. Morley, the vice president of the Parents' Association," she said emphatically, but then her curiosity seemed to get the better of her. "Did you say you were Violet's—*son?*"

"What's your name, young man?" the principal asked, equally intrigued. "Do you have some form of identification?"

Like the cop after he'd wrecked Liza's car. Rich people were endlessly obsessed with identity verification.

"I'm fifteen," he said. His birthday was in two days, at which point he'd be eligible for a legitimate ID. "Jonah Bendt. You can call Matt and ask him. But I still don't get— Wyatt, buddy, what's the matter?"

Wyatt pulled his head away and looked at Jonah. "Where's Mama?"

He had no fucking idea where Violet was, and he was shocked that she wasn't here, and it made him nervous, her absence, because forgetting didn't seem like something she did.

"She got stuck in traffic," he said without thinking. Wyatt continued to stare at him expectantly. "Yeah, it was— There was a crazy—this crazy accident and your mom got stuck on the other side of it. This big accident with a train and like a million cars, and a fire, and—"

The principal cleared her throat.

"Everyone was fine, though. And Violet—your mom was watching the whole thing from a few blocks away, but she couldn't move her car, right, because everyone else was stopped, too, and so she—she called me and told me to let you know that she's fine and she's trying to make it but if she can't then . . ." He glanced up at the secretary, who seemed like a better wing-woman than the principal. "What's your name?"

"Miss Ruth," she said, like that was a normal name to go by as an adult.

"If your mom can't make it, Miss Ruth is going to record the whole thing on my phone, and you and your mom and your dad can all watch it together. Does that sound good?"

Wyatt whispered something, his face once again buried in Jonah's shirt.

"Come again?"

"I can't do it by myself," he repeated.

"You won't be by yourself," he said, though he had a bad feeling about where this was headed. "I'll be there, and your whole class, and—Miss Ruth."

Miss Ruth beamed.

"No, I can't *sing* by myself. Mama promised to sing with me if I got too nervous."

"Yeah, except." He cleared his throat. "Yeah, except, man,

remember how we talked about this? I'm not a singer. You're the singer."

"I'm not the singer. *Mama* is the singer but I do it too because no one knows the song if it's just the music." Wyatt shook his head, his body beginning to tremble. This poor nervous kid.

"Hey, hey," he said. He said it into the top of Wyatt's head like he'd seen Violet do. "All right, man. Fine. I'll do it with you."

The moms surrounded him in droves after the Star of the Week performance, bringing with them an amalgamated cloud of perfume and a blinding rainbow of athleticwear.

"You two were *adorable* up there," one woman said. "I had no idea that Wyatt had an older brother; are you adopted?"

He'd gotten through the performance by numbing himself to the crowd and focusing only on Wyatt, his little brother with his teensy guitar. He had a weird moment at the beginning where he remembered hearing the song in the car with his dad—his *dad*-dad, his viaduct dad—but he pushed past it, toward a moment from last week, fixing the gnarly shower stall in the basement with his grandpa and watching David's face light up as he said, "Marilyn *loves* CCR." By the end of the first verse he'd kind of gotten into it, drumming the beat onto the edge of the teacher's desk, singing along with Wyatt without caring what his voice sounded like and without caring, for the most part, that he got a little choked up midway through. And he was proud of Wyatt, the first time he'd ever been proud of another person: this goofy kid who'd just been let down by his parents for the first time in his life and still pulled it together enough to sing a whole song in front of his class.

"You have a *lovely* voice," one of the moms said, and another, picking up seamlessly, asked, "Is that something you get from Violet's side? Or your dad's?"

"Where *is* Violet, by the way?" said another, a startled-looking woman with dark eye makeup and a visor. "She's been keeping a pretty low *profile* lately, but it seems unbe*lie*vable to me that she'd miss Star of the Week."

He was able to ignore them, mostly, by watching Wyatt commune with his classmates, all of whom seemed to like Wyatt as much as he did. But he was worried about Violet, despite everything, because for her to miss something like this did seem radically out of character, even though he wasn't entirely sure what her character was. He wasn't sure she knew what her *own* character was, to be honest, but she at least seemed pretty heavily swayed by the opinions of others, and he figured it had to be something pretty bad that prevented her from being here to fend off the stylish vultures and keep them from learning about him, her darkest secret.

He didn't like her, but he didn't wish her *dead*.

"She's not actually my mom," he said, knowing Wyatt was out of earshot. Being someone's family had something to do, he'd learned from watching his grandparents, with taking one for the team. "She and her—Matt, they were volunteering at the shelter where I live. And they took me out to lunch one day with Wyatt and Eli and we all just—hit it off."

"A shelter?" said one of the women, looking suddenly devastated.

"More like a group home," he said. "Lathrop House."

Were he some kind of precocious Disney-movie hero, he would have expounded on the importance of giving to those less fortunate, on the fact that nobody who lived at Lathrop House *chose* to live at Lathrop House, and that they could really use some new iPads for the computer lab, some more contemporary books in the library. But at the moment, all he wanted to do was scram before he had a chance to make anything worse, before Tall Hair called the cops or before it was revealed that

Violet had been crushed to death by a stop sign in the accident he'd made up to calm Wyatt down. Miss Ruth had assured him that Matt was on his way.

"Buddy," he whispered, pulling Wyatt aside, kneeling before him. "I've got to get back to school. But you kicked *ass* out there, okay?"

Wyatt smiled baldly, trusting him like kids deserved to trust adults, or fifteen-year-olds, whatever, like how he wanted Wyatt to be able to trust the world, though he hadn't been able to himself; and he held out his fist for Wyatt to bump.

Violet awakened and didn't remember falling asleep. Her head felt leaden, her esophagus raw from crying. She rose from the chair and stretched, feeling the stiffness in her body from sleeping in a ball. She wondered what regrettable thing her mother had prevented herself from saying when she hung up the phone. She felt her eyes fill again when she heard a strange buzzing sound: her phone, on vibrate, half-covered by a dish towel on the counter.

"Hey," she said, seeing Matt's name.

"Oh my God," he said. "Oh, for— God, are you okay, Viol? Jesus Christ."

"I'm fine," she said. "I fell—"

"I— You have no idea what I've been— Holy *shit*, Violet, I can't believe that you . . ."

She felt the same creeping dread as she had when she'd talked to her mother.

"I guess you forgot what was happening today," Matt said.

It thumped through her head like an extra heartbeat: *oh no oh no oh no.* "What?" She leaned against the table, looked over at her kitchen wall calendar. "Oh, God." Oh, poor Wyatt. Oh, her poor, tiny star, sweeter than anyone on the earth.

"They waited a while for you," Matt said. "They tried calling you."

She closed her eyes. "Did you go? Did he do it?"

"I was in a meeting. I left right after they called but traffic was hell."

"What *happened*?" she asked again.

"Jonah came."

Surprising and inevitable. It stilled her.

"They sang it together. Miss Ruth made a video for us."

Were they on solid ground, they both might have laughed at something like this. *Miss Ruth.* They both might have taken a moment to bask in how bizarre it was, their kindergartener's debut CCR performance, accompanied on vocals by his relinquished half brother, before an audience of women who'd be fueling their lunchtime conversation with the indiscretion for *months*, Bouffanted Gretchen and Ashton's Mom and Jennifer Goldstein-Visor.

But instead she was crying, and Matt sounded angrier than she'd ever heard him.

"Jesus, Violet. I *told* you something like this would happen. Plus I just left in the middle of a meeting with the DreamWorks guys."

"I was so tired," she said.

"Okay, but here's the— I'm not sure what's quite so tiring when the only thing you're required to do is not be a shitty mom."

"That's—that's an awful thing to say."

"Yeah, well, it's been pretty fucking awful for the last hour when I assumed you were *dead*, Violet, not *napping*."

"Did you tell Wyatt how sorry I am?"

"Of *course* I did," Matt said. "Jesus, have you told *me* how sorry you are? Will you tell Jonah? Christ. This is exactly what I've been trying to avoid. But he's in it now, you see that?

He made up this whole story about how you got caught in traffic. He saved us, Violet."

"I'm sorry," she said.

"You could try," Matt said, his voice eerily measured, "to sound sorrier."

The landscapers wouldn't come to cut down the ginkgo until spring, and he wasn't going to let it languish like it was, stripped of its dignity, dead branches drooping downward. Plus he had an apprentice now, in Jonah, who was strong and nimble and seemed to take pleasure in physical exertion. A branch fell and he bent to retrieve it, throwing it into the pile with the others. Jonah, fifteen feet up, killed the motor on the chainsaw.

"I forgot to tell you," he said. "I need this permission slip signed."

"What for?" He stepped forward as Jonah began his descent on the ladder.

"It's this tournament," he said. "This regional Krav Maga thing."

He did not pretend to understand the boy's unusual extra-curricular activity, but it seemed to be a good thing for him, a source of structure. "Regional sounds like a big deal."

"Yeah, kind of." Jonah met his eyes once, quickly, and appeared to be suppressing a smile. "I'm a finalist. Statewide. So I get to compete against—like, really good people."

"As a really good person yourself, it sounds like?"

Jonah shrugged.

"That's fantastic," he said.

"It's not for a couple months. April. Can I go?"

"Of course," he said. "I mean—as far as I— We should talk to Marilyn too. And—Violet? Or—well. I'm sure it won't be a problem. Can families come?" He shook out the stiffness in his shoulder and reached for the chainsaw. Jonah held the ladder for him as he climbed.

"I'm not sure. I guess so."

He made it to the branch above where Jonah had last been cutting and leaned back against the trunk, winded. "Well, find out. I'd like to see what all the fuss is about."

"You'd want to come?"

He looked down to see that the incredulity in Jonah's voice matched the expression on his face. He smiled. "Of course we would. Marilyn's conflict-avoidant, so she might want to pace around outside during the actual fighting, but we'd love to see what you're—" A belch rose in his throat and he colored. He revved up the saw and went to work on a branch, but about halfway through he was overcome by nausea. He turned off the saw, his lungs quickly filling with a rising panic. "Christ, it's hot, all of a sudden."

"It's like five degrees out here," the boy said.

He tried to laugh. "Of course. That's what I meant."

The world, at once, seemed finite and fleeting, the breath in his lungs limited. He was sweating through his sweater. His wife, twenty years old, above him beneath this very ginkgo tree. His daughters, again and again and again and again, coming into the world. His father exiting it. All of those things gone in an instant, nobody left to remember them but him and now no longer him, it seemed. Marilyn on all fours, just before Gracie was born. *Motherfucker.* The pain in his chest, sudden and crushing, insistent behind his sternum.

"Jonah, I'm going to drop this down. Don't try to— I'm just going to—" The saw fell from his hands and he heard it land on the cold ground with a sickening crack. "I just need to—"

"David?"

The lawn swam beneath him. The sharp pain behind his heart. "Sonofa*bitch.*"

"David, are you okay?"

The dog barked, muffled, from inside of the house.

"I need to—I need you to— If you can hold the ladder— I'm just not feeling—"

And then the dog: loud and ever-present, having pushed through the screen door.

"Call Marilyn," he said woozily. "But don't scare her."

"Fuck," Jonah was saying. "*Fuck*, get *away* from me, you—"

The barking.

"Tell her—" He felt half-formed and disoriented. He smiled. "Tell her she's the most fun I've ever had." And the sharpness grew sharper, and his vision began to blur, and he couldn't make his limbs move the way he wanted them to, and Jonah was yelling from the ground, and he wanted to tell the boy not to worry, that there was nothing he could do, but he found he couldn't really speak, either, because the pain was all-consuming.

"David!" the boy yelled.

The dog barked madly.

His gaze drifted downward. Jonah and Loomis, swirling in circles.

He'd read, of course, about life flashing before you in the final moments.

The last thing he pictured—as he fell from the ladder, as the world began to swim—was the beguiling cat-green of his wife's eyes.

Violet reentered Wendy's life in an exquisitely un-Violetesque fashion, her trembling voice over the phone spewing disclosure: "I have nowhere to live and now I'm late and I'm never late."

And Wendy's first shameful thought: *Well well well, look who's just as fucked-up as the rest of us.* She had been sunbathing nude on the roof of the brownstone and she sank back into one of their deck chairs and folded her legs into a pretzel, reveling in her pantilessness and the position of inarguable power her sister was placing in her lap. Violet had been brooding at their wedding nearly three months ago, still reeling from a breakup with her lame boyfriend, too heartbroken, apparently, to dredge up any occasion-appropriate happiness for Wendy, the glowing bride. And now Violet was knocked up. She reached for her sundress and slipped it over her head, suspecting that this was not a conversation she wanted to conduct naked.

"I have to take care of it," Violet said. "Jesus Christ, Wendy, I'm starting law school in a couple of months."

Of course she knew about this; of course there had been ample discussion of Violet's recent U of C acceptance at her parents' house when last she'd seen them. But Violet hadn't led with that sentiment; she'd begun with *I have to take care of it*, and Wendy wasn't sure if she was imagining the indecisive wobble in her sister's voice as she delivered that particular line.

"I mean, why?" she asked, and she marinated in Violet's resultant quiet, letting the midsummer breeze flutter the hem of her skirt.

"I just— I wasn't expecting for this to . . ."

"You could be siring the next Stephen Hawking," she said. And, at Violet's silence: "Or, I mean, not a great example, I guess. But—hey, there's a chance you and Mr. Express-for-Men Poindexter might enhance Dad's scientific genes in a way that none of the rest of us could."

Her sister remained quiet, and her heartbeat trilled.

Then: "Rob doesn't shop at Ex*press*, Wendy; I don't understand why you have to be so—"

"I'm just *saying*," Wendy said, "that you could be harboring a kid who comes out with the periodic table memorized."

Violet's silence, then, she recognized as the tearful kind, and she remembered the context, the content, the stakes.

"I'm just asking why this is so black-and-white for you. Because you don't seem particularly happy with the option you've chosen."

"Nobody's happy about having an abortion, Wendy."

"Maybe it's not your only option."

"I just— I've never felt so— But of course it's the most logical . . ."

"It's not always the most logical decision that's the right decision," Wendy said, feeling wacky and sage and somehow powerful, like their mother. But it was what she would have told herself. You didn't always *have* to do what other people expected you to do. She'd built an entire life around this. "I'm just saying that you can find a little leeway if you want to. Defer school for a year. Come here, if you want. God. I'm not saying that you have to *do* anything; I just mean that the thing that everyone else does isn't always necessarily the best thing."

"You have no idea how fucking *scary* this is for me," Violet said.

And so Wendy was triply surprised when her sister called her from the airport three days later.

"I don't know what I'm doing," Violet said, climbing beside her into the passenger seat of Miles's Audi.

"First time for everything," she said, but she took a second—in the O'Hare arrivals lane, with neon-vested sticks-in-the-mud ushering her car out of its idling place—to look her sister up and down. "You look *fulsome*," she said. "You actually look really good, Viol."

"You're sure Miles is okay with this?"

Her husband had been unbelievably accepting when she'd floated the idea by him, still fascinated, as an only child, by Wendy's mystical ties to her myriad siblings.

"Absolutely okay," she said. She glided the car into traffic, and she and Violet spent the stop-and-go ride home on the Kennedy talking about what was to come.

She'd pulled the lie about Paris out of her ass, and Violet, conversationally fluent from a French minor, had gone with it, and when they got to Hyde Park they sat drinking lemonade on the roof, Wendy in the hammock and Violet primly cross-legged in a wicker chair, both of them getting kind of silly from the sun and the circumstances.

"I bet they sell shitty black-market Chanel bags at Navy Pier," Wendy said. "You could send one to Mom."

"We could get Dad a beret," Violet said, and they both cracked up in the hysterical punch-drunk way you could do only with your sister.

It was in moments like this that Wendy remembered how much she loved her sister—her prissy, perfectionist, annoying-as-all-get-out sister—because Violet was the only person on the earth who had experienced the world in almost the exact same way, in real time, step for step, save for those first few months of life, but even then she'd been accompanied by Violet for most of the time, Violet growing inside of their mother.

And she felt a surge of pride for Violet—laughing, lovely Violet, head dipped back and throat exposed and a hand unthinkingly on her still-flat stomach, but even still the gesture reminded Wendy that all of this was not *quite* funny, was actually quite fucking terrifying, if you really gave it a lot of thought, but not giving it thought had been her idea in the first place, hadn't it? Violet doing something brave. Violet doing something because some part of her wanted to. She pushed her toes against the ground, setting the hammock aswing. Their laughter had died off.

"What'll we *do* about Mom and Dad, though?" Violet asked, and Wendy bristled at the strains of whininess in her voice.

But it was a fair question. Because their parents were, of course, only fifteen miles northwest, benevolently worried about Violet traveling abroad (even in *Europe*), expecting weekly long-distance phone calls and newsy handwritten letters and, probably, an excess of visits from Wendy to make up for the absence of their preferred child. She and Violet were both fairly certain that their parents wouldn't try to visit Paris; they still had Liza and Gracie at home, and their mother had thrown herself full-throttle into running the hardware store and was so deeply entrenched that it was unlikely she'd pull herself away for a vacation.

"God, I *should* be going to Paris," Violet said. "I should be doing something *exciting* before I . . ."

"Spend the rest of your waking hours negotiating contracts and staving off the advances of overstuffed Midnight-at-the-Viagra-Triangle predators in Canali suits?"

"I'm not sure," Violet said softly.

"I'll deal with Mom and Dad."

"Wendy, I . . ."

"Jesus Christ, how many fucking times do you want me to tell you that you're a legal adult who's allowed to make whatever decisions you want to make? I don't have some shrewd insider knowledge, Violet. I don't have any kind of assurance that everything's going to be—"

"I was going to say thank you," Violet said. "For—this. Whatever it is."

And people did not often thank Wendy, so her voice contained the hint of a question when she replied, "You're welcome."

Then for a while it was actually sort of fun, a pedestrian espionage. They figured out a way—a friend of Miles's who lived in Bretagne and accepted envelopes of prewritten postcards—to get correspondence from Violet to their parents with European postmarks. Violet moved into one of their guest rooms and at night they'd walk together along the lakeshore, out to Promontory Point, talking about everything and nothing. Wendy expounded on her sex life, and Violet pretended to be disgusted but asked sly follow-up questions that betrayed her curiosity; they assuaged each other's weak guilt over lying to their parents—parents *wanted* their children to be best friends, didn't they? And everything had unfolded from there, in the way that most of their interactions unfolded, with long stretches of defiance punctuated by bursts of tenderness, arcs of jealousy that tapered off with flurries of compassion. In the way that most of their interactions unfolded, except wholly different, huger and more extraordinary than either of them could begin to understand.

Wendy, on the occasions when she had to have dinner in the suburbs with their parents, played her part flawlessly, peppering David and Marilyn with fraudulent secondhand anecdotes about the personable sheep in Mont-Saint-Michel, betraying nothing of the fact that their little Francophile was in fact just a few miles away, watching *The West Wing* and reading about breathing exercises.

Unsurprisingly, Violet excelled—as she did with everything in her life—at pregnancy. Wendy would come home and find her sister sitting cross-legged at the kitchen table, one hand cupping her belly and the other holding a book—*What to Expect*, or *Let's Go: France*, or, during windows of peak dorkiness, *The University of Chicago Law Review*—a beautiful glow coming off of her face, glints of red in her messy brown hair. Violet seemed, despite the elemental desolation of her situation, *accompanied*. She was supplemented in a way that Wendy herself had never felt.

"I don't know," Violet said one night, beached on the loveseat. "I feel sort of—like, anointed." She wore her pregnancy well, seemed only to be getting prettier as she gained weight, rounded out, became slower in her movements.

"Calling yourself a saint is generally frowned upon, I think, in terms of being—you know, humble," Wendy said.

"I suppose what I mean to say is that I feel—well, blessed, kind of. Despite everything," Violet said. "I feel almost—whole."

"Call Mom and tell her," Wendy replied. "She'll be happy to know that all the money she spent sending us to CCD wasn't entirely for naught." She liked the sound of what Violet was saying, though, the idea of wholeness—and the implied whole*some*ness—that came along with childbearing. She wasn't sure she'd ever felt whole. She had a house and a husband and a kitchen with a built-in wine fridge, but when she donned the black backless Calvin Klein tomorrow night and went with Miles as Platinum Donors to the Shedd Gala, she would feel not like a woman but like a little girl playing at something. She would drink too much and, she hoped, not say anything embarrassing and later she would tumble into a cab and come home to Violet—who would likely be wearing sweatpants and doing the weird, private exercises she did with her pelvic muscles to prepare for the coming months, but who was *blessed* and *whole*.

It might be kind of nice, she thought, not for the first time, to be Violet.

. . .

There was something about being around Wendy that made her feel almost drunk. Or maybe the feeling was amplified by the fact that she hadn't had a drink in eight months. But she'd started to feel inexplicably weepy one night sitting cross-legged in Wendy's living room, feet falling asleep beneath her slightly swollen ankles. The baby, whoever it was, had been making her feel, alongside a sickly and unending indigestion, a strange euphoria lately, imbuing her with an unfamiliar sense of communion with the world around her, despite the fact that she was hiding from said world. But in the last few weeks she had begun to allow herself—*really* allow herself—to consider what might happen next. What came after her parting from this tiny bonfire of human collegiality and wonderment, this little person who wouldn't exist were it not for her. Were it not for her sister.

She missed her mother during these times—when she was kept awake with racing thoughts, when her belly hardened with Braxton-Hicks, when she actually dared to picture what it would feel like to hand her baby over to someone she'd never met and would never see again. What in the holy hell had she gotten herself into? She had huge-hearted and endlessly generous parents; they would have understood; they would have arranged their lives around her transgression in the way they did Wendy's; they would've taken her to Planned Parenthood or supported her if she'd decided to keep the baby.

She *could* call her mom, she knew. Even this late in the game. Even when she was so close to the finish line, filled to the gills with a baby whose face she couldn't picture. She tried to imagine what the phone call would sound like—Marilyn shocked and fretful, her words inflected, but a taskmaster, too, asking the questions neither Violet nor Wendy had asked, the crucial what-ifs, keeping Violet's best interest at the forefront all the time.

"Wendy," she said. Sometimes when she was a kid she'd

awaken from a nightmare with the feeling she had now—a rushing sound in her ears, her heartbeat in overdrive, and the loss-of-control sensation that would make her grip her bed-sheet as if it were some kind of lifesaving buoy. Tonight she gripped the arm of the couch with one hand while the other covered the baby, a kid who might have her eyes or hands or penchant for order, a kid who'd instinctively assume that she would be there when it breathed air for the first time, a kid who'd never been given a reason to think otherwise, who'd never been given a say in any of this.

"Wendy, are we . . ." *We didn't think this through.* "Who do you think's going to adopt him? Or her?"

Wendy stared at her for a long minute. She felt some of her panic receding, but she could tell it wasn't far away. She was due in two weeks—or thereabouts; she'd fudged the possible date of conception at her first prenatal visit, which Wendy had insisted on chaperoning. Who would she be a month from now, without the thrumming presence inside of her? She pictured herself then, empty-bellied, childless, training her body back into something she recognized, training herself to be the daughter her parents would recognize: law-school-bound, going through the motions, fresh from an enlivening year in Europe.

"I think you need to cede one to the powers that be," Wendy said.

Of course telling her parents had appealed to her less than Wendy's offer. Wendy's offer, one that promised excitement and eventual escape, appealed more to her simply by virtue of the fact that Wendy had made it. Because her parents were her parents, but Wendy was her sister, the bravest person she knew and the person who had always known her best in the world. It seemed ludicrous that anyone was supposed to make a decision about going forward with a pregnancy so early on, before she understood the immensity of the implications, before she knew what it felt like to have an animate being inside of her.

But would it not also be brave to *keep* the baby? To test her own limits, the limits of her body and her heart and her understanding of the world?

As though reading her thoughts, Wendy spoke again: "Don't fucking dare start thinking about that, Violet, because it'll drive you out of your mind."

There were footfalls on the stairs, and then Miles appeared, down from his study. "Ah," he said. "I'm interrupting."

"We're just pontificating," Wendy replied. Violet sipped her water, even more frightened than before, letting their weird domesticity wash over her.

"Raucous Thursday night around here," Miles said. "But I just graded thirty-eight papers, so I'm getting a drink."

"One for me too," Wendy called after him. "And get Violet a glass of wine. One of the lighter reds." She turned to Violet. "Relaxed muscles are better prepared for labor."

She still hadn't quite confronted the fact of impending labor, of how it would feel. She was enormous but didn't feel anywhere near ready to give birth. "So glad someone's aware of what controlled substances I'm allowed to consume." The sensation lingered, her nervy trepidation. What it would feel like to leave the hospital with a baby in her arms.

"You'll thank me later," Wendy said, the edge back in her voice. But then Miles returned, three glasses clustered in his hands, and he came to Violet first. He was deferential toward her; he acted almost as though he was the visitor. Tonight he sat beside her at the other end of the couch and lifted his glass to cheers them both.

"What'd I miss?"

"We've been discussing existential anointment and the grave peril of hypothetical thinking," Wendy said. Her jauntiness sounded forced.

"And how are *you* doing, Violet?" he asked solicitously.

She didn't know what to say. She'd been with them for over

six months, but it was Wendy who took her to doctor's appointments, who entertained her with Pavement albums and rice cakes and endless games of Scrabble, who facilitated shoddy contact with their parents, an elaborate setup involving *67 and prepaid calling cards, approximating—at this they'd both died laughing—Parisian background noises, clanging spatulas and softly playing Serge Gainsbourg. Wendy who made it all feel, somehow, like a game.

"Apparently I'm ceding to the powers that be," she said finally. How dare Wendy speak to her with such authority now, as though she deserved scolding, as though either of them had had any idea what they'd been getting themselves into six months ago? She felt the panic rise again but it was quelled by the baby's sudden movement, a reminder of the fact that she wasn't alone. That for now, at least, she had a person of her own.

Miles smiled. "Not much else to do, I suppose. It's funny, one of my students tonight actually—we were shooting the shit during our break, and she'd been adopted from Seoul as a baby, and she was talking about how grateful she was to have ended up where she did."

There was an uncomfortable pause before Wendy said, "Taking remedial night classes where an eccentric billionaire teaches her about inflation?"

Miles was the only person—besides Violet herself—who didn't flinch after Wendy made a joke. "I just think it's a brave thing that you're doing," he said. "Giving it up to people who—"

Her eyes were suddenly filled. She knew this would always be the decision in her life that made the least sense: why she hadn't just taken care of things at the clinic in Middletown. Why she'd hemmed and hawed for so long that by the time she called Wendy, it was just about too late for the clinic. What the fuck had she been thinking? Going through with a pointless pregnancy was not a Violet move; it was a Wendy move, ballsy and inexplicable.

"For Christ's sake, master of bedside manner," Wendy said.

Violet shook her head. "No, it's fine." Of course the adoption agency had found good parents for the baby—parents who could care for it better than she could, parents who *wanted* it.

"May I?" Miles asked, and she looked up, confused. He gestured to her.

"Oh." She could feel Wendy's gaze on her.

"Not if it makes you—" Miles began.

"No, sure." She forcefully ignored Wendy, now. "Go ahead. Not much to feel, but . . ."

He inched closer to her on the couch and held his hand out like he was waiting for her to stamp it. She grabbed it and placed it squarely at her navel.

"So if you—yeah, right here is about— I think that's a foot."

"Oh, wow."

She watched his face light up and some of his tightly wound awkwardness receded and she could see some of what she suspected Wendy saw in him, a kindness in the eyes. So long since she'd been touched by anyone besides her doctor. He looked up at Wendy and she watched them exchange something.

She sipped her wine, warm and foreign to her after months of herbal tea, and felt her panic pulsing dully in her ears as she tried to listen to them talk about an upcoming fund-raiser. When she finished her glass, she rose to go to bed. In the opulent guest suite, she sank down between the cool sheets. She squirmed around to accommodate the baby, thinking that maybe she could confront it tomorrow, consider what she was really doing. The presence inside her had been so unyielding, so sweetly trusting of her to ensure its safe passage. Maybe she was stronger than she thought. Maybe her real bravery could show itself with what happened next. Wendy had said it herself:

It's not always the most logical decision that's the right decision. She would give herself the remaining two weeks to consider all possibilities, to itemize what she was capable of. She drifted off, envisioning telling her parents, contemplating the road not taken.

An hour later, her water broke.

CHAPTER TWENTY-FOUR

She thought she knew fear. She'd been afraid for most of her childhood: of her mother's tenuous grasp on reality and her father's ability to turn a blind eye, of how huge and unforgiving the world often seemed. She suspected—but would never say—that David had happened in part because he made her feel safe.

And then she got pregnant with Wendy and it all started up again. She feared every potential outcome of her unborn child's life; and when the girls emerged from the womb she invented new things to fear without even trying. She feared sharp table corners and faulty electrical sockets, ruthless kindergarten classmates named Ashley and Heather, cars that drove too fast and teachers who missed important signals. She worried about them drinking as teenagers and she worried about them overdosing and then Wendy actually *did* overdose. She worried about losing them and then she did lose them, but she lost each one in a way that left both parties adult and largely unharmed; she lost them in a normal, suburban way that enabled her to still see them at major holidays.

Losing David, though—scarier, perhaps, than anything else, because it was the most likely. The thing that happened to the blood in her wrists when Jonah called her at the store at 4:46 p.m. on a Tuesday was nothing she'd felt before.

Of course, she thought, oddly serene. *This is what I've been afraid of all along.*

At every mile marker Jonah worried he'd be pulled over, that maybe Wendy hadn't gotten his text, that maybe she *had* gotten it and called the cops anyway about David's car. About David himself, please, Jesus Christ, let him be alive. He wasn't sure what his plan was. He'd just left, knee-jerk, because this—whatever it was that had happened—seemed far worse than the stupid thing with Liza's car. He'd taken driver's ed last semester, and David—following the dumb mailbox accident—had been giving him lessons, too, taking him all around Oak Park.

He'd heard one of the paramedics use the word *code*, and he was almost positive, from TV, that *code* meant *dead*, although they were still shocking David's chest with paddles.

"Hey, buddy, how about if you go grab your dad's wallet for us?" the male paramedic had said. "Everything's going to be fine."

And though it was in his historical experience that everything was not going to be fine if someone felt the need to *tell* you everything was going to be fine, he scurried inside anyway, the dog following him, not chasing anymore, rubbing his big dumb head as if in apology against Jonah's leg as he rifled through David's desk in search of the wallet. *Your dad.* It was then that he found the envelope with his name on it, a regular white letter envelope with *JONAH* across the front in his grandfather's blocky, doctory writing. It stilled him for a second, but then he shoved it into his back pocket and went, with Loomis at his heels, to check the kitchen counter.

He found the wallet there and brought it out to the paramedics, who had loaded David onto a stretcher. There was an oxygen mask on his face and a needle in his arm and they'd cut open his sweater to reveal the pale hairiness of his chest. He stopped in his tracks without meaning to, and the male paramedic came over to him and put a hand on his shoulder.

"We've got him stabilized and we're going to take him to the hospital. How about if you ride with us?"

He handed over the wallet and, still staring at his grandfather, shook his head. "I'll wait here," he said, though he wasn't quite sure why, and he watched them lift the stretcher, watched the bottoms of David's shoes as the doors closed, watched the red and blue lights blur purple against the red-brown brick of the house on Fair Oaks as the ambulance screamed away.

He felt like he'd failed, in some fundamental way, and on many levels. He'd allowed his fear of the dog to get in the way of his grandfather's need for his help. He'd been too frightened to ride in the ambulance because what if David *died* in the ambulance; what if the medic was just being nice and David was actually already *dead* and so he would just be trapped with a dead body? A braver person wouldn't have cared about these things. Maybe he'd used up all of his bravery with Wyatt at Star of the Week. He thought of Violet on Christmas, before she slammed her bedroom door in his face: *You're almost a fucking adult. There's no reason for you to try to ruin it for my kids.*

And so he ran upstairs to his bedroom, grabbed a few essentials—a couple of sweaters, some boxers and socks—and while he was in the closet he found the wine he'd stolen from Violet over the summer, so he grabbed that, too, because even in his panic he didn't want her to be able to use it against him. Then he called Marilyn and he texted Wendy and he filled Loomis's bowl with dry food and he grabbed David's keys from the hook by the door and he got the Jeep purring and he found his way carefully to 290W, because Wendy had taught him that if you went east, where they lived, you could get only so far before you ran into the lake.

So he was westbound, hours later, the highway pitch-black, his visibility limited to the scope of his headlights. He hoped he wouldn't hit a deer or a yeti or anything. He cranked the radio and kept the windows open, so he couldn't hear anything but the bass and the roar of the air outside. The noise was almost enough to distract him from the thoughts about his grandfather, who was possibly no longer alive, and who, if he *wasn't* alive, probably would have been if only Jonah had grabbed the ladder in time, if fucking Cujo hadn't chased him away. The noise almost erased the image he had in his head, David on the ground beneath the tree, eyes closed, arm at a fucked-up pipe cleaner angle, dark wetness pooling from the left side of his head. He stopped at a rest area in Nebraska to throw up. *Cardiac arrest*, the paramedic had said. And the arm was definitely broken. He wasn't sure about the blood.

He couldn't get rid of his phone—he needed it for the maps—but he'd turned it on Do Not Disturb, and he was afraid to check and see if Wendy had responded to his text, or see who had called him. He took only a minute's pleasure in the fact that he was certain *someone* had called him. That he was missing, and there were people who would care, even if they cared only because he had possibly murdered their dad, their husband, their grandpa. He thought of Wyatt and Eli, lucky little bastards who never had to worry about anything. He'd miss them, though. Goofballs. They probably wouldn't remember him after a month or two.

There was a strobe light going in his head, reminding him repeatedly of the worst parts of the day. The way David had dropped the chainsaw. Then the sickening sound of his body hitting the ground, a dull thump like the chainsaw but a thousand times worse. Christ. How harmless that stupid fucking horse-dog was. How the ladder had started to waver, and how he hadn't been there to catch it because he was running away from the dog. How the dog, as soon as David's body hit the ground—Jesus, the *sound* it made—immediately forgot about their impromptu game of tag and went to check on his master.

And possibly worse than anything else was how Marilyn's voice had sounded when he called her: sick with fear, trembling, bodiless, and—most notably—not remotely suspicious.

"Oh, sweetie, I—" A vacancy, like she was reading from a script in a language she didn't speak. "Are you okay? I'm so sorry you had to— I'm so glad that you're—" A sharp intake of breath, but not a sob. "I should get to the hospital," she'd said. "Oh, but I— He gave me a ride to work this morning."

"Maybe Wendy could drive you."

"Of course. Thank you." Now a sound that might have been crying, but when she spoke again her voice was steady. "You stay in one place for me, will you? I'll call Violet and—you can either go to her house, or stay home, or I'm sure Liza's going to want to come to the . . ."

"I'll call Liza for you," he offered, but she still didn't reply. "I said I'll— Marilyn?"

"Had he been complaining of chest pain? Tingling in his arm? Anything like that?"

"No."

"His eyes really weren't open? Not at all?"

"Not— It was hard to tell, I guess." He hesitated. "They were maybe a little bit."

He kept, based on the green signs he passed, making decisions that propelled him west. And in his consideration of where he might go—a sad inventory of people he knew on the entire earth—he remembered Oregon, home to the only Sorenson he'd yet to meet. He could leave David's car with her. And maybe she'd loan him some money. Enough so that slipping even farther away would be a cinch.

David looked smaller in the hospital bed, his skin pale against the green gown. He'd always been thin, her husband, but it was a thinness padded by muscle and browned skin and outerwear. Now he looked gaunt and wasted, which was ludicrous because she'd seen him just that morning, kissed him goodbye in the car when he'd dropped her at the store. The doctor had walked her through the sequence of events that had transpired: cardiac arrest, a fall from the ginkgo, resuscitative paddles by the firemen, an ambulance ride. He'd been dead, technically, for an indeterminate number of minutes. It seemed unconscionable that she hadn't been cosmically aware of this at the time. That she'd been adding up the register, humming "More Than a Woman," when he'd temporarily ceased to exist. And now: a medically induced coma. His body temperature lowered to subsequently lower his blood pressure.

"Mother of God," she said without meaning to. She went to him, touched his face, nearly recoiled at the chill of his skin, like he was already dead. *Still* dead. Wendy was now cowering behind her in the doorway. She was at once grateful for her presence and put out by it. Her husband smelled like hand sanitizer. She kissed his cool cheek and studied the monitors on either side of him, the bandage on his head, the bruising visible on the vulnerable exposure of his right arm, the institutional blue cast on his left.

"Jesus," Wendy whispered from behind her. It was normally her reflex, when her children were scared, to assure them that everything was fine, but she was light-years away from feeling maternal, couldn't bring herself to dredge up anything remotely comforting. She needed to be comforted in order for that to happen, and the only person who could comfort her had a catheter snaking out from under his thin green hospital blanket. On top of everything else, he'd been up in a tree at the time—that *fucking* tree, when he was having a fucking heart attack, her healthy jogging husband—and so he'd fallen, and there were two broken ribs and a broken arm, a messy laceration above his left eyebrow, and they weren't ready to rule out a concussion from his head hitting the ground. The person on whom she relied to process medical information was missing. The only prognosis she could devise was grim.

"Mom?" Wendy said.

Still she couldn't answer. Wendy, driving her to the hospital, had called the other girls, shocked voices blaring, one by one, from the speakerphone in her car. She hadn't retained many of the details but she kept thinking of what Gracie had said after Wendy gently delivered the news—that their father had a heart attack, and that he'd fallen and hurt himself, that he was in the hospital: *No he's not.* Matter-of-factly, not the least bit childlike. *No he's not.* As though what Wendy had said was unequivocally contrary to fact.

She should buy Gracie a plane ticket, she thought. Call and make sure she had the credit card information. How frightened her baby must be, all alone, all the way across the country. The nurses told her, after she'd awakened from the trauma of Grace's birth, that David had cared for the baby exclusively during the time she'd been unconscious. *My two,* she'd called them. Her prolonged stay at the hospital, watching her husband waltz their newest daughter around the room. *Find yourself a man who likes to hold babies,* she'd said to Liza once. *It's a sign of good character.*

She felt her shoulders shudder and realized she was crying. She seemed to have been split into a number of distinct entities: the physical self in the hospital room, the emotional self clinging to the physical self from the outside, the brain stalled somewhere in the early 1990s. She was experiencing the world in photographic flashes. A horrible thought: What if she was having a heart attack too? An even more horrible thought: at least she'd get to be with her husband, wherever he was.

David in their house in Iowa City, before the children were born, getting ready for work in the middle of the night, stalking naked around their bedroom looking for his clothes in the dark, trying not to wake her. David in a silly mood, humming to her, driving them home from dinner at his father's house, the girls asleep in the backseat of the station wagon, sleet sullying the windshield. David, walking with her in the rain in College Green Park the night she'd gone into labor with Wendy. When Jonah had called—where was he? Someone should call him too—he'd sounded frightened, had tactfully lied to her about David's eyes possibly being open before the paramedics arrived. And at the end of the call: "Marilyn, he said to tell you . . ."

And she'd braced herself, prepared to reject any of the painfully finite things he might say to her if he thought he'd never see her again: *I love you; if you ever need to adjust the water heater, you have to hit it on the left side a few times first, really give it a good thump with your fist.* "Wait," she said to Jonah, "I don't know if I—"

"He said to tell you you're the—" Jonah sounded embarrassed. "He said to say you're the most fun he's ever had."

At the time, she'd laughed aloud, surprised. Now she felt the crying escalate.

The hand on her back startled her.

"Mom," Wendy whispered, wrapping her into a hug. "Mom, it's okay."

2001

The contractions: one on top of the other, furious, merciless, and Violet felt herself turn into someone not quite human, a mammalian beast, growling, cursing.

"Remember what the book said." Wendy was somewhere beside her, an infuriating disembodied voice. "If you *resist*, you're making it harder on your*self*."

"Shut the fuck *up*."

"Almost there, Violet," said the hot doctor. It seemed utterly wrong that such an attractive man was allowed to oversee the undignified carnage of childbirth. "What say you help out this little one just a bit more, okay?"

She vomited into a bedpan, pushed against her will.

"Viol, I can see the head," Wendy said.

"Oh my God, don't *look* at me. *Fuck*."

And then what felt like an explosion.

"Violet," Wendy said. "Oh, wow, Violet."

To her, the baby's cries sounded Jurassic, a series of angry, desperate bleats. She fought the urge to cover her ears with her palms, like a child.

"Great job, Viol," Wendy said, trailing a few steps behind the nurse, who was taking the baby over to a scale. "Oh, Violet, he's—he's perfect."

He. *He*.

Wendy moved in efficaciously, perching next to her on the bed and taking one of her hands. "I know you're exhausted, but are you sticking with your plan? It's totally up to you."

"Yeah," she said hoarsely, still not opening her eyes.

"Yeah, you want to see him?"

She shook her head.

"You're sure?"

She nodded.

There was a beat before she felt her sister's forehead rest against their clasped hands. She heard her inhale sharply. Wendy stayed like that for nearly a minute and finally kissed her hand and raised her head: "Would it be okay if I—held him?"

This caused her to open her eyes, avoiding looking at the wailing mass being swabbed clean on a rolling cart across the room.

"Please." She closed her eyes again, feeling hot tears seep through her lids, and heard her sister murmuring to the nurse. The wailing quieted and the door closed.

When Wendy returned she slid neatly next to her in the bed.

"He's exquisite," she said, and then she held her little sister while she wept.

Wendy had expected the delivery to be disgusting—and she was right; it had included the most horrifying noises and antiseptic smells and animal moanings that she had ever experienced in her life—but as soon as they swaddled the gross little alien she could see clearly that he was amazing, with bizarrely intricate tiny features and perfect star hands. Once she had Violet's permission—her poor sister no longer looked lustrous and whole but deflated, bloated and bleary and more depressed than she'd ever seen another person look—Wendy was taken by one of the nurses to an empty delivery room and there she sat, in a hospital rocking chair intended for an exuberant new father, and cradled the baby's warm, near-nonexistent weight.

"Don't know how you do the voodoo that you do," she murmured.

Small children unnerved her then. So did school-age kids, come to think of it; and she couldn't *stand* teenagers. Once Liza had asked her, very earnestly, if it *counted as sex* if a guy fingered you (except she had said, in the roundabout fashion of unsophisticated youth, "Puts his—like up your—with his hand?"), and Wendy had just stared at her, horrified, and finally replied "It depends on the guy" and skittered away, far away from her dorky little sister with her lavender Converse and her boundless, embarrassing curiosity.

Babies, however, were different. Babies were soft and helpless and they smelled nice; they had tiny fingers and sweet blue eyes and they wore hilarious outfits that looked like little sacks. They trusted you; they held on to your forefinger when offered even if you had not introduced yourself to them and were about to relinquish them blindly to some ruddy strangers who had just flown in, frantic, from vacationing in Steamboat. They slept against your chest even though you had betrayed them, harbored their mother like a fugitive for six months in your fancy house and then just *let her* hand over custody. They snuggled into you and made snuffling noises even though you probably didn't smell that great because your sister had wakened you in the middle of the night and requested that you take her to the hospital *now* and didn't let you change out of your sporadically laundered Hole T-shirt. Babies were different, and she wanted one, a tiny perfect person, the most lasting tie to the world you could possibly ask for.

CHAPTER TWENTY-FIVE

Violet had tried to apologize to her mother at the hospital, but Marilyn had just hugged her fiercely and said *oh, honey* in a way she supposed was meant to absolve her. They'd moved on to bigger things. It was absurd to her that only a few hours earlier she'd been fighting with her mother and neglecting her tiny troubadour. She didn't feel comfortable leaving Wyatt with a sitter after she'd so let him down, so Matt had left work to take care of the boys—he now had a sympathetic excuse, she noted darkly, for walking out on the DreamWorks guys—and she was sitting next to Liza on a little bench outside of their father's room. Time was funny that way—sometimes it felt like her days took months to go by, days when the kids had colds or stomach bugs, days when the weather prevented them from going to the park; but entire years seemed to have passed since she'd woken up this morning.

Wyatt had been quiet when she picked him up from school, accepting her apologies and telling her that it was okay, that Jonah had known the words without having to be taught.

Jonah. "Who do we call about Jonah?" she asked now.

Beside her, Liza blinked, as though surfacing from underwater. In a chair across from them, Wendy kept her eyes fixed on the exit sign above their father's door. She had a strange momentary memory of being at the hospital with her sisters after Grace was born, their father skittish and their mother's fate uncertain. She hugged her arms tightly around her rib cage.

"Do we— I mean, is this Amber Alert territory?"

"He wasn't *kidnapped*," Wendy said.

"Okay, but he's an unaccompanied minor without a license. Isn't there a similar degree of—urgency?"

"He did total my car," Liza spoke up.

"That kid's been more mature than all of us for a long time," Wendy said, and though the statement struck Violet as somehow accurate, it annoyed her still.

"Being wise beyond your years doesn't make you a safe driver. It doesn't mean he's anywhere *near* equipped to steal Dad's car and just go—on the lam."

"He didn't steal Dad's car," Wendy said. "And could you stop acting like you give a single fuck about what happens to him? When's the last time you even talked to him? Christ."

"You guys," Liza implored. "Please, not now."

"We had an early Christmas with him," she said. "That's the last time I saw him."

"Great," Wendy said. "Room at the inn. Gold star for spending one evening with the kid you gave away."

"I'm actually trying to keep my blood pressure down," Liza said, "if that's something that matters to either of you."

Violet touched Liza's shoulder in apology. When she started speaking again, she was unsure of why. "I said awful things to him. He— I kicked him out of my house, kind of."

It was easier to think of this than try to recall the last time she'd seen her father. A weekend lunch at her parents' house a few weeks back. Something totally and unremarkably normal, her dad playing trains with Eli or pulling Wyatt in a wagon. Her mind kept, against her will, slipping to all the pitiful unknowns: the thoughts that must've raced through her father's head; how scared he must have been; the sheer indignity he must have felt at losing control of his own body like that, her handsome, stoic, formidable father.

"Let me guess, Mrs. Bridge," Wendy said. "He actually used one of your hand towels to dry his hands?"

Liza closed her eyes. "Wendy, God, please."

But Violet was unoffended, immune to her sister's toxicity. Maybe she could unburden herself of her own toxic memory, the one brought to life so vividly by her mother that morning. Wasn't that what sisters were for, the storage of shameful secrets? "He told Wyatt that Santa's not real."

Liza tsked. "I had to be the one to tell Gracie. Though she was about seventeen, not five."

"I lost it," Violet said. "And I made him leave. But he showed up at Wyatt's school today to help him. He's not— He's really a nice kid. We shouldn't just let him—"

"Jesus, we all *know* he's a nice kid," Wendy said. "Everyone but you has known for months that he's a nice kid. He's fine, okay? We're not calling in an Amber Alert, we're not going to the fucking FBI; he's fine, and we'll hear from him when we hear from him."

A vulturine man walked by, an oxygen tank trailing behind him, and Wendy leapt up when he passed. "Shit. It's like fucking Goblin Market around here. I'm going outside."

There was a time Violet would have gone with her. She wished she could now. Instead, she told herself she couldn't leave Liza alone. Liza, who had no one waiting for her at home; Liza, who—like Violet, once—was grappling with the fucked-up juxtaposition of gestating in the midst of—sorrow. Parting. Abandonment. Although, of course, their father could not leave them.

Liza opened her mouth, closed it again. "Violet, he wouldn't pass up an opportunity to meet— God. Another—you know, this person, would he?" She dropped her forehead into one hand. "Right? He wouldn't— He has to at least— God, I've been banking on him an*oin*ting this baby when it's born because otherwise—"

"Lize, it's going to be fine." She put her arm around her sister. Liza leaned heavily against her. She thought again of her father, standing with Gracie in his arms in their mother's vacated hospital room, pretending not to panic. "Come on. Someone should check on Loomis."

Liza lifted her head foggily. "Has anyone called Gracie?"

The smell of the hospital was beginning to make her feel sick. She rose, offering Liza a hand, suddenly anxious for the night air, and her reply, though not by any means intentionally unkind, was also unintentionally untrue: "I think Wendy was going to call her."

A shitty thing about living near the place you'd grown up was the likelihood of running into people from your youth, people who remembered you pigtailed or inebriated or pathetic. So Wendy wasn't *surprised* to see Aaron Bhargava, but she also wasn't terribly excited, especially because he was accompanied by his pregnant wife and a bug-eyed little girl wearing a tutu. She was smoking on a bench outside of the hospital, and as she saw them approaching from across the parking lot, she clung to the feeble hope that he wouldn't recognize her. People sometimes didn't. She was no longer coked out and twenty pounds underweight.

She kept her head down, adopted the distant brooding look of a person in deep contemplation, eyes locked on an engraved brick embedded in the sidewalk that read IN MEMORY OF GRETCHEN AND LARRY STANISLAUS. She wondered if they'd died together. If they were even a couple. Maybe a pair of incestuous siblings. An overly affectionate mother and son. A theatrical murder-suicide of a trainwreck woman and her sexy high school boyfriend.

"Wendy?"

She tensed involuntarily and let her gaze lift lazily upward with the sleepy nonchalance of a prolific thinker.

"I thought that was you," he said.

She couldn't pretend not to recognize him. He looked exactly the same as he had when they were sixteen. "Oh my God," she said. "Aaron." She rose, moved to hug him, realized she was still holding her cigarette, which the child was watching with interest. She could have stubbed it out but instead she simply retracted the hug, squared her body against the trio. The cigarette gave her an ally. And if she needed a quick getaway, she could light herself on fire.

"We're just heading in to a doctor's appointment," he said. "I was just saying to Jen that I would *swear* it was you, but— I mean, the odds."

"Astronomical," she said. They hadn't ended on bad terms, and it had been nearly twenty years, but she was surprised by how emotional it made her, seeing him, the first boy who'd treated her well.

"You look great," he said.

She knew she was supposed to be self-effacing, but her looks were about the only thing she had going for her at the moment, and she was too tired to counter. She dragged on her cigarette as Aaron turned to his wife: "Babe, this is Wendy Sorenson. Wendy, my wife, Jen."

"Eisenberg now, actually," she said, ducking her head to exhale before she reached to shake the woman's hand. "Nice to meet you."

"I've heard a lot about you," Jen said. "I mean that in the least sinister way."

Wendy decided immediately that she liked her, and this made her, just as immediately, resentful: of Jen, for landing Aaron

Bhargava when she herself could not; of Aaron Bhargava, for finding someone with a good aura and a functional womb.

"Eisenberg, huh?" Aaron said. He reminded her of a Labrador, pure myopic goodness. He made up for being so vanilla, she recalled, in bed. She looked again at Jen's belly.

"Of the West Egg Eisenbergs," she said absently. The Bhargavas regarded her with smiling bemusement. "And who have we here?" She gestured to the girl, whose big blue eyes were still following the trajectory of the cigarette.

Aaron laid a hand on the small head. "This is Evie," he said. "Can you say hi, honey?"

"Why do you have that?" Evie asked instead.

"Because it's been a long day."

"Sweetie, don't be rude," Jen said.

"It's a valid question," Wendy said. "One I should be asking myself more often."

"We're in a very inquisitive phase," Aaron said. "Do you have children?"

It was a simple enough question, but it still sometimes tripped her up. "I should head back inside," she said. "God, sorry, I spaced. I've been out here way longer than I meant to be."

"Everything okay?" Aaron asked.

"Uh-huh." She now turned to stub out her cigarette, pressing it into the little tower of sand. "Just my—" Her throat filled before it could emit the word *dad*. "My husband sprained his wrist. Golfing. Stupid." She apologized to Miles in her head; thanked him for saving her. She'd not told anyone yet that Jonah had texted her shortly after they arrived at the hospital: *ill give the car back. pls dont call cops. sorry for fucking everything up.* She was arguably the least emotionally stable person in her family; why did the universe insist on plaguing her anyway?

"It's so wild to see you," Aaron said, and this time it was he who reached to hug her, and, sans cigarette, she reciprocated, feeling the familiar way his muscles stretched taut across his back and his arms around her felt pleasantly like being in a straitjacket. "How're your sisters, by the way? How's Violet?"

She squeezed back for a couple of beats longer than was socially appropriate. "Superior to me in all ways," she said.

The fact that her father hadn't died made the need to go home feel even more pressing, but nobody had offered to pay for her ticket—her mother certainly would have, if asked, but Grace couldn't bear to seem so pathetic, couldn't bear to add one more thing to a to-do list whose contents she couldn't bring herself to think about.

She resented her sisters for being in Chicago, for also not thinking to bring her home. Then again, she couldn't believe how selfish she'd been, not coming home for Second Thanksgiving or Christmas, giving up what was possibly—God, please, not—her final opportunity to see her father. Violet had predictably insisted that she not let the accident get in the way of her schooling. Liza had been nice enough, but she'd sounded edgy and preoccupied, and Grace had felt the need to reverse their roles, act as though Liza was the one who needed taking care of; her baby was due in less than a month. And Wendy only expounded on her hatred of hospitals. So she was stuck, confined to her apartment. She'd started to text Ben a dozen times, but had ultimately decided against it.

She began to understand how some people could abdicate any commitment to normal human life. Layering one bad thing on top of another had the effect of making a person capable of nothing beyond drinking wine and smoking cigarettes, sitting on the balcony into the wee hours like some kind of pervy sitcom neighbor and coming in to watch documentaries about murderers.

When the doorbell rang, she had not showered since Sunday

and was eating stale pita chips she'd found in her pantry. She panicked, thinking first of her geriatric landlord, then of Ben Barnes, then of an elaborate deliveryman murder ruse (*Call Me Craig*, a documentary about the Craigslist Killer, was streaming from her laptop on the coffee table). She flattened herself against the couch, rolled onto the floor and crawled down the hall toward her bedroom, so the visitor couldn't see her. She considered that this might be what it looked like to hit rock bottom.

When she was safely in her bedroom, her phone dinged, like something out of a horror movie. How had this become her life, this abject fear of everything normal—a person ringing your doorbell; a well-adjusted boy expressing his love for you? She held her breath as she looked at the message: *hey its jonah ur nephew, i can see ur computer, can u let me in.*

She exhaled. She was weirdly not surprised, weirdly relieved about this unexpected visitor. She wouldn't be alone, at least. She rose from the floor. She would have to teach Jonah the art of the semicolon.

2002

Grace did not have a middle name, though her sisters got Evelyn, Rose and Ann.

"Oh, honey, I don't know," her mother said. "I guess we ran out of ideas."

She had been hoping for something more mystical. Perhaps the confession of a weighty decision her parents had made: "You just didn't need a middle name like your sisters, Gracie. You were special enough without one." She knew, of course, that her mother had nearly died when she was born, but it didn't seem that hard to come up with a name.

"You could have just named me after you," she suggested. She was making a genogram for social studies and sat before an impressive spread of glitter glue and Sharpies, staring at her mother disdainfully over her poster board.

Her mom, dubiously examining a batch of tomatoes she had just brought in from her garden, stopped to consider it. "It doesn't sound right," she said finally, and Grace had to agree that Grace Marilyn didn't have quite the singsongy cadence of Violet Rose.

"What about your middle name?" she suggested.

Her mother snorted, placing the best of the tomatoes into a colander to wash. "It was the least I could do to not curse you with a clichéd Irish name. Trust me. Less is more." She'd grown up Marilyn Margaret Frances Connolly. Grace conceded that, again, her mother had a point. She still felt robbed, though; she was consistently, across her genogram, inking in middle names with an icy blue Gelly Roll pen, and it seemed a great injustice that she didn't get to use it for herself.

"Who was your doctor?" she asked.

"Pardon?" Her mother's voice had sharpened.

"Thompson's named after his mom's doctor because he almost died when he was born."

"How romantic," her mom said, a meanness in her voice.

"Mom?"

Her mother was holding a tomato under a violent stream of water. "What?"

"What was your doctor's name?"

She paused, turned off the water. "Gillian," she said.

It was rhythmically unsatisfying, but the alliteration was pleasant. She left the space below her own name blank, and waited until school the next day to ink in the false middle name.

Her parents called her their afterthought. Sometimes her dad called her the Epilogue, which she preferred, because epilogues were deliberate and valuable. But epilogues also got the shaft, because they came after all of the important things had already happened. She had a faulty memory that seemed to consist primarily of events for which she had not been present. Sometimes, during family gatherings, she would muster up the courage to speak and say something like "Remember when that lady tried to fight Dad for his parking space at the zoo?" and inevitably—almost every time—one of her sisters would snort. All of her sisters snorted in disbelief with the same intonation, like a tribe of braying elephants.

If Wendy were the first to speak, she'd say something like "I do, Gracie, because I was there. You weren't." If it were Violet or Liza, the rebuttal would be equally weary but slightly kinder: "You were two, Gracie," or sometimes, embarrassingly, "You weren't even born, dude."

But she could see them, these memories, and this seemed a cruel cognitive trick. She could conjure with ease the memory of her father angling the station wagon into a tight spot in the parking lot of Brookfield Zoo, only to be assaulted when he emerged from the car by a woman in a *Sound of Music* sweatshirt who called him a swindler and demanded that he relinquish the space to her. Once she'd raised it, though, her sisters would fly free, sail along without her, cracking up at the dinner table over how David had offered, flustered, to move his car in order to let her have the spot and how Marilyn, already tired of being at the zoo though they had not yet entered its arched, lion-spotted gateways, got out of the passenger seat and said, "This day is harrowing enough as it is. Find another spot." This happened constantly, her family gliding down the rails of memories for which she had not been present. It was disconcerting, especially because some of the memories were less whimsical. She had lots of scary memories whose origins and/or validity were difficult to articulate—scary only in the sense that they diverted from the otherwise cheery, pristine norm of her other childhood memories, her mother's luminous smile and her father's strong hugs and her sisters' gentle laughter. She remembered Liza babysitting her once and showing her a big star that someone had drawn on the back of her neck. She remembered happening upon her mother, once, sitting on the back stairs smoking a cigarette, and she remembered asking, "Mama, who gave you that?" and her mother stubbing out the cigarette and saying, "A bad girl, sweet pea; come sit with me."

"I didn't mean we ran out of ideas," her mom said in the kitchen, coming over and kissing her head. "We had plenty of ideas. Dad just liked the sound of your name on its own."

She didn't have a middle name, and she didn't have her own

memories, and this was the trouble with being an epilogue. You got shoved at the end of the book before anyone gave you a chance to read it.

Violet's relationship with Matt was predicated on a series of never-ending conversations. Before she'd even kissed him for the first time, they'd spent six weeks of evenings together, racing to cover infinite ground: they both had families to inaccurately render and hard-nosed political positions to exaggerate and college roommates to slander; they had between them four decades of books to discuss and low-level secrets to divulge. She never wanted to stop talking to him. She was a 1L and he was a third-year. She approached her postgraduate education with a militancy attainable only by the crazy or friendless, but somehow Matt penetrated her formality; they met at a Studs Terkel lecture and spent several evenings on the patio at a dive on University Avenue, during which they drank a lot together and talked about their most beguiling idiosyncrasies. And then one night he kissed her by the Fountain of Time, and she couldn't remember feeling this happy—feeling happy at all, in fact—since before she'd gotten pregnant.

His normalcy frightened her, honestly. Because though she had been cultivating a similar image since she was ten years old, to find a man who seemed so entirely without defect seemed statistically unlikely. She met Matt seventeen months after she'd given birth. He laughed at her jokes but he also asked her serious questions: *Explain that; how do you feel about that?; convince me, Violet.*

They were lolling around in his bed one evening, Matt reading an article in *The Economist*. He was a difficult man to distract; his face was twisted in concentration and he was twirling his Uni-ball in a convincing display of absorption.

"Matt," she said, knitting and unknitting her fingers.

"Hmm." Not taking his eyes from the magazine, he reached for her hand.

"I don't want to—like, have a big buildup, but I want to talk to you about something."

With that he sharpened his gaze on her. "What?" Their relationship was still so new that this could have been an admission of a sex change or a tryst with one of his classmates, and she wondered where her confession was about to fall amid the ranks of betrayal or romantic wrongdoing. She shifted to face him. She loved Matt, already—she knew this—and it seemed pivotal that he know this about her, that he be aware of her most painful thing. She thought of her parents, who seemed to have been sharing everything with each other forever. Disclosure facilitated trust, did it not?

"So I've," she began, and then faltered.

"You sleeping with Professor Milman?" he asked. She would not realize until later what a gift it was to be able to joke about something like this.

"I had a baby," she said tonelessly, staring at a spot on his blue bedspread, and the statement hung unpleasantly in the air like the fumes of a passing garbage truck. "A year and a half ago. I broke up with my boyfriend and I found out I was pregnant right as I was graduating and I had the baby and I placed it with an adoption agency."

Matt was quiet for a moment, still holding her hand. And that had proven to be the most wonderful thing about their relationship, bar none—just the presence of another person, hanging on to you, even if it wasn't with any particular vigor or purpose.

"I'm not sure what to say," he said finally, gently, and so she just started talking. She talked about Wesleyan and her straitlaced boyfriend Rob, who was getting a PhD in biochem and who wasn't always very nice to her, about his cheating on her with a research assistant. She did not tell him about the night before Wendy's wedding, just a month before graduation when she'd been utterly crushed by the upset of her life plans: the Volvo in the parking lot, the acrobatic blue-eyed boy who'd come inside her and whom she hadn't seen since.

She talked about moving in with Wendy; she talked about selecting a discreet adoption agency; she talked about how she'd been too afraid to look when the baby emerged from her body and so she'd never actually seen her son; she talked about how empty she felt when she returned from the hospital to her room in Wendy's house.

"Wow," Matt said when she'd finished. "I can't imagine."

"No, you can't."

"But why didn't you—" he stopped. "Never mind." Matt had the nightstand of a fifty-year-old suburban father, glasses and Carmex and a well-worn paperback copy of *The Adventures of Augie March*, bottle of multivitamins and glass of water and earplugs to tune out his downstairs neighbors. Matt had had his life figured out since he was ten, Dartmouth and law school and recreational basketball on the weekends. She felt a chilly fear settle around her for the first time since she'd met him. Perhaps he wouldn't understand. Why had she ever thought he would? Why had she thought she could possibly explain to him—Mr. Perfect, sailing down the path—what had motivated her to make the decisions she'd made?

"Why didn't I what?" she asked.

"I just mean— It sounds crass to say about— I don't mean it in a— Why didn't you just have an abortion?"

She was quiet, considering it. It was, of course, the question she'd never fully answered in her own mind. The best she had was a number of fragments that were all loosely related but didn't quite add up to a finished whole. When they were in high school, she and Wendy would lie on the eave outside of Wendy's bedroom window and discuss their potential futures. As kids they'd spent hours playing MASH, sketching out elaborate hypotheticals, marriages to Dennis Quaid or Dennis Rodman, a mansion in Sacramento or an apartment in Queens, careers in food service or international relations. Wendy always made the riskier choices, populating her charts with wild cards, while Violet played it safe, everything in moderation. At the end of the game, Wendy would end up homeless and overburdened with children and married to Pee-wee Herman, but Violet would always have something more palatable, a decent salary and a safe but luxurious car, a stately suburban home inhabited by a manageable number of children who'd been fathered by Bono. It wasn't always the most logical decision that was the right decision. That would be a foreign concept to Matt, as it had been to her at the time. But she had wanted to be brave, an adjective no one had ever applied to her, especially when Wendy was around.

"Violet, I wasn't trying to—"

"No, I know." She picked up the Carmex, screwed and unscrewed its tiny lid. "It just—stopped being an option at a certain point. I can't really—explain it better than that. It's— Wendy. That's the best answer I've got."

"You haven't talked much about her," he said.

"It's complicated." She pulled her knees to her chest.

"She was the only person who knew about this?"

"Pretty much."

"I can't imagine ever doing something like that. I think it— That'd crush me, I think. I can't believe you're— It sounds horrible."

"It was horrible."

"Violet, I—"

How easy it would be for him to ruin everything right now, to say the wrong thing, to reveal that she was simply too flawed, that the choices she'd made when she was low and confused would follow her forever, ruining her prospects of happiness, of normalcy.

"I wish I could've been there for you," Matt said, and she felt some of the weight lift, because if Matt had been there, things would have been different, better; there wasn't a doubt in her mind about this.

"I'm telling you this because I think you deserve to know," she said. She issued a silent apology to the baby, for calling him a *this*, a thing, for slamming the door in his face like she was, for the second time, for so firmly locking the deadbolt after she'd already refused to look at him. "But I don't want to talk about it anymore, Matt, okay? It happened and it's over." If anyone could understand this, it was Matt, who thought he could will away nascent head colds simply by denying their existence, who'd trained himself to wake up at 5:45 each morning without an alarm clock. "If this—changes anything for you, I'll understand."

"It doesn't," he said.

"But you can't be *sure* that you won't feel differently in—"

"Are you trying to talk me out of being with you, Violet?"

"No, I just want to make sure you know what you're getting yourself into."

He kissed her. "I'm sure," he said.

CHAPTER TWENTY-SIX

GRACE was aware, for the first time, of having the upper hand with a member of her family, age-wise. She got to be the cool aunt, the autonomous elder with an apartment and a debit card and a couch on which transient visitors could crash. She'd clocked the power dynamic early—practically from the moment Jonah had entered her house, though he'd caught her braless and depressive and watching a docudrama about the Craigslist Killer.

"We finally meet," she said. "How'd you get my number? How'd you know where I live?"

"Your dad made me store everyone's info in my phone," he replied.

Having the upper hand allowed her to tamp her gut reaction, which was to burst into tears. "How is he?" she asked instead. "Why didn't anyone tell me you were . . ." But his appearance caused her to back off, the ghostly glow of his skin that betrayed a lack of sleep, nails bitten to the quick, fear on his face as though she might turn him away.

"Sit down," she said, feeling big-sisterly for the first time. "Let me get you some water." To be in the company of one of her family members, albeit one who was still technically a stranger, was an unspeakable relief; she was face-to-face with someone who'd been with her dad before everything had gone south. He looked less like Violet than she'd expected. She felt her eyes fill and turned away, pretending to busy herself with filing her single fork into a drawer. "You hungry?" she asked, then realized, quickly, that the stale pita chips had been the only remaining edible items in her house. She surreptitiously checked her bank balance on her phone. It was technically money allotted for the next two weeks of groceries, but the thought of riding on the bus with him to the market made her soul-crushingly exhausted.

So they ended up at the Comeback. The Irish bartender smiled when he saw her, waved from behind the bar. She felt herself flush.

"Who's that?" Jonah asked.

She flushed even more deeply, because it was not a promising personality trait to be on a casual-greeting basis with barroom staff. "No one."

"We can sit at the bar, if you want."

She narrowed her eyes at him. "You're fifteen years old, are you not?"

It was fun, playing the role of the patronizing older sister. She'd had such good teachers.

"Sixteen, actually," he said, and she thought she saw him suppressing a smile.

She studied his face. He did seem older than a high school sophomore, but he was still wearing those big Kleenex-box skater shoes and there was a waxy galaxy of acne across his forehead. "Let's take a booth," she said. "We have stuff to talk about."

He didn't protest, and they sat down together, the high backs of the booth muffling the bar's ambient noise.

"So you were with my dad. When it happened?"

He squirmed, fiddling with his straw wrapper. "Kind of."

"Wendy said you called the ambulance. Thanks for doing that."

"You don't have to *thank* me. I did what any normal person would do."

She leaned back, startled. "I just meant—"

"Sorry. Whatever. You're welcome."

"Can you tell me— I mean, was he— What *happened*, exactly, was he—"

"He was—like, he started acting really weird. Then he fell. It happened in, like, a nanosecond. Just, like, splat."

She shuddered. She couldn't quite bring herself to envision it, her formidable father dropping to the ground like a rag doll. It went against the rules of her cognition. It wasn't a thing that was supposed to happen.

"Sorry," Jonah said. "I didn't mean, like—*splat*."

"Can you stop saying that word?"

"Have you heard anything more?" He seemed to know almost nothing about her father's condition. When she'd told him, at her apartment, that her father was, at least, stable, if not conscious, some of the tension had flooded from his face; he'd looked like a kid for a second.

"I've tried calling my sisters," she said. "Nobody's answering. So I'm assuming— I mean, I don't really have a *choice* but to assume that no news is good news."

Their food arrived and Jonah dug into his burger as though he hadn't eaten since March. She picked listlessly at hers. Had she brought him here because the food was cheap, or because she hoped that Ben might show up? Then her stomach clenched anew, for allowing herself to even think about Ben, for the fact that she was at a bar with her teenage nephew just two days after her father had suffered a major heart attack. She reached for the vodka soda she'd ordered and casually set between them on the table, nodding at Jonah like *See? I'm cool. Have a sip.*

"My dad's in the hospital," she said, "and my whole family is with him and I've returned to the site of my recent breakup to get drunk with a teenager." She closed her eyes and pressed her forehead to the hard edge of the table.

"I wasn't sure where else to go," he said. "And I . . ."

"No," she said, and she reached across the table to touch his wrist, because she'd learned in the last two hours that you were allowed to be motherly with younger people. "It's actually really nice to have you here. Even if you won't tell me *why* you're here and why you have my dad's car and whether or not anyone knows you're gone."

"Who'd you break up with?"

She sighed, allowing him, once again, to dodge the subject, taking full custody of the cocktail. "It's stupid to even call it that. We weren't even really together."

Weakened by fatigue and vodka, she told him.

"He sounds like kind of a tool," Jonah said.

"He was being *honest* with me." She had never understood why men were so quick to throw each other under the bus. "How does that make someone a tool?"

"Sorry." He nodded toward the bar. "What's the deal with that guy?"

The Irish bartender was chatting with an older man by the top-shelf liquor, but it was undeniable that he kept glancing over at their booth. "Nothing's the deal." She pushed the drink across the table toward him. She could not recall if it was their third or fourth. Time had been moving weirdly since she'd gotten the call about her father.

"What'd you say his name was?"

She felt her face heat up again. "I didn't. Luke. Why?"

Jonah crunched an ice cube. "No reason."

"Can we talk about what happened?" she asked. "My father's in the hospital." Her voice broke, startling her, and Jonah, as well, apparently, because he sat up straighter.

"I wasn't— I didn't mean to . . ."

She paused, feeling a creeping sensation at the back of her neck. "Didn't mean to what?"

"I shouldn't have let him go up there in the first place. I'm like a thousand years younger than he is. I had one job and I couldn't even——"

"My dad's been climbing around our house for decades. There's no way you could have stopped him." She watched him, her sisterly upper hand now allowing her to feel a pang of sadness for him, this confused kid without a family, now caught in the tornadic swirl of hers. "And Jonah, he—— My dad *wanted* to hang out with you. That's just how he——" She faltered before using the word *is*. "My dad cares about like six things in the world. Spending time with us is one of them." The shift in the power dynamic, for whatever reason, was enabling her to speak without getting choked up. "My parents are crazy about you, Jonah. My dad asked you to help him with the tree for the same reason he used to ask me to rake leaves with him. So he could spend *time* with you."

His eyes were an unearthly blue and swimming with tears. "Yeah, but I—— It was the fucking dog. He got loose and he startled me and I would've been holding the ladder otherwise."

The creeping was replaced by a heavy sadness. "Jonah, it's just a thing that happened. What could you have done? Broken his fall? He still had a heart attack."

"But I should've been the one to go up there. I shouldn't have let him——"

"Jonah, I—— How bad did he look?" she asked, and her voice broke on the penultimate syllable. "Seriously. Don't tell me the——"

"Really bad," Jonah said, and he looked down, and he seemed like a little kid again, shoulders caved inward and hands pulled into the sleeves of his shirt.

She tried to imagine what that meant. She pictured her dad blue and bleeding; she wondered what it would sound like if he screamed. Her dad, who'd sat with newborn her in his arms, at her mother's bedside, not knowing if she'd ever wake up. Her dad, who'd never not been there. She closed her eyes and took a few breaths. "Why doesn't my family care that I'm alone here? Why are— I mean, no offense, but why are *you* the one who's here instead of one of my sisters? Why are they not calling? He's, like, my favorite person in the world."

"Sorry," Jonah said.

"It really is nice to have you here," she said finally. "It's nice to have a person who—looks like people who I look like. No one's been to visit me in a while."

"You think I look like your family?"

She cocked her head, felt it dip a little too much to the left, heavy with drink. "I do. Not—well, not in the way that my other nephews do. But you definitely seem *familiar* to me."

His eyes bored holes into the table before him. "Do you know anything about my dad?"

She realized anew how much differently from her this kid had experienced the world. To not know your father's *fate* was one thing, but to not know your father at all was another entirely. The curiosity reminded her, again, of how young he was, how lucky *she* was, grand-scheme.

"Violet had this boyfriend for a while," she said. He straightened to attention. "I don't remember his name, but I—I remember thinking at the time that he was probably really smart, but in hindsight it just seems like he might've been super douchey."

His face fell. She remembered both her audience and the carelessness of what she was saying, that if asked to describe her own father she could go on for hours, cataloging his nuances, his quirks, his favorite things, his dumbest jokes, all the times he'd been there for her, cared for her when she was sick, tucked her into bed, moved her into dorm rooms and apartments. Her dad, assembling the cheap Swedish heft of her bed. *It's in my dad contract.*

"I don't mean— I was in like second grade, so my memory isn't . . . And just because someone's dad is shitty doesn't mean that . . ."

"You aren't really the authority on shitty dads," he said.

"You're right," she said.

He glanced at her empty glass, then looked up at her. "You're in law school, right?"

She didn't answer.

"If you're in law school, why do you live in, like, a shed?"

Her eyes filled again, this time in shame.

"No offense or anything. It just seems weird that you— I don't know."

"I'm not—*in* law school, per se," she said. "Not exactly." All the times she could have confessed—*should* have confessed, prior to this. To be speaking the words aloud now, to the only member of her family younger and more helpless than she, was almost kind of funny. And then she took a breath—weak, terrified, and for the first time in ages in the company of someone who had some of the same genes she did. "I didn't get in anywhere. I've been lying to everyone. I *do* live in a shed. I have no idea what the fuck I'm doing."

Jonah looked sort of uncomfortable. "Wow. Your parents are, like, super proud of you. They talk about you all the time."

She bent her straw, angrily, into a knobby spiral. "That's funny," she said, "that they'd talk a lot about someone who they basically forgot existed."

"Dude," he said. "Your bedroom's like a shrine. Although I was *way* more impressed by your TV on the Radio poster than I was by the Coheed and Cambria, by the way."

She colored. "I was fifteen." Then, remembering her new role: "You'll have to dip back into the annals of your memory to recall what that was like."

"Seriously, it's like you're still a little kid. Like they're just waiting for you to come home and revive your Tamagotchi."

"Which is part of the problem," she said. "Everyone refuses to see me as an adult, and because they've been denying the fact that I can ever *be* an adult, I'm a total fucking mess."

"I actually saw it more as, like, two people who really like their kids and are sad they're not living in their house anymore," Jonah said. "It's actually really nice, I think."

She crumpled, at that, and after about fifteen seconds Jonah was sitting next to her, not the most comforting presence but trying nonetheless, patting uneasily at her shoulder with one hand and holding an ineffectual wad of napkins in the other. Finally, less because she was finished crying and more to put him out of his misery, she dried her eyes and snarfed in her snot.

"You're a really nice kid, Jonah," she said.

"I really have to pee," he replied with apology.

When he disappeared she tried to compose herself, checked her phone fruitlessly for nonexistent messages from her family members. She sent off identical texts to Wendy, Violet, and Liza: *Any updates? I feel really out of the loop.*

"Hey," Jonah said, appearing at her elbow. "That guy at the bar likes you."

"Excuse me?"

"He asked if I was your little brother."

"Ah, yes. Inquiring after one's siblings. The natural aphrodisiac."

"I can just tell. He seems nice. You should go talk to him."

She scoffed. "Okay, Casanova."

"I'm really tired anyway. I can go back to your house. I promise to let you in when you get home."

"You're acting as though I've already agreed to this." But she looked up, and Luke the Irish bartender met her eyes and offered her a genial little salute, and she was reminded of the night of her faux-breakup with Ben, how kind he'd been. She smiled at him.

"See you in the morning," Jonah said, snatching the keys from her hand, and he was gone before she could change her mind.

As she watched him go, her phone dinged with a reply—from Wendy; characteristically underwhelming: *All good. Go to bed.*

She shoved the phone in her pocket and made her way to the bar.

He knew he should probably call someone. Wendy. She'd give him an update. But if the update was bad, then *he'd* have to break the news to Grace, and he couldn't handle telling Grace.

It wasn't his fault. Was it? As Grace had said, it wasn't as though he could have cushioned David's fall. What had even *happened*? God, what if he'd watched someone die and didn't even know it? Watched *David* die. David, who was so dorky and dad-jokey, who worried so much about his daughters, who actually seemed to enjoy the time he and Jonah spent together rehabbing the sick basement shower and watching the Blackhawks. There was no way he'd forgive Jonah—obviously not if he was dead, but also not if he was alive and learned that Jonah had stolen his car and driven to Oregon and set his daughter up with an Irish bartender. Jesus.

A knock on the door caused him to jump nearly a foot in the air, even though he'd promised Grace he'd wait up. It was almost midnight. Fortunately, it hadn't sounded forceful enough to be a cop. He went to the door, holding one of Grace's pathetic string cheeses, and opened it to find a twenty-something guy in a Pearl Jam T-shirt. "Yeah?" he said, as though he had a leg to stand on, squatting in a city he'd never been to, on the lam, eating someone else's cheese.

"I— Did I get the wrong—" The guy looked past him, seemed to take stock of the photos, the curtains, all of Grace's little efforts to make her house look less like a psychiatric hospital. "Where's Grace?"

"Out."

"Who are you?"

"Who are *you*?" He missed these kinds of banal confrontations, he was surprised to realize, marking one's territory, the way he'd learned to fight with other guys at Lathrop House over who claimed which bed or what they'd watch on TV. He was good at it. *Wielding authority*, his Krav Maga instructor called it.

"Is Grace okay? Is she—"

"We're related," he said, because the guy seemed nervous, and he didn't want him calling the cops.

"You and Grace? Related how?" Then a moment of recognition. "Are you Jonah?"

It moved him, a little bit, that there was a stranger in Oregon who'd *heard* about him, who knew his name because his aunt had told him it.

"I'm Ben," the guy said, holding out his hand. "I'm a friend of Grace's. Is she around?"

"No." He released the handshake.

"Are you staying with her?"

"Just temporarily."

"She hasn't been answering my calls."

It struck him, then, that this was the breakup guy Grace had mentioned at the bar. The guy who'd dumped her. "I doubt she's coming home tonight," he said, and it took a minute for the guy's face to rise and fall with the realization.

"Oh," Ben said. "I— Do you know where she— Never mind. Nice to meet you, man."

"You too." He watched the defeated slump of the guy's back as he retreated. "I'll let her know you stopped by," he called, but Ben didn't turn around, just raised a hand in thanks and kept walking. He felt a little bad; he'd just been messing around, trying to fuck with the guy a little bit and see how much he could get away with—kind of, it occurred to him, like how he'd been trying to keep up with Ryan and had gotten carried away and blabbed about Liza's hookup. And he realized that he'd done it again, fucked things up for yet another member of the Sorenson family.

It was his sixteenth birthday. He hadn't told Grace because he hadn't wanted her to feel the need to do anything for him, and because he hadn't wanted to feel disappointed, as he always had, on every birthday of his post-viaduct life. Because he had been really looking forward to a dorky birthday with his grandma and grandpa, Marilyn's overcooked chicken and that Stones album she loved on the stereo, talk of his upcoming Krav Maga tournament, a chocolate cake with his name on the top. Just a quiet night with his grandparents, who never seemed disappointed to see him, their applause as he blew out his candles and made a wish for the coming year.

He remembered the envelope he'd found in his grandfather's desk, the one he'd been smashing in his back pocket for two days while he drove. He removed it, creased and crumpled. The letters were all caps except for the *J*, which had a big cursive loop at the bottom. He took a knife from Grace's kitchen drawer and slit the envelope open. A hundred-dollar bill fell out first, followed by a folded slip of paper.

> *Dear Jonah, at the start of your sixteenth year—happy birthday. Wishing you great things to come. Thank you for joining us. —David/Grandpa*
>
> *PS—Use this for something fun. & don't tell Marilyn; she thinks it's crass to give $$.*

How would it have felt to open this envelope across the big dining room table from his grandparents? How would it have felt to use part of the money for a new basketball hoop to replace the old one so he and David could shoot layups together in the evenings? How would it have felt to blow out his candles? Instead he was alone, as ever, everyone he knew in the world either ignorant of the fact that it was his birthday or separated from him by his own doing. This was what happened when you got too comfortable. Though Violet had rejected him before he'd had time to establish a comfort level, separated herself from him before they'd even met. Not to mention that if anyone in the whole fucking world should know when his birthday was, it was Violet. He allowed himself to acknowledge how fucking much it hurt that she didn't want him around. That if they could do it all over again, he'd want her to unfuck whoever his secret dad was and spare him this whole fucking existence. A couple of tears leaked from his eyes and he brushed them away angrily. No matter how much anyone else in the family accepted him, she never would, and he couldn't make himself stop wanting her to. But he had his emergency fund, plus an extra hundred dollars, plus a couple of twenties that Grace kept in a jar on top of her mini-fridge, and so he could get the fuck out of Dodge and pretend that this whole stupid year had never happened.

Marilyn was in a shallow sleep beside his bed—dozing, really, because she was still aware of the nurses' incremental visits and the green glow of the cardiac monitor—and there was a nervy ache in her neck whose presence she was nursing like a plant, leaning into it and setting the soreness ablaze, feeding it all of her negative thoughts.

A jump in the heart rate monitor pulled her from her fog, and she turned, without thinking, to her husband, right into the irritated nerve. She squeaked at the sudden spark of pain. But David was blinking. Animation, finally, on the face that she'd only vaguely recognized for the last two days. She rose and took his hand—which still, too, didn't feel quite like the hand she'd been holding since she was twenty, but they were getting there; they would get there.

"Love," she said, bending to kiss his forehead. Not until she watched a tear fall into his hair did she realize she was crying. "Oh, there he is. There you are."

He wasn't fully awake—drifting, still, on the beta-blockers—but as his eyes closed again, she felt him squeeze her hand, feebly, three times.

Grace felt incongruously victorious on the cab ride home from Luke's apartment. She was pleasurably sore between her legs. She'd lost her virginity to someone who seemed more or less like a decent person. She was eligible now to partake in the time-honored discussions of penises and pregnancy scares (though Luke had used a condom, of course, circumventing any need to explain that she wasn't on birth control like every other normal twenty-three-year-old girl).

She came home to an empty house. She dropped her bag, called out for Jonah, and then happened upon what looked like some weird cult idolatry on her kitchen table, three bottles of wine—fancy-looking wine, like Violet and Wendy drank, not Hodnapp's Harvest—and three Post-it notes covered with an adolescent scrawl. She felt the hair on the back of her neck stand up even before she read the words: *sorry if i fucked anything up. was trying to help. i took some cash from your jar but ill pay u back. tx for dinner. ben seems nice—j.*

No, no, no. She called out his name again, hoping it was some kind of joke.

ben seems nice.

"What the fuck," she said aloud. Wasn't the universe supposed to be gentler to her, given all that she had going on? She pulled on one of her dad's old sweaters, the pilfered, fraying articles she and her sisters fought over endlessly, and she sank down into her spot beside the fridge. She still felt a little drunk. It was just after three, which meant that it was just after five in Chicago. She dialed anyway.

"Goose?" Wendy sounded surprisingly alert.

"Hi," she said, and even on the one syllable her voice wavered. "Jonah was here. But I just got home and he's gone. And I'm really worried about Dad. And I just had sex with this Irish guy. I feel like everything's— Nothing's how it's supposed to— And I'm so far away." And then, because she no longer had the wherewithal to restrain them, the tears came, the type of crying that felt like throwing up.

"Oh, shit, Gracie. What did you just say about Jonah?"

She inhaled phlegmily. "He—showed up."

"In *Portland*?"

"I don't own multiple properties, Wendy. Jesus. Yes, in Portland."

"Oh my God, we've been—we've all been so worried. He drove to *Oregon*? He doesn't even have a learner's permit. He totaled Liza's car, you know that, right?"

"No, I actually *didn't* know that because nobody in this family tells me fucking anything. It's not like *I* told him to do any of this. I'd never even met him until tonight."

"Is he okay?"

"Well, he—he's not here anymore."

"What do you mean?"

"I don't know. I just got home and he left me some wine and an apology note."

"Apologizing for what?"

"He said he borrowed some cash and he was sorry if he fucked anything up and he—"

"He what? This is fucking unbelievable. I can't believe you didn't call us, Gracie."

"I can't believe none of you called *me*. You're all together there and I'm alone all the way across the country and I've been so scared and I— Nobody even responds to my messages. *The girls*. I'm a fucking girl, too, Wendy."

"Gracie—"

"And all I want is to talk to Dad and I'm afraid to call Mom because what if someone tells me he's dead? Jonah is as scared shitless about Dad as I am, and I just had sex with someone I barely know, and I think Jonah might have told the guy who broke up with me about it, and I just feel like—" She gasped wetly. "Everything's falling apart."

"Okay, Gracie. It's okay."

"It's *not* okay."

"It will be," Wendy said, sounding enough like their mother that Grace was almost comforted. "Goose, ah—this—person who you— Christ. The person you had sex with."

Her dad often joked, "Most people have a mother and a father. Gracie has *four* mothers and a father." She'd always had four women looking out for her, prodding her in different directions, regarding her with affectionate amusement or disdain or a patronizing kind of knowingness. But nobody had ever taught her anything constructive about being a woman, really. They never talked to her about sex, aside from her mother once giving her the Catholic rundown about how when you *made love* it should be with someone you loved very much (though even Marilyn had seemed a little bit skeptical during this delivery) and Wendy once using the word *orgasmic* and clarifying, after Grace had prodded her, that it meant *really, really good*. She felt momentarily bad for presenting this side of herself to her sister. She knew that she was relied on to keep the peace. She was the liaison of the family, the Lollipop Guild, the plump, kindly little diplomat who pretended not to notice when people were fighting at Christmas. She was the Sorenson mascot for youth and innocence and life that had yet to be irreparably marred by the gore of adulthood—or at least she *had* been, until about two hours ago. Or perhaps until eight months ago, when she pretended to get accepted to law school and started living a lie.

"Are you— Who *is* this person? He broke up with you right after he—" She knew this was the point where her sister would normally have used the verb *fucked.*

"No. Different guys," she said.

"What the fuck is going on in the Pacific Northwest, Gracie?" Wendy asked, and she felt herself laugh, which was—she realized then—exactly why she had called her oldest sister. "You're safe, right? You're— It was—God. Consensual? It was—it wasn't—?"

"It was consensual. I feel like— Wendy, I feel like such a dirtbag. I wasn't—I wasn't thinking clearly and I was upset and I'm starting to feel a little bit crazy, you know? When you're alone for so long that you—like, you stop being able to objectively see what's normal and what's not? Do you know what I mean?"

"Quite well, yes," Wendy said gently.

"I never fuck up like this," she said, and in the time it took Wendy to reply, she realized that this could possibly be offensive to her sister, *I'm not like you, the fuckup.* "I mean— Sorry."

Wendy snorted.

"I didn't mean—"

"For fuck's sake, Gracie. Come on. Start from the beginning," Wendy said, letting her off the hook, and so she did.

"It was my first time," she tacked on in almost a whisper.

"Oh, sweetie," Wendy said, sounding uncharacteristically motherly. "Okay. Well it's—it's normal for you to be feeling weird, I think." Grace heard a crashing noise. "Hang on. I'm getting a drink. I can't do this sober, Gracie, I'm sorry." More clinking, then the whoosh of a sliding door and the flick of a lighter. Wendy's voice was full of smoke when she spoke again. "Describe him," she said, "in detail. So I know what we're dealing with here."

When Grace had satisfied her curiosity, Wendy said, "So how was it?"

"How was . . ."

"The sex. I'm just going to have to get over the fact that you're an adult. I have to accept that. And it's important to talk about these things. So how was it?"

Grace swallowed. "Awkward? And . . . I don't know. It sort of hurt."

"Yeah, a lot of people say that."

"It didn't for you?"

"Oh my God, no. It was amazing."

"Seriously?" Another perk of calling Wendy was that her sister had enough tact to skate over the enormity of her lies for the time being, to focus at the moment on the most entertaining anecdote because everything else was too dark.

"It's actually— It's so funny we're talking about this, because I ran into— You must not remember Aaron Bhargava. Jesus, you're so young. He was my first *boyfriend*-boyfriend. And he was fucking gorgeous. He still is, it turns out. I just ran into him in the parking lot of the hospital."

"Seriously?"

"Isn't that a trip? Totally random. But he was a tennis player, and he—"

"Hey, Wendy? Is it okay for us— I feel selfish talking about this other stuff when—"

"Goose. If Dad finds out we spent our time weeping over him, he'll kill us. What would he be doing if he were awake right now?"

This incited a new surging of tears, but she bit down on her tongue. "Well, it's five a.m. your time, so he'd probably be running around the woods in that disgusting Wesleyan shirt."

"Let's say it's nighttime and you're sad and Dad's there. What would he tell you?"

"To— I don't know. Hang in there, I guess."

"Exactly. And he'd make a dorky joke and give you one of those awkward hugs that's, like, the best hug in the world, right?"

She nodded, sniffling, aware that Wendy couldn't see her.

"Hey. Do you want to hear about my virginity being ceremoniously taken by a hot fifteen-year-old tennis player or not?"

"I do," she whispered. She would tell Wendy everything— she was too tired to keep lying, and plus she'd already confessed to Jonah, so there was no use in further trying to keep it under wraps—but not until her sister told her this ersatz bedtime story. She curled up against the side of the fridge, hugging the cuffs of her dad's sleeves in her hands, resting the phone against her ear. Wendy had artfully, seamlessly steered the conversation to herself, which was another thing Grace had known she would do. Sometimes it was enough just to listen to voices that weren't your own.

2005

When Wendy got pregnant, there was shopping to do, all sorts of different ways to highlight her new assets, her adorable belly and her newly formidable rack. The joy she felt at loving her body—its roundness, its resilience, its fecundity—was wild, the wonder of fostering growth rather than starving herself into submission. She played both Brahms and Bowie to her belly at night, found inventive ways for her and Miles to continue making love, and joined a new moms walking group that lazily wandered a short stretch of 57th Street every Thursday before settling in for full-fat decaf macchiatos and discussions of sleep training.

Violet, perhaps understandably, was keeping her distance. She'd rallied, after the baby, after a while—springing from her sorrow with more vigor than Wendy figured was healthy—and started at the U of C, started dating a piece of driftwood named Matt, and she was back to her same old self, high-strung and high-functioning, none of the soft vulnerability she'd shown while living with them in Hyde Park, almost as though the whole year had never happened. But Wendy was very nearly too happy to miss her sister, too taken by all that was to come.

And then it happened, when she was exactly thirty weeks along, the baby as big as a butternut squash, and she awoke not to the feverish calisthenics of her daughter (by then it had been confirmed: *Ivy Eisenberg*) but to a troubling stagnancy, no movement at all, and she prodded anxiously at her belly and woke Miles and called her doctor, bordering on hysteria, saying, "I don't know how I know but I know something's wrong," and Miles took her in a cab to Prentice and the doctor confirmed that they couldn't find a heartbeat. What followed would forever remain a blur to her, because she forced herself to forget, but that didn't mean she couldn't remember, couldn't dredge it up in dark moments when she wanted to revel in the pain of it, in homage to her daughter.

They induced her, and she was hooked up to all manner of monitors except one to track the baby's heartbeat, which was when the shock started to wear off and the agony began to hit her, the realization that Ivy didn't have a pulse, because her heart didn't work anymore, because she was dead, dead inside of Wendy, and she threw up bile all over the hospital blanket, and this coincided with the medicine kicking in and the onslaught of the contractions, which were strident from the get-go, the pain requiring so much of her attention and her energy that she couldn't even cry during them.

Miles urged her to call her parents, but she insisted that he call Violet first. Dimly, through the pain, she heard snippets of him leaving her a message: *Would be good if you could come . . . Not sure what . . . Room 249; there's a sign on the door that . . .*

The contraction ended and she sat up straighter. "What sign on the door?" she asked.

Miles came to sit beside her, his eye contact steady and even. He took her hand. "It's—so people know, before they come in, that this isn't—that there are—special circumstances. That's the wrong word; I meant— Jesus Christ, I meant— I'm sorry." And he began to weep, the first time she'd ever seen him cry, the man with whom she'd forged this path, who'd lost their daughter too, who would do anything for her but could currently do nothing. "I hate this," he said. "Wendy, I . . . God, I hate this so much; I'm so sorry."

Hours later—the doctor and nurses had repeatedly encouraged painkillers but Wendy adamantly declined, needing to feel present, to marinate in the pain—Miles suggested again that they call David and Marilyn, and she finally agreed, but told him to tell them not to come until after the delivery, because she didn't want them there for what was happening now; Violet was the only person on the earth besides her and Miles who was meant to be present for this terrible occasion, but she hadn't answered the phone yet, though Miles continued to leave messages.

Kneeling in bed, knees wide, she began to feel the globe of the baby's head pressing against her cervix, and she cried out, brayed like a mare, past the point where she could stop herself from making noise.

"Where *is* she?" she asked when Miles came in from calling her parents.

He came over to her, rubbed her back until she swatted him away. "Your parents say they love you and they'll be here whenever you give them the go-ahead," he said. "Violet's holed up doing bar review, I guess. Your mom's trying to reach her."

And then Violet slipped from her mind, replaced by all-consuming physical necessity.

"Miles I think I have to— Would you tell the doctor that I— Jesus *fuck*."

The pushing was the worst part, because she was imagining the whole time—when she had the wherewithal to contemplate anything past the burning blaze between her legs—what the doctor and nurses would be like if she were delivering a *live* baby, a big, healthy baby like Violet's. Even though her sister's doctor knew that she was giving the baby up he had still been kind, heartening, making weak jokes to Violet as she got deeper and deeper into the throes of her labor and saying things like *You've got this, Violet,* and *Let's help out this beautiful baby, okay?* It almost felt like a sporting event, exciting even though it was also utterly depressing, even though neither athlete nor spectators would be a part of the baby's life beyond what took place in that room. But her own doctor looked grave and grayish and had not made any direct references to the fact that there was a *human body* in her birth canal, just an object, a *mass,* instead of who it really was: her beautiful Ivy unleashed into the outside world without a fighting chance, and it seemed so *unjust,* the fact that it could all be taken away like that, even when you did everything you were supposed to do.

She still expected the baby to cry when she was born. When she felt her slip out, she waited, primed—some biological conditioning, apparently, because everyone in the *room* seemed to be expecting it—for the sound of her wailing daughter, for the evidence that this entire terrible day had simply been a test to ensure she was cut out for motherhood. And she'd passed, hadn't she, declining ice chips and peppermints and additional pillows, denying herself pain relief and the comforting proximity of her parents? *I'm ready for you,* she thought to Ivy, through the silence in the room. *Look how ready I am for you.* Miles was stroking her forehead.

"Is she—" she said. "I don't— Wait."

"I love you," Miles whispered into her temple.

"No, but I— God. Oh, God." Her teeth began to chatter, and she felt a rising panic as the doctor, holding the baby low enough so that Wendy couldn't see, said, "Miles, would you like to cut the cord?"

"Sweetie?" he asked, but she didn't answer, and she felt him stand.

She and Miles sat together for hours holding her, a new sign apparently affixed to the door because nobody so much as knocked, and she couldn't believe how little Ivy weighed, how someone so light could still be so intricate. She was half the size of Violet's baby but no less breathtakingly, perfectly complex, tiny eyelids and ears, the smallest knees Wendy had ever seen.

"Sweetheart, do you think you'll be ready soon to . . ."

"To what?" she asked, her voice startling in the quiet. Miles put his arm around her.

"To—I'm not—say goodbye to her, honey."

"I have to throw up," she said, like it was a logical response, and Miles reached for the trash can beside the bed and she vomited violently, just a sick foamy bile again because her stomach was empty, devoid of everything.

What happened next—the doctor coming in, a nurse at her elbow—she refused to recall; she could only remember wailing like an animal and failing to find comfort in Miles for the first time in her life; she could not remember how her daughter stopped being in her arms; she could not remember refusing the doctor's offer to take photos; she could not remember saying goodbye.

At some point she fell asleep and when she woke up, Miles was gone and her mother was sitting next to her bed, holding her hand.

"Hi, sweetheart," Marilyn murmured. And Wendy replied *hi* and her voice sounded echoic and scary. "Miles ran home to get you a few things." And she marveled for a second, because what *things* could she possibly need? What on earth could he possibly be bringing her? "I love you, my girl," her mom whispered, reaching to smooth Wendy's hair away from her forehead.

"Is Dad here?" she asked, and her mom shifted uncomfortably.

"He's parking the car," she said. "He's nearby. How are you feeling pain-wise, sweetheart? Miles said they gave you a little morphine. Do you want more?"

She shook her head. She resented Miles for consenting to

the morphine on her behalf. The pain had been her new companion, her way of honoring the tiny person she'd failed to bring safely into the world. The gaping hole where Ivy should have been was molten and pulsing, and to dull it was disloyal.

"I wish I could take it all away from you, sweet thing," her mom said simply. It was a strange sentence, darkly poetic, one that with a subtle shift in vocal inflection could have been a curse instead of a sweet proclamation of motherly selflessness.

"Why isn't Violet here?" she asked, and her mother adjusted one of her blankets.

"She's—she has the bar exam coming up in a few months. She's in her—you know, her studying mode. I'm having a little trouble pinning her down."

It was an insultingly flimsy excuse. *Studying*, as though her sister had done something forgivable, as though she'd simply missed a family dinner and not the time Wendy needed her more than anything. She had wanted Violet beside her in the cab instead of Miles; she had wanted Violet to stand up to her cunt of a doctor, to whisper threateningly, *Have some goddamn respect*, because Violet was almost a lawyer and could do things like that. She had wanted Violet to be able to hold Ivy.

But by the time Violet got there, burst in at nearly ten at night wearing a raincoat and looking anguished, Wendy didn't want to see her anymore. Didn't want to talk about anything, didn't want the vibrancy of her sister to inflict its painful glow on the dark, depressing, sadistically fancy hospital room.

"Hey," Violet said, a crying-thickness already in her voice. "Wendy, I'm so, so sorry." Violet sank into the chair next to her and reached affectionately to tuck Wendy's hair behind her ear. "I'm so sorry I'm just getting here now," she said. "I came as soon as I could."

"It's not a big deal," Wendy said. "You shouldn't have even come." This was her strategy: mind over matter. It was all she had left and she vowed to adhere to it with militancy.

"Of course I came," Violet murmured, and she rubbed gently at Wendy's wrist with her fingers, touching, fretting, a rain-coated bundle of anxious kinetics. "I ran into Miles in the hallway," she said inanely.

"He just went to smoke." She twisted toward the window, away from her sister. "I would fucking murder a chaplain if I could have a cigarette right now."

Violet squirmed, looking at the door. "Can you—could you go outside? I could take you. I can sneak you out. You can wear my coat."

It was then that she noticed Violet's hands, clasped together over her chest: the glint on her left ring finger. Violet saw her looking and shoved them into the pockets of her raincoat. While Wendy was enduring the worst day of her entire life, Violet had gotten engaged.

"I can't just *leave*," she said. She probably could have, actually, but it still felt too soon, too soon to leave the last physical space she would ever share with her child. She couldn't think about where they'd taken Ivy, what wing of the hospital had been deemed appropriate for her daughter. "Christ, Violet. It's not that fucking simple."

"Of course," Violet said. "Shit, I'm sorry. I was just trying to— That was a dumb thing to offer." But it wasn't: it was a nice thing to offer, and Wendy wished for just a second that she could backtrack, say "sure, hand over the raincoat" even though it probably wouldn't fit her, slip down the hallways and out through the fire escape to smoke a cigarette with her gentle, worried, perfect sister. But Wendy was angry, because Violet was so *malleable*. Violet had it in her to be stubborn, forceful; but she checked those things at the door whenever she was around Wendy. And perhaps it was unfair to find these things irritating, because hadn't that been Wendy's ultimate goal? Wasn't that every sister's dream from the beginnings of consciousness, to have your siblings under a spell?

But this was the thing: sometimes being a sister meant knowing the right thing to do and still not doing it because winning was more important. Victory was a critical part of sisterhood, she'd always thought. And she was not winning today, by any conceivable stretch, so why the fuck not seize an easy conquest when you could?

"You can go, really. There's no need for you to be here."

Violet's face fell. "Oh—sure. Okay." She chewed on the inside of her cheek. "You know I came as quickly as I could, right? Matt and I were—" She winced. "I just got home and checked my machine. If I'd known, Wendy— I'm so sorry I didn't know."

"It's fine. You should go home." *Go, go, go. Go in case I want to start crying too.*

Violet grew paler. "Whatever you want, Wendy. But I'm happy to stay."

"There's really no reason. I mean, I have Miles here, so there's really no point."

"Okay, if—" Violet looked as though she'd been slapped. "I wanted to be here with you."

She refused to let Violet be the one with hurt feelings. "Thanks for coming," she said, "but I just expelled a dead baby from my vagina, so I'm not actually in the mood for company." She saw tears spring back to Violet's eyes, but her sister still leaned in to hug her. Wendy stiffened.

"Call me for anything, Wendy, okay? I'll just be at home. I'll be waiting for your call, okay? Just in case. Anything you need."

"There's not a single thing in the fucking world that I could possibly need."

Violet gathered the belt of her raincoat in her hands and turned to leave. "I love you."

Get out, get out, get out.

She paused at the door. "This is the worst thing and I'm so sorry," she said.

Wendy waited until the door clicked closed before she finally allowed herself to fall apart.

In the car on the way to the hospital, through halting downtown traffic, David held his wife's hand. He watched her sucking in her cheeks as she looked out the window, felt her rubbing her thumb against his palm. She'd been so excited. They'd *both* been excited, certainly, but he could tell that she was looking especially forward to grandparentage. She was not one of those women for whom the word triggered apprehension. She was fifty years old and delighted at the thought of changing diapers again, so long as she could return the wearer of the diapers to its wearied parents at the end of the day. She was thrilled by the prospect of having a tiny new person around, one who would not slam doors in her face or shun her like Gracie had begun to do as she slipped into the murky hormonal bath of early adolescence.

"We can just *play* with it," she'd said to him shortly after Wendy told them she was pregnant. They were in bed and he was feeling elderly, due to the fact that his daughter, his first baby, was going to have a baby of her own. Marilyn rested a hand on his chest. "You were always so good with them when they were babies," she said. They could smile now, at the fact that Wendy demanded, from nearly the moment she was born, to fall asleep in her father's arms. She would keep herself awake, fussing and burbling and occasionally shrieking in Marilyn's exhausted embrace, until David came home. And then she would snuggle into him and promptly conk out. It had made Marilyn weep on several occasions—out of fatigue and that irrational resentment that arose from being the spurned parent of a choosy infant—but that night in their bed she was charmed by the memory of his mystical baby-soothing arms. He pulled her against him and kissed her hair. "We get to do it all again," she murmured happily into his neck. "Except we get to send it home at the end of the day." The kids were Marilyn's life, parasite and sustenance, and he knew how much it thrilled her to think of them having kids of their own.

He hated driving in the city. Despite his early aversion to the suburbs, he now stayed in Oak Park unless forcibly extracted, ruing the seizure of the Kennedy and the hectic sludge of the Gold Coast. Stopped at a light, he turned to study her. She'd swept her hair into a messy bun and little strands had escaped, wispy blond with glints of gray.

"Remember the day Wendy was born?" he asked. "Remember that traffic on the way to the hospital?" There had been a storm, rain turning to sleet turning to snow, and then a terrible accident that left cars stalled for blocks, among them David's secondhand white Corvair. He'd worried about both his daughter being born in that car and himself being murdered in it, by his wife.

They glided east down Superior. She took his hand, pressing it to her cheek then holding it in her lap, rubbing at it with her thumbs as though it were some kind of anthropological artifact. Was it unseemly, thinking about that jubilant occasion amid such an awful one?

"It was a good day," she agreed.

At the hospital, he separated from her at the elevators, mumbling that he wanted to stop and speak to someone. His wife caught his sleeve.

"Someone who?" she asked. "Who do you know here?" She sounded suspicious and he colored. She was still holding his arm. "Honey, what is it?"

"I'd just like to talk to her doctor," he said.

"David, no."

"Just for a few minutes," he said. "I'd just like to know—I'd like to know what happened. Really." Miles's account had been brief and unsatisfying.

"You ask Wendy that," she said, softening. "You ask Wendy that when she's ready to talk about it. It's an invasion of privacy, sweetie."

"She's our daughter."

She hesitated.

"I'll meet you in a minute." He pressed the elevator button for her and kissed her cheek. "Tell Wendy I love her and I'm parking." The doors slid open and she stepped in. She lifted a hand to him as they closed.

So he interrogated Wendy's doctor, requested a meeting in the hospital cafeteria and grilled her about the specifics, about whether they'd done blood tests or planned on an autopsy, about how this possibly could have happened to such a young, healthy woman. The doctor regarded him patiently, sadly from across the table.

"Your daughter declined an autopsy," she said gently. "And there's no guarantee that it would be conclusive, anyway. You know that as well as I do. Wendy's blood pressure was normal. No hydrops in the—your granddaughter. I wish I could tell you something more comforting." She shook her head. "I'm so sorry for your loss, Dr. Sorenson. But Wendy's going to be fine. She can try again."

He was fairly certain she wouldn't, though. His eldest was not fond of trying again. Quashed efforts at anything—hula hooping, long division, SAT prep—had historically reduced her to angry tears, histrionic sessions of huffing and cursing and declaring things *idiotic*. Wendy didn't generally try again. She gave up and found a new thing that worked better for her, and she took that new thing and ran with it, threw herself into it with a fervor that made her forget previous failures. She'd run away from them all, from the shame of her teenage years, into the arms of Miles, and look where it had gotten her.

"I appreciate your time," he said, and she patted his arm.

"Your family is in my thoughts, Dr. Sorenson."

"Thank you," he mumbled. He sank back down at the table, twisting his wedding ring. This wasn't how things were supposed to be. Marilyn was supposed to be in her garden right now and Wendy was supposed to be safely at home with her husband and instead they were both on the second floor of this fancy downtown hospital, his girls, grieving the loss of someone neither of them had even had a chance to meet.

A tiny weight against her chest, avian and sleepily kinetic. The compliant pursing muscles of her mouth as she nursed. The rhythmic flexings of her star fruit fingers. The mystery of her infinite mind, housed inside her ever-growing brain. Her first daughter, the baby who'd just been *given* to her and David, to take home, with no consideration whatsoever of their ineptitude, their past darknesses, their own respective infantilities. Their Wendy Evelyn Sorenson, born at 12:26 a.m. on the fourteenth of December, nine pounds and nine ounces.

Thinking of Wendy as a baby, Marilyn sat by her daughter's bedside, held her hand, prayed with her. And Wendy—perhaps only because she was medicated—acquiesced.

"Mom," she said, and Marilyn turned to her on high alert, feeling an uncomely sense of pleasure given the dark circumstances because it felt like she and her daughter were *connecting* for the first time since Wendy's babyhood. "Mom, she was— She had a *face.*" Which was a silly thing to say, perhaps, because of course a thirty-week-old baby had a face, but in the utterance of the phrase she felt her daughter's broken heart and felt her own heart break in kind. "She looked sort of like Dad and she had a—she had an *expression* and I couldn't tell what kind of face it was; I couldn't tell what she was feeling."

One of the perils of having a daughter who was similar to you was that you were frequently at a loss for what to say. What could you possibly offer to a statement like that?

"I'm sure she was at peace, honey," she said, because she was—her feeble Catholicism had its merits sometimes. "How could she not be, sweetheart? Look at how much you loved her. Look at all you did for her."

Wendy, miraculously, accepted this lame assurance, and she did not protest when her mother climbed beside her in the hospital bed and held her.

Grace associated the arrival of bad news with the scent of burning bread. It began, she assumed, because her mother had given her the Sex Talk when they were driving down Roosevelt Road one afternoon, coming home from the city, and just as Marilyn uttered the words *making love* they drove past the Turano factory and the car was suddenly filled with the pleasant scent of a-bit-too-toasted French rolls, swirling around among abject mortification and unbridled disgust. Thenceforth she remembered all bad news being imparted to her this way. She got watered-down, after-the-fact, diplomatic versions of events that were unquestionably more confusing than the true versions.

The first time she got a straight story it came from her father. She had the sense that something was awry but she couldn't quite place what it was.

"We're going to the hospital to visit your sister," her father said, merging onto the expressway.

She turned to him, first confused and then embarrassed. Her dad, perhaps sensing this, took one hand from the steering wheel and ruffled her hair.

"You know how Wendy was going to have a baby, Goose?"

"Yeah." This was, in fact, what had prompted the burning-bread Sex Talk from her mom, Grace's inability to wrap her mind around the notion of sisters becoming mothers.

"Well, sometimes—sometimes a pregnancy doesn't *take*,

honey." Her father could be very awkward. She didn't know what he meant. She looked at him in the driver's seat, clutching the steering wheel more intently than usual. "The baby died, Gracie," he said. "It's a really terrible thing that happens. Sometimes people die before they're born."

She wanted to say *I don't get it* or *How is that possible?* or *What happens to all the cupcakes Mom and I just ordered for the baby shower?* but she also didn't want her dad to go into any detail; she didn't want a repeat of the Sex Talk, made significantly more awkward because it would be coming from her father.

"It's a sad thing, Goose." His voice sounded thin and wobbly. "Wendy and Miles are really sad. So are Mom and I. Wendy's going to be okay, but it's a really sad thing."

She didn't know babies *could* die. She knew, certainly, that people could, but babies weren't people, or not really. *Does this mean I'm not an aunt anymore?* she wanted to ask, and *Do you still get to have a name if you die before you're born?* She felt herself starting to cry, not because she was sad—though she was; it was a sad thing—but because she recognized, at twelve years old, that a part of her had died, too, the part that was normally spared these sorts of details. Because it was the first time her dad had ever told her *he* was sad and that seemed like a pretty seminal thing, the realization that your parents could feel sad or scared.

Her father squeezed her knee, not picking up on the selfish layers of her thoughts. They were on the Eisenhower bound for the hospital, nowhere near the Turano factory, but she smelled it anyway, burning bread, and she rested her head against the window and breathed.

CHAPTER TWENTY-SEVEN

The phone buzzed in Wendy's sports bra, and she answered, even though she was in the middle of core barre.

"Wendy?" And at the voice, her heart stalled. Took them long enough. Jesus Christ.

She slipped out into the hall. "Where the fuck *are* you? Where have you been?" She was finally allowed to exhale, finally allowed to reveal how fucking terrified she'd been since she'd heard he'd left Grace's house, despite the fact that she kept assuring everyone that he'd call when he was ready.

"I'm sort of in a jail."

"In *jail*?"

"In—like, *a* jail, not an actual cell, just, like, the location, technically, is a jail."

"I'd kill you if I wasn't so happy you're alive."

"I need— They said I need someone to come pick me up. I have your dad's car but I can't— They won't let me drive it."

"How did you get to *a jail*?"

"I got pulled over. One of the taillights was out. Sorry, Wendy. I wasn't—expecting this to happen."

"When you stole your grandfather's car and drove to fucking Oregon? Without a license? You weren't expecting to get pulled over and end up in *a jail*?"

"You can stop saying *a jail*; I get that you think it's funny."

"I love that you managed to evade capture when you were driving across the entire country but you ended up getting busted for something as stupid as a taillight."

"Wendy—"

"Where are you?" she asked. "Where, *technically*, is this jail?"

"Sort of in Montana."

"What, like, half-in, half-out?"

"In Montana."

"How'd you end up in Montana?"

The voice got smaller. "I got kind of lost, and then was thinking of—like, maybe Canada, but I realized I didn't have any ID with me."

"Jesus. Don't quit your day job." She sighed. "Are you safe? Can you stay in the—jail? I'll get the next flight."

She heard the murmur of a voice from the background. Then: "He wants to talk to you."

She closed her eyes, leaned against the wall, wondered if the heat coursing through her veins felt at all like what it felt like to be someone's mother. If her mix of terror and relief and hysteria and exhaustion had anything in common with loving someone, parentally, whether you were their parent or not. "Put him on the phone," she said. "And for fuck's sake, stay where you are. I'll be there as soon as I can."

Marilyn insisted on setting them up temporarily in the downstairs guest room.

"I didn't break my *legs*," he'd said irritably, as he had when she'd insisted on wheeling him out of the hospital in a wheelchair.

She had, both times, ignored him.

So David was sitting by the window in the easy chair his

wife had dragged from the living room, looking out into the yard, Loomis curled obligingly at his feet. His broken arm had shifted from hurting to itching in its cast, and he felt renewed and retroactive sympathy for eight-year-old Violet—*Dada, it's a mean itch*—who had broken her wrist falling off of the monkey bars. The discomfort in his chest had abated as well, but he still didn't feel like himself. His appetite was gone, which meant his energy was low, which meant he was less interested in doing things like showering, which meant that his hair felt waxy and his face like steel wool. Dressing was an ordeal, so he was wearing his bathrobe. He was embarrassed by himself. And feeling no insignificant degree of self-pity. And the fact that Jonah—who'd been missing now for nearly a week—had had to witness it all. For all David's years in practice, he'd never actually *seen* anyone having a heart attack. To have to experience that, to see it happening to your *grandfather*. He shuddered, and was reminded again of his infirmity by a niggling spark of pain in his shoulder—no longer the ache he'd been ignoring for months but a new kind of pain, a sprain, from the fall.

"Sweetie." Marilyn bustled in, bringing with her the static smell of cold. She kissed his head. She'd brought tea and toast, which she arranged on the end table beside him. "The Roths just got this unbelievable snowblower. Space-age. Like a Zamboni." She perched on the windowsill in front of him. "Dan did the driveway and the sidewalks for us." Certainly she wasn't rubbing it in on purpose, but she had to remember that he actually *enjoyed* shoveling snow, that it was yet another simple pleasure now denied to him. She retrieved his pill case from the nightstand—a day-by-day, like his elderly patients had, filled with a flamboyant amalgam of pills—and knocked the day's allotment into her hand. "You want water instead of tea?"

"It's fine," he said, taking them. Then, remembering: "Thanks, kid."

She smiled at him and smoothed his hair away from his forehead. "How about we get you showered today, huh? It might feel nice; it's so cold outside."

Infantilization aside, the thing he was having the most trouble thinking about was the simple fact of her being here, being *home*. It had actually taken him until recently to notice that she was home all the time, home to administer his meds and make him bland meals and lie in bed beside him and cheerfully read him notable news items.

"Did you draw up some kind of family leave policy?" he'd asked. "For powerhouse women to care for their one-armed husbands?"

She'd turned to a new page, not meeting his eyes. "I put Drew in charge."

"You *what*?"

"It just seemed easier that way." Then she'd looked up at him, smiling tiredly.

"You're taking a leave from work?" He'd felt a creeping sense of déjà vu. "Hang on, Marilyn, I didn't— I'm not going to let you—"

"It's done," she'd said, and she'd leaned over to kiss him on the shoulder. "I'll go back when we're ready. Once we've got you climbing trees again, huh?"

Now he'd adjusted to her being home, and, less so, to her tending to him.

"A shower," she said, sounding preoccupied, lost in her own mental calendar. "And then maybe something out of the house? The grocery. Or a movie, if you're feeling adventurous."

"Naah," he said. "I'm not in the mood."

"Well." She rose, her voice unnaturally chipper, and went about making their bed. "Sometimes it takes a little jump start to *get* in the mood. Let's get you in the shower, and it'll warm you up, and then you'll be all nice and clean and we can—"

"For Christ's sake, Marilyn, could you stop talking to me like I'm a toddler?"

She froze, leaning over to tuck in a corner of the sheet.

"I'm sorry," he said, though he didn't feel terribly sorry.

"No," she said, "that's—a reasonable request." She cleared her throat and went back to work on the bed. "It's just difficult for me to talk to you like an adult when you're behaving like a little boy. I have sort of a hard time equating that person with the husband I'm accustomed to."

"It's not fair for you to resent me for—"

"I don't resent you in the least." She said it so plainly that it startled him. She came over and stood in front of him again. "This is why we exist, isn't it? To be here for each other? The store isn't my top priority right now. Because I love you, and you being well is more important to me than anything else. You'd do the same for me, wouldn't you?"

"Of course."

"The only thing I resent is your complete unwillingness to look on the bright side."

"I could've *died*," he said, the first time he'd verbalized the thought.

She took his hands. "But you didn't. That *is* the bright side. You're here, and you're going to be okay. I'm just trying to help that along."

He took a slow breath, felt the warmth of his wife's hands in his. She was the only person he knew who could find an upside like this: medical recovery as a means of enjoying life, exploring new hobbies, *basking*. "Thank you," he said.

She smiled, smoothed his hair again. "You don't have to thank me. Hey, we're both unencumbered and not working, at the same time, for the first time *ever*. It's criminal for us to take that for granted."

"I guess we could go to the grocery."

"Oh, my adventurer." She bent to kiss him.

"*If* you agree to shower with me."

The phone rang and she rose to answer it, calling over her shoulder: "I'll give that some serious thought."

Liza's first word was, bafflingly, *David*. Not *Papa*, which was Wendy's, or *Ma*, which was Violet's, but *David*, two crisp syllables from her tiny handlebar-mustache mouth, *David*, at the dinner table, and her parents had looked at each other, fighting constantly at that time about money and mortgages and space and time management, and laughed, the tension of their difficult months momentarily extinguished.

What would her kid's first word be? *Despair*, she thought dully. *Injustice. Existential apathy. Gloom.* She was in her sunroom, marooned on the glider, marveling over her enormity and her isolation. The only reminder that she was not completely alone was the occasional thump she felt from within, the baby now too big to move around with much intent.

"I'm David and Marilyn's daughter," she'd say sometimes, introducing herself to family friends. Her kid wouldn't get to say that. *Undetermined Sorenson-Marks*, the kid would say. *As-yet-androgynous offspring of Liza Sorenson and Ryan Marks, two people who tried to settle but couldn't ever make it work.*

She shifted uncomfortably on the glider and a gripping in her torso took her breath away for a good thirty seconds. There was a warm, sharp-smelling fluid between her legs, seeping out of her onto the floor; when had her life become so gross, so undignified? This couldn't be it; of course it couldn't; she was supposed to have several more days; the sensation was so violent, hurt so much, had emerged out of nowhere, out of her indulgent self-pity.

Motherfucker; this was it. She thought she might throw up.

She thought of Dirk the tattoo artist, the musk from his arm-pits, the needle on her neck a 4 out of 10 on the pain scale. How naïve she'd been. She wanted her dad; she wanted a do-over. She picked up her phone and dialed.

"Mom?" she said. *David and Marilyn's daughter.* The relief of being able to call herself that. "Mama, I need you."

2006

Another wedding in his backyard. Another daughter married, on her way to building an autonomous life. Violet had friends and coworkers and a husband, now, and with him a large, vaguely agnostic extended family. But as pleased as David was for his little overachiever, at some point he became painfully aware of Wendy, who, as the night wore on, got progressively drunker. Between requisite dances with his wife and his other three daughters he kept an eye on her, saw her nearly topple a waiter trying to grab a flute of champagne, saw Miles chastise her and saw her rebuff him with a jab of her elbow. Saw the guests watching her similarly, warily.

"Someone needs to cut her off," Marilyn said. They were standing together by the ginkgo, taking a breather, thinking of their own inception, thirty years ago in this very same spot. "She's drawing attention to herself."

Wendy had pulled even further away from them—from everyone—since she'd lost the baby. *She's hurting*, he wanted to say to his wife, but he knew she already knew that. It was a mystery to him why the largest-hearted woman in the world had such a difficult time mustering active sympathy for their firstborn, especially when he knew how much time she spent worrying about her.

"Should I go get Miles and have him take her home?" she

asked. He smoothed the material of her dress between his fingers. She looked beautiful, had looked radiant all night; all his girls were glowing except for the one self-destructing in a folding chair over by the swing set.

"No," he said. How nice it would be to just stay over here with her, agree to dance with her to "Tennessee Waltz," sip at his scotch and feel good about life. "I'll go talk to her." His poor kid had been through so much. He kissed Marilyn's hair and handed her his drink. "Go remind our new son-in-law of your fictitious ties to the Irish mob."

She smiled a little at him but her gaze shifted to Wendy again and she wilted. "Bring her some seltzer," she said. "It might settle her stomach."

He nodded and set off across the lawn.

"Wendy," he said. He wished he didn't always sound like such a stickler. She looked up, her eyes watery and wandering, and she smiled.

"Daddy," she said. He squatted down before her. "Nice socks, dude."

"How about you come with me?" he said. Wendy attempted to glower at him. He took her elbow. "Humor me; come on." She shrugged and made an effort to stand. He helped her up and guided her slowly inside, through the kitchen and past the caterers, into his office, grabbing a liter bottle of Perrier from the counter on the way. "Have a seat," he said, leading her to the sofa.

She stumbled a little on her way down, and she laughed, a cackle that both scared him and reminded him of times when she was three, spinning around in his arms in their old backyard, unapologetically gleeful. He grabbed the ottoman from the foot of his armchair and dragged it over, sitting down before her. He uncapped the bottle of water and handed it to her.

"Daddy, I'm *fine*."

"Wendy, drink some water." He lifted the bottle to her lips and she moved to drink some, spilling a considerable amount down the front of her dress.

"You'd *die* if you knew how much this cost."

He reached for a tissue and blotted at her face.

"One thousand six hundred dollars," she said in an affected whisper.

"All right," he said. "Just try to relax." But relaxation was not what his daughter needed, he knew. She needed coffee and psychotherapy and a father who knew what to do besides dry her off with a Kleenex and tell her to relax.

"I know Matt's Mr. Savings-and-Bonds," Wendy said. "But I don't think it would have killed Violet to buy a dress that didn't look like it was from *Kohl's.*"

"Okay, now." It was what he always said when they did things that made him uncomfortable, when they tried to confide in him past a point that he understood. *Okay, now.* "It's her wedding day, Wendy. Try to be happy for her."

"I'm thrilled," Wendy said. "Mazel tov, Violet. We're all so fucking shocked that your life is turning out perfect." It had been six years since Wendy's wedding, since the day he'd observed Wendy looking, for the first time in her life, truly happy.

"I know you've had a hard year."

Wendy turned her face to him and he saw her make that frightening shift achievable only by the extremely intoxicated, a fluid leap from joviality to malevolence. "Do you, Dad? Do you know what a hard year I've had?" The final syllables bled together, an assonant slur that betrayed how far gone she was.

"Lower your voice." He felt his face getting hot. "Of course I do, Wendy. We all know."

"She could have waited," Wendy said.

He'd had the same thought. He'd mentioned it to Marilyn, wondered aloud if maybe Violet shouldn't put off the wedding for a while, if maybe it wasn't kind of unseemly to have a big party on the heels of your sister's stillbirth, but Marilyn had looked at him as if he had three heads and said, "It's been almost a year. And she's always wanted to get married in June."

So here they were, June sixteenth, in his office with a bottle of seltzer.

"You should be happy for your sister," he said.

"It's just not *fair*," she said. "She just gets to pretend none of it ever happened? Why can't *I* do that? You think I wouldn't like to do that? She just gets to act like everything's perfect and I'm the huge fuckup, but *she* fucked up too, Dad; Violet and her huge fucking *secret*, but I'm not the only person in this family who fucks things up, okay?"

"Nobody said that, Wendy. What are you talking about?"

She looked at him with an odd clarity for just a second before tilting her head up toward the ceiling again. "Just for-fucking-get it." And then she was crying and what could he do, then, besides hug her? He held her until she fell asleep and then he positioned her on her side on the couch in case she threw up, and then he went out front and got Miles.

"You might want to go keep an eye on her," he said, and his son-in-law shoved his hands in his pockets and toed the dirt like a teenager and then nodded.

"Thanks, David."

"Should I be worried?" he asked. He'd always liked Miles, albeit reluctantly, given how much older he was than Wendy. But he could tell how much the man loved his daughter, and he suspected, now, that Miles was probably the only thing keeping her from hitting rock bottom.

"I ask myself that hourly," Miles said. "I don't have a good answer."

He returned, disoriented, to the party, and he spun Gracie in circles and posed for photos and he kept saying, *Thanks, we're thrilled; we couldn't be happier; we're so proud of her*, and he didn't even notice when Miles guided Wendy out to their car and drove her home.

In bed that night, a night on which he should have been blitzed by his happiness, he was still thinking about his conversation with his eldest daughter.

"Wendy said something strange to me," he said.

Marilyn rolled to face him. "What?"

What huge secret? Not their Violet. Violet had nothing to hide. Violet, who'd gotten weepy during their requisite father-daughter dance to "Sweet Thing," who'd made *him* also get weepy during said dance, who appeared wholly at peace, lithe and unburdened, bound for an impressive career and married to a man she loved.

Marilyn was watching him, sleepy and affectionate, rubbing her foot between his calves underneath the blankets. Wendy had been completely obliterated. She hadn't even recognized her father's office. Certainly she hadn't meant anything by it. Certainly he didn't need to burden his wife, who'd had such a nice time, who was so beautiful and trusting. "Well, now I can't remember," he said lamely.

She smiled and reached to cup a hand to his face. "Too much to drink?" She scooted closer to him, twining her leg between his thighs, and she leaned in and kissed him before urging him onto his back and climbing on top of him, his lovely, oblivious wife, and he let her, kissed back and let her and pretended that what Wendy said hadn't set off an alarm bell somewhere deep inside of him.

CHAPTER TWENTY-EIGHT

"He's worried about germs," Marilyn said flimsily, acknowledging Liza's disappointment when she realized that David wouldn't be coming. A half hour earlier, as she banged around the house, throwing anything in her purse she thought might prove useful in the coming hours—playing cards, ChapStick, and, inexplicably, a flashlight—she'd stopped and fixed her gaze lethally on her husband. "You're being a child."

"I'd just be in the way."

"You don't deserve to have your ego massaged right now," she said, "but you know that's not true." Of course she knew he had other reasons. She couldn't *identify* the other reasons, but she knew they existed, and she knew they had to be weighing heavily on him for him to be protesting so forcefully, but she was too anxious to stop and try to get to the bottom of it.

"Can we drop this, Marilyn?"

"She needs you," she said.

"You'll be there."

"*I* need you."

"You would have lost your *mind* if your dad showed up when you were giving birth."

"My dad wasn't the dad to me that you are to the girls," she said. She felt a murky mix of grief and nostalgia and a fresh wave of sadness for Liza. "Our daughter is having a baby, David. Alone. She needs us."

But he wouldn't budge. So she was in the car with her daughter, the driver, for once, marveling at Liza's composure; the only evidence that betrayed Liza's unease was the way she'd suddenly go quiet, gripping the handle above the window.

"It's okay, love," Marilyn murmured, and she felt a pang of retroactive empathy for David, beside her in the hospital again and again. Of course there was nothing she could do. And Liza probably wanted to kill her, just as Marilyn had repeatedly wanted to kill her husband.

"Why didn't you *warn* me about this?" Liza asked, surfacing, letting go of the handle.

She rubbed Liza's shoulder, steeled her own nerves. "I didn't want to spoil the surprise."

There was a smell, when she and Liza were seen to the birthing room, powdery and sharp, that nearly brought her to her knees, not because it called up associations she was trying to repress, but because it reminded her of her husband, way back when, when the hospital smell was still a novelty, before it became part of him and then, gradually, part of their marital ether, like those proverbial frogs adjusting to the pot of boiling water. They navigated the next few hours together, whiling away the time, determining which nurses were their favorites. But she could tell, from Liza's inability to keep still or quiet, that the contractions were worsening.

"You want to lie down, sweetheart?" she asked, and Liza shook her head, going over to the window, looking at once immense and childlike, both frail and formidable.

Marilyn didn't notice the door opening behind her.

"How're we doing in here?"

She recognized the voice at once, knew it at the base of her skull. *David's not my patient; he's my friend.* She turned slowly, and she was ashamed to admit that the first thing she took note of was the fact that Gillian had a good deal more gray in her hair than when last she'd seen her.

How long had it been? At least a decade. Probably closer to two. She now existed without ties or context, appearing to Marilyn only in dreams or especially dark marital moments as the woman who'd once held the power to unravel all that she had worked to create. Her status as the doctor who'd delivered Grace, who'd pulled them both through that unexpected and terrifying time, had been demoted by what happened afterward. The night David told her that Gillian was leaving to start her own practice, she'd tabled her initial reaction—relief that it was over; anger that she had to feel relieved in the first place—but later fucked him vigorously and uncharacteristically, wakened him in twilight with her hand down his briefs, rejoicing, *mine mine mine*.

And yet here she was. She looked to Liza in surprise, but her daughter's face betrayed nothing—she recognized, from her own experience, the blank inwardness of Liza's gaze, that singular focus on the task at hand. All that mattered at the moment, and for the next indeterminate number of hours, was inside of her; the external world faded away.

"Marilyn." The look on the doctor's face was candidly benevolent, easy and amenable. She came over and opened her arms for a hug.

Marilyn embraced her loosely. "Gillian."

"I was just thinking about whether or not I'd run into you. I hoped I would."

Liza, from the window, detached incredulity, her voice gravel: "Oh, *fuck*."

It was her instinct—a physical tugging—to go to her daughter, to do what she could to absorb some of the pain as her own, but Liza had violently waved her off during the last few contractions.

"What are you . . ." *Doing here* would be a silly question, of course. *Does David know you're here* would be overly hostile. Who knew how many hours she'd be spending with this woman. Liza made a whinnying sound, and they both turned to regard her. "Sweetie, do you—"

"No," Liza breathed out, impatient.

"Full circle, huh," Gillian said softly, touching Marilyn's elbow.

Her psyche was being pulled so intensely in two directions— her shock at the sight of David's old friend, and the transmuted agony of seeing her daughter in so much pain—that she didn't feel she was fully partaking in either situation.

"I hear she's doing great," Gillian said, pulling her decidedly into the mental camp of her daughter's labor. Until now, only nurses had been checking in on Liza.

"Yes, she's a trooper."

"That runs in the family." Gillian squeezed her arm again. She didn't remember the woman being so touchy. "How's it going, Liza?"

Her daughter, once again in the land of the living, arched her back and shook her head, coming to lower herself onto the bed.

"Human existence is a ludicrous notion, isn't it, love?" Marilyn said.

"Indeed," Gillian said, though Marilyn hadn't been talking to her. She fiddled with one of the monitors. "David on his way too?"

Marilyn froze, unsure of how to answer. She wondered if the woman had ever completely stopped loving her husband, or if it was something that haunted her still. But she nevertheless resented Gillian's presence a bit, the fact that she was once again encroaching upon the privacy of their family, even if Liza had solicited it.

"David just had a heart attack," she said. "He's not really up for—such excitement."

Before Gillian could react, Liza asked, "Could you check me, Dr. Levin?"

She looked to her daughter in gratitude, tears in her eyes over all of it, the excess of emotion clouding everything about the current state of their lives, and she held Liza's hand as Gillian, once again, took their fate in hers.

It was astounding how much more slowly time passed when you weren't the one giving birth. Marilyn remembered, when her daughters were born, the hours seeming at once interminable and transitory, ticking away on an entirely different clock, but in the hospital with Liza, she was sharply cognizant of the sun going down and her phone battery dying, of the stale feeling in her mouth and the hungry rumbling of her stomach and the itchiness of her eyes, begging to close. Liza was getting more and more agitated—"Oh my *God*, Mom, could you stop *standing* like that?"—and so she took the opportunity to slip into the hall and call her husband, with whom she was not at all interested in speaking, but she knew he would want an update on Liza, and thus far she'd only sent him terse, informative text messages. Wendy had texted them both earlier to tell them that she'd found Jonah.

"Hey, sweetie," he said. "How goes it?"

Life seemed to be throwing them evenly divided deluges of good and bad; they were in a relatively good place now, new babies in transit and missing persons found, but she was unrested and irritable and she didn't have the energy to table her anger. "Well," she said, unable to keep the stiffness from her voice. "She's at seven centimeters."

"Oh, good; that's—"

"Gillian's been incredibly attentive," she broke in archly. "As thorough as ever."

He paused. "Oh, God," he said. She could practically hear his mind at work. "Marilyn, I'm— I feel like such a— I completely forgot."

"So you knew," she said. "You knew and didn't tell me."

"No, honey, I just— I planned to tell you; I kept meaning to but then everything happened with Jonah, and then with Ryan, and I just got distracted, but I— Liza wanted someone who— I don't know. Knows our family. Someone who can maybe understand—you know, that things are sometimes more complicated than they seem."

"We're not the *Mansons*. It's not like we have this big lumbering *secret* in our—"

"I was just trying to be supportive, honey, and I thought it might upset you so I was trying to figure out the best time to tell you, but other things kept—and then suddenly . . ."

In his trailing off, she was reminded of the bad deluge they'd just endured, the *worst* deluge, David in this same hospital, three floors down in the cardiac ICU. She massaged the bridge of her nose.

"It's not so much *her* that I'm angry about as the fact that you didn't tell me. And that you've developed this ridiculous *germs* paranoia and let me come here and get absolutely blindsided."

"I'm not at a hundred percent," he said, and in the softness of his voice she recognized real dejection. "I didn't think I'd have the energy to stick it out for a long labor, or like I'd be in any position to be of help when I—I still don't feel quite like myself, and it just didn't seem doable." This admission, coming from her stoic husband, was huge. "She's been through so much already. I want her to have this happy moment without worrying about me."

"Oh, love." She sighed. She glanced up to see Gillian coming toward her down the hall.

"I'm sorry I didn't tell you," he said. This oblivious man she'd fused lives with. "Believe it or not, it really did slip my mind."

"I forgive you," she said. "We can talk about how insane you are when I get home."

"Kiss Liza for me. Tell her I love her."

"I will."

"Tell yourself that too."

She smiled, keenly aware of Gillian, feet away. "You do the same."

"Sorry to interrupt," Gillian said when she hung up.

"Not at all."

"I brought you some coffee. We've got a long night ahead of us."

"Oh—thank you." She accepted the cup and took a sip, winced at the sweetness.

"Sorry. Old habit. I rely heavily on caffeine and sugar in times like these. Is it your first?"

"First what?"

Gillian smiled at her. "Grandchild."

"Oh. No. I have— Violet has two boys. Or—three, actually." She snagged on this. "Eli and Wyatt are still little guys. And Jonah is—well. Sixteen, now."

"How on *earth* do you have a sixteen-year-old grandchild?" Gillian asked, smiling.

"It's a long story," she said. "There's a lot going on in our family at the moment."

"I'm so sorry about David," Gillian said. "I had no idea, Marilyn. How's he doing?"

"He's recovering," she said. "Slowly. Steadily, physiologically. He's home; he's mobile. But I think it's— He's having a hard time feeling— Lord, it's the scariest thing in the world, our mortality, isn't it?" She was unprepared for the catch in her throat.

"One of the perks of my job is that I can just will myself into thinking that all we do is get born. Forget the rest. Though that's becoming harder and harder the older I get."

"I remember thinking how young you seemed, back then," Marilyn said.

"Gloves are off, I see." Gillian laughed.

"Oh, I didn't mean— I just mean it's funny how— Back then you seemed closer in age to my girls. Now you—well, we're contemporaries. I guess it all just evens out. How are things with you?"

"Things are good," Gillian said. "I'm healthy. I'm busy. I have two boisterous German shepherds and a fair amount of joy in my life."

It was strange to hear it in such frank, clinical terms, but Marilyn envied her, in a way, how she was so confidently able to itemize her happinesses, without earmarks or asterisks.

"I still think about you and David sometimes," Gillian said. "Your family. I'm pretty sure you're the origins of my unattainable standards of living."

Marilyn shook her head. "Ah. Oh, well, we—"

Gillian tactfully changed the subject: "Liza's an impressive young woman."

As if on cue, her daughter's voice: "Dr. Levin?"

Gillian abandoned her mug on the triage desk and Marilyn followed suit.

"The sugar was a good idea," she said, trailing the doctor back into her daughter's room, feeling her anxiety creep back in, but Gillian, going to Liza, didn't reply, had already moved on to the next thing.

2010–2011

Strange bruising on his abdomen, fatigue, significant weight loss. Wendy was astounded that she hadn't noticed, but then again she hadn't been noticing much of anything, and Miles was thin to begin with. The things she couldn't have seen—his elevated white count, for instance—were confirmed by the doctor, and these things yielded a theatrically grim prognosis and an immediate, aggressive treatment plan, chemo and radiation. It was almost laughable, how magnificently fucked they were, how such larger-than-life tragedy could befall a single family—and they were such a *small* family, God! She would never forgive herself for the distance she'd created between them after Ivy, for all the times she appreciated life without him.

For the first week, they barely talked, focusing on completing the necessary steps: paperwork, consultations, an alarming shopping list that featured ominous items like shower curtain liners and nonlatex gloves. And the night before he began his treatment, they sat on the roof together, twined in the loveseat under the comforter from their bed. She could feel, now, his boniness. They were still tiptoeing around the subject, still feeling license to be coy, avoidant as adolescents and afraid to discuss anything head-on.

"You could still easily die before me," he said. "You could

get struck by lightning. Or hit by a bus. Or—you know, Ebola. Swine flu. Endless possibilities."

"I'm glad you've given this so much thought."

He was drawing little circles around her belly button with his fingers.

"I'm supposed to be your cheerleader now, I think," she said. "Like—*you'll get through this; you're a fighter.*"

He raised his eyebrows expectantly.

"That's not how real people talk, is it?"

"Fuck if I know," he said.

"You will, though. You are." She felt such painfully strong, prematurely nostalgic love for him in that moment. She could either make a joke or break down. "What doesn't kill you makes you stronger," she said, and she felt Miles laugh.

"There's light at the end of the tunnel."

"You can't always get what you want."

"... but if you try sometimes ..."

"Your stairway lies on the whisperin' wind." She was laughing now too, something she hadn't done in ages. "It's the thrill of the fight, Eisenberg," she said.

He snorted. "Wait, who is that, Whitesnake?"

"How *dare* you? Survivor."

"Of course." He leaned his head against her shoulder.

"God doesn't give us more than we can handle," she said into the top of his head.

"Is *that* Whitesnake?"

She smiled. "My grandpa used to say that. But I always kind of liked it."

He hummed.

"Listen. I know we've been through some fucking shitty times, M, but I hope you know how much I— I know I haven't been the easiest person to be—married to." She would never forgive herself for shutting him out like she had after Ivy died, for withholding sex, for offhanded cruelty, for refusing to let him comfort her, for pretending that she was the only one who needed comforting. For falling asleep without him and luxuriating in the extra space. For ever, for a second, not wanting him around. She breathed in the smell of his hair. "And I could say it's not personal, but of course it's personal, because you're my—my *person*, and I—you know. What is it? The people we hurt the most are the ones we know won't abandon us?"

"Water under the bridge. As long as we're throwing around clichés."

"I love you. Just, like—fucking stupendously." The threat of crying returned, but this time she didn't specifically fight it.

"I love you cetaceanically and immeasurably, Wendy Eisenberg."

The only person on the planet who spoke to her as though she was of equal intelligence. She slipped her hand down the waist of his pants, wrapped her fingers around the warm familiarity of him. She wanted to fuse herself with him, to keep him earthbound with her.

Miles had grown quiet. "Things are going to be okay?" he asked.

The last time she'd seen him this scared was on the day Ivy was born. She had no fucking idea if things were going to be okay.

"Yes," she said.

"Okay."

"I *could* die before you," she ceded.

"I'd prefer it if you didn't." He kissed her breast. "But I appreciate your willingness."

Violet couldn't tell, when Wyatt was born, if her disorientation was simply a characteristic of routine new parenthood, or if all those who had come before—her own abandoned child and her sister's lost one—were leaving their mark on her prospects of happiness. Did other new mothers, after the blunted relief of the birth itself being over, have to search the twisted corridors of their insides, like those emotional intelligence assessments with the many-expressioned smiley faces, to determine what, precisely they were feeling? Other new mothers cried, of course, upon face-to-face acquaintance with their infants, but how many of them did so not entirely out of elation and exhaustion? How many of them felt another presence in the room, a pallor hanging over what was supposed to be one of the most enchanted moments on the human spectrum? Matt seemed not to notice, and she was glad that at least one person in the room was enjoying himself the way he was supposed to.

His parents were en route from Seattle, and hers were stuck in traffic. She knew she had to call Wendy; she knew her sister couldn't hear the news from their punch-drunk mother. She couldn't help but think of the message Miles had left for her the day Ivy was born. *Hey, listen, Violet, I have—the worst news.* And how Matt, who'd just proposed to her on a bench by the Fountain of Time, was standing behind her when she listened to it, how he'd opened his arms to hug her and how, with her face pressed against his chest, she let everything wash over her, her sadness for Wendy, her guilt for missing the calls, and—only inklings of this, at the moment, inklings she wouldn't allow to concretize until later—shame at the fact that she'd never intended to be there in the first place, whether or not Wendy had given birth as planned, to a healthy full-term baby. That she'd begun planning a trip to Seattle to meet Matt's parents in the vicinity of Wendy's due date. That she knew she couldn't do it, couldn't be there when her sister gave birth, no matter how much Wendy wanted her there, no matter how happy she was for Wendy and Miles, because the first time around had nearly killed her. That she *knew* she'd never be able to pay Wendy back for being there for her.

And alongside all of those awful thoughts, the dread crept in, because there was no way she could bow out of visiting Wendy given what had happened instead. That she would, again, have to share an empty birthing room with her sister. She'd feared the sensory memories she'd endure—from the iron-spiked smell, the unnatural whiteness of the sheets—and she'd feared what Wendy's grief would do to her own, how her sister's agony could potentially awaken all that she'd been keeping tamped down, still so fresh, then, and with such potential to unhinge her completely. But when she'd gotten there, Wendy hadn't wanted to engage with her at all. Her sister had been like she'd never seen her be before, which of course made sense, given everything, but still surprised her a little, Wendy's cold impassive tone and her insistence that Violet needn't have come, not to mention her—again, well-earned but still smarting—barbs of cruelty when Violet tried to comfort her. And of course much of this was owing to the trauma Wendy had endured before Violet arrived, but she couldn't help but know, deep in her gut, that Wendy was also, rightfully, angry with her, hurt by her absence and her betrayal. And while Wendy certainly couldn't have *known* of Violet's plans to avoid the birth, had things not gone so terribly wrong, she seemed to sense Violet's guilt, and the guilt itself seemed a kind of admission. To feel guilty was to know you'd done something wrong, and she'd felt guilty, and there was nobody on the planet who knew her better than Wendy.

Perhaps that was why it took her so long to muster up the fortitude to call her sister. Wyatt—far from lifeless and in possession already of an impressively complex mastery of REM sleep—was tucked against her, and Matt was stroking his tiny knee with one finger, and she took a deep breath and reached for the phone by her bedside and dialed.

Wendy arrived almost immediately—Violet couldn't help but think some part of her may have been trying to make a statement about sisterly obligations—bearing an ostentatious bouquet of dahlias and a box of Cuban cigars, which she dropped into Matt's lap without airs. She tossed her coat over a chair and glanced critically out the window for several seconds before she finally turned back to face them, fixing her gaze just above Violet's line of sight.

"Could you have gotten a worse view?" she asked.

"It's hideous, I know," Violet said uncertainly. She had deliberately chosen not to go to Prentice, though she would have liked to, because she'd been anticipating this moment, anticipating her sister having to return to the site of her own trauma, and had instead opted for a hospital on the North Shore, which had been a bitch to drive to during rush hour that morning. Its views, whether or not the ambient lakeshore spans of Northwestern, had not once entered Violet's mind.

"Dumpster art has its merit" was Matt's feeble contribution.

"So you're okay?" Wendy asked.

"Absolutely." Did other new mothers feel crushing guilt for being okay? She thought of how Wendy had squeezed in next to her in her hospital bed after the first baby was taken away, how she had eventually cried herself to sleep in Wendy's arms. Wyatt was asleep in her arms now, tightly swaddled and at the apex of adorable, and Wendy hadn't even looked in his direction. And it was hard for her sister, Violet was sure, but she'd come all the way there to—what? Insult the room?

"What do you think, Wendy?" Matt asked, his voice a touch more jaunty than Violet would have liked. She saw Wendy's gaze drift finally downward and land on Wyatt's sleeping face. There was a vague, nauseated smile on her lips.

"Mm." And then she looked back up at Violet and her voice, though strained, was free of all the irritating, tightly sealed airs to which she usually defaulted when she felt uncomfortable or defensive. "He's perfect." She sounded, in fact, stunned. "He's so—*big*."

She'd never seen Wendy's daughter, but she knew she had

been only three or so pounds. Her son, who had seemed until that moment to be the smallest person ever to have existed on the earth, was gargantuan in comparison to the photos of preemies she had seen online. Like just-hatched dinosaurs, iridescent and impossibly fragile. She felt a fleeting second of disgust with herself for safely, successfully giving birth to this enormous person when her sister had been robbed of the same opportunity. And then she felt an equally fleeting surge of anger toward Wendy for making her feel this way, for ruining her happiness.

"We're glad you're the first one to meet him," Matt said, covering for her, his voice now acknowledging the unbearable mix of elation and sorrow hanging heavily in the moment.

"Do you want to hold him?" she asked. Maybe it would be different because he was a boy. Violet had hoped Wendy would have an easier time of things because the situation did not entirely resemble what her own situation ought to have looked like.

"Sure," Wendy said finally. "Yeah."

Violet lifted her arms toward her husband and offered the baby. She watched as Matt placed him into Wendy's arms, and she watched as Wendy accommodated her posture around the baby, and she watched as something like contentment settled onto her sister's face.

"Hi," Wendy whispered. "Hey, there."

Matt sat on the edge of the bed and took Violet's hand, sensing her emotion before she felt it herself. It wasn't until she tried to squeeze his hand in thanks that she realized how tense she was, already gripping him viselike.

"He has Mom's nose," Wendy said to them, not lifting her eyes from the baby. Wendy, whose husband was currently undergoing chemo. Wendy, who'd been dealt the shittiest hand of them all. Wendy, who had lost so much, and whom Violet would always have failed, and who somehow found it in herself to be generous at this moment, though it couldn't have been easy.

"I hadn't noticed that," she said, brimming with gratitude. Perhaps they could let this moment play out like it would with normal sisters. Perhaps not everything, always, would be quashed by what had come before it. Matt rubbed the back of her hand with his thumb. The father of her child, to whom now— lest there was ever any doubt—she was indivisibly bound, the man who'd proposed to her on the very day Ivy was born. She'd allowed herself to be happy that night, for the first time in ages—what luck, that the person she loved loved her back, that the universe was giving her a pass, a chance to move on— only to have it shadow-darkened a half hour later by one of the worst things that could possibly ever happen. She remembered him standing behind her as she listened to Miles's messages. How elated they'd been—giddy, champagne-sloshed—and how quickly it was extinguished, her brother-in-law's voice on the machine getting hollower with each message, *Violet, please, you're the only one that she— Please just come; it's almost over.* And Matt, newly cemented into her life, waiting open-armed to comfort her. The sick juxtaposition of that: she'd gained Matt the day she lost her sister forever. And yet here they were, she and Matt and Wendy and her brand-new baby, and the air between them felt almost peaceful.

But then Matt was leaping from the bed, because Wendy had suddenly lurched forward.

"I'm going to be sick," she said, and she swiftly handed off Wyatt and was out the door, and moments after that, David and Marilyn arrived, and the world continued to turn, and Violet tried very hard to pretend that it wasn't her fault.

It was almost nine. Too early for bed. Grace stretched, cast aside the latest issue of *Teen Vogue* and went downstairs. She paused on the landing, feeling oddly bashful. Her parents were together on the couch, her dad stretched on his back and her mom sitting near his feet.

"Of course they'll find him guilty," her mom said. Loomis was curled up by her legs.

"In a perfect world. But it's always the most obviously guilty ones who—"

"You're such a cynic."

"One of us has to be." Her father nudged her mother with his foot and she smiled, pushing him away with her elbow. It occurred to her that if their family had followed the normal trajectory, without its Epilogue, her parents would be living alone now. She wondered if they ever thought about it like that, if they ever wished they could live their boring lives without a teenager overhead. But when her mother noticed her she didn't sound disappointed or bothered.

"What're you doing, honey?"

She realized she probably looked weird just standing on the stairs so she advanced into the living room, going over to pet Loomis. She squatted before him, just a foot or two away from her mom, and stroked at the wispy light hair on his belly. Intrigued initially by her entrance, he closed his eyes again and let out a contented snort.

"Nothing," she said.

"Ah," her mom said. "Well, we're watching *Law and Order*, if you'd like to join us."

Grace shrugged, settled back to sit beside Loomis.

"I know we're just your dorky old parents," her father said.

"But of course we'd love to absorb your presence," her mom said, reaching down to ruffle Grace's hair. "Glom on to our sweet lastborn while you're still under our roof."

"We'll live vicariously through your youth and vitality until you abandon us," said her dad, and Grace could tell it was becoming one of those moments when her parents were technically talking to you, their child, but were obviously talking to each other, lame overdone jokes to make the other crack up.

"Fine. God," she said. "I'll watch with you. Just stop." Her dad reached down with his socked foot and brushed at the ends of her hair with his toes and she squealed and jumped up. "Ugh, *Dad.* Are you *trying* to get rid of me?"

"Of course he's not," said her mom. "Get up here, little love. I know you're our wildly mature driver-in-training but I just want to touch that sweet head of yours before it goes off to rule the world." She looked up at them, so content with their station in life.

"Come on, Goose," her dad said. "Humor us before we're sent off to assisted living."

"Lord, you're morbid." Her mom nudged his legs away with her hand. "Move those feet. Make way for goslings."

There had never been anyone else on the entire earth who was so simplistically happy to be around her. But it was weird to be best friends with your parents, right? She rose slowly, self-consciously, and fitted herself between her mother and father, hugging her knees.

"Oh, my heart," her mom said, snaking an arm around her back. "The only daughter who will still indulge me in snuggles and horrible network television shows about sex crimes."

"Our lenient lifeline," said her dad, "who has not yet realized her parents are the lamest of the lame."

She wrinkled her nose, trying not to delight in their attention. "Can we just watch the show?"

"Our diplomat," her dad said, elbowing her gently. "I knew we made the right decision when we kidnapped you."

She'd seen Miles weeping and delirious and covered in his own shit. She would ask her mother this if she ever had the balls: How was it possible to love another person this much?

How was it possible that she didn't care, that the effluvia and the heartbreak became minor details? That the smells made her gag, but the feeling of his body beneath her hands—in the bath, on the toilet, being maneuvered into the movie-theater seat of his wheelchair—roused such throat-filling tenderness, the conviction that she'd been put on this earth to bolster the bulk, however insignificant, of another body? Not a baby, but her husband. Her person.

And the miracle when he started coming back to her, after more than a year—when it seemed that the drugs were working, when some magical antidote took hold in his veins, and suddenly he was making jokes again, putting on a little weight, staying awake beside her for an entire episode of *The Sopranos*, requesting that she wheel him out onto the deck some evenings so they could sit together in the breeze from the lake.

It wasn't always the worst of times, during that period. She'd cover him with kisses across his forehead, like her mom used to do when they were little. The first few times she'd gone for his mouth, but it had felt like kissing a corpse and so she moved upward, filling the space above his sleeping brown eyes, quiet kisses, dry ones, so he wouldn't, through his now-dubious cognition, mistake her for a dog.

Kisses, kisses, kisses, and then: the flutter. The sign of life in the eyes that made a well break open in her chest—he was *there*; he was *here*; he was *still*, still—and he'd reach to one of the perfect spots—the crook of her elbow, the insignificance of one of her breasts. And once: once! His hand found its way downward, fingers drowsy but nimble, hitting the target right out of the gate, with such precision that she assumed he had to still be sleeping, faking it, fluking it.

"Honey," she said. "Hey, Miles, honey." She paused, frozen, his hand in her most favorite bodily arrangement. "Are we?" she asked, and it felt to be its own sentence, unformed and syllabically lacking.

"I'm supposed to wear a condom."

She fell back away from him, this odd unsexy vestige of their old pre-Ivy life returning—*are you ovulating; is this a bad time; should we wait and see if.*

"Listen," she said. "The prospect seems unlikely."

"Because of the chemo."

"I'm going to interfere?"

"No," he said, and he gestured childishly at her nether regions. "The chemicals could be transmitted, and I'm unclear on what happens if that happens."

"I'm not worried about that."

"But for the future," he said quietly, and it did her in: that he was holding out hope that she'd long since abandoned; he still had visions of his continued vitality, of the progeny that would emerge therefrom.

She laid a hand across his forehead. "Thoughtful man."

"Do we have any?"

Two, among folded bills and business cards in her wallet, from before she'd met him.

"Do we ever," she said.

CHAPTER TWENTY-NINE

Wendy slapped at his wrist when he tried to mess with the radio dials.

"I refuse to tolerate your sad-sack prose poems when I'm rescuing you from your failed attempt at going on the lam," she said. They were driving his grandfather's Jeep, home to Chicago, through North Dakota.

"God, are you ever going to stop making fun of me for this?" He was grateful to her, though. She'd shown up when she said she would, and she'd brought him his Death Cab hoodie and stopped at Panda Express for lunch. It was kind of amazing, really, that he was able to do that—call someone to help him out of a jam, and have them buy him kung pao chicken and worry about whether he was warm enough. It was even more amazing that Wendy didn't seem angry. He clasped his palms together and stretched his arms, seeing her wince as his elbow joints popped. He pulled his hands inside of his sleeves and leaned his head against the window.

"Oh, this isn't going to be *truly* funny for about a decade," Wendy said. "These things take time. We haven't come close to peaking."

"Wendy, I didn't . . ."

"Why the fuck *did* you do this?" she asked conversationally. "Ten sentences or less."

He fiddled with the buttons on the armrest, accidentally opened his window a crack, letting in a deafening whoosh of air. He quickly closed it. "I was scared," he said. "I mean, first, initially, that—like, it was my fault that I—with your dad, that I— And then I just ended up in Portland, and at first I was just planning on dropping off David's car, or maybe staying at Grace's for a while, but then I sort of—fucked that up too. And I just figured it would be better for everyone if I wasn't around anymore."

"Oh, Jonah." She sounded sadder than he'd ever heard her sound, Hanna-level emotion.

"Is Grace, like—okay?"

Wendy took a minute to answer, cleared her throat. "Okay as in alive? Or okay as in doing anything remotely normal or healthy?" She shook her head. "Did she— What impression did she give you of what she's been up to out there? Of—law school?"

"I know she's been lying."

"I'm giving her one more week to call our parents, otherwise I'm ratting her out. Did you two hit it off?"

"Yeah, I think so. It was—like, kind of a weird time for her, but she— I like her."

Wendy smiled. "It's so funny to me that she's a real person now; she was so little for so long. You know she's closer to your age than she is to mine?"

"I owe her some money," he said, remembering.

"Oh my *God*, the blind robbing the blind."

"Are your parents mad at me?"

She took in a big breath and let it out. "They're relieved beyond words," she said, "which does not necessarily rule out residual anger. You missed almost two weeks of school."

School, strangely, had been the furthest thing from his mind, but now he felt an immediate, legitimate fear. "Is it—is that going to be a—"

"If anyone asks, you had mono," she said.

"Seriously?"

"I trusted that you were going to come back," she said.

He'd trusted her to come get him, he realized. And he didn't *care* if she was mad at him, at least not logistically, because if this family had taught him anything it was that people could get mad at each other and then make up again. And he'd fucked up so exquisitely—Liza and Ryan, Wyatt and Santa, dropping the ladder and stealing the car, Grace and Ben—but he hadn't been surprised by how kind Wendy was when he called her.

"Liza just had her baby too," Wendy added. "So I'm trying not to steal her thunder with news of our ancient mariner."

"Oh." He felt a strange pang of something. He'd never known a brand-new baby. He'd never known the *parent* of a brand-new baby. Before he'd met Violet, he used to try to imagine what it had been like the day he was born, if his mom had held him like normal moms did, if it had been hard for her to hand him over. Since meeting her, he'd had difficulty imagining her gently handling anything. "Is Liza okay?"

"Yeah, she's great. The baby's great. She's huge. Like nine pounds." Wendy's voice seemed not particularly level. "Kathryn Elizabeth Sorenson. She's calling her Kit."

He felt a tsunami of guilt in his gut. "Is—is Ryan around?"

Wendy looked at him again curiously. "I'm not sure. Why do you ask?"

"I just—" He was so tired. It was so nice to be sitting in a moving car and not be responsible for its motion. To have eaten the pot stickers that she'd known to order without even asking him. Wendy had picked him up and they were sailing comfortably across the northern plains and he felt, for the first time in ages, like he could fucking *relax*. Why not put it all on the table? "I think it might be my fault that he bolted. I didn't mean to say anything, but I—might have said something to fuck things up between them."

To his surprise, Wendy laughed. "God, you really made the rounds, didn't you? What did you do? Tell Ryan that Santa wasn't real?"

So Violet had spread the word, apparently. He wondered if she thought he was at fault for her dad's fall. He wasn't home free yet, not if Violet still hated him.

"I'm kidding. You know that wasn't your fault, right? Plus those kids could stand a few doses of reality. But seriously, what could you have possibly told Ryan that was such a big deal?"

Honesty was a good thing, right? And Wendy had always been honest with him. If he could get this off of his conscience, maybe they could all have a giant do-over.

"I didn't— It's not . . ."

Wendy's eyes flashed. *Gossipmongers*, David had called his daughters once, kindly. "Okay, then let me guess. I'm going to throw out a couple of options and you can just make a subtly indicative facial expression when I say the right one."

"You should be watching the road."

"Says the car thief I just picked up from *a jail*."

"I wasn't—"

"Ryan's transitioning."

He rolled his eyes.

"Torrid affair?"

He flinched without meaning to.

"Are you fucking kidding me?"

"No, I wasn't—"

"*Liza* cheated on him?"

"What makes you—"

"Because I'd be shocked if Ryan could muster the energy to get it up. Or leave the couch for long enough to find a willing candidate."

"Wendy, God."

"With *who*?"

"Wendy, please, I—"

"God, what is it with the women in this family?"

"Huh?"

She shook her head. "I promise to stop making fun of you for calling me from jail if you promise to tell me the details of this Liza scandal."

He fought a smile. "The *details* aren't my business to share with other people."

"Oh my God, you're this principled gentleman all of a sudden?" Wendy cracked up. "It's really pretty fucking astounding that you're Violet's kid, because she's the least funny person I've ever met in my life, whereas *you*, you total goon, are actually kind of a trip sometimes." He watched her smile fade a little as she stared ahead. "I will say I find it *intriguing* that you chose to call *me*," she said a minute later.

He squirmed. "I figured you'd be the one with the most free time."

She snorted. "I know I should take that as a dig, but having free time is actually pretty great. Not being tied down by kids who believe in Santa or boring husbands who make you want to sleep around?" Her voice was doing the wobbly thing again. "Definitely has its perks."

"You didn't want kids?"

"God, you say that like I'm some withered hag."

"I didn't mean—"

"It's probably not in the cards for me anymore, though; you're right." She paused, almost seeming to forget she was talking to him. "But it's not totally out of the question. I hail from fertile lineage. I probably have a few years left in me."

"Sorry," he said, embarrassed, thinking of her ovaries, thinking of her in her bedroom that night all those months ago, the ginger's face between her legs.

"You really only called me because you think I have no life?"

"I knew you'd come," he said simply. He knew that Wendy, despite having unceremoniously evicted him, cared about him, and could be relied on, if not always in the most conventional sense. She'd lied about him having mono so he wouldn't get in trouble. She'd bought a plane ticket and showed up in Assfuck-Nowhere, Montana, and flirted with the policemen, which mortified him, and got the pot stickers, and kept glancing over to make sure he was wearing his seat belt.

"I will," she said. "Anywhere, anytime. Though if you pull some shit like this again, I might make you publicly demean yourself before I rescue you. Flowery apologies and whatnot." She paused. "I had a daughter, actually. Miles and I did. Did Violet tell you that?"

He felt a kind of sadness he didn't recognize. "No."

"She didn't quite—make it."

"I don't— That sucks."

"It *does.*"

"When was she—did she—"

"She'd be eleven. It happened a few years before my husband got sick, actually."

"Seriously?"

"As a heart attack," she said, unsmiling.

He wasn't sure what to say. "What was her name?"

"Nobody ever asks me that," she said. "Her name was Ivy."

He became aware of the radio, Creedence Clearwater Revival again, not Wyatt's song but the one about being stuck in Lodi. "I'm really sorry, Wendy."

"Yeah. Thanks. You and me both." She sighed. "You know, it's funny; I— You know I was there when you were born, right? I was the first person to hold you, actually."

"You were?"

She reached to turn off the radio. "Listen, Jonah, I'm sorry. For—kicking you out. I wasn't— I was in over my head, and I blamed you, but it wasn't your fault."

His face heated up. "You did come pick me up from a jail."

She smiled. "Yeah, but that's not a fair— Like *ha ha, threw you out on the streets but then I bailed you out of the clink so it was all worth it in the end."*

"Your parents' house isn't exactly, like, the hood."

"It was a shitty thing to do. You're fifteen; you need—"

"I just turned sixteen."

"One way to make yourself seem more mature is to not remind people of your maturity." She paused. "Jesus Christ, we missed your birthday. Oh, Jonah."

"It's not a big deal."

"It's a *huge* deal. God, I didn't even— I'm sorry. I'm— Happy birthday, Jonah."

"Thanks. You were the first person to hold me?"

"Technically, yeah. Like you were caught by a nurse, but she handed you over to me."

"I never knew you were there."

"I guess that was the idea."

"Was I an ugly baby?"

She laughed. "I mean—at the time, I thought—but no. You were beautiful. You were just this tiny little *gem* that was suddenly a person in the world, out of nowhere. Like fucking magic."

"Thanks for—holding me."

"It was my pleasure," she said. Then: "Look, my dad's been really worried about you."

His heartbeat sped up. "He's not mad?"

"I mean, if *I* had taken his car and driven to Montana, I'd be toast. But my dad likes you a whole lot. You're like the belated younger brother I never got to appropriately resent."

He fought a smile.

"Probably shouldn't tell him *specifically* that I picked you up from a Montana jail."

"Okay."

"I don't understand why or how you sometimes manage to sound like an adult, but I appreciate it."

"Ditto." He felt, weirdly, like he might cry. Everyone's life was just as fucked-up as his was. Wendy, with her mean jokes and her wine and her questionable roster of d-bag hookups, had lost things too. Was possibly not as confident as she appeared.

"Jonah? There is nothing on this earth that would be made better by your not being around. Please set fire to that thought immediately. Run it over with a stolen car."

Nobody was who they appeared to be; everybody was struggling; money didn't make a difference; blah blah blah; he could spin all of this for some extra-credit what-I-contemplated-when-I-got-mono essay, but for right now he was focused on Wendy, his strongest link to the only family he had: Wendy, who had shown up; Wendy, who had held him before he'd even consciously been a person; Wendy, who had found him again in the first place, and taken him to that fancy restaurant patio to meet Violet almost a year ago.

"Violet is someone who resists interruption," she'd said, across from him at the table before Violet had shown up and then left again. "But she needs you in her life, whether she's aware of it or not." At the time he'd felt like collateral damage and he still felt sort of like that, but that was also probably how Grace felt, sometimes, like someone who wasn't quite old enough to be taken seriously but who people also turned to in times of crisis, someone with whom they shared things that were confusing or twisted or hard to process.

"You can't run away from this family," Wendy said now. "Take it from someone who knows."

He felt the heat blasting from the vents of the Jeep and he gave a lot of grateful thought to the fact that he was finally in a comfortable enough place to fall asleep, not driving a stolen car and not sleeping in said stolen car in a copse of trees in twelve-degree weather; not in an unfamiliar bed that smelled like someone else; not in the series of try-hard cots in the Interim Room at Lathrop House but instead in the soft bucket seat of a Jeep that smelled like someone he knew; homeward bound, God what a weird thing to say but he hardly had the where-withal to correct himself, so heavy were his eyelids, his head full of newfound knowledge, his belly full of egg rolls, and he didn't even notice falling asleep; he just drifted off, Wendy to his left, because he knew, somehow, that she'd get them home.

2011

On the plane home from Portland, having successfully deposited Gracie in her freshman dorm at Reed, Marilyn—who hated to fly—accepted her husband's proffered Benadryl, allowed herself to cry for a few moments and then dropped her head onto David's shoulder and fell asleep for the entirety of the flight. She dreamed of Grace, wide-eyed and vulnerable, tromping around the unfamiliar campus; she dreamed of Grace as a baby, strapped to her chest in a BabyBjörn, that specific wonderful weight of sleeping infant head on her breastbone.

When they arrived home, stopping on the way to pick up Loomis from the kennel, they both peered through the front door with hesitation. Loomis broke free of her grip on his collar and shoved ahead of them.

"After you," she said, and David went first, dropping the bags in the hallway.

"Huh," he said. Certainly that echo was normal—it wasn't as though Grace's presence had dramatically altered the acoustics of their house; it wasn't as though she was remotely large enough to absorb ambient noise—but it startled her still.

"Well." She'd cringed every time someone had made an empty-nester remark lately, but standing in the foyer she heard the words clanging around in her head. It wasn't even as though Grace had been a particularly *enjoyable* presence in the last few months—in the last few years, honestly. She was moody and temperamental and teenaged; she walked too hard on the stairs and spoke in affected hyperbole and made faces that suggested she thought her mother was a subpar life-form. But without her—without anyone—the air felt different; she heard Loomis crashing around upstairs, where he'd gone, she realized, straight up to Grace's room. She drew in her breath and it made a little sound.

"You okay?" David asked.

The dog skittered down the stairs, his nails clicking frantically against the hardwood, and presented himself at her feet, pushing his head between her knees.

"Where's your sister, buddy?" David asked Loomis, reaching to scratch behind his ears. She felt herself start to cry again and David looked up at her, squeezed her hip.

She stepped into his embrace, the dog pressed between them. "We knew this was coming. Why am I acting like it's a surprise that everyone's gone?"

"Because it *is* a surprise," he said. "How could it not be a surprise? Gracie's been in this house every day since she was born."

She rued his composure, but she'd seen his face when he hugged their daughter for the last time, knew that he was holding himself together for her benefit.

"Let's take the dog for a walk," David said. "This quiet's going to drive me nuts before I start to love it."

They were alone in their house—really alone—for the first time since Iowa City, she realized, since they'd first been married. This thought seemed to occur as well to David, who pushed her gently against the kitchen counter with his hips.

"Is there an empty nest joke about spring chickens?" he asked, his mouth near her ear, then moving down to kiss her neck.

She laughed, but then felt herself growing serious, here in

this familiar space with her husband again. The nest would never be empty so long as she was in it with him. They both stilled in the newfound quiet, and she met his eyes before lifting her face to kiss him, really kiss him, without having to worry about being interrupted.

Loomis, sensing his walk was being postponed, skulked away resignedly to chew on one of his discarded rawhides.

It was astounding to Violet how ignorant she'd been during her first pregnancy, how blithely and offhandedly she'd approached the whole process, blind to the boundless melancholy that awaited her after the birth—to say nothing of the breast engorgement, the ghoulish blood clots, the racing thoughts and spontaneous weeping, the afterpains that curled her into a ball in her bed at Wendy's house. Wendy sustained her, keeping her elbow-deep in painkillers and leaving trays of tea and toast outside of her door like a scullery maid. And this gave her the ability, then, to tune out everything besides her bodily horrors. She slept sometimes for twenty hours a day. She existed in a psychotropic fog, cabbage leaves on her breasts and archaic puffy pads between her legs, pretending she was dead, because denying the fact of her existence allowed her as well to deny the fact of all she'd allowed herself to lose.

With Wyatt, these same things happened—the soreness, the swelling, the hemorrhoids and stitches and ghastly emissions of blood—but they were secondary, perhaps even tertiary to their cause, this tiny perfect person she'd borne, this person who slept in fits and over whom insatiable hunger descended in seconds, this person for whose existence she was exclusively responsible. And the end-all love she felt for him—of course she loved him! God, how *intensely* she loved him—raised the stakes even higher, caused her to focus on him with such sleepless intensity that once she forgot to change her pad and bled onto the couch while feeding him, a woman who no longer had control over her most basic bodily functions. She endured these days with no medicinal aids, without so much as a single cup of coffee, because he deserved it, didn't he, her son; but also, convolutedly, though the other baby was ignorant of her goings-on, because she wanted to redeem herself, to be fully present for this intentional child in the way she hadn't been for the first baby. She had the luxury of a do-over, and she'd be damned if she took it for granted. She felt it was her comeuppance, the price she had to pay for so cavalierly abandoning her first child, for thinking that she could just go on like everything was normal.

For weeks she ignored it—lacked the wherewithal to acknowledge it, really, blinded by her exhaustion and her newfound routine, at once foreign and soul-annihilatingly boring. She wept while she nursed her son to sleep and pictured, sometimes, smothering him at sunrise, when she'd been up with him for hours already, but these wrongs would right themselves eventually, when Matt came home in the evenings and the three of them would curl together on the couch, she and her two most favorite people, and she would feel as though things were on an upward trajectory, but then they would all fall asleep, and by the time the baby woke her up she would forget about the bright spots. Endless hours spooling before her, Matt off to work, and she would be alone with Wyatt, aware constantly of his pressing need, so different than that of the first baby, so much more *dire*.

And so each day the sun would rise and everything would begin anew, the weeping and the smothering and the drifting away, until one evening when Matt got the baby down in his crib and came and cradled her against him and said, "Hey, sweetheart; I'm worried about you." And she'd resisted then, for weeks, indignant and offended, until one day when she was changing Wyatt and she looked down at his tiny defenselessness and thought, *I could do anything I want to him right now,* and the thought startled her so that she called her husband at work, and he came home within the hour, already in crisis mode, prepared to talk about *next steps* and *getting help.*

There was a diagnosis: quiet and crisp; and a subsequent cure: candy-colored and complex. She switched Wyatt to formula and began taking the pills. She became used to the way her husband tiptoed around her. She grew accustomed to the beige hum of her psyche, no longer in overdrive but now seemingly in no drive at all, out of gear, quietly churning as she cooed benignly to her baby.

"I'm sorry," she said to Matt one night, the two of them unsure of how their bodies fit together anymore, his arm wrapped around her abdomen, her abdomen clenching at his touch, mortified by her excess flesh and her newfound emptiness. At this point she was medicated enough to feel self-conscious, and the thing she hated more than anything was how helpless she felt, while still being entirely in control of her faculties.

"You have nothing to be sorry for," he said, his mouth pressed against her temple.

"I never would've hurt him."

"Oh, sweetie, I know that."

"I've never seen you be so *urgent* about anything before."

"I didn't recognize you, Viol. It scared me."

"It's just a lot," she said. "All of this."

"Of course it is. Violet, it— Everything's new, and constant, and—of course you were feeling overwhelmed. I'm just so glad you called me."

And it both appealed to her and repulsed her, how he was speaking about this so matter-of-factly, like they'd already gotten through the worst of it, like it was possible to move forward without glancing back at the past, like maybe this was simply a matter of chemicals, a physiological imbalance that had nothing to do with anything that had happened before.

"You can tell me anything," he said, but she couldn't bring herself to move her mouth, so she said nothing, so it wasn't true—*anything*—and the tiniest crack formed then, in their bed on a warm Wednesday evening, and she held herself responsible for all of it, everything, *anything*; and she committed, thenceforth, veins full of tonic, fallout be damned, to never frighten him in that way again.

CHAPTER THIRTY

Marilyn was the first one to witness the change in her husband, to see it before he'd even had time to realize it himself. David shifted when Jonah returned, culminating in the kind of smile—genuine, full of relief—that she hadn't seen from him in ages. They'd both been characteristically reticent at first: Jonah, though he'd consented to her hugging him for aeons straight in the foyer when he'd come in with Wendy, had simply held out a hand to David and said, "Hey, man." And David— only she, too, could hear the fullness in his voice—had replied, "Look who it is." And they shook, and that was that.

Later that night, the four of them sat together around the dinner table. Wendy, adhering thoughtfully to the dietary specifications of David's cardiologist, had ordered out a fancy and heart-healthy Mediterranean spread. Marilyn watched Jonah devour two folded-together pitas in three bites, like he hadn't eaten in years.

"Should I acknowledge the elephant in the room?" she asked, and her motley trio of family members looked up at her innocently over their plates.

"Honey," said David.

"My *God*, Mom," said Wendy.

"I'm sorry," said Jonah, and she focused her gaze on him, this sweet mysterious boy with the prematurely mournful eyes. "I freaked out and I figured it would be easier for everyone if—"

"Mom, I swear to you that Jonah and I *just* debriefed this in the car. Exhaustively. He's sorry. He's embarrassed. He's hungry. The Catholic trifecta. You've taught him well."

"This isn't something to joke about, Wendy." Amid the relief of having him back, she'd allowed herself to entertain all of the thoughts she'd been pressing into the depths of her mind since Wendy had assured her everything would be okay: even if it *were* okay, Jonah had still run away from them; in the wake of a terrifying, terrible event, he'd taken David's car and driven cross-country without a license; he'd behaved recklessly and childishly and disturbingly, and could this not, perhaps, have had something to do with their failure, as a family, to offer him any real permanence, from his jarring arrival into their lives to Violet's white-knuckled avoidance of him to Wendy's failure to give him a stable home? She and David had been good for him, she thought, but there was no such thing as good parenting, apparently, and so who knew what blind spots they had with him, what they'd overlooked. They were all capable of doing better. "Jonah, that was an incredibly irresponsible thing that you did."

"I know," he said.

"You can't imagine how scared we were. On top of what was already an unbelievably awful time. You can't ever do something like this again, okay?"

"I won't. I'm really sorry."

"Which is why we've decided to ground you," Marilyn said. David had tepidly engaged with her in this discussion, but he'd ultimately told her to do whatever she thought was best. "One month. Effective immediately."

"Mom, don't you think he's been through enough? Jesus Christ."

"Do you realize how *lucky* it is that he got pulled over? I

can't even think about what might have happened otherwise—
another accident, or if something had gone wrong with the car
out in the middle of nowhere, and—"

"He got pulled over because I hired somebody to go find
him," Wendy said. "Christ. Yes, it was dumb of him and, yes, it
was immature, but he's back and he's safe and it's not going to
happen again—right, Jonah?—so can we all just eat our fucking grape leaves in peace and let this horrible ordeal be *over*?"

She recalled Wendy making similar moves as a teenager,
dropping explosive lines like lit grenades in the middle of the
dinner table and watching gleefully as they detonated. Jonah
was staring at her, openmouthed.

"Don't look at me like that," Wendy said to him, pouring
herself more wine. "God knows why, but we're all quite fond
of you."

Jonah's face softened to the point where it almost seemed
like he might laugh. "I've never been grounded before," he said.

"I'll draw you a map of the escape routes," Wendy said.

"The comedic timing in this family leaves something to be
desired," David said.

"How's Liza?" Wendy asked.

"She's well." Marilyn didn't look at David. "Home with the
baby. Getting acclimated."

"She sent me a couple of photos. Kit looks slightly less like
the Crypt Keeper than the male babies born into this family."

She studied Wendy, surprised to hear her making this sort
of joke, and tried to smile at her. "Yes, she's darling, isn't she?"
It had just dawned on her that Kit was now occupying the space
intended for Ivy, the coveted first granddaughter. It filled her
with a guilty sadness.

"What do you think, Dad?" Wendy asked.

It snapped Marilyn out of her reverie. She stiffened. David
looked to her, seemingly for help, but she busied herself with
her salmon.

"Pretty cute," he said.

"Not that he'd know firsthand." She hadn't meant to say it, but perhaps public shaming would nudge him in the right direction. Wendy and Jonah glanced up, and David glared at her.

"You haven't met her yet, Dad?" Wendy asked.

"Doesn't anybody understand that babies are highly susceptible to infection?"

"Are you, like, radioactive now or something?" Wendy asked, and Jonah snorted.

"Casts are *full* of bacteria," David said, his posture caved rather dramatically around his own bandaged arm. "I'm just taking extra precautions."

"It's not as though Kit's going to be directly breathing in your cast bacteria," Marilyn said, breaking her own rule about mealtime conversational propriety.

"I don't want to talk about this anymore," David said, and the look he gave her—the fact that it was less angry than wounded—shut her up.

"I broke my arm in first grade," Jonah said. "The cast smelled so sick when they took it off."

"Thanks for ensuring that no person at this table is left with an appetite," Wendy said.

"*Thank* you," David said to Jonah. "Finally, another voice of reason."

It pained her to see him like this. She couldn't determine the origin of his objection to seeing the baby, but she knew it wasn't rooted in his fear of infection, however vigilant he'd been about germs when their own children were newborns.

"Dad," Wendy said. "It's kind of— I mean, like, shit happens regardless, right?"

A quiet fell over the table.

"Am I not allowed to say that? It's not like Liza's asked you not to come over, right?"

"No, she hasn't," Marilyn answered for him. She realized, with shame, that she was allowing her daughter's grief to get tangled up in her marital spat. "That's a good point, Wendy."

"Thank you," David said, "for all of this unsolicited feedback."

"Two fights in one dinner," Wendy said, raising her glass to Jonah. "Your welcome wagon has arrived."

Jonah went to shoot layups after dinner. His grandfather didn't look great. He was pale and thin, and there was a big blue cast on his arm, and his hair looked matted, like he hadn't showered in a while. He couldn't believe that Wendy had hired someone to find him. Sniper-level shit. He didn't hear the front door open.

"Jonah."

He jumped about twelve feet out of his skin, clutching the ball to his chest.

"Whoa, whoa, sorry." David sat on the stairs facing the driveway.

"Sorry, was I— I can— Am I making too much noise? I was just— Sorry. Sorry."

"Are you sorry about something? I couldn't tell." David smiled. "Just came out to say hello. You're doing nothing wrong. I wanted to thank you, actually."

Thanks for fucking up our lives. Thanks for breaking my arm. He dribbled the ball for something to do.

"I'm so sorry that you had to—see what you did. I can't imagine what that must have been like for you." David sounded almost teary, and it made him profoundly uncomfortable. "I didn't see it coming. Though arguably I should have. I— It's funny, the blind spots we have for ourselves. If any of my patients complained of shoulder pain, I'd have them go to the hospital straightaway." He rubbed at his forehead with his free hand. "I wanted to thank you for calling the ambulance. For calling Marilyn. For telling her—what you told her." Here he colored. "And I wanted to thank you for staying with me."

"But I didn't—"

"I would have died if you weren't there, Jonah. I don't want to scare you, but I want you to know that."

"But I wasn't— I didn't hold the ladder."

"Oh, kid. The ladder was the least of my worries."

"I should have—"

"You stuck around for when it counted," he said, "and none of this was your fault."

"I stole my birthday present," he blurted out. "From your desk. I was looking for your wallet for the paramedics. And I found an envelope with my name on it and I—took it. Because I thought— I wasn't sure if I was going to be coming back. Or if you . . ." *I decided to take it in case you died and couldn't give it to me.* God, what had he been doing?

But David laughed. "I'm glad you got it on time."

"It was really nice of you. Thanks. A lot. For—everything."

"It's our pleasure," David said. "You should move a little to the left of the net when you're making free throws. I'll show you when I get this thing off of my arm."

It dawned on Wendy later, when the vodka wasn't helping her to sleep and she was prostrate on her living room couch, thinking of her dad, of how he didn't want to meet Liza's baby and of how, similarly, Violet had decided, way back when, that she couldn't come to say goodbye to Miles.

The fragmented cognitive leaps of the intoxicated, the mess of the last few weeks: her infant niece, blind to the fact of her grandfather's incapacitation, the gray cast of his skin. Jonah, mysteriously missing and now returned. And, out of nowhere, the inquisitive little Bhargava girl, ignorant of her impending demotion by an incoming baby. Those big blue cyclone eyes

that came, Wendy knew, straight from her father, the hot graceful tennis player who'd once fucked her on the hard acrylic of
the court behind the baseball field. His agility, his dexterity,
the current running through him. The vulpine abilities of his
body, incongruous with the benign aesthetic magnetism of his
persona.

She sat up.

This: her punishment. *The grand reality-show reveal.* Because
Jonah was suddenly alive on Aaron's face, all over, the flattish
nose, the long lashes, the eyes—boundless blue typhoons—
that betrayed an intrinsic kindness even when their propri-
etor was being kind of a dick. And then—she colored, even
there, alone on her couch at three in the morning—his body,
long-limbed, lined with muscle, an olive cast to skin that didn't
freckle—though Aaron had a birthmark high on his left thigh,
just below the curve of his ass; she remembered that—and
overall, generally, an alluring self-possession. And those weird
inverted elbows. She pictured Jonah stretching beside her in
the passenger seat of the Jeep. Catlike reflexes. She'd always
assumed that that part of Jonah came from their dad. But—
well, David had just fallen from a tree, hadn't he?

Rob fucked his TA, Violet had said. *He fucked his TA and he
left me and now I'm late.* Utterly convincing. And why shouldn't
it be?

You're a goddamn sociopath, Violet had said to her more
recently, during their last substantive conversation.

She was blown away by the expansive cruelty of this act, not
just that Violet had slept with her ex-boyfriend—that, in itself,
hurt, of course, though she'd moved on by the time it occurred;
she'd unequivocally identified Miles as her intended—but that
she'd allowed Wendy to become so intimately acquainted with
the fallout, that she'd let the fallout become a part of their
shared history, that it had sparked so much more than either of
them ever could have anticipated. And all the while, Violet had

had her eyes on the prize, knowing the details, knowing their magnitude, knowing that with Wendy's aid she'd be able to land steadily on her feet.

She felt the need to sit, though she was already seated.

Because Violet—fucking Violet—had always known how to save face.

2013

Things had been stable for almost two years when the fever happened. Miles was teaching again, one class a week, and taking his daily walks to the lagoon by the Museum of Science and Industry. He'd been in remission for so long that Wendy had started to relax, loosen her shoulders, dare to think about the future. Finally, some luck, in among the rest of it.

But then one evening—she'd been running numbers for an upcoming Misericordia auction—he called to her from the living room: "Isn't the capital with the dense one, Scout?"

She felt the hair stand up at the back of her neck, and she rose and found him lying on the couch, face shiny with sweat. "Sweetheart," she said.

"If she sparkled the other one, you can't see her—"

"Miles." She knelt next to him, and she flinched when she felt how hot his forehead was.

He smiled thinly, eyes elsewhere, rolling upward.

"Fuck," she said. "Fuck, fuck." She ran for her phone. "No, no, no."

The doctor confirmed what she already knew. She half-listened as he explained the difference between recurrence and progression.

"We'll keep on fighting till the end," she sang under her breath in her Freddie Mercury voice, when the doctor finished talking, and he looked confused, and she laughed, and then she dipped her head down to her husband's arm and cried and cried.

Violet had invited Wendy to join her at Matt's parents' lake house on Mercer Island primarily because she thought her sister wouldn't come: *Look at this inconveniently located olive branch I've extended; don't feel bad if you can't reach it.* But her sister, as she was wont to do, surprised her by accepting at the last minute. She'd been alone there with Wyatt for the better part of the month, Matt flying in for long weekends, and she couldn't remember a time she'd felt more relaxed, waking with the sun each morning in a place where the air felt different, spending full days on the beach with her two-year-old, working her way through novel after novel, napping liberally. She worried about nothing beyond Wyatt's well-being, that he was fed and rested and not getting sunburned. Wendy's arrival threw a wrench into this system.

"Please tell me those are not Matt's sunglasses on the counter," she said. She'd just arrived and they were making lunch. Violet glanced over. There was a beat-up pair of black frames by the toaster; Matt had sensitive eyes and a terrible mind for keeping track of things.

"I'm sure they are," she said. "He picks them up at yard sales. He can't spend much time in the sun without them."

"Those are Prada sunglasses. Your husband bought himself Prada sunglasses."

"From a *garage sale*. Jesus, Wendy, lay off, okay?"

"Someone's pissy," Wendy said.

"Long day," she replied with less hostility, not wanting a fight. "You look wonderful."

"Thanks," Wendy said. "God, you look like hell."

She chewed, literally, at her tongue, containing all of the

acidic responses she had stored in her brain. She was trying to maintain her zen. "Thank you. Is your hair different?"

"One of Miles's friends gave me a Turkish spa workup as a gift. Which ended up being far less relaxing than it sounded. All of the *people*, you know? Naked bathhouse. *Communing*. Total nightmare. So I felt like I needed a week when I got home just to *recover*."

"Naked bathhouse?"

"I'll just say that I saw a stranger's *literal* vagina and I almost died."

"The life you lead. We drove to town yesterday and I considered that a huge victory."

"Becoming one with nature?"

"Sort of," she said. "Wyatt's gone crazy for swimming."

"I was reading about radioactivity in freshwater not too long ago."

"Well, if he's survived this long, I'm not too worried," she said, and then she realized her word choice and paled. This was what got her; this was what sucked her, every time, back into the nauseating stratosphere of being Wendy's bitch: this unplayable card, this awful, looming iceberg whose existence you could conjure without even realizing it. Wendy studied her, assessing the level of intent with which she'd made the statement. Then she stood up.

"Speaking of environmental toxins," she said, "let's go to the beach."

They went down to the shore for lunch. When they finished eating, Wyatt leapt up to resume work on his sandcastle but she stopped her son and beckoned him over to her, propped up on her elbows on a beach towel.

"Not yet, sweetie. Come sit with Mama for a few minutes before you go play. Let your tummy gobble up some of that peanut butter first." She felt Wendy's notorious side-eye and chose to ignore it. She, too, frequently hated how she sounded when speaking to her son, but she thought it was better than the alternative—her mother, for instance, who had talked to them all like tiny bureaucrats the moment they exited the womb. Wyatt, who'd skipped a nap, consented with ease, crawled into her lap and rested his damp head against her shoulder. "I'm pregnant," she said. It wasn't how she'd planned to do it but she was spurred by Wendy's silent judgment and by the shield of her drowsy little boy. Wendy was quiet for what felt like a long time.

"Oh," she said finally. "Well, I guess there have been more surprising announcements."

It was early to be telling people. As soon as she said it she wished she hadn't, was seized by an irrational fear that Wendy would somehow supernaturally ruin things.

"I wondered, actually," Wendy said. Her voice was clipped; she wasn't looking at Violet as she spoke. "You have that sort of puffy, sickly Jane Austen antiheroine thing going on."

"Just what every newly pregnant woman wants to hear," she said lightly, though the remark had hurt her feelings.

"Perfect timing," Wendy said. "As ever."

"I'm not sure what you mean."

"Was it an accident?"

She touched her belly, protective of her percolating person. "No."

"Well, you're nothing if not predictable."

She felt like a kid again, not in a good way.

"Remember when you didn't want kids?"

"Jesus Christ," she said, smarting from the impact of Wendy throwing it in her face so offhandedly. "God, Wendy, that was a—" It seemed like an especially unkind thing to say in front of Wyatt, even though he was dozing against her, even though he wouldn't know what it meant. "I was at a different place in my life," she said. She never got anything back from Wendy, not obviously, at least, and that was what made it so difficult. So *draining.* Because with your sister, it would have been *nice* every once in a while to hear an affirmation when you said, *I love you* or *I missed you* or *I was thinking about you today.* To feel some sisterly validation, some sort of sustenance when it counted. *Congrats on the new baby.*

"So Miles's cancer is back," Wendy said. "And we're done. Maybe six weeks, maybe six months. No more than that, probably."

She felt like she had been punched. *Not this. Not now; not ever, but especially not now.* She looked up at Wendy slowly.

"He insisted that I come here for a *break,* but I'm going to leave first thing tomorrow."

"Wendy. Jesus. Come here."

Surprisingly, Wendy complied, scooted indelicately off of her towel.

And that was what broke her heart and brought her to life: the image of her stoic sister doing something as undignified as scooting, being in a low enough place that she would finally accept comfort. She took Wendy's hand. "That is some fucking bullshit," she said.

Wendy glanced up at her. "Right?"

"Complete *bullshit.* I'm so sorry." She put an arm tentatively around her sister's shoulders. "They're sure?"

"It's spread," Wendy said. "Quickly. There has never on the earth been a time when it's less helpful to have a bazillion dollars. There's nothing they can do."

"I can't even imagine," she said, which was true.

"Bad fucking genes in that family," Wendy said. "Not like ours."

At this they both ventured to laugh.

CHAPTER THIRTY-ONE

It was ludicrous, of course, to be avoiding a baby, but he had his reasons, and once he'd put his foot down with Marilyn he felt the childish impetus to keep it there. He felt weak and geriatric. He knew he'd let Liza down by not coming to the hospital. He knew his cast excuse was a flimsy one. But he didn't want his granddaughter's first encounter with him to be like he was now. Feeble and dependent and hindered by his own mortality.

He was in his study, trying to rekindle his interest in honey fungus. He'd grown tired of the view from the guest room window. He'd felt himself to be fusing with the easy chair. He still couldn't read books one-armed. The computer seemed a logical outlet, a step up from daytime television, which he was resisting with a vengeance.

He heard the jingle of Loomis's collar, then footsteps.

"Dad?" In the doorway, again: Liza, this time with a baby in her arms. A baby, still at that tiny, perfect stage of babyhood, barely larger than a rabbit.

"Oh," he said. He rose from his chair. "Oh, Lize. Hi. I wasn't . . ."

"Mom around?"

"No, she's running errands."

"Well. I've got someone here who very much wants to meet you."

He was struck by how much Liza looked like her mother. He had a sudden image of Marilyn shortly after Wendy was born, standing in her bathrobe with the baby in the kitchen on Davenport Street, golden-haired and radiant with fatigue.

"Oh, I— You didn't have to come all the way here with—"

"I had this notion," Liza said. "Utterly ridiculous, but hear me out; this notion that you might be uncomfortable meeting her when you're not feeling quite like yourself."

He wasn't sure when the tears in his eyes had arrived, only that they were there now.

"So I figured I'd drop by. Because she's not allowed to become a fully legitimized person until she meets you, and she's getting kind of impatient."

"Lize, I—"

"I'm so sorry this happened to you," she said. "And I'm so glad you're okay."

"I just didn't want to—with the cast; she's susceptible to all kinds of . . ."

"Dad. Is that genuinely something you're worried about?"

"Well, I—"

"Because I trust you. I'll leave, if you really think she'd be at risk." She watched him steadily from the doorway with her mother's frank inquiry.

"Well, if you've come all the way here. I'm sure a couple of minutes wouldn't hurt. If she's swaddled."

"You're in luck. Have a seat."

"Right—here? In the office?"

"Would you rather go somewhere else?"

"I— No, I suppose this is fine."

Before he sat down, she came and hugged him, hard, both of them one-armed.

"Thanks for coming over, Lize."

Her eyes were shiny as she smiled at him, another face so like her mother's.

"All right," he said. "Let's see this kid. But you should probably spot me."

There was a flicker of apprehension on her face.

"Your mother and I did have four of you, Liza-lee. I can hold a baby with one arm."

She lowered the baby into his unbroken arm and he was struck by the featherweight familiarity. "David, meet Kit. Kit, David." She perched on the edge of his desk.

"Hello," he said, throat full. Perfect peanut. Tiny dollface. Already growing into her features. "Wow, Lize."

"She's something, isn't she?"

"To be sure."

The feeling he'd get holding his daughters when they were this small: it was like being drugged. He bowed his chin to smell the crown of her head and the act brought with it sparklers of synapses. Nights in bed with his wife, the babies between them. Walking with a fussy Wendy around the block at sunrise, trying to let Marilyn get some extra sleep. The way he could feel the tiny forming plates of Liza's skull beneath his lips as he hummed to her.

"Liza-lee," he murmured. "Look at this person you made."

"Isn't it wild?"

"The wildest." He glanced up at her. "Lize, I'm sorry I didn't— I should've been there with you."

"It's okay." She smiled. "I had a tag team."

He had also been not quite able to envision what it had looked like for Marilyn and Gillian to be together for all that time, in such intense and intimate circumstances. He cleared his throat, looking down at the baby again. "Liza, Gillian mentioned something to me a few months back. I've been— debating whether to ask you about it."

"I'd wondered if she told you."

"I'm so sorry if you ever thought—"

"I was distracting myself," she said, cutting him off. "I was looking for— I don't know. Evidence of something. Evidence that things weren't perfect between you and Mom."

"Of course they weren't. Aren't."

"But they're closer to it than they are for most people. And yet my point is that I don't care anymore. It was instantaneous when Kit was born. I can't *believe* the things I thought were important."

In his arms, the baby mewled, yawned, punched him good-naturedly with a tiny fist. He smiled. "Hey, honey, is Ryan— Has he . . ."

"We're talking," she said. "He's coming to meet her this weekend, actually. He really wants to be here for her, but it— We don't want to rush it, because things are actually going really well in Michigan, it sounds like. He's on new meds; he's got a new therapist; he has a group of friends out there now that are—I guess they're able to be there for him in a way that I wasn't because I had so much else going on, with my job, and—well, our family. I think we both wish he could be in the picture *now*, but I also know we're going to have to ease our way into things. Whatever *things* might look like. Neither one of us was—at our best, during this last year." Liza colored but neglected to further explain. "We've got a lot to figure out, I guess. But he sounds—good, actually. For the first time since . . . before we moved here."

"More importantly," he said, "how are *you?*"

She shrugged. "I'm taking it as it comes. One thing at a time." She fussed with Kit's blanket. "Some times are easier than others."

"My daughter, the wise young mother."

Liza laughed. "I just realized that I haven't actually referred to myself that way yet. As her mom."

"You'll have plenty of opportunities," he said.

The baby shifted in his arms, infinitesimally, as her mother had done so many years ago.

Last week he'd been halfway across the country in a stolen car but today he was hers, this awkward young man wearing shiny new Converse high-tops. In the car, they were silent. Jonah stared dispassionately out the window.

"How's school?" Violet asked. With Wyatt and Eli, this question was unfalteringly met by a steady stream of chatter, news of tiny nemeses and class gerbils named whimsically after historic figures.

Jonah simply shrugged. "I got a C in chemistry."

"You and me both," she said, though this was not actually true. He didn't smile. "Do you have a favorite subject? My mom tells me you're a pretty avid reader."

"Not really."

She inhaled slowly, gliding to a stop at a red light, and she recalled the dog park where her mother used to take them, the big grassy expanse where they'd spent hours as children with Goethe, chasing around shih tzus and pugs and huskies, reveling in their fur and their lack of inhibition. "How hungry are you?" she asked, flicking on her turn signal.

"Not very."

"Want to make a pit stop?" She glanced over to ensure he was warmly dressed.

"Whatever," he said, and she used it as an opportunity to flex her maternal muscles as her mother must have done all those years, accepting lackluster teenage feedback with the deluded enthusiasm of a clown.

"Let's get some air."

Out of the car, he followed her shufflingly. The dog park

had been turned into a playground for the nearby elementary school, a rambling space-age structure.

"Thought you might like an opportunity to go down the slides," she said, and he looked at her with horror. "I'm kidding." She took a seat on something that resembled a bench and he joined her, as far away from her as was physically possible. She watched him fold in on himself, elbows pressed into his rib cage and hands shoved deep into his pockets.

"I guess it's not really park weather," she said.

"I'm fine."

She shifted to face him. "I've been trying to figure out how to apologize to you. This has been—a difficult thing for me."

He raised his eyebrows.

"Not that it hasn't been for you. I just— You seem to be accepting all this with a good deal more grace than I am. And I figured I would try to explain myself and tell you that I'm not—you know, I'm not proud of how hard it's been for me. Or of the fact that I've been—you know, not the most willing to work on this. Us."

"Okay," he said.

"I want to thank you for helping out with Wyatt. For showing up at school like you did. I can't tell you how grateful I am."

"It's fine," he said. "It was—fun, kind of. He's a nice kid."

"Well, so are you."

"I'm not a—"

"Young adult; sorry." She paused. "Wyatt adores you." She faltered again, gearing up for what was next. "I'm sorry I got so angry with you at Christmas. I'm kind of—tightly wound. I get anxious when things happen beyond my orchestration. Particularly when my children are involved."

"I wasn't trying to ruin it for him," he said. "When I was a kid I always appreciated it when adults talked to me like I was a regular person instead of, like, a cat."

"Me too. And so does Wyatt." She paused. It had been Matt's idea, this time, for her to ask Jonah to dinner. Her husband had come to terms with Jonah following the Star of the Week incident, and when they'd sat down together to hash things out, Matt had stated it plainly: there was no turning back for them now, no turning a blind eye to Jonah, no chance in hell that they could keep going as they had been, trying to keep him separate from their life. It was critical that she do her best to fix all that had been broken along the way, he'd said. Critical that they forge on clear-eyed and candid, to avoid a pit like the one she'd fallen into after Wyatt was born. Matt was the patient pragmatist he'd always been, doing what he could to keep their family afloat despite a violent bout of turbulence, and the gratitude she felt for this was staggering, like the primal satisfaction of flopping into the grass after a long run.

"Look, Jonah, I—I didn't know who I was, when you were born. And I—to be honest, I haven't really known since. Your existence has had a huge impact on mine, even if—but I can't— Things would be so different, if you'd come back into my life and I was alone. But when you have kids, you have to—you know, table any kind of soul-searching. You've triggered a lot of old stuff for me, just by being here, and that's not your fault by any stretch, but I can't change the fact that it's hard for me. That it's going to be hard for me for—a while. Maybe forever. I don't know. But it didn't occur to me until recently that I'm making it a great deal harder by resisting it." Had Wendy not said as much to her, when she was in labor with Jonah? But Wendy had always been better than she at taking things as they came, rolling with the punches. She supposed it was that particular reflex that had gotten them into this situation in the first place. "I'd like for us to try and make this work. Is that something you're interested in?"

He squirmed. "Sure."

"That's going to require us to be candid with each other. And patient."

"Were you reading a book about this?"

She colored. "Just some stuff online."

Jonah smiled. "Bondingwithyoursecretkid.org."

She laughed in spite of herself.

"If we're being *candid*?" he asked. "I didn't drink the wine."

"Excuse me?"

"The wine I took. I was fucking with you. To see what you'd do. You're one of those people who—like, everything's so fucking perfect that sometimes it's just fun to, like, mess things up. Move a doily and see how you react."

"I don't own any *doilies*."

"Anyway, sorry. I gave it to Grace. I didn't—I just felt like having a little fun with you."

"At my expense, more like. Though I guess that's your job, isn't it?"

"Until I'm cleared to work at Baskin-Robbins," he said. Then: "What's my dad like?"

She froze.

"Assuming you even know who he is." There was that hint of combat she'd seen in him the first time they met, the prickly unabashedness that made her feel a surprising pride. Perhaps her litigious genes had found a foothold in the fibers of his being; perhaps she'd given him something valuable after all.

"Of course I know who he is," she said, trying not to sound offended because she assumed that was what he wanted. "Or I mean I—I knew who he *was*, back when—"

"He's *dead*?"

"No, no. I mean, not that I've heard. It's been—well, it's been sixteen years." She studied him. "Sixteen plus, I guess. Happy birthday, by the way. I can't believe I— Well, I didn't *forget*, you know. I never have." She had never forgotten the moment he was born; the memory existed in her like an extra organ; her body, healing from his birth, had created a space for it, for *him*, and though she could will herself not to think about it, she had always been certain of its presence.

Beside her, Jonah stiffened. "It doesn't matter."

"You were born at nine-fourteen in the morning. There hasn't been a year that's passed without my being cognizant of that exact time on January seventh. I don't— I know I've been a letdown in every possible way, Jonah, but I've never stopped thinking about you." She paused. "I'll make up for it next year, if you let me." And she was conscious, this time, of promising him longevity. She actually *hoped*, she realized, that they would have this to look forward to.

"Sure," he said. He was staring intently at the ground, but she could see from the tightness of his mouth that he was trying not to smile. "Chuck E. Cheese's. I'll see you there."

And there was something indescribably lovely about this, the baby who'd once jabbed with restless knees at your internal organs sitting beside you on a park bench and benevolently giving you shit, and it occurred to her that it was moments like these that made being alive feel worth it, little blips of contentment amid the mayhem and status quo.

She was not surprised when it was ruined: "What's my dad's name?" Jonah asked.

"I— Listen, Jonah, there's no one else on the earth who knows this, so I'm not one hundred percent comfortable with—"

"You're the one who brought up candor."

"And *patience*." She was aggravated, but there was a kind of pleasure to be found in the rhythm of their conversation, and as she saw Jonah come to life before her for the first time—the first time he was speaking to her like he did to Wendy, or her parents—she began to wonder if maybe she *could* be honest with him; he was, after all, the most deserving recipient of this information. And it bound her to him further; they were the two people on the earth to whom the details were most relevant. "I've never told anyone this," she said.

"I asked Wendy and Grace," he admitted.

"Wendy and Grace don't know anything. Nobody knows. As I said."

"Not even Matt?"

She reddened.

"Shit," he said. "That's, like, high-level fraud."

"It's not *fraud*. It's just—it's never really mattered." She realized how this sounded. "I mean, of course it *mattered*, but not—"

"Not if you never saw me again, as planned." She couldn't read his expression. "It's fine," he said. "I never expected that you'd be like super-stoked to see me."

"I never expected *to* see you. I never thought we'd be— But here we are. And of course I'm happy about that. Just because it wasn't something I planned on doesn't mean I don't welcome it."

He eyed her askance.

"I realize it may not seem like I welcomed it *at first*."

He snorted. "Convincing."

"Of course it mattered to me who your father was. Is. Matters. Jesus."

"That's all you're going to give me?"

She set her jaw, knitted her fingers together. "For the purposes of this conversation."

"What are the purposes of this conversation?"

She didn't answer right away. "I had this boyfriend in college," she said. "He was finishing his PhD when we were together. Biochemistry. An incredibly smart man."

"But?"

"Pardon?"

"It sounded like that's where you were headed."

"No buts," she said. She felt a prickle of agitation at his interruption. "We weren't meant to be together long-term. Which was a surprise to me, to tell you the truth." She'd caught his attention; he still wasn't looking at her but there was interest on his face, a lift in his eyebrows that reminded her of her mom. "We were together for almost three years," she said. "I was sure we would get married. But I was also— Well, I was twenty-one, so I was a complete dumbass."

A flicker of a smile from him. "So what happened?"

She hesitated.

"Look," he said, "all I know about him is that he maybe has a PhD and he dated a dumbass for three years. I'm not going to, like, send a bounty hunter after him." He kicked at the eco-friendly foam gravel substitute. "I don't like you that much."

He'd told the joke so self-consciously, with such affected disdain, that it brought tears to her eyes. He was a funny, thoughtful, inquisitive kid. She'd treated him so poorly. He hadn't asked for any of it. "He cheated on me," she said. "And we broke up."

"End of story?"

She swallowed. "More or less."

"Which means there's more."

She turned to face him, baldly, studying him without shame or tact, the way she did Wyatt and Eli, the way you were allowed to stare at another person only when they came from you. There was the loveliness in his face she'd seen when she first met him. Her father's forehead. Cheekbones that reminded her, residually, of a photo she'd seen of her maternal grandmother. So odd, how these tiny vestiges of earlier times could appear plainly on the landscape of a face, ghostly particles of people you'd never met.

"If I tell you this, I—need some form of assurance that you'll keep it between us." The odds of this were slim, she knew. Information had a way of trickling down, particularly in her family. But she owed him this much, and she owed it to him before it got tarnished by the anger of others involved. Jonah wouldn't be hurt by it in the way that Wendy or Matt would.

Jonah was, interestingly, the only one she'd yet to lie to. Here was her clean slate, her chance to begin anew with him.

"Do you want me to, like, sign something?"

She had not, of course, considered all possible avenues of fallout, but she knew with certainty that they would be lesser in magnitude than the decision she'd made with Wendy all those years ago.

"I made an error in judgment."

"With the scientist guy?"

"No. With—someone who'd—well, they'd broken up, but he'd dated my—for years. My best friend. So she would be— deeply hurt by this."

"Who's your best friend? Do you even *have* any friends?"

"You and Wendy share a sense of humor; do you know that?"

"Your mom says that too."

"I'm not quite ready to just— I'll tell you this, okay? I wasn't in love with this man. I never told him about you. But he was kind. Very thoughtful. Agile."

"*Gross,*" Jonah said, and she realized how he'd interpreted this and blushed wildly.

"Oh, God, I meant— No, he was an athlete. Not in— Christ. Like, a *sports* athlete."

"My father, the friendly *sports athlete.*"

She felt more connected to him, in that moment, than she ever had. He seemed to her a realist, and this struck her: there she was, within him. She was absent from the sharp contours of his body and the soft ease of his voice, but his practicality, his ability to accept the world as it was, had to have come from Violet herself. People were often disappointing. Their stories were unsatisfactory. She had come to terms with this years ago, and he was doing the same in a few-minute span on a suburban playground.

"Can I ask another question?"

"Oh, look, Jonah, I wonder if maybe we've covered enough—"

"Did you ever think about keeping me?"

She looked over at him, took a chance and put a hand on his shoulder. "All the time."

She worried he would ask her most feared follow-up question, *Do you regret not keeping me*, but he didn't, and he also didn't recoil at her touch.

CHAPTER THIRTY-TWO

Grace was going home. She had confessed to her parents—had arranged it with Wendy so her sister would be at the house on Fair Oaks when the call came, to act as a buffer. If she watched one more true-crime documentary, she worried she might take up serial murder herself. Her parents were in Chicago, and Loomis, and her sisters, and Jonah. And her new niece, just a few weeks old, too small still to understand how wildly disappointing her youngest aunt was. People who gave her a pass on her lackluster performance in life because she was the baby of the family and always would be. She gave them a perpetual excuse to feel superior simply by virtue of her lack of exposure to the world.

There was a line at Orion, so she lingered by the end of the counter, and Ben saw her and had to wait on four people before he could talk to her. Finally he took the last order and whispered something to his coworker, and then he removed his apron and joined her.

"Sorenson," he said awkwardly. "Long time."

She was already feeling herself starting to cry and she bit down on her tongue until the sensation went away. "Hi," she said. "Do you have a couple minutes?"

"Twenty-five," he said. "Not to brag."

"Can we walk?" she asked.

He turned to her, bemused. "Yeah, Sorenson. Whatever you want."

They walked together for a few minutes in silence, not looking at each other. Ben stopped to arch his back—he opened on Sundays and had presumably been on his feet for eight hours already—and then he turned to her. "So what's new? It's been—a while."

"Yeah," she said. "Nothing. I mean—some things." She was trying to pin down exactly how much Jonah had told him. "Sorry I've been a little—off the radar. Family stuff."

"Is everything okay?"

"Getting there," she said.

"I met your nephew."

"I heard. I— Ben, I'm sorry for—"

"I'm not allowed to care what you were doing that night."

"Of course you—"

"I'm not. That's not how this works."

"How *what* works?"

"This—whatever it is we have. We're—I don't know, we're just *friends*, I guess. I'm not allowed to be angry or curious or fucking *hurt* if you choose to spend the night with someone else. I'm not entitled to— God, I'm not sure we *are* friends anymore, even."

"I hope we are." She paused. "I made a mistake."

He stopped walking.

"It was a stupid, one-time thing. A bartender."

"Jesus. Not the guy from the Comeback?"

"Well, I—"

"The fucking *Irish* guy?"

"You don't have to say *Irish* like some kind of weird nationalist. He's just a regular person."

When he spoke again, his voice was strange: "Why are you telling me this? Why did you come here? Do you have any idea how cruel this is? You know you still haven't said a word to me about Christmas? I said some stuff and you just fucking—like it never even happened? How is it possible that you're this emotionally idiotic?"

"I'm sorry," she said. "I don't— This isn't who I am. I never wanted to— The thought of hurting you makes me want to— I was drunk, and I was scared, and I—"

"Scared of what?" His voice had quieted.

She waved her hands in front of her. "Everything. I don't know."

"Did you come here to tell me that you're going out with him now?"

"No. No, not at all." She paused. "I'm here to tell you I'm going to Chicago."

He stopped walking. "For—what? A visit?"

"No. I think I'm done here. Portland hasn't really . . . brought out my best. I'm going to live with my parents for a little bit." The tears were back, filling her throat, blurring her vision. "And maybe help out my sister, Liza; she's the one who—"

"Delusional psychologist? Dating the software developer with tattoo sleeves? Accidentally pregnant?"

She looked to him in gratitude. "Yeah, that's the one. She had her baby though."

"Congrats."

"Thanks? Good memory."

"Never tell me I don't pay attention," he said, sounding like someone's grandfather. It made her smile. "I've got all you Sorensons down. Violet's the one with the illegitimate love-child and the 'live, laugh, love' poster in her upstairs bathroom. Irish twin of your other fucked-up sister—Wendy, the heiress with the tragic past, who bought you eight-hundred-dollar luggage for your college graduation, which I still, by the way, think you should hock for spending money."

Grace smiled, listening to this boy construct her sister from memory—not necessarily Wendy as she really was, but Wendy as Grace had relayed her: the only portrait you could ever get, really, of one sister from another, tinged inevitably with jealousy and double standards and affection as deep and intractable as marrow.

He'd hung on her every word; no one had ever done that before.

He kicked a rock and paused to watch its trajectory down the sidewalk. "Your dad's a stoic family practitioner who's recently taken up landscaping in his retirement," he continued. "Your mom is a bombshell flower child who was romanced into a life of quiet domesticity. I can keep going, if you'd like. But as I mentioned, I've only got twenty-five minutes. More like twenty, now. Are you leaving, like, forever?"

"I'm not sure."

Ben stopped again, perched atop a U-shaped bicycle rack and watched her. "I'm not going to flatter myself and assume that your bailing has anything to do with me," he said. "But about Christmas . . ."

It occurred to her to interrupt him and apologize herself, but something stopped her.

"You hurt my feelings," he said. "But I know you weren't trying to. I like you so much, Grace." Had he ever called her *Grace* before? "And from where I stand, this should be the easiest thing in the world because I like you and I think you like me."

"I do."

"But it's *not* easy with you, and that makes me angry. I was trying to tell you how I felt, and you shit all over everything." She heard a flash of anger in his voice. "And then you, well—"

"This is all—these are all new things for me. I hate everything in my life right now except you. It's hard for me to imagine how you could possibly want to be a part of that. I know that's unattractive. I know it makes me hard to be around." She looked down and swallowed, trying to ease the throbbing in her throat. "I need to like more than one thing about my life. Including myself. That's allegedly how it works."

"So you're just skipping town?"

"I'm going—home. To regroup." It was her turn to stop walking. She found a pebble of her own, swung her leg, made contact. "I really like you," she said. "And I'm really going to miss you."

She took a breath and looked up at him; something in his face relaxed her, made everything feel less dire. Maybe another person couldn't irrevocably save you, but they could sometimes calm you down, and that felt like an exquisitely magical thing.

She kissed him then. She stepped forward and moved her face toward his face, this elusive, intimate act that had only ever before been done *to* her. He moved from his bike rack and leaned in and touched his hand to her face, and for exactly 1.5 seconds she wondered *is this really happening* and then she decided *yes, it is.*

And Ben Barnes, bless his heart, kissed her back.

2014

Wendy was only dimly aware, as her husband died, of the fact that she wished she weren't alone. She was mostly distracted by the process itself—the surprising tedium of it, the number of times she'd shamefully harbored thoughts like *Why can't this just end already*—but occasionally it occurred to her that it might be nice to have another conscious person around, someone to sit with Miles when she had to pee, someone to bring her coffee and Cheetos and news from the outside world. Her parents had both fought hard to come and help her, but she'd resisted that without fully knowing why—because her father had never quite approved of Miles? Because the last time she and her mother had been in the hospital together was after Ivy, and they hadn't been that close since? Gracie was in Portland; Liza was in Philly. Which left Violet, the most logical candidate for company, but Violet—it still made her blood boil, thinking about it—had demurred, claiming that her obstetrician had said she shouldn't be in the cancer ward so late in her pregnancy. She'd been so stunned to hear her sister lie in this way that she didn't even fight her on it, didn't point out that cancer wasn't contagious, that pregnant women spent plenty of time in hospitals, that the hospital was the final destination for most pregnant women, the Mecca. Her sister was avoiding her, as she had when Ivy was born. Too fragile to endure anything beyond the spotless arrangement of her own life. Taking full advantage of the fact that the universe wasn't fucking her over in the way it was Wendy.

But all of these thoughts were distraction, she supposed. Easier to think about than Miles, who was nearly unrecognizable beside her in the bed, his body wasted and gray, put through the wringer again and again, his eyes sunken into the hollows above his cheekbones, his thready pulse visible through the thin skin of his neck. The doctor had been saying it could be any time for three days. He'd last awakened exactly a week ago, and he'd been surprisingly lucid, weak but coherent, and she'd been so excited to see him conscious that she'd made a joke about how one of his nurses looked like a sea horse, and then he'd dipped back into sleep, so that was the last thing she'd said to her husband. The last thing she would ever say to her husband. She was holding his hand now, palm up, tracing his lines with her finger. Those had stayed the same, despite everything. The meat of his palms was gone, wasted into nothing, but the lines were still there, their familiar crosshatch.

She maneuvered her way into the bed beside him, careful not to jab him with an elbow or a knee.

"I'm not sure how to do this without you," she said, feeling foolish. Her words reverberated across the empty room. She'd turned the lights off, left on only a lamp in the corner. She lowered her voice to a whisper. "I'm not sure what I'm supposed to do."

They'd taken him off of the respirator. She listened to his breathing.

"You're the best thing in my life. Sometimes I think I used up all of my luck when I met you." She paused. "Worth it, though, I'd say. Despite everything. Because you were around to get me through everything else. I'm not sure how to get through this. I'm not sure what you'd say if you could say something right now."

The pain of losing him had become physical to her in the last few days. There was an ache in her stomach that she almost couldn't stand, a soreness she stooped her body around.

"Thanks for letting me dig your gold," she said, which she knew would have made him laugh. "Thanks for impregnating me. Thanks for teaching me that the expression isn't 'for all *intensive* purposes.' Thanks for marrying me. Thanks for the time you made me come four times in a row."

He didn't smell like himself, hadn't smelled like himself for months. She pressed her nose into the folds of his pajamas, trying to find something familiar. A whiff of skin. It was there, still, and it made her start crying.

"Thanks for taking care of me," she said, then: "I'm trying to think of an inspirational song lyric. Want me to do my Neil Young voice?"

This would have made him laugh, too, so she laughed for him.

"I love you behemothically, Miles Eisenberg," she said. She curled herself around his body, rested her head in the concavity of his chest. She fell asleep holding him. When she woke up, he was gone.

The thing about her doctor was true. Maybe not medically true, but Violet had been told that it would be unwise to visit such a seriously sick person when she was weeks from her due date. They'd chosen someone kind of new-agey, and Violet liked her for the most part but bristled at some of her bedside manner— beyond counseling avoidance of the hospital, she made frequent use of the word *yoni* and could not understand Violet's aversion to having Matt massage her perineum with olive oil. The doctor had said something about radiation and chemicals on the cancer ward, and she couldn't shake the image of herself accidentally touching the wrong light switch and transmitting something toxic through her skin into her bloodstream, all the way to the baby, who would subsequently emerge with horns or with no life at all, a husk of a baby, like Wendy's. You weren't allowed to vocalize worries like these.

It was also true that she found the doctor's orders to be a relief. This was the shameful part. She was glad—*glad!*—to be given medical advice that exempted her from having to be so close to death when her child was so close to being born. Another unforgivable thing.

But still she checked on her sister. That was something. She sent Wendy text messages, and she made brief phone calls—*daily*, always, despite the mundane but constant demands of her life. She kept this up until one night it wasn't her bladder that woke her but their landline. And she'd gone immediately. She left Wyatt with Matt and she drove to Hyde Park and she arrived at Wendy's house hours after Miles had died. And then, even then, when she'd arrived at Wendy's door, her sister had sighed and said, "Jesus, are you dramatic."

So it was Violet, not Wendy, the widow, who was weeping into their mother's arms later that night. It was Violet, after having been politely rejected from entering her sister's brownstone, who decided to drive to the house on Fair Oaks instead of all the way back up to Evanston, crying through the dodginess of Chicago Avenue between Kedzie and Austin, who practically fell through the door of her parents' house and collapsed into her mother's arms.

"I know, honey," her mom said. She made them some tea and Violet lay curled up on the couch with her head in her mother's lap.

"She wouldn't even *see* me," she said, whimpering. "I did—I'm doing the best I can."

"Calm down, love. Of course you are."

She intermittently cried and flirted with falling asleep against the warm, dusty sweetness of her mother's bathrobe.

"It was— My doctor said I shouldn't. I know that sounds— I know it's terrible but I—"

Her mom was smoothing a hand slowly, heavily, rhythmically over her hair. "It's not terrible," she said. "Violet, it sounds human and it's not terrible, all right? We do things for our family. You're looking out for yourself and your baby. There's nothing wrong with that."

"Did she let *you* come over to her house?"

"Just for a few minutes."

"Her own *mother*?" she said, indignant now, foolish with exhaustion.

"Your sister's been dealt a rough hand," her mother said, and before Violet could tell her that she'd heard that particular statement a hundred thousand times, she continued. "Pick your battles, sweetie, okay? You've got a lovely life." She patted Violet's belly. "You've got a beautiful little one on the way. Everyone's healthy. Focus on that."

She supposed her mother was simply trying to be optimistic— it was one of her more irritating traits—but something about the statement rubbed Violet the wrong way. Should she apologize for having a life so unmarred by tragedy? Should she feel sorry for the fact that she'd happened upon such *lovely* circumstances? Not to mention her own struggles, all the cherished parts of herself she'd sacrificed in order to build her lovely life.

"I just don't think it's fair that—"

"Darling." Marilyn's voice was colder, though she rested a hand on Violet's shoulder. "Your sister's just lost her husband. Let's give her a few days, okay?"

CHAPTER THIRTY-THREE

Marilyn had gone to yoga while pregnant with Grace, had adjusted the household bedtime so she got enough sleep, had choked down the vitamins she'd evaded the first three times around. And what did any of it matter anymore, really, because Grace was smoking on the roof just like the other kids had done, having just undulated her way back home on the waves of a major lie.

"Goose," she called, careful not to startle Gracie into falling off of the eave. "Come down here, please." She'd been stunned into speechlessness when their daughter had called to confess, when she'd revealed to them that she'd fabricated nearly a full year of made-up classes and fake ski vacations and fictional friends; she'd been at an utter loss for words until Grace finished recounting her duplicity, and then she'd said, "You get on a plane and get home *immediately*, Grace Sorenson," and she wished, for the first time, that David had given their lastborn a middle name, so that she could invoke it to more dramatic maternal effect.

Grace had arrived home last night, thin and jittery—"Huck Finn!" Wendy had greeted her—and then Wendy had stolen her away for dinner, presumably sparing Grace from their parental wrath for a few more hours. Grace had returned home at midnight and gone straight to bed. Now it was nearly noon, and Gracie padded barefoot onto the porch, a little vagabond who reeked of tobacco. Marilyn raised an eyebrow at her, patted the space beside her on the glider.

"You've always come to us," she said, trying to remain even-keeled despite her anger and her bafflement. "When you were having a hard time, you always— We've been here for you, haven't we? I just don't understand why you wouldn't . . ."

"I didn't want you to be disappointed in me. And you had so much else going on."

"The only times I'm ever disappointed in any of you are when you're deliberately doing things you know aren't in your best interest. Dad and I don't care if you go to law school or *clown* college, Gracie. Washburne Trade School. Haven't we made that clear?"

"Well, yeah, but like . . ."

"What?"

"I mean you gave me a lot of *attention.*"

She frowned. "I'm sorry, is that—a bad thing?"

"I just mean I've always been under more scrutiny than everyone else. Because you had more—time. To pay attention to me."

"So we didn't neglect you enough," she said dryly. There was no such thing as winning, as a parent.

"No, it's not— I didn't want to scare you. I feel terrible about what a disaster we all are. Wendy's like Miss Havisham. Violet was living a *way* bigger lie than I was when she was my age, and now she's just, like, this weird pod person. And Liza's basically a single mom. You and Dad are the only people in this family who have it figured out."

It struck her how universal this particular take on her marriage seemed to be, among all of her daughters, Gillian, her father-in-law: everyone that mattered on the outside assumed that she and David were bulletproof. Her kids would never fully understand her, just as she'd never fully understood her own parents and just as she, in close proximity to this girl, once a tiny baby who'd grown inside her body, would never fully understand her kids.

"It's okay to not know what you want," she said. "You're still so young. You can stay here for as long as you need, and you can figure out what's next and get your act together and think about what you've been doing for the last year. But the lying has to stop, Grace. It's a surefire way to guarantee your own unhappiness." She opened an arm to her daughter, half-expecting to be spurned. But Gracie tucked herself against Marilyn's side, like she'd done when she was little.

"I didn't even mean to— You know how sometimes things just happen?"

Marilyn closed her eyes, memorizing, as ever, the part in her daughter's hair. "Yes, I'm familiar."

The screen door opened, a rusty squeak, and David appeared. Beside her, Gracie curled her knees to her chest to make room for him on the glider.

"How worried are we about Gracie?" Marilyn asked him in bed that night. "One to ten."

"I don't know. Seven?"

"Seven's *high*."

"I'm generally at about a five with her, though, so you have to look at it relatively." When he'd gone to collect Grace at the baggage claim the day before he'd wanted to cry, because while it seemed like she'd aged years since she'd last been home, she also still looked so young, as wide-eyed and vulnerable as ever. His fury—at the way she'd denied them the only thing they'd ever asked of her, the *truth*—was replaced by sadness, which rested alongside his concern and his moderate irritation that she'd asked, once they were on Mannheim headed toward home, as though he were picking her up for a normal school break, if they could stop at Johnnie's Beef for Italian ice.

"Just when I was starting to feel so *smug* about everything," Marilyn said.

"Pride cometh before the fall."

"We've happened upon the nesting dolls of parenting," Marilyn said. "Every time we wash our hands of one, another materializes with a pack of Camels."

"That's the danger of mass-producing children, I guess."

"You were right," she said.

"Thanks," he replied. "About what?"

"About the fact that we're never going to—you know. Reach the finish line. With the kids. There's always going to be something."

They lay in silence for a few minutes, listening to the house settle, to the wind outside.

"I was thinking," he said.

"Were you?" She smiled. He could tell she was tired. "What about?"

"As long as we're still going full-throttle with the rest of the kids, I thought I might talk to Liza." He always felt nervous when proposing new ideas to his wife, not because she judged him but because she tended to support him wholeheartedly, advancing seeds of thought into full-grown blooms practically before the conversation was over. Marilyn got things done. If you ran something by her, you had to be prepared to do it. "I thought I might see if she could use a babysitter for the fall semester."

Marilyn's face lit up and she seized one of his hands, squeezing it to her chest. *"Really?"*

"I heard that degenerate girl next door with the big spikes in her ears was looking for work," he said, and Marilyn kicked his shin gently under the blankets.

"Honey, ask her. *Ask* her. Do it now. That's a terrific idea.

Call her. Sweetheart, she'll be *thrilled*. She's been so anxious about going back to work. Call her now. Where's your phone?"

"It's almost midnight, kid. Slow your roll."

"Slow my *roll*?"

"Gracie said it earlier. Bit of disaffected youth-speak."

"Well, call her in the morning, then. Will you? I think it's a fabulous plan."

It was sort of funny, if you thought about it, this poetic reversal of roles: his wife cycling off to work each morning at the hardware store while he spent his days swimming in the dull minutiae of babyhood. They weren't so old after all, were they?

"You're wonderful with the babies," she continued. "It'll be— I mean, tedious is an understatement; ask anyone. Ask Violet. Ask Lize. Ask *me*, if you don't feel I've adequately briefed you over the last forty years. But it'll be abbreviated. I'm guessing Lize is going to want to spend as much time at home with her as possible. And you'd be doing her such a favor, David; you'd be giving her such a gift."

"Well, not a gift. Do you think thirty-five dollars an hour is a fair asking wage?"

"Don't downplay this, honey."

"Think I can handle it?"

She smiled at him. "There's not a doubt in my mind."

He found her confidence deeply touching. He thought of her desperation in those early days, her panic and her disappointment, the paint fumes in the kitchen.

"But it made you miserable," he said without thinking.

Marilyn looked hurt. "No, it didn't."

"I mean, sometimes, didn't it?"

She let go of his hand and turned onto her back. "Sometimes, sure. I was in over my head, and I was exhausted to the point of insanity, but I—I mean, of course I was. But it was also—immensely gratifying, sometimes."

"I know this isn't the same thing."

She smiled faintly. "No, it's not."

"I didn't mean to say you were miserable," he said.

"Not hardly. It was a blast, day in and day out."

His turn to smile. "I just know that there were things you might rather have been doing."

"Is that ever not the case?" She sounded tired again.

"No, I guess not."

"It would be a good thing for you and for Liza. And especially for Kit. I'm sure you're wildly preferable to a daycare at a public university."

"Gee, thanks." He nudged her. "Did I offend you?"

She sighed. "Oh, a little. It's silly, though. I know what you meant."

"The girls and I are lucky to have you."

"Yes, they all turned out so flawlessly," she said. She sighed. "Jesus *Christ.*"

"I mean it," he said.

She faced him again and kissed him. "Sweet man."

He moved closer to her, slipped his hand beneath the back of her shirt and pulled her against him.

"Hey," she said, moving back to look at him. "I'm proud of you."

The word still meant so much to him, coming from her.

2014

Wendy had expected—*hoped*, perhaps—that Violet and Matt's new home would be located in an undesirable part of Evanston, but the house in front of which the cab deposited her—to bring her car was to commit to sobriety, which she couldn't bring herself to do, not when Violet was involved—was smack in the middle of a dense thatch of elm trees and mere blocks from the lake and stately and imposing and fabulous. Probably at least a couple million. It made her want to throw up. She considered slipping the driver a fifty and asking him to drive around for a few minutes while she smoked a cigarette, but then the front door opened and Violet appeared, ponytailed and smiling, kid on her hip.

"Thanks, Alan," she muttered to the driver. "May the rest of your day suck less than mine." He let her out and left her standing alone with Violet, who reached out with her free arm to hug her. Since when did Violet *hug*? She could feel her sister's bones through the thin, expensive knit of her summer-weight cashmere. Eli was—what? Four months? Five? How was she so skinny already? She'd been keeping a low profile for months—God, since Miles had died, twenty-six weeks ago to the day—and she'd been avoiding Violet more than anyone else, consenting to shopping trips on the Mag Mile when Gracie was home for break and attending tepid dinners at her parents' house but not much else. She'd ditched Matt and Violet's housewarming party last month and finally consented to this makeup only because Violet had threatened to bring the kids over to her house if she didn't.

"I'm so happy you're here," Violet said. She reeked of money and Kiehl's and suburbia. "You look wonderful. Wyatt's making you a sign as we speak."

"A sign?" Violet was making her feel huge and clumsy and inarticulate, the urban ogre who had emerged from her spinster cabin to make the rounds in the North Shore.

"A welcome sign," Violet said. "He's so excited to see you. So's this one, aren't you, babycakes?" She jostled Eli. He appraised her in the blank, unforgiving way of babies. "He's starving; he'll perk up in a little bit. Come in, come in. Wy? Buddy? Guess who's here?"

Her nephew appeared in the entryway of the kitchen bearing a piece of poster board larger than he was that read WELCOME WENDY in a messy spewing of glitter glue, the lack of punctuation giving it an air of comical indifference. "Hi," he said shyly, ducking behind the sign.

"Hey, Sheriff," she said. She liked this kid; he was thoughtful and funny and he had kind eyes. "Did you make that for me?" She nodded at his sign. "Or is there another Wendy coming over?"

Wyatt looked to his mother with concern, making sure. Violet winked at him, nodding.

"It's for you," he said.

"It's fabulous," she said. "It's the most spectacular sign anyone's ever made for me."

He brightened and then faltered. "It's not done yet. I'm just finishing the stickers." He hugged the board to his little body and skittered away from whence he'd come.

When she turned around she was confronted head-on by

Violet's exposed breast; her sister was sitting at the dining room table with her shirt lifted for the baby.

"Jesus *fuck*," she said, and Violet looked up at her, blunted and dazed, like a panda.

"What?" The baby latched on and Wendy turned her head away sharply.

"Oh my God, Violet, you have a *guest*."

It amused her a little, thinking that there were people on the earth who would reply to that with "You're not a *guest*; you're family." But being a guest trumped blood relation in their family, and so she was allowed to be a little pissy if she wanted, because she otherwise did not have anything resembling the upper hand. This small victory pleased her.

Violet opened her mouth and closed it again. She glanced down at the baby as though she were doing something workaday and normal, filling her gas tank or renewing her library books. Wendy couldn't help but voyeuristically delight in the silvery stretch marks that fleeced her sister's breast, the way that, unclothed, she looked less like perfection and more like a PSA.

But Violet was still so lovely. She looked at peace, half-naked in her cavernous dining room, providing sustenance to a skeptical infant. Violet, annoying as she was, could pull shit together. She was beautiful and capable and tranquil in a way that almost made Wendy feel dizzy. And her house smelled like jasmine.

"I got yelled at in a Starbucks last week," Violet said. "I'm a little sensitive."

"Well, he's kind of *old*, isn't he?" she asked. Violet cradled the baby closer. In truth, Eli still looked microscopic. She couldn't remember his birthday. She didn't know when it was appropriate for a person to stop breastfeeding; she'd shoved all of that knowledge out of her mind after Ivy. Wyatt was lurking in

the doorway with his stickers, and it seemed vaguely untoward that he was so comfortable with the sight of his mother's
exposed rack.

"We've talked about weaning but it's hard," Violet said.
"With his schedule."

She snorted. "Is he, like, a broker or something?"

Violet looked at her in a tired, bothered way that reminded
her of their mother. "It's harder than it looks, okay?" she said,
and though something in her voice bespoke a real kind of sadness, Wendy chose instead to be offended. It was something
you were allowed to do when all of the most important people
in your life had died.

"Yeah, I suppose I wouldn't have any idea, would I?" she
asked, slapping down the trump card. It was needlessly hostile;
she was a little embarrassed for herself.

"I'm sorry, Wendy." It was too easy with Violet. It was far
too effortless to get exactly what you wanted from her. "That
was a stupid thing to say. I'm tired. Forgive me."

"You don't *look* tired," she said, giving Violet something in
return. A seesaw, this sisterhood, and Wendy was the jerk who
jumped off early so the other person toppled into the sand.

Violet laughed, and whatever was askew had been righted.
"Well, that's blessedly kind of you to say. I got a facial yesterday. I was hoping it helped." Perhaps that was it: expensive self-
care. Something about her sister looked eerily different—her
face was the same, her body, but there was a shift in the way
she carried herself, in the way she seemed to be willing her face
into every expression it made.

Wyatt brought in his sign and Eli finished nursing and Violet rose to give her a tour of the house, which nearly made her
heave—it was so huge, so bright and open and orderly, artistic but not in a weird way, the house of normal, tasteful rich
people.

"There's the library; there's Matt's guitar room; there's the little tree house, I won't let Wy go in it yet, Matt says he's old enough but I can just see him falling out of one of those windows, can't you?" It was like a very boring episode of *Cribs*. Violet cracked open another door. "There's my office," she said.

Even Wendy couldn't get away with asking, *What the fuck do you need an office for?* so instead she chose a more diplomatic phrasing. "Are you working again?"

Violet looked a little sad. "I mean—not—not *practicing*, no." She swallowed. "But this is my space for—you know, pay-ing the bills, managing the boys' schedules and"—at this she blushed—"doing things for the preschool. Listen, I'm desper-ate to pee; can you take him for just a minute?" Violet pressed Eli suddenly into her arms and she held him awkwardly, arm's length away from her body. This kid she knew so little about. Dressed in a onesie with a necktie screen-printed on it. Healthy and perfectly formed.

It was all so simple for Violet; it was all so nauseatingly effortless. Her sister was, as always, so fucking *calm*, confi-dent that life would have her back and that everything was just *natural*. Wesleyan, the adoption, law school, Matt, the bar exam, marriage: *everything* was just *happening*. Things *hap-pened* to her sister, and the fact that they were happening to her seemed to be enough for Violet. She required no external stim-ulation because she was a knockout with an advanced degree and a dorky husband who probably ate her out on command, and everything that happened to her was just *life*. Violet took things in stride, Wendy had to hand it to her; but it always seemed kind of put-on, like *Oops, life's amazing*. Meanwhile, Violet treated Wendy like a piece of glassware, an antique beer stein that was very old, very ugly, and very breakable. But there were plenty of times—*most* times, really—that Wendy had not called her sister for help. She'd spared Violet from so much and her sister couldn't help but shove her fulfillment in her face.

At Violet's wedding, not long after they'd lost Ivy, she'd

passed out, inexplicably, on the couch in her father's study, and Miles had carried her to the car and taken her home. Violet had left the next morning for her honeymoon in Greece, and then she came back and worked at her impressive job and then she got pregnant and they had Wyatt and all of the chips kept landing precisely where they were supposed to land.

The baby squirmed, being held up in the air like he was, and she was forced to bring him closer to her, to rest him on her canted hip. "Hi," she said, trying. "Hey, there."

He felt strange, like a damp pile of laundry. He smelled nice, though, like Dreft and sleep and the subtle perfume Violet had worn since college. The last kid she'd really held for any significant amount of time was Grace. She'd been good with her, when she was feeling giving enough to allow her mother the satisfaction of help, would wake up in the night sometimes before their parents heard Grace crying and wander around the house with her, whispering stories into her uncomprehending ears, *Spencer Stallings is the dumbest person on the earth but he's so hot, Goose*, and *See this table? This table is from a hundred years ago; that's three hundred times as old as you.* She tried bouncing Eli, and he smiled at her, a dazzling baby smile, and reached for her necklace, taking it in a tiny fist.

"Isn't that a beautiful necklace?" she said. "Isn't it, mister?" He laughed, a great gremlin laugh, and she felt herself laughing too. "I know," she said. "I'm a riot." Her eyes drifted to a frightening calendar over Violet's desk, one that was the size of an overhead projector screen and color-coded, it appeared, by family member, Matt in blue and Wyatt in red and Eli in green, and Violet, appropriately, cloyingly, in purple. *Vinyasa. Shady Oaks Fun Run. Dr. Jacobi. Bongos by the Boatyard. Park day w/ Wilhelmina and Grayson.* It was like another language, the language of a crazy person, a boring, well-tended-to crazy person. She hoped, for Violet's sake, that Dr. Jacobi was a shrink.

"Careful with your necklace. He's hell-bent on destruction lately."

Eli turned at the sound of his mother's voice. The simple science of it made her ache. "Aren't you, little terrorist?" He reached out for Violet, suddenly straining against Wendy when seconds earlier he'd been so content. Everyone liked Violet more than they liked her. "I think I just heard Matt," Violet said, and she led the way back downstairs.

"Are there guys *and* gals in my house tonight?" Matt's voice rang out from the kitchen and she saw Violet lighten at the sound of it. "Wendy, hey, welcome." She watched as he went over to Violet. "Hi, honey." He leaned in close and kissed her.

Wendy looked away.

"Hi, love," Violet said.

She looked back in time to see Violet lift her face to kiss him again, then hand off the baby to him. "Wendy, some wine?"

"God, yes."

Matt was laughably bland—not even milquetoast, she'd joked once, but like a piece of bread that you *intend* to toast, but you forget to turn the toaster on—but it still made her insides twist when she saw him rolling up his shirtsleeves like Miles used to, one of the absolute sexiest pedestrian things a man could ever do, in her opinion. The baby looked even tinier against Matt, impossibly fair against the thatches of dark hair on his forearms. Wyatt appeared again, summoned from his picturesque playroom by the sound of his father's voice.

"*Daddy,*" he said.

"As we live and breathe," Violet murmured from over by the fridge.

"The *monster,*" Matt said, and she watched as he hefted Wyatt up using his free arm and pretended to gnaw at his shoulder. Wyatt squealed with laughter; her gut throbbed. "How did you get past the guards, huh?" Being in such close physical proximity to a man with such big, capable arms was enough to make her need to sit down. The man she was currently sleeping with, a young financial analyst named Todd, was blond and reedy, pleasurably fox-like in bed but unimpressive in his street clothes. Violet brought her an enormous glass of wine, nearly two times a normal ration, and she looked up with amusement, grateful for this break from the unbearable lovefest happening in her peripheral vision.

"Is it passé to make *Desperate Housewives* jokes? Jesus. So this is how you get through the day."

Violet blanched, then blushed, white to red. It was a cruel thing to say, maybe; judging by the look on Matt's face it was *definitely* a cruel thing to say. "We're celebrating," Violet said weakly after a moment, going to pour her own glass. "Honey," she said to Matt, and something in her voice changed. "I said we'd do the food for the pre-K open house next week; it's seven to ten on Tuesday so remember to be home on time. And Jax's birthday party is on Sunday at the pottery-painting place and I'd *really* love if you'd come with; I think a lot of dads are going to be there. I fixed that light in Wyatt's bathroom too. Oh! And I built the bookshelf while Eli was napping. It looks good, I think. You might have to check and see if all the screws are tight enough; I started to get that same backache before I finished. I might go to the chiropractor again next week."

If she wasn't mistaken, this domestic catalog was being recited for her. It was how Violet got her digs in—artfully, through the unassuming shields of other people.

And then her sister turned to her, swept over in her size-4 Sevens and her practical, stylish Sperry Top-Siders, and her frozen face had configured into something distinctly unkind.

"Cheers to desperate housewifery," she said, clinking her own full glass against Wendy's. She went over and kissed her husband again—her husband, who had seemed bored by her talk of bookshelves and back pain but who perked up at this intimate act. She took the baby and kissed his head and took a slug of wine, fixing her gaze on Wendy, buoyed on all sides by the undeniable aesthetic perfection of her circumstance. "It's really not so bad."

It wasn't fair that Violet got to live this life, that Violet got an able-bodied man who loved and took care of her, that her own body produced child after healthy child, that her house had a *guitar room*, that she was pretty much guaranteed to never be alone again. And it especially wasn't fair that Violet seemed unwilling to acknowledge any of this, to be grateful for the fact that she was doing okay when Wendy had been so cosmically fucked. That she was content enough with her superior standing in life that she could make jokes about it while canoodling with her husband in front of her recently widowed sister, the sister who had made her good life possible in the first place and would never, ever have what Violet had, despite all the money in the world. That Violet was apparently just fine with shedding any pretense of humility about how goddamn lucky she was.

This was why the next day Wendy called her attorney and asked whether he knew any private investigators, money no object, someone who could circumvent sealed adoption records.

CHAPTER THIRTY-FOUR

"It's kind of sad, isn't it?" Marilyn asked, beside him on the back stairs, voice barely audible beneath the whir of chainsaws. One of the biggest branches fell from the ginkgo, and David flinched.

He studied the atrophied bark, the familiar patch of grass beneath it. So odd, how well acquainted you could become with the physical details of your life without even realizing. If you'd asked him to recall, from a distance, the pattern of the exposed roots and the paltry sprinkling of tulips that encircled the trunk, he wouldn't have been able to tell you, but staring at it now was like looking at the complicated map of veins on his own hand, a visual memory that made his eyes well up.

It wasn't quite melancholy, what he was feeling. It was more mathematical than that, more of an itemization of intangible things, his life with his wife, the ground they'd covered together, how he still felt a little like he had when they'd lain beneath the ginkgo on that cold night in December: astonished by the fact of her presence alongside him.

"You okay?" she asked him, leaning her head against his shoulder. She'd been like this since the heart attack, constantly aware of how close they'd come to losing this life they'd built. It pained him a little to see the way she looked at him lately—

the way all of them looked at him, like he could expire at any moment. Old Tenterhooks, he'd called her, jokingly, last week, but she hadn't found it funny. Astonishing, also: the fact that he was still here to be beside her, watching the tree come down.

He wrapped his arm around her. "I'm very much okay, kid."

Between their two sets of parents, only his father had grown old enough to contemplate his impending obsolescence. What would Marilyn's dad think if he could see them here, weatherworn, the two kids he'd caught in flagrante now older than he'd ever been? He thought of making a joke—*the Dago prevails* or some such—but it struck him as unkind, and plus— he remembered—of course she wasn't following the train of thought inside his head, at least not to that degree of specificity. The landscapers were going at the trunk now, notching it deeply in specific areas so it would fall where there was only flat lawn. He felt Marilyn tense beneath his arm, then relax, angling her head more snugly against him, closing her eyes to the show before them, like when they'd be carrying in the girls from the car and they'd tuck their sleeping eyes away from the light.

His best friend, the most wonderful surprise life had ever lobbed his way.

"I am so unspeakably glad you're here with me," she said, and her breath warmed his chest, and his eyes filled, because the statement was not, upon reflection, so very different from his train of thought after all.

Violet couldn't recall a time when she'd actually, formally apologized to her sister. It wasn't how they operated. She was professionally averse to linguistically accepting blame, and it seemed as though it had never occurred to Wendy to say she was sorry for anything. In the elevator on her way up to the thirty-sixth floor, Violet nursed a renewed anger over this, anger tinged with envy, because going through life unburdened by guilt actually sounded pretty nice. They hadn't spoken, not really, since their phone call after Wendy had kicked Jonah out. They'd both thawed slightly when their father was in the hospital, but only for the purposes of civility, of not further upsetting their mother, of bonding, on some level, in order to karmically encourage David's recovery. It had been Matt who'd convinced her that she needed to make things right, who'd reminded her that Wendy was as much a part of things as she or Jonah; who'd acknowledged—setting aside his own reservations about her sister—that the only way she or Wendy would ever be able to truly move forward was if they cleared the air. She'd almost turned around a dozen times on her way, and she considered it once more as the elevator dinged open, but Wendy was already waiting in her doorway.

"Speak of the sacred," she said, "and she shall appear."

Violet could not assess her sister's level of levity. "You were talking about me?"

"Nope."

"Then how did you—"

"Jesus, the doorman buzzed me." Wendy ushered her inside. "Come in, I guess. Though it behooves me to point out that if I ever showed up at your house uninvited you'd have me tasered."

"Is now a bad time?"

"Not in the grand scheme."

She was half-annoyed and half-relieved that her sister had adopted this tonal affectation, speaking theatrically like some kind of genie. "I figured—you know, it was about time we talked about some things. Cleared the air."

"Great," Wendy said. "I love entertaining the emotionally maligned."

She relaxed at this. She wasn't going to have to apologize. She would allow Wendy the same courtesy. There was a relief in this stuntedness, the pleasant familiarity of your same old fucked-up family of origin.

"I've actually stopped drinking during the week, but the notion of being trapped alone in a room with you sober makes me want to decapitate myself," Wendy said. "No offense."

She poured them both wine and they went out onto the patio, Violet curling up cross-legged on the loveseat and looking out over the city, the swoosh of cars down Delaware and the arresting glitter of the lake. "How've you been?" she asked.

Wendy eyed her coolly. "Magnificent."

"Me too," she said, when Wendy didn't ask. "Things are actually really good."

"That's fucking great for you. A return to form."

"Wendy, I'm trying."

"Trying to *what*?"

"To—I don't know, to talk to you. To fix things."

"What does that even mean? Look how easy it was for you to just write me out of your life. We've never been *fixed*. I've resented you since you were born and you're perpetually high on the fact that your life's like a hundred thousand times better than mine."

"That's not true."

"You're also perpetually in denial about anything that doesn't look how you want it to."

"Jesus, Wendy, aren't I the one who's supposed to be angry?" She had never felt fully entitled to her emotions, not alongside her sister, who wore them proudly and impulsively. "Aren't you the one who fucked things up bringing Jonah back into the picture unannounced? Then kicking him out?"

"I fucked up one thing with him," Wendy said. "You fucked him over from day one."

This, of course, was what Matt knew she'd be facing if she tried to clean things up. Wendy had always been able to cut right to the heart, but she knew she had to steel herself against it now, to withstand her sister's venom in order to inhabit the new level ground she and Matt had decided to exist on. "That's really an awful thing to—"

"I ran into Aaron Bhargava when Dad was in the hospital. He said to say hi to you."

She nearly choked. She felt as she had on the beach on Mercer Island, gut-punched. *Not now.* She had never expected anything less than she'd expected this, not even when she'd shown up at the restaurant last spring and seen the back of Jonah's head.

"Jonah got his eyes."

She opened her mouth to say something but managed only a sharp intake of breath.

"The hypocrisy," Wendy said. "Jesus."

"I didn't— I was going to—"

"Is that what you're supposed to do to your sisters? Fuck their exes and then let them host you in their homes while you gestate and put the resulting children up for adoption?"

"We were so young," Violet said. It had been another life-time, that time, truly, regardless of how much it sounded like a line. They'd been different people, young and untarnished and stupid. She as much wanted to lay that era to rest as she genuinely couldn't remember it, couldn't recall what it had felt like to be the person she'd been.

"We weren't that fucking young. Jesus Christ. It's not like you took my fucking lipstick. You let me be there for you and you didn't even have the decency to be honest with me. And then you didn't even— God, I've been so royally *fucked*, Violet, and you didn't—"

"It's not like I *knew* what things were going to happen to you. And things going well for me has nothing to do with how they turned out for—"

"You didn't *ever* show up when I needed you, is what I was going to say, actually," Wendy said. Her voice was level and unadorned.

"Wendy, that's not—" But it was true. "You know, it's funny; I— Mom always used to tell me what a little caretaker I was when I was a kid."

"I remember," Wendy said. "It was super fucking irritating."

"I'm not sure what happened to me." Her voice wobbled. "I think I—I guess I just sort of shut down, when Jonah was born. I didn't have anything left to give."

"That's a cop-out," Wendy said. "It's not like they hand out little baggies of compassion at the outset and you have to ration it over the course of your life. You have to will yourself through the shit, Violet. Take one for the team on occasion. Like, for instance, when you've just lost a child and you're forced to put on a brave face for your little sister's wedding."

"It wasn't— God, Wendy, almost a *year* had gone by."

"Or," Wendy continued, sipping her wine, "when your sister's found out that you fucked her ex-boyfriend and he sired the baby you gave away, and she confronts you about that massive betrayal, and you muster up the strength to *not* be a total asshole who splits hairs about how closely on the heels of her stillbirth you decided to plan your wedding. That would be another example of taking one for the team."

"I think we allow ourselves to hurt the people we love the most because we know they won't abandon us." She couldn't help, sometimes, speaking in platitudes. They existed for a reason. And they came to her with more ease than anything else.

But Wendy, of course, wasn't having it. "Ah, tell me, please; what's the socioemotional wellness podcast du jour that you yanked that one from?"

"I'm just saying that when you've loved each other forever," she said, "like, literally, your whole life, you know it's harder to burn that bridge than it is to shore up the foundations."

"Christ, are you coming on to me? Also, I don't think that's, like, architecturally true." Wendy paused. "Were you ever going to tell me?"

"Yes, actually," Violet said. "Someday."

"Are you ever going to tell Jonah?"

"I haven't gotten—quite that far yet."

"What if I were to tell him?"

She looked up. "Wendy. Please. That's not— You wouldn't—"

"I'm fucking with you," Wendy said. "I actually like that kid a whole lot. I wouldn't traumatize him just to piss you off. He asked me about his dad when he was first staying with me. And I thought it was that sketchy Salad Fingers guy from Wesleyan. I still didn't tell him any specific details." Wendy paused. "Out of *respect* for you, because *at the time* I didn't realize you'd fucked my boyfriend."

"It was the worst thing I'd ever done," Violet said. "That's why I—I think part of me was trying to punish myself. By having the baby."

"You should've just gotten shitfaced and said a few Hail Marys like the rest of us. But if you had, I guess the little sensei wouldn't be here, so, you know."

She looked up at Wendy, hearing the surprising kindness in her voice.

"I honestly don't even— It's less about the fact that you slept with him and more, like, I more just think it's weird and shitty that you never *told* me," Wendy said. "I'm not even that angry. We'd been broken up for forever at that point; it's not like I— Aaron wasn't the person I was meant to be with. I knew that the minute I met Miles."

She saw, then, that Wendy's insertion of her husband into every conversation, no matter how seemingly irrelevant, had less to do with martyrdom than it did with love, with her sister's end-all, infinite love for the man she'd lost. That Wendy was, of course, in a great deal of pain, and probably always would be. "I'm sorry," she said softly.

"I don't think I've ever heard you say that before," Wendy said.

Her constant companion, guilty of everything and nothing. Matt had been correct in his assessment that both of them would be better off if they aired their grievances. To air culpability, to exchange apologies, to own up, together, to what they'd set into motion.

Wendy rose to get the bottle of wine. "You know what I've always wondered?" She topped off their glasses. "Do you think I was in the room when you were conceived?"

She met Wendy's eyes and she felt such wild relief at the mirth she found behind them.

"I could've been in their *bed*, even," Wendy said. "Have you ever thought about that?"

"That's disgusting."

Wendy dropped beside her onto the couch and brought her glass to her lips, smiling wickedly. "It's totally plausible. I wouldn't put anything past the two of them. They're probably at it right now."

"*Stop* it," she said, laughing. But then she remembered how Wendy had opened their conversation. "You've resented me since I was born?"

"You usurped my throne."

"But I mean it's not like I *asked* to be— I mean, God, don't you feel lucky that we got to grow up together? It hasn't been easy for me to not have you in my life, Wendy. I've missed you." She was reasonably certain she'd never said those words to her sister, either, and she was sadistically pleased to see that Wendy looked startled. "Have you—missed me?"

Wendy met her gaze evenly. "Sure," she said. "Sometimes."

She knew she wasn't going to get more than that, and also that getting it was monumental, coming from Wendy.

"I'd like to have you in my life again," Violet said. "If you'd like to be in it."

"Christ, you're dramatic."

"I'm sorry there have been times I wasn't there for you. I've been—having a hard time. Lately, and—for a while, I guess. I don't know. I put a lot of pressure on myself, Wendy, and it—it's harder than it looks, all right?"

"You've said that before. Do you realize how fucking sanctimonious that sounds?"

"I just don't feel like you've ever given me credit for how hard I try."

"Why am I responsible for giving you credit? Isn't that what your husband is for?"

"You're my closest friend, Wendy."

At this, Wendy laughed, loudly, but she didn't deny it.

"Isn't it okay to just call it? You've been the most important person in my life since I was born. We're—reliant on each other, are we not?"

Wendy didn't answer her question, didn't speak, in fact, until sometime later, and only then in order to respond to a comment that Violet made about how it felt like spring was finally coming; in the time between those things, the two of them sat, watching the dusky haze settle around them over the city, everything and nothing feeling like it might be okay, two lost girls watching the sky darken like they'd done on the roof of the house on Fair Oaks, sisters, Irish twins, contingent products of their parents, back before they realized that nobody ever had any idea what the fuck she was doing, just a couple of young women looking into the future, back in that nice soft space where they fit seamlessly together, way back before the world had grown so much larger than their grasp.

THE MIDST OF LIFE

December 10, 2017
Eight months later

"Did you hear Mr. Calhoun died?"

"Who?"

"The black history teacher."

Marilyn listened from the doorway, her daughters united, *ig*nited; everyone at the big table in the dining room, two leaves in the middle to accommodate them all.

"He wasn't the black history teacher."

"Yes he was."

"Oh my God, no he wasn't. I think he taught debate."

She went over to Grace and pressed a kiss into the top of her head. "You make sure nobody kills anyone else, all right, Goose?" And Grace smiled up at her, tranquil and tolerant, like the little Buddhist baby she'd once been, lording over the dinner table in her high chair.

It was almost mid-December, but it was the only time everyone had been available at once. Second Thanksgiving. She went back into the kitchen to tend to the turkey.

·   ·   ·

"No," Violet was saying. "He taught black history."

Wendy, who was only conservatively tipsy, was delighted to have regained the ability to fight with her sister in a way that wasn't fraught or loaded, and she sat back, arms folded, and appraised Violet. "That's racist," she said, and in her peripheral vision she saw Liza roll her eyes.

Violet scoffed. "How is that racist?"

"Because he was *black*. Just because you're black doesn't mean you automatically teach black history."

"But he *did*. It's not racist to say that if he actually was black and taught black history."

"Mr. Calhoun wasn't black; Mr. *Whiteman* was black."

"Now who's racist?"

On bad days, and from a close vantage point, Wendy's life could still be objectively described as jacked-up as all get-out, but she was trying, willfully, to stop letting the miasma take over. She'd never thought it would happen, but she found herself growing used to the oddity, letting it brand her benignly like a tattoo or a scar. Some people said it took a year for things to go back to normal. It had now, since Miles had died, been more than three, and she was beginning to accept that, for her, things would be indefinitely weird. She'd hosted Thanksgiving dinner for her parents and Gracie and Jonah at her place two weeks ago, when Liza was visiting Ryan's weird wind farm with the baby and Violet was hosting her own in-laws; Wendy had made craft cocktails with bourbon in honor of her grandfather and ordered takeout for everyone from Tavern on Rush. There were worse fates. There were still pockets of potential in her life; she was aware of this now in a way that she hadn't been previously. Shit got weird if she stopped to dwell on her capital-P Prospects: that she would never again find love like she'd found with Miles; that she didn't even *want* to; that her lack of college education would limit her in terms of professional endeavors; that she refused to be one of those sad-sack old botoxed ladies who started college in their fifties; that your memories of people began to loosen with time, even if you'd loved those people more than anyone else on the planet; that Miles was sometimes a blur to her unless she looked at his picture and that she could no longer conjure the complete image of her daughter in her arms, but that she remembered her perfect tiny face, every centimeter of her features. Life was never going to be what she wanted it to be, and she'd decided to pragmatically lower her bar in a way that would have horrified her teenage self. She was working her way through Miles's bookshelves, and she'd started taking Krav Maga three days a week at Jonah's suggestion, and she'd booked a spring break trip to the Philippines that she planned to give him for his birthday.

"This is one of the reasons I stopped litigating," Violet said, aware of her pulse, across from Wendy at the table. "I'm prepared to argue this into the ground."

"If you're cool with being delusional, go for it."

Violet was so rarely surrounded exclusively by women— all three of her sisters, her tiny niece asleep against Liza's shoulder—and she paused a moment to appreciate the energy of it, how different it was from the energy of her own dinner table. The boys in the next room playing Hungry Hungry Hippos— all three, Wyatt with a startling newfound height and Eli the affectionate honey blond moppet and Jonah, the earliest and latest addition to her roster, who was becoming more and more three-dimensional to her each time she encountered him: a dry wit, a diligent student, a discerning scholar of sad indie music; a contrarian, sometimes, and prone to moodiness before noon, but a trustworthy and fervently beloved babysitter to his half brothers. There was a relief in just trying to experience him as a person, no management or censorship. She felt lighter than she had in ages. The world as it was would almost never be the world you wanted it to be, and there was a certain pleasure in finding your space in the schism.

"Gracie, can you weigh in?"

"Neither of those people was there when I was. But there was this one guy—"

"Nobody cares."

"Wendy, Christ." She could admit it now, candidly: that she'd missed being able to laugh freely at Wendy's observations, always at once razor-sharp and utterly tactless.

"What? Sorry that I don't want to hear the annotated history of my high school faculty."

"It's only called faculty when it's a university."

"That's not true."

Grace's sisters—the braying elephants—were facing off across the table, as ever flying down the rails without her, leaving her cruelly in the dust, these two whose explosive closeness she would always envy, Wendy indeterminately intoxicated and Violet seeming a little sloshed as well, but both still relatively good-natured. She could stomach their mockery because she didn't hate herself quite as much as she once had, though she was twenty-four and living with her parents. Matt had gotten her a job as a paralegal at his firm. Her life did not currently suck, and that was progress.

Ben had, miraculously, joined them because he had an unexpected layover in Chicago after visiting his aunt in Boston. It wasn't like they'd *planned* to meet up, to have him meet her family. Their kiss—*her* kiss, her as-yet most major assertion of agency—had turned out to be the commencement of something, she wasn't sure what, lots of text messages and occasional phone calls, the easy amity of a person who listened and made you laugh. And now he was here, in her house, in Oak Park. She should go check on him, sequestered in the living room with the men, but she knew if she rose she would subject herself to more ridicule. Her sisters—with her at the table, fighting about someone she'd never heard of—were delighting in the amount of teasing there was to be done about Grace's first boyfriend-holiday, ignoring her protests that he wasn't her *boy*friend.

"He's just my person," she'd insisted to Wendy, earlier. "Or, not, like—just *a* person."

"Careful," Wendy said. "You'll flatter him to death."

But he was in her house, among her family—her other people—and this was emboldening, somehow. Her life had always been abundantly peopled—by her doting parents, by her indulgent sisters—but she now felt *accompanied* in a way she never had before, by a person who was choosing to feel beholden to her instead of simply scooting up the built-in rope of familial obligation. And it was striking, how much less alone that could make you feel, because of course to be peopled at all was a high-order gift, but to find people *beyond* your people was nothing short of miraculous, finding a person away from home who felt like home and shifted, subsequently, the very *notion* of home, widening its borders.

"You're being ornery." Liza felt the irritant of her sisters' voices deep in her molars.

"Somebody has to."

She and Ryan had only thus far spent time together alone, away from her family, in the form of his visits to Chicago to see the baby, in the form of one painfully long car ride with Kit, last month, to the northernmost point of Michigan, where Ryan met them to take them on a ferry to his friend's farm. This was his first visit to the house on Fair Oaks in over a year, and she knew his presence perplexed her parents and her siblings, but her mother had reached immediately to pull him into a hug; Liza had blushed and shrugged a little bit, holding the baby, who was in fact reaching for David, her daytime playmate, like a little octopus. And her mom had seemed wounded at first, by Kit's favoritism, but when Liza sheepishly passed the baby to her father, her mother leaned her head against his shoulder, both of them cooing to their granddaughter.

There was a difference, she'd begun to realize recently, between settling and ceding. She was still utterly baffled by the world around her but she felt at least more *comfortable* with her bafflement, distracted from it by her job and her romper-clad ten-month-old and the man with whom she'd started everything. Earlier, alone in the kitchen with her mother, she'd whispered, *I don't know,* and Marilyn had replied, *You don't have to know.* She had something with her daughter that she'd never had with anyone else, a kind of fever pitch, precisely the right note struck, sometimes, and during those times she could not imagine ever needing anything else from the world. At the table now, removed a bit from the conversation by a pleasant veil of exhaustion, her daughter asleep on her shoulder, she used her free hand to massage tiny circles into her jawline, a self-induced relaxation technique she'd found on a website for working single mothers.

"What the fuck is with you, Lize?" Wendy asked. "Are you high?"

She tilted her face down, pressed her lips to the top of Kit's head. "On life," she deadpanned, and Wendy laughed at her joke, which always made her feel a childish satisfaction.

Jonah felt himself getting fired up over the hippos, had to keep reminding himself that his opponent was only six and that it would be kind of a dick move to annihilate Wyatt at his own board game. Eli was sitting in his lap, bouncing with excitement, cheering him on. Wyatt was making the best face, scrunched up like a gargoyle, concentrating so hard on the game that he didn't seem to notice that his tongue was stuck almost all the way out of his mouth. His little brother. The world was such a weird fucking place.

Marilyn had begun to talk to him about college. Wendy had again offered to foot the bill. He'd not yet shared with either of them that he was reluctant to head off to college, that he couldn't quite picture leaving David and Marilyn, that he was the only member of the family who hadn't known them since he was born and that he was feeling a little bit greedy about his time with them, these people who woke him up when he turned off his alarm and made him pancakes on Tuesday mornings and stopped whatever they were doing to listen to him, even if he was just telling them he was going to bed.

"Your technique's a little off, man," he said to Wyatt, and he knew he would miss these little dopes, too, if he moved elsewhere. Nobody had written a book on how you were supposed to transition from being an orphan to having about seventeen thousand meddling nutcase family members. "It's a wrist thing," he said, demonstrating, as his grandfather did sometimes when they played basketball together. "You're going to want to hold the handle just a little bit to your right," he said, "and then you just have to *rail* on it, buddy, okay, like you've never wanted anything more than those marbles."

David was probably *killing the vibe*, as Gracie would say, but he couldn't help but ignore the football game in favor of watching, with interest, the handful of men who loved his daughters. They'd segregated themselves in that antiquated way, the women arguing at the table, the men crowded around the television. He was most intrigued by Grace's boyfriend—it pained him to even think the phrase, to think of their baby, partnered, but he grudgingly allowed himself to admit that he liked the boy, possibly even trusted him, ever since he'd seen him, when he thought no one was looking, kiss Grace with a reverent tenderness worthy of their Epilogue. Ben, Matt, and Ryan were together on the couch, visibly aware of how much space they were taking up and of the fact that their bodies weren't touching. He'd never really had to experience that kind of masculine awareness because he'd snapped into adulthood so early, because he and Marilyn had so securely fastened themselves to each other before either really had a chance to feel the awkward loneliness of being solo in the world. He sat in his chair near the bookshelves, halfway between the two groups, listening to the steady rise and fall of his daughters' voices and the static blare of the TV, too old to quite fit in with either set. He was aware of missing his wife, a thought that he dismissed as silly because she was, of course, in the next room.

Marilyn tried to tune out her daughters, adults in body if not in mind, while she peered dubiously at the turkey in the oven, which smelled okay but still looked frightening. She waged this battle annually. She closed the oven, unsatisfied, and drifted over to the back door, looking out at the yard and breathing in air that didn't smell like savory meat.

"I just went in to break up a brawl." Arms wrapped around her waist; hands rested on her abdomen. "But they broke it up *themselves*, before I could even open my mouth."

The ease of the remembering: how effortlessly she could conjure the feeling of their first time, her back melting in submission, her scalp prickling to attention, the chill of the ground through her clothes and the warmth of his early inelegance. She put her hands on top of David's and leaned back against him. "So who died? Mr. Calhoun or Mr. Whiteman?"

"Huh?"

She smiled. "Nothing. No one. Come here." She gripped his hand, unlatched the back door.

"What're you doing?"

"Abandoning our children." She pulled him outside and down the stairs. She settled on one of the steps and he followed more slowly, his long legs folding achingly into acute angles.

"Dinner smells good," he said.

She leaned her head against his shoulder. "Thank you."

"Good-looking crew in there too, huh?"

"Mm."

"A little annoying, though, if I may."

She snorted. "Yeah. Just a little."

"How did we ever live with all of them at the same time?"

She didn't reply. She worried about him constantly. She missed him preemptively.

The girls were all like David; the different similarities were becoming clearer to her by the hour with everyone home, some that she already knew—that she had recognized the moment they were born—and others that she had never noticed. Liza had the most elemental grip on him; she was pragmatic and suspicious and the very kindest kind of scientific. Violet had her father's loving all-business approach to her children. Grace had inherited his meticulous handwriting and his trepidation about merging with the surrounding world. Wendy—her eldest daughter nearly *forty*—possessed his art for making the absolute, most sardonic best out of the strange circumstances that had befallen her. And Marilyn in there somewhere, all over all of them, her optimism, her kinetic repression, her pluck, assured further by the pressure of her husband's hand around her right hip, by the buzz of voices, aggressive but playful, each knotted elaborately around her heart, through the screen door.

"Sure you're okay?" he asked.

"I am." His shoulder had felt the same against her face for

the entire time she'd known him. This man; her heart: maker of beds and terrible coffee, pain analyst and curmudgeon and unfaltering father; owner of strong arms and malleable convictions. Love of her life. She rubbed her cheek against the knit grain of his sweater. "Come here," she said.

"I couldn't be any closer unless I was sitting in your lap, kid." So much more confident than he'd been when they'd first met, emboldened by the years.

She lifted her face and kissed him, and the stairs squeaked beneath them, aging green paint that would flake off and embed forest flecks into their clothes; atrophied wood swelled with decades of rainstorms and snowstorms and pounded back into submission by a century of heavy footsteps, stomping teens and loping dogs and gardening semi-adults. They both felt the December chill through the insulatory dearth of their sweaters and David reached an arm around his wife's shoulders. They both turned slightly to a sound from the kitchen, the thump of the refrigerator door and the clink of glass.

"Refueling," David said, and she nodded against him. "Christ, those girls drink a lot of wine. I'll have to apologize to the recycling guy on Tuesday."

"He seems like a forgiving guy." She kissed him again.

"Think they're back at each other's throats in there?" he asked.

"Oh, probably. Let's not worry about it."

Those ancient stairs, those six-times-repainted stairs with layers of red and blue and yellow and brown and white and now their green, creaking ominously but never to the point of concern. Those ancient stairs upon which Marilyn had once laid herself strategically, fifteen years old and hoping the odd angles would allow her a more cohesive tan. Upon which the two of them had helped Gracie learn to work her tiny baby legs, adept then at walking on flat surfaces but not inclines. Upon which Wendy had probably done unspeakable things to boys with Napoleon complexes and offshore accounts. Upon which Liza and Violet had once erected a lemonade stand, blind to the fact that they were unlikely to attract customers by setting up shop in the backyard. Upon which now Marilyn was stretching out, arching her back uncomfortably on the stair beneath her husband and impelling him to join her.

"Old times' sake," she said, but he shook his head, moving his knees to accommodate her.

"My back's not cut out for this level of holiday whimsy, my dear."

She lay back flat, her husband's knees tented over her thighs in a corduroy bridge, and looked upward. They had five trees remaining in their backyard now, plus the stump of the tree David had put out of its misery: three ginkgoes and two oaks, all of which were older than they, older than her parents, older than anything. The ginkgoes had shed weeks ago but the oaks were different, always Marilyn's favorite: stragglers, late bloomers, the last to get their leaves and the last to lose them. There were a few remaining on the branches, misshapen hand-prints, hanging by a thread and waiting to fall.

Two seasons in Chicago, the old joke went. *Winter and construction.* But there were so many more, she thought. Dozens of seasons, some only a few hours long, idiosyncratic little pockets between the definitive stretch of autumn, the bright flash of spring. This season now, which may possibly last only a few moments, where you could wear a sweater outside in December and there were still a few leaves on the trees and the warmth radiating from the person next to you was enough to make it all bearable. And the season that would follow when they went back inside, their skin foggy from the cold air and the warm proximity of each other, their bodies overtaken as ever by their children, hands on their shoulders and eyes on their every move and voices in their ears, hands and eyes and voices that would never fully comprehend the complexity of their own origins; hands and eyes and voices that would be forever ignorant to what transpired on those stairs between David and Marilyn Sorenson, on their thirty-ninth Second Thanksgiving, literate in their own elusive language, their merged genes snaking through nearly every person inside the house on Fair Oaks.

"Hey, love," she said to him, imploring, but she wasn't sure what for.

He hummed in response, both echo and acknowledgment, and held out his open palm.

She shifted beneath her husband, reached up and took his hand.

ACKNOWLEDGMENTS

I have so very much gratitude for those who have helped me since the Sorensons first found their way into the world.

First, most, still, always: thank you to Tony and Sally Lombardo, my wonderful parents, for everything, forever.

Thank you infinitely to Ellen Levine, Alexa Stark, and Martha Wydysh, truly the most extraordinary advocates a gal could ask for.

To the boundlessly brilliant Lee Boudreaux: I will never get over my luck that this book found its way under your wing; thank you, thank you, thank you for everything. And thank you to Caitlin Landuyt, the far superior CL, for your abundant insights, editorial and astrological. In-house, thanks upon thanks to Todd Doughty, Sarah Engelmann, Julie Ertl, Ellen Feldman, Jason Gobble, Suzanne Herz, Emily Mahon, Cara Reilly, and Bill Thomas.

Booksellers and sales reps: you are the best kinds of people; thank you for making the literary world go 'round, and for helping me and *Most Fun* along the way.

To my family and to my friends and to every dog on the earth (but especially Renee): thank you for being.

And to readers, all: thank you for your time, eyes, and insight; I am ever grateful.

An Excerpt from *Same As It Ever Was*
by Claire Lombardo
Available from Doubleday in Summer 2024

It happens in the way that most important things end up having happened for her: accidentally, and because she does something she is not supposed to do. And it happens in the fashion of many happenstantial occurrences, the result of completely plausible decision making, a little diversion from the norm that will, in hindsight, seem almost *too* coincidental: a slight veer and suddenly everything's free-falling, the universe gleefully seizing that seldom chosen Other Option, running, arms outstretched, like a deranged person trying to clear the aisles in a grocery store, which is, as a matter of fact, where she is, the gourmet place two towns over, picking up some last-minute items for a dinner party for her husband, who is turning sixty today.

This one is a small act of misbehavior by any standards, an innocuous Other Option as far as they go: choosing a grocery store that is not her usual grocery store because her usual grocery store is out of crabmeat.

Afterward she will remember having the thought—leaving the first grocery empty-handed—that such a benign change to her routine could lead to something disastrous, something that's not supposed to happen. This is how Mark—scientific, marvelously anxious—has always looked at the world, as a series of choices made or not and the intricate mathematical repercussions thereof. Julia's own brain didn't start working this way until she'd known him for a substantial period of time; prior to that she'd always been content with the notion that making one decision closed the door on another, that there was no grand order to the universe, that nothing *really* mattered that much one way or another; this glaring difference in character is perhaps what accounts for the fact that Mark dutifully pursued a graduate degree in engineering while Julia neglected to collect her English and Rhetoric diploma from Kansas State.

Now, though, they've been together for nearly three decades and so she did consider—just a fleeting thought—that so cavalierly altering routine could result in some kind of dark fallout, but at the time she'd been envisioning something cinematically terrible, something she wouldn't have encountered had she just forgone the crab instead of driving fifteen minutes west, a cruel run-in with a freight train or a land mine, not with an eighty-year-old woman assessing a tower of kumquats.

Julia doesn't recognize her at first. She doesn't consciously notice her, in fact, nor does she stop; she's headed industriously past the organic produce to seafood, contemplating a drive-by to dry goods to see if they have anything interesting in stock; sometimes the stores in the farther-out suburbs have a more robust inventory. She's considering taking a spin around the whole store, checking out what else they have that hasn't been subject to the frenzied consumption of the usual suspects at her usual grocery, when it hits her; the woman's face registers in her brain belatedly, clad in the convincing disguise—that invisible blanket—of age.

Hers has not been a life lived under the threat of too many ghosts; there's only a small handful of people whom she has truly hoped to never encounter again, and Helen Russo happens to be one of them. So why does she find herself taking a step closer to the endcap of the dry goods aisle, getting out of the flow of traffic so she can turn to look back? It's been over eighteen years, which is somewhat astonishing both given the fact that they used to see each other at least once a week *and* given the smallness of her world, a world in which—as has been established—something as small as altering one's grocery plans can be considered a major decision.

She is unsure, as well, what moves her back to where she came from, but Helen's not in produce anymore, has progressed to the bulk section, where she is weighing out a bag of pine nuts. According to their accompanying sign, they are $16.75 for a half pound, and she remembers becoming aware of such extravagances during the afternoons she spent at the Russos' house, the heaviness of the cutlery, the paintings that looked suspiciously like originals, the bottles of wine she'd look up when she got home and find to have cost $58.

She is here procuring the ingredients for celebratory crab cakes, one of her husband's favorites. The thought of Mark sets off a momentary swirling of wooziness. She's carrying around an empty basket and, feeling somewhat ridiculous, she tosses in a purple orb of cabbage. In some ways Helen looks predictably much older than she remembers; in others—her optimistic ponytail, the glint of the big blue beads around her neck—she hasn't changed at all. Julia takes a few steps, then a few more. Normally she is the queen of evasion, treats her trips to the grocery like sniper missions, seeing how many faces she can avoid having to interact with; this does not mesh with whatever gregarious phantom has overtaken her body now, impelling her close enough to see the pair of drugstore cheaters propped on top of the woman's head.

"Helen?"

When Helen turns to face her, there's a curious vacancy in her gaze; her eyes trail slowly up and down. Julia thinks to consider how she looks; she runs a hand through her hair. She worries, momentarily, that she'll be mistaken for some kind of miscreant; she's wearing what Alma calls her *clown pants* and one of Mark's old button-downs; she likes to think the combination has miraculously resulted in something extemporaneously stylish, but it's likelier taken her in the opposite direction. It can be hard to tell, in the suburbs, whether an eccentrically clad woman carrying around a single organic cabbage is nomadic or expensively disheveled. She begins to consider how much she herself has changed since last they met, and the volume of those changes hits her forcefully and all at once; she is, upon reflection, more changed than not. She becomes nervily aware of her pulse pumping in her ears. It's entirely within the realm of possibility that Helen won't even *recognize* her—that old worry, so familiar to her, that you haven't meant to someone as much as they meant to you—but then Helen speaks.

"It couldn't be."

The heartbeat sound recedes, overwhelmed by the surrounding bustle, a woman arguing with the butcher, a man talking into an invisible earpiece, a child in a down vest singing shrilly about a baby shark. Helen's voice is remarkably unchanged; Julia is transported, not unpleasantly, to afternoons in the Russos' backyard, Helen—older, then, still, than Julia is now—imparting her parental platitudes, her pithy one-liners, her candid confessions, all with the confidence and ease of a person who actually enjoyed her life, astonishing to Julia at the time because she herself did not.

"Epic in scope—emotionally, psychologically and narratively. . . .
The literary love child of Jonathan Franzen and Anne Tyler."
—*The Observer*

When Marilyn Connolly and David Sorenson fo
in love in the 1970s, they are blithely ignorant of a
that awaits them. By 2016, their four radically diffe
ent daughters are in a state of unrest. Wendy, widowe
young, soothes herself with booze and younger me
Violet, a litigator turned stay-at-home mom, battle
anxiety and self-doubt; Liza, a neurotic and new
tenured professor, finds herself pregnant with a baby she's not sure sh
wants by a man she's not sure she loves; and Grace, the dawdling young
est daughter, begins living a lie that no one in her family even suspect
With the arrival of Jonah Bendt—the child placed for adoption by on
of the daughters fifteen years before—the Sorensons will be forced t
reckon with the rich and varied tapestry of their past: years marred b
adolescent angst, infidelity, and resentment, but also the transcenden
moments of joy that make everything else worthwhile.

"Rich, engrossing . . . spiked with sisterly malice. . . .
[Rendered] with such skill and finely tuned interest that it feels
like a quiet subversion of the traditional family saga."
—*The New York Times Book Review*

"A rich, complex family saga." —*USA Today*

Coming Summer 2024:

U.S. $19.00   Can. $25.99   Fiction
I S B N 978-0-525-56423-2

5 1 9 0 0

9 780525 564232

Cover design by Emily Mahon | Cover photographs: front © Mike Dobel/Arcangel; spine © xlibes/Shutterstock
Author photograph © Nina Subin | 𝕏 @ClaireLombardo 📷 @claire_lombardo
clairelombardo.com | vintagebooks.com | Reading Group Guide available at ReadingGroupCenter.com